DESMOND

Charlotte Smith

Ridley sculp.

Mrs Charlotte Smith.

Portrait engraved by Ridley and published in 1799 by Vernor & Hood.

DESMOND

Charlotte Smith

Edited by
Antje Blank
and Janet Todd

broadview literary texts

Canadian Cataloguing in Publication Data

Smith, Charlotte, 1749–1806
    Desmond
(Broadview literary texts)
Includes bibliographical references.
ISBN 1-55111-274-4
I. Blank, Antje, 1965- . II. Todd, Janet M., 1942- . III. Title. IV. Series.

PR3688.S4D4 2001   823'.6   C00-932877-7

Broadview Press Ltd. is an independent, international publishing house, incorporated in 1985.

North America:
P.O. Box 1243, Peterborough, Ontario, Canada K9J 7H5
3576 California Road, Orchard Park, NY 14127
Tel: (705) 743-8990; Fax: (705) 743-8353
E-mail: customerservice@broadviewpress.com

United Kingdom:
Thomas Lyster Ltd.
Unit 9, Ormskirk Industrial Park, Old Boundary Way, Burscough Road
Ormskirk, Lancashire L39 2YW
Tel: (01695) 575112; Fax: (01695) 570120
E-mail: books@tlyster.co.uk

Australia:
St. Clair Press, P.O. Box 287, Rozelle, NSW 2039
Tel: (02) 818-1942; Fax: (02) 418-1923

www.broadviewpress.com

Broadview Press gratefully acknowledges the financial support of the Book Publishing Industry Development Program, Ministry of Canadian Heritage, Government of Canada.

PRINTED IN CANADA

Contents

Acknowledgements

The editors would like to thank Judith Stanton for kindly making available her edition of *The Collected Letters of Charlotte Smith* (Bloomington: Indiana University Press, 2002). They are also grateful to the John Rylands Library, Manchester, for a copy of the text of *Desmond.*

Introduction

"Compelled to live only to write & write only to live"[1]

On 23 February 1765 Charlotte Turner, not quite sixteen, was married to Benjamin Smith, second son of Richard Smith, a wealthy London merchant with stock in the East India Company and sugar cane plantations on Barbados. Looking back nearly forty years later, Charlotte Smith would refer to the event as a moment when

> ... my father & my Aunt (peace to their ashes!) thought it a prodigious stroke of domestic policy, to sell me like a Southdown sheep, to the West India shambles, not far from Smithfield (& they would have done me a greater kindness if they had shot me at once) ...[2]

This ill-advised marriage, "worse than African bondage," would determine the course of Charlotte Smith's future.[3] Hastily contracted, it had been the means to rid the household of a young girl who squabbled with her new stepmother, a 40-year-old woman whose large dowry had been a vital addition to her father's dwindling fortune.

Charlotte was little prepared for life in a London merchant family. She had spent an affluent childhood at Bignor Park, the family estate on the picturesque Sussex Downs, and her early youth among fashionable London society; now she had to accustom herself to living in a gloomy second-storey flat in her father-in-law's house in Cheapside with relatives who she thought wanted refinement and education, frowned on her ignorance of housekeeping, and showed little understanding of her fondness for reading, writing, and drawing. Her hus-

---

[1] Charlotte Smith to Dr. Shirly, 22 August 1789.
[2] Charlotte Smith to Lord Egremont, 4 February 1803.
[3] *Ibid.*

band's character proved unstable; he was sometimes violent, frequently promiscuous, and habitually extravagant. Her father-in-law Richard Smith, however, took a great liking to Charlotte and recognized her literary talent, although he thought it would be put to best use in his counting-house. Charlotte declined becoming his paid clerk, but she continued to assist him in keeping the accounts until his death in 1776.

Only too aware of his son's expensive habits, Richard Smith attempted to provide for Charlotte and her family by bequeathing the bulk of his estate to her children. By 1776 she had given birth to nine children; one had died in his infancy, another—her eldest son—would die the following year. Unfortunately, neither Charlotte nor her surviving children would ever benefit much from their inheritance of £36,000; Richard Smith's will, which tied up his property in a trust, had been written without legal advice. Complications soon arose and the trust became the subject of a prolonged legal dispute which was settled only forty years later.[4]

Legal proceedings first came to a head in 1783 when it emerged that Benjamin Smith, carelessly performing his duty as executor to the will, had run up high debts and diminished the value of the trust by more than a third. Other members of the family and beneficiaries of the will sued; as a result, trustees were appointed and Benjamin Smith found himself in King's Bench Prison. Charlotte chose to share much of the seven months' term with her husband. Harassed with debts, she decided to write for money, beginning with a series of sonnets. The renowned publisher Dodsley to whom she turned doubted their marketability, but, encouraged by William Hayley, Smith published them at her own expense. Although she compiled her poems in the humiliating environment of a debtors' prison, she ensured with her title that the public was aware of her claim to a more genteel station in life: *Elegiac Sonnets, and Other Essays by Charlotte Smith of Bignor Park, Sussex* (1784).

The collection of sombre poems was immensely successful—in several ways. One immediate effect was, of course, financial, their profits contributing to Charlotte's and her husband's release from prison. In

---

[4] For a detailed clarification of Richard Smith's will, see Florence Hilbish, *Charlotte Smith, Poet and Novelist* (Philadelphia: University of Pennsylvania Press, 1941), 72–81.

the long term they established her reputation as a gentlewoman and author of serious verse and thus lent greater respectability to her later productions in a less prestigious but more lucrative genre—the novel. Within literary history, Smith's *Elegiac Sonnets* played a significant part in the revival of the sonnet form in the Romantic period. As they went through numerous subsequent editions, they swelled into a two-volume set, inspiring later poets such as William Wordsworth, Samuel Taylor Coleridge, and John Keats, and established the form as a proper vehicle for the expression of plaintive sentiment. Although many of the *Elegiac Sonnets* were explicitly autobiographical in their setting and mood, the public was still left in the dark about the specific legal, economic, and emotional causes of the poet's misfortunes—so much so that the gallant reviewer of *The Gentleman's Magazine* could state his preference for an imaginary distress, claiming he would have read her "exquisite effusions" with "diminished pleasure," could he have "supposed her sorrows to be real."[5]

Charlotte Smith's miseries, however, were only too real. Prison did nothing towards reforming Benjamin Smith. Soon he was in debt again, and his violent outbreaks escalated. On 15 April 1787, after 22 years of marriage, Charlotte Smith finally left him. "Tho infidelity and with the most despicable objects," she explained, "had renderd my continuing to live with him extremely wretched long before his debts compelled him to leave England, I could have been contented to reside in the same house with him, had not his temper been so capricious and often so cruel that my life was not safe."[6] Her sister noted that Smith made a futile appeal to one member of their family to make just terms of separation.[7] William, Smith's eldest son, had found employment in the civil service in India, and her second son Nicholas was about to follow him, but her remaining three sons and four daughters depended solely on their mother for their support. And with none of her marriage settlements providing for a separation and no legal arrangement to secure her fortune or her future income Charlotte Smith was left at the mercy of her husband Benjamin.

---

5   *The Gentleman's Magazine* (April 1786), 333.
6   Charlotte Smith to Joseph Cooper Walker, 9 October 1793.
7   Catherine Dorset's biographical sketch "Charlotte Smith" in Sir Walter Scott, *The Lives of the Novelists* (London: Dent, 1810), 321.

Under eighteenth-century patriarchal law a husband's power over his wife's person was absolute. He was authorized to confine or chastise her "within reason," her property and earnings were at his disposal. In return a husband was legally bound to supply his wife with a home, food, and clothes. The concept of the *feme covert*, the legal notion of the unity of person, denoting that "the very being and essence of the woman" was suspended during the coverture, meant a wife had no legal personality in common law, was unable to enter into contracts, sue or be sued, or instigate legal action. When marriages turned sour, women were left with few options. While a husband could file for a divorce on grounds of a wife's infidelity, she could only hope for a divorce in cases of bigamy, sodomy, or life-threatening violence. And without the safeguard of a private separation deed, a married woman leaving her husband risked forfeiting her maintenance without gaining either legal or financial autonomy. William Blackstone, eminent representative of British jurisprudence in the eighteenth century, declared that this blatantly discriminatory legislation actually paid homage to women's delicate and gentle natures: "even the disabilities, which the wife lies under," he stated, "are for the most part intended for her protection and benefit. So great a favourite is the female sex of the laws of England."[8]

But Charlotte Smith had little cause to think herself a particular favourite of the British laws. Soon after their separation Benjamin Smith went into hiding in Scotland to escape all court proceedings investigating his debts and pocketing of trust money. There he continued to live, as Charlotte Smith resentfully observed, "on the interest of my fortune, with a Woman he keeps," leaving her to find means of supporting herself and her numerous children.[9] Smith had four potential sources of income: her own fortune, her sons' annual remittances, her father-in-law's entangled trust, and her pen.[10] The interest payments

---

8   William Blackstone, *Commentaries on The Laws of England* (London, 1829), vol. i, 444.

9   Charlotte Smith to Thomas Cadell, Sr., April 1792. Apparently Benjamin Smith set up an odd *ménage à trois*. He was living with a Mrs. Miller, probably his cook or housekeeper, and her niece. With the latter he fathered a child which, in his will, he tried to foist off on Charlotte.

10   For a detailed record of Smith's earnings throughout her career see Judith Stanton, "Charlotte Smith's 'Literary Business': Income, Patronage, and Indigence" in *The Age of Johnson: A Scholarly Annual*, ed. Paul J. Korshin (1987), 375–401.

on her marriage settlements were an unreliable support: sometimes they were withheld by the trustees, frequently Benjamin Smith would sneak back to England and cash them in. Her two eldest sons working in the civil service in India sent home money but these payments, like the ships they came on, usually arrived late and irregularly. Much of the proceeds from Richard Smith's sugar plantations on Barbados were apparently embezzled. Had the numerous parties to the will settled their claims, the legacies due to her children would have spared her sons their perilous military careers and raised her daughters' chances of making advantageous matches. With this in mind, Charlotte Smith exerted herself to bring about a final settlement. Frequently her efforts were thwarted by Benjamin Smith: whenever she would try to secure an income out of the trust for her three children born after Richard Smith's death and thus not mentioned in the will he would exercise his legal powers to oppose her attempts until he had been handsomely paid off. Circumstanced as she was, it is hardly surprising that Smith felt she had no choice but to become a "slave of the Booksellers."[11]

In the years following her separation from her husband Smith churned out eleven novels, added to successive editions of the *Elegiac Sonnets*, produced two further volumes of poetry, and ended her career with the publication of four educational books for young people, a natural history of birds, and a history of England. Smith's professional career unfolded against the background of continuous financial pressures, a lingering depression, and a "gouty" complaint, probably rheumatoid arthritis, which progressively paralyzed her body and settled in her hands, making writing increasingly painful. Yet she never quite relinquished her hope of a trust settlement and continued publishing to maintain a standard of living suitable to her children's expected inheritance. Their tragic lives also bore heavily on Smith, emotionally, and ultimately, financially. In 1793 her son Charles Dyer lost his leg in the siege of Dunkirk and returned home crippled. In 1794 her daughter Anna Augusta, married to a French emigrant, gave birth to a child that died within a day, and subsequently fell into a consumptive decline from which she died the following year. In 1800 her youngest daughter Harriet, who had visited her brothers in India

---

11   Charlotte Smith to Joseph Cooper Walker, 9 October 1793.

hoping to meet with a wealthy husband there, returned suffering from a dangerous fever which left her subject to delirious fits. In 1801 Charles travelled to Barbados to settle trust business, contracted malaria, and died. The same year, her daughter Lucy's wastrel husband died, leaving Smith to care and provide for their three young children.

The Life in the Works

The difficulties of authoring trite sentimental plots when harassed by the exigencies of a distressing personal life were considerable, judging from Smith's depiction of the creative process in the autobiographical character of Charlotte Denzil, the novelist in *The Banished Man* (1794):

> After a conference with Mr. Tough, [a creditor] she must write a tender dialogue between some damsel, whose perfections are even greater than those "Which youthful poets fancy when they love," and her hero ... But Mr. Tough's conversation, his rude threats, and his boisterous remonstrances, have totally sunk her spirits; nor are they elevated by hearing that the small beer is out; that the pigs of a rich farmer, her next neighbor, have broke into the garden, rooted up the whole crop of pease, and not left her a single hyacinth.... She is divested from such reflections however, by hearing from her maid that John Gibbon's children over the way, and his wife, and John himself have all got the scarlet fever; and that one of the children is dead on't, and another like to die.... Compassion for these unhappy persons is now mingled with apprehensions for her own family.... The rest of the day is passed as before; her hero and heroine are parted in agonies, or meet in delight, and she is employed in making the most of either; with interludes of the Gibbin's family, and precautions against importing the infectious distemper into her own. (ii, pp. 225–9)

Nonetheless, Smith did produce the romantic, happily-ever-after texts that the publishers and the public demanded. All her novels are firmly within the popular genre of the feminine novel of sensibility.

The boundaries for women's fiction in the second half of the eighteenth century were narrowly drawn; narratives were expected to centre on the courtship plot, featuring a chaste and flawless heroine—frequently an orphan or of obscure parentage, but invariably of refined birth, and preferably aristocratic—subjected to repeated melodramatic distresses until eventually rescued and reinstated in society by the virtuous hero. Smith followed the pattern, but with little zeal, protesting against the insipidity of the contemporary heroine and complaining of a trivialized mode that confined her fiction within a domestic sphere.[12] Her formal discontent regularly surfaces in her writings. At times she heightens the sentimental ingredients to parodic extremes. At other times her objectionable radical politics are voiced through her male characters. Occasionally she inserts narratives of female desire, where "fallen" women somehow avoid their conventional punishment; and frequently she includes tales of female discontent and male despotism which deconstruct the redemptive values of the foregrounded romance and question the legitimacy of male authority in public and domestic life.

Many of Smith's marginal plots are thinly veiled accounts of her own life. This was not uncommon; weaving personal experience into fictional plots was a feature of women's sentimental novels, especially for those using the form for political purpose. Yet neither Mary Hays nor Mary Wollstonecraft exploited this potential self-representation and self-exoneration with as much determination as Smith. Muddling the personal with the political, and the sentimental with the professional, she deliberately blurred all boundaries between the private and the public. An important facet in the culture of sensibility which she put to clever use was the exaltation of motherhood; emphatically she cast herself in the role of the injured wife and devoted mother who sacrificed her entire life and career to the well-being of her large family. All

---

12   In *Marchmont* (1796) Smith stressed how "difficult" it was for a novelist "to give to one of his heroines any very marked feature which shall not disfigure her!" (I/177) Later on in the same novel the hero who, hard-pressed for money, contemplates writing novels has to learn that "any tendency to political discussion, however liberal or applicable, was not to be tolerated in a sort of work which people took up with no other design than to be amused at the least possible expence of thought." (II/229)

her works, whatever genre—poetry, fiction, children's literature, letters, prefaces—were employed to convey this image.[13]

Of her powerlessness before the law Charlotte Smith was painfully aware. At one point she moaned: "All voice, all opinion is taken from me."[14] But she fought back, trying to reclaim the voice denied her in the legal discourse with the methodical use of her writings as a forum to publicize her case. In the early years of her career she was, after all, one of the most popular and widely-read novelists in Britain, and she capitalized on her status to pressure her adversaries. Discussing the craft of writing only briefly, her prefaces, couched in the language of sensibility, effectually became a serialized autobiographical narrative in which Smith kept the public up to date with the latest developments in the lawsuit. The trustees were featured as gothic arch-villains who persecuted her family and hoarded the money legitimately her children's, while she was a sentimental heroine, a wronged and defenceless woman. The sentimental pose, attracting a readership nurtured on tearful tales of female suffering, also helped veil the fact that she was venting her aggression and vilifying her enemies in a manner hardly deemed proper or ladylike. The stock elements of apologia and feminine modesty also indicted patriarchal authority: she was venturing into the literary marketplace only because her husband and his relatives had robbed her children of their fortune, and her works are defective only because she had no respite from their cruel oppression.

The autobiographical thread continues through the fictional plots. The social discrimination Smith experienced as a separated wife turned her into an avid advocate for legal and egalitarian reforms. Acutely

---

13 For an excellent study of Smith's method of marketing her *Elegiac Sonnets* through the spectacle of herself as a distressed woman, see Jacqueline Labbe's article "Selling One's Sorrows: Charlotte Smith, Mary Robinson, and the Marketing of Poetry" in *The Wordsworth Circle*, 25:2 (1994): 68–71. Smith's private letters to friends, publishers, and trustees share common characteristics with her public writings: when not upraiding her husband and her enemies in the lawsuit, they utilize the same sentimental vocabulary. Frequently, as Sarah Zimmerman observes, Smith "interjects requests for better financial terms and advances into narratives that read like novels." Smith contemplated the publication of her letters but William Hayley strongly urged her not to, deeming this project "not suitable to the dignity of her literary character." See Zimmerman, "Charlotte Smith's Letters and the Practice of Self–Presentation" in *The Princeton University Library Chronicle*, 53:1 (1991): 65.

14 Charlotte Smith to Lord Egremont, 7 January 1803.

aware that her own miseries originated in the partiality of contemporary marriage and property laws, Smith set about exposing women's legal, economic, and sexual exploitation: many of her approved female characters are blameless middle-aged wives burdened with abusive husbands who wreak financial havoc wherever they go, and young innocent heroines stripped of their property and social position by pillaging relatives and sharkish lawyers. As the years ground on and Smith's frustration and bitterness over her lawsuit heightened, her onslaughts on patriarchal authorities in general, and "legal banditti" in particular, grew ever more scathing.[15]

That her satire was anything but inadvertent and impersonal was a fact Smith readily pointed out; but whether her public attacks on her husband and the trustees, the latter powerful members of the establishment, made her more enemies or friends is difficult to gauge. She herself firmly believed in the beneficial influence of her published word, and in 1794, thinking the trustees were yielding to her pressure, she triumphantly wrote:

> By the generous interposition of Lord Egremont & the public flogging I have given the Villainous Men who have for so many years reduced me to a state of mendicity [sic] (or what is as bad, to the necessity of writing for bread) and by their fears, which are well founded, that what I have said is only an *antepast* of *what I will say*, I am now in more hopes than I have hitherto been that My children's Estate will be forced out of their hands; & then I trust I shall never again have occasion to solicit advances—nor to write a line.[16]

Her sanguine hopes proved unfounded. Still, her self-portrait as a woman in distress did, initially at least, succeed in gaining her the much-needed support of influential men. William Hayley, William Cowper, and the third Earl of Egremont chivalrously came to her defence, while publishers willingly co-operated to secure her earnings from her acquisitive husband and his rapacious creditors. Yet soon many tired of her seemingly interminable woes and the public began to resent the

---

15 *Marchmont*, ii, 71.
16 Charlotte Smith to Thomas Cadell, Jr., and William Davies, 16 September 1794.

manner in which she paraded her sufferings and eulogized her own character. Anna Seward, a poet herself, came to scorn Smith for her "boundless vanity" and the "indelicacy" in holding up to "public contempt" the man "whose name she bears."[17] Other critics, similarly disturbed by Smith's unfeminine display of aggression, disapproved of her attacks on the status quo.[18]

As time passed, politics also worked against her. The storming of the Bastille in 1789 and the ensuing political reforms of the early phase of the French Revolution met with widespread support in England, particularly among aristocratic liberals, middle-class reformers, Dissenters, political thinkers, and sentimental writers. But many English sympathizers were gradually alienated as moderate political goals became more radical and republican and the means of achieving them more bloody. In the volatile years following the execution of Louis XVI and the declaration of war in early 1793, Britain defined itself in increasingly reactionary and patriotic terms. Clinging more than ever to the status quo, the public turned against any kind of reform, now often branded "French principles." With francophobic sentiment running high, any author who endorsed liberal visions or was known to have espoused the revolutionary cause was attacked with open hostility and even risked legal prosecution for seditious activity under the "Two Acts" of 1795.

Not surprisingly many writers yielded to the pressure and renounced their "French principles" to hail the stability of the British constitution. The publication of *Desmond* (1792), documenting Smith's radical enthusiasm and naive faith in the virtue of the French leadership, was particularly untimely, closely followed as it was by the reversal in revolutionary politics that put an end to the constitutional phase. Initially, contemporary reviewers unanimously praised Smith's novel, commending the introduction of political matter which made

---

[17] Anna Seward to Mrs. Hayley, 11 January 1789. Seward's indignation was probably kindled in part by the overwhelming success of Smith's *Elegiac Sonnets*, to which she scornfully referred as those "poetical whipt syllabubs, in black glasses" (Seward to Theophilus Swift, 9 July 1789).

[18] The *Critical Review*, XXIV (September 1798): 84, for example lamented that "Mrs. Smith should degrade her productions with personal satire" and the obituary in the *Universal Magazine*, VII (March 1807): 260, condemned her for "lash[ing] with pointed severity, the profession of the law, in a manner that shewed more ill–nature than good sense."

Desmond "tower far above the common productions of the day."[19] Yet only a few months later the political climate had changed dramatically and Smith found herself in a precarious dilemma. Though she was deeply dismayed at the ferocity of the Jacobin dictatorship, their betrayal of the democratic ideals of the Revolution did not blind her to the defects of the constitution in Britain. In the dedication to her blank verse poem *The Emigrants* (1793) she explains that the worst effect these incidents had had on the British was that

> by confounding the original cause with the wretched catastrophes that followed its ill management; the attempts of public virtue, with the outrages that guilt and folly have committed in its disguise, the very name of Liberty has not only lost the charm it used to have in British ears, but many, who have written, or spoken, in its defence, have been stigmatized, as promoters of Anarchy, and enemies to the prosperity of their country.

Refusing to recede into the romantic realm of her popular and more conventional earlier novels *Emmeline* (1788), *Ethelinde* (1789), and *Celestina* (1791), in which she had steered clear of political disquisition, Smith stayed true to her progressive beliefs. Espousing the libertarian ideals of a radical sensibility, she continued to publish fiction of a decidedly subversive nature that promoted principles of universal benevolence and condemned institutionally authorized oppression, be it in social, racial, or gender relations.

However, threatened with indigence and wary of the conservative mood among her audience, Smith *did* tone down the radicalism that had characterized the authorial voice in *Desmond* and adopted more oblique techniques to express her views. So that in *The Old Manor House* (1793) she displaced her plot into the past of the American War of Independence, which allowed her to remind her readers of a fact that had slipped from the minds of many anti-Jacobins: that a republic based on the revolutionary ideals of equality and liberty had been successfully established. In *The Emigrants, The Banished Man* (1794), and *Marchmont* (1796), she picked up the theme pivotal to reaction-

---

[19]   *European Magazine,* XX (July 1792): 22.

ary propaganda—the Jacobin government's savage persecution of its own citizens—and related the sufferings of the French *émigrés* to those whom legal oppression and corruption in England had reduced to a similar existence, that of exiles in their native country.

The Young Philosopher (1798) marked a decisive return to frank radical fiction. With no hope of possible social change, a break with the reactionary patriarchal structures of England seemed the only solution. And so the "philosopher" Delmont seeks the freedom of America, leaving his native country where "the miseries inflicted by the social compact greatly exceed the happiness derived from it" and where

> for a great part of the year my ears are every week shocked by the cries of hawkers, informing who has been dragged to execution; and where, to come directly home, it is at the mercy of any rascal, to whom I have given an opportunity of cheating me of ten pounds, to swear a debt against me, and carry me to the abodes of horror, where the malefactor groans in irons, the debtor languishes in despair. Is or is not this picture true? (IV/394)

Not surprisingly, by the late 1790s the taint of Jacobinism stuck and earned Smith a rank among Richard Polwhele's band of "Unsex'd Females."[20] Sales of her novels had been dropping for a while and eventually she had to resort to less risky genres: educational books for which publishers did not pay much. In 1798 her expectations were raised when her influential patron George Brian, third Earl of Egremont, took over the trusteeship. But he too eventually failed her; exasperated at the entangled state of a trust mismanaged and fiercely litigated over for more than two decades, and weary of the obstinate determination with which Smith pursued her cause, he withdrew his support. Piqued at the confidence with which she gave him detailed injunctions as to how to proceed and questioned every decision taken by his steward,

---

[20]   Richard Polwhele, *The Unsex'd Females* (London, 1798). Polwhele lamented that "charming SMITH resign'd her power to please" and "suffer[ed] her mind to be infected with the Gallic mania." But Smith was spared the malignant abuse hurled at Mary Wollstonecraft, Mary Hays, and Helen Maria Williams, undoubtedly because her emphatic self-representation as a dedicated mother had ruled out suspicions of sexual licentiousness.

he left her innumerable letters, packed with business minutiae, unanswered. Worse still, he withheld the annual £70 interest payments on her marriage settlements—an income even the previous much-loathed trustees had usually granted her. By the beginning of 1803 Smith was destitute: she complained she could barely afford food and had no coals to heat her cottage, the cold severely affecting her joints. To settle her debts she sold her treasured collection of 500 books but still owed £20 for which she feared being sent to jail. Still the fabulously rich earl, who reportedly lived on £52,000 a year, refused to assist her. The arthritis had by then virtually immobilized her; jokingly she remarked to a friend that it was not

> likely I shall now ever be able to do more than vegetate for my few remaining years or months in this or some other solitude. It is literally vegetating, for I have very little locomotive powers beyond those that appertain to a cauliflower.[21]

During her last years Smith repeatedly voiced her wish to move to Lake Leman, the pastoral world of Jean-Jacques Rousseau's *Nouvelle Héloïse*, and wave goodbye to England, a country which, she observed, "has not protected my property by its boasted Laws, & where, if the Laws are not good, I know nothing that is."[22] On 23 February 1806 Benjamin Smith died in a debtors' prison and some money reverted to Charlotte. By then she was far too ill to execute her plan. On 28 October 1806 she died, only eight months after her husband, and seven years before Richard Smith's estate was finally settled.

Desmond: *letters to the Right Honourable Edmund Burke*

In 1791, four years after she had fled from her husband, Charlotte Smith began work on the epistolary novel *Desmond*, which was to become her most overtly polemical text. *Desmond* has to be read in dialogue with the "Revolution Controversy."[23] The core conservative text

---

[21] Charlotte Smith to Sarah Rose, 5 March 1804.
[22] Charlotte Smith to Joseph Cooper Walker, 25 March 1794.
[23] The term is used by Marilyn Butler in *Burke, Paine, Godwin, and the Revolution Controversy* (Cambridge: University Press, 1984).

in this pamphlet war of the 1790s was Edmund Burke's sentimental best-seller *Reflections on the Revolution in France* (1790), celebrating aristocratic ideals of benevolent paternalism, patrilineal succession, and chivalry. Scores of middle-class radicals responded with their visions of a society of greater economic and legal equality, based on civic freedom and individual merit. Smith, however, was the first to join in the intellectual discussion of the Revolution in France with a novel, and one of the first to extend the concept of social equality to gender issues.

Desmond is the only epistolary novel among the eleven Smith published, and although she had doubts whether she would succeed "so well in letters as in narrative" (45) she felt the form fundamental to the argument. Literary history traditionally classified epistolarity as an essentially feminine model. A woman's special talent was seen to reside in her natural ability to produce the ideal epistolary style—unpretentious, ingenuous, emotional, and spontaneous—a style praised in Alexander Pope's eroticised imagery as "so many things freely thrown out, ... thoughts just warm from the brain without any polishing or dress, the very *déshabille* of the understanding."[24] This fiction of the letter's artlessness dominated contemporary epistolary theory which subordinated the composed to the unplanned, the rational to the emotional. Men, according to these criteria, could learn to appropriate the idealized female voice by shedding their scholastic rhetoric (the opposite was, of course, deemed impracticable); the most famous eighteenth-century epistolary heroines Pamela, Clarissa, Fanny Hill, and the *Nouvelle Héloise* Julie were all products of this kind of authorial transvestism.

During the 1990s feminist critics have argued that this celebration of women's natural gift for epistolarity actually reduced female literary authority, keeping feminine expression within the confines of the domestic, the personal, and the romantic. However, it was not until Mary Favret's ground-breaking *The Romantic Correspondence*, drawing attention to the letter's potential for political agitation, that the accepted fiction of the letter's "feminine" origins as such was challenged.[25] Drawn to the epistolary genre and its legitimate "looseness" and "spon-

---

24 *The Correspondence of Alexander Pope*, edited by George Sherburn (Oxford: Clarendon Press, 1956), vol. i, 160.

25 Mary Favret, *Romantic Correspondence. Women, Politics and the Fiction of Letters* (Cambridge: University Press, 1992).

taneity," which made it an ideal medium for polemicists wishing to stage themselves as driven by sincere exasperation and absolute conviction, most of the contenders in the Revolution Controversy assumed the guise of the personal letter for their publications. Edmund Burke capitalized on the form of the letter in his *Reflections* and, though addressing a wide public, he maintained the pretence of an epistolary discourse, so apparently excusing the expression of personal sentiment and subjective opinion. In reality, of course, the *Reflections* is a carefully thought-out, structured, and sophisticated piece of propaganda, reworked over nearly a year to appear impulsive. The first to respond to Burke was Mary Wollstonecraft, whose *Vindication of the Rights of Men* (1790) likewise made use of the letter form. Written hurriedly, her rhetoric had the emotional immediacy distinguishing epistolary discourse and, compared to *Reflections,* was probably more genuinely so. Charlotte Smith, too, was acutely aware of the potential of the letter. At one point Wollstonecraft suggests she had been taken in by Burke's device when she grudgingly allowed him to be at heart a "good" man who had fallen victim to his own boundless vanity and irrational passions.[26] Smith, however, relentlessly exhibited Burke as a corrupt opportunist who coolly prostituted his rhetorical gift; she focused on the man, formerly a friend of the people, champion of American independence, and critic of royalty, who went on to publish an apologia "in favour of despotism" (182). Seeing through Burke's manipulative use of sentimental language, her hero Desmond reads *Reflections* as Burke's attempt to shroud his blatant sell-out of political principles with his carefully contrived emotiveness of epistolary discourse: "he advances opinions, and maintains principles absolutely opposite to all the professions of his political life," dressing up "contradictions with the gaudy flowers of his luxuriant imagination"(360).

Yet, as Desmond slyly observes, Burke's writing also provoked a storm of uninvited responses, calling forth in the defence of "truth and reason" all "the talents that are yet unbought (and which, I trust, are unpurchasable) in England" (183)—herself of course being one of them, Charlotte Smith implied. This, however, her enemies were quick to doubt, and soon after the publication of *Desmond* reports spread of

---

[26]   Mary Wollstonecraft, *Political Writings,* ed. by Janet Todd (Oxford: Oxford University Press, 1994), 5.

her being in the pay of the pro-revolutionary factions. Smith's friend William Cowper firmly refuted the allegations though he, feelingly sympathetic to her predicament, actually seemed to take less umbrage at the charge than at the fact that she *hadn't* been rewarded for a job this well done:

> There goes a rumour likewise which I have with equal confidence gainsaid, that Mrs. Smith wrote her Desmond bribed to it by the democratic party, by whom they say she is now actually supported. I could only reply to this, that I would to heaven, for her own sake and the sake of her many children, the assertion were founded; but there are certain circumstances in her case which are by no means symptoms of any such felicity.[27]

Desmond is closely linked to *Reflections* in several ways: the epistolary discourse of the former mimics and parodies the structural concept that underlies the latter. It is surely no coincidence that the names of Edmund Burke and that of his addressee De Pont are echoed in the correspondents Erasmus Bethel and Desmond. Furthermore, Burke's pattern of the experienced mentor admonishing a wayward student also informs the plot of *Desmond,* but to the contrary effect: in Smith's novel the disciple is given ample space to defend the revolutionary cause while a sermonizing Bethel has to grapple with the fact that his epistolary remonstrances and instructions have little impact on Desmond's actions. Turning the educational process on its head, Smith depicted aged experience succumbing to youthful change and made Bethel come round to Desmond's trust in the virtues of both Geraldine and the French Revolution.

Like Burke, Smith used epistolary discourse to suggest the letter's immediacy and authenticity, pitting fictive eyewitness accounts against unfavourable and fake representations: her heroine Geraldine Verney, after her passage to Dieppe, reports to her sister Fanny that "all religion is not abolished in France—they told me it was despised and trampled on; and I never enquired, as everybody ought to do, when such

---

[27] William Cowper to William Hayley, 21 May 1793, in *The Letters and Prose Writings of William Cowper*, ed. James King and Charles Ryskamp (Oxford: Clarendon Press, 1984), vol. iv, 341f.

assertions are made—Is all this true?" (325). The question of false and truthful representation is a key issue in *Desmond* which caricatures enemies to the Revolution in France as almost pathologically averse to historical truth. As in the world of state politics, where the Home Office spun its fledgling network of spies and agents, the fictional world of *Desmond* is infiltrated by a web of informants and gossipers whose national and personal "news" proves equally unfounded. Here, Jane Austen's "neighbourhood of spies" is busily at work: rumour spreads not only uncommonly fast but through obscure and unknown channels. Anti-Jacobins who "exaggerate with malicious delight, all the mischief they hear of, and represent the place ... as a scene of anarchy, famine, and bloodshed" (322) assiduously circulate with equal "malicious delight" reports of the heroine's adultery. Eventually, Smith suggested, just as the "truth" of Geraldine's virtue will triumph over scandalous gossip, the truth of her representation of the events in France will triumph over Burke's bloodcurdling *Reflections* and other manipulative fictions fabricated by hirelings in the pay of the conservative government. It is of course an irony of history that, with hindsight, even the most sanguinary representations of the early revolutionary events gave only a faint conception of the real horrors perpetrated by the Jacobin Committee of Public Safety.

Smith's political critique in *Desmond* has to be read as a pointed refutation of Burke's ideology as expressed in *Reflections*. One of his fundamental tenets was an unqualified veneration for the past, demanding deference to the English constitution on the grounds that it represented an accumulation of the wisdom of ancestral generations. Mary Wollstonecraft in her *Vindication of the Rights of Men* had discredited the wisdom of the ancestors Burke revered by drawing attention to the fact that they had lived in "dark" times dominated by "the grossest prejudices and most immoral superstitions." Smith in contrast pointed out the arbitrary nature of Burke's canon of venerable forefathers.[28] Countering the common assertion that the arguments brought forward in favour of the French Revolution were all "novelties," *Desmond* traces them back to the works of the English philosophers Milton and Locke, "great men, towards whom we have been taught to look with acquies-

---

[28] Wollstonecraft, *Political Writings*, 11.

cence and veneration (183). Burke, to lend tangible substance to his reverence for traditional structures, had frequently depicted monarchical constitutions as noble and venerable castles. Smith incorporated his architectural imagery into the ideological argument of *Desmond*: following Wollstonecraft's motto—"why [i]s it a duty to repair an ancient castle, built in barbarous ages, of Gothic materials?"—the reformist Montfleuri pulls down the "original structure" of his ancestral home, preserving nothing but what was "actually useful to himself" (112) as a symbolic act signalling his break with absolutist rule and aristocratic extravagance.[29] Thinking Burke's ideology of stasis through to its logical conclusion, Desmond predicts a gloomy future for the emblematic castle that is the British constitution:

> ...if every attempt to repair what time has injured, or amend what is acknowledged to be defective, is opposed as dangerous, and execrated as impious; let us go on till the building falls upon our heads, and let those who escape the ruins, continue to meditate on the prodigious advantage of this holy reverence, and to boast of the happiness of being Englishmen! (208f)

The electoral system, lauded in *Reflections* as "perfectly adequate," is condemned by Smith for functioning chiefly through electioneering bribes and resulting in oppressive taxation, sums the Crown raised to finance its parliamentary influence with the disposal of pensions.[30] Naturally Erasmus Bethel's confession of his own political corruption feeds back into Desmond's representation of Edmund Burke as the Tory party hack.[31] The satiric subplot depicting Sir Robert Stamford's meteoric rise from an unscrupulous country attorney to a corrupt but titled Member of Parliament is an additional wry comment on Burke's

---

[29] Wollstonecraft, *Political Writings*, 41.

[30] Edmund Burke, *Reflections on the Revolution in France*, ed. Conor Cruise O'Brien (London: Penguin Classics, 1986), 146.

[31] In the *Vindication of the Rights of Men* Wollstonecraft had touched upon another dark spot in Burke's political career when in November 1788 his eagerness to "taste the sweets of power" (26) had induced him, the avid defender of hereditary monarchy, to collect statistics from mental institutions on the unlikelihood of King George III's recovery from insanity and to plead impassionedly for his deposition — in favour of the Prince of Wales who had promised him the post of Paymaster-General. And

celebration of aristocratic lineage. In *Desmond* "showers of new coronets" fell "daily" on more or less deserving heads until nobility "mushroom[ed]" on rather dubious soil (61, 317). Apart from blasting Burke's nostalgic ideal of an ancient nobility, Smith, like Wollstonecraft, took exception to his notion of class-bound virtue. Countering Burke who thought the "bare idea of liberal descent inspires us with a sense of habitual native dignity," Wollstonecraft believed in the degenerating effects of rank and riches.[32] Smith, too, reasoned that prosperity contracted feelings of empathy. "How few do we meet with," Desmond ponders, "who can feel for miseries they cannot imagine, and are sure they can never experience?" (208). A sardonic portrait of the English nobleman in Lord Newminster as a selfish, dissipated, ignorant moron, naturally violently opposed to the egalitarian reforms in France, underpins Smith's argument.

Smith exposed the degeneracy of the nobility but she equally censured avaricious, middle-class *nouveaux riches* for their espousal of a capitalist culture rooted in economic inequality. After years on the receiving end, Smith had come to hate the alliance of money and power that left the disenfranchised out in the cold. It was this critique of property that pitted Smith against Burke. His harangue against the National Assembly had specifically singled out for attack the *Tiers État* whose members were largely professionals of the lower bourgeoisie. Burke had claimed that men who possessed no wealth of their own would naturally have only one thing on their mind: "lust of plunder."[33] Smith in turn made the point that this insatiable "lust of plunder" was in fact an earmark of the propertied classes: where Burke had sent his revolutionary professionals on a rampage through aristocratic and Church properties, Smith depicted respectable members of the ruling class putting entire estates in the service of lavish self-indulgence, their exploitative hedonism echoing the parasitic irresponsibility of *ancien régime* feudal *seigneurs*. Property and "liberal descent," far from breeding benevolent rule, originated and resulted in social oppression, Smith argued.

---

intriguingly in 1794, only two years after the publication of *Desmond*, when Burke was heavily in debt, he accepted an annual pension of £2,500 from Pitt for thirty years' service to the country.

[32] Burke, *Reflections*, 121.

[33] Burke, *Reflections*, 135.

Burke's *Reflections*, however, is not the only political publication to which *Desmond* is intertextually linked; Nicola Watson first noted that the documentary effects of the epistolary mode in *Desmond* seemed designed "to replicate the impact of Williams's *Letters from France*."[34] On her return to England in late 1790, Helen Maria Williams, the celebrated sentimental poet and fashionable salonière, had published her *Letters Written from France in the Summer of 1790*, an emotive chronicle of the revolutionary spectacles she had witnessed. Williams herself advertised her spontaneous eyewitness accounts as a counter to the distorted reports circulated by French emigrant aristocrats that described "every street ... blackened with a gallows, and every highway deluged with blood."[35] And indeed, the British public eagerly read Williams's *Letters* as a source of information on the current state of French affairs. Smith, too, was keen to get hold of them soon after their publication and, considering their popularity, it is not implausible she attempted to capitalize on their fiction of fact, immediacy, and authenticity. [36] Particularly so as it seems doubtful—despite her contrary claim in the preface—that she spent any time in France after the winter of 1785, when she and her husband fled his creditors to a derelict chateau in an isolated region of Normandy.

There are striking thematic parallels between Williams's *Letters* and Smith's *Desmond*. Like Williams who opened her chronicle with a rush of enthusiasm, Smith has her epistolary hero arrive just in time for the Paris celebrations of the *Fête de la Fédération*. He too is overwhelmed by the festive gaiety spread throughout the city. In this first letter from Paris Desmond aims to animate his correspondent Bethel

---

34 Nicola Watson, *Revolution and the Form of the British Novel 1780–1825. Intercepted Letters, Interrupted Seductions* (Oxford: Oxford University Press, 1994), 36.

35 Helen Maria Williams, *Letters from France* (New York: Scholars' Facsimiles and Reprints, 1975), volume i, 217.

36 In a letter to her publisher Smith asked him to send her copies of Williams's *Letters from France* and her novel *Julia* as soon as they were out (Charlotte Smith to William Davies, 19 February 1790). It is unclear how well acquainted the two authors were; Smith gave William Wordsworth a letter of introduction to Helen Maria Williams but there is no proof of any further correspondence between the two women. That, in any case, *Desmond* was targeted at a similar audience as Williams's *Letters* is corroborated by the fact that their publishers G.G. and J. Robinson placed an advertisement of Williams's second volume of *Letters* into the second edition of Smith's *Desmond*.

with sympathetic feeling, translating the tremendous political upheavals that had revolutionized the French constitution into a melodramatic narrative of hit-and-run casualties. Reporting that now the "utmost care" was taken of the common people, he recalls the frequent incidents when "proud and unfeeling possessors" of "those splendid equipages" felt "their rapid wheels crushing a fellow creature, with emotions so far from those of humanity, as to have said, '*tant mieux, il y a toujours assez de ces gueux*'" (88). Williams had made a similar episode symbolize aristocratic oppression: Madame Pompadour's coach once ran over an old woman, prompting the mistress of Louis XV to fling "a louis d'or out of the window" and say "with the utmost sang-froid, '*voilà de quoi la faire enterrer; allez, cocher.*'" "Is it possible," Williams exclaimed, "to hear this incident without rejoicing, that a system of government which led to such depravation of mind is laid in ruins?"[37]

Though *Desmond* and *Letters from France* have much in common thematically, methodically Smith's concept represents an exact inversion: where Williams had imported the feminized "discourse of the sentimental novel into what is avowedly a politico-historical document," Smith inset the Revolution Controversy into the plot of sensibility.[38] *Desmond* was already firmly grounded in the sentimental tradition. The literary predecessors of Smith's protagonists were the heroes of three eponymous works of epistolary fiction, Frances Sheridan's *The Memoirs of Sidney Bidulph* (1761), Jean-Jacques Rousseau's *Julie, ou La Nouvelle Héloïse* (1761), and Johann Wolfgang von Goethe's novel *The Sorrows of Young Werther* (1774). In many ways *Desmond* is a happier retelling of all three novels. Geraldine, for example, may remark wistfully, "I have *no Faulkland*!" (334), yet readers, having the advantage in accessing Desmond's sentiments, know her Faulkland is already

---

37   *Letters from France*, volume ii, 52. Charles Dickens, too, in *A Tale of Two Cities* (1859), had used a melodramatic account of a child run over by an aristocrat's carriage to condemn the *ancien régime*: the Marquis' carriage "dashed through streets and swept round corners, with women screaming before it, and men clutching each other and clutching children out of its way." When a little child is run over and killed, Monseigneur tosses the child's distraught father a gold coin and remarks indifferently: "It is extraordinary to me, ... that you people cannot take care of yourselves and your children. One or the other of you is for ever in the way. How do I know what injury you have done my horses?" (ch. vii, "Monseigneur in Town")

38   Watson, *Revolution and the British Novel*, 31.

waiting in the wings. Not only does Desmond love her with the arduous devotion of Sheridan's feeling hero but, like Faulkland, he too has fallen victim to his susceptibilities and another woman. But Geraldine has learnt her lesson from "poor" (334) Sidney's lot and marries her lover in spite of his liaison with Josephine de Boisbelle.[39] Bethel compares his ward to Werther (299), and Desmond indeed shares the throbbing sensitivities, despondent world-weariness, and dark melancholy of Goethe's legendary hero—albeit he is spared his paradigm's suicidal end. Desmond himself prefers to see himself in the literary context of Rousseau's heady love scenes among the rustic mountain idylls of Switzerland: his tour of the Pays de Vaud was surely not an effective panacea to cure him of his passion, and probably not meant as such. Smith's romantic plot, centring on the hero's unconsummated love for the married Geraldine and his behind-the-scene affair with her French *Doppelgänger* Josephine, adapted, with a slight change to the cast of the love-triangle, Rousseau's notorious best-seller in which the heroine Julie bedded the hero and married another. *Desmond* even replicated Rousseau's scandalous construction of desiring yet virtuous femininity—though Smith chose an opportune doubling of Geraldine to allow for the impeccably chaste ending whilst providing a marginal space to dramatize female sexual expression.

Operating from within the romance tradition, Smith strove to brace her fictional narrative with factual information and historical realism. Accordingly, obvious sentimental material is often neglected in favour of political disquisition. This is the case with the pitiful tale of Montfleuri's two sisters who, not pretty enough to make profitable barters in the marriage market, were immured in convents to save family expenses. Their story was relegated to the text's periphery, while Smith chose to focus on the National Assembly's ecclesiastic reforms of Catholic institutions. So, too, the life story of the Breton vassal Merville. This account, Smith claimed, was a "free translation" (151) of a French pamphlet—but since no such pamphlet seems to have existed, this could well have been another ruse to lend greater historical realism to her narrative, the tone of which is largely informative, in spite of the sentimental potential of Merville's miseries.[40]

---

[39] For further textual parallels see vol. iii, note 32.

[40] Many of the details in Smith's description of the conditions in English county jails

Moreover, Smith ensured that the romance plot of *Desmond* embodied a political argument in its own right. Like Williams, who had always insisted that her love of the French Revolution was the natural result of her feminine sensibility, Smith similarly tried to make her literary venture into the public domain of international politics palatable to conservative critics by grounding her interest in unobjectionable domestic affections. "Women it is said have no business with politics"; but "why not?" she counters, "have they no interest in the scenes that are acting around them, in which they have fathers, brothers, husbands, sons, or friends engaged?" (45). Smith's incorporation of the public within the private was particularly intriguing in its anticipation of the narrative mechanism propelling *Desmond*: after all it is the tyranny that Geraldine Verney experiences at home that directs her thoughts towards the social and legal injustices perpetrated in the public sphere, just as her story necessitates readers outraged by the fictional sufferings of the ill-used wife to extend their emotional sympathies to the political arena and the very real miseries of the socially oppressed.

At first the character of Geraldine, the epitome of suffering duty so popular with eighteenth-century sentimental fiction, might seem curiously at odds with the radical agenda of *Desmond*. However, Smith's use of her heroine is clearly subversive of those ideals of femininity conventionally invested in the archetypal virtue in distress. Eleanor Ty notes that, undercutting the lessons of conservative polemicists such as Hannah More and Jane West, Smith demonstrates that female meekness led only to "further exploitation," rather than "to reform in the male figure of authority."[41] But Geraldine is more than a parodic exaggeration of the orthodox Griselda figure, she is also one of Smith's studied—and definitely not parodic—attempts at literary self-presentation and self-exoneration. Gauging from her biography and her letters Smith rarely evinced that meek docility with which her heroine submitted to her husband's unreasonable commands. But through Geraldine Verney she conveys an exalted picture of herself as the

---

and the oppressive economics of *ancien régime* feudalism are reminiscent of John Howard's *The State of the Prisons* (1777–84) and Arthur Young's *Travels in France* (1792).

[41] Eleanor Ty, *Unsex'd Revolutionaries. Five Women Novelists of the 1790s* (Toronto: University of Toronto Press, 1993), 139.

virtuous, dutiful wife to an undeserving dissolute husband. The function of Geraldine is analogous to that of the eulogized Mrs. Stafford in *Emmeline*, the first novel Smith published after separating from her husband. At the time the correspondence between Mrs. C. Stafford and Mrs. C. Smith was deemed too obtrusive by some, a criticism Smith heeded, for in *Desmond* the autobiographical clue is not as overt but certainly as unmistakable: Geraldine's children George, Harriet, and William share their Christian names with Smith's eldest surviving son, her youngest daughter, and son.

Smith's handling of the heroine is extraordinarily shrewd; as Chris Jones succinctly put it, Geraldine is her "Trojan horse."[42] Having drawn her as a paragon of female virtues, Smith subsequently makes her violate laws of feminine propriety almost effortlessly: like the heroine in *Emmeline*, Geraldine assists in the secret lying-in of the "fallen woman" Josephine, and even takes care of the baby girl. She also comments freely on the political situation in France; through her Smith conveys a favourable reading of the Paris fishwomen's march to Versailles, the incident that had composed the gruesome centrepiece to Burke's *Reflections*, and which even Wollstonecraft later condemned.[43] Travelling past a fertile Normandy landscape, Geraldine declares that the 1789/ 90 food shortage in the capital had been a royalist conspiracy to starve the people into submission. She justifies the violence erupting from this economic need:

> While humanity drops her tears at the sad stories of those individuals who fell the victims of popular tumult so naturally excited, pity cannot throw over these transactions a veil thick enough to conceal the tremendous decree of justice, which, like "the hand writing upon the wall," will be seen in colours of blood, and however regretted, must still be acknowledged as the hand of justice. (326)

---

[42] Chris Jones, *Radical Sensibility. Literature and Ideas in the 1790s* (London: Routledge, 1993), 163.

[43] Wollstonecraft, *A Historical and Moral View of the Origin and Progress of the French Revolution* (1794) in *Political Writings*, 343.

This is an uncommonly radical statement. Smith's liberal contemporaries generally offered psychological explanations for mob violence, excusing it by citing the oppression suffered. Arthur Young in his *Travels in France* (1792), for example, had argued that "when such evils happen, they surely are more imputable to the tyranny of the master, than to the cruelty of the servant."[44] But Smith goes much further by characterizing the murders committed as being justified.

Yet in stark contrast to her budding radical sympathies, Geraldine continues to comply with conduct-book constructions of the dutiful wife; eventually, however, for objectives so baneful they impugn the very ideology of propriety she seems to embody. When her husband is wounded and sends for her, she promptly sets out on a perilous journey through provinces racked by counterrevolutionary rebellions. This act of bravery, however, is not inspired by her solicitude for him. As Diana Bowstead pointed out, the "emotional impetus" driving Geraldine is "suicidal despair."[45] Geraldine candidly voiced her death-wish in the mournful "Ode to the Poppy." This poem, in its melancholic world-weariness akin to the mood of Smith's own *Elegiac Sonnets*, praises opium's "potent charm":[46]

> Might sorrow's pallid votary dare,
> *Without a crime, that remedy implore,*
> Which bids the spirit from its bondage fly,
> I'd court thy palliative aid no more...
>
> (340, my emphasis)

Although Enlightenment thinkers like David Hume and William Godwin supported the right of an individual who found life unbearable to end it, suicide in England was still judged a sin and a crime. That Geraldine should meet with her death in the observance of her wifely duties was, on the one hand, an astute comment on the destructive effects of society's exacting conceptions of feminine self-effacement. On the other, her journey gained a truly subversive

---

[44] Arthur Young, *Travels in France during the Years 1787, 1788, 1789* (London, 1890), 322.

[45] Diana Bowstead, "Charlotte Smith's *Desmond*. The Epistolary Novel as Ideological Argument," *Fetter'd or Free? British Women Novelists 1670–1815*, ed. M. Schofield and C. Macheski (Athens, Ohio: Ohio State University Press, 1986), 260.

[46] In fact the ode was written by Smith's close friend Henrietta O'Neill.

dimension bearing in mind that she uses the mask of the exemplary wife to commit "without a crime" an act that was damned as anti-Christian, an act that remains essentially anti-social and individualistic. This indeed makes Geraldine Verney a veritable "Trojan horse" to the conservative camp.

The story of Geraldine's marriage is a frank indictment of patriarchal ideology epitomized in Burke's ideal of benevolent domination. Envisioning the events of 1789 as a sentimental family drama, *Reflections* presented the French Revolution as a child's unnatural rebellion against an affectionate father's lenient rule. In *Desmond* Smith took up the parallel, analogously linking the head of the state and the head of the household, but then featured the oppression resulting from abusive and inadequate male authority, familial and public. The domestic tyranny Geraldine suffered is explicitly equated with the political tyranny undergone by the French people under the *ancien régime* (303), a link that is reinforced with Verney's enlistment in the counterrevolutionary armies. The political discourse of *Desmond* is skilfully interwoven with depictions of Geraldine's deplorable situation; hence John Locke's quoted dialectic on a people's right to overthrow a government failing to secure the welfare of its subjects serves as a legitimization of matrimonial rebellion, both Geraldine's potential and Smith's own accomplished revolt. Domestic and state politics coupled, Smith demands, in a manner both subtle and unequivocal, the liberation of women.

Like Wollstonecraft, whose *Rights of Woman* was published the same year, Smith employed a discourse of colonial slavery to condemn women's legal, economic, and sexual subjugation. On her way to Paris, where she is to meet the Duc de Romagnecourt to whom Verney has sold her, Geraldine equates her husband's power over her body with that of a plantocrat's over his slave: to her sister she admitted to feeling such a (sexual?) dread of her husband that there was "no humiliation" to which she had "not rather submit" than that of considering herself "as his slave" (316). The sexual abuse routinely inflicted on female slaves by white colonialists must have been a well-known and disturbing fact to Smith's audience, not least since the publication of Olaudoh Equiano's autobiographical slave-narrative.[47] Against this awareness of the sexual vul-

---

[47]   *The Interesting Narrative of the Life of Olaudoh Equiano* (1789).

nerability and commodification of the female body, the drama of Geraldine's marriage unfolds. In recurrent episodes debating female education, the economics of the marriage market, and suits for criminal conversation (damage payments for husbands of adulterous wives), *Desmond* foregrounds the multifarious social and legal customs objectifying women. Thus Verney's conduct no longer appears an isolated instance of matrimonial tyranny but rather the tip of an iceberg, the symptomatic manifestation of the *feme covert* concept that had pervaded the whole consciousness of eighteenth-century British culture.

By the time *Desmond* was published, even the French Revolution had done little to establish women's equality. Changes in the legislation allow the reformist Montfleuri to release his two sisters from their cloistral "entombment," but to "break the cruel bonds" which enslave Josephine to "one of the most worthless characters in France" (92) proves far more problematic. For Geraldine Verney, her mirror-image Josephine de Boisbelle, and their creator Charlotte Smith, liberty would primarily have meant the personal liberty to divorce. In France, the Legislative Assembly's pioneering decree of 20 September 1792 instituted reforms which made divorce readily available to women. But this brief spell of women's equality lasted only until 1804 when the new *Code Napoléon* did everything to reconsecrate patriarchal powers. In England, women's right to divorce was not legislated until a century later.

The eighteenth-century culture of sensibility had given rise to a host of humanitarian campaigns. Penning sentimental verse in support of the abolitionist cause was widely deemed a respectable occupation for the liberals of Smith's time—Helen Maria Williams was celebrated for her poems in support of conquered Indians and slaves—but Smith reminded her contemporaries that they need not look as far as the West Indies to find food for their philanthropic zeal. Exploring the sexual politics of her society, Charlotte Smith condemned a patriarchal system that reduced women's bodies to purchasable commodities. She challenged her readers to question the moral authority of an establishment that prided itself on a liberal democratic parliament but relegated its entire female population to a position of social, economic, and sexual subjugation, little better than that of colonial slaves.

Charlotte Smith: A Brief Chronology

1749 *May 4*   Charlotte Turner born

1752   Charlotte's mother Anna Towers dies; her father Nicholas Turner travels to the continent leaving his three children in the care of his sister-in-law Lucy Towers

1764 *Aug. 30*   Charlotte's father marries the wealthy Miss Meriton

1765 *Feb. 23*   Charlotte marries Benjamin Smith

1766   First of twelve children is born

1767   Richard Smith, Charlotte's father-in-law, marries her aunt Lucy Towers

1776 *Oct. 13*   Richard Smith dies, leaving estate worth about £36 000

1783 *Dec.*   Benjamin Smith in debtors' prison for seven months; Charlotte Smith accompanies him

1784   *Elegiac Sonnets and Other Essays* published

    Winter   Charlotte and Benjamin Smith flee to Normandy to escape their creditors

1785 *Spring*   Charlotte Smith and her family return to England

1786   *Manon Lescaut* appears

1787   *The Romance of Real Life* appears

    Apr. 15   Charlotte Smith leaves her husband and moves to a cottage near Wyhe

1788   *Emmeline, or The Orphan of the Castle* published

1789   *Ethelinde, or The Recluse of the Lake* published

1791   *Celestina* published

1792   *Desmond* published

    Aug.   Charlotte Smith spends two months at William Hayley's villa in Eartham; in the company of William Cowper and George Romney she writes the first volume of *The Old Manor House*

1793   *The Old Manor House* and *The Emigrants* published

    July   Daughter Anna Augusta marries de Foville, a French emigrant

    Sep. 6   Son Charles is wounded and loses his leg in the siege of Dunkirk

    Sep. 10   Charlotte Smith's friend Henrietta O'Neill dies

1794		*The Wanderings of Warwick* and *The Banished Man* published
1795		*Rural Walks: in dialogues: intended for the use of young persons* and *Montalbert* published
	Apr. 23	Anna Augusta dies
1796		*A Narrative for the Loss of the Catharine, Venus and Piedmont transports, Rambles Farther. A continuation of Rural Walks,* and *Marchmont* published
1797		*Elegiac Sonnets,* vol. II, published
1798		*The Young Philosopher* and *Minor Morals, interspersed with sketches of natural history, historical anecdotes, and original stories* published
		Charlotte Smith's patron, Lord Egremont, takes over trusteeship of Richard Smith's estate
1799		*What is She?* premiered
1800–1802		*The Letters of a Solitary Wanderer: containing narratives of various description* published
1801		Son Charles dies of malaria while settling trust business on Barbados
		Daughter Lucy's husband dies penniless, leaving Smith responsible for the support of Lucy and her three young children
1803		Charlotte Smith destitute
1804		*Conversations Introducing Poetry: chiefly on subjects of natural history. For the use of children and young persons* published
1806		*History of England, from the earliest records, to the Peace of Amiens, in a series of letters to a young lady at school* published
	Feb. 23	Benjamin Smith dies in a debtors' prison
	Oct. 28	Charlotte Smith dies and is buried at Stoke Church near Guildford
1807		*The Natural History of Birds, intended chiefly for young persons* and *Beachy Head: with other poems* published posthumously
1813 *Apr. 22*		Richard Smith's estate is finally settled

Works by Charlotte Smith

1784	*Elegiac Sonnets and Other Essays*
1786	*Manon Lescaut* (translation from the French, withdrawn by publisher after accusations of literary plagiarism)
1787	*The Romance of Real Life* (translation from the French)
1788	*Emmeline, or The Orphan of the Castle*
1789	*Ethelinde, or The Recluse of the Lake*
1791	*Celestina*
1792	*Desmond*
1793	*The Old Manor House* and *The Emigrants, a poem, in two books*
1794	*The Wanderings of Warwick* and *The Banished Man*
1795	*Rural Walks: in dialogues: intended for the use of young persons* and *Montalbert*
1796	*A Narrative for the Loss of the Catharine, Venus and Piedmont transports, Rambles Farther. A continuation of Rural Walks,* and *Marchmont*
1797	*Elegiac Sonnets,* vol. II (subscription edition)
1798	*The Young Philosopher* and *Minor Morals, interspersed with sketches of natural history, historical anecdotes, and original stories*
1799	*What is She? A comedy in five acts* (attr. to Smith)
1800–1802	*The Letters of a Solitary Wanderer: containing narratives of various description*
1804	*Conversations Introducing Poetry: chiefly on subjects of natural history. For the use of children and young persons*
1806	*History of England, from the earliest records, to the Peace of Amiens, in a series of letters to a young lady at school*
1807	*The Natural History of Birds, intended chiefly for young persons* and *Beachy Head: with other poems*

Further Reading

Bartolomeo, Joseph. 'Subversion of Romance in *The Old Manor House.*' *Studies in English Literature, 1500–1900* 33.3 (1993): 645–57.

———. 'Charlotte to Charles: *The Old Manor House* as a Source for *Great Expectations.*' *Dickens Quarterly* 8.3 (1991): 112–20.

Bowstead, Diana. 'Charlotte Smith's *Desmond*: The Epistolary Novel as Ideological Argument.' *Fetter'd or Free? British Women Novelists, 1670–1815.* Ed. M.A. Schofield & C. Macheski. Athens, Ohio: Ohio University Press, 1986. 237–63.

Bray, Mathew. 'Removing the Anglo-Saxon Yoke: The Francocentric Vision of Charlotte Smith's Later Works.' *The Wordsworth Circle* 24.3 (1993): 155–8.

Brooks, Stella. 'The Sonnets of Charlotte Smith.' *Critical Survey* 4.1 (1992): 9–21.

Conway, Alison. 'Nationalism, Revolution, and the Female Body: Charlotte Smith's *Desmond.*' *Women's Studies* 24.5 (1995): 395–409.

Curran, Stuart. 'Romantic Poetry: The I Altered.' *Romanticism and Feminism.* Ed. Anne K. Mellor. Bloomington: Indiana University Press, 1988. 185–207.

Doody, Margaret. 'English Women Novelists and the French Revolution.' *La Femme en Angleterre et dans les Colonies Americaines aux XVIIe et XVIIIe siècles.* Société d'études anglo-américaines des XVIIe et XVIIIe siècles. Lille: Pub. de l'Univ. de Lille III, 1976. 176–98.

Elliott, Pat. 'Charlotte Smith's Feminism: A Study of *Emmeline* and *Desmond.*' *Living by the Pen: Early British Women Writers.* Ed. Dale Spender. New York: Teachers College Press, 1992. 91–112.

Flanders, W. Austin. 'An Example of the Impact of the French Revolution on the English Novel: Charlotte Smith's *Desmond.*' *The Western Pennsylvania Symposium on World Literatures, Selected Proceedings: 1974–1991.* Ed. Carla E. Lucente. Greensburg: Eadmer, 1992. 145–50.

Fletcher, Loraine. *Charlotte Smith: A Critical Biography.* London: Macmillan, 1998.

Foster, James R. 'Charlotte Smith, Pre-Romantic Novelist.' *PMLA* 43 (1928): 463–75.

Hilbish, Florence M. *Charlotte Smith, Poet and Novelist (1749–1806).* Philadelphia: University of Pennsylvania Press, 1941.

Hoeveler, Diane Long. *Gothic Feminism: The Professionalization of*

Gender from Charlotte Smith to the Brontës. Liverpool: Liverpool University Press, 1998.

Hunt, Bishop C., Jr. 'Wordsworth and Charlotte Smith.' *The Wordsworth Circle* 1 (1970): 85–103.

Jones, Chris. *Radical Sensibility: Literature and Ideas in the 1790s*. London: Routledge, 1993.

Kennedy, Deborah. 'Thorns and Roses: The Sonnets of Charlotte Smith.' *Women's Writing* 2.1 (1995): 43–53.

Labbe, Jacqueline M. 'Selling One's Sorrows: Charlotte Smith, Mary Robinson, and the Marketing of Poetry.' *The Wordsworth Circle* 25.2 (1994): 68 –71.

McKillop, Alan Dugald. 'Charlotte Smith's Letters.' *The Huntington Library Chronicle* 15 (1952): 237–55.

Mei, Huang. *Transforming the Cinderella Dream: From Frances Burney to Charlotte Brontë*. New Brunswick: Rutgers University Press, 1990.

Rogers, Katherine. 'Inhibitions on Eighteenth-Century Novelists: Elizabeth Inchbald and Charlotte Smith.' *Eighteenth-Century Studies* 11.1 (1977): 63–78.

Schofield, Mary Anne. '"The Witchery of Fiction": Charlotte Smith, Novelist.' *Living by the Pen: Early British Women Writers*. Ed. Dale Spender. New York: Teachers College Press, 1992. 177–87.

——. *Masking and Unmasking the Female Mind: Disguising Romances in Feminine Fiction, 1713–99*. Newark: University of Delaware Press, 1990.

Scott, Walter. *The Lives of the Novelists*. London: Dent, 1910.

Spender, Dale. *Mothers of the Novel: 100 Good Writers before Jane Austen*. London: Pandora, 1986.

Stanton, Judith Phillips. 'Charlotte Smith's "Literary Business": Income, Patronage, and Indigence.' *The Age of Johnson* 1 (1987): 375–401.

Ty, Eleanor. *Unsex'd Revolutionaries: Five Women Novelists of the 1790s*. Toronto: University of Toronto Press, 1993.

Wilson, C.S. and J. Haefner, eds. *Re-Visioning Romanticism: British Women Writers 1776–1837*. Philadelphia: University of Pennsylvania Press, 1994.

Wright, Walter Francis. *Sensibility in English Prose Fiction 1760–1814: A Reinterpretation*. Urbana: University of Illinois Press, 1937.

Zimmerman, Sarah. 'Charlotte Smith's Letters and the Practice of Self-Representation.' *Princeton University Library Chronicle* 53.1 (1991): 50–77.

Note on the Text

The first edition of *Desmond* was published in three volumes by G. G. J. and J. Robinson in 1792. In the same year there swiftly followed a second edition and a Dublin edition. A French translation *Desmond, ou l'Amant philanthrope* was published in four volumes in 1793. The copy-text for this edition is the second edition published by Robinson with the corrections by Charlotte Smith. The editors have retained Smith's punctuation but regularized it silently where it confounded meaning. All other grammatical corrections have been recorded in the endnotes. The footnotes included in the text are Charlotte Smith's.

DESMOND

Charlotte Smith

DESMOND.

A

NOVEL,

IN THREE VOLUMES,

BY

CHARLOTTE SMITH.

SECOND EDITION.

VOLUME I.

LONDON:
PRINTED FOR G. G. J. AND J. ROBINSON,
PATER-NOSTER-ROW, 1792.

Preface

In sending into the world a work so unlike those of my former writings, which have been honoured by its approbation, I feel some degree of that apprehension which an Author is sensible of on a first publication.

This arises partly from my doubts of succeeding so well in letters as in narrative; and partly from a supposition, that there are Readers, to whom the fictitious occurrences, and others to whom the political remarks in these volumes may be displeasing.

To the first I beg leave to suggest, that in representing a young man, nourishing an ardent but concealed passion for a married woman; I certainly do not mean to encourage or justify such attachments; but no delineation of character appears to me more interesting, than that of a man capable of such a passion so generous and disinterested as to seek only the good of its object; nor any story more moral, than one that represents the existence of an affection so regulated.

As to the political passages dispersed through the work, they are for the most part, drawn from conversations to which I have been a witness, in England, and France, during the last twelve months.[1] In carrying on my story in those countries, and at a period when their political situation (but particularly that of the latter) is the general topic of discourse in both; I have given to my imaginary characters the arguments I have heard on both sides; and if those in favour of one party have evidently the advantage, it is not owing to my partial representation but to the predominant power of truth and reason, which can neither be altered nor concealed.

But women it is said have no business with politics. — Why not? — Have they no interest in the scenes that are acting around them, in which they have fathers, brothers, husbands, sons, or friends engaged! — Even in the commonest course of female education, they are expected to acquire some knowledge of history; and yet, if they are to have no opinion of what *is* passing, it avails little that they should be informed of what *has passed*, in a world where they are subject to such mental degradation; where they are censured as affecting masculine knowledge if they happen to have any understanding; or despised as insignificant triflers if they have none.

Knowledge, which qualifies women to speak or to write on any other than the most common and trivial subjects, is supposed to be of so difficult attainment, that it cannot be acquired but by the sacrifice of domestic virtues, or the neglect of domestic duties. — *I* however, may safely say, that it was in the *observance*, not in the *breach* of duty, *I* became an Author;[2] and it has happened, that the circumstances which have compelled me to write, have introduced me to those scenes of life, and those varieties of character which I should otherwise never have seen: Tho' alas! it is from thence, that I am too well enabled to describe from *immediate* observation,

> 'The proud man's contumely, th' oppressors wrong;
> The laws delay, the insolence of office.'[3]

But, while in consequence of the affairs of my family being most unhappily in the power of men who *seem to exercise all these with impunity*, I am become an *Author by profession*, and feel every year more acutely, '*that hope delayed maketh the heart sick*,' I am sensible also (to use another quotation) that

> —————————'Adversity——
> Tho' like a toad ugly and venomous,[4]
> Wears yet a precious jewel in its head.'

For it is to my involuntary appearance in that character, that I am indebted, for all that makes my continuance in the world desirable; all that softens the rigour of my destiny and enables me to sustain it: I mean friends among those, who, while their talents are the boast of their country, are yet more respectable for the goodness and integrity of their hearts.[5]

Among these I include a female friend, to whom I owe the beautiful little Ode in the last volume; who having written it for this work, allows me thus publicly to boast of a friendship, which is the pride and pleasure of my life.[6]

If I may be indulged a moment longer in my egotism, it shall be only while I apologize for the typographical errors of the work, which may have been in some measure occasioned by the detached and hurried way, in which the sheets were sometimes sent to the press when I was at a distance from it; and when my attention was distracted by the troubles, which it seems to be the peculiar delight of the persons who are concerned in the management of my children's affairs, to inflict upon me. With all this the Public have nothing to do: but were it proper to relate all the disadvantages from anxiety of mind and local circumstances, under which these volumes have been composed, such a detail might be admitted as an excuse for more material errors.

For that asperity of remark, which will arise on the part of those whose political tenets I may offend, I am prepared. Those who object to the matter, will probably arraign the manner, and exclaim against the impropriety of making a book of entertainment the vehicle of political discussion. I am however conscious that in making these slight sketches, of manners and opinions, as they fluctuated around me; I have not sacrificed truth to any party — Nothing appears to me more respectable than national pride; nothing so absurd as national prejudice. — And in the faithful representation of the manners of other countries, surely Englishmen many find abundant reason to indulge the one, while they conquer the other. To those however who still cherish the idea of our having a *natural* enemy in the French nation; and that they are still more *naturally* our foes, because they have dared to be freemen, I can only say, that against the phalanx of prejudice kept in constant pay, and under strict discipline by interest, the slight skirmishing of a novel writer can have no effect: we see it remains hitherto unbroken against the powerful efforts of learning and genius — though united in that cause which *must* finally triumph — the cause of truth, reason, and humanity.

CHARLOTTE SMITH.

London,
June 20, 1792.

DESMOND

LETTER I

TO MR BETHEL

June 9, 1790

Your arguments, my friend, were decisive; and since I am now on my way — I hardly know whither, you will be convinced that I attended to them, and have determined to relinquish the dangerous indulgence of contemplating the perfections of an object that can never be mine. Yes! — I have torn myself from her; and, without betraying any part of the anguish and regret I felt, I calmly took my leave! — It was five days ago, the morning after she had undergone the fatiguing ceremony of appearing, for the first time since her marriage, at court on the birth-night.[7] —

I had heard how universally she had been admired, but she seemed to have received no pleasure from that admiration — and I felt involuntarily pleased that she had not. — Her husband — I hate the name — Verney, had already escaped from the confinement, which this ceremony of their appearances had for a day or two imposed upon him, and was gone to I know not what races. She named the place faintly and reluctantly when I asked after him; and I did not repeat the question. There was, however, another question which I could not help asking myself; does this man deserve the lovely Geraldine? — Alas! — I know he does not; cannot: the sport of every wild propensity or rather of every prevailing fashion, (for it is to that he sacrifices rather than to his own inclinations) I have too much reason to believe he will dissipate his fortune, and render his wife miserable. — But is it possible she can love him? — Oh, no! it is surely not possible — When through the mild grace and sometimes tenderness of her manner, I remark the strength and clearness of her understanding; when I observe, how immediately she sees the ridiculous, and how quickly her ingenious and liberal mind shrinks from vice and folly — I believe it impossible that the hour can be far distant, if indeed it is not already arrived, when the flowers, with which the mercenary hands of her family, dressed the chains they imposed upon her, will be totally faded; and when, whatever affection she now feels for him, if any does exist, will be destroyed by the conviction of Verney's unworthiness — Ah! where will then an heart, like hers, find refuge against the horrors of such a destiny — Would to heaven I had become acquainted with her before that destiny was irrevocable — or that I had never known her at all.

When I was admitted to her dressing-room the last time I saw her — she was reading; and laid down her book on my entrance — I was ill, or had appeared so to her, when I had seen her a few days before — She seemed now to recollect it with tender interest — and when, in answering her inquiries, I told her I intended going abroad for some months, I should have thought — had I dared to indulge the flattery of fancy — that she heard it with concern: 'we shall not then see you this year in Kent,' said she, 'I am very sorry for it': — she paused a moment, and added, with one of those smiles which give such peculiar charms to her countenance, 'but I hope you will regain your health and spirits — and I think we shall certainly have you among us again in the shooting season.' — I know not what was the matter with me, but I could not answer her; and the conversation for some moments dropped.

She resumed it after a another short silence, and asked me when I had seen her brother? — 'He talks,' said she, 'of going to the continent also this summer, and I wish you may meet him there — your acquaintance could not fail of being advantageous in any country, but particularly a foreign country, to a young man so new to the world as he is; and one, so unsettled in all his plans, from temper and habit, that I am ever in pain least he should fall into those errors, which I every day see so fatal to those who enter into the world unexperienced like him — without a guide. — Should you happen to meet with him abroad, I am sure you have friendship enough for us all, to direct him.' —

I seized with avidity an opportunity of being serviceable to any one who belongs to her — I had not seen Waverly for some time, and I imagined he was gone back to Oxford; but I assured her, that if Mr Waverly could make it convenient to go when I did to Paris, I should be extremely glad to be useful to him, and happy in his company.

Pleased with the earnest manner in which I spoke, she became more un-reserved on this subject. 'You know a little of my brother,' said she, 'but it is impossible, on so slight an acquaintance, to be aware of the peculiarities of his temper — peculiarities that give me so many fears on his account. — It is not his youth, or the expensive style in which he sets out, that disquiet me so much as that uncommon indecision of mind, which never allows him to know what he will do a moment before he acts; and some how or other he always continues, after long debates and repeated changes, to adopt the very worst scheme of those he has examined. I may say to you that this defect originated in the extreme indulgence of his parents — A very considerable part of my father's estate would have gone into another branch of the family, had he not had a son — and it happened his six eldest children were daughters, so that when this long wished-for and only son was born, he became of more consequence to my father and mother than the rest of their family; and we, his three sisters, who survived, have through our lives hitherto uniformly seen our interest yield to his. — But, believe me, we should never have murmured (at least I can answer for myself) at whatever sacrifices have been made, had they contributed to render him really and permanently happier; but the continual enquiries that were made of what he would do, and what he would like, while nothing was ever offered to him but variety of gratification, have, I think, coincided with his natural temper to produce that continual inability, to pursue any study or even any pleasure steadily. — My father's death, and his being of age, have rendered him master of himself and his fortune; but he cannot resolve what to do with either of them, and my apprehensions are, that he will fall into the hands of those who will determine for him, and dispose of both, rather for their own advantage than for his. I have therefore encouraged, as much as possible, his half-formed inclination to go abroad — but he talks so vaguely about it, and varies so much in his projects, that I doubt whether he will ever execute any of them. — If you really would allow him to accompany you — yet I know not how to ask it, your society would perhaps determine him to the journey, and prevent his meeting any of those inconveniencies to which young travellers are exposed.'

I believe my lovely friend mistook the expression which my eager acquiescence threw into my countenance, for what might be produced by the embarrassment of wishing to escape with civility from an unwelcome proposal — for she hesitated — yet, without giving me time to reply, said, 'but perhaps I am taking a very improper liberty with you — I ought to have recollected, that in this expedition you have probably a party, to which any addition may be unwelcome; and that you have so slight an acquaintance with my brother' —

I interrupted her. — 'It is enough for me, that he is your brother — that alone would make me wish to render him every service in my power — even if I had never seen him.' — I had said more than I ought; more than I intended to say. — I felt instantly conscious of it, and I now confusedly hurried into professions of personal regard for Waverly, far enough from being sincere; and assurances, that, as I went for change of air and scene, which my health and spirits required, I should make no party, unless it was with one friend, to whom my society might be useful — 'and when that friend,' added I, 'is your brother.' — I was relapsing fast into the folly, of which, but a moment before, I repented. — I saw her change colour, and for the first time since the rise of this attachment — which will end only with my life — I had said, what to a vain woman might have betrayed it.

Geraldine seemed now solicitous to change the conversation; but this I would not do, till I had made her promise to write to her brother, as soon as she could learn where he was, and mention to him my intended journey, and my readiness to begin it with him immediately.

I assured her, that if I met Waverly before I left London, I would endeavour to fix his departure with me, and giving her my address, that he might write to me at Margate, reluctantly, and with pangs, such as are felt only when 'soul and body part' — I bade her adieu!

She looked concerned, and gave me her lovely hand, which I dared not press to my lips — but, as trembling, I held it in mine, she wished me health and happiness, a pleasant journey, and a prosperous return, in that soul-soothing voice which I always hear with undescribable emotions. — More tremulously sweet than usual, it still vibrates in my ears, and I still repeat to myself her last words — 'Farewell, Mr Desmond, may all felicity attend you.'

Now, you will call this wrong, ridiculous, and romantic. — But spare your remonstrances, dear Bethel, since I obey you in essentials, and am going from England, rather because you desire it, than because I am convinced that such an affection as I feel, ought to be eradicated. — Do you know against how many vices, and how many follies, a passion, so pure and ardent as mine, fortifies the heart? — Are you sure that the evils you represent, as attending it, are not purely imaginary, while the good is real? — I expect, however, a heavy lecture for all this, and it were better not to add another word on the subject.

Your's ever, with true regard,

LIONEL DESMOND

I forgot to add, that though my journey is certainly decided upon, because I hope to find, in the present political tumult in France, what may interest and divert my attention; yet, I will not fail to deliver to your relations the letter you enclosed in your last — and to avail myself of it as an introduction to Mrs Fairfax, and her family, as soon as I arrive at Margate. — You imagine that the charms of one or other of your fair cousins will have power enough to drive, from my heart, an inclination which you so entirely disapprove — though I am too well convinced of the inefficacy of the recipe, I try it you see — in deference to your opinion — just as a patient, who knows his disease to be incurable, submits to the prescription of a physician he esteems. — As soon as I have delivered my credentials you shall hear from me again.

LETTER II

TO MR DESMOND

Hartfield, June 13, 1790

Yes! — you have really given an instance of extreme prudence — and, in consequence of it, you will, I think, have occasion to exert another virtue; which is by no means the most eminent among those you possess; the virtue of patience. — So! — you have really undertaken the delightful office of bear-leader — because the brother of your Geraldine cannot take care of himself — and this you call setting about your cure, while you continue to dispute, whether it be wise to be cured or no — and, while you argue that a passion for another man's wife may save you from abundance of vice and folly, you strengthen your argument to be sure wonderfully, by committing one of the greatest acts of folly in your power. — And as to vice, I hold it, my good friend, to be a great advance towards it, when you betray symptoms (which no woman can fail to understand) of this wild and romantic passion of yours, or, as you sentimentally term it, this ardent and pure attachment — an attachment and an arrangement, I think, are the terms now in use. I beg pardon if I do not always put them in the right place.

But seriously — do you know what you have undertaken in thus engaging yourself with Waverly? — and can you bear to be made uneasy by the caprices of a man who is of twenty minds in a moment, without ever being in his right mind? — Your only chance of escaping, as you have now managed the matter is, that he will never determine whether he shall go with you or no. — Some scampering party will be proposed to a cricket-match in Hampshire, or a race in Yorkshire: one friend will invite him to a ball in the West of England, and another to see a boxing-match in the neighbourhood of London: and while he is debating whether he shall make any of these engagements, or which, or go to France with you, you will have a very fair opportunity of leaving him — unless (which from the style of your last letter I do not expect) you should yourself change your resolution on the best grounds; and find your romantic and your patriotic motive for a journey to France, conquered at once by the more powerful enchantments of one of my fair cousins.

While, from your fortune's being entrusted to my management by your grandfather till you were five-and-twenty, I considered myself as your guardian, I forbore to recommend to you either of these young women, because they were my relations — But now as you are master alike of yourself and of your estate, yet are still willing to attend (at least you say you are) to the opinion of a friend who has lived fourteen years longer in the world than you have, I am desirous that you should become acquainted with them, and that you should judge fairly, since that must be to judge favourably, of women who are so universally and justly admired; who certainly are most highly accomplished; and who have fortunes to assist whomsoever they marry, in supporting them in that rank of life to which they will do so much honour — This you call an extraordinary style of advice, from a man who, in the noon of life, has renounced that world, whose attractions he recommends to you: but that, at hardly nine-and-thirty, I have no longer any relish for it, arises, not from general misanthropy, but from particular misfortune; and against those calamities of domestic life that have embittered *my* days, I wish to guard yours — by giving you some of my dearly-bought experience.

You have talents, youth, health, person and fortune — a good heart and an ardent imagination — these, my dear Desmond, are advantages very rarely united, and when they do meet, all the first are too often lost by the fatal and irregular indulgence of the last. This is what I fear for you — but my lecture must terminate with my paper — my good wishes ever follow you; let me hear from you soon — and believe me ever

Yours,

E. BETHEL.

LETTER III

TO MR BETHEL

Margate, June 16, 1790

My visit to your friends is paid, and I met such a reception as I might expect from your recommendation. — Would I could tell you, that it has answered all the friendly expectations, or rather hopes, you formed of it: but you expect an ingenuous account of my sentiments in regard to these ladies; and you shall have them.

Mrs Fairfax has been certainly a very fine woman, and even now has personal advantages enow to authorise her retaining those pretensions, which it is easy to see she would, with extreme reluctance, entirely resign. — It is however but justice to add, that her unwillingness to fade, does not influence her to keep back the period when it is fit her daughters should bloom — she rather runs into the contrary extreme; and with a solicitude, which her maternal affection renders rather an amiable weakness, she is always bustling about, to shew them to the best advantage; and, as she is perfectly convinced that they are the most accomplished young women of the age, so she is very desirous of impressing that conviction on all her acquaintance — For the rest I believe she may be a very good woman; and have only to object to a little too much parade about it; and that she talks rather too loud — and rather too long.

My first introduction to her was not at her own house: for entering one of the libraries about two o'clock on Thursday noon, I observed, that the attention of the few people who so early in the season assemble there, was engrossed by a lady who was relating a very long story about herself, in a tone of voice, against which, whatever had been the subject, no degree of attention to any other could have been a defence. I was compelled therefore, instead of reading the paper where I was anxious to see French news, to join the audience who were hearing — how her lease was out, of an house she had in Harley-street, and all the conversation held between herself, her landlord, and her attorney about its renewal; but how at last they could not agree; and so she had taken another in Manchester-square, which she described at full length — 'The Dutchess,' continued she, 'and lady Lindores, and lady Sarah, were *all so delighted* when they found I had determined upon it — and lady Susan assured me it would delay at least her winter's journey to Bath — Oh! my dear Mrs Fairfax, said lady Susan, you have no notion now, how excessively happy we shall all be, to have you so near us — and your sweet girls! — their society is a delightful acquisition — Miss Fairfax's singing is charming, and I so doat upon Anastatia's manner of reading poetry, that I hope we shall see a great deal of both of them.' —

Though I at once knew that this was the lady to whom I was fortunate enough to have a letter of recommendation in my pocket, it was not easy with all that *mauvais honte* with which you so frequently accuse me, to find a favourable moment to make my bow and my speech, between the end of one narrative and the beginning of another, with such amazing rapidity did they follow each other; and I should have retired without being able to seize any such lucky interval, if this inexhaustible stream of eloquence had not been interrupted by the sudden entrance of a young man who seemed to be one of Mrs Fairfax's intimate acquaintance, and who said he came to tell her, that a raffle, in which she was engaged at another shop, was full, and that her daughters had sent him to desire she would come.[8] 'There is nobody now, madam, to throw,' said this gentleman, 'but you and I; and Miss Anastatia being the highest number, thinks she shall win the jars — but as for me, I cannot go back this morning, for I am engaged to ride' — 'Oh, but I desire you will,' replied Mrs Fairfax, 'it wont take you up a minute, and I will have it decided — for I hate suspence.' — 'Yes, madam,' said another gentleman who had been among the listeners, 'you may hate it — but there is nothing that Waverly loves so much, if one may judge by the difficulty he always makes about deciding upon every thing — and if the determination of the raffle depends upon him, you will hardly know who the jars are to belong to this season.' — 'I protest, Jack Lewis,' cried Waverly, whom I now immediately knew, though his cropped hair and other singularities, of dress had at first prevented my recollecting him — 'I protest you do me injustice — I am the steadiest creature in life — and I would go now willingly — but upon my soul I'm past my appointment.'

'And what signifies your appointment?' replied the other — 'What signifies whether you keep it or no?' Why, that's true,' answered my future fellow-traveller, 'to be sure it is of no great consequence, neither — so if you desire it, I'll go with you, Ma'am, though really I hardly know.' — He was beginning to hesitate again, but Mrs Fairfax took him at his word, and they went out together. However, before they had reached the place where the possession of the China jars was to be decided, I saw Waverly leave the lady, and go I suppose to keep the engagement, which he allowed a moment before was of no consequence. As for myself, as soon as I recovered from the effects of the first impression made by Mrs Fairfax's oratory, which perhaps the weakness or irritability of my nerves rendered more forcible than it ought to be, I collected courage enough to follow her; and in a momentary pause that succeeded her losing her raffle, which would now have been finally settled, she said, had Waverly been present, I advanced and delivered your letter.

She received it most graciously; and even retired from the groups she was engaged in, to read it. I took that opportunity of addressing myself to Miss Fairfax, who is certainly a very pretty woman: she seemed however cold and reserved; and, I thought, put on that sort of air which says — 'I don't know, Sir, whether you are in style of life to claim my notice.' These little doubts, however, which I readily forgave, were immediately dissipated, when her mother appeared with your letter in her hand — and said, 'Margarette, my dear, this is Mr Desmond — the friend and ward of Mr Bethel. I am sure you will be as rejoiced as I am in this opportunity of being honoured by his acquaintance.' — I saw instantly, that the young lady recollected, in the friend and ward of Mr Bethel, a man of large, independent fortune. — The most amiable expression of complacency was immediately conveyed into her countenance; and, as I attended her and her mother home, I perceived that two or three gentlemen, who came with her also, and towards whom she had before been lavish of her smiles, were now almost neglected, while she was so good as to attend only to me — At the door of their lodgings I took my leave of them, after receiving the very obliging invitation to dine with them the next day. Anastatia was not with them. Miss Fairfax told me, that, as soon as she had thrown for the jars, she went home, 'for Anastatia,' said she, 'is excessively fond of reading and reciting — and, her reading master, a celebrated actor at one of the theatres, happening to be here by accident, she would not lose the opportunity of receiving a lesson.' 'She does excel, assuredly,' said the elder lady, 'in those accomplishments, as Mr Desmond, I think will say, when he hears her.' — I expressed my satisfaction at the prospect of being so gratified, and then took my leave.

Yesterday morning I saw Waverly, who seemed to embrace, with avidity, the project of going with me to Paris — I represented to him the necessity of his knowing, precisely, his own mind, as I cannot remain here more than four or five days. — He assures me, that nothing can prevent his going, and that he will instantly set about making preparations. — Indeed, my good friend, you were too severe upon him. — He is young, and quite without experience; but he seems to have a good disposition, and an understanding capable of improvement. — There is too, a family resemblance to his sister, which, though slight, and rather a flying than a fixed likeness, interests me for him; and in short, I am more desirous of curing than of reckoning his faults.

He dined with Mrs Fairfax yesterday, where I was also invited, and where a party of nine or ten were assembled. The captivating sisters displayed all their talents, and I own they excel in almost every accomplishment. — I have seldom seen a finer figure, taken altogether, than the younger sister, and indeed, your description of the personal beauty of both, was not exaggeration. — To their acquirements, I have already done justice: yet, I am convinced, that, with all these advantages, my heart, were it totally free from every other impression, would never become devoted to either.

It would be nonsense to pretend to give reasons for this. — With these caprices of the imagination, and of the heart, you have allowed that Reason has very little to do.

One objection however, to my pretending to either of these ladies, would be, that very degree of excellence on which you seem to dwell. — Always surrounded by admiring multitudes; or, practising those accomplishments by which that admiration is acquired, they seem to be in danger of forgetting they have hearts — appearing to feel no preference for any person, but those who have the sanction of fashion, or the recommendation of great property; and, affluent as they are themselves, to consider only among the men that surround them, who are the likeliest to raise them to higher affluence or superior rank.

Of this I had a specimen yesterday — Waverly seems to have an inclination for Miss Fairfax, and as he and I were the two young men in the party of yesterday, who seemed the most worthy the notice of the two young ladies, I was so fortunate as to be allowed to entertain Miss Anastatia, while Waverly was engaged in earnest discourse by Miss Fairfax, who put on all those facinating [sic] airs which she so well knows how to assume. — I saw that poor Waverly was considering whether he should not be violently in love with her, or adhere to the more humble beauty, for whom he had been relating his *penchant* to me a few hours before, when the door suddenly opened, and a tall young fellow, very dirty, and apparently very drunk, was shewn into the room[9] — The looks of all the ladies testified their satisfaction: and they all eagerly exclaimed, 'Oh! my lord, when did you arrive, who expected you? how did you come?' — Without, however, attending immediately to these questions, he shook the two young ladies hands; called them familiarly by their Christian names; and then throwing himself at his length on a sopha, he thus answered — 'Came! — why, curse me if I hardly know how I came here — for I have not been in bed these three nights — Why, I came with Davers, and Lenham, and a parcel of us. — We were going to settle a wager at Tom Felton's — But rat me, if I know why the plague we came through this damned place, twenty miles a least out of our way. — How in the devil's name do ye contrive to live here? Why, here is not a soul to be seen.' — Then, without waiting for an answer to this elegant exordium, he suddenly snatched the hand of the eldest Miss Fairfax, who sat near him, and cried, 'But, by the Lord, my sweet Peggy, you look confoundedly handsome — curse me if you don't. — By Jove, I believe I shall be in love with you myself — What! — so you have got out of your megrims and sickness, eh! — and are quite well, you dear little toad you, eh?'

— The soft and smiling answer which the lady gave to an address so impertinently familiar, convinced me she was not displeased with it; the mother seemed equally satisfied; and I saw, that even the sentimental Anastatia forgot the critique on the last fashionable novel, with which she had a moment before been obliging me; and cast a look of solicitude towards that part of the room, where this newly-arrived visiter, whom they called Lord Newminster, was talking to her sister in the style of which I have given you an example — while poor Waverly, who had at once lost all his consequence, sat silent and mortified, or if he diffidently attempted to join in the conversation, obtained no notice from the lady, and only a stare of contemptuous enquiry from the lord — As, notwithstanding the favour I had found a few hours before, I now seemed to be sinking fast into the same insignificance, I thought it better to avoid a continuance of such mortification, by taking my leave. Waverly, as he accompanied me home, could hardly conceal his vexation — yet was unwilling to shew it: while I doubt not but Mrs Fairfax and the young ladies were happily entertained the rest of the evening by the delectable conversation of Lord Newminster.

I shall probably write once more from hence.

Your's, ever and truly,

L. D.

LETTER IV

TO MR DESMOND

Hartfield, June 20, 1790

I am sorry my prescription is not likely to succeed. I had persuaded myself that the youngest of my fair cousins, was the likeliest of any woman of my acquaintance, to become the object of a reasonable attachment. — Surely Desmond you are fastidious — you expect what you will never find, the cultivated mind and polished manners of refined society, with the simplicity and unpretending modesty of retired life — they are incompatible — they cannot be united; and this model of perfection, which you have imagined, and can never obtain, will be a source of unhappiness to you through life.

I told you in a former letter, that I would endeavour to give you a little of my dearly-bought experience. — You know that I have been unhappy; but you are probably quite unacquainted with the sources from whence that unhappiness originates — In relating them to you I may perhaps convince you, that ignorance and simplicity are no securities against the evils which you seem to apprehend in domestic life; and that the woman who is suddenly raised from humble mediocrity to the gay scenes of fashionable splendour, is much more likely to be giddily intoxicated than one who has from her infancy been accustomed to them.

At one and twenty, and at the close of a long minority, which had been passed under the care of very excellent guardians, I became master of a very large sum of ready money, and an estate the largest and best conditioned that any gentleman possessed in the county where it lay. — I was at that time very unlike the sober fellow I now appear — and the moment I was free from the restraint of those friends, to whose guardianship my father had left me, I rushed into all the dissipation that was going forward, and became one of the gayest men at that time about town.

With such a fortune it was not difficult to be introduced into 'the very first world.'[10] The illustrious adventurers and titled gamblers, of whom that world is composed, found me an admirable subject for them; while the women, who were then either the most celebrated ornaments of the circle where I moved, or were endeavouring to become so, were equally solicitous to obtain my notice — and the unmarried part of them seemed generously willing to forget my want of title in favour of my twelve or thirteen thousand a year. — I had, however, at a very early period of my career, conceived an affection, or according to your phrase, an ardent attachment to a married woman of high rank — but I had at the same time seen enough of them all, to determine never to marry any of them myself.[11]

Two years experience confirmed me in this resolution; but by the end of that time I was relieved from the embarrassment of a large property. — In the course of the first, the turf and the hazard table had disburthened me of all my ready money; and, at the conclusion of the second, my estate was reduced to something less than one-half.[12] — I then found that I was not, by above one half, so great an object to my kind friends as I had been — and, when soon afterwards I was compelled to pay five thousand pounds for my sentimental attachment —

when the obliging world represented my affairs infinitely worse than they were, and I became afraid of looking into them myself, I found the period rapidly approaching when to this circle I should become no object at all.[13]

My pride now effected that, which common sense had attempted in vain; and I determined to quit a society into which I should never have entered. — I went down to my house in the county where almost all my estate lay; sent for the attorney who had the care of my property, and with a sort of desperate resolution resolved to know the worst.

This lawyer, whose father had been steward to mine, and to whom at his death the stewardship had been given by my guardians, was a clear-headed, active and intelligent man: and when he saw himself entrusted with fuller powers to act in my business than he had till then possessed, he set about it so earnestly and assiduously, that he very soon got successfully through two law-suits of great importance; raised my rents without oppressing my tenants — disposed of such timber as could be sold without prejudice to the principal estate — sold off part of what was mortgaged to redeem and clear the rest; and so regulated my affairs, that in a few months, from the time of his entirely undertaking them, I found myself relieved from every embarrassment, and still possessed of an estate of more than five thousand pounds a year. The seven that I had thrown away gave me however some of the severe pangs that are inflicted by mortified pride. — Nabobs and rich citizens became the ostentatious possessors of manors and royalties in the same county, which were once mine; and some of my estates — estates that had been in my family since the conquest, now lent their names to barons by recent purchase, and dignified mushroom nobility.

I fled therefore from public meetings, where I only found subjects of self-reproach, and made acquaintance with another set of people, among whom I was still considered as a man of great fortune; and where I found more attention, and, as I believed, more friendship than I had ever experienced in superior societies.

More general information and more understanding I certainly found; and none of my new friends possessed a greater share of both than my solicitor, Mr Stamford — He had deservedly obtained my confidence; and I was now often at his house, which his family seemed to vie in trying to render agreeable to me.

His wife was pleasing and good humoured, and he had several sisters, some married and two single, who occasionally visited at his house; and it was not difficult to see, that in the eyes of the latter, Mr Bethel, with his reduced fortune, was a man of greater consequence than he had ever appeared to the high born damsels among whom he had lived in the meridian of his prosperity.

I was not however flattered by their attention or attracted by their coquetry — They were pretty enough, and not without sense, but they had both been very much in London; and I thought too deeply initiated, if not into very fashionable societies, yet into the style of those which catch, with imitative emulation, the manners and ideas those societies give. — Mr Stamford seemed desirous of giving both these ladies a chance of success with me, for they were alternately brought forward for about twelve months — at the end of which time they were both perhaps convinced that they had neither of them any great prospect of it, for then the family of a widow sister was invited, none of whom I had ever seen, or hardly heard mentioned before.

The father of this family, a lieutenant in the army, had married the eldest of Stamford's sisters, when he was recruiting in the town where she then lived — by which he so greatly disobliged the friends on whom he depended, that though he had a very large family, they never afforded him afterwards the least assistance; and about two years before the period I now speak of, he had died at Jamaica, leaving his widow and seven children, with very little more than the pension allowed by government to subsist upon. — Of these children the two eldest were daughters; who, from the obscure village their mother was compelled to inhabit in Wales, were now come to pass the winter at the house of their uncle in a large provincial town. — On entering one morning Stamford's parlour, in my usual familiar way, I was struck with the sight of two very young women who were at work there; the elder of whom was, I thought, the most perfect beauty I had ever seen. — When I met Stamford, I expressed my admiration of the young person I had just parted from, and enquired who she was — He told me she was his niece, and briefly related the history of his sister's family.

At dinner, as Stamford invited me to stay, I could not keep my eyes from the contemplation of Louisa's beauty, which the longer I beheld it, became more and more fascinating. The unaffected innocence and timidity of her manners, rendered her yet more interesting

— she knew merely how to read and write; and had, till now, never been out of the village, whither her mother had retired when she was only six or seven years old — and her total unconsciousness of the beauty she so eminently possessed, rivetted the fetters which that beauty, even at the first interview, imposed.

Her uncle was not, however, so blind to the impression I had received: yet he managed so well, that, without any appearance of artifice on his part, I was every day at the house; and, in a week, I was gone an whole age in love. I soon made proposals, which were accepted with transport. I married the beautiful Louisa — and was for some time happy.

Mr Stamford had immediately the whole management of my fortune, in the improvement of which, he had now so much interest; and in his hands it recovered itself so fast, that, though I made a very good figure in the country, I did not expend more than half my income. — The money thus saved, Stamford put out to the best advantage — and I saw myself likely to regain the lost consequence I so much regretted: a foolish vanity, to which I sacrificed my real felicity.

Stamford, who had all the latent ambition that attends conscious abilities, as a man of business, had, till now, felt that ambition repressed by the little probability there was of his ever reaching a more elevated situation. — But he saw and irritated the mortified pride which I very ill concealed, and, by degrees, he communicated to me, and taught me to adopt those projects, by which he told me I should not only be relieved from this uneasy sensation, but rise to greater consequence than I had ever possessed. — 'You have talents,' said he, 'and ought to exert them. — In these times, any thing may be done by a man of abilities, who has a seat in Parliament. Take a seat in the House of Commons, and a session or two will open to you prospects greater than those you sacrificed in the early part of your life.' — I took his advice, and the following year, instead of selling, at a general election, the two seats for a borough which belonged to me, I filled one myself, and gave the other to Stamford; who, conscious as he was of possessing those powers, which, in a corrupt government, are always eagerly bought, had long been solicitous to quit the narrow walk of a country attorney, and mount a stage where those abilities would have scope.[14]

In consequence of this arrangement, I took a large house in town; where Stamford and his family had apartments for the first four or five months. — At the end of that time, he had managed so well, that he hired one for himself. — Artful, active, and indefatigable, with a tongue very plausible, and a conscience very pliant, he soon became a very useful man to the party who had purchased him. Preferments and fortune crowded rapidly upon him, and Stamford, the country attorney, was soon forgotten, in Stamford the confident of ministers, and the companion of peers.

I was not, however, entirely without acquiring some of the advantages he had taught me to expect — I obtained, by what I now blush to think of, (giving my voice in direct opposition to my opinion and my principles,) a place of six hundred pounds a year; which, though it did little more than pay the rent of my house in town, was, as Mr Stamford assured me, the foretaste of superior advantages. — But, long before the close of this session of Parliament, I discovered, that far from being likely to recover the fortune I had dissipated, I was, in fact, a considerable loser in pecuniary matters. — Alas! I was yet endeavouring to shut my eyes against the sad conviction, that I had sustained, a yet heavier and more irreparable loss; domestic happiness, and the affection of my wife.

Dazzled and intoxicated by scenes of which she had till then had no idea, Louisa, on our first coming to town entered, with extreme avidity, into the dissipation of London — and I indulged her in it, from the silly pride of shewing to the women among whom I had formerly lived, beauty which eclipsed them all. — They affected to disdain the little rustic, whom they maliciously represented as being taken from among the lowest of the people. — The admiration however with which she was universally received by the men, amply revenged their malignity; but, while it mortified them, it ruined me.

Louisa lived now in a constant succession of flattery, by which perhaps a stronger mind might have become giddy. — She had princes at her toilet and noblemen at her feet every day; and from them she soon learned to imagine, that had she been seen before she threw herself away on me, there was no rank of life, however exalted, to which such charms might not have given her pretensions. — That love, which till this fatal period she seemed to have for me — that gratitude of which her heart had appeared so full (for I had provided for all her family), even her affection for her children, was drowned in the intoxicating draughts of flattery, which were every day administered to her — and when the time came for our returning into the country, she returned indeed with me, but I carried not back the ingenuous, unaffected, Louisa; whose simplicity, rather than her beauty, had won my heart. — Ah! no! — I saw only a fine lady eager for admiration; willing to purchase it on any terms; and sullen and discontented when she had not those about her from whom she had been so accustomed to receive it. — That happiness was lost to me for ever. I had long been conscious, but I still hoped to preserve my honour — and that I might detach my wife from those by whose assiduity it seemed to be the most endangered, I determined to make a journey into Italy. — She neither promoted or objected to the scheme; but a few days before that, which I had fixed on to begin our journey, she left the house, and put herself under the protection of a man who disgraces the name he bears.

I pursued the usual course in these cases. I challenged and fought with him — I was slightly, and he was dangerously wounded; and by way of further satisfaction I heard, that my wife attended him in his illness, and as soon as he was able to travel, accompanied him to the south of France.

I then thought of pursuing that method of vengence, which had some years before been successfully employed against myself; and had begun the preliminary steps towards it, when Stamford, the now prosperous uncle of my wife, undertook to dissuade me — He represented to me that any money I could obtain, would only be considered as the price of my dishonour — and that such a publication of misconduct in the mother of my children would be very injurious to them, particularly to my little girl that therefore it would, upon every account, be better to suffer him to negociate an accommodation with — I stopped him short, without hearing to its close, this infamous and insulting proposal — and desired him to leave my house; no longer doubting, from comparing this with other instances that now occurred to me, that he had sold the person of his niece to her seducer, with as much *sang froid* as he had before sold his own conscience to the minister.

Impressed by this opinion, and being too well convinced of the futility of those chimerical plans with which he had lured me from independence and felicity, I determined never more to hold converse with him; and to divest myself, as soon and as compleatly as possible of all regret, for a worthless and ungrateful woman. — I therefore took all my affairs into my own hands, accepted the chiltern hundreds, and selling my seat for the remainder of the seven years, I resigned at once my place at court, and my place in parliament; for by the latter I now felt, that I had unworthily obtained the former.[15] — Then, letting the family house where I had resided in the neighbourhood of Stamford, I settled myself at this smaller place; the only property I possess at a distance from my native county.

Here I have now lived nearly eight years, and between the education of my children, and the amusement afforded me by my farm, I hope I shall end those years at least not so unhappily as they began. — Of the woman once so beloved, I can now think with sorrow and pity rather than resentment, for she is dead — and I wish her errors to be forgotten and forgiven by the world, as I have forgiven, though I cannot forget them. — Though released by her death from any matrimonial engagement, I have no intention again to hazard my happiness, but apply all my time in improving the remains of my estate for my son; to render him worthy to enjoy it — and to educate my daughter in such a manner, that although she promises to possess her mother's beauty, she may not be its victim. — For this purpose it will soon become necessary for me to quit occasionally the solitude where I have regained my peace, and return to those scenes among which I lost it: for I am determined my little Louisa shall see the world before she is settled in it; that she may learn to enjoy it with moderation, or resign it with dignity.

In looking forward, my dear friend, to this period, now not very remote, I have thought that a wife of yours would be the person to whom I should best like to entrust so precious a charge as my charming girl on her first entrance into life. — Thus you see, that I had, in recommending a wife to you, no very just claim to the disinterestedness of which I have sometimes boasted — but so goes the world. I have tired myself, and exhausted my spirits, by this detail of what I always avoid recalling, when it can serve no purpose but to renew fruitless regret — May, however, the narrative which has cost me some pain, serve to convince you, that such women as the two Fairfaxes, are much less likely to sacrifice their honour on the altar of vanity, than the rural damsel from the Welch mountains or northern fells. I hope to hear from you, as you promise, once more before you depart — It is impossible to help again offering my congratulation on your fortunate choice of Waverly for a travelling companion — nor can I avoid admiring the effect of *family likeness.*

Adieu! your's ever,

E. BETHEL

LETTER V

TO MR BETHEL

June 25, 1790

You are very good to have taken so much trouble, and to have entered on a detail so painful to yourself for my advantage — Be assured, my good friend, I feel all my obligations to you on this, and on innumerable occasions; and that I should pay to your opinion the utmost deference were not my marrying now, perhaps my ever marrying at all, quite out of the question — for I believe I shall never have an heart to bestow; and without it I can never solicit that love, which, so circumstanced, I can neither deserve nor repay.

You tell me, Bethel, that I vainly expect to meet the cultivated mind and polished manners of refined society, united with the simple and unpretending modesty of retired life, while the idea I have thus dressed up as a model of perfection, will embitter all my days — It will indeed! — But it is not the search that will occupy, or the *idea* that will persecute me — it is the reality, the living original of this *fair idea,* which I have found — and found in possession of another — Yes my friend — Geraldine unites these perfections — and adds to them so many others, both of heart and understanding, that were her person only an ordinary one, I could not have known without adoring her. I will not, however, dwell upon this topic — for it is one on which you do not hear me with pleasure, and it is not fit that *I* indulge myself in what I feel while I write about her — though I can only do so while I write to you, for no other person on earth suspects this attachment, nor do I ever breathe her name to any ear but yours.

I force myself from this subject then; though there is not in the world another that really fixes my attention an instant: not one that has any momentary attraction, unless it be the transactions in France. — I am waiting here for Waverly, who is gone to Bath, to take leave of his mother: a measure which, on her writing to him to desire it, he adopted with only two debates — whether he should go round by London, to bid adieu to his dear Nancy, a nymph who lives at his expence; or proceed directly to Bath. — As I foresaw that his dear Nancy might chuse to visit the Continent too; or might apprehend his escape from her chains, and therefore prevent his going himself, I most strongly enforced the necessity of his obeying his mother's summons in the quickest way possible; declaring to him, that, if he detained me above a week, I must absolutely go without him — This, as he is now very eager for the journey, and speaks no French, so that he would be subject to many difficulties in travelling alone, at length determined him to go straight to Bath and return immediately; on which conditions I agreed to wait a week where I am, though, since I must go, I am extremely impatient to be at Paris — and would have made this sacrifice of time to nothing but the service of Geraldine in serving her brother.

Since I wrote to you last, I have passed part of several days with Mr Fairfax's family, without seeing cause to change my opinion of any part of it. — But all my observations tend rather to confirm that which I formed on my first introduction. — The foolish vanity, whence originates so many stratagems to heighten the consequence; that affectation which carries them into the superior ranks of life, to applaud and flatter there, that they may acquire, in their turn, greater superiority over that class where fortune has placed them, and be looked up to as the standards of elegance and fashion, because they live so much with the nobility; and the sacrifices they are ever ready to make of their own dignity, in order to obtain this: such conduct, I say, has something in it so weak and so mean, that no accomplishments, beauty, or fortune could tempt me to connect myself with a woman who had been educated in such a course of unworthy prejudice. — Surely, my friend, if you have ever remarked this *mal de famille*, you, who have not much reason to venerate the influence of aristocracy in society, would not have supposed that either of these ladies, even if they would deign to accept my fortune in apology for my being only Mr Desmond, (with hardly a remote alliance to nobility) could have given me in marriage that felicity, which I am sure you wish I may find.[16] — You have probably, therefore, suffered this trait of character, though it strongly pervades the whole family, to escape you.

Yesterday morning Miss Fairfax was so obliging as to invite me to be of a party she had made to ride out; or rather allowed me to attend her, together with Waverly and another gentleman, who neither of them came — I however waited on her by her own appointment at the hour of breakfast, and found her sitting at the tea-table, with her mother, her sister, and the Lord Newminster; who, notwithstanding his complaints of the dulness of the place, had returned thither after having settled his wager. — He was stretched upon a sopha — with boots on — a terrier lay on one side of him, and he occasionally embraced a large hound, which licked his face and hands, while he thus addressed it. — 'Oh! thou dear bitchy — thou beautiful bitchy — damme, if I don't love thee better than my mother or my sisters.' — Then, by a happy transition, addressing himself to the youngest Miss Fairfax, he added, 'Statia, my dear, tell me if this is not a divinity of a dog — do you know that I would not part with her for a thousand guineas?' 'Here Tom,' speaking to the servant who waited, 'give me that chocolate and that bread and butter' — the man obeyed, and the noble gentleman poured the chocolate over the plate, and gave it altogether to the divinity of a dog — 'Was it hungry?' cried he — 'was it hungry, a lovely dear? — I would rather all the old women in the country should fast for a month, than thou shouldest not have thy belly-full.' — The ladies, far from appearing to think this speech unfeeling or ridiculous, were lavish in their praises of the animal; and Miss Fairfax, who seems more desirous than her sister to attract the attention of its worthy owner, said, 'my Lord, do you think she has had enough? — shall I give her some more chocolate? — or send for a plate of cold meat?' She then caressed the favourite, and fed it from her fair hands; while I, who had been a silent and unnoticed spectator since my first entrance, contemplated with more pity than wonder, this sapient member of our legislature; who having, at length, satisfied the importunity of one of the objects of his solitude, turned to the other, and hugging it with more affection than he would probably have shewed to the heir of his titles, he cried, 'my poor dear Venom when will you pup? — Peggy! — will you have one of her puppies? — they are the very best breed in England. — Damme now, do you know, my cursed fellow of a groom lost me the brother to this here bitch a week or two ago — and be cursed to his stupid soul — and now I have got none but Venom left of that there breed.' At this period his lamentation was suddenly suspended by the door's being opened, and the entrance of a figure who gave me the idea of a garden set on its end, and supported by two legs. I found it, however, on a second view, a person I had often seen; and immediately recognized him to be General Wallingford; who, as soon as he could recover his breath, which seemed to have been lost for a moment by exertion and agitation, thus began:

'So Madam! — so! — this is astonishing — this last news from France — This decree fills up the measure of that madness and folly which have always marked the conduct of that beggarly set who call themselves the National Assembly![17] — The evil is however now so great, that it must, it must absolutely cure itself: this decree is decisive — they have crushed themselves.' — Mrs Fairfax now enquired what it was? 'Why — I have letters, Madam,' replied the General, 'from my friend Langdale, who was passing through Paris on his way to Italy, (for as to making any stay there now, it is impossible for a man of fashion so far to commit himself as to stay in such a scene of vulgar triumph and popular anarchy) Langdale, saw too much of it in three days; and his last letter states, that by a decree passed the nineteenth of June, these low wretches, this collection of dirty fellows, have abolished all titles, and abolished the very name of nobility.' — 'The devil they have?' cried Lord Newminster, raising himself upon his elbow, and interrupting a tune he had been humming, a *mezza voce*; 'the devil they have? — then I wish the King and the Lords may smash them all — and be cursed to them.[18] — I wish they may all be sent to hell — Now damme — do you know if I was King of France for three days, I would drive them all to the devil in a jiffy.'

The more sagacious General cast a rueful look at the wise and gallant projector of an impossible exploit; and then, without attempting to demonstrate its impracticability, he began very gravely to descant on the shocking consequences of this decree. Sentiments in which Mrs Fairfax very heartily joined. — 'It will be impossible, I fear,' said the General, 'at least, for some time, for any man of fashion to reside pleasantly at Paris, which I am extremely sorry for, for it is a place I always used to love very much; and I had great inclination to pass the autumn there. — For my part, I've never observed, but that the people had liberty enough. — Quite as much, I am convinced, as those wrongheaded, ignorant wretches, that form the canaille ought to have, in any country. 'Tis a very terrible thing when that corrupt mass gets the upper hand, in any country; but, in the present instance, the misery is, that certain persons among even *les gens comme il faut*, should be absurd and senseless enough to encourage the brutes, by affecting a ridiculous patriotism, and calling themselves the friends of the people.'[19]

'Rot the people,' — cried the noble Peer: 'I wish they were all hanged out of the way, both in France and here too. — What business have a set of blackguards to have an opinion about liberty, and be cursed to them? Now General I'll tell you what, if I was a French nobleman now, and had to do with them, damme if I did not shew the impudent rascals the difference. — By Jove, Sir, I'd set fire to their assembly, and mind no more shooting them all, than if they were so many mad dogs.'

Though it was used on behalf of his own system of politics, the extreme ignorance and absurdity which this language betrayed, made the General decline answering or approving it; but he was infinitely attentive to the more pathetic lamentations of Mrs Fairfax, which were thus expressed. — 'Well! I really think, my dear General, that in my whole life, I never *was* so shocked at any thing, as at what you tell me: Heavens! how my sympathising heart bleeds, when I reflect on the numbers of amiable people of rank, compelled thus to the cruel necessity of resigning those ancient and honourable names which distinguished them from the vulgar herd! and who are no longer marked by their titles from that canaille with which it is so odious to be levelled. — They might, in my mind, as well have robbed them of their property, and have turned them out to perish in the streets, if indeed that is not done already.'

'No;' replied the General, 'that has not happened yet, but doubtless it will; and, indeed, they might as well have done it at once; for they have made Paris so insupportable to people of fashion, that it must, of course, become a mere desart. — Nobody of any elegance of manners can exist, where tradesmen, attornies, and mechanics have the *pas*.[20] — The splendour of that beautiful capital is gone: the glory of the *noblesse* is vanished for ever.'

'Come, come, my dear General,' answered the lady, 'let us hope not. A counter-revolution may set all to rights again, and we may live to see these vulgar people punished for their ridiculous ambition, as they deserve. My heart, however, bleeds *to a degree* for the *noblesse*, particularly for two most intimate friends of mine, women of the highest rank, who are, without doubt, included in this universal *bouleversement.*[21] — It was only this last winter, when one of them, la Duchesse de Miremont, who was then in England, you know, said to me — Ah! *ma très chere & très amiable madame Fairfax, je vous en responds que —*'

The lady had, in an instant, forgotten the calamities of her foreign friends in her eagerness to display her own consequence; but I found it impossible to attend, with patience, to the rest of the dialogue between her and the General, and was meditating how, with the least appearance of rudeness, I could make my escape, when Miss Fairfax's horses were brought to the door, and my servant immediately afterwards arrived with mine. — She rose to go; and, turning towards Lord Newminster said, with extreme softness — 'Does not your Lordship ride this morning?' 'No, my dear Pegg,' answered he, yawning in her face as he spoke; 'I cannot undertake the fatigue, for I was up eight o'clock to see a set to between the Russian and Big Ben, who are to fight next week for a thousand.[22] — I sparred a little myself, and now I am damned tired, and fit for nothing but a lounge. Perhaps I may meet you in my phaeton an hour hence or so; that's just as the whim takes me.' — The Lady then, in the same gentle tone cried — 'Oh creature! equally idle and ferocious!' — while he folded his arms, and re-settling himself, with his two dogs upon the sopha, declared that he felt himself disposed to take a nap.

The old General, more gallant and more active, notwithstanding his gout and his size, now led Miss Fairfax to her horse; and, as he assisted her to mount it, he seemed to whisper some very tender sentence in her ear; if I could guess by the peculiar expression of his features, while I had nothing to do but to wait while all this passed, and when the ceremony was finished, to ride silently away by her side, — We had hardly, however, quitted the town, when the young Lady thus began: — 'This is really very frightful news, Mr Desmond, that General Wallingford has brought us to-day. — Do you not think it extremely shocking?' 'No, Madam, not at all: I own myself by no means master of the subject, but from all *I do know*, I feel myself much more disposed to rejoice at, than to lament it.'

'Impossible, Mr Desmond! — Surely I misunderstand you! — What! are you disposed to rejoice that nobility and fashion are quite destroyed?'

'I am glad that oppression is destroyed; that the power of injuring the many is taken from the few. — Dear Madam, are you aware of the evils which in consequence of the feudal system existed in France? A system formed in the blindest periods of ignorance and prejudice; which gave to the *noblesse*, not only an exemption from those taxes which crushed the people by their weight, but gave to the possessors of *les terres titrès*, every power to impoverish and depress the peasant and the farmer; on whom, after all, the prosperity of a nation depends.[23] — That these powers are annihilated, no generous mind can surely lament.'

'I hope,' replied Miss Fairfax, with more asperity than I thought my humility deserved — 'I hope, Sir, I am not ungenerous, nor quite ignorant, neither, of the history of France. But I really must own, that I cannot see the matter in the light you do. — Indeed, I can see nothing but the most horrid cruelty and injustice.' —

'In calling a man by one name, rather than by another! — My dear Miss Fairfax, the cruelty and injustice must surely be imaginary.' — 'Not at all, in *my* opinion, Sir,' retorted my fair antagonist. — 'A title is as much a person's property as his estate; and, in my mind, one might as well be taken away as another — And to lose one's very birth-right, by a mob too, of vulgar creatures. — Good Heaven! I declare the very idea is excessively terrific: only suppose the English mob were to get such a notion, and in some odious riot, begin the same sort of thing here!'

'Perhaps,' replied I, (still, I assure you, speaking with the utmost humility) 'perhaps there may never exist here the same *cause*; and, therefore, the *effect* will not follow. — Our nobility are less numerous; and, till within a few years, that titles have become so very common, they were all of that description which could be ranked only with the *haut noblesse* of France. They are armed with no powers to oppress, individually, the inferior order of men; they have no vassals *but those whose service is voluntary*; and, upon the whole, are so different a body of men from that which was once the nobility of France, as to admit no very just comparison, and no great probability of the same steps ever being taken, to annihilate their titles; though they possess, in their right of hereditary legislation, a strong, and to many, an obnoxious feature which the higher ranks in France never possessed. — However, we will, if you please, and merely for the sake of conversation, suppose that the *people*, or, if you please, the *vulgar*, took it into their heads to level all those distinctions that depend upon names — I own I see nothing in it so very dreadful: it might be endured.'

'Yes, by savages and brutes, perhaps,' replied the Lady, with anger flashing from her eyes, and lending new eloquence to her tongue; 'but I must say, that I never expected to hear from a man of fashion, a defence of an act so shamefully tyrannous and unjust, exercised over their betters by the scum of the people; an act that must destroy all the elegance of manners, all the high polish that used to render people, in a certain style, so delightful in France. By degrees, I suppose, those who can endure to stay in a country under such a detestable sort of government, will become as rude and disgusting as our common country 'Squires.'

I saw by the look with which this speech was delivered, that I was decidedly a common country 'Squire. — 'Unhappily,' replied I, 'my dear Miss Fairfax, the race of men whom you call common country 'Squires, are almost, if not entirely annihilated in England; though no *decree* has passed against them — A total change of manners has effected this.' I was going on, but with great vivacity she interrupted me. —

'So much the better, Sir, they will never be regretted.'

'Perhaps not, Madam, and as we are merely arguing for the sake of conversation, let me just suppose that the same thing might happen, if all those who are now raised above us by their names, were to have no other distinction than their merits. — Let me ask you, would the really great, the truly noble among them (and that there are many such nobody is more ready to allow) be less beloved and revered if they were known only by their family names? On the other hand, would the celebrity of the men of *ton* be much reduced? For example, the nobleman I had the honour of meeting at your house to-day. — He is now, I think, called Lord Newminster. Would he be less agreeable in his manners, less refined in his conversation, less learned, less worthy, less repectable, were he unhappily compelled to be called, as his father was before he bought his title, Mr Grantham?'

I know not whether it was the matter or the manner that offended my beautiful aristocrate, but she took this speech most cruelly amiss, and most inhumanely determining to avenge herself upon me, she replied, with symptoms of great indignation in her countenance, 'That she was truly sorry to see the race of mere country 'Squires *did* still exist, and *that*, among those where, from fortune and pretensions, she should least have imagined they would be found. (This was me.) That as to Lord Newminster, by whatever name he might at any time be called, she should, for her part, always say and think, that there were few who so compleatly filled the part of a man of real fashion among the nobility; and not one, in any rank of life, who, in her mind, possessed a twentieth part of his good qualities.

The manner in which this was uttered, was undoubtedly meant to crush at once, and for ever, all the aspiring thoughts, that I, presuming on the strength of my fortune, might per-adventure have dared to entertain. — Overwhelmed by the pretty indignation, as much as by the unanswerable arguments of my angry goddess, I began to consider how I might turn or drop a discourse where I was so likely to suffer for my temerity, when I was relieved by the appearance of a carriage, at a distance, which, she said, she knew to be Lord Newminster's phaeton; and, without any further ceremony than slightly wishing me good morrow, she cantered away to meet it — leaving me, as slowly I trotted another way, to congratulate my country on the pure notions of patriotic virtue with which even its women are impressed; and, on such able supporters of its freedom, as Lord Newminster in the upper, and General Wallingford in the lower House. — Alas! my opposite principles, however modestly and diffidently urged, have lost me, as I have since found, for ever, that favour, which, without being a man of fashion, I was once so happy as to enjoy from your fair relations: for whenever, in the course of the next two or three days, I happened to meet them, I was so slightly noticed, that I apprehend our acquaintance will end here. — Condole with me, dear Bethel; and, to make some amends, let me soon hear from you.

I have had, very unexpectedly, a letter from Mr Danby, my mother's sole surviving brother; who, absorbed in his own singular notions and amusements, has hardly seemed to recollect me for many years. — He has heard, I know not how (for I have long had no other communication with him, than writing him an annual letter, with an annual present of game and venison, since I became of age) that I am going to France; and he strongly remonstrates upon the danger I shall incur if I do, both to my person and my principles. — He entreats me not to try such a hazardous journey; and hints, that his fortune is too large to be despised. — I don't know what this sudden fit of solicitude means; for though I am the only relation he has, I never had any reason to think I should benefit by his fortune; and your care, my dear Bethel, has precluded the necessity of my desiring it. I shall answer him with great civility, however, but certainly make no alteration in my plan.

Adieu! my friend — fail not to write if you hear any thing of the family of Verney.

Your's ever,
LIONEL DESMOND

LETTER VI

TO MR BETHEL

Calais, July 4, 1790

I had waited for Waverly the week I had promised to wait — the last day of that week was come; and I was going to enquire for a passage to Calais or Dunkirk, when I met Anthony, his servant, in the street. The poor fellow was covered with dust, and seemed half dead with fatigue. 'Well Anthony, where is your master?' 'Oh! lord sir,' answered he, 'my master has changed his mind about going to France, and sent me post from Stamford in Lincolnshire, Sir, where he is gone with some other gentlemen to an house, one Sir James Deyburne has just by there. — Sir, I have hardly been off the saddle for above six-and-thirty hours; and we had no sooner got down there, than master sent me off post to your honor; to let you know, Sir, that he could not, no how in the world, go to Paris with you at this time.' —

'But did he not write?' 'Why, no Sir, he was going to write I believe, but somehow his friends they persuaded him there was no need of it: so, Sir, he called me, and bid me, that I should deliver the message to you, about his not coming, the soonest I possibly could: and so, I set off directly, and he told me to say that he should write in a very little time; and he hoped he said, that I would make haste, to prevent your honor's waiting for him.'

I had at this moment occasion to recollect, how nearly Waverly was related to Geraldine, to prevent my feeling some degree of anger and resentment towards him. — I sent, however, his poor harassed servant to my lodgings, where I ordered him to refresh himself by eating and sleeping; and then went to see about my passage to France.

I afterwards sauntered into one of the libraries, and took up a book; but my attention was soon diverted, by a very plump, sleek, short, and altogether, a most orthodox figure; whose enormous white wig, deeply contrasted by his peony-coloured face, and consequential air, declared him to be a dignitary, very high, at least, in his own esteem. — On his entrance he was very respectfully saluted by a little thin man in black; whose snug well-powdered curls, humble demeanor, and cringing address, made me suppose him either a dependent on the plump doctor, or one who thought he might benefit by his influence — for he not only resigned the newspaper he was reading, but bustled about to procure others: — while his superior, noticing him but little, settled himself in his seat, with a magisterial air — put on his spectacles, and took out his snuff-box; and having made these arrangements, he began to look over the paper of the day; but seeing it full of intelligence from France, he laid it down, and,

'As who should say I am Sir Oracle,'

he began an harangue, speaking slowly and through his nose.[24]

''Tis an uneasy thing,' said he, 'a very uneasy thing, for a man of probity and principles to look in these days into a newspaper. — Greatly must every such man be troubled to read of the proceedings, that are going forward in France — Proceedings which must awaken the wrath of heaven; and bring down upon that perfidious and irreverent people its utmost indignation.'

The little man took the opportunity the solemn close of this pompous oration gave him, to cry — 'very true, Doctor, your observation is perfectly just: things to be sure have just now a very threatening appearance.' 'Sir,' resumed the grave personage, 'it is no *appearance*, but a very shocking reality. They have done the most unjust and wicked of all actions in depriving the church of its revenues.[25] — 'Twere as reasonable, Sir, for them to take my birth-right or your's.'

'I thought, Doctor,' said a plain looking man, who had attended very earnestly to the beginning of this dialogue — 'I thought, that the revenues and lands of the church, being the property of the state, they might be directed by it into any channel more conducive, in the opinion of that state, to its general good; and that it appearing to the National Assembly of France, that this their property was unequally divided, and that their bishops lived like princes, while their curates* had hardly the means of living like men, — I imagined —'

'You imagined, Sir? — And give me leave to ask what right you have to imagine? — or what you know of the subject! — The church lands and revenues the property of the state! — No, Sir — I affirm that they are not — That they are the property of the possessors, as much, Sir, as your land and houses, if you happen to have any, are your's.'

'Not quite so, surely, my good Doctor,' replied the gentleman mildly — 'My houses and lands — if, as you observe, I happen to have any, were probably either acquired by my own industry, or were my birth-right. — Now Sir' — He would have proceeded, but the Divine, in an angry and supercilious manner interrupted him — 'Sir, I wont argue, I wont commit myself, nor endeavour to convince a person whose principles are, I see, fundamentally wrong. — But no man of sense will deny, that when the present body of French clergy took upon them their holy functions — that then they became, as it were, born again — and — and — and by their vows —'

'But, my worthy Sir, those vows were vows of poverty. — They were vows, by which, far from acquiring temporal goods, the means of worldly indulgencies, they expressly renounced all terrestrial delights, and gave themselves to a life of mortification and humility. — Now, it is very certain, that many of them not only possessed immense revenues, wrung from the hard hands of the peasant and the artificer, but actually expended those revenues; — not in relieving the indigent, or encouraging the industrious; but in gratifications more worthy the dissolute followers of the meretricious scarlet-clad lady of Babylon, than the mortified disciples of a simple and pure religion.'[26] Then, as if disdaining to carry farther an argument in which he had so evidently the advantage against the proud petulance of his adversary, the gentleman walked calmly away, while the Doctor, swelling with rage, cried, 'I don't know who that person is, but he is very ignorant and very ill-bred.' — ''Tis but little worth your while, Doctor,' cried the acquiescent young man, 'to enter into controversial discourse with persons so unworthy of the knowledge and literature which you ever throw into your conversation.'

---

*   Curés-rectors.

'It is not, Sir,' answered the Doctor: 'it were indeed a woeful waste of the talent with which it has pleased heaven to entrust me, to contend with the atheistical pretenders to philosophy, that obtrude themselves but too much into society. — However, Sir, a little time will shew that I am right, in asserting, that a nation that pays no more regard to the sacred order, can never prosper; — but, that such horrible sacrilegious robbery, as that wretched anarchy, for I cannot call it government, has been guilty of, will draw down calamities upon the miserable people; and that the evil spirit, which is let loose among them, will prompt them to deluge their country with blood, by destroying each other.'

'So much the better, Doctor,' cried a fat, bloated figure, in a brown riding wig, a red waistcoat, and boots — 'so much the better — I heartily, for my part, wish they may.' This philanthropic personage, who had till now been talking with an old lady about the price of soals and mackerel that morning at market, now quitted his seat, and squatting himself down near the two reverend gentlemen, proceeded briskly in his discourse, as if perfectly conscious of its weight and energy. — 'Yes, Doctor, I vote for their cutting one another's throats, and so saving us the trouble. — The sooner they set about it, the better I shall be pleased; for, as for my part, I detest a Frenchman, and always did. — You must know, that last summer, I went down to Brighton, for I always go every summer to some of these kind of watering places. — So, as I was observing, I went down to Brighton, in the month of August, which is the best part of the season, because of the wheat-ears being plenty: but, I dont know how it happened, I had an ugly feel in my stomach.[27] What was the meaning of it I could not tell; but, I quite lost my relish for my dinner, and so I thought it proper to consult a physician or two on the case; and they advised me to try if a little bit of a sail would not set things to rights; and told me, that very likely, if I went over the water, I should find my appetite. — So, Sir, I determined to go, for riding did me no good at all; and so of course I was a little uneasy. — So, Sir, I even went over the herring pond. — I was as sick as a horse, to be sure, all night; but, however, the next morning, when we landed on French ground, there was I tolerably chirruping, and pretty well disposed for my breakfast. — Oh, ho! thinks I, this will answer, I believe. — However, I thought I would lay by for dinner, for the Monsieur at the inn told us he could let us have game and fish. — But lord, Sir, most of their provisions are nothing to be compared to ours; and what is good they ruin by their vile manner of dressing it. — Why, Sir, we had for dinner some soals — the finest I ever saw, but they were fried in bad lard; and then, Sir, for the partridges, there was neither game gravy, nor poiverade, nor even bread sauce.[28] — Faith, I had enough of them and their cookery in one day; so, Sir, the next morning I embarked again for old England. However, upon the whole, the thing itself answered well enough, for my appetite was almost at a par, as I may say, when I came home. But for your French, I never desire to set eyes on any of them again — and indeed, for my part, I am free to say, that if the whole race was extirpated, and we were in possession of their country, as in justice it is certain we ought to be, why, it would be so much the better — We should make a better hand of it in such a country as that a great deal. — I understand, that one of the things these fellows have done since they have got the notion of liberty into their heads, has been, to let loose all the taylors and tinkers and frisseurs in their country, to destroy as much game as they please. Now, Sir, what a pity it is, that a country where there is so much, is not ours, and our game-laws in force there.[29] — And then their wine; I can't say I ever saw a vineyard, because, as I observed, I did not go far enough up the country: but, no doubt, we should manage that matter much better; and, upon the whole, considering we always were their masters, my opinion is, that it would be right and proper for our ministry to take this opportunity of falling upon them, while they are weakening each other; and, if they will have liberty, give them a little taste of the liberty of us Englishmen; for, of themselves, they can have no right notion of what it is — and, take my word for it, its the meerest folly in the world for them to think about it. — No, no; none but Englishmen, free-born Britons, either understand it or deserve it.'

Such was the volubility and vehemence with which this speech was made, that the Doctor could not find any opportunity to interrupt it. — Whatever was his opinion of the politics of the orator, he seemed heartily to coincide with him in the notions he entertained on the important science of eating. He therefore (though with an air of restraint, and as if he would cautiously guard his dignity from the too great familiarity with which the other seemed to approach him) entered into another dissertation on the French revolution, anathematising all its projectors and upholders, with a zeal which Ernulphus might envy; and, in scarce less charitable terms, branding them with the imputation of every hideous vice he could collect, and ending a very long oration with a pious and christian denunciation of battle and murder, pestilence and famine here, and eternal torments hereafter, for all who imagined, aided, or commended such an abomination.[30]

The gentleman who had visited France for the reformation of his appetite (and who had formerly, as I learned afterwards, kept a tavern in London, and was now retired upon a fortune) seemed unable or unwilling to distinguish declamation from argument, or prejudice from reason — He appeared to be delighted by the furious eloquence of the churchman, whom he shook heartily by the hand. — 'Doctor,' cried he, 'I am always rejoiced to meet with gentlemen of your talents and capacity; you are an honour to our establishment; what you have said is quite convincing indeed; strong, unanswerable argument: I heartily wish some of my acquaintance, who pretend to be advocates for French liberty, were to hear you — I believe they'd soon be put to a non-plus — You'd be quite too much for them, I'm sure. Pray, Doctor, give me leave to ask, what stay do you mean to make in this place? I shall be proud to cultivate the honour of your acquaintance. If you are here next week, will you do me the favour to dine with me on Wednesday? — I've a chicken-turtle, which promises well — the first I've received this season, from what I call my West-Indian farm; a little patch of property I purchased, a few years since, in Jamaica.[31] — As to the dressing of turtles, I always see to that myself, for I am extremely particular; though, I must say my negro fellow is a very excellent hand at it — I have lent him more than once to perform for some great people at t'other end of the town. — If you'll do me the pleasure, Doctor, to take a dinner with me I shall be glad; and, indeed, besides the favour of your company, I would fain have the four or five friends that I've invited for that day, to hear a little of our opinion upon these said French matters.'

Though the Doctor had, till now, hesitated and seemed to doubt whether he did not descend too much from his elevated superiority, in encouraging the forwardness of his new acquaintance; this proposal, flattering at once his pride and his appetite, was irresistible. — He, therefore, relaxing from the air of arrogant dignity he usually wore, accepted very graciously of the invitation to assist in devouring the chicken-turtle, and then these two worthy champions of British faith and British liberty, entered into conversation on matters, which, seen as it should, were neither last nor least in their esteem. This was an enquiry into the good things for the table, that were to be found in the neighbourhood; in praise of many of which, they were extremely eloquent. — The Doctor complained of the scarcity of venison, but added, that he expected an excellent haunch in a few days, from a nobleman, his friend and patron; of which, Mr Sidebottom (for such was the name of this newly acquired friend) was requested to partake. — This request was, of course, readily assented to, and they, at length, left the shop together, having settled to ride to a neighbouring farm-house, where Mr Sidebottom assured the Doctor, that he had discovered some delicate fat ducks and pigeons, of peculiar size and flavour. — 'I even question,' said he, 'whether there will not be, in about a week's time, some nice turkey powts.[32] — The good woman is very clever about her poultry, and if she has had tolerable luck since I saw her, they must now be nearly fit for the dish.' — In this pleasing hope, the two gentlemen departed together. I followed them at a little distance, and saw them accosted by a thin, pale figure of a woman, with one infant in her arms and another following her. Her dress was not that of a beggar, yet it bespoke extreme indigence. I fancied she was a foreigner, and my idea was confirmed when I heard her speak. She stepped slowly, and, as it seemed, irresolutely, towards the two prosperous men, who were going in search of fat ducks and early turkeys; and, in imperfect English, began to relate, that she was a widow, and in great distress. 'A widow,' cried Mr Sidebottom, 'why you are a Frenchwoman; what have you to do here? And why do you not go back to your own country? This is the time there for beggars — they have got the upper hand. Go, go, mistress; get back to your own country.' — The poor woman answered, that she had travelled towards Dover with her two children, in hopes of getting a passage to France; but that they having been ill on the road, her little stock of money was exhausted; 'and therefore,' said she, 'I was advised to come hither, Sir, in hopes of procuring, by the generosity of the company who frequent this place, wherewithal to pay my passage to France; for unless I can produce enough for that purpose, no commander of a vessel will take me.'

'And let me tell you, they very properly refuse,' said Mr Sidebottom; 'you had no business that I know of in England, but to take the bread out of the mouth of our own people; and now I suppose you are going to join the fish-women, and such like, who are pulling down the king's palaces.'[33] — The unhappy woman cast a look of anguish on her children, and was quietly relinquishing this hopeless application, when the Doctor, more alive to the tender solicitations of pity than Mr Sidebottom, put his hand into his pocket, and then, in a nasal voice and in a magisterial manner, thus spoke: 'Woman! though I have no doubt but that thou art a creature of an abandoned conduct, and that these children are base born; yet, being a stranger and a foreigner, I have so much universal charity, that, unworthy as I believe thee, I will not shut mine heart against thy petition. If thou art an impostor, and wickedly imposest upon that charity, so much the worse for thee. I do my duty in bestowing it, and the wrong rests with thee! Here! Here is — sixpence! which I give thee towards thy passage! Go, therefore, depart in peace; and let me not have occasion to reprove thee to-morrow for lingering about the streets of this place; where, as people of fortune and consideration come for their health, they ought not to be disturbed and disgusted by the sight of objects of misery. I don't love to see beggars in these places; their importunity is injurious to the nerves. Let me hear of you no more — Our laws oblige us to provide for no poor but our own.'

The Doctor having thus fulfilled two great duties of his profession, those of giving advice, and giving alms, strutted away with the worthy Mr Sidebottom; who wisely considered that the turnpike through which he must pass in his tour after good dishes, would demand the small money he had about him: he therefore forebore to add to the bounty of the Doctor towards the unfortunate petitioner, who, feeling some degree of alarm from the remonstrance she imperfectly understood, remained for a moment gazing on the six-pence, which she yet held in her hand. She then clasped the youngest of her children to her breast, took the hand of the other as he clung to her gown, and burst into tears. In a moment, however, she dried her eyes, and, leaning against the rails of the parade, she cast a despairing look towards the gay groups who were passing, yet seemed examining to which of them she might apply with most hope of success. At this moment I approached nearer to her, but she did not see me till I spoke to her in French, and inquired, how I could assist her. The voice of kindness, in her own language, was so soothing, and I fear so new, that she was for some moments unable to answer me. The simplicity of the narrative with which she at length satisfied my inquiry, convinced me of the truth of all she related.

She told me, that her husband, the son of a reputable tradesman at Amiens, had married her, the daughter of a very inferior one, against his father's positive injunctions, who had thereupon dismissed him from the business to which he had been brought up, and left him to the world: that thus destitute, with a wife, and soon afterwards a child to support, he had accepted the offer of an English gentleman to accompany him to England, 'where he behaved so well,' continued she, 'that his master, who was a good man, became much his friend, and hearing he had in France a wife and child, whom he loved, he not only gave leave, but money to have us fetched over. Some months after, Sir, the gentleman married a very rich lady from the city, who wished him to part with his French servant: but though he prevailed upon her to let him keep a person who had been very faithful to him, the lady never liked him. In less than a twelvemonth after his marriage, my husband's master was taken ill of a fever and died. My husband sat up with him many nights, and by the time his master was carried to the grave, he fell ill himself of the same distemper; and his lady being afraid of the infection, hurried him out of the house to the lodging where I and my children lived. There he lay dreadfully ill for three weeks, during which time the lady sent a physician to him once or twice, but afterwards went into the country, and thought no more about him; so that we had nothing to support this cruel illness, but what my husband had saved in his service; which, with a wife and two children to keep out of his wages, to be sure, could not be much. He got through the fever, Sir, but it had so ruined his blood, that he went almost immediately into a decline; and it is now three weeks since he died, leaving me quite destitute with these two children. I applied for help, in this my utmost distress, to the widow of his late master, in whose service he certainly lost his life. After waiting a great while for an answer, she sent a gentleman to me with a guinea, which was, she said, all she should ever do for me; and she advised me to get back to France. This, by the assistance of the gentleman that brought me this money, who touched with pity for my situation, raised for me, among his friends, above a guinea more, I attempted to do; but on the road my children fell sick, and my money was all expended in procuring them assistance: so that now I have no means of reaching France, where, if I could once get, I hope my parents, poor as they are, would receive me, and that I should be able some way or other to earn my bread and my children's.'

I hope it is unnecessary to say, that I immediately set the widow's heart at ease on this score; and undertook to pay for her's and her children's conveyance.

Yesterday evening then I embarked. The wind was against us, and the sea ran extremely high: but I was impatient to be gone; and though the master doubted whether he could cross to Dunkirk, I was impatient, and pressed him to get under *weigh*, which he did, notwithstanding the unpromising appearance of the weather.[34]

I sat upon deck, looking towards the shore, when I saw, though we were by this time at a considerable distance from it, a group of people who seemed to be making signals to the men in the vessel. I bade the master observe them, and he distinguished, by his glass, a boat attempting to put off, in which he told me he imagined some other passengers, who had arrived after we had come on board, might be. He requested, therefore, that I would give him leave to lay to and wait for it, which I readily granted; and as the waves were now extremely high, we continued, with some apprehensions, to watch the boat, which was a very small one, and which often entirely disappeared.

At length, by the great exertion of the fishermen who were in it, the boat came along side, and one of the men hailing the master, told him he had brought a gentleman and his two servants, who were but just arrived from London in great haste, for a passage to France.

Three rueful figures did indeed appear in the boat; and, in the first of them that was helped up the side of the vessel, I recognised Waverly!

Sick to death, wet to the skin, and, I believe, not a little frightened by the tossing of the boat, he could not immediately answer the questions I put to him. At length he told me, that the day after he had sent off Anthony he altered his mind, and set out post to overtake me before I sailed. 'But now,' said he, 'I wish somehow I had not come till next week; for setting off in such a hurry, I have not brought my horses and carriages as I intended; and have only that portmanteau of cloaths with me.' I was almost tempted to tell him he had then better return on shore, and wait for the accommodation he thus regretted. But I thought of Geraldine, and detesting myself for my petulance, began to condole with, instead of blaming the half-drowned Waverly, whom I immediately advised to change his cloaths and go to bed; for he suffered extremely from the motion of the vessel, and again wished himself on shore. On the shore, however, to which, in less turbulent weather, a little encouragement might have sent him, he had now no inclination to venture, but took my advice and retired to the cabin; from whence Anthony came up in a few moments with a letter in his hand, which he said his master had forgot to give me. I looked at the direction — it was the writing, the elegant writing, of Geraldine. I opened it with trembling hands, and a palpitating heart. Heavens! does she write to me? Dare I hope she remembers me? — I have employed every moment since in reading and in copying it, that you may see how elegantly she writes, though I cannot part with the original. With what delight I retrace every word she has written; with what transport kiss the spaces between the lines, where her fingers have passed! But you have no notion of all this, and will smile contemptuously at it, as boyish and romantic folly. — My dear Bethel, why should we call folly that which bestows such happiness, since, after all our wisdom, our felicity depends merely on the imagination? I feel lighter and gayer since I have been in possession of this dear letter, the first I ever received from her! Waverly's little foibles disappear before its powerful influence. It is like a talisman, and hides his faults, half of which I am ready to think virtues, since without his indecision I should never have received it. Oh! with what zeal will I endeavour to execute the charge my angelic friend gives me to watch over the conduct of her brother. He is really not a bad young man; and I particularly rejoice at his being here, as I have learned from him, this morning, that the people with whom he went from Bath into Lincolnshire are gamblers, who have won a considerable sum of money of him. From such adventures, I hope to save him in future; and admitting it possible that his unsettled temper may sometimes occasion me some trouble, I shall remember that he is the brother of my adorable Geraldine, and the task will become a pleasure. — Farewell, my friend, you know my address at Paris. I shall go on this evening to Amiens, where I shall, perhaps, be detained a day by the affairs of my poor *protegée* and her children, who must be put into some way of subsistence before I leave them.

I am, ever, my dear Bethel,

Faithfully your's,

LIONEL DESMOND

LETTER VII

Paris, July 19, 1790

I have now, my dear Bethel, been some days in this capital, without having had time to write to you; so deeply has the animating spectacle of the 14th, and the conversation in which I have been since engaged, occupied my attention.[35] — I can now, however, assure you — and with the most heart-felt satisfaction, that nothing is more unlike the real state of this country, than the accounts which have been given of it in England; and that the sanguinary and ferocious democracy, the scenes of anarchy and confusion, which we have had so pathetically described and lamented, have no existence but in the malignant fabrications of those who have been paid for their mis-representations.

That it has been an object with our government to employ such men; men, whose business it is to stifle truths, which though unable to deny, they are unwilling to admit; is a proof, that they believe the delusion of the people necessary to their own views; and have recourse to these miserable expedients, to impede a little the progress of that light which they see rising upon the world. You know I was always interested in this revolution; (you sometimes thought too warmly) and I own, that till I came hither, I was not sufficiently master of the subject, to be able to answer those doubts which you often raised, as to the permanency of the new system in France — But I think, that candid and liberal as you are; and with such principles of universal philanthropy as you possess, I shall now have no difficulty in making you as warmly anxious, as I am, for the success of a cause which, in its consequence, involves the freedom, and, of course, the happiness, not merely of this great people, but of the universe. I had letters of introduction to several gentlemen here; among others, to the *ci-devant* Marquis de Montfleuri — a man, in whom the fire of that ardent imagination, so common among his countrymen, is tempered by sound reason, and a habit of reflection, very unusual at his time of life, to a native of any country, but particularly to one of this; where corruption has long been a system, from the influence of which, it was hardly possible for young men of property and title to escape.[36] — Montfleuri, however, though born a courtier, is one of the steadiest friends to the people — and it is from him that I have heard a detail of the progress of this great event, on which, I believe, you may depend; and I will, in my two or three next letters, relate it in his own words.

In the mean-time, my friend, I have infinite pleasure in describing to you the real state of Paris, and its neighbourhood — where there is not only an excellent police, but where the natural gaiety of the people now appears without any restraint, and yet, certainly, without any disorder; — where the utmost care is taken of the lives of the commonality, of whom a great number perished yearly in Paris, by the furious manner in which the carriages of the *noblesse* were driven through the streets, where there are no accommodations for the foot passenger — and where the proud and unfeeling possessors of those splendid equipages (the disappearance of which has been so much lamented in England) have been known to feel their rapid wheels crushing a fellow creature, with emotions so far from those of humanity, as to have said, *tant mieux, il y à toujours assez de ces gueux.**' Is it not natural for a people, who have been thus treated, to retaliate with even more ferocity than has been imputed to them? — and can it appear surprizing, that when the remark has been made, that there are now fewer magnificent carriages in the streets of Paris than there were formerly, they have answered, '*mais il y'en a encore trop?*†'

One of the greatest complaints which the discontented here have made — one, on which the eloquent declaimers among us have the most loudly insisted, is the levelling principle which the revolutionists have pursued. — Certainly, it is a great misfortune to the nobility to

---

* 'So much the better, there are always enough of those shabby rascals.'

    I know not whether, in the numerous anecdotes of this kind, that have been collected, it has ever been related, that a very few years since, as a young Frenchman of fashion — one of 'the very first world,' was driving through the streets of Paris, with an Englishman, his acquaintance, in a *cabriolet*, in the *rue St Honoré*, which is always extremely crouded, his horse threw down a poor man, and the wheels going over his neck, killed him on the spot. — The Englishman, with all the emotions of terror, natural on such an incident, cried out — Good God, you have killed the man! — The *charioteer* drove on; saying, with all possible *sang froid* — '*Eh bien, tant pis pour lui*' — Well then, so much the worse for him.[37]

† 'But there are still too many.'

be deprived of the invaluable privilege of believing themselves of a superior species, and to be compelled to learn that they are men.

I was assured, in London, that I should find Paris a desert — How true such an assertion is, let the public walks, and public spectacles witness; places, where such numbers assemble, as are hardly ever seen collected in London, (unless on very extraordinary occasions) yet, where even in the present hour, when the ferment of the public mind cannot have subsided, there is no disorder, no tumult, nor even that degree of disturbance, which the most trifling popular whim excites among us.

It is, however, at these places, the people are to be seen, and not their oppressors. — And if it is only these latter that constitute an inhabited country, Paris will remain, perhaps, deserted, in the eyes of those who are descibed by General Wallingford and Mrs Fairfax — as 'people of fashion' — *les gens comme il faut* — While the philosopher, the philanthropist, the citizen of the *world*; whose comprehensive mind takes a more sublime view of human nature than he can obtain from the *heights* of Versailles or St James's, rejoices at the spectacle which every where presents itself of newly-diffused happiness, and hails his fellow man, disencumbered of those paltry distinctions that debased and disguised him.

Such a man — with heart-felt satisfaction repeats that energetic, and in regard to this country, *prophetic* sentence of our immortal poet.

'Methinks I see in my mind a noble and puissant nation, rousing herself like the strong man after sleep; and shaking her invincible locks: — Methinks I see her, an eagle mewing her mighty youth, and kindling her undazzled eyes at the full mid-day beam; purging and unscaling her long abused sight at the fountain itself of heavenly radiance, while the whole flock of timorous and noisy birds, with those that love the twilight, flutter about, amazed at what she means, and in their envious gabble, would prognosticate a year of sects and schisms.*' — After this, my friend, I will now add a word of my own. — My next letter will give you some of the conversation of Montfleuri. When shall I hear from you? — And when will you indulge me with some

---

* Milton on the liberty of unlicensed printing.[38]

account of your neighbours? — Pray forget not what, even in this scene, is still nearest the heart

Of your's,

L. DESMOND

LETTER VIII

TO MR BETHEL

Paris, July 20, 1790

Montfleuri, with whom I have passed many pleasant and instructive hours since I have been here, has desired me to go with him to his estate on the banks of the Loire, about fifteen miles from Lyons, where business will soon call him. From thence, he proposes taking me to the *chateau* of his uncle, the *ci-devant* Count d'Hauteville in Auvergne, where I am to witness the pangs of aristocracy, reluctantly and proudly yielding to a necessity which it execrates: and my friend, afterwards, accompanies me to Merseilles, where, I believe, I shall embark for Italy, or, perhaps, for the Archipelago — I know not which — It depends on I know not what. (There is a sentence a little in the Waverly style). — I was, however, going to say, that it depends on the state of my mind, whether my absence from England shall be longer or shorter: — If I could return to see Geraldine happy, and not to regret that she is happy with Verney: — If I could feel, when I behold her, all that disinterested affection, which the purity of her character ought to inspire, without forming wishes and hopes that serve only to torment me, I would return through Italy in a few months to England. — You tell me absence will effect all this, and restore me to reason. — I rather hope it than believe it; and even, amidst this interesting scene, I catch myself continually carrying my thoughts to England, and imagining where Geraldine is — and enquiring whether she has not new sources of uneasiness in the encreasing dissipation of her husband.

What attractions for me has her very name! — It is with difficulty I recall my pen, and my wandering spirits, to endeavour to recollect, whether I told you how much disturbed poor Waverly was at the French post-horses and carriages, with which we travelled from Dunkirk; and how often he cursed his improvident haste, which had made him set out without his own horses and carriages. — At Abbeville, he seemed strongly disposed to have sent Anthony back to have fetched them; and, at Amiens, still more inclined to return and bring them himself; nor had he quite settled the debate when I came back from an absence, that was occasioned by the settlement of my poor *protegée* and her children, which I managed with less diffculty than I expected. — All this trifling I could bear from Waverly, and forgive it as boyish folly. — But it provokes my spleen to see a fellow have no more idea of the importance of the present period in France. — If ever he can be brought to think about it at all, it is only to raise a debate, whether he should have resigned his title calmly, had he been a French nobleman? — which usually terminates in the wise declaration, that he should have thought it a little hard.

Now will you pique yourself upon your sagacity in foreseeing that I should be sometimes peevish at the foibles of my fellow-traveller: it is, however, merely a transitory displeasure, and one thought of Geraldine dissipates it at once. — Since we have been at Paris, there is so much to engage him, that he has been very little with me; and here are several Englishmen of his acquaintance, who have taken the trouble of deciding for him, off my hands; all my care being to help to keep him, as much as possible, from the gaming houses, in obedience to his sister's wishes, which are my laws.

While he saunters away his time in a morning in the *Palais Royale*, and in the evening at the theatres, and in suppers with the actresses, I am deeply, and more deeply interested by the politics of the country.[39] — Montfleuri passes much of his time with me; and, therefore, I will give you a sketch of his character and his history.

He is now about five-and-thirty, a fine manly figure, with a countenance ingenuous and commanding. — He has been a fop, and still retains a something of it in his dress and manner; but it is very little visible, and not at all disgusting; perhaps, less so than that negligence which many of his countrymen have lately affected, as if determined, in trifles, as well as in matters of more consequence, to change characters with us.[40] The father of Montfleuri died in America, and as an only son, he was the darling of his mother; who, being anxious that her daughters, of whom she had four, might not be an incumbrance on an estate which his father had left a good deal embarassed, compelled the second and the youngest of them to become nuns; and married the eldest and the third, who were remarkably beautiful, to the first men who offered. — Montfleuri had no sooner the power by the new regulations, than he took his youngest sister, who is not yet eighteen, from the convent, where she was on the point of taking the vows; and, to the second, who has taken them, he offers an establishment in his own house, if she will leave her monastery, which is near his estate in Lyonois.[41] — To conquer her scruples and to prevail upon her to return to his house, is part of his immediate business in that country. — His mother, whose mistaken zeal he reveres, and for whose fondness, however unjust, he is grateful, has been dead a few months, and left him at liberty to follow the generous dictates of his heart.

It is not so easy for him to break the cruel bonds which that fatal partiality put on his other sister; I mean the third, for the eldest is a widow. — This third sister, who is called Madame de Boisbelle, I have seen; and, in finding her a very lovely and interesting woman, have, with extreme concern, heard that her husband is one of the most worthless characters in France, where, however, he is not at present, being a *fier aristocrate*, and having quitted his country rather than behold it free.[42]

Madame de Boisbelle, is now, therefore, at the hotel of her brother, with Mademoiselle Montfleuri, his younger sister; and they are to go with us to Montfleuri in a few days.[43]

I was yesterday with Montfleuri at a visit he made to a family of fashion, where, in the evening, people of all parties assemble; and where the lady of the house piques herself upon being a *bel esprit*, and giving to her guests the utmost freedom of conversation.[44] When we went in, a young *abbé*, who seemed to have an excellent opinion of his own abilities, was descanting on the injustice of what had been done in regard to the clergy. — The sneering tone in which he described the National Assembly, by the name of '*ces Messieurs qui ont pris la peine de nous reformer*,'* and the turn of this discourse, made it evident, that under a constrained or, at least, an affected moderation and candour, he concealed principles the most inimical and malignant to the revolution. — His discourse was to this effect.

'In every civilized country, there is no doubt of the supremacy of the church; more especially in this, where, ever since the baptism of

---

* Those gentlemen who have taken the trouble to reform us.

Clovis, it has made one of the great principles of the state.[45] — All ecclesiastical property, therefore, ought undoubtedly to be sacred; and, to invade it, is to commit sacrilege. I will not go into scriptural proofs of this axiom, I will only speak of the immorality and injustice of those measures which have been taken against it. It is well known, that much of the revenues of the church arise from gifts; from legacies given by Clovis and his pious successors; or, by other high and illustrious persons, to raise houses of piety, where the recluse and religious might pray for the repose of the souls of those eminent persons. — To fulfil these purposes, a certain number of men, renouncing the honours and emoluments of the world, have given their lives to this holy occupation; and is it not just they should enjoy the lot they have thus chosen in peace? Is it not just that, if they have resigned the pleasures of this world, they should be allowed its necessaries, while they are smoothing the passage to, or securing the happiness of the other, for those, who trust to their sanctity and their prayers? — Besides, permit me to remark, that many of the monastic estates have been waste lands, which have been cultivated and reclaimed by their former possessors; that, among the various societies of religious men, many have well earned their support, by undertaking the education of youth, while others have been employed in the charitable office of redeeming slaves from captivity. — Perhaps there might be some little disproportion between the emoluments possessed by the superior and inferior clergy; but it was always possible for these latter to rise by their zeal and good conduct; and, I must be permitted to think, that *messieurs nos reformateurs*, have not enough considered what they were doing; when instead of rectifying, with a tender hand, any little errors in the ecclesiastical order, they have destroyed it; instead of pruning the tree, they have torn it forcibly up by the roots. — If the nation was distressed in its revenues, by — by — by I know not what cause, the clergy offered four hundred million of livres* towards its assistance — a generous and noble offer, which ought to have been accepted.' — The *abbé* ceased speaking with the air of a man, who thought he had not only produced arguments, but such as it would be impossible to controvert. Montfleuri, however, who seemed of another opinion, thus answered him.

---

* Making upwards of 16 and half millions sterling.

'You have asserted, Sir, that in all civilized countries, the church forms a supreme branch of the legislature. — This is surely not the fact: I will not, however, enter into a discussion of how far it is so in other countries, or how far it ought to be so in any, but reply to the arguments which you have deduced from its power in our own. — You must allow me to remark, that the antiquity of an abuse is no reason for its continuance — And if the enormous wealth of the clergy be one, it ought not to be perpetuated, unless better reasons can be brought in its favour, than that it commenced at the conversion and baptism of Clovis; who, guilty of horrible enormities, and stained with blood, was taught to hope, that by erecting churches, and endowing monasteries, the pardon of heaven might be obtained for his crimes: and, in doing so, he certainly did not make a bad bargain for himself; for it cost him only that of which he robbed his subjects. It was with their toil and misery he thus purchased the absolution which the monks gave him for murder and oppression — It was their tears, and their blood, that cemented the edifices he raised.*

I believe the same may be said of the foundations made by those monarchs, whom you call his pious successors. The weak bigot Louis the Seventh — the ferocious sanguinary monster Louis the Eleventh, are, I suppose, among the most eminent of the list.[46] — Of what efficacy those prayers might be, that were thus obtained, I shall say nothing, since that is matter of opinion. — It is plain, however, that the nation does not now believe them useful to its welfare, and there-fore, with great propriety, turns into another channel, that wealth, which it no longer deems beneficial in this. I think you will not deny that the most useful of the clergy are the *curés*, who live on their cures; whose time should be given up to the really christian and pious pur-poses of instructing the poor, visiting the sick, and relieving the tem-poral necessities of their parishioners, by such means as they possess; though it too often happened that they had hardly wherewithal to supply themselves with the necessaries their humble manner of life required:[47] — An error, in the distribution of money appropriated to the church, which, in the present system, will, I apprehend, be

---

* Some sentences here are drawn from a little French pamphlet, entitled, *'Lettre aux Aristo-theocrate Français.'*[48]

remedied. I cannot agree with you, that the tree is torn up by the roots: I should rather say, that its too luxuriant branches, which prevented the production of wholesome fruit, are reformed; and the whole reduced nearer to the proportion, which may secure it from being destroyed by the storms that pass by, through the disproportion of its head. — You have, Sir, declined entering into those scriptural proofs of their sacred nature, which you intimated were to be brought in support of the ancient establishments; a fortunate circumstance for me, as on that ground I must have felt my inferiority. — But, from what I know of the subject, I have always supposed, that whatever spiritual resemblance there might be between the primitive fathers of the church and their present successors, there was certainly very little in the temporal conditions. It does not appear ever to have been the expectation of the saints and martyrs, that those who followed them in their holy calling, should become temporal princes, or possess such immense revenues as the higher clergy enjoyed in this country, of whom, you know, Sir, that there were some whose yearly incomes amounted to eighty, an hundred, two, three, four hundred thousand livres a year.

As to that rank of them who lived in convents, I will not enquire whether piety or idleness decided their vocation — I will believe that it may, in numerous instances, have been the former motive — and that in others, the unhappy, or the guilty, might seek, in these retreats, shelter from the miseries of life, or leisure to make their peace with heaven. — But men, carried into religious retirements by such motives, would probably be content with mere necessaries of life, which are not taken from them: it is not therefore these men who complain. — To the monks, I am disposed to allow all you can urge in their favour, as to the education of youth, and the redemption of prisoners, though these merits, and particularly the latter, have been much disputed (probably from the *misrepresentations* that have been made of the manner of executing these charges) — I will go farther, and enumerate one obligation the world owes them, which you have overlooked, or do not think it of consequence enough to mention; — I mean, that to them we are indebted for the preservation of those precious relics of antiquity, which, but for the security which superstition enabled them to give, would have perished in the ferocious turbulence of the dark ages. But, Sir, with all the disposition imaginable, to allow the monastic institution all the honour they can assume, I still cannot be of opinion that the good works they have given birth to, even in their utmost extent, balance the various evils which these communities occasion to the nation that supports them. As to the mendicant orders, surely the suppression of them cannot be complained of. — The vow of poverty taken by *capucins, recollets,* &c. &c. may now be executed in humble privacy, for which the state will provide during the lives of those who have taken these vows, and they will no longer be in a degraded condition of life, which must be a continual tax to the pious, while it gave to the light-minded a subject of ridicule, and to the indifferent, of disgust. I need hardly insist on the miseries to which monastic vows, made at a time of life when no civil contract would be binding, have condemned individuals of both sexes.[49] — Wretches, who having thus thrown themselves, yet living, into the tomb, have afterwards existed only to curse their being. — I will not retouch the disgusting pictures that have been so frequently exhibited, of the wretchedness, or the vices that have prophaned these dark recesses, built for far other purposes; nor enlarge upon the deluges of blood, the variety of tortures by which the monks have established their power over the ignorance and apprehensions of mankind. — What then should prevent a nation from re-assuming grants; which, admitting they were originally given to good purposes, have long since been perverted? Certainly, Sir, you cannot assert, that *le haut clergé*, the higher rank of ecclesiastics in our day, whose declined authority and lessened revenues you regret, resemble, in any instance, those apostles who professed poverty and humility, and went about doing good? — Though I am, on the other hand, ready to admit of their resemblance to their more immediate, though still remote predecessors, the bishops who lived as long ago as the reign of Louis le Debonnair.[50] One of our historians* speaks of them as being, at that period, 'men who were, for the most part, become great lords, possessing vast domains and many vassals; and, while they governed the minds of the people, entirely devoted to a court: — men, whose ample revenues enabled them to gratify every worldly inclination, and to enjoy luxu-

---

* Millot.[51]

ries which soon made them lose sight of their spiritual duties, and neglect their original vocation.' —

A young man, whom I had not till now noticed, took advantage of a pause to interrupt Montfleuri. — 'Well,' said he, in English, and what then? it proves that those worthies knew how to live: and, I am sorry with all my soul, that their successors, the old bucks of our own times, are thrown out as they are. — When I was at Paris last, I was always sure of a *couvert* at the table of an archbishop, and an excellent table it was: then, at that time, there were many of the *haut clergé* who gave comfortable, and even elegant establishments to two or three women, to whose parties one was always welcome.[52] — Now there is an end of all that — the poor bishops are gone upon their travels, and their *cheres amies* upon the town; which, in regard to its society, I am sure is very far from being improved: for, instead of the agreeable sort of people one used to converse with, one now only meets queer fellows; who *bore* one to death with long preachments about their freedom, their constitution, and the rights of the people; and, after all, I don't see that any of these things are much changed for the better. — As to the people, that is, the *canaille*, of whose happiness there is so much talk, I don't think, myself, that they are so much happier than they were before.[53] Indeed, I have heard it affirmed by those who are much more interested in the matter, and more acquainted with it than I am, that they are not at all happier since this boasted revolution, not at all better off.' —

Montfleuri, who had, I saw, conceived a very mean opinion of this individual, of a nation he loves and esteems, answered very calmly — 'The objection you have made, Sir, to the reduction of the higher clergy; the evils you have deduced from it are certainly most convincing — In regard, however, to the opinions which have, you say, been delivered by good judges of the subject on the happiness of the people; perhaps, the best way of ascertaining the justice of those remarks, would be to refer you to the people themselves, as being alone competent to decide.

'Enquire of them, whether they are not better for being relieved from the *taille*, from the *gabelle*, from the imposts levied at the gates of every town, on every necessary of life;[54] for the relief they have obtained from those burthens that were imposed upon them, because they were poor; while their illustrious compatriots were exempt, because they were noble.* Ask the aged peasant, who is no longer able to labour for his own subsistence; ask the mother of a group of helpless children, if they are not the happier for being assured, that the son, the husband, on whom their existence depends, cannot now be torn from the paternal cottage; and, to execute some ambitious scheme of a weak king or a wicked minister, be enrolled against their inclination in a mercenary army? — Let the soldier, who is now armed for the defence of his country, a country sensible of the value of the blood he is ready to shed for its freedom, tell you whether he is not happier for the consciousness that he cannot be compelled to carry devastation into another land as a slave, but shall hereafter guard his own as a freeman: ask the husbandman, whose labours were coldly and reluctantly performed before, when the *fermiers-general,* and the intendants of the provinces, devoured two-thirds of their labour, if they do not proceed more willingly and more prosperously to cultivate a soil from whence those locusts are driven by the breath of liberty?[55] Enquire of the citizen, the mechanic, if he reposes not more quietly in his house from the certainty that it is not now liable to be entered by the *marechaussées,* and that it is no longer possible for him to be forcibly taken out of it by a *lettre de cachet,* in the power of a minister, or his secretary, his secretary's clerk, or his mistress?[56] Let the voice of common sense answer, whether the whole nation has gained nothing in its dignity, by obtaining the right of trial by jury; by the reform in the courts of judicature; where, it is well known, that formerly, every thing was given to money or to favour, and to equity and justice, nothing? — As to the prejudice that all these alterations have been to the manners of society, to that, indeed, I have nothing to say. — I must lament that, in shaking off the yoke, we have been so long reproached for wearing, we have not taken care to preserve, unfaded, all those elegant flowers with which it was decorated. The complaint, perhaps, is well founded, for I have heard it before; and, particularly from the ladies of your country, Sir; to whom,

---

* Ce gouvernement serait digne des Hottentots, *says* Voltaire, dans lequel il seroit permis à un certain nombre d'hommes de dire, c'est à ceux qui travaillant à payer — Nous ne devons rien payer, parceque nous sommes oisifs.[57]

I am afraid, the name of a Frenchman will hereafter give no other idea than that of a savage; a misfortune which, as I greatly admire the English ladies, nobody can more truly regret than I shall. — But I shall tire you, Sir, by thus dwelling on a subject which you have just observed is very *ennuyant*; and, therefore, will leave you to Monsieur l'Abbé de Bremont, whose ideas, on public matters, seem more happily to meet your own.'[58]

Montfleuri then walked away, and, with me, joined the party of the Lady of the house, who was at play in another room. — The conversation, round the table, took another turn, and we soon afterwards went away; and, as the evening was warm, strolled into the Luxembourg Gardens, where my friend continued, as I will relate in a future letter, to speak on the predisposing causes of the revolution — and on its effects.[59]

I am so late now, as to the post, that I have only time to entreat you to write to me immediately, that I may receive your letter before I leave Paris, which will be within these fifteen days. — The ten last have past without my receiving a single line from you. — Adieu! dear Bethel,

Your's truly,
LIONEL DESMOND

LETTER IX

TO MR BETHEL

Paris, August 4, 1790

It is very uneasy to me, my dear Bethel, to be so long without hearing from you. — I am willing to believe, that you are absent from Hartfield, and wandering with my little friends, Harry and Louisa, on one of your usual summer tours; and that, therefore, you have not received my letters, and know not whither to direct. — I would, indeed, rather believe any thing than that you have forgotten me, unless it be, that illness has prevented your writing. Waverly has had only two letters from his youngest sister since he left England; and they hardly mention the Verney family, as Fanny Waverly is with her mother at Bath, where they usually reside.

Were my heart less deeply interested for my friends in England, I should be quite absorbed in French politics; and, could those friends be even for a little while supplied by foreign connections, the family of Montfleuri would be that where I should chuse to seek them. — But the tender interest I feel for some individuals in England, no time, no change of scene can weaken. My heart

> 'Still to my country turns with ceaseless pain,
> And drags at each remove a lengthening chain.'*

I will not indulge this train of thought: it will be better to continue to relate the conversation I had with Montfleuri in the latter part of that evening, of which I described the beginning in my last letter.

As we walked together towards the Luxembourg Gardens, he asked me if I knew the young Englishman, whose argument, in defence of the enormous revenues of the bishops, was so very convincing. — 'Not even by name,' answered I; 'and so far am I from wishing to enquire, that I would I could forget having heard such frivolous folly in my native language.' — Montfleuri smiled at the warmth with which I spoke. 'I can forgive,' said he, 'the short view of an unexperienced boy just come from his college, or the trifling inconsequence of a mere *petit maitre*, who knowing nothing beyond what the saunterers in a coffee-house, or the matrons of a card-table have taught him to repeat by rote, talks merely as a child recites his lesson, without being capable of affixing one idea to the sentences he utters.[60] — Such people are perfectly harmless, or rather bring into ridicule the cause they attempt to defend. But, when I meet, as too often I have done, Englishmen of mature judgment and solid abilities, so lost to all right principles as to depreciate, misrepresent, and condemn those exertions by which *we* have obtained that liberty they affect so sedulously to defend for themselves; when they declaim in favour of an hierarchy so subversive of all true freedom, either of thought or action, and so inimical to the welfare of the people — and pretend to blame us for throwing off those yokes, which would be intolerable to themselves, and which they have been accustomed to ridicule us for enduring; I ever hear them with a

---

* Goldsmith.[61]

mixture of contempt and indignation, and reflect with concern on the power of national prejudice and national jealousy, to darken and pervert the understanding.

'All, however, that I have ever heard from such men, has served only to prove to me, either that they fear for their own nation the too great political consequence of ours, when our constitution shall be established; or know and dread that the light of reason thus rapidly advancing, which has shewn us how to overturn the massy and cumbrous edifice of despotism, will make too evident, the faults of their own system of government, which it is their particular interest to screen from research and reformation. — But how feeble are all the endeavours of this political jealousy on one hand, and the yet obstinate prejudices of papal superstition on the other, to obscure this light in its irresistible and certain progress; more rapid and more brilliant from the vain attempt to intercept and impede it. — "*Ne sentez vous pas,*" says Voltaire very justly — "*Ne sentez vous pas, que ce qui est juste, clair, évident, est naturellement respecté de tout le monde, & que des chimeres ne peuvent pas toujours s'attirer la même vénération?*"*

'The sudden change that has taken place in this country, from the most indolent submission to a despotic government, to the adoption of principles of more enlarged liberty than your nation has ever avowed, appeared so astonishing, and so unaccountable, to those who beheld the event at a distance, that they believed it could not be permanent. Our national character, a character given us by Caesar, and which we are said still to retain — that vehement, fierce, and almost irresistible, in the beginning of an action, we are soon repulsed and dismayed — encouraged the persuasion, that the revolution would prove only a violent popular commotion; and that when our first ardour was abated, the spirit of our ancient government, taking advantage of this well-known disposition of the French people, would gradually resume its influence; and perhaps, by a few concessions of little consequence, induce us to submit again to that system, which a momentary frenzy had suspended.[62] But I, who, though as dissipated as most men, was

---

* Are you not sensible, that what is just, clear, and evident, must be naturally attended to — And that chimeras cannot always be held in veneration?

neither an unobserving or disinterested spectator of what was passing, have for some years seen, that our government was approaching rapidly to its dissolution, and, that many causes unknown, and unsuspected, were silently uniting to accelerate its ruin.

'The advocates for despotism consider the reigns of Henry the Fourth, and Louis the Fourteenth, as evidences in favour of their system: but allowing that the former was an excellent man, and worthy to be entrusted with the power of governing a great people (which can hardly be allowed to Louis the Fourteenth), what a black and hideous list of regal monsters may be brought to contrast the most favourable pictures that can be drawn of these monarchs![63] The various murders and assassinations which stain the annals of the last princes of the House of Valois; and, above all, the massacre of St Bartholomew, reflect disgrace on a nation, which, even at that dark period, could tolerate and obey such ferocious tyrants, and still more, on the sanguinary superstition which gave them a pretence to commit these enormities.[64] The same bigotry, however, delivered his insulted country from the last of this odious race*; but it opposed, in his successor, a man who seemed born for the political salvation of his people, and who became afterwards the best king that France ever boasted. — Brought up like the mountaineers, over whom only it was once likely he should reign, his heart had never been hardened, nor his frame enervated by the flatteries or luxuries of a court. — He had not been taught, that to be born a king is to be born something more than man.

'The admirable dispostions he had received from nature, were so much improved in the rigid school of adversity, in which so many years of his life were passed, that his character was fixed, and prosperity and power could not destroy those sentiments of humanity and goodness which made him, throughout his whole reign (even amidst the too liberal indulgence of some weaknesses and errors) consider the happiness of his people as the first object of his government. But his life was imbittered, and his endeavours for the good of his subjects continually opposed, by the restless suspicion, and encroaching ambition of the priests of that religion, to which, to save the effusion of his people's blood, he was a reluctant, and perhaps, not a very sincere con-

---

* Harry the Third.

vert: till at length the same execrable fanaticism raised against him the murderous hand of Ravaillac, and with him perished the hopes of France; a nation that, had he lived, would probably have possessed prosperity and happiness, with a considerable portion of political liberty.[65]

'The treasure that the wise oeconomy of the Duc de Sully had amassed for him, to carry on his projects, which would have secured a long and universal peace, were instantly, on his death, dissipated among the hungry and selfish nobility that surrounded his widow*.[66]

'The early part of the reign of the weak and peevish bigot his son, Louis the Thirteenth, was marked by a faint attempt to restore something like a voice to the people, by a convocation of *les etats généraux*†.[67]

'But this was rather an effort of the nobility against the hated power of the Italian favourites, the Conchinis, than meant to restore to the people any part of their lost rights.[68]

'The whole of this reign was rendered odious by the continual wars on the subject of religion, which deluged the country with blood; by the factions, which existed even in the family of the prince upon the throne; where the mother was armed against her son, the son against his mother; and the brothers against each other: — all practising, in turn, every artifice that perfidy and malignity could imagine; and sacrificing every thing to their own worthless views.[69] — When to these ruinous circumstances was added an ambitious aristocracy, ready on every occasion to take advantage of the weakness of the monarch, and the discord in his councils, it is easily seen that nothing but the resolute courage, and strong talents of Richelieu could have prevented the total destruction of France as a monarchy.[70] It would, but for him, have been broken into small republics, and small principalities. The first would have been possessed by the Huguenots, and the latter by the principal nobility; who, when ever they opposed the court, and flew into rebellion, revolted not against measures, but men.[71] — It was the favourites of Louis the Thirteenth that provoked them, and not the encreasing oppression of the people: — the unhappy and plun-

---

*   Mary of Medicis.[72]
†   The last assembly of that description that was called in France.

dered people, who equally the victims of the monarch, the nobles, and the priests, were pillaged and destroyed by them all.

'But the thick cloud of ignorance which covered Europe, was yet but slowly and partially rolling alway. It was during this period that Galileo was imprisoned in Italy* for his discoveries in astronomy; and that Descartes was accused of impiety and atheism.[73]

'The reign of Louis the Fourteenth was more propitious to knowledge. — His encouragement of science and literature has, in the immortality it has conferred upon him, led many writers to forget the ostentatious despot, in the munificent patron. — Fascinated by his manners, dazzled by the magnificence of his public works, and elated by his victories, his people felt for him the most enthusiastic attachment, and loved even his vices; vices which the servile crowd of nobles around him, found it their interest to imitate and applaud; while the priests also made their advantage of these errors, obtaining by them the means of dictating to a man who was at once a libertine and a *devoté*.[74] — The revocation of the edict of Nantz; the cruel and absurd persecution of the Protestants, were among the follies that they led him to commit; and depopulated and impoverished his country, which, at his death, soon after the close of an unsuccessful war, was in a state of almost total bankruptcy.[75] Yet, so bigotted were we then to the system of passive obedience, so attached to unlimited monarchy, that throughout the long reign of his great-grandson,† the murmurs of the people were feeble and disregarded; though their burthens were intolerable, though they were imposed by a prince who, without any of the virtues of his predecessor, had more than his vices; and, though the sums thus extorted from the hard hands of patient industry, were either expended in disgraceful and ill-managed wars, or lavished in the debaucheries of the most profligate court‡ that modern Europe has beheld.[76] From the infamous means that to support all this were then

---

* 'There I visited,' says Milton, 'the celebrated Galileo, then poor and old, and a long time a prisoner in the dungeon of the Inquisition, for daring to think otherwise in astronomy than his Franciscan and Dominican licensers thought.'[77]

† Louis the Fifteenth.[78]

‡ See la Vie privée de Louis XV.[79]

practised to raise money; from the heavy imposts that were then laid on the country, France has never recovered; but, perhaps, in the *discontents* which these oppressions created, silent and unmarked as they were, the foundation was laid for the universal spirit of revolt, to which she is now indebted for her freedom.

'In the mean time, the progress of letters, which Louis the Fourteenth had encouraged, was insensibly dispelling that ignorance which alone could secure this blind obedience. — The president Montesquieu had done as much as a writer, under a despot, dared to do, towards developing the spirit of the laws, and the true principles of government; and, though the multitude heeded not, or understand not his abstract reasoning, he taught those to think, who gradually disseminated his opinions.[80] Voltaire attacked despotism in all its holds, with the powers of resistless wit: — Rousseau with matchless eloquence: — and, as these were authors who, to the force of reason, added the charms of fancy, they were universally read, and their sentiments were adopted by all classes of men.[81]

'The political maxims and oeconomical systems of Turgot, and the application of these principles by Mirabeau, excited a spirit of enquiry, the result of which could not fail of being favourable to the liberties of mankind:[82] and such was the disposition of the people of France, when the ambitious policy of our ministry sent our soldiers into America to support the English colonists in their resistance to the parent state.'[83]

I here interrupted my friend, by remarking, that so deep is the resentment which the English still entertain against his nation for this interference, that I had heard many rejoicing over the most unpromising picture they could draw of the present state of France; and, when they have imagined the country deluged with blood, and perishing by famine, have said — 'Oh! the French deserve it all for what they did against us in America.' —

'And yet, my dear Sir,' answered Montfleuri, 'these good countrymen of your's are a little inconsiderate and inconsistent; inconsiderate in not reflecting, that the interference which seems so unpardonable, was the act of the cabinet, not of the people, who had no choice, but went to be shot at for the liberties of America, without having any liberty of their own; and, inconsistent, inasmuch, as they now exclaim against the resolution we have made to deprive our monarchs of the power of making war; a power which they thus complain has been so unwarrantably exerted — These are some of the many absurdities into which a resolution to defend a pernicious system, betrays its ablest advocates. However, our court has found its punishment. Blinded by that restless desire of conquest, and their jealousy of the English, which has ever marked its politics, our government did not reflect that they were thus tacitly encouraging a spirit subversive of all their views; nor foresee, that the men who were sent out to assist in the preservation of American freedom, would soon learn that they were degraded by being themselves slaves; and would return to their native country to feel and to assert their right to be them selves free.

'I was then a very young man: but my father, who was a colonel in the regiment of Nassau, and who died in America, took me with him in despite of the tears and entreaties of my mother. — I saw there such scenes as have left an indelible impression on my mind, and an utter abhorrence for all who, to gratify their own wild ambition, or from even worse motives, can deliberately animate the human race to become butchers of each other. — Above all, it has given me a detestation of civil war; for the fiercest animosity with which the French and English armies have met in the field, was mildness and friendship in comparison of the ferocity felt by the English and Americans, men speaking the same language, and originally of the same country, in their encounters with each other. I saw, amidst the almost undisciplined Americans, many instances of that enthusiastic courage which animates men who contend for all that is dear to them, against the iron hand of injustice; and, I saw these exertions made too often vain, against the disciplined mercenaries of despotism; who, in learning to call them rebels, seemed too often to have forgotten that they were men. How little did I then imagine, that a country which seemed to be devoted to destruction, could ever be in such a state as that in which I have since beheld it — Yes, my friend, I revisited this country two years since, in which fourteen years before, I had served as an ensign, when it was the seat of war. — I see it now recovered of those wounds, which its unnatural parent hoped were mortal, and in the most flourishing state of political health.

'What then becomes of the political credit of those who prognosticated, that her productions would be unequal to her wants; her legislatures to her government. — I know not how far the mother-country is the worse for this disunion with her colonies — but, I am sure, they are the better; and, nothing is more false than that idea of the veteran statesman, that a country, under a new form of government, is destitute of those who have ability to direct it. — That they may be unlearned in the detestable chicane of politics, is certain; but, they are also uncorrupted by the odious and pernicious maxims of the unfeeling tools of despotism. Honest ministers then, and able negociators will arise with the occasion. — They have appeared in America; they are rising in France — they have, indeed, arisen; and, when it is seen that talents and application, and not the smile of a mistress, or a connection with a parasite, give claims to the offices of public trust, men of talents and application will never be wanting to fill them.'

Montfleuri here paused a moment, and a sentence of Milton's, of whom you know I am an incessant reader, immediately occurred to me as extremely applicable to what he had been saying; I repeated it to him in English, which he understands perfectly well.

'For, when God shakes a kingdom, with strong and healthful commotions, to a general reforming, it is not untrue that many sectaries and false teachers are then busiest in seducing: but yet more true it is, that God then raises, to his own work, men of rare abilities and more than common industry; not only to look back and revise what hath been taught heretofore, but to gain further, and go on some new and enlightened steps in the discovery of truth.'*

Here our conference was ended for this time, at least, on politics. We took a few turns among the happy groups who were either walking, or sitting, to enjoy the most beautiful moon-light evening I ever remember to have seen; and I then returned to my hotel, and went to my repose, determined to indulge the pleasing hope of having letters from England on the morrow, as it was post day; but, I am again most severely disappointed. — Waverly, however, has letters from his sisters — they lay on the table in the room where we usually sit, for he is gone with, I know not what party, to Chantilly. — I see that one of them is directed by the hand of Geraldine. — I have taken it up an hundred times, and laid it down again — It is sealed with an impres-

---

*   Milton on the Liberty of unlicensed Printing.[84]

sion of the Verney arms — It is heavy and seems to contain more than one or two sheets of paper: perhaps, there is a letter in it for me. — Yet, why should I flatter myself? — The other letter is from Fanny Waverly — I recollect her hand, for it a little resembles her sister's. — Would to heaven Waverly were come back — He went on a sudden, and named no time for his return; and my time, these last two days, has been wasted in the most uneasy expectation; for I can think of nothing but the purport of these letters. — If they assure me of the health and content of Mrs Verney, for I will try to break myself of calling her Geraldine (because I always long to add *my* to that beloved name) — I will endeavour to account, dear Bethel, for your silence, by believing that you are travelling with your children; and set out as chearfully as I can, with Montfleuri and his sisters, on Monday, which is the day fixed for our departure. — I hoped a few days ago, that I had determined Waverly to go with us, but he has since made some new acquaintance, and has probably new schemes.

Adieu! You know me to be ever
most faithfully your's,
LIONEL DESMOND

LETTER X

Montfleuri, August 29, 1790

After being once more compelled to change my plan on account of the indecision of Waverly, who did not return to Paris till some days after he had written to me to say, he should be there, he arrived, and I saw these letters, which alone would have induced me to wait. — But I was extremely mortified to find, that instead of an account of Geraldine herself, it was only a long letter about health and prudence, which Mrs Waverly, who has the gout herself, has employed her daughter to write for her to her son. In a postscript, however, she adds some trifling commissions on her own account, which, as Waverly set out the next day for Rheims, with the same scampering party with whom he was just returned from Chantilly, he left for me to execute. Judge whether I did not undertake them with pleasure, with delight, and whether I regretted the two days longer that were thus passed in her service at Paris. — This circumstance gave me an opportunity of writing to her. — And so, my dear Bethel, I shall have a letter from her before I quit this place, whither I have entreated her to direct. Do not now give me one of your grave, cold lectures — and blame me for the inconsistency of flying from my country to conquer a passion which I still take every opportunity of cherishing. — Without this affection, I feel that my life would sink into tasteless apathy; and I cannot, my rigid Mentor, discover the immorality of it, in its present form. On the contrary, I am convinced, that my apprehensions of rendering myself unworthy of the esteem, which, I now believe, Geraldine feels for me, acts upon me as a sort of second conscience. — What ought not that man to attempt, who dares hope ever to become worthy of her heart? — But I dare not; nor do I ever trust myself with so pre-sumptuous a thought. — Her friendship, her esteem, may be mine — But I am getting into regions, where your cold and calm philoso-phy cannot, or will not follow me.

I return, therefore, to mere matter of fact; and to thank you for your long-expected and long wished-for letter. — It is tolerably inter-spersed with lectures, my good friend — but I thank you for them, because I know they are the effusions of anxious friendship — and still more, I thank you for the account you give me of yourself, your children, and all other friends, for whom you think I am interested, except the Verney's whom you cruelly leave out of the list — and rela-tive to them, therefore, I form many uneasy conjectures; so that, in-stead of saving me from pain, you have inflicted it. My apprehensions, probably, go beyond the truth; but Geraldine is unhappy, I know she is. — In every English newspaper that I have seen since I left London, there is some account of Verney's exploits upon the turf — and of his winnings or his losings. — Some of Waverly's acquaintance, whom I accidentally conversed with at Paris, spoke of him in terms of high approbation; as, to use their own cant, 'a devilish dashing fellow — a good fellow' — and such epithets as convinced me he is sacrificing the happiness of that lovely woman to the glory of being talked of — the only species of fame which seems to give him any pleasure.

I am now at Montfleuri, in the Lyonois. — Had I not felt, as I travelled hither, a strange, uneasy sensation, which I acknowledge to be a weakness, in reflecting on the encreasing distance between me and Geraldine; and had I not very uneasy apprehensions about her brother, who is gone with a set of very dissipated boys, they hardly know whither themselves, my journey to this place would have been one of the most agreeable I ever made.

I have twice before travelled the direct road from Paris to Lyons. — Montfleuri, who is the most chearful companion in the world, has himself a great taste for rural beauty, and therefore, though every part of this country is, of course, well known to him, he had particular pleasure in turning out of the road to shew me any view, or building, which he thought worth my observation. Our journey, by this means, was of eight days continuance — and eight days have been seldom more pleasantly passed.

I have said very little hitherto of Montfleuri's two sisters, who are with us; and who are by no means objects to be passed in silence, in the account you wish to have of my wanderings. — Though I, you know, 'bear a charmed heart,' and therefore cannot, like our friend Melthorpe, enliven my narrative with details of my own passions for a sprightly French-woman, or an elegant Italian.[85] I am persuaded, that were I to be shewn, in succession, the most celebrated beauties of all the kingdoms through which I shall pass, I thus should still apostrophise Geraldine:

> 'I scorn the beauties, common eyes adore,
> The more I view them — feel thy charms the more.'[86]

But I am talking of her instead of Madame de Boisbelle, who is very beautiful and very unhappy, two circumstances that cannot fail to make her extremely interesting. Perhaps she is rendered yet more so by the unfailing variety of her manner. There are times when her naturally gay spirits sink under the pressure of misfortune. Sometimes her ill-assorted marriage, which has put her into the power of a man altogether unworthy of her; the embarrassment of his affairs, and the uncertainty of her fate, recur to her in all their force; and she escapes from company, if it be possible, to hide the languor and depressions she cannot conquer. During our journey, however, this was not easily done; and I often remarked with pain, these cruel reflections fill her fine eyes with tears, and force deep sighs from her bosom. — But this disposition was as a passing cloud obscuring the brilliancy of the summer sun. — The moment her attention is diverted from this mournful and useless contemplation, by some new object, or yields to the tender raillery of her brother, who is extremely fond of her, the gayest smiles return again to her expressive countenance; her eyes regain their lustre, and she passes almost instantaneously from languid dejection, to most brilliant vivacity. — Without having ever had what we call a good education, Josephine (for I have learned from her brother, and at her own desire, to drop the formal appellation of Madame de Boisbelle) Josephine has much of that sort of knowledge which makes her a pleasant companion; and a fund of native wit, which, though it is rather sparkling than impressive, renders her conversation very delightful. — She has a pretty voice, and plays well on the harp. — Yet all she does has so much of national character in it, that it would become only a French woman, and I think I should not admire one of my own countrywomen, who possessed exactly the person, talents and manners of my friend's sister. — I do not know whether you perfectly understand me, but I understand myself; though, perhaps, I do not explain myself clearly.

The little mild Julie is yet too young to have any very decided character. — The religious prejudices which she received in her early infancy (for at nine years old her mother determined to make her a nun) have sunk so deeply in her mind, that I much doubt whether they will ever be erased. This has given to her disposition a melancholy cast, which, though it renders her, perhaps, interesting to strangers, her brother sees with concern. — I perceive that there is, at times, a very painful struggle in her mind, between her wish to obey and gratify him in entering into the world, and her fears of offending Heaven by having failed to renounce it; and, I am afraid, there are moments which any absurd bigot might take advantage of, to persuade her, that she should yet return to that state whither Heaven has summoned her.

Julie, however, is extremely pretty, though quite in another style of beauty from her sister. — Waverly admired her, on first seeing her, as much as it is in his nature to admire any woman; and, for three days, I fancied it possible that the fair and pensive nun might fix this vagrant spirit. I even began to consider, how (if the affair should become more serious) Geraldine, as much as she wishes her brother married, would approve of his chusing a woman of another country, and another religion from his own; and, I had settled it with myself, to give no encouragement to the progress of his attachment, till I knew her sentiments. — I might, however, have saved myself all my wise resolutions; for Waverly immediately afterwards making some fortunate additions to his number of English acquaintance (Mr Chetwood, the able advocate for episcopalian luxury is one) has since passed all his time among them; and seems to have lost, in their company, every impression that the gentle Julie, and her fascinating, though very imperfect English, had made. — He has promised, either to come hither within ten days, or to meet me at Lyons in the course of a fortnight; but I do not expect that he will do either the one or the other.

I do not know whether you love the description of places, or whether I am very well qualified to undertake it, if you do. — However, I will endeavour to give you an idea of the habitation of Montfleuri, and of the country round it, where his liberal and enlightened spirit has, ever since he became his own master, been occupied in softening the harsh features of that *system of government, to which only the poverty and misery of such a country as this could, at any time, be owing.*

The *chateau* of Montfleuri is an old building, but it is neither large nor magnificent — for having no predilection for the gothic gloom in which his ancestors concealed their greatness, he has pulled down every part of the original structure, but what was actually useful to himself; and brought the house, as nearly as he could, into the form of one of those houses, which men of a thousand or twelve hundred a year inhabit in England.

Its situation is the most delicious that luxuriant fancy could imagine. — It stands on a gentle rise; the river there, rather broad than deep, makes almost a circuit round it at the distance of near half a mile. — The opposite banks rise immediately on the south side into steep hills of fantastic forms, cloathed with vines. — They are naturally indeed, little more than rocks; but wherever the soil was deficient, the industry of the labourers, who are in that district the tenants of Montfleuri, has supplied it; and the wine produced in this little mountainous tract is particularly delicious. These pointed hills suddenly sink into a valley, or rather a narrow pass, which through tufts of cypress that grow among the rocks, gives a very singular view into the country beyond them. — Another chain of hills then rise; and these last were the property of a convent of monks, whose monastery is not more than a mile from the house of my friend. — In the culture of these two adjoining ridges of vineyards, may be seen the effects of the management of the different masters to whom they belong. — The peasants on the domain of Montfleuri are happy and prosperous, while in the line of country immediately adjoining to his, though the good fathers have taken tolerable care of their vineyards, there is every where else the appearance of a languid and reluctant cultivation. — On the top of one of the highest of these hills is the ruin of a large ancient building, of which the country people tell wonderful legends. I have never yet explored it, but it is a fine object from the windows of this house; and I rejoice, that Montfleuri, who has purchased the estate of the convent, will now be able to preserve it in its present romantic form, from the farther depredations of the neighbouring hinds, who, whenever their fears yielded to their convenience, were in habits of carrying away the materials for their own purposes; and have, by those means, done more than time towards destroying this monument of antiquity. — I, who love, you know, every thing ancient, unless it be ancient prejudices, have entreated my friend to preserve this structure in its present state — than which, nothing can be more picturesque: when in a fine glowing evening, the almost perpendicular hill on which it stands is reflected in the unruffled bosom of the broad river, crowned with these venerable remains, half mantled in ivy, and other parasytical plants, and a few cypresses, which grow here as in Italy, mingling their spiral forms among the masses of ruin.

The whole of the ground between the house and the river, is the paternal estate of Montfleuri. — It is now divided, the lower grounds into the meadows, and the higher into corn inclosures, nearly as we separate our fields in England. — The part most immediately adjoining to the house he has thrown into a paddock, and cut those long avenues, which in almost every direction pointed towards the house into groups of trees: breaking as much as possible the lines they would yet describe, by young plantations of such trees as are the most likely, by their quick growth, to overtake them in a few years. — But, I am not quite sure, that I do not wish he had left one vista of the beautiful and graceful Spanish chestnut remaining. — I know this betrays a very gothic and exploded taste, but such is the force of early impressions, that I have still an affection for 'the bowed roof' — the cathedral-like solemnity of long lines of tall trees, whose topmost boughs are interlaced with each other.[87] — I do not, however, defend the purity of my taste in this instance; for nature certainly never planted trees in direct lines. — But I account for my predilection, by the kind of pensive and melancholy pleasure I used to feel, when in my childhood and early youth, I walked alone, in a long avenue of arbeal, which led from a very wild and woody part of the weald of Kent, to an old house my father, at that period of my life, inhabited.[88] I remember the cry of the wood-peckers, or yaffils, as we call them in that country, going to roost in a pale autumnal evening, answered by the owls, which in great numbers inhabit the deep forest-like glens that lye behind the avenue. — I see the moon rising slowly over the dark mass of wood, and the opposite hills, tinged with purple from the last reflection of the sun, which was sunk behind them. — I recall the sensations I felt, when, as the silver leaves of the aspins trembled in the lowest breeze, or slowly fell to the ground before me, I became half frightened at the encreasing obscurity of the objects around me, and have almost persuaded myself that the grey trunks of these old trees, and the low murmur of the wind among their branches, were the dim forms, and hollow sighs of some supernatural beings; and at length, afraid of looking behind me, I have hurried breathless into the house.

No such sombre tints as these, however, shade the environs of Montfleuri's habitation. Ever since he became master of this place, which, till then had been very neglected, he has been endeavouring to bring it as nearly as possible to those plans of comfort and convenience which he saw were followed in England, and of which, it must be acknowledged, the French, in general, have not hitherto had much idea. In this pursuit, he has succeeded much better than I ever saw it done in France before; and were it not for a few obstinate and prominent features that belong to French buildings, which it is almost impossible for him to remove, it would be easy for me to imagine myself in some of the most beautiful parts of England. — A little fancy would convert the vineyards into hop-gardens (if hops could be supposed to grow on such eminences); nor would they be much injured by the comparison; for, when the vine of either is in leaf, the hop, seen at a distance, has the most agreeable appearance. — At other times, neither the one or the other are, as far as the beauty of the landscape is considered, very desirable objects.

At this season, however, when the peasantry around the *chateau* of Montfleuri are preparing for the vintage — when the people, happy from their natural disposition, the effect of soil and climate — happy in a generous and considerate master; (and now more rationally happy, from the certainty they enjoy, that no changes can put them, as once it might have done, into the power of one who may not inherit his virtues) when they are making ready to avail themselves of this joyous season, the expression of exultation and content on their animated faces, is one of my most delicious speculations.[89]

Montfleuri, whose morality borders, perhaps, a little on epicurism, imagines, that in this world of ours, where physical and unavoidable evil is very thickly sown, there is nothing so good in itself, or so pleasing to this Creator of the world, as to enjoy and diffuse happiness. He has therefore, whether he had resided here or no, made it the business of his life to make his vassals and dependents content, by giving them all the advantages their condition will allow. — The effect of this is, that instead of squalid figures inhabiting cabins built of mud, without windows or floors, which are seen in too many parts of France (and which must continue to be seen, till the benign influence of liberty is generally felt,) the peasantry in this domain resemble both in their own appearance, and in the comfortable look of their habitations, those whose lot has fallen in those villages of England*, where, the advantages of a good landlord, a favourable situation for employment, or an extensive adjoining common, enable the labourers to possess something more than the mere necessaries of life, and happily counteract the ef-

---

* The English have a custom of arrogantly boasting of the fortunate situation of the common people of England. — But let those, who, with an opportunity of observation, have ever had an enquiring eye and a feeling heart on this subject, say whether this pride is well founded. At the present prices of the requisites of mere existence, a labourer, with a wife and four or five children, who has only his labour to depend upon, can taste nothing but bread, and not always a sufficiency of that. Too certain it is, that (to say nothing of the miseries of the London poor, too evident to every one who passes through the streets) there are many, very many parts of the country, where the labourer has not a subsistence even when in constant work, and where, in cases of sickness, his condition is deplorable indeed — realizing the melancholy, but just picture, drawn in Knox's Essay, No. 150, entitled, 'A Remedy for Discontent.'[90] — Yet we are always affecting to talk of the misery and beggary of the French — And now impute that misery, though we well know it existed before, to the revolution; — To the very cause that will in a very few years remove it.

fects of those heavy taxes with which all those *necessaries* of life are loaded.

Oh! my friend! let those of our *soi-disant* great men who love power, and who are, with whatever reluctance, compelled at length to see, and the hour is very rapidly approaching, when usurped power will be tolerated no longer, — let them, if nothing but the delight of governing will satisfy them, have recourse to the method Montfleuri has pursued; and then, the best and sincerest of all homage, the homage of grateful hearts may be theirs.[91] — I am convinced, that not even the family pride which, in feudal times, actuated the Irish and Scottish clans, could produce, in the cause of their chieftains, a zeal so ardent and so steady, as that with which the dependents of Montfleuri would defend him at home, or follow him into the field, were there occasion for either.

It is, indeed, a singular sight, to observe the mutual attachments that exist between this gay and volatile man, and his neighbours, whom he will not allow to be called dependents, since no beings, he says, capable of procuring their own subsistence are dependent. — He enters, however, with rational but warm solicitude into the interests of the humblest of them, and should not, he says, be happy if there was among them an aching heart which he had neglected to put at ease, whenever it depended on him.

The neighbourhood, however, of the *seignory* which belongs to the monks, was, till now, a great impediment to all the plans which his benevolence suggested to him. — These reverend fathers encouraged in idleness, those whom Montfleuri was endeavouring to render industrious; and, the alms given away at the gates of the convent, without affording a sufficient or permanent support to the poorer class of his people, were yet enough to give them an excuse for indolence, and a habit of neglecting to seek their own subsistence. In many other instances too, the influence of the monks has counteracted that of Montfleuri. — It is not quite three years since he lost nearly a third of the adults, and a fourth of the children of his villages, by a malignant small-pox that broke out among them; for the monks had taught the people to believe, that inoculation, which he had long earnestly wished to introduce, was an impious presumption offensive to heaven.

These men, however, are now dispersed. Those who adhere to the monastic vows, are gone into other communities; others have taken advantage of the late change to return to that world which they had reluctantly renounced; and one only, among two-and-twenty, accepted the offer which Montfleuri made to those whom he thought the most respectable among them; and whom he, therefore, wished to save from any inconveniences that might attend an involuntary removal. — This proposal was to fit up one of the wings of the house (which he had destined for other purposes) for the reception of those who chose to stay; and of supplying to them, at his own expence, every gratification to which they had been accustomed, that their reduced income did not enable them to enjoy. — Most of those to whom this generous offer was made, treated it either with resentment or scorn: father Cypriano, a Portuguese, who has lost all attachment to his own country, or for some reason or other does not wish to return to it, accepted the proposed accommodation, with some little changes, according to a plan of his own. — He told Montfleuri, that though he had no great attachment to any of the members of the society, yet that there would be something particularly comfortless in residing alone, where he had been accustomed to see so many of his brethren around him; and that, though he in reality courted solitude in preference to society, it was not exactly there he wished to enjoy it; but, that if Montfleuri would allow the workmen employed about the house to raise for him, in a sequestered spot which he pointed out, a sort of hermitage after a plan of his own, he would be happy to avail himself of his bounty, and to end his days on his estate. — I need hardly say, that my friend most readily acceded to his wishes; and, during his late absence, father Cypriano has, on the rocky borders of the river, which are there concealed by some of the thickest woods I have ever seen in France, built an hermitage exactly corresponding to the ideas I had formed of those sort of habitations from Don Quixote or Gil Blas.[92] — It is partly an excavation in the hard sand rock that rises above the river. It is situated about two hundred yards from it, and is partly composed of rough wood, which supports the roof, and enlarges the site of the building (if building it may be called.) The outward room is paved with flat stones, and the inner is boarded; there, is his little bed, his crucifix, and two chairs. — The other apartment contains only a table; the seats of turf and moss, that surround it; and a sort of recess where he puts his provisions, which are furnished him daily from Montfleuri, with an attentive liberality, of which the good anchoret even complains, though he never refuses it. — Montfleuri tells me that there is something singular in the history of this venerable man, with which he is not acquainted; but that, as he seems very communicative, he will endeavour, some day when we are together, to engage him in an account of his life.

This anchoret, as a being to which we are never accustomed (unless it be to a hired or to a wax hermit in some of our gardens), has led me away strangely from what I was going to tell you of the use to which Montfleuri has destined the dissolved monastery.

He has fitted it up as an house of industry; not to confine the poor to work, for he abhors the idea of compulsion, but to furnish with easy and useful employment, such as by age, or infirmity, or infancy, are unfitted for the labour of the fields. — And here also means that the robust peasant may, when the rigour of the season, or any other circumstance deprives him of occupation abroad, find something to do within. Nothing, however, in the way of manufactures is to be attempted, farther than strong coarse articles, useful to themselves, or in the culture of the estate. — I think the sketch Montfleuri has given me of his plan an admirable one. It is yet only in its first infancy; but, if it succeeds, as I am sure it must, I will establish such an house on my own estate, whenever I settle there.

Whenever I settle there! — Ah! Bethel, that expression recalls a thousand painful ideas from which I have been vainly trying to escape. — Alas; I shall never settle there! or, if ever I do, it will be as a solitary and insulated being, whose pleasures will soon become merely animal and selfish, because there will be none to share them: — a being who, though weary of the world, will find no happiness in quitting it. — Methinks I see myself rambling at four or five-and-fifty, over grounds which I shall have none to inherit; and surveying, with the dull eye of torpid apathy, improvements which, when I am gone, there will be none to admire; and which will then, perhaps,

'Pass to a scrivener, or a city knight.'[93]

Yes, I shall be, I doubt not, that forlorn and selfish being an old batchelor; one, who having no dearer ties to sweeten his weary existence, is surrounded by hungry parasitical relations, or is governed in his second childhood by his house-keeper.

You will smile, I suppose, at this apostrophe, and would even laugh, when you know the moment at which it occurs — when the lovely, the bewitching Josephine herself, is waiting for me to walk with her;

and, 'in these sportive plains, under this genial sun, where, at this instant, all flesh is running out, piping, fiddling, and dancing to the vintage, and every step that's taken, the judgment is surprised by the
imagination.'* — How shall I resist her? — The first grapes are to be
gathered in a few days on the opposite hills; the peasants singing the
liveliest airs, have been this evening carrying up their implements for
this delightful operation; — Julie and her brother are gone already to
see them; and Josephine sent me, a few moments since, a note, in which
she gaily reproaches me for want of gallantry in thus making her wait
this lovely evening. Oh! were it but Geraldine who expected me! —
were it Geraldine who waited for me, to lend her my arm in this little
expedition! — I have once or twice, as Madame de Boisbelle has been
walking with me, tried to fancy her Geraldine, and particularly when
she has been in her plaintive moods. I have caught sounds that have,
for a moment, aided my desire to be deceived. — But, as the lady
herself could not guess what made me so silent and inattentive, some
sudden *etourderie* not at all in harmony with my feelings; some trait,
in the character of her country, has suddenly dissolved the charm, and
awakened me to a full sense of the folly I was guilty of.[94]

But I see, at this moment, Josephine herself, who condescends to
beckon to me, and to express her impatience at my delay. — Farewell,
my friend, I shall hardly write again from hence.

Ever your's most faithfully,

LIONEL DESMOND

LETTER XI

TO MR DESMOND

Hartfield, September 20
'In those sportive plains, and under this genial sun, where, at this instant, all flesh is running out piping, fiddling, and dancing to the vintage; and every step that is taken, the judgment is surprised by the

---

*   Sterne.[95]

imagination.' — With the lovely Josephine beckoning to you as you sit at your window! — and reproaching you for want of gallantry! —

Bravo, my friend! — This will do — I see, that though my first advice did not succeed, my second infallibly will. — 'Go, search in England for some object worthy of those affections which, placed as they are now, can only serve to render you miserable — Or if that does not do — if you are become, through the influence of this romantic attachment, too fastidious for reasonable happiness — go abroad, dissipate your ideas, instead of suffering them to dwell continually on a hopeless pursuit; and you will find change of place and variety of scenes are the best remedies for every disease of the mind.' — Thus I preached; and I now value myself on the success of my prescription, though I did not foresee this kind Josephine, who will undoubtedly perfect the cure. — At your age, my good friend, a lovely and unfortunate woman — who probably tells you all her distresses — who leans on your arm, and whose voice you endeavour to fancy the tender accents of Geraldine — will, I will venture to prophecy, soon cease to please you, notwithstanding you 'bear a charmed heart,' only in the semblance of another. — And as to any engagements, you know, such as her having a husband, and so forth, those little impediments 'make not the heart sore' in France.[96] In short, I look upon your cure as nearly perfected, and by the time this letter reaches you, I doubt not, but that you will have begun to wonder how you could ever take up such a notion, as of an unchangeable and immortal passion, which is a thing never heard or thought of, but by the tender novel writers, and their gentle readers. — Madame de Boisbelle seems the woman in the world best calculated to win you from the absurd system you had built; and had you been a descendant of Lord Chesterfield's, and his spirit presided over your destiny, he could hardly have led you to a scene so favourable to desultory gallantry, and so fatal to the immortality of your attachment, as the house of Montfleuri.[97]

Thus, believing your cure certain, I venture to tell you what I know of Verney. — You will still, perhaps, receive it with concern; but it will no longer awaken your quixotism. — You will not, I think, now offer Verney half your estate to save his wife from an uneasy moment; or strip yourself of nine or ten thousand pounds to supply his deficiencies at Newmarket, where the next meeting would probably create the same deficiency, and, of course, the same necessity.

Verney, then, I am sorry to say, has at length parted with his estate in this country: I am more sorry to say, that he has parted with it to Stamford, to whom, as I have been lately informed, it has been long mortgaged.

The final settlement of this matter, which has, I find, been sometime in agitation, has happened only within this month; and in consequence of it, Mr Stamford, or, I should rather say, Sir Robert Stamford, for he is almost as lately raised to the dignity of a Baronet, took possession, about ten days since, of the house, which he bought ready furnished, and he is, for the present, living there with his family. I am not, as you will easily believe, much delighted with this, either on his own account, or because of the stile of living which he will introduce into the country. A very small part of his grounds adjoins to my wood-lands. — He is said to be a very great savage in regard to game; and though I care very little myself about that perpetual subject of country contention, it will be very disagreeable to me to have my tenants subject to the vexations of this petty tyrant. — I do not know whether I have told you of the places he now enjoys, nor how they have enabled him to encrease the splendour of his appearance, or the luxury of his table, by which he strengthens his interest. In the latter, it is said that he excels, from talents and taste; and that more good dinners have of late been eaten at his house for the benefit of the English government, by those who are intrusted to carry it on, than have ever before been prepared for the like purposes. — He is supposed to be one of those fortunate persons, who, being deep in the secret, are enabled to take advantage of every fluctuation, to which the proceedings of ministry give rise, in the value of the public funds; and by this means principally, to have secured beyond the reach of fortune, that wealth which he has so rapidly, and, in the apprehension of many people, so wonderfully accumulated. — He has already, since his immediate neighbourhood gives him a considerable degree of interest with the tradesmen of W————, been courting their favour with a meanness, equal to that arrogance with which he treats all who are, or may be, his equals; and from whom he expects nothing equal to the cringing servility with which he fawns upon his titled friends, and those who have helped to raise him to his present seat; or the junto, by whose united strength he means to keep it. —

I have forgotten poor Verney's affairs in my account of this great man; but I own the incident of his coming into this neighbourhood has vexed me, more, perhaps, than it ought to do. — I shall not feel it very pleasant to absent myself from those public meetings, which, as a magistrate, I have thought it my duty to attend, because *Sir Robert* will now take the chair on account of his new rank. — Yet, certainly, I shall as little like to meet a man, by whom I know I have been grossly and irreparably injured; and whose private and public character are equally hateful to me. — To him, I may well address the lines of Shakespeare,

> ————————————————————'Your heart
> 'Is crammed with arrogancy, spleen, and pride;
> 'You have by fortune, and your friends high favour,
> 'Gone lightly o'er low steps — and now are mounted
> 'Where powers are your retainers.'[98]

I believe, my friend, it is a weakness to be disturbed at such a man. — I will name him then no more; but to proceed to tell you all I know farther of Verney, which is merely, that the money he received from Sir Robert, more than what his estate was already mortgaged for (which did not amount to above six thousand pounds) was immediately paid away to satisfy debts of honour; and that he is now raising money on his northern estates, in which he finds some difficulties on account of his wife's settlement. This I hear from such authority, that I cannot doubt the truth of it. — I enquired of my informer, why, if Verney had discharged *such* considerable debts of honour by this last transaction, he had immediate occasion to encumber his Yorkshire estates? — My acquaintance laughed at my calling six thousand pounds a considerable debt, and told me, that if that sum had paid all the demands that were the most immediately pressing on his friend Verney, which he knew they did not, that he would have occasion for at least as much again for the October meeting; and therefore, was trying to raise all he wanted at once. — This was said by no means in the way of a secret, or, as of a design of which Verney had any notion of being ashamed; and the young man who related it to me, and who is one of the set to which he belongs, spoke of it rather as complaining, that it was a confounded shame, that as Verney had married a girl of no fortune, or next to none, he should have been drawn in to make such an unreasonable settlement upon her, as prevented his raising money upon his estates. I am very sorry for Mrs Verney; but I have long foreseen this. — She will, undoubtedly have too much firmness of mind, and attention to the interest of her children, to give up her settlement; and it will always afford the family a certain degree of affluence. — You may assure yourself, that were the whole treasures of the East to find their way into the pocket of her husband, he would finally possess no more, for there is nothing but the impossibility of parting with it, that can ever keep any property whatever in his possession.

So much, dear Desmond, for private news from England. As for public news, you probably receive it from those who are better qualified than I am to speak upon it. — You know I am not by any means partial to our present arrangements: yet, as I do not yet see the success of the new modes of government that have been taken up in France, I am not so sanguinely looking out for changes, as you seem to be. — Perhaps this coldness is owing to the observations I made in my short and unfortunate political career. — I saw then such decided selfishness in all parties, so little sincerity, so little real concern for the general good in any, that it imprest me with an universal mistrust of all who profess the science of politics. — Your friend, Montfleuri, however, seems to be sincere. — But for many of those whom the *abbé* termed *messieurs les reformateurs*, they appear to me to be wavering and divided in their councils, and breaking into parties, which occasions me again to entertain some doubts of the permanency of the revolution. — I am certainly a warm friend to its principles. — I only hesitate to believe, that there is steadiness and virtue enough existing among the leaders, to apply those principles to practice. — I conclude, therefore, as I began, with a quotation from Sterne — and I say with uncle Toby — 'I wish it may answer.'[99]

I have no expectation of hearing from you very soon again, as from your last letter, this seems likely to be long in reaching you. — But I am persuaded, that the interest you take in French *politics* on one hand; and, on the other, the interest the fair Josephine takes in your's, will restore to you your gay spirits — and to me my rational friend.

You know I remain, ever,
Most faithfully your's,
E BETHEL

LETTER XII*

TO MR BETHEL

Hauteville, in Auvergne,
Sept. 14, 1790

Reluctantly — Oh! how reluctantly, I quitted, three days since, the chearful abode of Montfleuri, where every countenance beamed with pleasure and content, for this mournful residence: — a residence, where mortified and discomfitted tyranny seems to have taken up its sullen station; and with impotent indignation to colour with its own gloomy hand every surrounding object. — The Comte d'Hauteville is the brother of Montfleuri's mother; and though they are as opposite in their principles, and in their tempers, as light and darkness, Montfleuri has so much respect for his uncle, and so much goodness of heart, as to fulfil a promise he required of him, when the latter left Paris, that he would come to him for ten days. — Unable to endure a country, where his power, and as he believes, his consequence is diminished, Monsieur d'Hauteville is preparing to quit France. — His nephew thinks he can dissuade him from this resolution, and reconcile him to the terrible misfortune of being free among freemen, instead of being a petty tyrant among slaves — while the Comte himself entertained hopes that he would convert his nephew, or, at least, lessen his extravagant zeal for that *odious* democratic system he has embraced. — That both will fail in these their expectations, is already very evident. — I must give you, however, a sketch of our journey, and of our reception, to enable you to form some idea of this place, and of its possessor.

We set out in my chaise — neither of us in very gay spirits, though those of Montfleuri are not very easily depressed. But our taking leave of Josephine and Julie, who with tears saw their brother depart, though he is so soon to return; — the melancholy which he knew hung over this house, and perhaps the heavy atmosphere, which just then prevailed, contributed to make him pensive, and from the same causes that render a Frenchman of his disposition grave, an Englishman naturally feels disposed to hang himself. I had, besides the additional vexa-

---

* Written before the receipt of the foregoing.

tion of leaving the house of Montfleuri, without having received, as I expected, a letter from Mrs Verney during my stay there.

The beginning of our journey, therefore, was dismal enough. — Towards evening, we stopped at the convent where Montfleuri's other sister is a professed nun. I was not permitted to see her; but he returned in worse spirits than he set out, exclaiming against the odious superstition, that had condemned so amiable a young woman, to so many years of rigid confinement, (for she is a Carmelite) and has given, he says, to her mind, a tincture of sadness, which he fears it will always retain.[100] When he comes back, it is to be decided, whether or no, she quits her convent. — He has a small property near the little town of Aique-mont, where, as he had some business to settle, we remained all night; and where, I have occasion again to remark, the affection which all who are connected with him feel for Montfleuri. — We did not quit Aique-mont till late the following day. The weather was so unusually warm, that we travelled slowly; and it was the evening of yesterday before we approached the end of our journey.

The country through which we travelled, was, in many parts, beautifully romantic; but, within about three leagues of the *chateau* d'Hauteville, it opens into one of those extensive plains that are very frequent in Normandy, though not so usual in this part of France. — Over these dead flats, a straight road usually runs for many miles, and the dull uniformity of the prospect is broken only by the rows of pear or apple trees, which are planted upon it in various directions.

A few plantations of vines had here an even less pleasing effect. — In some of them, however, people were at work; but we no longer heard the chearful songs, or saw the gay faces that we had been accustomed to hear and see in the Lyonois. — At length, Montfleuri pointed out to me, at the extremity of this extensive plain, the woods, which he said surrounded the habitation of his uncle. — The look of even ill-managed cultivation soon after ceased; and over a piece of ground, which was grass, where it was not mole-hills, and from whence all traces of a road were obliterated, we approached to the end of an avenue of beech trees: they were rather the ruins of trees; for they had lost the beautiful and graceful forms nature originally gave them, by the frequent application of the ax; and were, many of them, little better than ragged pollards.

A few straggling trees of other kinds, that had been planted and neglected, were mingled among the rows of beech on either side; but were, for want of protection, 'withering in leafless platoons.' — Not a cottage arose to break the monotony of this long line of disfigured vegetation. — Nothing like a lodge, animated by the chearful residence of a peasant's family, marked its termination; but the paling, which had once divided it from the plain, had either fallen down for want of repairing, or had been carried away by the country people for fuel, in a country where it seemed to be particularly scarce.

Slowly, and through a miserable road, we traversed this melancholy avenue, without seeing, for some time, a human creature. — It seemed to lengthen as we went, and had already lasted above a mile and a quarter, when we observed a figure quickly walking towards us, with a gun on his shoulder, whom I, at first, supposed to be the Count himself. The man seemed, by his step and manner, to be in eager pursuit of something; but I could perceive, by his action, that, on observing an English chaise, he changed the object of his attention, and advanced towards us in a sort of trot, which, from his lank figure and grotesque habit, had a very ridiculous effect.

Under a full dress coat, of a reddish brown, and which had once been lined with sattin, appeared a waistcoat of gold-flowered brocade, the flaps reaching to his knees, and made, I am persuaded, in the reign of Louis *ci-devant le Grand*.[101] — What appeared of his breeches, under this magnificent *juste au-corps*, was of red velveret, forming a happy contrast to a pair of black worsted stockings. — The little hair which grew on each side of his temples had been compelled, in despite of its reluctance and incapability, to assume the form of curls, but they seemed to have fled, *d'un manière la plus opiniatre du monde*, from his ears.[102] A little hat, like what I recollect having seen in caracature prints, under the name of *Chapeau à le Nevernois*, covered the rest of his head; but this, as he approached us, was deposited under his arm, notwithstanding the incumbrance of his gun.[103]

'This is a curious fellow,' said Montfleuri to me, as I approached him, 'he is my uncle's confidential servant, and more singularly original than his master — a tremendous aristocrate, and miserable at the loss of dignity which he believes he has sustained.' — Then addressing himself to the man, who was by this time very near us, 'Aha! my old friend, Le Maire,' cried he, 'how are you? — How is Monsieur d'Hauteville?' — The old man, not at all satisfied with the manner of this address, stepped back, laid his hand on his breast, and, with a cold and formal bow, replied, 'that he had the honour to assure Monsieur le Marquis de Montfleuri, that Monseigneur le Comte d'Hauteville was as well as, under the present melancholy circumstances of the kingdom, any true Frenchman could be.' — There was something so very ludicrous in the method and matter of this answer, that Montfleuri did not attempt to resist his violent inclination to laugh — an impoliteness in which I could as little forbear to join. — 'Well, well, Monsieur le Maire,' cried Montfleuri, 'I am glad to hear my uncle is only indisposed from his national concerns — So open the chaise door, my old friend, and I will walk up to the house with this English gentleman, who has been so good as to accompany me.'

Le Maire turned his little fierce black eyes upon me, as Montfleuri announced me to be an Englishman, and, with a look which I could not misinterpret, muttered something as with a jerk he shut the chaise door — 'Ah curse those English, no good ever comes where they are.'

'Well, but Le Maire,' said Montfleuri, 'what are you shooting at this time in the evening? what were you so eagerly pursuing when we first saw you?' — 'Partridges, Monsieur le Marquis, partridges; I saw a great number of them feeding round the house just now, young ones, hardly able to fly, and I was resolved not one of them should escape.'

'Mais à quoi bon cela?' enquired Montfleuri, 'of what use will that be, since if they are so young they are unfit to eat?'

'A quoi bon Monsieur le Marquis?' replied the old domestic, very indignantly;* 'Mais c'est que je ne veux pas, qui'ly reste, dans le domaine un seul perdrix pour ces gueux du village; qui ont la liberté

---

* Why is it, because I would not have remain on the whole estate, one single partridge for those beggarly rogues of the village, who have the infamous liberty of killing the birds on my lord's grounds. I'll spare them the trouble, rascals as they are, of taking game; and, if I met them — I should do their business.'
  'But how do their business?' 'Why, Monsieur le Marquis, perhaps I might fire a few shot among those scoundrels.' — 'You have, then, a decided call for exhibiting on the lanthorn post?' — 'Be it so: I had rather be hanged than live where those fellows are my equals, and have the liberty of hunting.'

infâme de chasser sur les terres de Monseigneur le Comte d'Hauteville
— Ah! je les épargnerai bien, ces marauds, là, la peine de prendre le
gibier, & si je les rencounterai, je ferai bien leur affaire.'

'Mais comment leur affaire?' said Montfleuri. — 'Eh! Monsieur le
Marquis,' answered Le Maire, 'c'est que je pourrais bien, donner
quelque coups de fusil à ces coquins.'

'Tu as donc une vocation décidé pour la lanterne?' — 'Soit, Monsieur le Marquis, j'aimerai mieux être pendu par ces gens detestables,
moi, que de vivre où ils sont mes égaux, & où ils vont à la chasse.'
'You see, now,' said Montfleuri, turning to me, 'the style which even
the domestics of the *noblesse* assumed towards the peasantry and common people. — This fellow has imbibed all the insolent consequence
of those among whom he had lived; and, though *roturier* himself, con-
ceives, that he derives from the honour of being the idle valet to a
nobleman, a right to despise and trample on the honest man who draws
his subsistence from the ground by independent industry.'[104] By this
time we were arrived at the gate of the *cour d'honneur*, which is surrounded on three sides by the *chateau*.[105] — There had once been a
straight walk, leading from the termination of the avenue to the steps
of the house, but it was now covered with thistles and nettles: the steps
were overgrown with green moss, and when the great door opened to
let us in, it seemed an operation to which it was entirely unaccustomed.

Le Maire, however, extremely solicitous for the dignity of his master, had hurried in before us, and sent one servant to wait at this door,
and a second to shew us the way to the apartment where Monseigneur
was to receive us. — This was in a *salle à compagnie*, on the first floor,
where, after passing through three other cold and half-furnished rooms,
we, at length, arrived.[106] — The Count, who is a handsome man, above
sixty, received me with cold politeness; and his nephew with a sort of
sullen kindness. It seemed as if he at once embraced him as a relation,
and repulsed him as an enemy. — About half an hour after our arrival, I heard that the Count was to send, the next day, a courier to
Clermont, by whom I might dispatch letters to England. — I had this
and two or three others to write; and, I thought that it was better to
let the Count and his nephew begin their political controversy without the presence of a third person. For these reasons, as soon as supper was over, which was very ill dressed, and served in very dirty plate,
I desired to be conducted to my apartment. Having mounted a very

broad staircase of brick and wood, and passed through a long corridor, which seemed to lead to a part of the house very remote from that I had left, I was shewn into a sort of state bed-chamber; one of those where comfort had formerly been sacrificed to splendour, but which now possessed neither the one or the other: and, on opening the door, I was sensible of that damp, musty smell, which is usually perceived in rooms that have been long unfrequented.

The wainscoting was of cedar, or some other brown wood, finely carved; the hangings of a dull and dark blue Lyon's damask; a high canopy bed of the same, stood at one end of the room; and, at the other, was a very large glass reaching from the ceiling to the floor; but which, by the single candle I had, served only to reflect the deep gloom that every object offered. — A great projecting chimney of blood coloured marble, over which another mirror supported a large carved trophy, representing the arms of the family; a red marble table, and four or five high backed, stuffed chairs, covered with blue velvet, completed the furniture of the room; which, floored as it was with hexagon bricks, composed, altogether, one of the most funereal apartments I ever remember to have been in.

I sat down, however, and wrote my letters; but having done them, I felt no inclination to sleep, and therefore, opening the *croisée*, I leaned upon the iron railing, which, in houses built as this is, forms a clumsy sort of balcony to every window.[107] — The day had been unusually close and sultry; and with the night, the thunderstorm, produced by the heated atmosphere, approached. — I now heard it mutter at a distance, and soon after saw, from the south-west, the most vivid lightening I ever remarked, breaking from those majestic and deeply-loaden clouds, which the brightness of the moon above them made very visible. — In a country so level as that is, for many miles round the *chateau* d'Hauteville, the horizon is, of course, great and uninterrupted, and I saw to advantage the progress of the storm; a spectacle I have always had great pleasure in contemplating.

When the imagination soars into those regions, where the planets pursue each its destined course, in the immensity of space — every planet, probably, containing creatures adapted by the Almighty, to the residence he has placed them in; and when we reflect, that the smallest of these is of as much consequence in the universe, as this world of our's; how puerile and ridiculous do those pursuits appear in which we are so anxiously busied; and how insignificant the trifles we toil to obtain, or fear to lose! None of all the little cares and troubles of our short and fragile existence, seem worthy of giving us any real concern — and, perhaps, we never truly possess the reason we so arrogantly boast, till we can thus appreciate the real value of the objects around us.

Heaven knows, my dear Bethel, that I am far enough from enjoying this philosophic tranquillity. — I have entrusted you with my waking reflections — Dare I ask your indulgence for the wild wanderings of my mind, when reason resigned her seat entirely to 'thick-coming fancies.'[108]

When the hurricane had entirely subsided, and the rain-drops fell slowly from the roof, I still continued at the window, for my thoughts were fled to England, and I had only a confused recollection of where I was, till I found myself extremely cold, and turning, saw my candle expiring in the socket. I then recollected, that it was time to go to my bed, and to seek in sleep, relief against the uneasy thoughts that had dwelt upon my mind about Geraldine. On looking, however, towards it, it again seemed so comfortless and gloomy, that I fancied it damp; and though no man possesses a constitution more fortified against such accidents, or cares less about them, I had no inclination to undress myself; or, though I was weary, to sleep. I wished for a book, but I happened, contrary to my usual custom, not to have one in the small portmanteau I had brought from Montfleuri; and having nothing to divert my attention from the cold gloom that surrounded me, I became tired of hearing the dull murmurs of the sinking wind howl along the corridor — and I, at length, determined to try to sleep.

Still, however, the notion of the dampness of the bed deterring me from entering it, I took only my coat off, and wrapping myself in a flannel powdering gown, I threw myself on the embroidered counterpane, and soon after sunk into forgetfulness. I know you will say I am as weakly superstitious as a boarding-school miss, or as 'the wisest aunt telling the saddest tale' to a circle of tired and impatient auditors.[109] — I am conscious of all this, yet I cannot help relating the strange phantoms that haunted my imagination.

I believed myself at the same window as where I stood to observe the storm; and, that in the Count's garden, immediately beneath it, I saw Geraldine exposed to all its fury. — Her husband seemed at first to be with her, but he disappeared, I know not how, and she was left exposed to the fury of the contending elements, which seemed to terrify her less on her own account, than on that of three children, whom she clasped to her bosom, in all the agonies of maternal apprehension, and endeavoured to shelter from the encreasing fury of the tempest. — I hastened, I flew, with that velocity we possess only in dreams, to her assistance: I pressed her eagerly in my arms — I wrapt them round her children — I thought she faintly thanked me; told me, that for herself, my care was useless, but that it might protect them. — She was as cold as marble, and I recollect having remarked, that she resembled a beautiful statue of Niobe, done by an Italian sculptor, which I had admired at Lyons.[110]

While I was entreating her to accept of my protection, and to go into the house, I suddenly, by one of those incongruities so usual in sleep, fancied I saw her extended, pale, and apparently dying on the bed, which I had myself objected to go into, with the least of the children, a very young infant dead in her arms. — Distracted at such a sight, I seized her hand — I implored her to speak to me — She opened languidly those lovely eyes, which I have so often gazed on with transport — they were glazed and heavy — yet, I thought, they expressed tenderness and pity for me — while, in a low, tremulous voice — she bade me adieu! adieu, for ever!

I now shrieked in frantic terror — I tried to recall her to life by my wild exclamations — I would have warmed, in my bosom, the cold hand I held, when she gently drew it from me, and pointing to her two children, whom I now saw standing by the side of the bed, clinging to a young woman, who was, I fancied, Fanny Waverly, she said, in a yet lower, and more mournful tone — 'Desmond! — if ever you truly loved me, it is there you must shew your affection.' — I then saw the last breath tremble on those lovely lips — it was gone — Geraldine was lost for ever! — And, in an agony of despair, such as, thank Heaven, I never was conscious of waking, I threw myself on the ground. — The violence of this ideal emotion restored me to myself. — I awoke — my face bathed in tears, and in such confusion of spirits, that it was long before I could recall myself to reason, and to a clear conviction, that all this was only a dream. So strong was the impression, that I dared not hazard feeling it again by sleeping. — I therefore put on my great coat, and as the moon now shone in unclouded radiance, I went down into the garden, and wandered among the *bosquets* and *treillage* that make its formal ornaments.[111] — Still the figure of Geraldine pursued me, such as I had seen her in this distressing vision — Still I heard her voice bidding me an eternal adieu! — I would have given the world to have had some human being to have spoken to, that these imaginary sounds of plaintive sorrow might have vibrated in my ears no longer, but I was ashamed of awakening Montfleuri, had I known where to have found him — And my servant Warley, I had left at Montfleuri, to bring my letters after me.

I continued, therefore, to traverse this melancholy garden — sometimes resolving to conquer my weakness, and return to my bed, and then shrinking for the apprehensions of being again liable to the terror I has just experienced. At length, I heard the clock of the church strike three — I followed the sound for two or three hundred paces, through a cut walk that led from the garden towards it, and entering the church-yard, which is the *cimetière* of a large village, I was again struck with a circumstance that had before appeared particularly dismal.[112] I mean, that there are in France no marks of graves, as in England,

'Where heaves the turf in many a mouldering heap.'[113]

Here all is level — and forgetfulness seems to have laid her cold oblivious hand on all who rest within these enclosures.

No object appears in the mournful spot I was now contemplating, but a cross, on which a dead Christ painted, and representing life, as closely as possible, was suspended: the moon-beams falling directly on this, added to the dreary horrors of the scene. — I stood a few moments looking on it, and then was roused from my mournful reverie by the sound of human voices and of horses feet. — I listened, and found these sounds came from the farmyard, which was only two or three hundred paces before me. — Hither I gladly found my way, and saw the vine-dressers, and people employed in the making wine, preparing for their work, and going to gather the grapes while the dew was yet on them. Rejoiced to find somebody to speak to, I entered into conversation with them, and for a moment dissipated my ideas — I followed them to the vineyard, assisted in their labours, and was equally astonished and pleased to hear, how rationally these unenlightened men considered the blessing of their new-born liberty, and with what manly firmness they determined to preserve it.

There was among them a Breton, who appeared to have more acuteness and knowledge than the rest: with him, I shall take an opportunity of having farther discourse.

It is now one o'clock at noon. — I have had an hour's conversation with Montfleuri — I have paid my morning compliments to the Count — I have been amused with the ridiculous anger of Le Maire, whom Montfleuri has been provoking to display it, on the subject of the abolished titles — Yet, even after all this, the impression I received in my sleep is not dissipated — Yet, I am certainly not superstitious. — I have, assuredly, no faith in dreams, which are, I know, but

'The children of an idle brain,
'Begot of nothing but vain phantasy,
'And more inconstant than the vagrant winds.'*[115]

I shall hear from England, perhaps, tomorrow, or Friday, and then be able to laugh at my weakness, as much as you have probably done in reading this. I hear the Count's courier is ready to set out for Clermont. I must, therefore, hastily bid you, dear Bethel, adieu!

LIONEL DESMOND

†LETTER XIII[114]

TO MR BETHEL

Hauteville in Auvergne, Sept. 30, 1790

Montfleuri came into my room yesterday morning with letters in his hand, which he had just received from his own house. — I asked eagerly for mine, but there was none, and my servant yet remains waiting for them. — I expressed, perhaps too forcibly, what I felt — impatience and disappointment; when Montfleuri, as soon as these emotions had a little subsided, asked me gaily, 'whether I had many near and dear relations in England, for whose health I was so extremely solicitous as to injure my own by my anxiety?' — I replied, 'that though

---

* Shakespeare.
† Written before the receipt of Bethel's last letter.

I had very few relations, and with those few seldom corresponded, yet, that I had friends to whom I was warmly attached.' — 'And some lovely and fond woman also, I fancy,' interrupted he; 'for, my dear Desmond, the friendship, however great, that subsists between persons of the same sex, creates not these violent anxieties. — Ah! my good friend, I fancy you are a very fortunate fellow — As to my two sisters, they seem, by their letters, to be quite enchanted with you; and Josephine (whose tears, indeed, at our parting, I did not before attribute *all* to my own account) declares in this letter, that if I do not soon return with my English friend, she and Julie must rejoin us here, notwithstanding their dislike to this melancholy place; for, that since we have left Montfleuri, it is become so extremely *triste*, that they are half dead with lassitude and *ennui*.[116] You remember, I dare say, hearing fine sentimental speeches from Josephine about the charms of solitude and the beauties of nature. — Now nature was never more beautiful than it is at this moment in the Lyonois; yet is my gentle Josephine most marvellously discontent. Desmond, do tell me how you manage to bewitch the women in this manner?'

I was neither gay enough to enjoy this raillery, or coxcomb enough to believe that Madame de Boisbelle regretted me at Montfleuri. — Indeed, I rather felt hurt at her brother's speaking of her thus lightly; but with him this vivacity is constitutional. — He has besides, from education, habit, and principles, much freer notions than I have about women. — He again enquired of me of what nature was my English attachment — a question I declined answering; for the name of Geraldine is not to be prophaned by his suspicions, or even his conjectures. — Were I to say that my passion for her is as pure and holy as that of a fond brother for a lovely and amiable sister, which I am *almost* sure it is, he would turn my Platonism into ridicule; or, if he could be persuaded to believe that such a passion exists, he would think that she was a prude, and that I am an ideot; and to this, though I can forgive it, because he does not know Geraldine, I will not expose myself.

I heartily wish the time fixed for our stay here were expired — I am weary of the place — The frigid magnificence in which we live is very dull, and the perpetual arguments between the Count and his Nephew, are sometimes, at least, distressing. — The former, with that haughty obstinacy that endeavours to set itself above the reason it cannot combat, defends, with asperity and anger, those prejudices, in obedience to which he is about to quit his country — though could he determine to throw them off, he might undoubtedly continue at home, as much respected, and more beloved than ever he was in the meridian of his power.

The dialogues, which he is fond of holding with Montfleuri, have not unfrequently been carried on with so much warmth on his side, as to alarm me, least they should produce an open rupture; for what the old Count wants in soundness of argument, he makes up in heat and declamation. — His nephew, however, has so much good temper, and such an habitual respect for him, that he never suffers himself to be too much ruffled; and d'Hauteville, after the most violent of these contentions, is under the necessity of recollecting, that it is on his nephew he must depend for the care of his pecuniary concerns (a matter to which he is by no means indifferent) when he goes into the voluntary exile to which he chuses to condemn himself. He also recollects, that he owes to Montfleuri a considerable sum of money, part of his mother's fortune; which, together with the arrear of interest, he has always evaded paying by the chicanery of the old laws; and, he now fears, that when equal justice is established this claim may be revived and enforced by Montfleuri. — Thus it is rather interest than affinity that prevents his breaking with his nephew; and that compels him, with averted and reluctant ears, to hear those truths which Montfleuri speaks to him, with the same coolness, and as much divested of considerations of personal interest, as his nephew would speak before a conclave of cardinals, or, if it could be collected, of emperors.

To-day, after dinner, Montfleuri happened to be absent, and the Count taking advantage of it, began to talk to me, whom he wishes to win over to his party, on the subject nearest his heart — the abolition of all titular distinctions in France. — He went back to the earliest records of the kingdom to prove what I never doubted — the antiquity of titles, as if that were an irrefragable proof of their utility. — 'My God, Sir!' cried he, 'is it possible — that you — that you — who are, without doubt, yourself of noble blood.' — 'Pardon me, Sir,' said I, 'for interrupting you, but if that be of any weight in the argument you are going to use, it is necessary to tell you, your supposition is erroneous — I am not noble. — My ancestors, so far as I ever traced them, which is indeed a very little way, were never above the rank of plain country gentlemen; and, I am afraid, towards the middle of the last century, lose even that dignity in a miller and a farmer.' — 'Well, Sir,' continued the Count, in whose esteem I had gained nothing by this humble disclosure of my origin; — 'Well, Sir, however that may have been — you are now, I understand, from the Marquis, my nephew, a man of large fortune and liberal education — and therefore, in your own country, where *noblesse* is not so much insisted upon, you have, undoubtedly mixed much with men of high birth, and eminent consideration' — 'Really, Sir, you do me an honour in that supposition, to which I am not very well entitled. — With us, it is true, that a considerable fortune is a passport to such society; and had I found any satisfaction in enlisting myself under the banners of either of those parties, who are always contending for the good of old England, I might have been admitted among the old and middle-aged, who are busied in arranging the affairs of the public; or among the young, who are yet more busy in disarranging their own. But having no taste for the society of either the one or the other, I can boast of only one titled friend in my own country; and he is a man whom I love and honor for the virtues of his heart, not for the splendour of his situation. — Possessing an illustrious name and a noble fortune, he has a dignity of mind, and a sensibility of heart, which those advantages not unfrequently destroy. Could we, among our numerous nobility, boast of many such men, their conduct would be a stronger argument in favour of the advantages of a powerful aristocracy, than the most dazzling shew of a birth-day exhibition, or the most plausible vindication of titular distinctions that we have ever yet heard. — There may, for aught I know, be others equally respectable for their private virtues, but they have not, fallen within my observation; and judging therefore, of the greater part of them through the medium of public report, I have felt no wish to approach them nearer.' 'However you may think of individuals, Sir,' said the Count, 'you surely are not so blinded, so infatuated, by the doctrines that have obtained most unhappily for this country, as not to feel the necessity that this order of men should exist. — You must know, that the wisdom of our ancient kings created this distinction, that is to say, they thought it expedient to raise the brave and valiant above the common level of mankind, by giving them badges and titles of honour, in order to mark and perpetuate their glorious deeds, and stimulate, to emulation, their illustrious posterity. — Now — if these well-earned rewards are taken from their descendants — if these sacred distinctions be annihilated, and the names of heroes past, be erased from the records of mankind — I assert, that there is an end, not only of justice, but of emulation, subordination — all that gives safety to property, or grace to society — and the world will become a chaos of confusion and outrage. — What! — shall a man of trade, a negociant, an upstart dealer in wine, or wood, or sugar, or cloth, approach one in whose veins, perhaps, the blood of our Lusignans and Tancreds circulates: — the same blood which, in the defence of our holy religion, was shed in Palestine.[117] — I say, shall a mushroom, a fungus, approach these illustrious descendants of honoured ancestors, and say, "Behold, Oh! man of high descent, I am thy equal, my country declares it!"'

Indignation here arrested the eloquence it had produced, and gave me an opportunity of saying, 'My dear Sir, the united voices of common sense, nature, and reason, declared all this long ago, though it is only now you are compelled to hear them. As to the degradation of *Messieurs*, the present descendants of your Lusignans and Tancreds, if it be a degradation to be accounted only men, I really am much concerned for them; but for the ill effects it otherwise produces, inasmuch as such motives fail as might excite them to equal these their great progenitors, I cannot understand that there is in that respect much to regret. — The days of chivalry will never, I apprehend, return: the ravings of a fanatic monk will never again prevail on the French to make a crusade. — Nay,' added I, smiling, 'there seems but little probability that they will soon be called upon to take arms, in a cause which has in later times appeared of greater moment. — I mean, rescuing what one of your writers calls *le vain bonneur du pavillon**, from the arrogant superiority of us presumptuous islanders. The real value of both these objects, for which so much blood has been wasted, seems to be better understood; the real interest of humanity to appear in its proper light. Since, therefore, we no longer have occasion to follow the example of those heroes who have bled for either — why contemplate them with such blind reverence? I suppose, Sir, you will not say, that

---

* The vain honour of the flag, which, till within a few years, the English have always insisted on having struck to them in the Narrow Seas.[118]

the frantic expeditions to the Holy Land, preached by Peter the Hermit, answered any other purpose than to depopulate and impoverish your country and mine.[119] Nor will you maintain, that either France or England have gained any thing but taxes and poverty by the continual wars with which we have been harassing each other, through a succession of ages. Surely then it is time to recall our imaginations from these wild dreams of fanaticism and heroism — time to remove the gorgeous trappings, with which we have drest up folly, that we might fancy it glory. — The tinsel ornaments we have borrowed as the livery of this phantom, are become tarnished and contemptible — Let us not regret then, that the hand of sober reason tears off these poor remaining shreds, with which virtue *disdains* to attempt encreasing its geniune lustre; with which selfishness and folly *must fail* to hide their real deformity. — Have patience with me yet a moment,' added I — 'have patience with me yet a moment — while I ask — whether you really think, that a dealer in wine, or in wood, in sugar, or cloth, is not endued with the same faculties and feelings as the descendant of Charlemagne; and whether the accidental advantage of being able to produce a long pedigree (which, notwithstanding the infinite virtue ascribed to matrons of antiquity, is, I fear, often very doubtful) ought to give to the noble who possesses it, a right to consider every lower rank of men as being of an inferior and subordinate species?'[120] —

'So, Sir,' — angrily burst forth the Count — 'So, Sir! — I must from all this, conclude, that you consider your footman upon an equality with yourself. — Why then is he your footman?'*

'Because — though my footman is certainly so far upon an equality with me, as he is a man, and a free-man; there must be a distinction in local circumstances; though they neither render me noble, or him base. — I happen to be born heir to considerable estates; it is his chance to be the son of a labourer, living on those estates. — I have occasion for his services; he has occasion for the money by which I purchase them: in this compact we are equal so far as we are free. — I, with my property, which is money, buy his property, which is time, so long as he is willing to sell it. — I hope and believe my footman

---

* This argument has been called unanswerable.

feels himself to be my fellow-man; but I have not, therefore, any apprehension that instead of waiting behind my chair, he will sit down in the next. — He was born poor — but he is not angry that I am rich — so long as my riches are a benefit and not an oppression to him. — He knows that he never can be in *my* situation, but he knows also that I can amend *his*. — If, however, instead of paying him for his services, I were able to say to him, as *has* been done by the higher classes throughout Europe, and is still in too many parts of it — "you are my vassal — you were born upon my estate — you are my property — and you must come to work, fight, die for me, on whatever conditions I please to impose;" — my servant, who would very naturally perceive no appeal against such tyrannical injustice, but to bodily prowess would, as he is probably the most athletic of the two, discover that so far from being compelled to stand on such terms behind my chair, he was well able either to place himself in the next, or to turn me out of mine.[121] — "*Ceux qui disent que tous les hommes sont égaux," says Voltaire — "Ceux qui disent que tous les hommes sont égaux, disent la plus grande vérite, s'ils entendent que tous les hommes ont un droit égal à la liberté, à la propriéte de leurs biens, & à la protection des loix. — Ils se tromperaient beaucoup, s'ils croyaient que les hommes, doivent être égaux par les emplois, puisqu'ils ne le sont pas par leurs talens.'"

'Voltaire!' impatiently exclaimed the Count, 'why always Voltaire? — One is perfectly stunned with the false wit and insidious misrepresentations of that atheistical scribbler.'

Against the defender of the family of Calas; the protector of the Sirvens; the benefactor of all mankind, whom he pitied, served, and laughed at; the Count now most furiously declaimed, in a long and angry speech, which, as it possessed neither truth or argument, I have forgotten.[122] — Towards the close of it, however, he had worked him-

---

* Those who say that all men are equal, say that which is perfectly true; if they mean that all men have an equal right to personal and mental liberty; to their respective properties; and to the protection of the laws: but they would be as certainly wrong in believing that men ought to be equal in trusts, in employments, since nature has not made them equal in their talents.[123]

self into such a state of irritation, that he seemed on the point of forgeting that on which he so highly values himself— *Les manières de la vieille cour.*[124]

The entrance of a man of the church, whose diminished revenues had yet had no effect, either in reducing his figure, or subduing his arrogance, made a momentary diversion in my favour.

But the Count was now heated by his subject; and, being reinforced with so able an auxilliary, he returned to the charge. — He related the subject of our controversy to his friend, who, while he spoke, surveyed me with such looks, as one of the holy brotherhood of the Inquisition may be supposed to throw on the unhappy culprit whom he is about to condemn to the flames on the next *auto de fé.*[125] — In a manner peculiar, I trust, to *la vieille cour ecclesiastique,* he gave me to understand, that he considered me as an ignorant atheistical boy; and, that his abhorrence of my principles was equaled only by his contempt for my country and myself.[126] — 'Voltaire,' said he, 'Voltaire, Monsieur L'Anglois, is a wretch with whose name I sully not my mind; a monster whose pernicious writings have overturned the religion and the government of his country.' The manner in which this was said, brought to my mind an expression which Voltaire puts himself into the mouth of such a character. — 'Ah! nous serions les maîtres du monde, sans ces coquins de gens d'esprit.'* I continued to listen to the discourse which the Count now resumed; the purport of which was to convince me, that the decree of the nineteenth of May, was subversive of all order, and ruinous alike to the dignity and happiness of a state.[127] — At length he stopped to recover his breath, and gave me an opportunity of saying, 'If, Sir, I might be once more permitted to quote so obnoxious an author† as him of whom we have just been speaking, I should say, that "Le nom est indifférent; il n'y a que le pouvoir qui ne le soit pas.‡" — If the *name* of *noblesse* was so connected with the *power* of oppression, that they could not be divided, the nation had a right to take away both; if otherwise, it might, per-

---

* Ah! we should be masters of the world, were it not for those rascally wits.'
† Voltaire.
‡ The name is immaterial; it is the power only that is of consequence.

haps, have been politic to have divided them, and have left to the French patricians, these *sounds* on which they seem to feel that their consequence depends; together with the invaluable privileges of having certain symbols painted on their coaches, or woven on their furniture; and of dressing their domestics in one way rather than in another. — A great people who had every thing on which its freedom and its prosperity depended to consider, must surely have seen such objects as these with so much indifference, that had they not been evidently obnoxious to the spirit of reform, they would have left them to the persons who so highly value them; persons who resolve to quit their country because they are no longer to be enjoyed in it. — The framers of the new constitution, had they not been well convinced of the inefficacy of mere *palliation*, would not, certainly, by destroying these distinctions (matters in themselves quite inconsequential) have raised against the fabrick they were planning, the unextinguishable rage and hatred of a great body of men; but would have left them in quiet possession of these baubles so necessary to their happiness.'

'Hold, Sir,' cried the Count, whose impatience could no longer be restrained — 'Hold, Sir, and do not speak thus contemptuously I entreat you, of an advantage which it is very truly said, no man undervalues who is possessed of it. — You, Sir, have owned that your family is *roturier* — How then, and at your time of life, when the real value of objects cannot have been taught you by experience; how then can *you* pretend to judge of that which is appreciated by the wisdom of ages, and has been held up as the reward of heroic virtues. — Baubles! — Is it thus you term the name a man derives from his illustrious ancestors — Baubles! — Are the honours handed down to me, from the first d'Hauteville, who lived under *Louis le Gros*, the sixth in descent from Charlemagne, to be thus contumaciously described by the upstart politics of modern reformers?'[128]

I was really concerned to see the poor man so violently agitated, and replied, 'My dear Sir — I allow much to the pride derived from ancestry — Where the dignity of an house has been supported, as I doubt not, but that *you* have supported yours: but let me on the other side say, that there are but too many who certainly inherit not, with their names, the virtues of their progenitors. You recollect a maxim of Rochefaucault's on this subject, which, as I remember to have heard, that he is a favourite author of your's, you will allow me to bring forward in support of my argument — "Les grands noms abaissent au lieu d'élever, ceux qui ne savent pas les soutenir*." Besides, how many are there, both in your country and mine, who are called noble, who cannot, in fact, refer to the examples of a long line of ancestry, to animate them, by example, to dignified conduct. — How very many, who owe to money, and not *hereditary merit*, the right they assume to look down on the rest of the world! It is true, that for the most part, that world repays their contempt; and it is from the vulgar only, who venerate a new coronet, which is generally "*twice as big as an old one*" — that they receive even the "*knee homage*," this valued appendage gives them. "Les Rois font des hommes comme des pieces de monnoie; ils les font valoir ce qu'ils veulent, & l'on est forcé de les recevoir, selon leurs cours & non pas selon leur véritable prix†.'"

'Let such men, then,' said Monsieur d'Hauteville, 'let such be erased, with all my heart, from the catalogue of noble names. — Indeed, it is well known, that we never consider such as belonging to our order. — I argue not about them — but for those, whose blood gives them pretensions to different treatment. — Ah! Monsieur Desmond, if it were possible — but it is not — for you to understand my feelings, you would comprehend, how utterly impossible it is for me, at my time of life, to continue in this lost and debased country, to drag on an existence, from which every thing valuable is gone, and which is consequently exposed to indignity and scorn — Would they not erase my arms? change my description? tear down the trophies of my house?' — These ideas seemed so deeply to affect the Count, that his respiration again became affected; his eyes appeared to be starting from his head; and he assumed so much the look of a man on the point of becoming insane, that I thought it more than time to conclude a conversation, that I should not have continued so long, had he not seemed to desire it.

---

* 'Great names degrade, instead of raising, those who know not how to support them.' — Maxime 94, de Rochefaucault.[129]

† Kings give value to men as they do to coin. They mark them with what stamp they please; and the world receives them according to this imaginary estimate, and not according to their real value. — Rochefaucault, Maxime 158.

With inveterate prejudice, thus fondly nursed from early youth, it were hopeless to contend — In the mind of Monsieur d'Hauteville, this notion of family consequence is so interwoven, so associated with all its ideas, that, as the ivy coeval with the tree, at length, destroys its vital principle, this sentiment now predominates to the extinction of reason itself— 'These prejudices,' says an eminent living writer*, 'arise from what are commonly called false views of things, or improper associations of ideas, which, in the extreme, become delirium, or madness; and is conspicuous to every person, except to him, who actually labours under this disorder of mind.'

I withdrew therefore, as soon as I could, leaving Monsieur d'Hauteville with his friend; who, I am sure, had his looks possessed the power imputed to those of the Basilisk, would then have concluded my adventures.[130] — As I passed through the last anti-room, and turned my eyes on the drawing of a great *genealogical* tree, which covers one side of it, I could not help philosophizing on the infinite variety of the modes of thinking among mankind — The difference between my consideration of such an object, and that bestowed on it by Monsieur d'Hauteville, struck me forcibly. Had I such a yellow scroll, though it described my descent from Adam or Noah, from a knight of the flaming sabre, or a king of the West Saxons — I should probably, on the first occasion that such a material was wanted, cut it into the angular slips, and write directions on the back of these parchment shreds, for the pheasants and hares that I send to my friends — while Monseigneur le Comte d'Hauteville is going to leave his native country, because the visionary honour he derives from this record, are not ostensibly allowed him in it — Exclaiming, poor man! to the National Assembly, 'Oh! ye have —

> 'From my own windows torn my houshold coat;
> 'Raz'd out my impress; leaving me no sign
> 'To shew the world I am a gentleman†'

I hear conclude this long letter, though I shall not seal it to-nght, because I have here much time on my hands, and cannot employ it

---

*   Priestley's Letters to a Philosophical Unbeliever.[131]
†   Shakespeare's Richard the Second.[132]

better than in writing to you; and because, I hope to dispatch by the same conveyance that takes this, an answer to those which I hope to have from you — for surely, my servant will be here to-morrow or Tuesday, with the letters that I have so long expected to be directed to the *chateau* de Montfleuri, from England; and which I now await, with hourly and increasing impatience.

Vale — Vale et me ama.[133]

L DESMOND

LETTER XIV*

TO MR BETHEL

Hauteville, in Auvergne,
Oct. 2, 1790

Did I not name to you a Breton, who had something in his air and manner unlike others of the peasantry? — Whenever I have observed him, he seemed to be the amusement of his fellow labourers: there was an odd quaint kind of pleasantry about him; and I wished to enter into conversation with him, which I had yesterday evening an opportunity of doing. — 'You are not of this part of France, my friend?' said I — 'No, Monsieur — I am a Breton — and now, would return into my own country again, but that, in a fit of impatience, at the excessive impositions I laboured under, I sold my little property about four years ago, and now must continue to 'courir le monde, & de vivre comme il plaroit à Dieu.' — Sterne has, I think, translated that to be upon nothing.[134] My acquaintance did not appear to be fond of such meagre diet, 'But, pray,' said I, 'explain to me, what particular oppressions you had to complain of, that drove you to so desperate, and, as it has happened, so ill-timed a resolution.'

'I believe,' replied he, 'that I am naturally of a temper a little impatient; and it was not much qualified by making a campaign or two against the English.[135] The first was in a ship of war, fitted out at St Malo's — or, in other words, Monsieur, a privateer;[136] for though I

---

*   Written before the receipt of Bethel's last letter.

was bred a sailor, and loved fighting well enough, I was refused even as *Ensigne de vaisseau**, on board a king's ship, *because I was not a gentleman* — My father, however, had a pretty little estate, which he inherited from his great, great grandfather — But he had an elder son, and I was to scramble through the world as well as I could — They wanted, indeed, to make me a monk; but I had a mortal aversion to that *métier*†, and thought it better to run the risque of getting my head taken off by a cannon ball, than to shave it — My first debut was not very fortunate — We fell in with an English frigate, with which, though it was hopeless enough to contend, we exchanged a few shot, for the honour of our country; and one of those we were favoured with in return, tore off the flesh from my right leg, without breaking the bone — The wound was bad enough; but the English surgeon sewed it up, and before we landed, I was so well as to be sent with the rest of our crew to the prison at Winchester — I had heard a great deal of the humanity of the English to their prisoners, and supposed I might bear my fate without much murmuring; but we were not treated the better for belonging to a privateer. — The prison was over-crowded, and very unhealthy — The provisions, I believe, might be liberally allowed by your government, but they were to pass through the hands of so many people, every one of which had their advantage out of them, that, before they were distributed in the prison, there was but little reason to boast of the generosity of your countrymen. To be sure, the wisdom and humanity of war are very remarkable in a scene like this, where one nation shuts up five or six thousand of the subjects of another, to be fed by contract while they live; and when they die, which two-thirds of the number seldom fail to do — to be buried by contract[137] — Yes! — out of nine-and-twenty of us poor devils, who were taken in our little privateer, fourteen died within three weeks; among whom, was a relation of mine, a gallant fellow, who had been in the former wars with the English, and stood the hazards of many a bloody day — He was an old man, but had a constitution so enured to hardships, and the changes of climate, that he seemed likely to see many more — A vile fever that lurked in the prison seized him — My hammock (for

---

*   Answering, I believe, to our midshipmen.

†   Trade — profession.

we were slung in hammocks, one above another, in those great, miserable rooms, which compose, what they say is, an unfinished palace) was hung above his, and when he found himself dying, he called to me to come to him — ''Tis all over with me, my friend,' said he — 'N'importe one must die at some time or other, but I should have liked it better by a cannon ball[138] — Nothing, however, vexes me more in this business, than that I have been the means of bringing you hither to die in this hole — (for, in fact, it was by his advice, I had entered on board the privateer) However, it may be, you will out-live this confounded place, and have another touch at these damned English.' National hatred, the strange and ridiculous prejudice in which my poor old friend had lived, was the last sensation he felt in death — He died quietly enough, in a few moments afterwards, and the next day I saw him tied up between two boards, by way of the coffin, which was to be provided by contract; and deposited in the *fossé* that surrounded our prison, in a grave, dug by contract, and of course very shallow, in which he was covered with about an inch of mould, which was by contract also, put over him, and seven other prisoners, who died at the same time![139] — My youth, and a great flow of animal spirits, carried me through this wretched scene[140] — And a young officer, who was a native of the same part of Britany, and who was a prisoner on parole, at a neighbouring town, procured leave to visit the prison at Winchester, and enquired me out — He gave me, though he could command very little money himself, all he had about him, to assist me in procuring food, and promised to try if he could obtain for me my parole, as he knew my parents, and was concerned for my situation — But his intentions, in my favour, were soon frustrated; for, on the appearance of the combined fleets in the Channel, the French officers, who were thought too near the coast, were ordered away to Northampton, while, very soon afterwards, a number of Spaniards, who had among them a fever of a most malignant sort, were sent to the prison already over-crowded, and death began to make redoubled havock among its wretched inhabitants[141] — Of so dire a nature was the disease thus imported, that while the bodies that were thrown overboard from the Spanish fleet, and driven down by the tide on the coasts of Cornwall and Devonshire, carried its fatal influence into those countries, the prisoners, who were sent up from Plymouth, disseminated destruction in their route, and among all who approached them; thus becoming the instruments of greater mischief, than the sword and the bayonet could have executed. Not only the miserable prisoners of war, who were now a mixture of French, Spanish, and Dutch, perished by dozens every day; but the soldiers who guarded them, the attendants of the prison, the physical men who were sent to administer medicines, and soon afterwards, the inhabitants of the town, and even those of the neighbouring country began to suffer — Then it was that your government perceiving this *blessing of war* likely to extend itself rather too far, thought proper to give that attention to it, which the calamities of the prisoners would never have excited. A physician was sent down by Parliament, to examine into the causes of this scourge; and in consequence of the impossibility of stopping it while such numbers were crowded together, the greater part of the French, whom sickness had spared, were dismissed, and I, among others, returned to my own country. I, soon after, not discouraged by what had befallen me, entered on board another privateer, which had the good fortune to capture two West-India ships, richly laden, and to bring them safely into l'Orient, where we disposed of their cargoes; and my share was so considerable, that I determined to quit the sea and return to my friends — When, in pursuance of this resolution, I arrived at home, I found my father and elder brother had died during my absence; and I took possession of the little estate to which I thus became heir, and began to think myself a person of some consequence. In commencing country gentleman, I sat myself down to reckon all the advantages of my situation. — An extensive tract of waste land lay on one side of my little domain — on the other, a forest — my fields abounded with game — a river ran through them, on which I depended for a supply of fish; and I determined to make a little warren, and to build a dove-cote. I had undergone hardships enough to give me a perfect relish for the good things now within my reach; and I resolved most piously to enjoy them. — But I was soon disturbed in this agreeable reverie — I took the liberty of firing one morning at a covey of partridges, that were feeding in my corn; and having the same day caught a brace of trout, I was sitting down to regale myself on these dainties, when I received the following notice from the neighbouring *seigneur*, with whom I was not at all aware that I had any thing to do.

'The most high and most powerful *seigneur*, Monseigneur Raoul-Phillippe-Joseph-Alexandre-Caesar Erispoé, Baron de Kermanfroi, signifies to Louis-Jean de Merville, that he the said *seigneur*, in quality of Lord Paramount, is to all intents and purposes invested with the sole right and property of the river running through his fief, together with all the fish therein; the rushes, reeds, and willows that grow in or near the said river; all trees and plants that the said river waters; and all the islands and aits within it — Of all and every one of which the high and mighty lord, Raoul-Phillippe-Joseph-Alexandre-Caesar Erispoé, Baron de Kermanfroi, is absolute and only proprietor — Also, of all the birds of whatsoever nature or species, that have, shall, or may, at any time fly on, or across, or upon, the said *fief* or *seigneury* — And all the beasts of chase, of whatsoever description, that have, shall, or may be found upon it.' — In short, Sir, it concluded with informing me, the said Louis-Jean, that if I, at any time, dared to fish in the river, or to shoot a bird upon the said *fief*, of which it seems my little farm unluckily made part, I should be delivered into the hands of justice, and dealt with according to the utmost rigour of the offended laws. To be sure, I could not help enquiring within myself, how it happened, that I had no right to the game thus fed in my fields, nor the fish that swam in the river? and how it was, that heaven, in creating these animals, had been at work only for the great *seigneurs*! — What! is there nothing, said I, but insects and reptiles, over which man, not born noble, may exercise dominion? — From the wren to the eagle; from the rabbit to the wild-boar; from the gudgeon to the pike — all, all, it seems, are the property of the great. 'Twas hard to imagine where the power originated, that thus deprived all other men of their rights, to give to those nobles the empire of the elements, and the dominion over animated nature! — However, I reflected, but I did not resist; and since I could no longer bring myself home a dinner with my gun, I thought to console myself, as well as I could, with the produce of my farm-yard; and I constructed a small enclosed pigeon-house, from whence, without any offence to my noble neighbour, I hoped to derive some supply for my table — But, alas! the comfortable and retired state of my pigeons attracted the aristocratic envy of those of the same species, who inhabited the spacious manorial dove-cote of Monseigneur; and they were so very unreasonable as to cover, in immense flocks, not only my fields of corn, where they committed infinite depredations, but to surround my farmyard, and monopolize the food with which I supplied my own little collection, in their enclo-

sures. As if they were instinctively assured of the protection they enjoyed as belonging to the *seigneur* Raoul-Philippe-Joseph-Alexandre-
Caesar Erispoé, Baron de Kermanfroi; my menaces, and the shouts of
my servants, were totally disregarded; till, at length, I yielded too hastily
to my indignation, and threw a stone at a flight of them, with so much
effect, that I broke the leg of one of these pigeons; the consequence of
which was, that in half an hour, four of the *gardes de chasse** of
Monseigneur appeared, and summoned me to declare, if I was not
aware, that the wounded bird which they produced in evidence against
me, was the property of the said *seigneur*; and without giving me time
to either acknowledge my crime, or apologize for it, they shot, by way
of retaliation, the tame pigeons in my enclosures, and carried me away
to the *chateau* of the most high and puissant *seigneur* Raoul-Philippe-
Joseph-Alexandre-Caesar Erispoé, Baron de Kermanfroi, to answer for
the assault I had thus committed on the person of one of his pigeons
— There I was interrogated by the Fiscal, who was making out a *proces
verbal*; and reproved severely for not knowing or attending to the fact,
so universally acknowledged by the laws of Britany, that pigeons and
rabbits were creatures peculiarly dedicated to the service of the nobles;
and that for a vassal, as I was, to injure one of them, was an unpardonable offence against the rights of my lord, who might inflict any
punishment he pleased for my transgression[142] — That indeed, the
laws of Beauvoisis pronounced, that such an offence was to be punished with death; but that the milder laws of Britany condemned the
offender only to corporal punishment, at the mercy of the lord — in
short, Sir, I got off this time by paying a heavy fine to Monseigneur
Raoul-Philippe-Joseph-Alexandre-Caesar Erispoé, Baron de
Kermanfroi, in the midst of his greatness. — Soon afterwards,
Monseigneur discovered that there was a certain spot upon my estate,
where a pond might be made, for which he found that he had great
occasion; and he very modestly signified to me, that he should cause
this piece of ground to be laid under water, and that he would either
give me a piece of ground of the same value, or pay me for it according to the estimation of two persons whom he would appoint; but,

_____

   *   Game-keepers.

that in case I refused this just and liberal offer, he should, as Lord Paramount, and of his own right and authority, make his pond by flooding my ground, according to law.

'I felt this proposal to be inconsistent with every principle of justice — In this spot was an old oak, planted by the first de Merville, who had bought the estate — It was under its shade that the happiest hours of my life had passed, while I was yet a child, and it had been held in veneration by all my family — I determined then to defend this favourite spot; and I hastened to a neighbouring magistrate, learned in the law — He considered my case, and then informed me, that, in this instance, the laws of Britany were silent, and that therefore, their deficiency must be supplied by the customs and laws of the neighbouring provinces — The laws of Maine and Anjou, said he, decide, that the *seigneur* of the *fief*, may take the grounds of his vassal to make ponds, or any thing else, only giving him another piece of ground, or paying what is equivalent in money — As *precedent*, therefore, decides, that the same thing may be done in Britany, I advise you, Louis-Jean de Merville, to submit to the laws, and, on receiving payment, to give up your land to Monseigneur Raoul-Philippe-Joseph-Alexandre-Caesar Erispoé, Baron de Kermanfroi.

It was in vain I represented that I had a particular taste, or a fond attachment to this spot. My man of law told me that a vassal had no right to any taste or attachment, contrary to the sentiments of his lord — And, alas! — in a few hours, I heard the hatchet laid to my beloved oak — My fine meadow was covered with water, and became the receptacle for the carp, tench, and eels of Monseigneur — And remonstrances and complaints were in vain! — These were only part of the grievances I endured from my unfortunate neighbourhood to this powerful Baron, to whom, in his miserable and half furnished *chateau*, I was regularly summoned to do homage 'upon faith and oath' — till my oppressions becoming more vexatious and insupportable, I took the desperate resolution of selling my estate, and throwing myself again upon the wide world. — Paris, whither I repaired with the money for which I sold it, was a theatre so new, and so agreeable, to me, that I could not determine to leave it till I had no longer the means left of playing there a very brilliant part. When that unlucky hour arrived, I wandered into this country, and took up my abode with a relation, a farmer, who rents some land of Monseigneur the Count d'Hauteville, and here I have remained, at times, working, but oftener philosophizing, and not unfrequently regretting my dear oak, and the first agreeable visions that I indulged on taking possession of my little farm, before I was aware of the consequences of being a vassal of Monseigneur Raoul-Philippe-Joseph-Alexandre-Caesar Erispoé, Baron de Kermanfroi, and indeed sometimes repenting that I did not wait a little longer, when the revolution would have protected me against the tyranny of my very illustrious neighbour.'

De Merville here ended his narrative, every word of which I found to be true; and I could not but marvel at the ignorance or effrontery of those who assert that the *noblesse* of France either possessed no powers inimical to the general rights of mankind, or possessing such, forebore to exert them. The former part of his life bears testimony *to the extreme benefits accruing from war, and cannot but raise a wish, that the power of doing such extensive good to mankind, and renewing scenes so very much to the honour of reasonable beings, may never be taken from the princes and potentates of the earth.* I thus endeavour, dear Bethel, by entering into the interests of those I am with, to call off my thoughts from my own, or I should find this very long space of time, in which I have failed to receive letters from England, almost insupportable.

At the very moment I complain, I see my servant Warham approaching the house — I fly, impatiently, to receive news of Geraldine, of you, of all I love; and hope to have a long, a very long letter to write, in answer, to-morrow, to those I expect from you — We go back to Montfleuri the next day: this will therefore be the last pacquet you will receive from hence.

LIONEL DESMOND

Note. The latter part of this narrative is a sort of free translation of parts of a little pamphlet, entitled, 'Histoire d'un malheureux Vassal de Bretagne, écrite par lui-même,' in which the excessive abuses to which the feudal system gave birth, are detailed.[143]

*LETTER XV

TO MR BETHEL

Montfleuri, October 10, 1790

What did I say to you, dear Bethel, in my letter of the 29th of August, that has given you occasion to rally me so unmercifully about Madame de Boisbelle; and to predict my *cure*, as you call it — I cannot now recollect the contents of that letter; but of this I am sure, that I never was more fondly attached to the lovely woman, from whom my destiny has divided me, than at this moment; or ever saw the perfections of other women with more indifference — Were it possible for you, my friend, to comprehend the anguish of heart which I have felt ever since your last letters gave me such an account of the situation of Verney's affairs — you might be convinced, that time, absence, and distance, have had no such effect in altering my sentiments; and that the sister of my friend Montfleuri, were she even as partial to me, as some trifling occurrences I have related, may have led you to imagine, can never be to me more than an agreeable acquaintance. — Far from being able to detach my mind from the idea of Geraldine's situation — I have undergone continual raillery from Montfleuri, for my extreme dejection, ever since I heard it — If these distressing scenes should become yet more alarming, I shall return to England. — There I shall, at least, learn the progress of that ruin, which, though I cannot wholly prevent, I may, perhaps, soften to her, for whose sake alone, I deprecate its arrival — Restless and wretched, I left Hauteville, hardly conscious of the progress of my journey; and since I came hither, have had a return of that lurking fever which made my health one pretence for my quitting England.

Montfleuri is not here, but was detained by business at Aiguemont. — I expect him to-morrow; and shall then determine whether to bend my course southward with him, or northward, on my return to England. I cannot describe to you how wretched I am. — Surely, you never loved, or you would not ridicule feelings so acute as mine — Nor would

---

* Answer to letter xi.

you suppose that I should think about my fortune, if the sacrifice of any part of it could secure the peace and competence of a being for whom I could lay down my life. I intended to have continued a little narrative of all that happens to me — of the persons I meet — and of the conversation I hear — but your raillery has changed my purpose. Of whom can I speak here, but of Josephine and Julie; and if I tell you that they wept with pleasure on my arrival, and have since exerted themselves, with unceasing solicitude, to divert the melancholy they cannot but perceive — you would again renew that strain of ridicule about the former, which I so little like to hear — This prevents my telling you of a walk which Josephine engaged me to take with her last night to the ruin on the hill, of which, I believe, I gave a slight description in some former letter — nor will I, for the same reason, relate the conversation that passed there — when seating herself on a piece of a fallen column, she began, after a deep sigh and with eyes swimming in tears, to relate to me the occurrences of her unfortunate life.

Could I help listening to such a woman? — Could I help sympathizing in sorrows which she so well knows how to describe? — Alas! when she complains that her mother betrayed her into marriage with a man, for whom it was impossible she ever could either feel love or esteem — when she dwells on all the miseries of such a connection, on the bitterness with which her life is irrecoverably dashed — the similarity of her fate to that of Geraldine, awakens in my mind a thousand subjects of painful recollection, and fruitless regret — My tears flow with hers; and she believes those emotions arise from extreme sensibility, which are rather excited by the situation of my own heart.

This kind of conversation so entirely engrossed us last night, that I heeded not the progress of time; and the sun had been for some time sunk behind those distant mountains that bound the extensive prospect from the eminence we were upon, before I recollected that we had a river to cross, and a very long walk home.

When these circumstances occurred to me, I suddenly proposed to Madame de Boisbelle to return — She had then been shedding tears in silence for some moments, and starting from the melancholy attitude in which she sat, she took my hand, and gently pressing it, said, as I led her among the masses of the fallen buildings that impeded our path — 'To the unhappy, sympathy and tenderness, like your's is so seducing, that I have even trespassed on the indulgence your pity seems willing to grant me — I, perhaps, have too tediously dwelt on incurable calamities, and called off your thoughts too long from pleasanter subjects and happier women! — I answered — (not, I own, without more emotion than I wished to have shewn) that I had indeed listened —

Dear Bethel, I here broke off, on receiving intelligence that a messenger from Marseilles had a pacquet to deliver to me. I hurried to meet him, and received from a man sent express, the letter I enclose, from Anthony, Waverly's old servant.

As I am not sure that my presence in England can be useful to Geraldine, and have some hopes that at Marseilles, it may yet save her brother, I shall therefore hasten thither; but, at the earnest entreaty of the ladies of this family, I shall wait till noon to-morrow, by which time Montfleuri will certainly be returned. I have therefore dispatched my servant to the next post-house to order four horses hither to-morrow — I have no hope that Waverly will yield to reason; but his fluctuating character, which is usually so much against him, is here my only reliance — Direct your letters, till you hear from me again, to the care of Messieurs Duhamel and Bergot, at Marseilles; and do not, I beseech you, my dear friend, trifle with my unhappiness, but give me as exact an account as you can collect of Verney's affairs. As soon as possible I hope to hear from you.

Your's affectionately, ever,

LIONEL DESMOND

LETTER XVI*

TO LIONEL DESMOND, ESQUIRE

SIR, Marsales, Oct. 7th, 1790

Hoping you will excuse this freedom — this is to let you know, that Master changed his mind as to joining your honours party at my lord the Count of Hotevills as he promised faithfully, and instead thereof,

---

* Inclosed in the foregoing.

set out with the gentlemen as he was with for this place; where they have introduced him to a family as is come to settle near here since the troubles in the capitol; which is, a mother, a son and two daughters. And master have lived with this family all's one as if it were his home — I know no harm of the females — they are handsome young women — that is the two daughters: but the son, tho he appears so grand and fashinable, is as I hear a sort of a sharping chap — or what we call in England a black legs — He has won a good deal of money of master, as I have reason to think; but that does not altogether signify so much as the intention they have persuaded him into amongst them, to marry one of the mam-selles; which if something does not happen to make him change his mind he will certainly do out of hand — I can assure you honour'd Sir, I never knew master so long in the same mind ever since I have been in his service as upon this occasion — And I thought proper to let you know, because I am certain that my old lady, nor no part of his relations could like of this thing, and particularly his sister Mrs Verney, who said so much to him in my hearing about being drawn in to marry, and advised him by all means to consult you, before ever he resolved upon any scheme whatever — I was so bold as to tell this to my master, who was not angry indeed with me, as he is a very good natured gentleman: but he ask'd if so be I thought that he was to be always a child in leading strings.

I thought it best, seeing this affair is still going on, to advertise your honour of it; and if you think it proper to put an end thereto by your interference I think that there is no time to be lost.

From, Sir,
Your dutiful humble servant
to command,
ANTHONY BOOKER

END OF THE FIRST VOLUME

DESMOND.

A NOVEL,

BY

CHARLOTTE SMITH.

SECOND EDITION.

VOLUME II.

LONDON:

PRINTED FOR G. G. J. AND J. ROBINSON,
PATER-NOSTER-ROW, 1792.

DESMOND

LETTER I

TO MISS WAVERLY AT BATH

Upper Seymour Street, Nov. 10, 1790

Why did I flatter myself, dearest Fanny, that the numberless distresses which have lately surrounded me, would either bring with them that calm resignation which should teach me to bear, or that total debility of mind that should make me forget to feel, all their poignancy? — Is it that I set out in life with too great a share of sensibility? or is it my lot to be particularly wretched? — Every means I take to save myself from pain — to save those I love — on whom, indeed, my Happiness depends, serves only to render me more miserable. How ill I have succeeded in regard to my brother, the inclosed letter will too well explain.

Why did I ever involve Desmond in the hopeless task of checking his conduct? — I am so distressed, so hurt, that it is with the utmost difficulty I write. However, as the generous exertions of this excellent young man have, for the present, rescued my brother from the actual commission of the folly he meditated, though perhaps at the expence of a most valuable life, you will communicate to my mother this very unfortunate affair, and desire her directions in regard to recalling her son.

Perhaps I ought to say all this to her myself: but I am really so shaken by this intelligence, that it is not without great difficulty I can write to you. — My fortitude, which you have of late been accustomed to compliment, has, I know not why, quite forsaken me now: and, methinks, I could bear any thing better, than that such a man as Desmond should be so great a sufferer from his generous attention to a part of my family.

I have been very ill ever since the receipt of this melancholy letter; and it is only to-day, though I received it on Thursday, that I have had strength enough to forward it to you. I am now so near being confined, that the people who are collected about me weary me with their troublesome care, and will not let me have a moment to myself.

It would have been a comfort to me, my Fanny, to have had your company at this time. But I know that this incident will add to the reluctance with which my mother would have before borne your absence from her; and, therefore, I will not again name it, nor suffer myself to make those complaints, in which we (I mean the unhappy) too frequently *indulge* ourselves, without considering that this querulous weakness is painful to others; and, to ourselves, unavailing: — for, alas! it cures not the evils it describes.

As to Mr Verney, he has never been at home since the October meeting, nor have I ever heard from him.[1] — His friend, Colonel Scarsdale, called at my door on Tuesday, and was, by accident, admitted. — He made a long visit, and talked, as usual, in a style which I suppose I might admire (since all the world allows him to be very *charming*), if I could but understand what he means. However, though I am so tasteless as not to discover the perfections of this wonderful being, I endured his conversation from three o'clock till half past five; in hopes that, as he is so much connected with Mr Verney, I might learn from him where my husband is. — But he laughed off all my enquiries unfeelingly enough; and all I could collect was, that Mr Verney is now, or at least was a few days since, at the house of one of their mutual friends in Yorkshire. — I anticipate the remark you will make upon this — you, who are so little inclined to spare his follies, or, indeed, those of any of your acquaintance; and it is too true, that when he is at home, it makes no other difference to me than that of destroying my peace without promoting my happiness. I check my pen, however — and when I look at my two lovely children, I blame myself for being thus betrayed into complaints against their father. — Alas! why are our pleasures, our tastes, our views of life, so different? — But I will stifle these murmurs; and, indeed, I would most willingly drop this hopeless subject for ever. Let me return to one that gives, at least, more favourable ideas of human nature, though it can only be productive of pain to me — I mean — to poor Desmond. — Oh! Fanny, what a heart is his! — How noble is that disdain of personal danger, when mingled with such manly tenderness — such generous sensibility for the feelings of others! — When we saw so much of him in Kent the first year of my marriage, we used, I remember, to have little disputes about him — but they were childish. Do you not recollect, that when I contended for Lavater's system, I introduced him in support of my argument?[2] — His was the most open, ingenuous countenance I had ever seen; and his manners, as well as all I could then know of his heart and his temper, were exactly such as that countenance indicated. You then, in the mere spirit of contradiction, used to say, that this ingenuous expression was often lost in clouds for whole hours together; and that you believed this paragon was a sulky sort of an animal. — Did you believe that such a striking instance of disinterested kindness towards your own family would so confirm my opinion? — Yet while I write, he suffers — perhaps dies! the victim of that generous and exalted spirit which led him to hazard his life, that he might fulfil a promise I, who have so little right to his friendship, drew from him — a promise that he would be attentive to the conduct of my brother!

Indeed, Fanny, when my imagination sets him before me wounded, in pain, perhaps in danger (and it is an image I have hardly lost for a moment since the receipt of this cruel intelligence), I am so very miserable, that all other anxieties of my life, multiplied as they have lately been, are unheeded and unfelt. — But why should I write thus — why hazard communicating to you, my dear sister, a portion of that pain from which I cannot myself escape?

I will bid you good night, my Fanny. It is now six-and-thirty hours since I have closed my eyes — I will try to sleep, and to forget how very very long it will be before I can hear again from Marseilles.

Write to me, I conjure you — tell me what are my mother's intentions as to sending for my brother home: and be assured of the tender affection of your

GERALDINE VERNEY

P.S. Did you ever hear of this Madame de Boisbelle? and do you know whether she is a widow or married? — young, middle-aged, or old? — She is sister to Mr Desmond's favourite French friend, Montfleuri; and, if she has any heart, must have exquisite pleasure in softening, to such a man as Desmond, the long hours of pain and confinement. — I suppose he has forgotten that I read French tolerably. However, perhaps, it was better to let the surgeon write. — How miserable is the suspense I must endure till the arrival of the next letters!

LETTER II*

TO MRS VERNEY

Marseilles, 17th Oct. 1790

MADAM,

It is at the request of Mr Desmond, that I take the liberty of addressing you. His anxiety, on your account, has never forsaken him in the midst of what have been certainly very acute sufferings; not unattended with danger.

It may be necessary to enter into a detail of the causes that prevent his writing himself, on a subject, which nothing but the impracticability of his doing, would, I am sure, induce him to entrust to a stranger.

It is now four days since I received a summons to attend, at the distance of three miles from the city, an English gentleman, who had, on that morning, been engaged in an affair of honour. I had not till then the honour of knowing Mr Desmond — whom I found very terribly wounded by a pistol shot in the right arm. — The ball entering a little below the elbow, had not only broken but so shattered the bone, that I am afraid the greatest skill cannot answer the consequences — Besides this, there was a bullet, from the first brace of pistols which were fired, lodged in the right shoulder; which, though it was so situated as to be extracted without much difficulty, greatly increases the inflammation, and of course the hazard of the other wound, where the sinews are so torn, and the bone in such a state, that the ball could not be taken out without great pain. I did all that could be done, and Mr Desmond bore the operation with the calmest fortitude. I left him at noon, in what I thought as favourable a way as was possible under such circumstances; yet I found, on my return in the evening, that he had a great deal of fever; and I am concerned to say, this symptom has ever since been increasing. — Though much is certainly to be hoped for from the youth, constitution, and patience of the sufferer — I can by no means say I am certain of a fortunate event.

The dispute, in consequence of which this disagreeable accident happened, originated, I find, about your brother, Mr Waverly; who,

---

* Enclosed in the foregoing to Miss Waverly.

entangled by the artifices of a family well known in this country, had engaged to marry one of the young ladies — a step which was thought by Mr Desmond, as indeed it was universally, very indiscreet. — The interference of Mr Desmond to prevent it, brought upon him the resentment of the lady's brother, the young Chevalier de St Eloy; and the duel ensued.

I found, very early in the course of my attendance, that the mind of my patient was as much affected as his body; and that the greatest pain he felt, was from being rendered incapable of writing to you, madam. — He at length asked if I would be so good as to write what he would dictate, as it was the only way by which he could communicate his situation to you. His advice is, that the relations of Mr Waverly recall him immediately to England. He is now at Avignon; but notwithstanding what has happened, Mr Desmond seems to think him by no means secure from the artifices of a family that has gained such an ascendency over him. — I made notes with my pencil, as I sat by his bedside, and indeed promised to adhere to the words he dictated; but I think it my duty, madam, in this case, to tell you my real sentiments, and not to palliate or disguise my apprehensions. — As soon as the affair happened, I sent, by Mr Desmond's desire, an account of it to his friend, whose house, in the Lyonois, he had, I found, recently left; and to-day this friend, Monsieur de Montfleuri, arrived here express, with his sister, Madame de Boisbelle. — They both seem extremely interested for the health of my patient, and have attended him, ever since their arrival, with unceasing assiduity. — He appears pleased and relieved by their presence; and indeed I imagined that he would rather have employed one of them to have the honour of writing to you; but he said Monsieur de Montfleuri could write but little English, and his sister none.

I believe, madam, that to receive the honour of your commands, would be particularly gratifying to my patient, of whom I most sincerely wish that I may be enabled, in a few days, to send you a better account.

I am, madam,
Your most obedient
and most humble servant,
WILLIAM CARMICHAEL

LETTER III

TO MR DESMOND

Bath, Nov. 15, 1790

I never was so distressed in my life, my dear Desmond, as I was at the account of your accident; which I received yesterday from Miss Waverly. — I came hither about ten days ago by the advice of my friend Banks, who thinks the waters will decide, whether the something I have about me is gout or no; and thought of nothing less than of receiving intelligence here, that you lie dangerously wounded, at or near Marseilles, in a quarrel about Waverly. — This is no time to preach to you. — But I beg, that immediately upon the receipt of this letter, you will let me know if I can be of any use to you; and, if I can, be assured that nothing shall prevent my coming to you instantly. I hope you know, that I am not one of those who can, with great composure, talk over and lament their friends' misfortunes, without stirring a finger to help them. — My life, which has long afforded me no enjoyment worth the trouble of living for, is only of value to me as it may be useful to my children, and the very few friends I love. — You once, I remember, on an occasion of much less importance, scrupled to send for me, because you said you knew it was in the midst of harvest. — It is now in the midst of the wheat season; yet, you see, I am at Bath; and if a trifling, half-formed complaint, which is not serious enough to have a name, could bring me thus far from home, surely the service of my friend Desmond would carry me much — much farther.

I shall be extremely uneasy till I hear from you, and would, indeed, set out directly, if I could imagine you are as ill as Miss Waverly represented you. — But besides that, her account is inconsistent and incoherent. I know all misses love a duel, and to lament over the dear gallant creature who suffers in it. — This little wild girl seems half frantic, and does nothing but talk to every body about you, in which she shews more gratitude than discretion. — Your uncle, Danby, who is here on his usual autumnal visit, has heard of your fame; and came bustling up to me in the coffee-house this morning, to tell me, that all he had foreseen as the consequence of your imprudent journey to France, was come to pass; that you were assassinated by a party whom your politics had offended; and would probably lose your life in con-

sequence of your foolish rage for a foolish revolution. — I endeavoured, in vain, to convince him that the affair happened in a mere
private quarrel — a quarrel with an *avanturier*, in which you had engaged to save a particular friend from an improper marriage.[3] — The
old Major would not hear me. — He at length granted, that instead
of being assassinated, you *might* have fought, but that still it must
have been about politics; and, to do him justice, he judges of others
by himself, which is the only way a man can judge. — Very certain
it is, he openly professes it, that he never loved any body well enough
in his life, to give himself, on their account, one quarter of an hour's
pain. — The public interests him as little — he declares, that he is
perfectly at ease, and therefore cares not who is otherwise; and as to
all revolutions, or even alterations, he has a mortal aversion to them.
— Miss Waverly tells me she has written to you, by desire of her
mother, to thank you for your very friendly interposition, and has
given you an account of all your connexions in England. — This I
am very sorry for, because I am afraid she can give you no account
of the Verney family that will not add to the present depression of
your spirits. Indeed she cannot, with truth, speak of their situation
favourably; and, if truth could say any thing good of Verney, Miss
Waverly seems little disposed to repeat it. — She is naturally satirical, and hates Verney, to whom she thinks her sister has been sacrificed; so that, whenever they meet, it is with displeasure on her side,
and with contemptuous indifference on his: — but Fanny, whenever
she has an opportunity of speaking of him, takes care that the dark
shades of his character shall have all their force. — Allow, my dear
Desmond, something for this in the account you may, perhaps, hear.
— Let me have early intelligence of you, I conjure you; and I again
beg you to remember, that you may command the presence, as in
any other way the best services, of

Yours most faithfully,

E. BETHEL

LETTER IV

TO MR BETHEL

Marseilles, 29th Nov. 1790

I use another hand, my dear friend, to thank you for your letter of the fourteenth, which reached me yesterday. — Your attentive kindness in offering to come to me, I shall never forget; though I do not avail myself of it, because I know such a journey can be neither convenient or agreeable to you; and because it is in your power, in yours only, to act for me in England, in an affair on which the tranquillity of my mind depends: tranquillity — without which the progress of my cure will be slow; and that single reason will, I am persuaded, be enough to reconcile you to the task I now solicit you to engage in.

A letter from Miss Waverly, which I received by the same post that brought yours, has rendered me more than ever wretched. Good heavens! in what a situation is the woman, so justly adored by your unhappy friend, at a moment when he cannot fly to her assistance! — She had lain-in only ten days, when her sister wrote to me. — There are two executions in the house, one for sixteen hundred, the other for two thousand three hundred pounds. Verney is gone, nobody knows whither. — And Geraldine, in such a situation, has no father, brother, or friend to support her. — Yet the natural dignity of her mind has, it should seem, never forsaken her.

A little before her confinement she wrote to thank me for my friendship for her brother, and to deplore its consequences — (O Bethel! for how much more suffering would not her tender gratitude overpay me!) but of herself, of her own uneasiness, she said nothing; nor should I have known it but for Fanny Waverly; whom her mother has, at length, sent to the suffering angel, and who has given me a dreadful detail of the supposed situation of Verney's affairs — I say supposed, because there is nothing certainly known from himself; and these debts were only discovered by the entrance of the sheriff's officers. I cannot rest, my dear Bethel, whilst Geraldine is thus distressed. My thoughts are constantly employed upon the means of relieving her; but, a cripple as I am, and so far from England, I must depend on you to assist me. — Since then you were so good as to offer to come hither, I hope and believe you will not hesitate to take a shorter journey, much more conducive to my repose even than the satisfaction of seeing you. — Go, I beseech you, to London — enquire into the nature of these debts; and, at all events, discharge them; but concealing carefully at whose entreaty you take this trouble; even concealing yourself; if it be possible. — I send you an order, on my banker, for five thousand pounds; and if twice the sum be wanted to restore to Geraldine her house, and a little, even transient repose, I should think it a cheap purchase.

Do not argue with me, dear Bethel, about this — but hear me, when I most solemnly assure you, that far from meaning to avail myself of any advantage which grateful sensibility might give me over such a mind as hers, it is not my intention she shall ever know of the transaction; and I entreat you to manage it for me accordingly. While I find her rise every moment in my esteem, I know that I am becoming — alas! am already become unworthy hers.[4] — Do not ask me an explanation; I have said more than I intended — but let it go. — The greatest favour you can do me, Bethel, is to execute this commission for me as expeditiously as possible; and it will give you pleasure to hear, that I am so much better than my surgeon expected from the early appearances of my wound, that it is probable I shall be able to thank you with my own hand, for the friendly commission I now entreat you to undertake. I am already able to move my fingers, though not to guide a pen. My arm, however, is yet in such a state, as renders it very imprudent, if not impossible for me, to leave the skilful man, who has, contrary to all probability and expectation, saved it from amputation; which, at first, seemed almost unavoidable. Montfleuri wishes that I may remove to his house, in the Lyonois, as a sort of first stage towards England; but I have been already too much obliged to him, and his sister, Madame de Boisbelle. He attended me himself day and night, while there was so much danger, as Mr Carmichael apprehended, for many days after the accident; and since he has been absent, his sister has with too much goodness given me her constant attention. Montfleuri has been to Paris, and returned only yesterday. He sees my uneasiness since the receipt of Miss Waverly's letter — Madame de Boisbelle too sees it; and what is worse, my medical friends perceive it, from the state of my wound; so that, as it is impossible for me, my dear friend, either to conceal or conquer it, my sole dependence for either peace of mind, or bodily health, is on your friendly endeavours to remove it.

How long, how very long, will the hours seem that must intervene before I can hear that this is done! and what shall I do to beguile them? Montfleuri talks to me of politics, and exults in the hope that all will be settled advantageously for his country, and without bloodshed. I rejoice, most sincerely rejoice, in this prospect, so favourable to the best interests of humanity; but I can no longer enter with eagerness into the detail of those measures by which it is to be realized. — One predominant sensation excludes, for the present, all the lively interest I felt in more general concerns, and while Mrs Verney is ——— ——— but it is not necessary, surely, to add more on this topic. — No, my dear Bethel, you will, on such an occasion, enter into my feelings from the generosity of your own heart: and whatever that little touch of misanthropy, which you have acquired, may lead you to think of human nature in general — you will after my asseverations on this subject, and, I hope, after what you know of me, do justice as well to the disinterested nature of my love, as to the sincerity of that friendship, with which

I ever remain
most affectionately yours,
LIONEL DESMOND

LETTER V

TO MR DESMOND

London, Dec. 17, 1790

The moment I received your letter I hastened from Bath, where I then was, to London; determined to execute your commission to the best of my power, though I neither approved it, or knew very well how to set about it. — Do not imagine, however, my dear Desmond, that I have a mind so narrowed by a long converse with the world, or an heart so hardened by too much knowledge of its inhabitants, as to blame the liberality of your sentiments, or to be insensible to the pleasure of indulging them. — But here there is a fatal and inseparable bar to the success of every attempt you can make to befriend Mrs Verney and her children; and the facility with which Verney finds himself delivered from one difficulty, only serves to encourage him to plunge into others, till total and irretrievable ruin shall overtake him.

I was aware of all the difficulties of the task you set me; for it was by no means proper that the smallest suspicion should arise as to the quarter whence the money came that paid off those demands, which must otherwise have brought all the effects Verney had at his town-house to sale within a very short time. — I have a friend in the law who, to great acuteness, adds that most rare quality, in an attorney, of strict integrity. — To him I confided the business, and he has managed it so well that Mrs Verney is again in uninterrupted possession of her house; and believes, as does Verney himself, that Mrs Waverly advanced the money, but keeps it concealed lest it should subject her to future demands. Of the means by which all this was done, I need not enter into a detail — You will be satisfied to know it is done, and that the pride and delicacy of Geraldine have not suffered. — You will be better pleased, perhaps, to hear something of herself. — I thought I might call there as an aquaintance; and though I received intelligence at the door, that Mrs Verney was not well, and saw no company but her own family, I sent up my name, and was immediately admitted.

I found her in her dressing-room, so pale, so languid, so changed from the lovely blooming Geraldine of four years since, that I beheld her with extreme concern. — Yet however unwilling I am, my friend, to encourage in you the growth of a passion productive on all sides of misery, I am compelled to own, that this charming woman, in the pride of early beauty, never appeared to me so interesting, so truly lovely, as at the moment I saw her. — In her lap sleeping the little infant of a month old — The boy of which I have heard you speak with so much fondness, sat on the carpet at her feet, and the girl on the sopha by her. — In answer to my compliments, she said, with a sweet, yet melancholy smile — 'This is very good indeed, Mr Bethel, and like an old friend. — How are your two sweet children? — are they in town with you? — It would give me great pleasure to see them.' — I answered her enquiries about Harry and Louisa in the usual way; and she then, with a sort of anxiety in her manner, for which I could easily account, talked for a moment on the common topics of the day; which almost unavoidably led me to speak of France. — She sighed when I first named it; and, with a faint blush, exclaimed — 'Ah! Mr Bethel! how can I think of France without feeling the acutest pain, when it instantly brings to my mind what has so lately happened there to our excellent friend, Mr Desmond?' — A deeper colour wavered for a moment on her cheek; her voice trembled; but she seemed by an effort to repress her emotion, and continued: — 'Were you not a most candid and generous minded man, Mr Bethel, I should fear that you would almost hold me in aversion, for having been, however unintentionally, the cause of your friend's very dreadful accident. Believe me, nothing in my whole life (and it has not certainly been a fortunate life) has ever given me so much concern as this event. All who love Mr Desmond (and there are few young men so universally and deservedly beloved) must detest the very name of those who were the means of hazarding a life so valuable, and of exposing him to suffer such pain and confinement, perhaps such lasting inconvenience — for I fear' — and her voice faltered so as to become almost inarticulate — 'I fear it is far from being certain that he will ever be restored to the use of his hand.'

That idea seemed so distressing to her, that she looked as if she were ready to faint. — I hastened, you may be assured, to relieve her apprehensions; and assured her, that not only your hand would be well, but that you thought yourself infinitely overpaid for the inconvenience you had sustained in your rencounter with the Chevalier de St Eloy, since you had been the means of saving her brother from a marriage so extremely improper. Then, to detach her thoughts from what I saw they most painfully dwelt upon, your hazard and sufferings, I gave her an account I had learned from Mr Carmichael* of the family of St Eloy; and as I found this still affected her too much, because it excited her gratitude anew towards you, by whose interference Waverly had escaped from a connexion with it, I made a transition to the affairs of France; and knowing how well she could talk on every subject, had a wish to draw her out on this.

The little I could obtain from her would have convinced me, had I needed such conviction, of the strength of her understanding, and that rectitude of heart which is so admirable and so rare. — Yet, with all this, there is no presumption; none of that anxiety to be heard, or that dictatorial tone of conversation that has so often disgusted and

---

* In a letter that does not appear.

repulsed me, in women who either have, or affect to have, a superiority of understanding. Geraldine affects nothing: and, far from appearing solicitous to be considered as an oracle, she said, with an enchanting smile, towards the close of our conversation — 'I know not how I have ventured, Mr Bethel, to speak so much on a subject which, I am very willing to acknowledge, I have had not opportuntity of knowing well. — Mr Verney, you know, is no politician; or, if he were, he would hardly deign to converse on that topic with a woman — for of the understandings of all women he has the most contemptible opinion; and says, "that we are good for nothing but to make a shew while we are young, and to become nurses when we are old." — I know that more than half the men in the world are of his opinion; and that by them, what some celebrated author has said, is generally allowed to be true — that a woman even of talents is only considered by man with that sort of pleasure with which they contemplate a bird who speaks a few words plainly — I believe it is not exactly the expression; but, however, it is the sense of it, and, I am afraid, is the general sense of the world.'⁵

I could not forbear interrupting her, to assure her, that if such an opinion were general, mine was an exception; for that I was convinced, ignorance and vanity were much more fatal to that happiness which every man seeks, or ought to seek, when he marries, than that knowledge which has been insidiously called unbecoming in women. — I was going on, for I found myself absolutely unable to quit her, when her husband and the Lord Newminster, whom you described to me at Margate some months since, entered the room together.

Verney, who has naturally a wild, unsettled look, really shocked me. — To an emaciated figure and unhealthy countenance, were added the disgusting appearance of a debauch of liquor not slept off, and clothes not since changed. — The other man was in even a worse state: but as he was not married to Geraldine, I looked at him only with pity and disgust; while, towards Verney, I felt something like horror and destestation.

Geraldine turned pale when he was announced; and said, in a low voice, as he came into the room — 'This is very unexpected; I have seen Mr Verney only once for these last five weeks.' — I would have retired, but she added, with an half-stifled sigh — 'Oh! no! do not go; you hear he has his friend Newminster with him, and probably will not stay five minutes. — But if he should,' added she, as if fearing she had spoken too much in a tone of regret and complaint — 'if he should, he will, I am sure, be happy to see his old friend Mr Bethel.'

At this instant Lord Newminster, followed by Verney, entered. — The former appeared stupid, from the effects of his last night, or rather morning's carousal; but Verney, who has just heard that the creditors, who had the executions in his house, were paid, and the bailiffs withdrawn, was not in a humour to be reserved, or even considerate. — Without speaking to his wife, he shook hands with me, and cried — 'Damme, Bethel, how long is it since I saw you last? I thought you were gone to kingdom come. — Here's Newminster and I, we came only last night from his house in Norfolk. — Damme, we came to raise the wind together; for I have had the Philistines in my house, and be cursed to them! who had laid violent hands on all my goods and chattels, except my wife and her brats; but some worthy soul, I know not who, has sent them off. — I wish I could find out who is so damned generous; I'd try to touch them a little for the ready I want now.'

Oh! could you have seen the countenance of Geraldine, while this speech was uttering! — she was paler than ever; and was, I saw, quite unable to continue in the room. — She therefore rose, and saying her little boy was awake, who had continued to sleep in her lap during our conversation, she walked apparently with very feeble steps out of the room; the two other children following her. — 'Away with ye all,' cried the worthless brute their father; 'there, get ye along to the nursery, that's the proper place for women and children.' — The look that Geraldine gave him, as she passed to the door, which I held open for her, is not to be described — It was contempt, stifled by concern — it was indignation subdued by shame and sorrow. — 'Good morning to you, Mr Bethel,' said she, as she went by me — 'I know not how to thank you enough for this friendly visit, nor can I say how much my obligation will be increased, if you will have the goodness to repeat it: pray let me see you again before you leave London.' — I assured her I would wait on her with pleasure; and I felt extremely unhappy as the door closed after her, and I saw her no more. —

'Well, now, Bethel,' said the husband, 'let me talk to you a little: tell me — are not your horses at Hall's, at Hyde Park Corner?' I answered, 'Yes.' — 'Aye? then you're the man I want; — you've got a hellish clever trotting mare, one of the nicest things I've seen a long time; — have you a mind to sell her?'

'Certainly no.'

'I am sorry for it, for I want just such a thing. Don't you remember a famous trotting galloway I had, two years ago, that I bought at Tattersall's, that would go fifteen miles within the hour?[6] — I've lost him by a cursed accident, and I want one as speedy. — Damme, Bethel, I'll give you a hundred for your little mare, and I'll be curs'd if that is not fifty more than she's worth.'

'I shall not sell the mare, Mr Verney,' answered I very coldly; 'so let us talk of something else. — Pray tell me what is this story which you touched upon, a little unfeelingly I thought, before your wife, of an execution in your house.'

'An execution — by heaven I'd two, and that old twaddler, mother Waverly, for the first time in her life, has done a civil thing, for she paid them off the other day. — If my wife had not lain-in though, I suppose, and been so much alarmed as they told me she was, so that the good old gossip was afraid of the consequences, I believe she'd have seen me at the devil before she'd have drawn her purse-strings: so 'twas well timed, and now I only wish she'd keep the child, for I'd incumbrances enough of small children before.'

'Good God! Sir,' said I, 'is it possible that, having married such a woman as Mrs Verney, and having such lovely and promising children, you can neglect the one, and call the other incumbrances?'

'Poh!' replied he carelessly, 'I don't neglect her; — but children — when one has a house full of them, as I think I am likely to have, pull confounded hard; and as to their promising, I know nothing that they promise, but to grow up, to pull harder still, and find out that I am in their way before I have a mind to relinquish the enjoyments of this life.'

'Why, then, since you must have been aware of all these contingencies, did you marry?'

'Why — what a senseless question! Because I was a green-horn, drawn in by a pretty face, and a fine figure. The old woman, her mother, had the art of Jezebel, and I was a raw boy from College, and fancied it very knowing to marry a girl that all the young fellows of my aquaintance reckoned so confounded handsome. Besides, a man must marry at some time or other.'

'That,' said the Peer, who seemed suddenly awaked from his stupor, by a position so contrary to his sentiments — 'that I deny — 'tis a damned folly, and nobody in his senses will commit it.' He then talked in a manner too gross, and too offensive, for me to repeat upon paper; and concluded with expressing his pity for poor Verney; and protesting, that for his own part, though he saw half the fashionable girls in town angling for him, he should keep his neck out of such a damned yoke.

I repressed the contempt and indignation which it was impossible to help feeling; and addressing the illustrious orator — 'It is unfortunate, my Lord,' said I, 'that these are your sentiments, since by them the world is likely to be deprived of the worth you might transmit for its general benefit, and your country, in particular, of talents which might adorn its legislature. — Your Lordship's contemporaries must, I am sure, reflect with concern on the little prospect there thus remains, that your virtues and abilities will not descend to dignify the future annals of the British senate.'

'Oh! the devil may take the British senate for me,' answered he; 'I never put my head into it, but when I am sent for on some points that there are doubts about; and then, indeed, I go, if ministry desire it: but otherwise, I don't care a curse for their damned politics. — As long as I keep the reversion of the sinecures my father got for me, and two or three little snug additions I've had given me since for the borough interest I'm able to carry them; not one single guinea do I care for their parties or their projects.'7 — Then suddenly dismissing the subject, this *hereditary patriot* turned to his friend Verney, and said — 'Well, but, Dicky boy, what's the hour? — As you've paid your humble duty to Madam, should we not be off? — I've ordered my horses to be at my own door at six, and I have promised Caversfield to be with him by half past seven to dinner — We must not bilk him, as he has made the party on purpose for us.' 'I am ready,' replied Verney, 'for I shall not dress at home.' He then arose, as if he were going; but Miss Waverly, who had been out the former part of the morning, now entered; and while I spoke to her, Mr Verney called to his servant to give him some directions about his clothes, and Lord Newminster stretched himself on the sopha, and went very composedly to sleep.

To any young woman, however slight may be her pretensions, the marked neglect of a man of Lord Newminster's age is usually sufficiently mortifying: but to Fanny Waverly, who has been accustomed to excessive flattery and adulation ever since she left the nursery, this rude inattention must have appeared insupportably insulting; and I forgave the little asperity there was in her manner, when she said to me, with a smile of indignant contempt, and pointing to Newminster, who was, I really believe, in a sound sleep — 'An admirable specimen of the manners of a modern man of fashion!'

Verney, who had been giving directions to his servant at the door of the room, now returned to it — 'Aha! little Fanny,' said he, 'are you there? — How dost do, child? — Hohoop, hohoop, Newminster, it is time to go, my lad — come, let us be off.'

'Have you seen your wife, Sir?' said Miss Waverly very gravely. — 'Yes, my dear Miss Frances,' replied he in a drawling tone of mimicry, '*I have* seen my wife, looking for all the world like Charity and her three children over the door of an hospital.'

'She should not only *look* Charity,' retorted Fanny smartly, 'but *feel* it, or she would never be able to endure your monstrous behaviour.'

'Pretty pettish little dear,' cried he, 'how this indignation animates your features! — Anger, Miss Fanny, renders you absolutely *piquant* — My wife now — my grave, solemn, sage spouse, is not half so *agaçant* with her charity and *all* her virtues.'[8]

'That she possesses *all* virtues, Sir, must be *her* merit solely, for never woman had so poor encouragement to cherish *any*. — When one considers that she *suffers you*, her *charity* cannot be doubted: her *faith*, in relying upon you, is also exemplary; and one laments that, so connected, she can have nothing to do with *Hope*.'

Fanny Waverly then left the room; and as I was going before she came in, I now bowed slightly to the two friends, and went out at the same time. — When we came into the next room she stopped, and would have spoke; but her heart was full — she sat down, took out her handkerchief, and burst into tears.

'I beg your pardon, Mr Bethel,' said she, sobbing, 'but I cannot command myself, when I reflect on the situation of my poor sister and her children; when I meet that unfeeling man, and know, too well, what must be the consequence of his conduct.'

She was prevented by her emotion from proceeding, and I took that opportunity of saying, 'There is nothing new, I hope, my dear

Miss Waverly! nothing, just at this moment, to give you deeper concern, or more uneasy apprehensions for Mrs Verney?'

'Oh! no,' replied she, 'nothing very new — since the two executions which have been here this fortnight, cannot be called very recent circumstances. They were paid off by I know not what means, and the officers who were in possession of the effects dismissed only yesterday. Yet to-day this unhappy man returns; and returns with an avowed intention, as his confidential servant has been saying below, to raise more money. Oh! Mr Bethel, could you imagine all my sister has endured in this frightful period, during which she has only once seen her husband — could you imagine what she has endured, and have witnessed the fortitude, the patience, the courage she has shewn, while suffering not only pain and weakness, but all the horrors of dreading the approach of ruin for her children! you would have said, that the remembrance of that personal beauty, for which she has been so celebrated, was lost and eclipsed in the admiration raised by her understanding.'

'In my short conference with her,' answered I, 'all this was indeed visible, and could not escape the observation of one already impressed with the highest opinion of your sister from the report of Mr Desmond.'

At the name of Desmond, a deep blush overspread the face of the fair Fanny. Not such as that which wavered for a moment on the faded cheek of her lovely sister, when the blood, for a moment, forsaking the heart, was recalled thither by a consciousness that it should not express too warmly the sentiments that sent it forth — Fanny's blush spoke a different, though not less expressive language; and the tears that were trembling in her eyes, were a moment checked while she clasped her hands together, and cried eagerly — 'Desmond! — Oh! how I adore the very name of Desmond! — To him — to your noble friend it is owing, Mr Bethel, that while I lament the fate of a sister, I do not weep over the equally miserable destiny of a brother.'

I have seen Fanny Waverly in the ballrooms at Bath admired by the men, and envied by the women; and, with all the triumphant consciousness of beauty, enjoying the voluntary and involuntary tribute thus paid to her: but I never till now thought her so handsome, for I never till now thought her interesting — So much more attraction does unaffected sensibility lend to personal perfection, than it acquires from the giddy fluttering airs inspired by selfish vanity — Yes, indeed, my friend, Fanny Waverly is a very charming young woman; and I was so much pleased with every thing she said of you, and of her own family during the rest of our short conversation, that I have since indulged myself in fancying that it is not at all impossible for you to transfer to her the affection which, while you feel it for her sister, cannot fail to render you unhappy, and which, perhaps, may be attended with fatal consequences to the object of your love. — If your attachment to Geraldine is really as pure and disinterested as you have often called it, it might equally exist were you the husband of her sister; and such an alliance would put it much more in your power than it can ever be otherwise, to befriend and assist her and her children — But I know this is an affair in which you will tell me the heart is not to be commanded; and therefore I will no longer dwell upon it, than to repeat, that were you to see Fanny Waverly now, you would think her not inferior to her sister in personal beauty (though I own it is of a different character), and you would be convinced that she is not as you once believed, destitute of that feminine tenderness, without which I agree with you that mere beauty is powerless.

And now, my dear Desmond, let me speak of the 'thick-coming fancies,' with which you so strangely tormented yourself at Hauteville — I have been so much alarmed by your accident since, and have had so many subjects on which to think and write, that I have not touched upon your dream, which you surely are not superstitious enough to dwell upon — you, who are so little subject to the indulgence of prejudice, and who are not unfrequently ridiculing others for being too deeply impressed

'With all the nurse and all the priest has taught.'[9]

But why is it that the strongest minds — those who dare examine whatever is offered to them with acute reason, and who reject all, however, it may be sanctioned by custom, or rendered venerable by time, that reason refuses to accede to, shall yet sink under the influence of images impressed on the brain by a disturbed digestion, or a quickened circulation? Alas! my friend, there appears to be a strange propensity in human nature to torment itself; and as if the physical inconveniencies with which we are surrounded in this world of ours were not enough, we go forth constantly in search of mental and imaginary evils. — This is nowhere so remarkable as among those who are in what we call affluence and prosperity. — How many of my acquaintance, who have no wish which it is not immediately in their power to gratify, suffer their imaginations to 'play such tricks with them' (I use an expression of Dr Johnson's, whose imagination was surely not exempt from the charge) that they are really more unhappy and more truly objects of compassion than the labourer, who lives only to work, and works only to live! — I do not however, my dear friend, mean to say, that you are one of these. — Your active spirit and feeling heart secure you for ever against this palsy of the mind — but, perhaps, from the charge of indulging other extravagancies you are not wholly exempt — This attachment to Mrs Verney, which has given a peculiar colour to your life for three years, and which you still cherish as if your existence were to become insipid without it, is surely a weakness and an impropriety, which such an understanding as yours ought to shake off. — But I will say no more on a topic that is I know irksome to you; and indeed I am too apt to offer advice to those I esteem, without sufficiently considering, that we none of us love to take what we are all so eager to give — I cannot however drop the subject without remarking, that when in the same letter you describe your reflections on the puerility and inconsequence of the objects that mankind are so anxiously occupied in obtaining, and in the next page relate the terrors occasioned by a dream, the faintest shadow of those fleeting shades, which it seems so absurd to be moved by; I can only repeat, as one is continually compelled to do — Alas! poor human nature!

You have obliged me very much by the sketches you have sent me of the people you have conversed with, and the scenes to which you have been witness. — In answer to your remarks and narratives, I observe, that it is an incontrovertible truth, allowed even by those who have written professedly against it, that a revolution in the government of France was absolutely necessary: and, that it has been accomplished at less expence of blood, than any other event, I will not say of equal magnitude, (for I know of none such in the annals of mankind) but of such a nature, ever cost before, is also a position that the hardest prejudice must, in despite of misrepresentations, allow. But while I contemplate, with infinite satisfaction, this great and noble effort for the universal rights of the human race, I behold, with apprehension and disquiet, such an host of foes arise to render it abortive, that I hardly dare indulge those hopes in which you are so sanguine, that, uncemented by blood, the noble and simply majestic temple of liberty will arise on the site of the barbarous structure of gothic despotism.[10]

To say nothing of those doubts which have arisen from the want of unanimity and steadiness among those who are immediately entrusted with its construction, I reflect with fear on the force that is united to impede its completion, or destroy it when complete. Not only all the despots of Europe, from those dealers in human blood, the petty princes of Germany, to the sanguinary witch of all the Russias, but the governments, which are *yet called limited monarchies*, and even those which still pass as republics — in every one of these the governments, well we know, pay the venal pen and the mercenary sword against it — some openly; the others as far as they dare, without rousing, too dangerously, the indignation of their own subjects.[11] — In all these states, there are great bodies of people, whose interest, which is what wholly decides their opinion, is diametrically opposite to all reform, and, of course, to the reception of those truths which may promote it. — These bodies are formed of the aristocracies, their relations, dependents, and parasites, a numerous and formidable phalanx: hierarchies, whose learning and eloquence are naturally exerted in a cause which involves their very existence: an immense number of placemen and pensioners, who see that the discussion of political questions leads inevitably to shew the people the folly and injustice of their paying by heavy taxes for imaginary and non-existing services: — crowds of lawyers, who, were equal justice once established, could not be enriched and ennobled by explaining what they have themselves contrived to render inexplicable: — and last, not least, a very numerous description of people, who, being from their participation of these emoluments, from family possessions, or from successful commerce, at ease themselves, indolently acquiesce in evils which do not affect them, and who, when misery is described, or oppression complained of, say, 'What is all this to us? we suffer neither, and why should we be disturbed for those who do? — 'Chi ben sta, non si muove*,' says the Italian proverb. — In short, my friend, I do not, as some politicians have affected

---

* Those who are well situated desire not to move.

to do, doubt the virtue of the French nation, and say they are too corrupt to be regenerated — I doubt rather that European states in general will not suffer them to throw off the corruption, but unite to perpetuate to them what they either do submit to, or *are willing to submit to* themselves — I rather fear that liberty, having been driven away to the new world, will establish there her glorious empire — and to Europe, sunk in luxury and effeminacy — enervated and degenerate Europe, will return no more.

Let me, dear Desmond, hear soon from your own hand, that you are content with the success of my negociation, and with this long account of those for whom you are interested. Let me learn also your future designs, as to returning to England, or staying on the Continent, and above all, that you continue to believe me, with sincere attachment,

Yours affectionately,

E. BETHEL

Continue, I beg of you, to write by another hand till you can use your own, and let me have the sketches of such conversation as you may have during your convalescence — I mean those on political or general topics, and not, of course, the more *refined* and *sentimental* dialogues which you may hold with *Madame de Boisbelle.* — By the way, I do not quite understand what you mean by saying in your last letter, that you become every day more unworthy the esteem of Geraldine — *You surely think very humbly of yourself.*

LETTER VI

Marseilles, 8th Jan. 1791

The first letter I was able to write, was to Geraldine. — This, my dear Bethel, is the second; and it is with extreme pleasure I thank you for your immediate attention to my request, and the propriety with which you seem to have conducted so troublesome a commission — I thank you too for your long letter, and the account, painful as it is, of the scene you saw at Verney's — Gracious heaven! why is it that such a cruel sacrifice was ever made? But I dare not trust myself on this subject, and have made an hundred resolutions never to mention it more; yet, how avoid writing on what constantly occupies my mind? — how dismiss from thence, even for a moment, what weighs so heavy on my heart? Let me, however, assure you, Bethel, that though I have no hope, I had almost said no wish, ever to be more to this lovely, injured woman, than a fond, affectionate brother — yet, that I will never marry Fanny Waverly. I believe that the advantageous picture you have drawn of her is not a flattering one. — I admire her person, and think well of her understanding. — The symptoms of sensibility and of attachment to her sister, which you discovered in her, certainly add those attractions to her character, in which I know not why it appeared to me to be defective. — If I had a brother whom I loved, and whom I wished to see happily married, it would be to Fanny Waverly I should wish to direct his choice. — But for myself — No, Bethel, it is now out of the question; we will speak of it then no more; but I will hasten to thank you for those parts of your long and welcome letter that were meant to detach my thoughts from those sources of painful and fruitless regret, which I am, perhaps, too fond of cherishing. — Fain, very fain would I shake them off, my friend, but I cannot — nay, I am denied the consolation of talking to you on paper of all I feel. — I have often been very unhappy, but I never was quite so wretched as I am at this moment. My anxiety for the fate of Geraldine tears me to pieces; and I cannot return to England immediately, where I should, at least, be relieved from the long and insupportable hours of suspense which the distance now obliges me to undergo — If I could not see her, at least I could hear once or twice a week of her situation, and might, perhaps, be so fortunate as to ward off some of those misfortunes to which from her husband's conduct she is hourly exposed. Do not, however, be alarmed on account of my health. I believe I could now travel without any hazard; but there are circumstances which render it difficult for me to quit this part of France immediately. — My friend Montfleuri presses me extremely to return for some time to his house, and I once proposed doing so, but now I cannot do that; but shall, I believe, as soon as I am quite well enough to be dismissed from the care of Mr Carmichael, go by slow journeys towards Switzerland, and from thence to Italy — This, however, depends upon events; and you will see by the manner in which this is written, that I do not at present boast of so perfect a restoration to health as to make any immediate determination necessary.

I perfectly agree with you in the statement you have made of those causes which have made many of the English behold the French revolution with reluctance, and even abhorrence. To those causes you might have added the misrepresentations that have been so industriously propagated. All the transient mischief has been exaggerated; and we have in the overcharged picture lost sight of the great and permanent evils that have been removed — All the good has been concealed or denied; and the former government, which we used to hold in abhorrence, has been spoken of with praise and regret — This is by no means wonderful, when we consider how many among ourselves are afraid of enquiry, and tremble at the idea of innovation — how many of the French, with whom we converse in England, are *avanturiers*, who seize this opportunity to avail themselves of imaginary consequence, and describe themselves as men suffering for their loyal adherence to their king, and as having lost their all in the cause of injured loyalty — We believe and pity them, taking all their lamentable stories for granted — whereas the truth is, that no property has been forcibly taken from its possessors — none is intended to be taken — and these men who describe themselves as robbed, had, many of them, nothing to lose. — Half the English, however, who hear of these fictitious distresses, are interested in having them credited, and cry, 'These are the blessed effects of a revolution! — these private injuries arise from the rashness and folly of touching the settled constitution of a country!' — while others, too indolent to ask even the simple question — 'Is this true? — *are* the individuals thus injured?' shrink into themselves, and say, 'Well! I am sure we have reason to be thankful that there is no such thing among us.'

But though I have long been thoroughly aware, both of the interested prejudice and indolent apathy which exist in England, I own I never expected to have seen an elaborate treatise in favour of despotism written by an Englishman, who has always been called one of the most steady, as he undoubtedly is one of the most able of those who were esteemed the friends of the people — You will easily comprehend that I allude to the book lately published by Mr Burke, which I received three days since from England, and have read once.[12]

I will not enter into a discussion of it, though the virulence, as well as the misrepresentation with which it abounds, lays it alike open to ridicule and contradiction. — Abusive declamation can influence only superficial or prepossessed understandings; those who cannot, or who will not see, that fine sounding periods are not arguments — that poetical imagery is not matter of fact. I foresee *that a thousand pens will leap from their standishes* (to parody a sublime sentence of his own) to answer such a book.[13] — I foresee that it will call forth all the talents that are yet unbought (and which, I trust, are unpurchaseable) in England, and therefore I rejoice that it has been written; since, far from finally injuring the cause of truth and reason, against which Mr Burke is so inveterate, it will awaken every advocate in their defence.

One of the most striking of those well-dressed absurdities with which he insults the understanding of his country, is that which forcibly reminds me of the arguments in favour of absolute power, brought by Sir Robert Filmer in that treatise, of which Locke deigned to enter into a refutation.[14] — This advocate of unlimited government derives the origin of monarchies from Adam, and asserts, that 'Man, not being born free, could never have the liberty to choose either governors or forms of government.'[15] He carries, however, his notion of this incapacity farther than Mr Burke: according to him, man, in general, having been born in a state of servitude since Adam, can never in any case have had a right to choose in what way he would be governed — Mr Burke seems to allow that some such right might have existed among Englishmen, previously to the year 1688, but that then they gave it up for themselves and their posterity for ever.

It was mightily the fashion when I left England, for the enemies of the revolution in France, to treat all that was advanced in its favour, as novelties — as the flimsy speculations of unpractised politicians — or the artful misrepresentations of men of desperate fortunes and wild ambition. *Precedent*, however, which seems gaining ground, and usurping the place of common sense in our *courts*, may here be united with sound reason — if reason be allowed to those great men towards whom we have been taught to look with acquiescence and veneration.

'When fashion,' says Locke, 'has once sanctioned what folly or craft began, custom makes it sacred, and it will be thought impudence or madness to contradict or question it.'[16] This impudence and madness seems by the venal crew, whose interest it is that *no questions* should arise, to be imputed to all who venture to defend the conduct of the patriots struggling for the liberties of France. Mr Burke now loads them with the imputation, not only of impudence and madness, but with every other crime he can imagine, and involves in the same censure, those of his own countrymen who have dared to rejoice in the freedom of France, and to support the cause of political and civil liberty throughout the world.[17] Now, without committing myself to enter into any thing like an argument with so redoubtable an adversary; and with a view solely to escape the censure of *broaching novelties*, let me quote a sentence in Locke on civil government, which, among the few books I have access to, I happen to have procured. In speaking of conquest, he says,

'This concerns not their children (the children of the conquered); for since a father hath not in himself a power over the life and liberty of his child, no act of his own can possibly forfeit it; so that the children, whatever may have happened to the fathers, are free men; and the absolute power of the conqueror reaches no farther than the persons of the men who were subdued by him, and dies with them; and should he govern them as slaves, subjected to his absolute power, he has no such right of dominion over their children — he can have no power over them but by *their own consent*; and he has no lawful authority while force, not choice, compels them to submission.'[18]

If conquest does not bind posterity, so neither can compact bind it. Mr Burke does not directly assert, whatever disposition he shews to do so, that nothing can be changed or amended in the constitution of England, because the family who now are on the throne derive their sacred right (through a bloody and broken succession) from William the bastard of Normandy; but he maintains, that every future alteration, however necessary, is become impossible, since the compact made for all future generations, between the Prince of Orange and the self-elected Parliament who gave him the crown in 1688 — So that, if at any remote period it should happen, what cannot indeed be immediately apprehended, that the crown should descend to a prince more profligate than Charles the Second, without his wit; and more careless of the welfare and prosperity of his people than James the Second, without his piety; the English must submit to whatever burthens his vices shall impose — to whatever yoke the tyranny of his favourites shall inflict, *because* they are bound, by the compact of 1688, to alter nothing which the constitution then framed, bids them and their children submit to *ad infinitum.*

I have been two days writing this letter, with a weak and trembling hand. I now, therefore, dear Bethel, bid you adieu! I entreat you to write to me as often as possible, for if I quit this place, your letters will follow me. — I recommend to you, as the most essential kindness you can do me, to attend to that interest, which is infinitely dearer to me than my own; and with repeated acknowledgments of all your kindness on a thousand other occasions, but above all on the last, I entreat you ever to believe me

Yours, most gratefully and
affectionately,
LIONEL DESMOND

LETTER VII

TO MRS VERNEY

Bath, 11th Feb. 1791

I was uneasy, my dear Sister, at your not writing, and since you have written, I am more uneasy still. The account you give me of yourself and the baby frightens me — Dreary as the season is, I now join with you in wishing you in the country. — I beg your pardon if my frankness offends you; but I cannot help saying, you know too well, that your husband really cares not where you are, and will not oppose your going if you desire it, but will, probably, be glad to have you out of the way. — My dear Geraldine, it gives me the severest pain to be compelled to write thus, and to break the injunction you have so often laid on me, not to speak my thoughts so freely of Verney. — Your health is at stake, and I forget every thing else. After all, what do I say that you have not yourself said internally a thousand times, though your delicate sense of duty (duty to such a man!) makes you acquiesce in patient silence, under injuries that would have made nineteen women in twenty fly out of his house, and play the deuce in absolute desperation? — How is it possible that you can help being conscious of your perfections, and of his deserving them so little? — Can you fail to feel, and to compare? — It is impossible but that you must at

———————'That fate repine,
'Which threw a pearl before a swine.'[19]

There is a quotation from *me*, which you will allow to be, at least, a novelty. It will hardly, however, procure my pardon for its pertness, and therefore, I pray you, my dear Geraldine, to forgive me; or, if you are a little angry, I will learn to bear it, if you will but exert yourself (if exertion be necessary) to go into the country and be well.

You do not say a word of Mr Desmond, and *I* can think and talk of nobody else. — In hopes of hearing something of him, I have endured the misery of long conversation with that odd old animal his uncle, Major Danby. — The formal twaddler loves to tell long stories, and can seldom get any body to hear them, unless he can seize upon some stranger who does not know him; and these becoming every day more scarce, he has taken quite a fancy to me, because he finds I listen to him with uncommon patience, and do not yawn above once in ten minutes. The gossipping people here (of which heaven knows there are plenty) have already observed our *tête-à-tête*, and begin to whisper to each other that Miss Waverly has hooked the rich old Major — I like of all things that they should believe it, and am in hopes of being in the London papers very soon among the treaties of marriage. — What do you think Desmond would say to it? — Do you think he would like such a smart young aunt? — Poor fellow! — I have not been able to get at much intelligence about him, and what I have heard is very painful — His uncle has only heard lately, that his health is much impaired by long confinement, and that he is yet unable to travel towards England; but I hope the old croaker made the worst of it to me — He persists in saying, that his nephew could not have met with such an accident in England, as if people here did not shoot one another every day, for reasons of much less moment, or for no reason at all. — But though I have attempted, whenever he would hear me, to represent this, and to explain and dwell upon the generosity of Desmond's conduct, I have not yet succeeded in convincing him, that it was friendship to my brother, and not any political matter, that involved his nephew in this dispute. — The good Major, indeed, cannot comprehend how friendship should lead another to incur danger; for he had never in his life that sort of feeling, which should make him go half a mile out of his way to serve any body. This I have frequently heard from those who knew him as a young man; and I believe sensibility and philanthropy are qualities that do not increase with years — He retains now nothing of the ingenuous freedom of the soldier, but all the hardness which a military life sometimes gives; and in quitting it, he keeps only the worst part of a profession, that is said to make bad men worse — I don't know why I have said so much about him, unless it is because I have nothing to say of Desmond, and yet cannot entirely quit the subject. — He provoked me this morning in the pump-room, by standing up, and in his sharp, loud voice, giving an account, to two or three people that were strangers to him, of the accident that had happened to his nephew in France. An old, upright woman, who was, I immediately saw, a titled gossip, listened for some time very attentively, and then enquired, in a canting sort of whine, if the affair had not been owing to *the troubles?* — The Major, delighted to have a Lady Bab Frightful interest herself in his story, began it again; and I ran out of the place, half determined, that not even the wish I cannot help feeling to hear now and then of Desmond from him, should tempt me again to enter into conversation with this story-telling old bore.

My mother, who generally agrees to the opinion of her acquaintance, if they happen to be rich, and who is not unwilling to have the obligation Desmond has laid us all under, lightened by supposing some part of the quarrel with the Chevalier de St Eloy to have originated in a difference of political opinion, really encourages the Major in his notion; and when they get together, I lose my patience entirely. To your enquiry, how my mother is in health, I can assure you, I have not seen her so well these last eighteen months, and she is now so often in company, is at so many card parties abroad, and has so many parties at home, that, without having been much missed, I might have staid with you much longer. However, I did what appeared to us to be my duty in returning, and I must not regret it, though very certain it is, that all the maternal affections of my mother are more then ever engrossed by her son. — She is now impatiently expecting his arrival, and questioning every body she sees, about the probable length of his voyage from Leghorn. — It is amazing to me, that with all this tenderness and anxiety for him, she feels no gratitude, or so little, towards the man, without whose interposition he would never have returned at all. — I also wonder it does not occur to her, that it is far from being certain he did embark at Leghorn the time he proposed to do so. — For myself, I should not be at all surprised to hear from him at Rome, nor indeed to learn that he was again the captive of Mademoiselle de St Eloy. — Let me not, however, my sister, add anticipated to the real evils with which you seem destined to contend. — All will yet be well — Desmond will return in perfect health, and brighter days await us. Let me hear from you at least twice a week, and believe me ever, with true affection, your

FANNY

LETTER VIII

TO MISS WAVERLY

Sheen, near Richmond, Feb 19th, 1791

I have delayed answering your letter, my Fanny, till to-day, though I have been in possession of it above a week. Languor alone would not have caused this omission; but I have been busied in my little removal to a lodging I have taken here, as Dr Warren declared it to be necessary, both on my own account, and on that of the infant I suckle, that I should remove from London. Mr Verney, I know not why, resolutely opposed my going into Yorkshire, nor could my entreaties, or the opinion of the physician, obtain any other answer, than that my going thither would be inconvenient to him. — I have, alas! no longer the house in Kent to which I was so attached, and therefore, rather because it is my duty to try to live than because I wish to live — rather for the sake of my poor children than my own — I employed a friend in this neighbourhood to look out for apartments for me, where I could have accommodations for my three children, three servants, and myself. — Such he fortunately found in a tolerably pleasant situation, and at a reasonable price; a consideration to which I must no longer be indifferent.

Small, however, as the difference is, between my living here or in Seymour-street, and careless of my being either at one place or another, as you too justly observe Mr Verney to be; I own I remarked, and remarked with redoubled anguish of heart, that this additional expence, though pronounced to be absolutely necessary to my existence, and that of his child, is submitted to with reluctance by Mr Verney. — I check myself, Fanny — I will not murmur — and I will even reprove you, my sister, for encouraging me in those repinings, which, though I cannot always repress, I know it is wrong to indulge. — Do not, my love, teach me to yield too easily to a sensibility of evils, which, since they are without remedy, it is better to bear with equality of mind, and with resignation of heart. — Alas! mine is but too apt to feel all the miseries of its destiny — but my children and my duty must and shall teach me to submit unrepiningly to fulfil the latter, for the sake of the former. — Their innocent smiles repay me for many hours of anxiety; and while they are well around me, I believe I can bear any thing.

You conclude your letter cheerfully, my Fanny, as if you would dissipate the concern which the former part of it must give me on account of Mr Desmond. — Alas! the former part is all real, and the latter only the prophetic hope of a sanguine imagination — 'Desmond will return in perfect health, and brighter days await us.' — If he should *not* return, or not return in perfect health! — Amiable as Mr Desmond is, and interesting as he must be to every one of his acquaintance, I certainly should not feel so extremely anxious about him (as my solicitude for my children is as much as I am well able to bear), were it not for the unhappy circumstance that continually haunts me — I mean, that I involved him in this fatal affair, and that whatever ill consequences finally attend it, will be imputable solely to me. It is this, and this only, that renders me more unhappy about him than you or any of his friends have reason to be, however great your regard for him; and it is this, that, if the event should in any way be injurious to him, will overcast my days with regret and anguish that must be all my own; for none can share, because none can feel it as I shall. — How lightly you can talk, my dear girl, of his uncle, even a moment after naming the intelligence you have collected from him about Desmond! But *you* have no reason to reproach yourself for *his* misfortune — *your* heart is not weighed down by any of your own. — You cannot, and indeed ought not to look forward, as I do, to scenes of future sorrow. — Long, very long, may it be, before you may be compelled to do it — or rather, may nothing but rich and luxuriant prospects ever offer themselves to the eyes of my Fanny!

But I beseech you to check your vivacity when you meet Mr Danby, and be content to listen to his tiresome stories a little longer, if listening to them is the tax you must pay for hearing of his nephew. *I* could attend to the most tedious legend with which self-consequence ever persecuted patience, were I but sure that some authentic information, as to the real state of Desmond's health, would close the narrative. Such information, without any tax being demanded for it, I used to obtain from his friend Mr Bethel; but I have now no means of seeing him, as he is gone back to his house in Kent — that house so near the place which I cannot help regretting. — Had it not been sold, I could have gone thither now, and have seen Mr Bethel continually. He is an excellent man, and is so much attached to Desmond, that it is pleasant to hear him speak of him: indeed he is the only person who does justice to those noble qualities of heart and understanding that Desmond so eminently possesses, but of which three parts of the world know not the value.

Yet I know not whether it was only my being myself in dreadfully low spirits, when I last saw Mr Bethel, or whether he was himself in a distressed state of mind; but methought he spoke in a very reluctant and desponding way about Desmond, though he assured me that he was entirely out of danger of any kind from the wound, and that the loss of the use of his hand was no longer apprehended. — But I found that Mr Bethel knows nothing certainly of Desmond's future intentions; and if he did not deceive me about his health, there is assuredly some other circumstance relating to him that makes Bethel uneasy — He said much of the friendship Monsieur de Montfleuri had shewn to Desmond in attending him, and of his sister too; that Madame de Boisbelle, who has, it is said, been his nurse the whole time. I supposed, when I first heard of her attendance on Mr Desmond, that she had been a widow, as it seemed unlikely she could otherwise have been sufficiently at liberty for such an exertion of friendship; but Mr Bethel informed me she is married, but very unhappily; and that her husband, a bankrupt both in fame and fortune, is an emigrant, and is either in Germany or England — Mr Bethel says the lady, who is extremely beautiful, is now entirely dependent on the Marquis de Montfleuri her brother, whom she cannot oblige more than by the attention she has shewn to his friend — How fortunate she is in having such a brother! how doubly fortunate in being allowed to shew her gratitude to him, by giving her *sisterly* attendance to such a man as Desmond! — Beautiful and accomplished as Mr Bethel describes her to be, methinks I envy her nothing but the opportunity she has had to sooth his hours of pain and confinement. I used to think once, that Desmond had a very friendly regard for me, but now, in how different a light he must consider us! — *I* have been the cause of his sufferings — it has been the enviable lot of Madame de Boisbelle to soften and alleviate them — Mr Bethel says he calls her Josephine. — If her good fortune should still prevail, and her husband should not return from the hazardous exploits in which, it is said, his political principles are likely to engage him, she will, perhaps, become his Josephine; for I have persuaded myself that his long stay in France is now more owing to the tender gratitude he must feel for this lady, than to any necessity he is in, on account of indisposition, to remain there.

And now, my Fanny, indeed, I cannot conclude without availing myself of my *eldership* once more, to entreat that you would consider whether it would not be better to check that flippancy with which you are too apt to accustom yourself to speak of our mother. Admitting that she has the foibles you represent, of courting the rich — of being too partial to her son — it is not her children who should point them out to the observation and ridicule of others. — Believe me, my sister, there is nothing so injurious to that delicate sensibility which you really possess, as indulging this petulance. — By degrees, it will become habitual; and the little asperities, which you now give way to only, perhaps, in writing or in speaking to me, will soon be so much matter of course that you will forget their tendency, and be insensible of their impropriety. — It is true, that I have not lived so much longer in the world as to be able to speak much from experience; but, from the little I have seen of that world more than you have, I think I may venture to assert, that where families are divided among themselves — I mean, where the father or mother disagree with the children, or the brothers and sisters with each other, there is something very wrong among them all; and I protest to you, that were I a man, not beauty, wit, and fortune united, should engage me to marry a woman who shewed a want of duty and gratitude towards either of her parents, but particularly towards her mother. — Were I madly in love, I am convinced, that any thing like the ridicule of a daughter so directed, would produce a radical and immediate cure.

Here let me drop the subject, I hope, for ever: and to begin one that, I trust, will make amends for any little pain this may have inflicted, let me tell you, that since I have been here, I have found my health and that of my baby sensibly amend, and that I now hope I shall not be compelled to wean him.[20] Though I am not happy, though I know I never can be so, I have, at least, obtained a transient calm. The agitation occasioned by the late painful events, is gradually, though slowly subsiding. I can now return to my books with attention less distracted, and have been reading a description of some of the southern parts of Europe, particularly of the Lyonois, &c. — I should like extremely to see those accounts which I find Mr Desmond sends to his friend Bethel, because he has so much taste, and is so intelligent a traveller. — There was no possibility you know of asking in plain terms for this indulgence: I hinted it as much as I dared, though Bethel did not, or perhaps would not understand me. — But to return to myself, and what you would think melancholy, though it is not to me an unpleasing way of passing my time — dreary as the season yet is, I have betaken myself to my solitary walks in the fields that surround this house, which, for a situation so near London, is extremely pleasant, and quite retired — I find the perfect seclusion, the uninterrupted tranquillity I enjoy now, soothing to my spirits, and of course beneficial to my health. If I do but hear favourable accounts from the continent, and nothing new happens embarrassing in the pecuniary affairs of Mr Verney, I shall be soon restored to as cheerful a state as I am now likely ever to enjoy. — Assist the progress of my restoration, my dearest Fanny, by frequent letters, since I cannot have the delight of your company; and cheer with your vivacity, which I love (even in reproving its wildest sallies),

Your affectionate

GERALDINE

I had but just sealed my letter, when a pacquet was brought me from Desmond himself — Yes, my Fanny, a letter written with his own hand, and not with so much apparent weakness as one would imagine. — I hope there is nothing improper in the excessive pleasure this letter gives me. — Gratitude can surely never be wrong, or, if it can be carried to excess, its excess is here pardonable. — I know not what I would say, my spirits are so fluttered. — This welcome letter has been very long in coming, I will send you a copy of it in a post or two — Heaven bless you, my Fanny!

LETTER IX

TO MR DESMOND

Hartfield, March 18, 1791

I was in hopes, my dear Desmond, that long before this I should have spoken to you once more in England, instead of directing to you in Switzerland. Your letter of the 30th January* bade me sanguinely hope this, and therefore I forbore to write; but instead of seeing you restored to health, to tranquillity, and your country, I receive a melancholy letter from the *pays de Vaud.* — Yet you assure me that your arm no longer reminds you of your accident, and I trust to your assurances, as well as to the evidence of your handwriting. — You tell me also, that your health is much amended. Why then, my friend, this extraordinary depression of spirits? — I own I am made uneasy, extremely uneasy, in observing it, and cannot help lamenting that your time, your talents, and your temper, are thus wasted and destroyed. — Is it, that this fatal passion still obscures your days? or is there, as indeed I strongly suspect, is there some other source of uneasiness more recent, to which I am a stranger? It has been a rule with me, even while you were, in some measure, under my guardianship, never, dear Desmond, to intrude upon you with officious enquiries, nor to ask more of your confidence than you chose to give me. — Friendship, like the service of heaven, should be perfect freedom: yet forgive me, if for once I intrude upon your reserve with curiosity that arises solely from my regard for you. — Is there in this any circumstance, the pain of which I can remove? If there is, I will be satisfied with such a partial communication as may enable me to be of use to you, without enquiring into particulars you may wish to conceal.

I send you, with other books, one that now engrosses all the conversation of this country, and which, from its boldness and singularity alone, and, written as it is, by an obscure individual†, calling himself the subject of another government, could never have attracted so much attention, or have occasioned to the party whose principles it decid-

---

*   Which does not appear.

†   Paine.[21]

edly attacks, such general alarm, if there had not been much sound sense in it, however bluntly delivered. — As I had rather hear your opinion of it, than give you my own, I will leave the discussion of politics, to tell you of what passes among your acquaintance. — This neighbourhood is almost wholly occupied by the improvements which Sir Robert Stamford is making at Linwell, the place so regretted by Mrs Verney. — The beautiful little wood which overshadowed the clear and rapid rivulet, as it hastens through these grounds to join the Medway, has been cut down, or at least a part of it only has been suffered to remain, as what he calls a collateral security against the northeast wind to an immense range of forcing and succession houses, where not only pines are produced, but where different buildings, and different degrees of heat, are adapted to the ripening cherries in March, and peaches in April, with almost every other fruit out of its natural course. — The hamadryades, to whom I remember, on your first aquaintance with the Verney family, you address some charming lines of poetry, because it was under their protection you first beheld Geraldine — the hamadryades are driven from the place, which is now occupied by culinary deities. — The water now serves only to supply the gardeners, or to stagnate in stews for the fattening of carp and tench: heaps of manure pollute the turf, and rows of reed fences divide and disfigure those beautiful grounds, that were once lawns and coppices. — Every thing is sacrificed to the luxuries of the table; and the country neighbours, though many of them possessed the usual elegancies and superfluities of modern life before, are compelled to hide their diminished heads, when Sir Robert Stamford gives an entertainment. — Riches, however unworthily acquired, are a sure passport to the 'mouth of honour,' not only of the common herd of those who are called 'gentlemen and ladies,' but to the titled and the high born, who, while they court new-risen opulence, envy, and yet despise the upstart who has obtained it.[22] — I never meet this great man myself, as our former connections, and our present estrangement, are so generally known, that we are never invited together; but he is almost always the subject of discourse, at parties where I *do* go, and always spoken of with wonder: for hardly a week passes in which some new improvement in luxury does not excite admiration at his boundless expence, which, from such a man, is supposed to be supported by a great fortune; for, as he has raised himself, it seems unlikely that he should so little understand the value of money, as to squander it thus profusely, if he had not a great deal of it. To those, who are more in the secret, all this ought not perhaps to be wonderful. Yet, though I know the very extent of Stamford's abilities, and know that he has nothing like eminent talents, though perhaps an acute and active mind; I have, I own, now and then been tempted to wonder at his extraordinary and rapid rise, and have joined the old ladies, who talk him over, in pronouncing him *a wonderfully lucky man*. — When I hear of the ostentation with which he displays those acquisitions, which are beyond the reach of others — when I am told, that men of the first rank come to eat his good things, and praise his skill in collecting them — when I learn that the Minister sends for him express, and that no resolution of importance is adopted without consulting him — and recollect how very few years are passed since he was a country Attorney, and rode more miles for half-a-crown than a postillion — I cannot always repress a degree of astonishment, and say,

> 'We know the thing is neither new nor rare,
> 'But wonder how the devil it got there*!'

It is pleasant enough to hear the conversations that sometimes pass about this man at the dinner and tea tables. — The awe that the superiority of riches creates, represses the malignity that envy engenders, though with so much difficulty represses it, that it is every moment obliquely appearing. — For my own part, I regard this man with so much contempt, that the only pain I now feel from his residing in my immediate neighbourhood, arises from my regret for the loss of Mrs Verney, whose society indeed I had not learned to relish when I was deprived of it. This confession is imprudent, perhaps, my friend, and encouraging that unhappy prepossession which I have always blamed: but truth extorts it from me; and the more I see of the usual dull round of country visits and country conversation, the more I regret the time when I was sure to find at Linwell, a woman who, to the softness of manners of her own sex, unites a strength of understanding which we believe peculiar to ours, and who, with so capable a head, has a heart so admirably tender. — You will be alarmed, perhaps, Desmond, at

---

* Pope.[23]

the warmth of my panegyric; and fancy, that in endeavouring to cure you, I have myself caught the infection — but be at peace, my friend, on that score. — Though Geraldine, in the two last conversations I had with her, has made me a sincere convert to an assertion of yours, which I used to deny, that he who has once seen and loved her, could never divest himself of his attachment; yet I am no longer liable to feel this fatal infatuation in the excess you do, and am only sensible of such regard for her, as a father or brother might feel. — I own, that even the depression of spirit which her unhappy marriage occasions, is not without its charms. — But when I see her struggling to palliate what he will not allow her to conceal, the wild absurdities and ruinous follies of her husband — when I see her mild endurance of injuries, and that her patience and sweetness are vainly endeavouring

> —————————'To spread
> 'A guardian glory round her ideot's head*,'

I feel respect bordering on adoration, and set her above Octavia, or any of the fair examples in ancient story.[24] — Yes, my dear Desmond! I not only acquit you of folly, but have more than once caught myself building for you delightful *chateaux en Espagne*, which, however, I will not feed your sick fancy by sketching: for Verney's life, notwithstanding his irregularities, is a very good one; and it were therefore much wiser in me to direct your thoughts to the former and more rational advice I gave you, when I expressed my hopes that you might in time carry your affections to the very lovely and animated Fanny Waverly, who, if I am any judge of the female heart, from the countenance, and the manner, would not let you despair, and who, as she is very far from suspecting your partiality to her sister, perhaps, puts down to her own account the extraordinary exertions of friendship which you have made for her family, in becoming the travelling friend of her brother.

I do not hear that Waverly has yet made his appearance in England, though I have enquired of several of my acquaintance, who are lately come from Bath, and who tell me that his mother, Mrs Waverly, is distressed by his long delay, and the uncertainty of what is become

---

* Hayley.[25]

of him; and that she is compelled to have a party with her all day, who engage her at cards, in order to detach her mind from this insupportable anxiety. — Fortunate resource! — How these good folks are to be envied, who can in tranquillity solace, in affliction console themselves with a rubber! 'A blessing on him,' quoth Sancho, 'who first invented the thing called sleep! it covers a man over like a cloak.'[26] — A blessing, say I, on him who first invented those two-and-fifty squares of painted paper! they blunt the arrows of affliction, '*and reconcile man to his lot**.'

While the elder lady of the Waverly family is thus diverting the pangs of maternal disquietude, and the younger trying to think less of a certain sentimental wanderer, by flirting, to use her own phrase, with all the smartest men at Bath, who assiduously surround her — Geraldine remains in perfect retirement at a lodging near Richmond, with her children, and only two servants. — She has no carriage with her, and never goes out but to walk with her little ones; and having wisely declined all visitors, she has not, I hope, yet learned that all Verney's town-carriages and horses, except only a post-chaise, which somebody re-purchased for him, are lately sold. — He is himself gone into Yorkshire, whither he absolutely refused to suffer her to go, when country air was prescribed for her health; and it is reported, and I fear with truth, that he has established an hunt there, of which he bears the greatest share of the expence, though it is said to be at the joint charge of himself, Lord Newminster, and Sir James Deybourne. The arrangement at Mooresly Park is said (and still I believe with too much foundation) to consist of three of the most celebrated courtezans, who are at this time the most fashionable, and of course the most expensive — every one of these illustrious personages appropriating one of these ladies for the time of their residence. This has been going on ever since the month of January, and is to end only with the hunting season. — You will wonder, perhaps, how I got at all this intelligence; but my solicitude for Geraldine conquers the dislike I have to enter into that sort of conversation which is called gossipping; and I happen to have an acquaintance at W————, a spinster somewhat past the bloom of life, and who, very much against her inclinations, has hitherto remained

---

*   Cowper.[27]

unsapped by caresses, unbroken in upon by tender salutations.* This lady, though without fortune, is of a good family, and, being allied to some great people, and having contrived to make herself useful to others, she is received alternately at several fashionable houses, where she flatters the lords and ladies; sits with the young misses, while their masters are with them; and reads aloud to the blind or sick dowager, who loves a newspaper or a novel: but though she is thus three parts of the year among her illustrious friends, she chooses always to reserve a home, which happens to be a small, neat lodging at W———, where she has been many years an occasional inhabitant.

Now it chanced, that when first Geraldine was married, and came a lovely, blooming creature of eighteen into this neighbourhood, this Miss Elford was among her earliest visitors. — It is said, that a young and handsome married woman is generally an object of dislike to ladies who are

> 'Withering on the virgin thorn,
> 'In single blessedness.†'

But Miss Elford, as if to contradict so invidious an assertion, was seen to take a peculiar and lively interest in the welfare of her dear friend Mrs Verney (for a dear friend she soon became); and her good humour, which had before been but little remarked, became now very eminent. — The change was accounted for partly by the acquisition she had made of so pleasant an acquaintance as Mrs Verney, whose house, within a mile of the town, was extremely convenient to her, and whose coach and servants were always at her command; and partly by the supposed attention of a very handsome clergyman, who, having two years before given up a fellowship at Oxford to marry a very pretty woman, whom he passionately loved, had within twelve months lost her, and now had accepted a curacy at a distance from the scene of his past happiness and misfortune, and, in attempting to dissipate his grief, had mixed much in the society of the neighbourhood, and had appeared particularly pleased in that of Miss Elford, who passed for 'a most sensible woman.' — When Verney settled at Linwell, this

---

    *   Sterne.[28]
    †   Shakespeare.[29]

gentleman, Mr Mulgrave, was continually at the house, where Miss Elford frequently resided also, and where (especially after Verney gave him a living which happened to fall at that time) it was supposed their intended union was rapidly advancing to its conclusion; when suddenly Mr Mulgrave grew cold and reserved, and the mortified Miss Elford lost once more the prospect of an immediate and fortunate establishment.

Though, till then, Mrs Verney had been, in her estimation, the best, sweetest, dearest creature in the world, the excessive fondness of Miss Elford declined from this moment; and as she could not suffer herself to think that she had been premature in reckoning on the impression she had made on Mr Mulgrave, or that she wanted the captivating talents necessary to fix that impression when it *was* made, she took it into her head that Mr Mulgrave had conceived an improper affection for Mrs Verney; and though there was probably not the least grounds for this idea, she has cherished it ever since, and consequently hates Geraldine, with an inveterate malignity, which no other cause could raise, or could sustain. — Still, however, she conceals this hateful sentiment under the semblance of friendship. — She laments, most pathetically, the hard fate of 'that sweet woman' — sheds crocodile tears over the ruinous extravagancies of Verney (of which, however, she has always the earliest intelligence), and tells every body how long she foresaw these fatal propensities in the husband of her charming friend before they broke out — talks of the vanity of all sublunary plans of happiness, and thanks her good God! for having placed *her* lot where she is not exposed to these heart-rending vicissitudes. — This good little gentlewoman, then, great part of whose life, I really believe, passes in collecting and dispersing accounts of the failures, failings, faults and follies of her acquaintance, has been of late more than usually active; and as she finds I listen to her with a greater degree of attention than I used to afford her, and is not aware of the motive I have for doing so, I see she entertains a thousand wandering fancies relative to my assiduity, and eagerly exerts herself to obtain its continuance. — I am a widower, about her own age — I have children, who may want the care of such a discreet person — I may myself desire a rational companion — Of all these considerations it is really wonderful to remark the effect, and to observe how amiable, discreet, and reasonable my prude affects to be. — I am sorry to encourage hopes which I am afraid I cannot, even for your service, my dear Desmond, realize; but as I have no other means of obtaining such intelligence as you want, and such as indeed appears to me absolutely necessary to enable either of us to assist in dispersing those heavy clouds of calamity that are continually hanging over her for whom we are both so anxious, I hope I am justified in availing myself of the information so readily given me by my neighbour. — I wish I could add, that the picture I have drawn of Verney's conduct owes its darkest touches to the sharp hands of malignant envy, through which it has passed. — But on enquiring of other people, who are quite disinterested, and who really admire and regret the lovely victim of his follies, the circumstances and proceedings of Verney are represented in the same way.

I have had within this last week some symptoms that threaten a return of the gout (if gout it be) that has so long hung about me; and as my friend Banks, on whose skill I have a great reliance, persists in saying that my future enjoyment of life depends on my having a regular fit, I shall, if these flying complaints are not soon dissipated, go again to Bath as soon as my Lent corn is in the ground, which three weeks will complete. — We have hitherto had a remarkably fine season, and my farming is likely to go on most prosperously. — Harry is doing well at Winchester, and the masters assure me he will be a very clever fellow. — I shall take Louisa with me, and put her to school at Bath for the time I continue there, which will probably be three months. — Long, long before that time, my dear Desmond, I hope to hail your return to England, and to tell you personally how truly I am

Your attached and faithful

ERASMUS BETHEL

LETTER X

TO MR BETHEL

Lausanne, April 10th, 1791

Your letter, with a paquet of books, reached me here, my friend, by the hands of our old acquaintance Ashby, who took them up on his way, and delivered them safely to me three days ago. — How shall I, how ought I to reply to such friendly enquiries, such generous offers as yours? — I can find no words that answer my idea of all I ought to say to thank you — none that seem adequate to excuse that want of confidence, perhaps you will think of gratitude, which I must seem to shew, when I say, that though I am very certainly most unhappy, it is impossible for me to avail myself of your friendship towards the alleviation of my unhappiness, impossible for me even to communicate its source. — Notice not, therefore, my despondence, my dear Bethel; its cause cannot be removed, and whatever may be its consequences, be assured that I deserve them all — Every word I write on this subject gives me inexpressible pain; and therefore I know you will pardon my beseeching you not to renew the topic, assuring yourself, that if at any future time I can properly take advantage of your counsel and your friendship, there is not on earth the man to whom I would so readily apply.

I will not, however, in any instance deceive you. My late accident, my present state of health, are neither of them the cause of my remaining abroad — The uneasiness I suffer is not solely on account of Geraldine, though your last letter has increased and rendered almost insupportable the solicitude I feel for her. Yet amidst all the anguish with which my mind dwells on the calamities that surround her, it is most soothing and consolatory to hear from yourself that she has found a friend in you; and that, being a convert to the united power of goodness, understanding, and beauty, you have been taught by their invincible attraction, to pity, and even to approve the attachment you were so lately disposed to condemn and ridicule, and which you so lately and undeservedly gave me credit for having conquered.

In lodgings at Sheen, with only her children with her! — one of the houses, that in which she used to delight, sold — the other, the ancient house of her husband's family, inhabited by his courtezans, and his dissolute companions!

Yet, amid all this, instead of returning evil for evil, what is her conduct? — She goes to a cheap retirement; she is occupied only in the care of her children. Instead of the retaliation which we see so usually adopted by young and beautiful women, whose husbands neglect and ill treat them, it seems as if *her* patient sweetness increased in proportion to the provocation she receives. Accursed be he who shall attempt to degrade a character so noble, to sully a mind so angelic! Never will

I be that man. — But if I continue in this strain, I shall get into those regions of heroics that are, you say, beyond the reach of your reasonable and calm comprehension. So we will talk of something else; and in order to convince you that I can occasionally play the Mentor, instead of being always your Telemachus, I am going to give you something very like a lecture.[30] — My dear Bethel, why do you suffer that Sir Robert Stamford to occupy and inflame to resentment a mind like yours? — When you regret that the place where I first saw Geraldine, and where I have so often repeated

> 'Benedetto sia 'l giorna, e'l mese, e l'anno
> E la stagion e'l tempo, e l'ora e'l punto,
> E'l bel paese, e'l loco ov'io fui giunto
> Da duo begli occhi, che legato m'hanno*,'

is sold, I understand all your friendly emotions, and rejoice that you enter with such enthusiasm into those feelings which, till you were more acquainted with Geraldine, you treated as romantic puerilities. — But when the fungus growth of this arrogant upstart has so much share in your indignation, I am hurt, that the elevated spirit of my friend can be ruffled by a being so utterly contemptible.

> 'Small things make mean men proud.†'

Can you then wonder, that to such a man his sudden, and, as he well knows, his *undeserved* exaltation is matter of ostentatious triumph? But does it make him respectable in the world? and does not even the basest part of that world, while it courts, despise him? — Leave him then, my friend, to waste, in swinish excess, sums which he has earned by doing dirty work, at the expence of those who are now called the 'swinish multitude‡,' hundreds of whom might be fed by the superfluities of his luxurious table. — Leave him to the wretched adulation of the fawning parasite, who can stoop to admire his fine places, and be repaid by the delicacies of his table. Leave him to be an example of how little merit is required in our country to reach the highest posts of profit

---

   *   Petrarch.[31]
   †   Shakespeare.[32]
   ‡   Vide Mr Burke's description of the people.[33]

and confidence — an example of a placeman filling useless places — of a pensioner paid for the mischief he has assisted in doing to the nation, whose governors have thus rewarded him. — But let not *your* mind, possessing, as it does, all the upright principles, the generous independence that once characterised the English gentleman, be disturbed by the disgusting insolence of such a being, while you feel that the humblest labourer who cultivates your ground is a more honest and a more respectable man.

In reading the book you sent me, which I have yet had only time to do superficially, I am forcibly struck with truths that either were not seen before, or were (by men who did not wish to acknowledge them) carefully repressed. They are bluntly, sometimes coarsely delivered, but it is often impossible to refuse immediate assent to those which appear the boldest; impossible to deny, that many others have been acceded to, when they were spoken by men, to whose authority we have paid a kind of prescriptive obedience, though they now have called forth such clamour and abuse against the author of 'the Rights of Man.' — My other letters from England are filled with accounts of the rage and indignation which this publication has excited. — I pique myself, however, on having, in my former letter, cited against Burke a sentence of Locke, which contradicts as forcibly as Paine has contradicted one of his most absurd positions. I know, that where sound argument fails, abusive declamation is always substituted, and that it often silences where it cannot convince. I know too, that where the politics are obnoxious, recourse is always had to personal detraction. I therefore wonder not, that on your side the water, those who are averse to the politics of Paine, will declaim instead of arguing; and those who feel the force of his abilities, will vilify his private life, as if that were any thing to the purpose.[34] I do, however, wonder that these angry antagonists do not recollect, that the clamour they raise, serves only to prove their fears; and that if the writings of this man are, as they would represent, destitute of truth and sound argument, they must be quickly consigned to contempt and oblivion, and could neither be themselves the subject of alarm, or render their author an object of investigation and abhorrence: but the truth is, that, whatever may be his private life (with which I cannot understand that the public have any concern), he comes, as a political writer, under the description given of a controvertist by the acute author to whom Monsieur d'Hauteville has so terrible an aversion.

'A-t-on jamais vu un plus abominable homme? Il expose les choses avec une fidélité si odieuse; il met sous les yeux le pour & le contre avec une impartialité si lâche; il est d'un clarté si intolerable, qu'il met les gens qui n'ont que le sens commun, en état de douter, & même de juger*.'

I frequent no society here willingly, as I find my mind by no means in a state to attend to the common occurrences of life without fatigue, and that both my spirits and health suffer by the exertion which a man is obliged to make in company for which he does not care a straw. However, as Ashby had been very obliging to me in bringing my pacquets from Marseilles, and depended on me for introduction here, I went with him yesterday to the house of a man of some consideration, where there is generally the best company of the place assembled, and where there then happened to be, among many others, French and Swiss, two Englishmen; one a Mr Cranbourne, who has accompanied, in their travels, several men of rank, and now is returning to England with a Lord Fordingbridge, whose minority is just ended, and who is returning to England to take his seat in the house of peers.

Mr Cranbourne, who was, I find, bred to the law, has all that supercilious and dogmatical manner which an education for the bar very frequently gives. — He asserts with violence, and maintains with obstinacy; and though the world doubted either of the profundity of his judgment, or the power of his eloquence, so that he was unfee'd and unretained during the course of those years that he called himself a counsellor, he is so perfectly convinced of his eminence in both, that he is on all occasions, not a pleader, but a decider, and sits self-elected on the judgment-seat, on every occasion of controversy. — His travels, without diverting him of the querulous asperity of the bar, have made him a solemn coxcomb in every other science; and he prides himself on having formed his present pupil on his own model, and declares that he will make a superior figure as an orator in the British senate.

---

*   Was there ever such an abominable fellow: He exposes the truth so odiously; he sets before our eyes the arguments on both sides with such horrible impartiality; he is so intolerably clear and plain, that he enables people who have only common sense, to doubt, and even to judge. — Voltaire.

The boy, who has thus been taught to consider himself as a miracle of elegance and erudition, unites the flippant airs of a young man 'of a certain rank' — with the sententious pertness of an attorney's clerk just out of his time. — I found him, on our entrance, standing in the midst of a circle, declaiming against the French government, and pouring forth a warm eulogium on Mr Burke. — The lordling affects an Italian accent, and to have forgotten the harsh tones of his native language, when he deigns to speak it. — 'Pray,' said he, 'tell me, you who know, what is this other book — this answer to Burke, that I have been bored with — Somebody wanted me to read it, but I had neither patience nor inclination. — It seems from the account other people have given me, to be very seditious: I wonder they don't punish the author, who, they say, is quite a low sort of fellow. What does he mean by his Rights of Man, and his equality? What wretched and dangerous doctrine to disseminate among the lazzaroni* of England, where they are always ready enough to murmur against their betters! I hope our government will take care to silence such a demagogue, before he puts it into the heads of *les gens sans culottes*, in England, to do as they have done in France, and even before he gets some of the ragged rogues hanged[35] — *They* rights! poor devils, who have neither shirts nor breeches!'

You have accused me of lying by in company, even where the conversation has turned on topics that interest me most. I own I had done so now, partly from depression of spirits, and partly from the reluctance I felt to engage in 'wordy war' against prejudice and absurdity.[36] — I now, however, ventured to enquire of Lord Fordingbridge, whether these men whom he called lazzaroni, might not be urged to revolt by those very miseries which exposed them to his contempt? and whether such extreme poverty and wretchedness did not shew the necessity of some alteration in the government where they existed? — If government be allowed to be for the benefit of the governed, not the governors, surely these complaints should be heard. 'Why, what would you have government do?' answered he — 'How can it prevent such sort of things? — Ours, for example, against which these stupid dogs are

---

* Lazzaroni, a word descriptive of people reduced to the utmost poverty and wretchedness.

complaining in libellous pamphlets and papers, by what means can it obviate these discontents? — Would you have the Minister keep a slop-shop, to supply the *sans culotes* with those necessaries *gratis?*'[37] — This convincing argument, which the whole company applauded with a loud laugh, gave my right honourable adversary such confidence in his own powers, that, without permitting me to reply, he proceeded: — 'I insist upon it, that there is no cause of complaint in England: nobody is poor, unless it be by their own fault; and nobody is oppressed. As to the common people, the mob, or whatever you please to call them; what were they born for but to work? And here comes a fellow and tells them about their rights — They have no rights — they can have none, but to labour for their superiors; and if they are idle, 'tis their own faults, and not the fault of the constitution, in which there are no imperfections, and which cannot by any contrivance be made better.' —

'Your lordship,' answered I, 'whose comprehensive mind probably looks forward to the time when you will yourself make one of that illustrious body that Mr Burke describes as the Corinthian pillar of polished society, has, I dare say, in travelling through other countries, made the government of your own your peculiar study; and, by contrasting it with those you have seen, you have learned to appreciate its value.[38] — That it is superior to most, perhaps to all of them, I am willing to allow; yet I cannot pronounce it to be without imperfections, where I observe such dreadful contrasts in the condition of the people under it. — Who can walk through the streets of London without being shocked with them? — *Here*, a man, who possesses an immense income which has been given him for his servile attendance, or his venal voice; an income, which is paid from the burthensome imposts laid on the people, is seen driving along in a splendid equipage; his very servants clothed in purple and fine linen, and testifying, by their looks, that they "fare sumptuously every day"[39] — There, extended on the pavement, lies one of those very people whose labour has probably contributed to the support of this luxury, begging wherewithal to continue his degraded existence, of the disgusted passenger, who turns from the spectacle of his squalid wretchedness. — In our daily prints, this shocking inequality is not less striking. — In one paragraph, we are regaled with an eulogium on the innumerable blessings, the abundant prosperity of our country: in the next, we read the melancholy and mortifying list of numberless unhappy debtors, who, in vain, solicit, from time to time, the mercy of the legislature, and who are left by the powers who *can* relieve them, to linger out their unprofitable lives, and to perish, through penury and disease, in the most loathsome confinements, condemned to feel

> —————"The horrors of a gloomy gaol,
> Unpitied and unheard, where misery moans;
> Where sickness pines; where thirst and hunger burn,
> And poor misfortune feels the lash of guilt*."

To-day, we see displayed in tinsel panegyric, the superb trappings, the gorgeous ornaments, the jewels of immense value, with which the illustrious personages of our land amaze and delight us — To-morrow, we read of a poor man, an ancient woman, a deserted child, who were found dead in such or such alley or street, "supposed to have perished through want, and the inclemency of the weather;" and is it possible to help exclaiming,

> —————"Take physic, pomp —
> Expose thyself to feel what wretches feel;
> So shalt thou shake the superflux to them,
> And shew the heavens more just†!"

The young peer, who had shewn more patience than I expected, now interrupted me — 'All this is very fine, Sir,' said he; 'but give me leave to say, that it is all common place declamation (that was true enough), and does not go to prove that the form of our government is defective — Misery exists every where, and is intended to exist: even according to your own quotation, it is allowed —

"And shew the heavens more just."

It is heaven so decides then, and by no means the fault of governments — It is the lot of humanity, and cannot be changed.' 'Thus it is,' answered I, 'that we dare to arraign our God for the crimes and follies of man — that God, who certainly made none of his creatures to be miserable, nor called any into existence only to live painfully,

---

*   Thomson.[40]

†   Shakespeare.[41]

and perish wretchedly. But when the blind selfishness of man distributes what Providence has given; when avarice accumulates, and power usurps, some have superfluities, which contribute nothing to their happiness, others hardly enough to give them the means of a tolerable existence. — Were there, indeed, a sure appeal to the mercies of the rich, the calamities of the poor might be less intolerable; but it is too certain, that high affluence and prosperity have a direct tendency to harden the temper. How few do we meet with who can feel for miseries they cannot imagine, and are sure they can never experience! — How many, who have hearts so indurated by their own success of fortune, that they are insensible to generosity, and even to justice! — How many more, who would, perhaps, be in some degree alive to the sensations of humanity, if their business or their pleasures allowed them time to think — but who are so occupied by either the one or the other, and so little in the habit of attending to disagreeable subjects, that they shrink from the detail of poverty and sorrow, and would be disgusted with those who should attempt to intrude with such images

"On ears polite!"[42]

'Well, Sir,' cried my lord, in whose hands the rest of the company continued to leave an argument in which they thought he had greatly the advantage — 'well, Sir! and what then? — Have we not laws, by which our poor are amply, magnificently provided for?'

'That they were intended to be so, I believe,' answered I; 'but how those laws are perverted, let the frequent, the meritorious, but unsuccessful attempts to amend them, bear witness. — Their abuse, the heaviness with which they press on one part of the community, without relieving the other, are amongst the greatest evils we complain of; but here, as in twenty other instances, every attempt at redress is silenced by the *noli me tangere*, which our constitution has been made to say, and which has been echoed, without enquiry, by all who have either interest in preserving the inviolability even of its acknowledged defects, or who have been brought up in prejudices, that make them believe that our ancestors were so much wiser than we are, that it is a sort of sacrilege to doubt the perfection of the structure they raised, and to imagine an edifice of greater strength and simplicity. — If these prejudices are enforced and continued — if every attempt to repair what time has injured, or amend what is acknowledged to be defective, is opposed as dangerous, and execrated as impious; let us go on till the building falls upon our heads, and let those who escape the ruins, continue to meditate on the prodigious advantage of this holy reverence, and to boast of the happiness of being Englishmen!'[43]

'I should be glad, Sir, since you, at least, seem to have none of this respect,' said the young lawyer, and who now thought he had been silent long enough — 'I should be glad if your sagacity would point out some of those other defects in the structure of the English constitution, which, doubtless, you have discovered.'

'That is not very difficult,' I replied; 'and I should begin by saying, that its very foundation is defective, from the inequality of representation (were that assertion not allowed by every one as an incontrovertible truth; and had not there been such repeated mockeries, such frequently renewed farces acted, to amuse us with pretended efforts at a reform, which never were intended, nor can ever be carried into effect, but by the unanimous and determined perseverance of the people) — To drop the metaphor, let me turn to another very common subject of acknowledged complaint — I mean the penal laws — laws, by which the property and the life of the individual are put on an equal footing, and by which murder, or a robbery to the amount of forty shillings, are offences equally punished with death. — Is it possible to reflect without horror, on the numbers that are every year executed, while every year's experience evinces, that this prodigality of life renders the punishment familiar, and prevents not crimes? — Is there a session at the Old Bailey, where boys from fifteen to twenty are not condemned? — boys who, deserted from their infancy, have been driven, by ignorance and want, to violate the laws of that society, which

"Shakes her incumbered lap, and throws them out*".

Why do we boast of the mildness and humanity of laws, which provide punishment instead of prevention? And can we avoid seeing, that while they give up yearly to the hands of the executioner greater numbers than die the victims of public justice in all the other European

---

* Cowper.[44]

countries reckoned together; we must, in spite of our national vanity, acknowledge, either, that the English are the worst and most unprincipled race of men in Europe, or, that their penal laws are the most sanguinary of those of any nation under heaven?[45] Attempts have been made to remedy this enormity, which I cannot help calling a national disgrace; but, like every other endeavour at partial correction of abuses, these humane efforts have been baffled on the usual principle, that nothing must be touched, nothing must be changed' — 'Really, Sir,' said Mr Cranbourne, 'you are a most able advocate for beggars and thieves.'

'At least, Sir, I am a disinterested one, for I plead for those who cannot see me — but it is not for beggars and thieves, as you are pleased to say, that I plead — it is for the honour of my country — for the reform of the laws, which occasion beggars and thieves to exist in such numbers; while we ostentatiously boast, that those laws are the best in the world. Nor is it only the penal laws that seem to want alteration; allow me to observe, that from the continual complaints of the defects of our law, as it relates to the protection of property, it does not seem to deserve the praise of superiority which we arrogantly claim. — We hear every day of suits in which even success is ruin; and we know, that far from being able to obtain in our courts that speedy, clear, decisive, and impartial justice, which from their institution they are designed to give, a victory (obtained, after being sent through them all) is often much worse than a retreat — the remedy more fatal than the disease. — So conscious are even the lawyers themselves of this, that if one of them (as *may happen*) has a personal regard for his client, and is willing to wave pecuniary advantage in his favour, such a lawyer will say — "Do any thing — submit to any compromise — put up with any loss, rather than go to law." — One of our courts is called that of Equity, where the widow, the orphan, the deserted and unhappy of every description (who have money), are to find protection and redress; yet it is too certain, that such are the delays, such the expences in this court, that the ruinous tediousness of a Chancery suit is become proverbial — the oppressed may perish, before they can obtain the remedy they seek; and where, under the direction of this court, litigated property is to be divided, it continually happens, that, by the time a decision is obtained, there is nothing to divide. — The poet I just now quoted, says,

—————————"In this rank age,
Much is the patriot's weeding hand required*."

But, alas! — especial care is taken, that neither reason nor patriotism
shall touch too rudely

"The *toils* of law, where dark, insidious men
Have cumbrous added to perplex the truth,
And lengthen simple justice into trade†."

And yet

"How *glorious were the day that saw these broke,*
And *every man within the reach of right*‡!"

'As to your poets,' cried Mr Cranbourne superciliously — 'there is
no bringing argument against their flowery declamation: fine sounding words about rights and liberties, are imposing to superficial
understandings, but cannot convince others — fine flourishing words
are not arguments.'

'Nor does there,' said I, 'need arguments on what I have asserted
— they are matters of fact, and not of speculation or opinion — truths,
which cannot be denied, and which it would require some skill to palliate.'

'As to truth, Sir, it is not always proper to speak it; nay, it is not
always safe to the well-being of a state — The question, I think, is,
not whether a thing be exactly comformable to your Utopian and impracticable schemes, but whether it be expedient. — We know that
truth is not expedient, and that it is the business of government to enforce obedience, without which it would not go on; not to listen to
the reasoning of every wild dogmatist, who fancies himself a philosopher, and able to mend what is already good. — All such should be
prevented from disseminating their pernicious doctrines, which serve
only to make men discontented with their situation, to raise murmurs,
and to clog the wheels of government.'

---

*   Thomson.[46]
†   Thomson.
‡   Ibid.

This sentence, which was most consequentially delivered, was applauded by all the party. As I had nothing to offer against it, but that truth which had just been pronounced to be inexpedient, I declined the contest, saying only, 'If truth is not to be spoken, Sir, in a government calling itself free, lest it should be understood by the people who are governed, and prevent their freely supplying the oil that facilitates the movement of the cumbrous machine — if facts, which cannot be denied, be repressed; and reason, which cannot be controverted, be stifled; the time is not far distant, when such a country may say, Adieu, liberty! — Let them, therefore, if they are content to do so, begin with expelling those who dare speak truth, and are so impudent as to reason — "Tous ces gens qui raisonnent sont la peste d'un état*." I then left my adversary to enjoy the triumph of his imaginary superiority, and wandered away alone, indulging contemplations, mournful contemplations, on far other subjects. — The moment I am in solitude, the image of Geraldine in distress, Geraldine contending with irremediable misfortunes, recurs to me; and other subjects of regret add bitterness to my reflections. Perhaps, therefore, I should so wisely to mix more in society, where I must of course

> "Disguise the thing I am,
> By seeming otherwise."[47]

But I am so poor at dissimulation, that the pain of attempting it is more harassing than the thoughts I would fly from.

Write to me very frequently, my friend; and remember as he wishes to be remembered,

Yours ever, most affectionately,

LIONEL DESMOND

---

* Voltaire — "All these reasoning people are the very curses of a government."

LETTER XI

TO MRS VERNEY

Bath, April 20, 1791

I am not surprised, my dear sister, but I am very sorry you had a visit from your husband, and his foreign and English companions. — I foresee no possible good that can arise from it; though I will not affect so much prescience as to point out exactly the evils I apprehend; one of which, however, you must yourself see, I mean the expences that Verney will be drawn into to give himself consequence among these, his new friends. But, perhaps, he may be content to exhibit his Yorkshire house, with some of the inhabitants he had lately there, to do its honours, and may spare you, notwithstanding what he said about your going down thither. — Believe me, I would not have named this circumstance, as you have so often reproved me for speaking with asperity of Verney, could I have supposed it possible that you can be ignorant of the party who were so lately collected there, or of the real reason which made him oppose your going thither with your children, when the country was pronounced absolutely necessary for you by your physicians. Forgive me, pray, if I thus renew disagreeable recollections; but I do not love you should now go where such people held so lately their profligate societies — I do not love that my Geraldine should appear a neglected and unhappy wife, presiding in the same scenes that so recently witnessed the orgies of Verney, Scarsdale, Deybourne, and Newminster, with abandoned prostitutes. — Shall I go farther, and add, that I do not love my Geraldine should be where Scarsdale is at all? — You have often yourself observed his behaviour; and, as he knows you cannot fail to understand it, surely it is inconsistent with your character to allow him an opportunity of repeating it. Do not go to Moorsly Park, my sister, if you can avoid it; and if it cannot otherwise be evaded, without a violation of what you think your duty — obedience! — unqualified obedience! — I will contrive, that my mother shall make a point of your coming hither; a request which Verney will not refuse, since he believes that he owes to her the discharge of those two most troublesome debts (though it certainly was not by her they were discharged); nor, were some little gratitude out of the question (which, perhaps, with him it might be), would he, however impolitic he is, hazard offending my mother, while he feels the daily probability of his being under the necessity of asking other pecuniary favours.

Let me hear, by an early post, that you determine on this, or some other equally proper scheme. — Again let me ask your forgiveness, if I have said too much; and I entreat you to impute it to the tender affection I bear you, which is, you know, inherent, and has grown up with me from my first consciousness of existence. — Alas! if I did not love you, what else should I have to love in the world? My other sister is so much older, that I have always had my affection for her 'chastised by fear,' and she is now afar off, and time and distance are cruel enemies, even to the ties of blood.[48] — My brother! — alas! does he care for any of us, and is it possible to waste one's affection on apathy and indecision? — My mother! I trust, I venerate and regard her, as my only parent. I think myself indebted to her for the trouble she has taken during my infancy and my childhood, and for that portion of regard which she is able to spare me (since I believe the affections are involuntary) from her son; but I have felt too much awe, to be sensible towards her, of that sympathetic and gentle affection which unites me to you — to you, my Geraldine, whose soft temper is ever ready, even amidst your friendly chidings, to plead for your flippant Fanny, while *her* heart finds respondent sentiments only in yours. — Ah! would to heaven I dared entrust you with one, which is —— but no: you have too many troubles of your own — Never, never, may your tenderness for me add to their number!

Your uneasiness about my brother is now, I hope, relieved, at least so far as depends on knowing where he is. — My mother, however, is so far from feeling herself contented at the accounts he has sent her of his journey to the Archipelago, and his Grecian importations, that she is, if possible, more uneasy and more restless than she has been since his absence. For my part, I think he is quite well at Venice, with his Cypriot, as he would be at Paris, or in London, with any connection of the same sort, that he might form at either of those places; and certainly we have much less reason to be dissatisfied, than if he had added to our family alliances, by a union with that of the illustrious house of St Eloy.

That name brings to my mind, or rather to the end of my pen, another name — I mean, that of Desmond. His uncle, who is still here, is grown quite coy upon that subject, though willing enough to talk to me upon any other; or if I continue, at any time, to oblige him to speak upon it, his answers are peevish, short, and unsatisfactory. — I protest I am half inclined to believe the venerable veteran is in love with me himself, and is jealous of my grateful recollection of his nephew. — Oh! how I should be delighted to have the power of teasing this old petrifaction! But, alas! my dear sister, all is exerted in vain: the heart of the Major is composed of such impenetrable stuff, that, I believe, there is no plaguing him any way.

Now do I long to tell you a little of what is passing here; but, I know, the gossip of this place is rather irksome than pleasing to you; and I am often rather reproved than thanked, for endeavouring to amuse you with the events, real or imaginary, which occupy us here, and give us the requisite supplies of conversation for the tea and card parties. But, indeed, my Geraldine, if you deprive me, by your rigid aversion to what you call detraction, of such a resource, I know not what there will remain for me to write about, and to fill those long letters which alone satisfy you. I must not say much of any of our own family, because you say it is pert, and undutiful, and I know not what. If I could repeat only good of the people I am among, you would let me fill quires of paper about them: but, as it is, if I report only what I hear, you accuse me of being so spitefully scandalous as the dowagers, who sit in tremendous committees on the reputations of the week — You know, I never am allowed to converse with any of the literary people I meet, as my mother has a terrible aversion to every thing that looks like a desire to acquire knowledge; and for the same reason, she proscribes every species of reading, and murmurs when she cannot absolutely prohibit the fashionable, insipid novel.

There is so much enquiry of the sage, matronly gentlewomen of her acquaintance, who are, as she believes, deep in the secret, as to *what* books are proper, who are the authors, and whether there be 'any offence in them;' that, by the time these voices are collected, I find more than half I propose reading absolutely forbidden. — Novels, it is decided, convey the poison of bad example in the soft semblance of refined sentiment — One contains an oblique apology for suicide; a second, a lurking palliation of conjugal infidelity; a third, a sneer against parental authority; and a fourth, against religion. Some are disliked for doctrines, which, probably, malice only, assuming the garb of wisdom, can discover in them; and others, because their writers have, either in their private or political life, given offence to the prudery or the party of some of these worthy personages, whom my mother, relying on their reputation for sanctity and sagacity, chooses to consult; and thus I am reduced to practise the *finesse* of a boarding-school miss, and to hide these objectionable pages, from an inquisition not less severe than that which the lovely Serena* sustained; or I must confine myself to such mawkish reading as is produced, 'in a rivulet of text running through a meadow of margin,' in the soft semblance of letters, 'from Miss Everilda Evelyn to Miss Victorina Villars.[49]' — How then, my sister, am I to find any thing to say but of living characters? or how can I help being satirical against those who will not let me be sentimental? — I might, indeed, read history; but whenever I attempt to do so, I am, to tell you the truth, driven from it by disgust. — What is it, but a miserably mortifying detail of crimes and follies? — of the guilt of a few, and the sufferings of many; while almost every page offers an argument in favour of what I never will believe, — that heaven created the human race only to destroy itself, and that, in placing the various species of it in various climates, whence they acquired various complections, habits, and languages, their Creator meant these men should become the natural enemies of each other, and apply the various portions of reasons he has allotted them, only in studying how to annoy and murder each other.

But I am wandering, in my wild way, from the point; and, in my complaints, that the pretty, soothing tales of imagination are prohibited, while the hideous realities of human life affright me, I had nearly forgotten what I was going to say, which is not at all scandalous — Oh no! — it is, on the contrary, an event at which you will rejoice. — Your old friend, Miss Elford, has, at last, met with a lover, who really purposes to become her husband. — He is a physician; very well looking, and twelve or fourteen years younger than herself. — She is in love! — Oh! undescribably in love — and the Doctor foresees, in her extensive connexions, advantages likely to arise to him in his profession, that will, he thinks, more than counterbalance the trifling wants of fortune, beauty, and youth. — I dare not paint to you the ridiculous love scenes that this tender pair exhibit. — You have seen Miss

---

* Triumphs of Temper.[50]

Elford in love once before, and can, perhaps, imagine how she expresses now a still more ardent passion; and with what airs of antiquated co-quetry she recalls the Doctor to his allegiance, if, peradventure, she detects his eyes wandering towards any of the younger and handsomer part of the company. — The idea here is, that they are to be married very soon; and I really wish they may, if it be only in the hope, that Miss Elford, in having a husband of her own, will be so engaged by her own unexpected good fortune, as to let the rest of the world remain for some time unmolested. I cannot help it, my dear sister, if, in despite of your gentle admonitions, I do hate this little, shrivelled, satirical Sybil.[51] — It was from her, I find, that the history of my brother's adventures with the St Eloy family got abroad here, with numberless additional circumstances that never happened; and it is of her that my mother learned, what I wished to conceal from her, the parties that Verney lately had in Yorkshire. — Oh! if you could have heard how she canted about 'her dear, her amiable Mrs Verney,' while she could not disguise the pleasure she took in describing your husband's foibles — you would have been convinced of what I always told you; that under uncommon hypocrisy she conceals uncommon malignity. — As to myself, I find she goes about talking of me in such terms as these: 'Did you see dear Miss Waverly at the ball last night? — Was she not charming? — I think she never looked so well; and really I begin to be a convert to the opinion of those, who said, last year, when she first came out, that she was quite as handsome as her second sister, Mrs Verney, the celebrated beauty — Mrs Verney, poor, dear creature! — (I have an amazing regard for her, and have loved her from *our childhood*, though she is two or three years younger than I am!) Mrs Verney is a little altered, though still so very young — Poor thing! — troubles, like hers, are great enemies to beauty, which is but as the flower of the morning. But however she may be changed in appearance, she is still most amiable — indeed, more so, as to gentleness of temper, than Miss Waverly — though *she* is a sweet girl, and has no fault, except, perhaps, a little, a very little too much vivacity, which it is the great object of my worthy friend, her mother, to check; judging, indeed, very truly, that a young person, so much followed and admired, cannot be too reserved and cautious.' — Yes! and in consequence of this impertinent opinion, this odious tabby (who says she is only a year or two older than you, though she will never see forty again) has made my mother so full of fears and precautions, that I am neither to read any books but those that are ordered by the Divan, of which she is deputy chairwoman, or to speak to any men but old fograms, such as Major Danby; or men of large fortune.[52] — My mother need not be so apprehensive; first, because I have not the least inclination to set out for Scotland with any of the insignificant butterflies, whom I like well enough to have flutter about me in public; and secondly, because, if I had such a fancy, there is not one of them who has the least notion of marrying a young woman without a fortune, or with a very small one. — Even the fortunate beings who are not proscribed, men who can make a settlement, have, for the most part, but little inclination to encumber themselves with a portionless wife) and among them all, I know none who answer my ideas of what a man ought to be. — Alas! there is but one in the world whom I should select as the hero of my romance, if I were in haste to make one.

But you must give me leave to detest Miss Elford a little; though, indeed, I have not in my heart room for many other sentiments than those of anxiety and tenderness for you, my dear Geraldine. Write soon, and explicitly, of your intentions, to

Your affectionate and faithful

FANNY WAVERLY

LETTER XII

Seymour Street, 27th April, 1791

Yes! my sister, I knew of the way in which Mr Verney lived when he was last in Yorkshire, though I never mentioned it, and had some hope it might have escaped my mother's knowledge and yours. — Alas! Fanny! I *cannot* be ignorant, however I desire to appear so, of the extreme bitterness of the lot to which I am condemned: but while you love me — while my charming children are well — while my mother thinks of me with some interest — and let me add, while I have a few friends, whose regard is so well worth possessing, I will not sink under it; but will support myself by the reflection, that I do my duty, and, at least, deserve a better fate. — I now hasten to the other parts of your letter. — You will see, by the date of this, that I am returned to London — and you well know how much against my inclination. — However, it was thought better than going into Yorkshire; and fortunately for me, the Duc de Romagnecourt, who is become Mr Verney's most intimate friend, discovered, that he had no inclination to go at this season into so remote a part of England. — However, Mr Verney determines to entertain him here in a style which may do honour to his hospitality; and as frequent dinners are to be given, and the Duke professes himself dissatisfied, even with the most luxurious table, where ladies do not preside, I have been compelled to quit my quiet lodging, and am to remain here till —— indeed, I know not till when; for Mr Verney is as unsettled in his plans, even as my poor brother himself, and without the docility which Waverly has, who will generally allow some other person to decide for him, and then believes, for a few hours, that he has followed his own inclination.

All you say about Col. Scarsdale is very true. — It is impossible not to see, however I have endeavoured to misunderstand him, that his pretended friendship for Verney does not prevent his forming designs, which you may assure yourself excite only my contempt, and add abhorrence of his principles to personal aversion. — I now see a great deal more of him than I do of Mr Verney; for though we have apparently inhabited the same house these three days, we have met only once, even at table, and that was yesterday, when a magnificent dinner was given to his friends. — Col Scarsdale, however, is very obligingly willing not to consign me to solitude: but, since he is always admitted by Mr Verney's direction, and knows I am never out, he takes the opportunity of sauntering up to my dressing-room, where he plays with the children, picks up my thread-paper, insists upon bringing me new music, and on reading to me some novel or poem, with which he is generally furnished. — If coldness, and apparent disgust, could have put an end to attendance so improper, and so uneasy to me, it certainly would not have continued beyond the second morning; but today is the third, on which, in despite of myself, I shall probably be condemned to endure it. — He affects extreme uneasiness at the state of Verney's affairs (though, till lately, he has endeavoured to laugh off my solicitude about them, whenever I ventured to express it), and has given several intimations, that his friend has formed an attachment to some expensive woman — hints, that I determine never to understand. — But, when I thus evade the subject I wish not to hear of, he sighs, walks about the room, and, as if unable to repress his emotions, cries,

'I love Verney from my soul; but, in this instance, I cannot excuse him, though I pity him, for being so insensible of his own happiness! — I believe he is the only man in England who has so little taste.'

This, they say, is such a common *finesse*, and has been used so often, that I rather wonder the Colonel, who piques himself on his peculiar talents in gallantry, has not recourse to some less hackneyed expedient. — I must put an end to such sort of conversation, however, though I do not know how to do it; as my speaking to Verney (if he did not laugh at it, as he probably would) might be attended with unpleasant consequences. — To-morrow the whole party dine here again; and I have promised Mr Verney to go to Ranelagh with them, and Miss Ayton, who is so good as to come to me whenever these engagements are made, that I may not be the only woman.[53] — Oh! my Fanny, would you were with me! — Nothing could so sooth my sufferings, as having you, to whom I might weep at night, when I have been compelled to conceal all day, under affected tranquillity, the anguish of a breaking heart. — I shall own to you, my dear sister, that notwithstanding the resolutions I made at the beginning of my letter, to be patient and tranquil, there are moments when I most sincerely wish that I and my babies were all dead together. — What will become of us, if, as I greatly fear, there will soon be nothing left but my settlement, between their father and utter ruin? If it ever does come to that, of which, from the hints dropped by Scarsdale, I expect every day to hear, I shall, if I have any such power, give it up to him; for I cannot bear his distress, while I have the means of relieving it. — However, perhaps, it may not be so bad as Scarsdale, with some very unworthy view of his own, seems inclined to represent it. But, from him, I have heard of such losses at play, upon the turf, and in bets of other sorts, that if only half of what he says be true, it is impossible this poor infatuated man can go on long. — I need not say how greatly his expences are increased by the present set of acquaintance he has got into. — I have spoken of it to him at the only moment I had an opportunity, and his answer was — 'Pooh! don't give yourself any concern about that — I know what I am about, and shall take care to be no loser, but very much otherwise.' This, I suppose, meant, that he doubted not his success at play against the French noblemen, two of whom are men of very large fortune. — But how degrading is such a scheme! — how unworthy of a man professing any honour or principle! — Enough, my Fanny, perhaps too much on this cruel topic — I will try to talk of other things.

I cannot help smiling at your account of my old aquaintance Miss Elford, whom I have heartily forgiven, not only for the stories she once sent forth about Mr Mulgrave, which I never knew she had done till lately; but for the little air of triumph she assumes in relating, that 'poor, dear Mrs Verney is already altered in her appearance, though so young!' — Ah! it is very true, indeed, my love. — I not only forgive her, but am really very glad she is at length likely to enter happily into that state which has always been the great object of her laudable ambition. — She will now, I trust, bear less enmity towards her young married friends (how seldom, alas! the objects of well-founded envy), or towards those whose youth and charms seemed to give them a chance which she herself despaired of. — I wish, however, she would not beset my mother with stories of Mr Verney, which serve only to make her uneasy, without producing any benefit to us.

You say, that my mother certainly did not pay off those two debts that so sadly distressed us five months ago. — Who then could it be? — Since I have been convinced it was none of my own family, I have been, I own, very solicitous to discover to whom such an obligation is owing; and, in the indiscretion of my curiosity, I have applied to Col Scarsdale, who, without directly asserting it, has given such answers, as would (if I did not believe him incapable of such an action, even from *interested* motives) have led me to imagine it might be himself. — Surely this cannot be? — I wish it were possible to know.

You ask me, my Fanny, after Mr Desmond. — Alas! I know nothing satisfactory of him; and have sometimes been so anxious to hear of him, as to think of writing to Mr Bethel — Yet a fear of its having a singular and improper appearance, has always deterred me. What is your secret, my dear sister, which you will not communicate, lest it should add to my troubles? — Does it, as I guess, relate to Desmond? — Oh! how happy, how enviable, would the lot of that woman be, who, inspiring such a man with esteem and affection, should be at liberty to return it! — Need I say, that it is the wish of my heart, my Fanny might be that fortunate creature? Yet, let me not assist in cherishing an hope that may serve only to imbitter her life — I have heard it hinted (but it is long since, and, perhaps, came from no very good authority) that he is already attached, with the most ardent affection, to that Madame de Boisbelle, who so assiduously attended him in his illness; and that his continuing so long abroad, is owing to his unwillingness to leave her. — I have collected this intelligence partly from Col Scarsdale, who has some correspondence abroad, and partly from my servant Manwaring, whose husband is an old friend of Warham's, Mr Desmond's servant, and now and then has a letter from him. — Upon putting all the circumstances together, I am compelled to give that credit to their united evidence, which I should not have given to the Colonel alone, who seemed to triumph mightily in being able to relate, that my excellent and *virtuous* friend, as he sneeringly calls Desmond, is entangled in an adventure with a married woman. — Perhaps, however, this is all the invention of malice, or the painting of ignorance — malice, that will not allow it *probable* mere friendship should exist between two persons of different sexes; and gross ignorance, that cannot imagine it *possible*. May heaven bless Desmond, whatever are his prospects and connexions! and may he be as happy as he deserves to be! I feel, too sensibly, the weight of our obligation to him whenever his name is mentioned, whenever I think of him. Perhaps, I feel it the more, because (you only excepted) none of my family seem to feel it at all. My brother, I fear, never writes to him; and has probably committed follies as great, though not so irretrievable, as those from which Desmond delivered him. Mr Verney is continually making Desmond's quixotism the subject of his ridicule (a talent which he manages generally so as to attract ridicule himself); and my mother seems rather sorry that Desmond is wiser than her son, than obliged to him for having exerted that wisdom in his behalf. How long, my dear Fanny, has your reading been under proscription? We used to read what we would, when we were girls together, and I never found it was prejudicial to either of us: but my mother seems to have been listening (notwithstanding her dislike of women's knowledge) to some of those good ladies, who, by dint of a tolerable memory, and being accustomed to associate with men of letters, have collected some phrases and remarks, which they retail in less enlightened societies, and immediately obtain credit for an uncommon share of penetration and science. — But if every work of fancy is to be prohibited in which a tale is told, or an example brought forward, by which some of these ladies suppose, that the errors of youth may be palliated, or the imagination awakened — I know no book of amusement that can escape their censure; and the whole phalanx of novels, from the two first of our classics, in that line of writing, Richardson and Fielding, to the less exceptionable, though certainly less attractive inventors of the present day, must be condemned with less mercy, than the curate and the barber shewed to the collection of the Knight of the sorrowful Countenance; and then, I really know not what young people (I mean young women) will read at all.[54] — But let me ask these severe female censors, whether, in every well-written novel, *vice*, and even *weaknesses*, that deserve not quite so harsh a name, are not exhibited, as subjecting those who are examples of them, to remorse, regret, and punishment — And since circumstances, more inimical to innocence, are every day related, without any disguise, or with very little, in the public prints; since, in reading the world, a girl must see a thousand very ugly blots, which frequently pass without any censure at all — I own, I cannot imagine, that novel reading can, as has been alleged, corrupt the imagination, or enervate the heart — at least, such a description of novels, as those which represent human life nearly as it is; for, as to others, those wild and absurd writings, that describe in inflated language, beings that never were, nor ever will be, they can (if any young woman has so much patience and so little taste as to read them) no more contribute to form the character of her mind, than the grotesque figures of shepherdesses, on French fans and Bergamot boxes, can form her taste in dress. — Who could, for a moment, feel any impression from the perusal of such stuff as this, though every diurnal print puffed its excellence, and every *petit-maître* swore it was quite the thing — exquisite — pathetic — interesting?

'The beautiful, the soft, the tender Iphigenia closed not, during the tedious hours, her beauteous eyes, while the glorious flambeau of silver-slippered day sunk beneath the encrimsoned couch of coral-crowned Thetis, giving up the dormant world to the raven-embrace of all-o'erclouding night. — When, however, the *matin*-loving lark, on russet pinions floating amid the tiffany clouds, that variegated, in fleecy undulation, the grey-invested heavens, hailed with his soul-reviving note the radiant countenance of returning morn; the sweet, the mild, the elegantly unhappy maid turned towards the roseate-streaming East those sapphire messengers, that expressed, in language of such exquisite sensibility, every emotion of her delicate soul; and, with a palpitating sigh, arose. — She clad her graceful form in a close jacket of Nakara satin, trimmed with silver, and the blossoms of the sweet-scented pea, intermixed; her petticoat was of white satin, with a border of the same; and on her head, half-hiding and half discovering her hyacinthine locks, she carelessly bound a glowing wreath of African marygolds and purple China-aster, surmounting the whole with a light kerchief of pink Italian gauze, embroidered by herself in lilies of the valley. — She then approached the window, and in a voice, whose dulcet gurglings emulated the cooings of the enamoured pigeon of the woods, she sighed forth the following exquisitely expressive ode.'

Now do you think, my dear Fanny, that either good or harm can be derived from such a book as this? — Loss of time may be, with justice, objected to it, but no other evil. — A sensible girl would certainly throw it away in disgust: a weak one (who would probably not understand half if it, could it be understood at all) cries, 'Dear! — how sweet! — Charming creature! — A light kerchief of pink Italian gauze, embroidered with lilies of the valley! Her voice, the dulcet gurglings of the enamoured pigeon of the woods!' — And then, meaning only to enquire, whether this amiable Iphigenia was happy or no? she sits down to have her hair curled — reads as fast as the roseate rays, and azure adventures, will let her, to the end — and, forgetting them all, dresses herself and goes to Ranelagh, or the Opera, where she tells some little cream-coloured beau what a dear, divine novel she has been reading; but of which, in fact, she has forgotten every word.

I own it has often struck me as a singular inconsistency, that, while novels have been condemned as being injurious to the interest of virtue, the play-house has been called the school of morality. — The comedies of the last century are, almost without exception, so gross, that, with all the alterations they have received, they are very unfit for that part of the audience to whom novel-reading is deemed pernicious: nor is the example to be derived from them very conducive to the interests of morality; for, not only the rake and the coquette of the piece are generally made happy, but those duties of life, to which novel-reading is believed to be prejudicial, are almost always violated with impunity, or rendered ridiculous by 'the trick of the scene.' — Age, which ought to be respected, is invariably exhibited as hateful and contemptible. — To cheat an old father, or laugh at a fat aunt, are the supreme merits of the heroes and heroines; and though nothing is more out of nature than the old man of the stage — I cannot be of opinion, that the scene is a school of morality for youth, which teaches them, that age and infirmity are subjects of laughter and ridicule. — Such, however, is the taste of the English in their theatrical amusements. — And now, when the very offensive jest is no longer admitted, portraits of folly, exaggerated till they lose all resemblance, harlequin tricks, and pantomimical escapes, are substituted to keep the audience awake, and are accepted in place of genuine wit, of which it must be owned there is 'a plentiful lack' (with some strong exceptions, however) in our modern comedy.[55] — All this is very well, if we take it as mere amusement; but what I quarrel with is the canting fallacy of calling the stage the school of morality. — Rousseau says, very justly, 'Il n'y a que la raison qui ne soit bonne à rien sur la scene*.' — A reasonable man would be a character insupportably flat and insipid even on the French stage; and, on the English, would not be endured to the end of the first scene. — Even those charming pieces which are called dramas, such as Le Père de Famille, L'Indigent, Le Philosophe sans le scavoir, would, however well they might be translated, adapted to our manners, and represented, lull an English audience to sleep, though they exhibit domestic scenes, by which morality and virtue are most forcibly inculcated; and such as, by coming 'home to the business and bosoms' of the younger part of the audience, might be, indeed, lessons in that school, which our theatre certainly does not form; though the careful mothers, who dread the evil influence of novels, carry their daughters to its most exceptionable representations.[56]

In regard to novels, I cannot help remarking another strange inconsistency, which is, that the great name of Richardson (and great it certainly deserves to be) makes, by a kind of hereditary prescriptive deference, those scenes, those descriptions, pass uncensured in Pamela and Clarissa, which are infinitely more improper for the perusal of young women, than any that can be found in the novels of the present day; of which, indeed, it may be said, that, if they do no good, they do no harm; and that there *is* a chance, that those who will read nothing, if they do not read novels, may collect from them some few ideas, that are not either fallacious or absurd, to add to the very scanty stock which their usual insipidity of life has afforded them. — As to myself,

---

*   It is reason only that is worth nothing on the stage.[57]

I read, you know, all sorts of books, and have done so ever since I was out of the nursery, for my mother had then no notion of restraining me. — Novels, of course, and those very indifferent novels, were the first that I could obtain; and I ran through them with extreme avidity, often forgetting to practise my lesson on the harpsichord, or to learn my French task, while I got up into my own room, and devoured with an eager appetite the mawkish pages that told of a damsel, most exquisitely beautiful, confined by a cruel father, and escaping to an heroic lover, while a wicked Lord laid in wait to tear her from him, and carried her to some remote castle. — Those delighted me most that ended miserably, and, having tortured me through the last volume with impossible distress, ended in the funeral of the heroine. — Had the imagination of a young person been liable to be much affected by these sort of histories, mine would, probably, have taken a romantic turn; and at eighteen, when I was married, I should have hesitated whether I should obey my friends' directions, or have waited till the hero appeared, who would have been imprinted on my mind, from some of the charming fabulous creatures of whom I had read in novels. — But, far from doing so, I was, you see, 'obedient — very obedient;' and, in the four years that have since passed, I have thought only of being a quiet wife, and a good nurse, and of fulfilling, as well as I can, the part which has been chosen for me.[58] — I know not how I have slid into all this egotism, from a defence of novel-reading. — It has, however, served to detach my thoughts from subjects of 'sad import;' and I have written myself into some degree of cheerfulness.[59] Before I relapse, therefore, I will bid you, my beloved Fanny, adieu!

GERALDINE VERNEY

LETTER XIII

TO MR DESMOND

Bath, May 17th, 1791

In pursuance of my promise, which, though it was, perhaps, indiscreet to give it, I hold sacred now that it is given; I write to you, my dear friend, to relate an history that cannot but wound you most cruelly, and add to that melancholy despondence too visible in your last letters. — I believe I told you* that Geraldine was suddenly returned to London, at the request of her husband, and that his style of living at his house in Seymour-street, far from having been reduced by the late untoward circumstances that befel him there, was more extravagant and profuse than before. — He was supposed to have won considerable sums of money from the Duke de Romagnecourt, and some other Frenchmen of fortune, emigrants in England; and it was to do the honours of his house to these new friends, that his wife, who could no longer plead the excuse of ill health, was compelled, in obedience to his wishes, to leave her quiet retirement at Sheen, and return to witness follies she could not check, and to see the progress of ruin it was impossible for her to prevent.

In my way through London, about three weeks ago, I called at her door, merely to make an enquiry after her, and not expecting to see her. — The servant, however, whom I spoke to, informed me she had been some days in London, was then at home, and would, he believed, see me. I sent up my name, and, on entering the room, was gratified by the expression of pleasure which I saw on the countenance of Geraldine, who, instead of receiving me with the formality of mere aquaintance, held out her hand to me, and called me her good friend.

The features of a gentleman, who was sitting with her, wore, I thought, a very different meaning. — This was Colonel Scarsdale, who looked at me as if he at once contemned me as a rural 'Squire, and disliked me as an unwelcome intruder — while the evident preference that Geraldine gave me by addressing all her conversation to me, and enquiring solicitously about you, seemed every moment to increase his displeasure. Still, however, he staid — now humming an air — and now making a violent noise with the little boy, for whom he affects the most extravagant fondness; and though I wished very much to have some conversation with Geraldine, in which, notwithstanding her reserve, I might have learned more of her real situation than I can gather from public report — I found the Colonel determined to stay too; and that he was so much domesticated in the house, that he dressed there, and was, that day, to make one of a large party that were coming to dinner. — As I was under the necessity of leaving London early

---

* In a letter which does not appear.

the next morning, I had no opportunity of attempting another interview with her; but as soon as I arrived at Bath, I waited on her mother
and her sister, and fortunately found the latter at home alone.

Fanny Waverly received me with great pleasure, and was not less
early and eager in her enquiries after you, than Geraldine had been
two days before. — When I told her that you were, from your own
account, so far recovered of your accident, that you talked of leaving
off the sling in which your arm had been confined — her eyes spar-
kled with pleasure; but when I added, that you spoke less favourably
of your general health, and had no thoughts of returning soon to England, she evidently drooped in dejection; and when I led the discourse
towards Geraldine, as I immediately did, she dissolved in tears.

She told me, that the situation of her sister gave her the most cruel
alarms; that Verney was most undoubtedly ruined beyond remedy; and
that she feared his real reason for having brought back Geraldine to
his house, was, a hope of persuading her to give up her settlement, and
enable him to sell his Yorkshire estate, which, said she, 'I have too
much reason to believe my sister will consent to. — Nor is this all my
fear — Geraldine is young, and very lovely. — Every man of intrigue,
who sees such a woman neglected, or even worse treated by her husband, is ready to form designs for himself. — I know there are, at this
time, many such surrounding my sister; and though the purity of her
heart, the excellence of her understanding, and her excessive tenderness for her children, are securities for her conduct, which I cannot a
moment doubt; yet, I have such an opinion of Verney, that I am not
certain he is not capable of the most infamous proceedings, even towards his wife, if, by such, he could obtain the means of supporting a
little longer the wild career, which his mad infatuation represents as
the only one worthy of a man of fashion.'

This remark, added to what I had made in town on the behaviour
of Colonel Scarsdale, and my opinion of Verney, which is not at all
better than that Fanny entertains of him, startled me extremely. — 'If
such, my dear Miss Waverly,' said I, 'are your apprehensions for your
sister, surely your mother, or your brother, ought to interfere, before
they can be realized — Surely, they ought to rescue this excellent and
lovely woman from the power of a husband, of whom such horrors
can be suspected.' — 'Alas! Mr Bethel,' replied she, 'how can I mention such dreadful ideas to my mother? who, conscious, I believe, that

Geraldine was the victim of duty, and married only in compliance with her and my father's wishes, now endeavours to escape the conviction, that she has condemned her to the most dreadful of all destinies, and will not see or hear, if she can by any means escape it, what is, unhappily, too evident to the rest of the world. — Wrapt up as her whole soul has ever been in my brother, she has always thought, that in marrying her daughters in what is called a prudent way, that is, to men of large fortune, she had taken sufficient trouble about them. She never considered whether there were any other sources of unhappiness than want of money; nor did it ever occur to her, that, in giving Geraldine to a man of fortune and family, she overlooked circumstances in the character of Verney (though, when he married, his character was not developed) that might make her daughter liable to all the distresses and inconveniencies of poverty. — To be convinced that it is so, is to be convinced, that she has wanted either judgment or tenderness, and she takes refuge in cards and company against the reproaches of her own heart. — I have ventured, however, since I received some hints of the probability there was that Geraldine would be persuaded to part with her settlement, to implore my mother's attention to a circumstance so destructive: but she impatiently answered, that I talked nonsense; for that the trustees to her marriage-articles would take especial care to prevent her committing such a folly. — As to any other fears I entertain, such as those I have just now mentioned, my mother would treat them as a romantic chimera of mine, and resent my supposing them probable or possible. — How then can I venture to make representations to my mother, which would, probably, be ill received and fruitless? or which, were she to attend to them a moment, she would, perhaps, find some occasion to condemn as futile, because she would dislike to do that which, if she allows them well founded, she ought to do — I mean, to take her daughter to her own house, as the only proper asylum, if she is compelled to quit that of her husband. — This, however, I know my mother will avoid; for Geraldine will never leave her children, and my mother dislikes their noise, and the trouble they occasion in an house; and she is, in short, for why may I not speak the truth to you? just at that period of life, when the character retains little that is feminine, but a love of trifles, and a redoubled attachment to some one weakness that has long been cherished. — Such is her violent partiality to my brother, for whom (notwithstanding the little encouragement his entrance into the world has given to such hopes) she looks forward towards titles and dignities, which she imagines his fortune will command, and his merit deserve. — There are some hearts, Mr Bethel, that have not room for more than one strong affection — Such, I suppose, is my mother's. — The rest of it, which her daughters might have occupied, is filled with trifling objects — and —— but I believe you will think me very wrong,' continued she, 'and, perhaps, I have already said too much. — I meant, however, to account to you for omitting to do what certainly appears most rational under the apprehensions I have ventured to express to you.'

I was so much struck by the manner, as well as the purport, of this answer — so concerned for the situation of Geraldine — and so affected by the tender interest her sister thus expressed, that I could neither find words immediately to do justice to my feelings, nor, in my mind, any remedy for the unhappy circumstances that excited them. — Your charge, my dear Desmond, to use your fortune without scruple, in the service of Geraldine, cannot here be executed; for to her it would be worse than useless, while her husband would derive from it the means of continuing his career of vice and folly. Yet something should be done, and done immediately, to save her sensible heart from the anguish it must endure for her children — to spare her the mortification and misery she must feel in seeing herself at the mercy of a wretch, who is believed capable of such actions as Fanny Waverly, I fear with too much reason, represents him as likely to practise. As I wished to have time to reflect on what measures were the most proper, since of her own family there seemed so little to hope, I took leave of Miss Waverly, and returned to my lodgings; but my thoughts dwelt in vain on the subject. — I saw no way in which it was proper, or even possible, for the most disinterested friendship to interfere between a man and his wife. — If Verney is determined to ruin himself and her, I see not by what means it can be prevented, or on what pretence even her own family can separate them, while he chooses she should remain the victim of his dissipation, or hopes to derive, from the admiration she excites, the power of continuing it; for to such a plan Fanny Waverly undoubtedly alluded; and I have since heard, that Scarsdale, who has been long trying to recommend himself to the favour of Geraldine in vain, has found it much easier to embarrass her husband's affairs so much, as to have a prospect of obtaining that influence over her from necessity, which from any other motive he could never obtain. — But I think, if I know any thing of the spirit and temper of that incomparable woman, she will spurn, with detestation, a monster who pursues the gratification of his passions by perfidy so atrocious. — There was a time when, new to the world, and unhackneyed in the ways of men, I should have felt indignation at the mere representation of such characters as those of Verney and Scarsdale, and should have thought it a misanthropic libel on human nature. — But, alas! I know that such men do exist; and I know that it is very difficult to save Geraldine from them, if they unite in destroying her peace and her reputation. — I here break off, to keep an appointment I have made with Fanny Waverly, to meet at a bookseller's shop, and walk together. You will smile, or rather, you would smile at any other time, in figuring to yourself your sage Mentor making an assignation with a sprightly girl of nineteen or twenty. — But this is the only way by which I can obtain an opportunity of talking with her alone — and I am one of the favoured few, whom her discreet mother allows to converse with her. Louisa, who is a great favourite, and who loves Miss Waverly extremely, is, however, to make a third in our party.

May 18th, 1791

Well! my friend — I am returned from my *tête-à-tête* with this young beauty, and with an aching heart, but aching from other motives than those of love. — The week that has elapsed since I last conversed with her about Geraldine, has produced some of the events she then expected, and others of which she had no apprehension.

Waverly, your travelling companion, is suddenly returned to England, while his mother and his sister thought him at Venice, with a nymph whom he had brought from the Isle of Cyprus, whither he went with some other young Englishmen. — Some misadventure, by which he lost the lady, disgusted him with their society; and meeting at Genoa with a Captain of a merchantman just coming to England, he embarked, after half an hour's debate, with only one of his servants, leaving the others with his baggage to follow; and having a very quick passage, he landed near London; and in fourteen hours arrived at Bath, to the extreme satisfaction of his mother, who received him as if the whole time of his absence had been passed in refining his manners, and cultivating his understanding. — I believe (though Fanny does not say so) that there is no very visible improvement in either; but that he has picked up, at every place, some small specimen of the reigning follies, without having dropped those that he had acquired before he set out. But his mother, who believes he had completed the course of study and education which is requisite to a man of fortune, and 'of a certain style,' is now most eagerly solicitous to have him married; and Fanny tells me, that, from every appearance at present, it is highly probable that, by the mutual endeavours of the two elder ladies, Mrs Fairfax and Mrs Waverly, this great event may be accomplished. — The eldest Miss Fairfax (your fair aristocrate, at Margate) is the lady whose happy destiny it will be to fix this fluctuating lover.

This is a matter of importance no otherwise than as it occupies entirely the maternal feelings of Mrs Waverly, and prevents her giving any attention to the situation of her daughter Verney, and will as certainly be a reason against her affording her even that pecuniary assistance which I greatly fear she may now want; for the catastrophe of Verney's affairs, so long foreseen, is at length arrived. — The sudden increase of expence which he rushed into in London, ended in his giving up the lease of the house, and all its furniture, to his creditors; and it is advertised for sale on the 30th instant. — Geraldine and her children have of course left it; but not to go to Mooresly Park, which is made over for a term of years, with the furniture and stock, to Colonel Scarsdale, as is said, towards the discharge of a considerable debt of what is called honour. — Verney himself, who seems totally insensible to the sufferings of his wife, and has left her to struggle against them alone, is either gone or going to Germany with the Duke de Romagnecourt, and his party, who are about to join the exiled French Princes. — Fanny Waverly told me, with many tears, that her sister was gone into a small lodging at Kensington; for those at Sheen, humble as they once appeared, she now thought too expensive for her; that she did not intend to remain so near London, but to find some cheap retirement in a distant county, where she might conceal her sorrows from those to whom the sight of them would be oppressive. — Thus, my dear Desmond, I have executed the most uneasy task I ever undertook, that of relating the calamities that seem likely to overwhelm our charming friend. — Be not, however, in pain about her immediate situation, as to money. — I have settled with Fanny Waverly the means of being for the present her banker, without her knowing that any but her own family execute this office — And I have entreated this amiable girl to endeavour to obtain leave of her mother to go to her sister in this hour of bitter distress. — This, however, is a permission that Fanny has already solicited in vain; nor can she obtain of Mrs Waverly any other attention to the cruel situation of Geraldine, than what the old lady thinks necessary to prevent the circumstances she is under from bringing any sort of disgrace on the rest of the family, and injuring her present projects in regard to her son, which are alone near her heart.

I direct this to St Germains, where your last letter tells me you will, by this time, be arrived, to remain some time — I cannot imagine why, and do not ask — as if you had chosen I should know, you would probably have told me. — However, my business is to forward this letter to you, by as quick a conveyance as possible. — I luckily have an opportunity of doing so, by a servant belonging to an aquaintance of mine, who is going to rejoin his master at Paris. I shall be impatient to hear from you — Let me soon have that satisfaction; and let me hear that the despondence is gone, which, at your age, and with your character, is a weakness you ought not to indulge. Adieu!

Most faithfully yours,

E. BETHEL

LETTER XIV

TO MISS WAVERLY

May 29th, 1791

At length, my Fanny, I begin to recover. — It is now three days since I have been settled at my new abode; and returning tranquillity, I mean outward tranquillity (for that of the heart and spirit can never more be mine), gives me a little time to collect my troubled thoughts —

'And on the heat and flame of my endurance,
Sprinkle cool patience*.'

---

* Shakespeare.[60]

But be not uneasy about me — I am not ill: — I am only languid from the severity of my past sufferings, and that languor is every day decreasing.

My two eldest children are quite well; and my little George is as gaily playing on the turf here, as he used to be on that of the lawn at Linwell, or the park at Mooresly — places, of which I once hoped he would be the inheritor. — But of my disappointed hopes my lovely boy is unconscious! — yet he continually brings tears into my eyes, by asking, why we came hither? — what is become of his papa, of the servants, and the horses, whose names they had taught him, and of the maid who used to wait upon me? — I endeavour to divert these infantine enquiries as much as I can, for they affect me more than even my own melancholy reflections. Fortunately it is a season when he is easily amused. I send him out with his sister and his maid into the surrounding meadow, where, after their maid has dressed their hats with cowslips, orchisses, cuckoo-flowers, and golden-cups — my Harriet brings home her lap full of these 'gay children of the May,' and, in her imperfect language, says, they are for 'dear mama.'

While my little prattlers are absent, I hang over the cradle of my infant William, whose health has again been sadly disordered by all the anxiety I have endured. Yet, for his sake, I endeavoured to repress those acute feelings with which my heart was torn to pieces; but such was their nature, that it was impossible my health should not be affected, and, of course, that of the child, whom, under such circumstances, I have, perhaps, done wrong to continue nourishing at my breast, especially as I think he has never recovered the first shock he received, when, at his birth, I first knew so much, and so suddenly, of the disarranged state of Mr Verney's circumstances. — Compared with the loss of my child, every other evil would be as nothing; yet, perhaps, I ought not to wish him to live, since to live is but to suffer. — But again, my dear sister, I check these mournful thoughts, with which I ought not to oppress you; and again I assure you, that when none of these apprehensions assail my heart, I am not so unhappy as you say you fear I am. If I obtain resolution enough to look calmly at the change which has befallen me, I see much less to regret than most people would discover. The only pleasure I have lost in losing high affluence, is that of having the power to befriend the unhappy, to whom I can now give only my tears; but, for the rest, what have I lost that I ought to lament? — The turbulent and joyless societies which Mr Verney loved, were to me only fatiguing and disagreeable. The parties of fashionable men that he continually collected, offered me neither rational conversation, nor permanent friendship: — and the women, with whom I was, in consequence of these connections, compelled to associate, were so insipid, or so vain, so devoted to the card-table, or occupied by the rage of being admired, that their acquaintance gave me as little pleasure as mine seemed to give them; and our intercourse was, after two or three formal dinners, reduced to the slight civility of sending cards to each other four or five times in a winter. The fineries in which Mr Verney's vanity dressed me out (he called it love, I think, for a little time) never gave me a moment's pleasure; and when, last year, Colonel Scarsdale persuaded him that I ought to be presented, and appear sometimes at court, I was perfectly convinced that such ceremonies were for me the heaviest punishments that could be devised: and, indeed, few of those whose pride or interest made their attendance on them more frequent, were apparently more delighted than I was; for they seemed universally to feel, under all the apparent gaiety and splendour, the influence of the daemon *Ennui* —

'That realm he rules, and, in superb attire,
Visits each earthly palace*.'

Now, I believe, my Fanny, I am for ever exempt from being a visiter where this hideous phantom holds his eternal reign; and he will not, I trust, seek me in the farm-house I now inhabit, and which I am going to describe to you.

The situation of it is charming. — It stands on a rising ground, among meadows, of which poetry, in the most flowery language, could hardly exaggerate the beauty. Through these yellow meads the Wye takes its 'sinuous course,' till its progress is concealed by projecting hills, or rather mountains, rising beyond the meadows; their summits bare and rocky, their sides clothed with woods, which, at this time, exhibit every varied tint of vivid and early vegetation.[61] — Forgive me if I borrow here the aid of a poet, whose powerful pen, with more than the magic of the pencil, brings whatever he describes immediately before the eye.

---

* Hayley.[62]

No tree in all the grove but has its charms,
Tho' each its hue peculiar; paler some,
And of a wannish grey; the willow such,
And poplar, that with silver lines his leaf;
And ash, far stretching his umbrageous arm;
Of deeper green the elm; and deeper still,
Lord of the woods, the long-surviving oak;
Some glossy-leaved and shining in the sun;
The maple, and the beech of oily nuts
Prolific; and the lime at dewy eve
Diffusing odours*.'

Beneath these varied woods are a tract of orchards, now covered with bloom, giving completely the idea of the

'Primavera candida e vermiglia†.'

A cottage or two, almost embosomed among the trees, are marked rather by the smoke arising from their chimneys, than by their concealed thatch; but thus dimly seen, they give cheerfulness to the landscape. — Behind the house, the country wears quite another aspect. It rises abruptly into small knolls, too steep for the plough, and, from the nature of the soil, not much worth cultivation, since it is in the lower part of a black moor; and the hillocks are of a yellow sand, producing little but the heath and the whortle-berry‡ — the higher ridges, furze, or thorns, with here and there, in the hollows, tufts of self-planted oaks.

From this rude tract of country the garden of this house is divided, in some parts, by an old wall, in others by a thick hedge of yew and holly, the growth of centuries: for this is an old manorial residence; and, besides the long row of firs, of very ancient date, that shade part of the garden, has many marks of having been once the abode of opulent possessors, who ornamented it in the taste of the days in which they lived. The last improvements in the house appear to have been

---

*   Cowper.[63]

†   Petrarch.[64]

‡   Whortle-berry, or hurts. Vaccinium Myrtillus.

made in the time of Elizabeth and James the First; but those in the garden are rather, perhaps, in the style that was imported from Holland by William, when he was sent for to secure the liberty of Englishmen, and teach them to curtail that of their trees — I mean the taste which decorated our gardens with rows of evergreens, formally planted, and cut into the imagined shapes of men, peacocks, and sundry other forms —

'Gorgons and Hydras, and Chimeras dire.'[65]

The last inhabitant of the house was an old and rich farmer, who had not relish for these monuments of former elegance; but the wife of him who now rents it, and of whom I hire my apartments, told me, with great exultation, that *she* had caused one of the men, at his leisure hours, to clip them into their former beauty, and 'make them fit to be seen, all's one, as folks say, they used to be in the old Squire's time.' — But, as this rustic sculptor of vegetables is not very expert in his art, the box, the holly, and the yew, have lost all resemblance to themselves, without finding any other. — In the borders beneath them, however, there are a great many flowers, whose roots have survived those who planted them, and these are even scattered over the rough parts of the enclosure, which is given up to the culinary productions, or left wholly uncultivated,

'Along the waste, where once the garden smiled,
And where still many a garden flower grows wild*.'

And it is among these, which are now peeping through the grass, or blooming, unseen, among the thyme, balm, and lavender, that I, in my melancholy meditations, repeat

'The tender rose which seems in Winter dead,
Revives in Spring, and lifts its dewy head:
But we — the great, the glorious, and the wise!
When once the hand of death has clos'd our eyes —†'

. . . .

---

*   Goldsmith.[66]
†   Idyllium of Moschus on the death of Bion.[67]

Or rather, the lighter comment of a very agreeable French authoress on this text, which concludes with

'Mais hélas! — pour vouloir revivre,
La vie est-il un bien si doux?
Quand nous l'aimonstant, songeons nous
De combien de chagrins sa perte nous delivre?
Elle n'est qu'un amas de craintes, de douleurs,
De travaux, de soucis, de peines,
Pour qui connoit les miseres humaines,
Mourir n'est pas le plus grand des malheurs*.'

But I am getting again into reflections, which I blame myself for indulging; and moralizing, when I undertook to give you a picture of my abode.

The house itself is very old. Wide, projecting casements, divided by heavy stone work, a great brick hall, and

'Passages that lead to nothing,'[68]

may give you some idea, and perhaps a dreary idea of the sort of house. — The farmer and his family inhabit the northern end of it, which was once the servants' apartments, kitchen, and buttery. The rooms, however, which I have taken, are not so forlorn as from the general air of the house you would suppose. I have a parlour wainscoted and carpeted. The chimney, indeed, is very large, but, at this time of the year, is

'With flowers and fennel gay†,'

and will, I dare say, look very well with a blazing wood fire in it. — Above, I have a very good bed-chamber for myself, and one, still better, immediately adjoining, for my children: these are papered, and, though not in a very modern style perhaps, they are clean and warm. I have desired some great, old family-pictures, with which both these and the parlour were disfigured, might be removed; and I shall supply the places of these heroes, who bled in the civil wars (as I guess

---

* Les Fleurs, Idylle par Madame des Houlieres.
† Goldsmith.[69]

by their wigs and their armour), and the dames whose simpering charms rewarded their prowess, but whose very names are now forgotten (sad lesson to human vanity!), with rude brackets of wood, on which I shall put flowers, and between them shelves for the books I have brought with me. — These little arrangements serve to occupy my mind; and I forget the conveniencies and luxuries of which I am deprived, in contriving how I may still obtain those few, which (perhaps from singularity of taste) are more necessary to my content, than the side-board of plate, the elegant furniture, and handsome carriages I have parted with.

I think more of their late thoughtless owner, poor Verney! — Yet why do I speak of him in a tone of pity, when he is probably much happier than I am? — I have had no other letter from him since our hasty parting in London, than that wherein he very briefly assented to my proposed retirement; and said, though not in direct terms, that if I did not embarrass him about money, I was at liberty to do with myself and my children whatever I thought good.[70] — I will not comment on this — I will endeavour not to think of it. — I turn always with painful pleasure, to *some other* subjects; but to *one* I think with pleasure only. I am happy to hear Mr Bethel is at Bath, that you have such long and pleasant conversations with him, and that his charming girl is so much with you. He is a man whom I have always regarded and esteemed for his own sake, as well as because he was so excellent a guardian, and is so warm a friend to Mr Desmond. You hear that Desmond is at St Germains: that place is, I suppose, the residence of Madame de Boisbelle, when she is not with her brother. But Mr Bethel tells you that Desmond is quite restored to health, and only occasionally wears his arm in a sling — may he soon lose even that recollection of his painful adventure! — I must now, my Fanny, bid you adieu. My letter is very long; yet I have written it all while my little William has been sleeping, and my other charmers walking with their maid in the shade of one of the woods, which a rustic bridge thrown across the river puts within our reach. — It is now near their hour of dinner, and I see them from my window crossing the meadow: I go to meet them, and help to bring them home, as I see, by his actions, that George complains of being tired, and solicits his Peggy to carry him as well as his sister. I will seal my letter on my return, as it cannot go to the post till tomorrow.

I did not imagine, my Fanny, in leaving my letter unsealed this morning, that I should have to add to its contents, the history of a circumstance that has surprised me a good deal.

On my meeting my children in the field below the house, their maid told me, that Master George had tired himself so by playing with a gentleman whom they had met, and with a great dog he had with him, that she could hardly get him home. I enquired who the gentleman was, and heard that they had seen him reading in the wood; and that the dog, which was a large water-spaniel, having ran [sic] towards the children, and somewhat alarmed the little girl, his master, who was as Peggy described him, 'one of the most handsome gentlemen she ever set eyes upon,' had come up to them, and asked very eagerly, whose children they were? and hearing that their names were Verney, he had taken them both up and kissed them: that the little boy looked earnestly at him, and then returned his fondness; and that once, in playing with him, the gentleman called him George, as if he had known him before. — I desired the maid to describe the figure of this gentleman, that I might know if it were any of my acquaintance. She said, 'that he was a tall, and (according to her phrase) quite a *grand-looking man*, though not *lusty*, but rather *thinnish*; he had dark eyes, brighter than any diamonds, and brown hair; but that he looked a little pale, as if he was sick; and, though he seemed in his way somehow like an officer, that he was left-handed.' — Till now, I had formed, I own, a vague, and yet a very uneasy idea, that this stranger, who knew the name of my little boy so well, might be Colonel Scarsdale: but this description did not at all answer his person; and then I recollected, that if it had been him, George would have known him, and indeed the maid also, who has been so lately accustomed to see him every day. — I then supposed it might be some of the neighbouring gentlemen, and bade Peggy describe him to the farmer's wife and servants, which she has just done, and tells me that there is no such person in this country that they know of, and that the nearest gentleman's seat is above seven miles off. — I have again been questioning Peggy, as this stranger's having so much noticed the children has made a great impression on my mind. She says, she is sure, from his manner, that it is some gentleman who had been acquainted in the family, because he seemed so fond of them, and 'somehow glad to see them;' and that he asked George if he often walked in that wood, and whether his mama ever walked there? — 'And to be sure, Ma'am,' remarks Peggy, 'it must be somebody that knows you, or how should he enquire after the children's mama? for I never told him whether they had a mama or a papa, or who belonging to them.'

The more questions I ask, the more I wish to know who this is, and whether it is really any man whom I have formerly known, who happens accidentally to be in this country. If it is, he will probably, since he knows where I am, call upon me; and if it is not, of what importance is the circumstance at all? — Thus I have endeavoured to reason myself out of the restless curiosity that has disturbed me, perhaps foolishly enough, the whole of the remaining day. — It is now night — a calm, a lovely night! without a moon indeed, but with the canopy of heaven illuminated with countless myriads of 'planetary fires!' such a night, my Fanny, as some of those in which we used, during the first year of my marriage, to be induced by Desmond to wander in the coppice-walks and shrubberies that surrounded the lawn at Linwell.[71] — Alone, as I am here, I must not, venture so far from the house. But I may traverse the grass-plat before it, and listen to the nightingales, of which numbers salute me every evening with their song from the opposite woods — their delicious notes, softened and prolonged by the echos from the bridge and the water. One, only one, seems to have taken up his lonely abode in the garden here — Alas! I could be romantic enough to fancy it the spirit of some solitary and deserted being like myself, that comes sympathetically to hear and sooth my sorrows.

Let me tell them, then, to this visionary visitant, rather than to my Fanny; and now, in wishing her a good night, wish too, that her slumbers may bring to her mind, without disturbing it, the image of her

GERALDINE

LETTER XV

TO MISS WAVERLY

6th June, 1791

The opportunities I have of sending to the post are so few, my dear sister, that though I write whenever I have any thing to say which I imagine you wish to hear, or whenever it relieves my heavy heart to pour out its sorrows to you, yet I know my letters do not reach you regularly; and I have, from the same cause, the mortification of waiting some days for yours, after they arrive at the post-office of the neighbouring town.

You may, perhaps, be anxious to know if I have again heard of the stranger whose notice of my children seemed so extraordinary, and, I own, for the following day or two gave me some uneasiness. — He was probably, however, only a traveller of taste, invited by the beauty of this part of the country at this season, to make an abode of a day or two at some little neighbouring public-house or cottage; a circumstance which my landlord here tells me is not unfrequent. It was, perhaps, the loveliness of my little ones that attracted his attention, and not any previous acquaintance with their family; and for the familiarity with which he seemed to treat them, much of it possibly is the mere fancy of Peggy, who, though a very good girl, is as likely as any other to add to a story she tells, from a natural love of the marvellous. — I say thus much about this adventure, lest what I told you in my last letter should raise any uneasy ideas in your mind; for I know you have a hundred fancies about Colonel Scarsdale, and suppose that he is a sort of modern Lovelace: but, believe me, my Fanny, that character does not exist now; there is no modern man of fashion, who would take a hundredth part of the trouble that Richardson makes Lovelace take, to obtain Helen herself, if she were to return to earth.[72] And Scarsdale is a man so devoted to the acquisition of fame in his own style of life, that with *my* change of fortune, *his* pursuit ends. — It would have added something to the glories he already boasts in the annals of gallantry, if he could have carried off Verney's wife from her husband, her children, and her fame; but now that she is banished from the circles where she was talked of and followed — now that she is forgotten by the idle flutterers who surrounded her for a few months, she is too humble, and too inconsiderable, to be any object to such a man, and is, she thanks Heaven, sheltered by her obscurity from his insolent pretensions.

I have little more to say to-day, but that my precious William is better, and my apprehensions about him subside again. — I impatiently wait to hear how my brother's love affair proceeds, though, in my last letter, I omitted to mention his name, engaged as I was by the multiplicity of trifles; but this is not owing to any indifference about him. — I love my brother, and should rejoice in his being happily married; though he seems to have forgotten that he has a sister, whose comfortless destiny should at least secure to her the common civilities of life from her own family, if they cannot spare her any share of their affections. — Alas! how easily do common minds make to themselves excuses for forsaking and forgetting the unhappy! — Were I again to appear (which Heaven forbid!) in those societies whose members now think me sunk below them — what insulting pity — what contemptuous condolences I should receive! — In proportion as I was once thought the object of envy, should I now be that of ill-concealed triumph and malignant scorn, under the semblance of sympathy and concern. — When these thoughts arise, you cannot imagine how well pleased I am, that I am here.

> —————————————————'Are not these woods
> More free from peril than the envious court*?'

And, as I hide myself in them, I regret nothing but your company, my sister; and yet I ought not to wish you with me, when you are where the young and happy ought to be, amid that world which has, at your age, and with your unblighted prospects, so many charms.

Farewell, for the present! it is a delicious evening, and I will now venture to walk out and enjoy it. — How forcibly every such scene brings to my mind our morning walks, our evening rambles in Kent, and the pleasant little trios we used to make with Mr Desmond, who has so much taste, and so much genuine enthusiasm! — I wonder whether he is as much gratified by the charms of Spring at St Germains, as he used to be in England. I should rather fear not; at least, that he

---

* Shakespeare.[73]

is less likely there to find companions who understand him, and can participate his pleasure: for the French ladies in general have, I believe, very little notion of that species of delight that arises from contemplating the simple beauties of nature. — A few days will soon make it a twelvemonth since I saw Desmond, and of that time he has sacrificed more than half to his disinterested friendship to my brother. But I have repeated this so often to myself, that, perhaps, I have as often obtruded it upon your recollection.

I have found in the opposite woods one of the most singular and most beautiful spots that I ever saw. It is a little hill, or rather three or four hills that seem piled together, though the inequality of their forms is concealed and adorned by the variety of trees with which they are covered. Many of these are ever-greens, such as holly and yew; and just where their shade is the darkest, they suddenly recede, and from a stony excavation bursts forth a strong and rapid stream of pure and brilliant water, which pours directly down the precipice, and is lost in the trees that crowd over it. — A few paces higher up, from a bare projection of rock, darts forth another current equally limpid; and having made itself a little bason, which it fills, it hastens over the rugged stones, that are thus worn by its course, and, dashing down the hill for some time in a different direction, meets the former stream: united, they make a considerable brook, and hasten to join the Wye; not, however, till two or three other little wandering currents, that arise still nearer the summit of this rocky eminence, which seems to abound in springs, have found their way to the same course. — Of these unexpected gushes of water you hear the murmurs often without seeing from whence they arise; so thickly is the wood interwoven over the whole surface of the wild hill. A narrow, and hardly visible path, however, winds around it, quite to its summit, which is less clothed than the rest, and where, on two roots, that the hand of time, rather than the art of man, has twisted into a sort of grotesque, rustic chair, I sit; and, listening to the soothing sounds of the water, as it either steals or rushes beneath, I can see through the boughs great part of the farm-house I inhabit, and nearer, the grey smoke of cottages without the wood, curling among the mingled foliage. — It is, my dear sister, in this sequestered nook that I am going to wander, and to think of you as the most pleasing contemplation in which I can indulge myself: once more, then, a good night.

Gracious heaven! — Am I in the delirium of one of those fever-ish visions, which, with undescribable sensations of pain, pleasure, and wonder, reconcile, for a moment, impossibilities; or am I really awake? — I have seen him. — Desmond, whom I believed to be in France! whom I had not the least idea of meeting in this remote country! whom I even doubted whether I should ever see again, that I might say how truly sensible I was of the debt of gratitude I owed him! — But I will try to recollect myself enough to relate, instead of exclaiming —— Yesterday evening, I had finished, as I believed, my letter to you, and had seen my children put to bed. It was not yet eight o'clock; and the sun, though sunk beneath the opposite hills, tinged the whole landscape with that rosy light which it is impossible to describe. I did not take a book with me, as I usually do when I walk alone, because it was so late that I meant, instead of saunter-ing, as I love to do, to take my walk and return. However, when I reached the wood, I was tempted, by the perfect tranquillity of every thing around me — the fragrant scents that floated in the air — the soothing song of innumerable birds — and the low murmurs of the water, to gratify myself with a view of my favourite little hill, which I had never yet seen in an evening. — I reached the top; when, stretched on the ground, his head resting on his arm (from which a book seemed to have fallen) as it hung over the branch of the rude chair I before described to you, I saw a gentleman who appeared to be sleeping — I had no idea of his face, for his hat and his hair con-cealed it; nor did I stay to see if I recollected his figure; but, con-cluding that this was the same person who had been met by the children, I was returning very hastily, from an impulse that had more of fear in it than his general appearance ought to have raised, when his dog, which lay by him, ran forward towards me: at the same mo-ment the gentleman raised his head. — I saw Desmond leap from the ground, and, though in as much confusion as I was, he instantly approached me — 'Mrs Verney!' was all he said; and even to that I had nothing for a moment to reply, till he added — 'I am afraid I have alarmed you.' — 'You have indeed,' answered I — 'for to meet any one here was very unexpected — To meet you!' — I did not know what I would say; but he seemed now to have recovered himself, and finished the sentence for me — 'was more unexpected still!' — 'It was indeed, for I thought you were in France.'

He gave no answer to this, nor did he account for his being in a part of the country where I don't remember to have heard he had any acquaintance or connexions; but, simply begging of me to forgive the momentary alarm he had involuntarily been the occasion of, he said, 'Since I *have* had, however unexpectedly, the happiness of meeting you, Madam, will you allow me to have the honour of attending you to your home?' — I hesitated, I know not why; and then said, 'Certainly.' — We began slowly to descend the winding and steep path, which is crossed by roots, and interrupted by pieces of rocks. It was now, from the lateness of the hour, also obscure; and he, of course, offered me his arm, which I accepted indeed, but not with that easy confidence I used to have in our early rambles three years ago. —— It was now that I first observed a black crape round his neck, in which he flung his right arm, while he assisted me to descend with his left — I shuddered, but I could make no remark on that circumstance. He seemed no more disposed to converse than I was; and we were silent till we reached the orchard, surrounding a cottage, through which the path leads by a stile through the meadows, and over the bridge. He seemed to know the way, as if he had been long accustomed to it. — I then disengaged my arm, and he went first: but, in reaching the other side of the stile, my foot slipped, and I should have fallen; but Desmond, who had advanced three or four steps, flew back and caught me. He trembled so, that it was impossible to help remarking it. I feared that in endeavouring to save me, he had hurt his arm; and I almost involuntarily expressed my apprehensions. — He assured me he had not received the slightest injury, and again offered me his left arm, on which I again leaned, and, with very little conversation, and that little consisting of broken and incoherent sentences, we at length reached the house.

There were candles in my little parlour, and the table was prepared for my simple supper. I asked him, of course, to partake of it; he replied, in a low voice, that he seldom supped at all, but could not refuse to sit down. — Peggy came in to wait, and he placed himself opposite to me.

It was then, and not till then, my Fanny, that I observed the extraordinary alteration in the countenance of Desmond. He has lost all that look of health and vivacity which we used to remark — pale, thin, almost to emaciation; his eyes still radiant indeed, but expressing dejection; or if they, for a moment, assumed any other look, it was that of anxiety. He spoke sometimes very low, at others with that sort of quickness which is observable when people wish to end embarrassing conversation. And when I mentioned his wanderings, or his friends in France (which I at length collected courage to do), he gave me slight answers, and changed the conversation as soon as possible.

As this evasion of every topic that led him to speak of his foreign connexions was every moment more striking, the cause of it at length occurred to me. — I trust I am not suspicious, or inquisitive; and certainly am neither desirous of prying into the actions of my friends, nor disposed to blame those of Desmond, to whom I owe so much: but I have now no doubt that this reserve arises from his having been accompanied to England by Madame de Boisbelle; and having taken, in this neighbourhood, some residence for her, on account of its being so retired. If this is the case, he was probably hurt and distressed in meeting here one of his acquaintance; and it accounts at once for his manner, which, though I cannot well describe it, appears very extraordinary.

This idea no sooner struck me, than I felt hurt at the pain I thus unintentionally had given him, and particularly at having asked him, as I had done some minutes before, and merely for something to say, how long he proposed staying in this part of England? an enquiry which he answered, after some hesitation, by saying it was uncertain.

As I now dreaded that every question, however apparently inconsequential, might lead him to suppose me impertinently curious, we both sat silent; and I believe he was meditating how to put an end to an interview which was, perhaps, at once tedious and distressing to him: yet I observed, when I dared observe his countenance, that he looked at me with eyes full of concern and pity, which I impute to the goodness of his nature — He felt sorry to see me in a situation so different from that which I was placed in when our acquaintance began; an acquaintance that, I cannot endure to think, has been productive to him only of personal and mental uneasiness.

At length, after an hour and a half, the only time of my life that I ever passed in Desmond's company unpleasantly, he arose to go, and, with a solemnity that yet had more dejection than formality in it, he said he must wish me a good night. — I was on the point of asking him a very natural question, 'If he had far to go home?' but I checked myself, and did not increase, by any question, the embarrassment he seemed to be under, when, hesitating and faltering, he said, 'May I be permitted, Madam, to pay my respects to you once more before I — — May I be allowed the honour of waiting on you once again?' — I had surely no pretence to refuse this: he knows I am never engaged; and he knows that I am, or ought to be, more obliged to him than to any other human being. — I could not assuredly, therefore, decline or evade what I however wished he had not asked; as I not only see him so changed as he is, both in appearance and in spirits, with concern; but fear, from his deportment, that the attention which he perhaps thinks himself under the necessity of shewing me, may put him into difficulties with the lady to whom he has attached himself. I have other uneasy sensations about it; but, however, I could only say, in answer to the permission he requested, that I should always be glad of Mr Desmond's company, whenever he would so far honour me. — He sighed, and thanked me; but added, 'I shall not, Madam, intrude much on your indulgence, for in a very few days ———' He hesitated again, and I could not help repeating, 'In a few days! do you leave the neighbourhood in a few days?' — 'I believe so,' said he — 'Yes; I believe I *must* go within a few days: Will you then suffer me to call to-morrow? and may I be gratified with a sight of your children?' — I said, 'Yes.' And then, without naming the hour at which he would call, he left me.

Thus, my Fanny, ended this very extraordinary interview; for, extraordinary it certainly is. — I know not from whence Mr Desmond last came, or whither he is going — I know not where he has taken up his present abode. — I could not, however, forbear marking from my window the way he took when he left me; and, as long as I could discern his figure through the obscurity of the night, he seemed to return through the fields, and over the bridge, the same road as he came with me. — I left the window (from whence, I hope, there was nothing wrong in my thus observing him) — I left it only to retire to my pillow and my tears, which flowed more than usual this evening; yet I know not why, unless the suddenly meeting an acquaintance, a friend, who has certainly a great claim to my gratitude and good wishes, had more than usually fatigued my spirits; for, as to the rest, why should I be thus agitated by a circumstance in which I have no immediate interest? — Whether Mr Desmond be travelling through this country alone, or whether he is retired hither with any companion, what have I do to with it? or why should I think of him farther than ever to follow him with my grateful wishes?

It is now eleven o'clock. I have left my bed since a quarter past five, for to sleep was impossible. Ever since the hour when *I thought* it probable Mr Desmond (who knows I am an early riser) might come, I have been expecting him; but, perhaps, he has changed his mind, or his friend may have engaged him. — It is market-day at the neighbouring town, and I have an opportunity of sending this letter, or rather this enormous pacquet, to the post, by my honest farmer, who has just sent in to say he is going. I therefore seal it, and will endeavour to reason away this ridiculous flutter, which the idea of a visiter gives me (probably because I have been of late so little used to company), and sit quietly down to finish a view I am doing for you, of the prospect from my windows; in the progress of which, hitherto, I have, contrary to my usual custom, pleased myself.

Farewell, my dear sister! — Perhaps my commissioner may, on his return from town, bring me what would now be the most soothing and consoling to my spirits, a letter from my Fanny.

GERALDINE VERNEY

LETTER XVI

TO MR BETHEL

From Bridge-foot, a small cluster of Cottages
in Herefordshire, June 8th, 1791

When a man knows, my dear Bethel! that he is acting like a fool, the most usual way is to keep it to himself, and to endeavour to persuade the world that he is actually performing the part of a wise man: but I, who am, as you have often said, a strange, eccentric being, and not much like any other, am going to do just the reverse of this, and to acknowledge my folly without even trying at palliation. Nay, I accuse myself of having the *appearance* of something much worse than folly, which is ingratitude to you: but, as this is in appearance only, it is the former accusation alone to which I shall plead; and much eloquence will be necessary to supply the defect of *reason*, which I know you will think my conduct betrays, when you see my letter dated from such a place, and are told that it is within half a mile of the residence of Geraldine. — Have patience, however, till I can relate the cause of all this; and though I was neither bred to the bar, where, for money, our learned in the laws undertake

'To make the worser seem the better reason*,'

nor am *naturally* endowed with the faculty of doing so, I shall at least be able, I think, to convince you, that no motive injurious either to my friendship towards you, or my more tender affection for Geraldine, has led me to visit her in a way that may be called clandestine, or to conceal from you my journey and my intentions; though, to say the truth, I did not mean to inform you of it till I saw you; nor should I have done so, but for the accidental circumstances of having first met her lovely children, and then her lovely self.

'How then,' you ask, 'were you concealed in her immediate neighbourhood, without any intention of either? — Incredible folly!' — Such, however, *were* my intentions. — I allow, if you please, all the folly; but I insist upon it, that there was no sort of harm in such a gratification as I proposed to myself, by which myself only (if romantic attachment can hurt a man) was alone likely to be hurt, and for which, therefore, I should hold myself accountable to no one, my dear friend! — not even to *you*, if I did not feel that your sincere and generous attachment to me deserves all that confidence which I can repose in you, in matters that relate only to *myself*. — Your last letter describing the total ruin of Verney, and the dispersion of his family, completed the measure of that uneasiness I had long sustained on account of Geraldine. It was in vain I endeavoured to reason myself out of it. I find that seven-and-twenty is not the age of reason, or at least where the heart is so deeply concerned. — There were a hundred causes why I had rather have gone, at the moment I set out, to Nova Scotia, or even to Nova Zembla, than to England. But the idea of Geraldine deserted in distress! — of Geraldine in poverty and sorrow! obliterated every other consideration in the world; and within four-and-twenty hours after the receipt of your last letter, which found me at St

---

*   Milton.[74]

Germains, I set out post, without taking even Warham with me, or saying whither I was going; and in six-and-thirty hours afterwards was at Dover, from whence I made my way, as quickly as I could, to the post-town in Herefordshire, near which I had learned (it matters not by what means) that Geraldine had, with her children, fixed her humble abode.

I told the people at the inn where I put up, that, being in an ill state of health (an assertion to the truth of which my figure and countenance bear some testimony), I was directed by my physicians to travel; and had been advised to bend my way towards Wales, staying some little time at any place where the face of the country appeared agreeable, or the air salubrious. — I added, that I should stay, perhaps, a week or ten days in this neighbourhood; but as it was not for their interest to find out a private lodging for me, I applied, for that purpose, to the hair-dresser, who professed, over his shop-window, to 'dress ladies and gentlemen in the very newest London fashion.'

This very intelligent personage informed me, that what I wanted was at present somewhat hard to be met with; for, that 'the pleasantest, and almost only lodging *near* that town (which was, however, about six miles off, or rather better) was lately taken by a lady and her children, for a year certain.' — I affected to be struck with the description he gave of the pleasantness of the situation, on the banks of the Wye; and asked, if he thought any cottage in the neighbourhood of the house he described, could afford me a bed-chamber? I cared not how humble and plain, if it were merely clean; — saying farther, that as health was my pursuit, money was no object to me; and that, therefore, I would give any person who could find such an accommodation for me, a handsome present for their trouble; and would hire the apartment for a month certain, though I possibly might not remain in it a week.

My honest barber, whose zeal for my service was now completely awakened, set forth immediately to see what could be done for me; and, in the afternoon, returned to say, that, in a very clean cottage, he had found a decent bed-chamber, which I instantly set off on foot to see — walking not much like an invalid. I found the humble thatched cottage was one among a group of five or six, which are situated among orchards, at the foot of that range of woody hills which are immediately opposite the farm-house inhabited by Geraldine. — There was no ceiling to the room but the thatch and rafters, and no curtains to the bed; yet the chamber was clean, and I determined to take immediate possession of it.[75] — I therefore ratified my bargain, to the great delight of the old man and his wife, who alone inhabited the cottage; and having satisfied my conducter, even beyond his expectation, I engaged him to return to the town for my baggage, and to attend me every day with a lad from the inn, from whence I am supplied with provisions.

I then retired to my lowly couch, and slept better than I have done since the receipt of your letter, in the certainty that, by the rising sun of the next morning, I should see the house where the loveliest and most injured woman on the earth hides her undeserved misfortunes.

You will believe me, my friend, when I protest to you, that this satisfaction, and that of witnessing her real situation (which I hoped to do without her knowing I was near her), were the only gratifications I proposed to myself: for many days I enjoyed it, and was content; nor did I voluntarily seek any other satisfaction.

'There are,' says St Preux, in those inchanting Letters of the incomparable Rousseau, 'but two divisions of the world, that where Julie is, and that where she is not.'[76] — I forget the French, and I have not the book here. To the force of the sentiment, however, I bear witness. — *To me* the world is divided into only two parts; or rather, to me, it is all a blank where Geraldine is not. Yet, my friend, is this declaration no contradiction to what I often, and particularly of late, asserted, that I have *now* (if indeed I ever was weak enough to indulge it) not the remotest hope of her ever rewarding an attachment with which, as I know it is wrong, I wish not that she should *even be acquainted*. — But, if you have ever truly loved, can you, Bethel, blame me for indulging that delicious, and surely that blameless sensation, which is derived from watching over the peace and safety of a beloved object, from whom we do not even hope a return? While I could open my eyes in a morning and see the sun's first beams enlighten the opposite heath, and fall on the roof of Geraldine's habitation, making its high clusters of heavy, antique chimneys, visible among the firs and elms that surround it — I used to say to myself, '*There she is!* — There, she will soon awaken to fulfil her maternal duties; to cultivate, to strengthen, or adorn the purest of minds by some useful or elegant occupation. — She is, if not happy, at least tranquil; and now and then, perhaps, bestows a thought, and a kind wish, on her friend Desmond.'

Indeed, Bethel, with this satisfaction (romantic, and even ridiculous as it would, I know, be thought by those who could not understand the nature of my affection for Geraldine) I should have been perfectly content; and having for a little while indulged myself in it, I should have sought you at Bath, have made you a confession of my folly, and then, after having given a few days to friendship, have again gone back to France; for England is not my country, when I can hear only, in whatever company I go into, of Geraldine's unhappiness, and the folly, extravagancies, and utter ruin of her husband.

This was my project: I lingered, however, from day to day, finding happiness, I could not easily determine to relinquish, in catching, now and then, at a window, which I fancied to be that of the room where she slept, the distant view of a figure which I persuaded myself was hers. — The window was only partly seen; the tall elms, which grow round a sort of court immediately before the house, hid it half; and though, when the setting sun played on the casement, I could more distinctly see it, I found, that if I would really satisfy myself with the certain view of Geraldine, I must seek some spot, where, from its elevation, I could, by means of a small pocket telescope, have an uninterrupted view of these windows.

I confined myself, however, to the house all day. — You know I never am weary of solitude, nor am ever destitute of employment: these days, therefore, appeared neither tedious nor unpleasant, since, at their close, I was to be engaged in seeking for the means of satisfying my wishes; and since I could, as they passed, look out of my low and narrow casements towards the habitation of Geraldine, and whisper to myself — '*She is there.*'

At length, in the woods that skirt the feet of these hills, which would, about London, be accounted inaccessible mountains, I found a little shady knoll, to which the gush of innumerable streams of water attracted me. — I ascended by the almost perpendicular path, which seems to have been traced only by boys in their excursions after birds, or by the sheep that sometimes feed here; and reaching the top, I had the satisfaction to find, that though it was surrounded on all sides by trees, so as to form the most perfect concealment, they were low towards the top; and that a little rocky crag, that hung over the twisted roots of an old thorn and a blighted ash, afforded me a view of many of the windows of Geraldine's residence; at a greater distance, indeed, than from my cottage, but much less obscured by the intervening objects. — Here, then, I resolved to pass some part of all the few days that I had determined to stay here.

Four days since, I was returning, about one o'clock, from this my morning occupation, when the heat of the morning, and the freshness of the grass in that part of the wood through which I was passing, induced me to throw myself on the ground, and continue the perusal of a book I had with me, on which I was extremely intent, when I heard the prattle of children: but as I had often seen such little rustic wanderers in the woods, I heeded not the circumstance; till suddenly, Flora running forward, I heard an infant scream at her approach. — I raised my eyes, and saw a maid-servant with the two elder children of Geraldine! — I started up to prevent the little girl's being more alarmed by the dog; and as I wished not to betray myself, I enquired the name of the children — yet in a way so confused, that I believe the servant thought my manner very strange. — I supposed it impossible, after an absence of twelve months, that George could recollect me; but he certainly did, though my name was no longer familiar to him; for, after looking at me earnestly a moment, he returned my embraces, and even hung round my neck. — What delight! to press to my heart this lovely fellow, so dear to me on account of his mother. — I was so charmed with him, and with the eagerness he shewed to continue with me, that I am afraid I more than once forgot my precaution: however, the children at length left me. I imagined the servant would conclude, that it was some person of the neighbourhood, and would think no more about it — I continued my usual rambles therefore in the woods, but not at those hours when it was probable I should again meet them.

Convinced that Geraldine was less uncomfortable in her new situation than my fears had led me to suppose; having been now above a week in the neighbourhood, and fearing my remaining there much longer might raise some suspicions, that I would not for millions of worlds excite — I began to think of quitting it, and had once or twice determined to stay only *one* day longer; yet, when the day of departure came, put it off till the next. — But on Thursday I resorted to the spot where I usually passed the evening. The weather was uncommonly lovely — I had, during the preceding day, taken my walk, at an hour when I fancied Geraldine was at her dinner, round her garden, and was effectually concealed by a thick hedge of cut evergreens; but I was happy enough to be mistaken, as to her hour of dining — She came out with her children — I saw her within ten paces of me — She spoke cheerfully — I heard once more that enchanting voice — I dared hardly breathe, lest she should be alarmed; but as soon as I could escape unperceived, I crossed among the high furze and hollow ways of the common, and returned home by a road remote from that which led from her residence to my cottage.

The delicious impression, however, which the sight of Geraldine had left on my mind, the uncommon beauty of the evening, united to that of the scene, contributed to sooth my mind. — I sat down, and began to read; but every thing that took my thoughts from her was insipid — I let my book fall, and fell into a *reverie*. — But I own, my dear friend, that the pleasing dreams in which I was indulging myself were interrupted by the recollection of your frequent remonstrances, and particularly by that question which you have so often repeated — 'What I meant by all this?' — My heart, however, could answer without hesitation, that I meant no injury to any human being — Nor, unworthy and undeserving as Verney is, would I wish to rob him of the affections of his wife, admitting it possible he could possess them. — Thus far my conscience clearly acquitted me (would to heaven it could do so in every other circumstance of my life!): and I had settled it with myself, that while I avoided giving any such evidence of my attachment to her, as might tend to cast a reflection on the fair and unimpeached fame of the lovely woman for whom I felt it, I might yield to its influence with impunity. — I know you will declare against any such inference; but I had convinced myself I was right, and lamented that I had ever left England, under the idea of curing myself of a passion which constituted the charm of existence; since, by doing so, I have, without losing whatever uneasiness may occasionally embitter that attachment, created for myself others, which will not soon be dissipated — In these sort of contemplations I had some time been lost, when suddenly my dog roused me. — I looked up, and saw Geraldine herself, who, having perceived me, was hastily retreating from the sight of a stranger in a place so remote.

Could I, Bethel, then avoid speaking to her? — It was impossible — I flew forwards to meet her — I apologized for the alarm I had occasioned her — I entreated leave to attend her home; though, when she accepted my assistance to conduct her down the declivity, on the summit of which we met, I trembled so that I could with difficulty support myself. — She seemed amazed at meeting me; but after some time recovered herself, and asked, in the way of conversation, several of those questions, which, from any other person, or in any other situation, would have been indifferent: but I could not answer them with the ease she put them; and I am sure I behaved like an idiot; for on a sudden she grew cold and reserved, and, I fancied, wished me away, though I could not collect courage enough to go. — At length, conscious of the foolish figure I made, sitting silently opposite to her, and afraid of entering into any conversation, lest it should lead to topics I could not determine to speak upon, I collected resolution enough to wish her a good night, and ask leave to see her again to-day. — This she granted in the same distant way that she would have granted it to a common acquaintance; and I left her, half frantic, to think that I am perfectly indifferent to her, though, three hours before, I was declaring to myself that I harboured not a wish to be otherwise.

It is now near eleven o'clock — I find I have an opportunity of sending this to the post — I dispatch it, therefore, and hasten to take one last look, for such, indeed, I mean it should be; and if I can gain courage to talk to her as a sister, who can feel for and pity my errors and my weakness, I think that, whatever I suffer in tearing myself from her, I shall yet, after I have once got over the pangs of an interview, which may be the last I shall enjoy for years, be more easy than I have been for many months. — Adieu, dear Bethel — I feel as anxious as if the fate of my whole life depended on the next three hours; but perhaps it does.

Yours faithfully,

LIONEL DESMOND

P.S. I shall not, certainly, stay here above a day longer — I think not — as, after I have taken leave of her, upon what pretence can I linger in the neighbourhood? Yet, as I have not determined, whether I shall reach you at Bath by the cross-country road, or go first to London, and for a day or two into Kent; in short, as I have not determined what I shall do, and, probably, shall fluctuate *à la* Waverly till the hour of my setting forth — you may as well direct hither; because I shall leave orders at the post-house, whither my letters are to be forwarded. Who said, that sorrow had anticipated the injury of time; and that the beautiful and once admired Geraldine had lost all her personal attractions? — To me, she appears a thousand times lovelier than ever; and were it merely her form and face to which my heart yields homage, it would be more than ever her captive.

LETTER XVII

TO MISS WAVERLY

June 9, 1791

I have seen Mr Desmond again, my Fanny; and if he had before a claim to my regard, it is now heightened into as much esteem as I can feel for any human being. — Yes! he is unhappy; and it is to me, as to a sister and a friend, he communicates his unhappiness. — Ah! what would I not do to relieve from its solicitude, that noble and ingenuous heart, which places such confidence in me? — But of this enough. — I only say thus much, to vindicate him from my unjust and improper suspicions, of having come here clandestinely, on account of the foreign lady, of whom we heard so many idle reports. — Desmond is alone, and quits this neighbourhood to-day. — He talks of visiting his friend Bethel, who is at Bath; and soon afterwards of returning to France. — If he goes to Bath, you will see him; but I, perhaps, shall see him no more for some years — as those years, with me, are, probably, to pass in this remote solitude; where, it would be violating the common rules which the world expects us to observe, were I to receive his visits, how innocent and brotherly soever they would assuredly be.

While I yet write, he crosses the bridge on horseback; and George, who is astonishingly fond of him, has run out, with his maid, to meet him. — Desmond gets off; he puts the dear little boy on his horse; and, with one arm round him, he makes Peggy lead the horse forward. — I hear the laugh of infantine delight even hither. — There is nothing, Fanny, in my opinion, so graceful, so enchanting, in a young man, as this tenderness towards children. — It becomes every man, but none more than Desmond; who is never so amiable in my eyes, as when he is playing with George — and my little girl, she now lisps out his name; and, though she has seen him only twice, is a candidate for a seat on his knee; and turns towards him those sweet blue eyes, without that pensive look that her delicate countenance generally expresses; as if she knew, even in babyhood, her fate to be marked with sorrow. — But my noisy boy, and his friend, are at the door. I hear Desmond say, he is come to bid him good-bye; and the child enquires, why he goes, and when he will come again. — I must go to wish him a good journey, and deliver him from the little, wild interrogatories of his playfellow. —

He is gone! and I feel ridiculously low — I say, ridiculously, though, I trust, I do not give way to an improper sentiment. — But why should it be wrong to admire and esteem an excellent and amiable man, from whom I have received more than brotherly kindness? — Why, indeed, should I question the propriety of this regard, because I am married? — Does that prevent our seeing and loving excellence wherever found? — and why should it? — To disguise these sentiments, would be to acknowledge them to be criminal — I rather glory in avowing them, because I am conscious they are just, pure, and honourable. — Why, indeed, should I hide, or apologize, for the tears I even now shed, when I think that I may never see Desmond again? — What a treasure is a friend, so disinterested, so noble-minded, as he is! And why should I not regret him? — How soothing, to a sick heart in solitude and sadness, is the voice of kindness, administering the consolations of reason and good sense, dignified with all the graces of a polished mind! — Such have I heard from Desmond, in our last conference; and can I help regretting, that I shall hear them no more?

But it is not to you, my Fanny, I ought to excuse myself (if, indeed, it could be necessary at all) for my regard, nay, I will call it my affection, for our admirable friend — not, though I feel his departure as a privation, just at this moment, can I lament having seen him. — I find that there is a possibility that I may be of use to one of his friends, in some disagreeable circumstance; and with what delight shall I embrace an opportunity of being useful to any of his acquaintance or connexions! — Farewel, my dear sister — I am unable to write a long letter to-day. — I will go to my books, and to my walk in the wood; for those are resources that, I find, sooth me to tranquillity; while the complaints of George, that Mr Desmond is gone, and that he shall not ride any more, and his little innocent questions, when he will come again? and if he is gone to see papa? quite overcome my spirits. I will write a longer letter in a day or two, though I shall have now very little to say.

June 10th, Six in the Evening

What is to become of me now; — An express from the neighbouring post town, accompanied by a French servant, has just delivered me the enclosed letter from Mr Verney — I enclose it; for I have not strength or time to copy it. — Oh! Fanny, what shall I — ought I to do? — In truth, I know not! — How unfortunate, that Desmond is gone, and that I cannot have the benefit of his advice! — Gracious heaven! what does fate intend to do with this miserable, persecuted being?

LETTER XVIII*

Paris, May 22, 1791

MY DEAR,

My very worthy friends, Monsieur le Duc de Romagnecourt, and Monsieur le Chevalier de Boisbelle, are this day setting off for England on a journey, relative to the affairs of the King of France, their master. They are returning to Paris directly; and, having heard me express a wish to see you here, have undertaken to escort you over; and the Duke himself attends you with this. — I desire therefore, that you will set off with him, as soon as you conveniently can. — As to the children, I think, travelling with them will be inconvenient to you; and should suppose your mother would take them for the time you are abroad; or, perhaps, you might leave them very safe in the care of their servants. — You will do as you like about bringing servants for yourself; but, I think, you will find English women only encumbrances, and may hire French maid servants here: as to men, as we shall live altogether at the Duc de Romagnecourt's, his *suite* of servants will be ours.[77] I shall expect the

---

*   Enclosed in the foregoing.

pleasure of your arrival with impatience, where all things are going on well for the suppression of the present vile proceedings.

> I am, my dear,
> Yours affectionately,
>
> RICHARD VERNEY.

I repeat my question, my sister — What ought I to do? — Good heaven! what an inconsiderate man is Mr Verney; and, I am sorry to add, how unfeeling! — Leave my children! — Accompany strangers to Paris! — The former I will not do; and surely I ought not to do the latter: but on something I must determine; for, I understand, from the French servant, to whom I have been speaking, that this Duke is actually waiting at the inn, at the neighbouring town, and expects to be asked hither. — What wildness — what madness, in Mr Verney, to propose such a scheme! — Whither can I turn me? — Oh! would to heaven Desmond were not gone! — Write to me instantly — Yet how shall I put off my determination till I receive your answer? — how evade going? — for surely I ought not to go. — I believe it will be best to write a letter of excuse to this French nobleman; saying, how impossible it is for me to undertake a journey so suddenly. — Surely, Mr Verney cannot mean —— But I will not distract myself with useless conjectures, with suppositions more tormenting than the miserable realities. I send this to the town, on purpose to have it reach you by the earliest post; but I tremble so, that I fear it is hardly legible. The Chevalier de Boisbelle has not, I find, taken the trouble to come down hither with his noble friend. Surely he cannot be gone in search —— But, again, I am bewildered and distracted. — Pity, and instantly relieve, your very unhappy

> GERALDINE

LETTER XIX

TO MR BETHEL

> Ross, June 11, 1791

By this time, my friend, you expect me at Bath; and there I should certainly have been Monday next, if I had not been, by a most singular and unexpected accident, stopped here.

I took leave of Geraldine yesterday morning — I left her situated in a place, where if she enjoyed not that affluence and prosperity to which she has been accustomed, she was, I thought, tranquil and content. — She bade me adieu with the tenderest friendship, yet with that guarded expression of it that her situation demanded. I blessed her for the generous kindness she shewed me; I respected the reserve her circumstances made it proper for her to adopt. — I thought by her eyes — and were there ever eyes more expressive? that she was sorry to see me depart, yet knew that it was proper I should go. — Such sensations, in a more violent degree, I also felt. — To tear myself from her was now more difficult than I ever yet found it; but I knew it would be injurious to her to stay; and never did my propensity to self-indulgence conquer my sense of what I owed to the disinterested tenderness I bear her.

It was necessary then to go — and I dared not tell her how cruelly I felt the necessity; I affected some degree of cheerfulness; I played with her lovely boy, and tried to disguise, though I believe ineffectually, the contending sensations with which I was agitated — at length I left her. As I looked back, I beheld her at the window as long as she could see me, for the little fellow would not be content to quit it while I was in sight; and she held him in her arms. — At length the descent of the bridge hid her from my view — I then hastened on to this place, which is about ten miles from her habitation, for hither I had directed my portmanteau-trunk to be sent from my cottage; and here an horse, I had purchased some days before, waited for me — as I found it easier and pleasanter to have an horse of my own, now that I am able to ride, than to go in a post-chaise, or by any other conveyance. — I was then giving some directions about the forwarding my trunk, and was just going to mount my new purchase in the yard of the inn; when a berlin, apparently belonging to a foreigner of distinction, attended by three French or Swiss servants, drove to the door — an appearance which, though about the affairs of others I have not much curiosity, I own excited it strongly. — I stopped therefore, and saw alighting from the carriage a man about three or four-and-forty: he seemed to be a person of rank; but he wore, with some strong symptoms of his own consequence, that bewildered look which I have often observed in travellers who are unacquainted with the language and manners of the people they are among. — He spoke French to the landlord and the waiter, who not having the least idea of what he said, were as much distressed as he was. A person, however, soon after made his appearance, who seemed to be a sort of travelling companion, and who undertook to be his interpreter; but so miserably did he execute this office, that the honest Welchman and his people were more puzzled by his incomprehensible English, than they had before been by the French of his superior. — The shewy equipage, and the number of attendants, however, raised so much respect in the breasts of the landlord and his household, that they were extremely desirous of accommodating their great customers, if they could but find out what they wished for.

The first idea that occurs to an Englishman, on such an occasion, is a good substantial dinner. This, therefore, by such signs as he thought most likely to elucidate his meaning, the master of the inn proposed; and as there is a language in all countries by which eating or loving may be expressed, this was at length assented to. The gentleman attendant, or, as the landlord called him, t'other Mounseer, was shewn into the larder; which, though it was not quite so well furnished as that of the Bear at Bath, or some others of equal fame, yet appeared very satisfactory; and a certain number of dishes were ordered to be prepared, to the satisfaction of both parties.

As there was something excessively comique in the distress of the landlord and his wife, who could get no more intelligence from the strange servants than from their master, I could not forbear staying a little to be amused with it. I had nothing to do better, and was indifferent whether I set out before dinner or afterwards on my solitary journey: but I had yet another motive for staying than to witness this odd scene. I thought I might be of some use to these foreigners, by explaining to the people what they really wanted, or what house they came in search of; for they enquired for some place or person in the neighbourhood, about whom or which the people could comprehend nothing.

The landlord, however, seemed fully persuaded, that after so good a dinner as had been ordered, matters must clear up: infinite, therefore, was the bustling and fussing to have this ready. — The weather was hot; and the landlord, with his wig half off, a good round, plump Welch head, a fiery red waistcoat, and his pompadour Sunday coat, exerted his broad squat figure to the utmost; while his wife put on her best plaited cap with pink ribbands, a fine flourished shawl, and a pea-green flounced stuffed petticoat, under a flowered cotton gown drawn up; and notwithstanding this elegance (all to do honour to the British females before outlandish gentlemen), she was as anxiously superintending the roasting and boiling, as if she was providing in her common array for the ordinary of a market-day, on which the custom of her house depended.

At length the dinner was ready, and the landlord marched in with it: but he had not remained long in the room before he left it; and came puffing into that where I sat, in redoubled consternation. — 'Oh lord, Sir,' said he, 'do you understand French? — Lord, Sir, if I ben't quite, as one may say, at a non-plush; not one syllable more can I make out from that there gentleman that fancies how he talks English, than that he is come to fetch away some lady, that he calls Madam something, and will have it that she's here. — Lord, Sir, I'm quite floundered for my share, and knows no more what he'd be at than my little Nan there in the cradle. — I wish, for my share, folks would speak English; for why — such lingo as these foreigners use is of no service in the world, and only confounds people, ready to drive them crazy — Then they gabble so plaguy fast, that there's no catching a word by the way, even to guess a little by what they would be at. — Sir, if your honour has a smattering of their tongue, and would not think it too great a condescension, seeing they are Frenchmen, to make yourself known to them, 'twould be doing me a great service, if so be you'd just give me an item of their intentions — for my wife she's teasing me like a crazy woman, to know if they want beds made up, and if they do, whether their beds are made like as ours are? — I says to her, Why how the murrain now, Jenn, should I know? but I'll go ask yon gentleman, perhaps he can let us in to the right of the thing, which to be sure I should be glad of; for, Sir, they say that one of these is a duke.' — To stop this harangue, which seemed not otherwise to be near its conclusion, I assured my landlord that I knew a little of their tongue; and if he would order one of their servants to me, I would send them in a message expressive of my wish to be of use to them if in my power.

In consequence of this, their answer informed me, that the Duc de Romagnecourt was much honoured and flattered by my attention, and requested the happiness of seeing me. — Judge, dear Bethel, of the astonishment, the mixture of wonder, indignation and confusion, with which I learned that Mr Verney is become the intimate friend of this Duc de Romagnecourt; that it is with him he resides at Paris, and that it is under his escort he has sent for Geraldine to join him there.

If I had heard that I was, at one blow, reduced from affluence, to depend on the bounty of upstart greatness — dependence which of all other species is most hideous to my imagination; if I had been told that I had no longer a friend in the world, nay that Bethel himself had forsaken me, I think I should not have felt a sensation of greater anguish and amazement. — Monsieur D'Auberval enquired of me if I knew Madame Verney. Though I saw by the Duke's manner that *he* was the person interested, I knew not what to answer; and my embarrassment must have been visible, if they had not imputed part of it to my natural *diffidence* as an Englishman, and (as they thought) an Englishman of inferior rank; for they saw I had no servants with me, and seemed to wonder how a person who travelled in his own country without a *suite*, should be so perfectly versed in the language of theirs. — I now, however, understood the purposes of their journey; and under pretence of making some enquiries, I withdrew to consider of what I ought to do.

To interfere between Geraldine and her husband (I cannot write his name with patience) was at least improper — To give her notice that I was still near her, was impertinent, and making myself ridiculously of consequence in an affair where my protection was not perhaps requisite. This Duc de Romagnecourt — though he had the air of a veteran *debauché*, and though his conversation, little as I heard of it, confirmed the idea his appearance impressed — *might* be a married man, a man of respectability and honour — at least he was one to whom it was evident Mr Verney chose to entrust his wife; and what right had I to interfere?[78] How could I indeed do so, without its being known that I had been privately residing in her immediate neighbourhood, and encouraging a belief that I had some fancied authority to exert that influence which only a brother, or some very near relation, is supposed to have a right to exert? The more I considered the man, this Duc de Romagnecourt, his behaviour, his conversation; the more improper, nay impossible, it seemed for Geraldine to set out with him on such a journey: yet I did not see how I could, with propriety, save her from it by my direct interference. I therefore determined to

give the Duc de Romagnecourt the direction he requested me to procure for him; to trust the first reception of such a proposal to the sense
and prudence of Geraldine; and to await where I was the event of the
letter which, by a servant of his own, he sent her from her husband. It
contained, as the Duke informed me, an injunction to set off immediately with him for Paris. — I affected merely to know there was such
a lady as Madame Verney in the neighbourhood; and having now made
up my mind, I returned to these worthy friends of Verney's, gave them
the address they desired, and saw the French valet set out accompanied by a guide from the inn. — It is impossible to describe to you
what I felt while these men were absent; nor the effort with which I
supported the conversation that the Duc de Romagnecourt invited me
to engage in. — However, I commanded myself as much as possible,
as it was absolutely necessary to prevent any suspicion of my being
particularly interested for Mrs Verney; and I wished to lead him to
speak of her, which he perhaps would not have done with so little reserve, if he had suspected that I was aquainted with her.

It is not very difficult, after having seen a good deal of this best of
all possible worlds, to enter into much of a man's character, even from
a first interview. — I soon learned that the Duc de Romagnecourt was
a man of very high fashion and a very great fortune in France; that he
was very much confided in by the court, and of course extremely averse
to the claims of the people; that he execrated the struggle they had so
successfully made for their liberties, and now visited England with a
view to engage in favour of an opposite system (which, he said, would
soon have *le dessus** again), those among us whose interest it was most
effectually to crush every attempt at reform. He hinted, that in his
way through London he had succeeded in the negociation beyond his
hopes; and that he was to have a farther confirmation of the support
that had been promised him on his return, which he proposed immediately, *avec la charmante femme*, whom he expected to conduct.[79]

Proud, profligate, and perfidious; accustomed to entertain high
ideas of self-importance; and seldom finding any of his inclinations
resisted, because he had power and money to purchase their indulgence; the Duc de Romagnecourt was but little disposed to conceal

---

* The upper hand.

his principles or his views. — I learned, that when he was in England some few months since, he saw and admired Geraldine, to whom he had been introduced by her husband. I understood that Verney was under very great pecuniary obligations to this man, who now actually supports him in France; and the inference I drew from the knowledge I thus obtained of the character of the one, and the necessities of the other, was too dreadful. I recoiled with abhorrence from its immediate impression; but still it returned with undiminished anguish, and every word uttered by the Duc de Romagnecourt served only to confirm my apprehensions, and increase my uneasiness.

I determined that, whatever might be the consequence, no consideration upon earth should induce me to quit the country, while this most illustrious personage remained in it; and having made that resolution, I awaited, with as little anxiety as possible, the return of the messengers who were sent to Geraldine.

I had, indeed, very little occasion for any other exertion than that of patience; for the Duke, with all the forward consequence of which we accuse (and sometimes justly accuse) his countrymen, entered, nothing doubting my approbation, into a history of himself. — His rank, his fortune, his seats, were described: nor was he more guarded on the subjects of his politics or his amours.

In regard to the first, he was, I found, a most inveterate enemy to the revolution — deprecated the idea of any degree of freedom being allowed to the inferior ranks of men in any country; yet owned that he had, with the duplicity that was adopted by many of his compatriots, appeared to yield to a torrent they could not resist: but while they seemed to go with the stream, he hinted that measures were taking effectually to turn its course; and he triumphed in the discomfiture of the reptiles who had thus dared to aspire to the privilege of freemen; and saw, in his mind's eye, the leaders of this obnoxious *canaille* languishing out their miserable lives in the most dreary dungeons of the new-erected Bastile. Such was the colour of his politics. — His love, ever successful, and without thorns, was, as he represented it, *toujours couleur de rose*.[80] He scrupled not to hint, in terms that could not be misunderstood, that he had been very highly favoured by some of the most exalted ladies of the French court; that he was an universal favourite; and that there was no woman in this country, or his own, who could long remain insensible of his powers of pleasing, when he chose to make a point of gaining their favours. In this style — (and I listened to him with contempt that stifled my indignation) — he ran on for some time; till the wine he drank, much heavier than that he was usually accustomed to, began to have a very visible effect on him. — His companion, a Monsieur d'Auberval (though I understand another person came over with him), was even more inebriated than himself — And I learned, from what they together discoursed, that Verney had no intention of meeting his wife at Paris, but was going to Metz with some other French noblemen deeply embarked in the cause, whatever it is, that now engages their intriguing spirit; and that Mrs Verney was, after some stay at a magnificent seat of the Duc de Romagnecourt's, about five leagues from Paris, to follow her husband to Metz. — In short, dreadful as the confirmation of my fears was, I had no longer to doubt but that Geraldine was sold by the wretch who dares call her his wife.

Nothing but the reflection of what I owed to Geraldine could have restrained me from expressing the indignation I felt. — It was, however, necessary to dissemble. — I am a wretched hypocrite; nor could I even in this emergency have succeeded, if my companions had been very accurate observers. — At length, after some hours of such tortures as I thought it hardly possible to feel and exist, the men who had been sent to Geraldine with her husband's letter returned, and brought to Monsieur de Romagnecourt a note, written in French, of which this is the substance:

'Mrs Verney presents her compliments to the Duc de Romagnecourt; and as it is quite out of her power, on account of ill health, and from other circumstances, to leave England immediately — and equally so to quit her children, who must necessarily be very inconvenient companions to him, she must beg leave to decline the honour he intends her of a place in his carriage on his return to Paris; and the letter with which she takes the liberty of troubling him to Mr Verney, will account to him for her delaying her journey.

'Mrs Verney is sorry the small house and establishment she has here, make it impossible for her to receive the Duc de Romagnecourt at her present residence; and oblige her to take this method of thanking him for the civility he intended her.'

Bridge-foot Manor-farm,
June 11th, 1791

Though the purport of this note was exactly what I expected from the presence of mind and good sense of Geraldine, and though I was relieved from my first anxious apprehensions as to the terror she would be in on receiving it, I had yet but too many fears to contend with. I saw that Monsieur de Romagnecourt was mortified for the moment, but by no means so much discouraged as to desist from his pursuit; and after reading the note over twice or thrice, admiring the elegance of the writing, and the purity of the French, which, he said, was such as not one in a thousand of his countrywomen could have produced, he strutted about the room, though with somewhat less dignity than usual, for he could hardly stand; and then calling her a lovely prude, he determined to try, the next morning, what his own irresistible presence could do towards thawing the ice of this cold English beauty; and in this disposition I left him at one in the morning.

I saw that any attempt to dissuade him from such a scheme would be fruitless; and indeed I thought it best to let her positive and personal refusal convince him at once that his presumptuous and insolent proposal must be abortive. — Still it was painful to me, to think that Geraldine must be insulted by hearing it. — I knew, that elevated as her mind is above those frivolous and unworthy apprehensions to which women fancy it an amiable weakness to yield; yet, that such an address, from such a man, in a place where she was entirely unprotected, and the application coming from her husband, could not but be altogether most distressing to her. — Though I could not save her from it, it was possible to soften the shock, by giving her notice of it, and assuring her that there was within her reach a man who would lay down his life, rather then see her exposed to any unworthy treatment.

Sleep was with me entirely out of the question. — At the earliest dawn of the morning I was on horseback, and directed my course to my former residence, the cottage. — My ancient host and his wife were just making their homely breakfast, on brown bread and cyder, when I entered their kitchen. They were rejoiced, yet amazed, to see me; and I was compelled, once more, to have recourse to stratagem, to conceal the real motive of my second visit. — I told them I had found myself not so well after I left their house, and had therefore returned from Ross, to abide with them a few days longer.

I then considered in what way I should announce to Geraldine the visit she was to expect; and I concluded, that I would go to the house and send up my name. — Slowly and pensively I began this short walk. — I dreaded for her the uneasiness I was about to inflict: I dreaded for myself, that I should betray, in a way too unequivocally expressive of my sentiments, all I felt. — To tell her that I apprehended her husband had consigned her to another, was to intimate to her a degree of infamy almost too shocking to be imagined, and that of a man with whom she was perhaps to pass her life, and who was the father of her children: yet, to let her, for a moment, think of obeying him, which it was possible she might do, if it struck her as being her duty, was still more dreadful; and I saw there was nothing to be hoped for, but from that rectitude of understanding which I have always remarked in her. But I even dreaded the excess of those strict principles which I have often known to impel her, contrary to her own wishes, and her own sense of propriety, to follow the dictates of those who, conscious as she must be of their mental inferiority, had, she thought, a right to her compliance.

As soon as I could distinctly discern the windows, I saw they were already open, though it was yet early. — The morning was lovely; but my mind was too much occupied to suffer me to enjoy it. I knew Geraldine used to walk early in the little court that is before her apartments: but now there were no traces of her having been out; nor did I hear the voice of my little playfellow cheerfully greeting my return, as, I own, I had fondly anticipated. — All seemed mournfully silent: yet I thought I heard some footsteps moving softly about the house. I tapped at the old, thick, carved door with my stick; for there is no knocker — Nobody answered. — I repeated it — still no answer. — At length, after waiting near a quarter of an hour at the door, I lifted up the iron latch, and opened it. — I crossed the brick hall, but saw nobody. — The door of the parlour, where Geraldine usually sits, was a-jar; I pushed it gently open, and was struck with a group of figures, which exactly brought to my mind that which had been so forcibly and painfully impressed on it by my dream at Hauteville.

Geraldine was extended on an old-fashioned cane sopha, or what is I think called a settee, supported by cushions of green stuff; and with her right arm she clasped the youngest of her children, who appeared to my terrified imagination to be dying, as its head reposed on her bosom, while her tears fell slowly on the little pallid face: the girl, unconscious of her mother's anguish, sat upon the pillow behind her, playing with some flowers; and the eldest boy had seated himself by her in his own little chair, and was holding her left hand, and looking mournfully at her and his brother. Fixed to the spot by grief and amazement, I dared hardly breathe lest I should too suddenly alarm her. Her eyes were shut, and I only saw by the tears that fell from them, that she was not in a state of insensibility, for my entrance did not seem to disturb her — she supposed it to be the maid.

In a moment, however, the little boy turned round and saw me, and, screaming my name in an accent of transport, as he eagerly ran towards me, Geraldine opened her eyes, and repeated, 'Desmond! gracious heaven! Desmond!'

As soon as I could disengage myself from the caresses of the child, I approached. — 'I am destined,' said I in faltering accents, 'I am destined to disturb and alarm you: can you forgive me for this intrusion?' — I hesitated — I hardly knew what I would say. She gave me however her hand as she rose: involuntarily I could have pressed it, for the first time in my life, to my trembling lips, but I dared not; and I remained holding it still in mine, while she said, after a pause of a moment — 'Never was the sight of a friend more truly welcome.'

The cordiality of this reception (for her eyes, heavy as they were, confirmed the purport of her words) restored me to some degree of confidence and composure. I took a chair, unbidden; she begged I would forgive her for attending to her child, who was, she apprehended, dangerously ill. — I enquired how long it had been so, and she replied —

'I am grown so very weak, Mr Desmond, I mean, that I am so much disposed to be what the fine ladies call nervous, that I am no longer fit for a nurse: every foolish accident discomposes me, and of course injures my nursling. — I have been extremely alarmed for the life of this ill-starred baby, within these few hours; but I hope my fears have exaggerated the danger.' I had no need to ask what it was that had so much distressed her; yet I did not like abruptly to tell her that I was already acquainted with it. She did not however lead to it, and we remained for some moments silent, while little George clung about me, and said he loved me dearly for coming back.

'Ask Mr Desmond, my love,' said Geraldine, as if glad to have the means of thus questioning me — 'ask him why he came back when we were afraid he was quite gone?'

'It was,' answered I, 'to prevent your being alarmed by the suddenness of a visit from another person, which will, even when you are prepared for it, be, I believe, disagreeable enough.' She grew more pale at these words. — 'You mean the Duke de Romagnecourt?' — I answered, 'Yes;' and, relating briefly what had passed, except that part of our conversation that raised my suspicions about her husband's having literally sold her (with which it was impossible for me to overwhelm her), I asked what she would do to evade the importunities of a man who seemed to suppose his wishes were not to be counteracted, and to believe he need not only appear to obtain them?

The dignity of conscious worth, thus deserted by its protector, gave spirit for a moment to her languid countenance. 'If Mr Verney,' said she — but she checked herself, and, hesitating a moment, said with less vivacity — 'If this nobleman gives himself the trouble to come hither, which, however, I most earnestly wish he may not, my answer will be very positive, and very short. — I am extremely obliged to you for giving me notice of his intentions; but if you could prevent his coming —'

It did not, at that moment, appear to her that *my* interference was liable to a thousand misconstructions — but before she had finished the sentence, this occurred to her very forcibly; and she added — 'But I beg your pardon for my inconsiderate folly. This cannot be — he must come — I must undergo, unfit as I am, the irksome ceremony of seeing him, and of giving him my positive refusal.'

'And if he should afterwards persist?'

'Impossible — he surely cannot intend it.'

I then gave her a specimen of his conversation, which I had, till now, mentioned only in general terms. — She was much affected at the idea, that the strange and unmanly conduct of Verney had exposed her to a scene so improper, and so extraordinary — And I saw her turn her eyes, expressive of the most acute maternal anguish, and filled with tears, on her children, particularly on the little one in her arms: but even in this moment she uttered no complaint against their cruel father, though I saw her bosom heave, as bitter reflections on his conduct swelled her heart almost to bursting.

Oh, Bethel! why could I not, at that moment, have taken this lovely, injured woman and her children openly under my protection? — Why could I not aver that ardent, yet sacred passion I feel for her? — Alas! instead of daring to own it, and to offer her my life, I was struggling, perhaps inefficaciously struggling, to make all I said, all I proposed, appear as the dictates of mere friendship; and to persuade her, that, from a mere friend, she might, nay ought to accept my counsel, if she could not my offers of service. — After a farther conference of half an hour, during which I said all that might, without too much alarming her, put her upon her guard against the Duke de Romagnecourt's projects, I was preparing to take my leave, when she asked me if I had breakfasted? — I never once recollected that I had not. — She ordered breakfast to be brought, and, I saw, made an effort to be cheerful: but it was evidently forced; her eyes anxiously followed the child, as the maid carried it out of the room. — I remarked, that notwithstanding the particular conversation in which we were engaged during breakfast, she listened to every noise above stairs, and went out twice to enquire after it. — It was proper I should go — for I knew I must be an inconvenient interruption to her: yet I had not said all I wished to say, and could not determine to depart.

On her return the last time into the room, she smiled on me with angelic sweetness, and asked if I forgave her abrupt rudeness? — She then sat down again — endeavoured once more to regain her composure; and enquired at what time I thought it probable she might be oppressed by the honour that threatened her? — As she thus again introduced the subject, I collected resolution enough to tell her that my fears of her sufferings did not end with this visit — for that I thought the noble foreigner very likely to persevere in his entreaties, and leave nothing unattempted to enforce them. — At the word *enforce*, on which I laid a strong emphasis, she smiled, and asked me if I thought he would really enact a French Sir Hargrave Pollexfen, and carry her to Paris without her own consent?[81] — I answered very gravely, that though that could hardly be done, yet that she might, and I was afraid would find the Duke a visiter of great perseverence, and one who would not, without great difficulty, be dissuaded to recede from a point which, he thought, he had her husband's authority to persist in.

She looked at me, as if to examine whether I meant more than I said — I suppose I looked as if I did. — But again she endeavoured to laugh off the fears which she would willingly believe groundless. —

'I cannot imagine,' said she, 'why you have taken it into your head that this man would give himself so much trouble — I dare say he will make a fine speech or two, be *au desespoir* that he cannot have the happiness of my company, and content himself with shrugging up his shoulders at my want of common sense, in preferring this *pays triste & morne* with my children, to the delights of a journey to Paris with him.'[82]

'I wish,' replied I, 'it *may* end so, my dear Madam.'

'But you doubt it?'

'I do, indeed.' — I then gave her some stronger reasons, drawn from my observations of the preceding evening, *why* I doubted it — 'You are,' said I, 'quite unprotected here: you have not even a man-servant, who might shut your doors against impertinent intrusion.' — She allowed this; and when I asked her whether I had her permission to remain at the cottage I had before inhabited, till I saw the event of this visit? a faint blush, which spoke a thousand grateful, yet fearful sensations, was visible on her cheek. — But checking her fear, her pure and noble mind yielded only to gratitude: she gave me once more her lovely hand. — 'It is worthy of you,' said she with enchanting frankness, 'to make so generous an offer. I accept it, rather to quiet your apprehensions than my own; but it must be upon condition that you run no risk of embroiling yourself with this extraordinary visiter of mine.' — I assured her I would not; and having obtained permission to wait on her for half an hour in the evening, I took my leave.

And now, my dear friend, I have written this volume since — I have seen from my windows the carriage of Romagnecourt go to her house. Impatiently I awaited its return, which was not for an hour and a half — and now I go to enquire the result; and as I shall send this immense packet away to-day, and shall have no opportunity to write again for some time, I leave you to comment on the strange story I have related, and to blame, for so I doubt not but you will (since chivalry is no more), this romantic knight-errantry

Of your faithful

LIONEL DESMOND

You see I conclude cheerfully, which I account for by telling you, that whenever I am to see Geraldine, I feel in heaven; and I hope to see her this evening restored to quiet, for her child was better when I left her. (Indeed I believe her tenderness greatly exaggerated his danger); and I hope the noble Duke has departed peaceably with his final answer. Yet, till I am assured that she is completely relieved from his insolent importunities, my heart, I find, must be subject to frequent fits of anxieties and indignation.

END OF THE SECOND VOLUME

DESMOND.

A NOVEL,

BY

CHARLOTTE SMITH.

SECOND EDITION.

VOLUME III.

———————

LONDON:

PRINTED FOR G. G. J. AND J. ROBINSON,
PATER-NOSTER-ROW, 1792.

DESMOND

LETTER I

TO MR BETHEL

Bridge-foot, June 13, 1791

Though there has not been time for you to answer my former letters, I am growing extremely impatient to hear from you; but till I do, though I fear you will blame all I have done, I must beguile the anxiety of the situation I am now in, by continuing my narrative.

I went on the evening of yesterday, at the time Geraldine had appointed, to her house. — So far from rejoicing in the final dismission of her importunate French visiter, as I hoped to have found her, she appeared extremely alarmed at his determined perseverance; and under the greatest apprehensions of another visit from him on the following morning. — She repeated, with symptoms of great disquiet, the conversation she had held with him: and his eager remonstrances, on her positively refusing to accompany him; mingled with what he believed the most irresistible adulation, left me no doubt as to his views; nor of the compact made with Verney, by which he assured himself he should carry them into effect. — Though the whole of this odious transaction did not seem to have struck Geraldine as it had done me, I see that she suspects but too much of it; and such, indeed, was the language the Duc de Romagnecourt held, that of his designs she could not be ignorant. — She evaded, however, repeating the extravagant speeches which made them so evident, with modest dignity; but, as this was no time to conceal from her any part of my apprehensions, I ventured to ask her — whether she could be blind to the real motive of this importunate interference; and, if it was not very visible that the Duke's pretended friendship for Mr Verney, was only a passion for her personal charms. — She owned that it appeared so; and then added, that during the time she was under the cruel necessity of remaining in London, where the acquaintance began, she perceived that this foreigner had considered the sums he lost to Verney, as a sort of passport to her favour; and had then addressed her in a style, which only the lighter manners of his country, and his total ignorance of her real character, could have induced her to tolerate a moment: but she had believed, that on returning to France he had thought no more about her.

I could have told her, that the impressions she made, even when those impressions were only those of her personal loveliness, were not easily erased: but I was in such a state of mind, that I dared hardly speak at all, least I should too evidently betray, what in her present situation would have been doubly improper. — Her distress distracted me; and I knew not how to relieve it but by a direct address to the Duke, from whence I saw many ill consequences, and she others; to which *I* should have been entirely indifferent. — I understood that this unfeeling suitor, had dared not only to express his contempt for all those ties which she held sacred, but to ridicule Verney; judging, perhaps, that it was impossible she could love him; and that her shewing she despised him, (which was a sentiment he thought she could not conceal,) would be a very important point in his favour. — 'It is now,' said she, 'it is now that I feel, in all its bitterness, that humiliation to which the conduct of Mr Verney has reduced me. — This man dares thus address me, because I am fallen from the situation in which I once moved, and he supposes that my mind is humbled with my fortune.' — She had hitherto restrained her tears, but they now fell on her bosom. — Had so many drops of blood been drawn from my heart, I should have felt them less painfully. — Blame me not too severely if the sense of what Geraldine suffered (she, at whose feet the world should be prostrate) my cursed situation which rendered my attempting to relieve her so hazardous to her fame — the dread of her continuing defenceless and unprotected as she was, to be exposed to proposals so insufferably insolent; the effect which I saw this state of uneasiness had on her health, and a thousand other reflexions, crouding together into my mind, threw me off my guard. — By heaven, Bethel! I was in a momentary phrenzy — and forgetting that to avoid encreasing her discomfort was the object nearest my heart, I yielded to the violence of such mingled and distracting emotions; and, I believe, looked and behaved like a madman.

I was almost immediately checked, however, by the effect this sally of ungoverned passion had on Geraldine. — She seemed as one thunderstruck for a moment; then recovering her presence of mind, she put her hand gently on my arm; and, with a countenance where what she felt for herself, was lost in the expression of solicitude for me; she said — 'My good friend! what is the meaning of all this? — Do not suffer your concern for me to overcome you thus. — Above all things, you *must* promise me that you do not personally appear in this affair. — Give my your advice — I know it will be that of the kindest and most brotherly friendship, and I will follow it: but I must insist upon your relinquishing every idea of speaking to Monsieur de Romagnecourt. — To any other proposal you shall make, I ought to attend.' — The manner in which this was uttered, restored me instantly to myself. I was ashamed of the expressions of vengeance against Romagnecourt, and of rage at my own situation, that I had used. — I felt all their impropriety, and regretted that I had uttered them: yet the emotions which gave them birth were as strong as ever; and, while I repented, I could not apologize for them. — I remained silent, till Geraldine, in a voice yet more soothing, enquired, what I would advise her to do, since it was too certain that no common means of repressing unwelcome importunity had any effect on the arrogant perserverance of Monsieur de Romagnecourt. — For he had told her, that he should remain at least a week in the neighbourhood, in expectation, that she would change in his favour, a resolution so hastily adopted.

'Good God! exclaimed I, is it impossible to escape seeing this man? is it impossible to deny yourself? On what pretence does he claim a right to molest you?' — 'On that,' she replied, 'of being sent by Mr Verney.'

'But has he no sense of propriety, none of the respect he owes you?'

'Alas!' answered she, 'it is, I think, too certain that I shall suffer much more persecution before I am released from him: but be that as it may, you may be assured, Desmond, that the idea of your personal danger, which could not fail to arise from any application to Mr de Romagnecourt, is infinitely more terrifying to me, than any apprehensions I entertain for myself; and, after all, why should I be thus uneasy at impertinence which cannot last many days; and which can only harrass and fatigue my spirits, but not do me any material injury?'

'And is it not then (Geraldine, I had nearly said) is it not a material injury, dear Madam, to be subjected for hours and days to hear such sort of conversation as that with which this man presumed to address you? and is not your deigning to admit a second and a third visit, giving him reason to hope you will finally be less inexorable than you declare yourself? — Presuming as he is, a very little of what he will interpret as encouragement, will render his insolence insupportable. — I own, that if I, who have not the happiness to be allied to you, and have certainly no right to influence you, should interfere on this occasion to deliver you from his importunity, (which, I believe, it would not be difficult to do) such an interference might give occasion to disagreeable misconstructions: but surely it were better to hazard those, which, perhaps, in this remote place, might not happen, than to leave you a day, an hour, exposed to the intrusion of this assuming and arrogant foreigner. — Would it be consistent with the friendship, the esteem, you are so good as to allow me to profess; (and I hope I need not say how sincerely I profess it) to leave you in a predicament, in which, were you my sister, I could not bear that you should remain a moment?'

I saw this argument had a visible effect on Geraldine — but, shall I own, that at this moment my selfish heart bounded with delight at the idea that I was not indifferent to her; and regardless of the additional pain *she* must feel from a preference against the indulgence of which her principles would revolt — I dared to taste delight, which no consideration had, for a moment, power to restrain. — She remained silent; and then said with a deep sigh — 'I thank you most truly, Desmond, for supposing me your sister — Ah! would to God I were indeed so! — Had I such a brother, I could not be exposed to a situation so cruel — I should then have a protector! But as it is, (and her tears fell fast) I am deserted by all those on whose guardianship I have a claim. — To your generous — your more than brotherly friendship, I am already but too much indebted. — Were there not an infinite number of objections, I could not bear to encrease this debt; but, as it is, the bare idea of any interview, on the subjects of his visits here, between you and Monsieur de Romagnecourt, is intolerably dreadful; and I entreat you never to name it again.'

'Something, however, must be done.' said I; 'for unauthorised, as I am, to speak to Monsieur de Romagnecourt, *I* can as little bear his insults to you — insults, from which it is the indispensable duty of every man of honour and feeling to defend you.'

'You terrify me to death!' answered she — 'Promise me — I insist upon your promise, that of such a measure as applying to this French man yourself, you will think no more.'

'Promise me then,' said I, 'that you will think of some way of avoiding his future visits.'

'I know of but one, and that —— that is, at present, impracticable.'

'Name it, however, for heaven's sake.'

'It is', said she, hesitating — to go to Bath to my mother; but besides other considerations, which render such a journey, at present, almost impossible — I have reason to fear that I should be at this time an unwelcome visiter — My brother is, as Fanny's last letters tell me, on the point of being married into a family, whose favour, prosperity alone can conciliate. — For this desired union my mother has long been labouring; and should my presence, depressed and humbled as I am, impede it — I know, too well, that I should be a most unwelcome visiter — Unwelcome to every one but my Fanny.'

This cruel reflection conquered, for a moment, her equality of mind; deep sighs and tears choaked her. Oh! Bethel! to behold the woman I adore in such a state, without daring to relieve, or even to participate her sorrows! — There is on earth no condition so painful. — I internally cursed her detestable relations; (of whom all but her sister are so unworthy of her) and, for a little time, was too much affected by her anguish, to be able to speak. — At length, I said — 'But it is not possible for you to be in lodgings where you need not be under the necessity of meeting this ridiculous Fairfax family. — You may escape from hence, for a time, to return again when your pursuer is baffled.'

'A journey, with such a family, to Bath,' said she mournfully, 'and lodgings, when I arrive there, are expences which my mother would assuredly murmur at. Perhaps you are not aware, that though it was found impracticable for me to give up my settlement, as I most willingly would have done; yet, that I have nothing during Mr Verney's life, but a trifling allowance by way of pin-money, which *I* have never asked for, and *he* has never paid. Though he could not sell his estate with my jointure secured upon it, yet it is sequestered. — Colonel Scarsdale inhabits the house for a certain number of years; and the income is his. — Verney has, therefore, left himself destitute, and thus improvident, on his own account. — Is it wonderful he should be so on mine and his children?'

'Oh!' thought I, 'had he been *only* improvident — equally improvident, it were well! — but for himself he thinks but too much; and you, Geraldine, are the destined sacrifice!'

But this, though I thought it, I dared not say. I shall make my letter endless, if I relate all that afterwards past. — Alas! my friend! I found, that notwithstanding the precaution with which you promised to supply her, by means of her sister, she had been of late so inadequately furnished with money, that she had not enough to pay what must be paid for her apartments, were she to quit them, and to answer the expences of her journey. At length, she consented to my supplying her with what was necessary for this purpose, to be repaid, as she believes, by her mother; and the apartments, (having paid for the present half-year,) she still retains; and thus it is settled, that if she cannot to-morrow dismiss this very improper and importunate visiter, she quits this place, and you will see her, my friend, at Bath. On my part, that no remarks may be made on our being in this retired spot, or travelling together, I shall see her only to a place of safety, probably as far as Gloucester, and then go into Kent for a few days; after which, there will surely be no impropriety in my joining you at Bath, (as I have always intended to do) even though Geraldine *should* be there. — She has promised to write to me — (I trust there is no harm in that) I shall hear how long her stay is likely to be. — If Waverly's marriage takes place, and all her own family look as cool upon her, as there is reason to fear they will, she will, perhaps, hasten to bury herself again in her beloved solitude. At all events, *my* stay at Bath must be short, as some business, from which I cannot disengage myself, will absolutely require my presence in France early in July; and then, perhaps, I shall take leave of England *for ever*.

The breath of scandal has never yet injured the spotless character of Geraldine. You, who know, that my love for her has a just claim to be called *true* love, because it seeks only her good — You, my friend, before you condemn me, will ask yourself, whether *I* am likely to commit any indiscretion that will really injure her fame? — You will not, after having so reflected, blame me for what has passed since I have been here. — I could not act otherwise — And after all, who is to report my being here at all? — Those foreigners do not know me even by name — They do not know that I am acquainted with Geraldine. — Her departure cannot be imputed to me; and though I foresee that you will now find a hundred reasons to condemn me — I value myself on having acted, as you would have acted, had you been so situated.

Farewell, dear Bethel, till I meet you. — You will, perhaps, see the lovely subject of this letter almost as soon as you receive it. From you, and from her sister, she will hear the soothing voice of friendship and tenderness — And I recommend her to those good offices from you, which, from her own family, I am afraid she will not receive.

Ever your's, faithfully,

LIONEL DESMOND

LETTER II

TO MISS WAVERLY

Gloucester, June 16th, 1791

I stay here a day, my Fanny, to recruit my exhausted spirits, after the variety of agitations I have been exposed to. You have, by this time, received my two last letters; and know the strange visit that has driven me from my peaceable abode; though I would have continued there in despite of importunities and impertinence, which could not have lasted long, if I had not dreaded Mr Desmond's interference, which seemed hourly probable; and which nothing but my determining to put myself under the protection of my family, could have long prevented.

My account of the second and third visits of the Duc de Romagnecourt*, would convince you that he was not easily to be repulsed; nor would Desmond be persuaded that I ought patiently to endure this transient evil. — I saw consequences attending *his* applying to Monsieur de Romagnecourt, of which I could not bear the idea without terror. — Any measure, therefore, was to be adopted rather than hazard it; and yet I foresee, that if even his present interference, and his friendly attention to me, be known, inferences may be drawn as false towards him, as unfavourable to me. Alas! my Fanny, the prospect every way around me is darkening; and in the storms that are on all sides gathering, I shall probably perish. Desmond was so good as to insist on accompanying me as far as this place on horseback — He then immediately left me; and is gone into Kent. I am very sure, my

---

* In a letter which does not appear.

sister, by your last letter*, that you blame me for the circumstances that have occurred since Mr Desmond's residence in the neighbourhood of my retirement; and I own that such adventures befalling a married woman, separated from her husband, are very likely to raise, even in the most candid minds, suspicions of her conduct. — You, however, surely know me too well to harbour them a moment; and if I were not bound by all the ties of honour and gratitude to secrecy, I could at once convince you, that no improper attachment to me, has been the cause of Mr Desmond's journey, hither. — Still, as it is impossible that this is at present to be explained, I wish that as little may be said of it as possible.

I know not how I find resolution to proceed from day to day in this career of misery. — My children, for whom I ought to live, alone support me; nor have I in the world another motive to wish my existence prolonged, unless it be your affection, my dear Fanny. — Do not, therefore, now when I most want it, do not let it fail. You will receive this letter a few hours before my arrival. — Let me find at the Bear at Bath, a note from you, to say where you have taken lodgings for me; when I shall see you, and when I may be permitted to pay my duty to my mother. — Surely, however, she may be occupied with the approaching festivities which are intended for the more beloved and more prosperous part of her family, she will not refuse some maternal kindness to her unfortunate child, whose unhappiness is not of her own creating — and who, though she returns poor and desolate, like the Prodigal in Scripture, has nothing wherewith to reproach herself; nor occasion to say, 'Lo I have sinned against heaven, and in thy sight.'[1]

Perhaps, my dear Fanny, your ill-starred Geraldine will not long trouble you. — 'There certainly is such a distemper,' says Fielding, 'as a *broken heart*; though it is not mentioned in the bills of mortality.'[2] — Till that calamity robs mine of every sensation, it will be fondly attached to you.

GERALDINE VERNEY

---

* Which does not appear.

LETTER III

TO MR DESMOND

Bath, June 21, 1791

I am again undertaking to execute a very unpleasant task. — But my friendship for you, Desmond, is of a nature which withstands even — what shall I call it? not unkindness, nor duplicity; for I believe, from my soul, you are incapable of either, — but that want of confidence which ought to subsist between us, and in which you certainly failed when you came to England, and went into Herefordshire without informing me of your intentions. — The consequences of this imprudence, for such it surely was, have been more uneasy to the object of your solicitude than you are aware of: but though I am still vexed, and a little angry with you, because I think you acted unlike yourself, it is impossible to see her, without feeling so much interested, that every other consideration is absorbed in anxiety for her. — Geraldine is, indeed, an excuse for every failure towards *me*; but when that failure has injured her, I cannot allow of the apology; and the task of chiding you for your indiscretions, and relating their effects, falls on me most unwelcomely.

Early yesterday, I received a hurried and confused note from Miss Waverly, beseeching me to see her, by some means or other, in the course of the morning. — I answered that I would be at a bookseller's, where we sometimes have, you know, made these *assignations*, within an hour. — I was punctual to my appointment, and and in a few moments after, Fanny arrived, wrapped in a large morning cap, and a cloak, tied round her neck, which were, however, insufficient, even with the deep veil that depended from her bonnet, to conceal that her eyes were swollen with weeping, and that her whole frame was in extreme agitation. She seemed unable to speak when she came in; but recovering herself, she asked if I would walk with her, as she had much to say to me. — We took the shortest way to get out of town, and proceeded in profound silence, till we reached the fields. — She then put into my hands her sister's last letter, dated from Gloucester, and told me, that she had obeyed, as well as she dared, her directions, and had provided a lodging for her; but that her mother was extremely displeased with the journey, and had heard, by some means or other, for which it was very difficult to account, that Mr Desmond had been some time concealed in the neighbourhood of her residence at Bridge-foot, and was the person who had advised her to quit it for Bath, instead of complying with Mr Verney's wishes, and going to France, with a nobleman of very high rank, a married man, a man of the very first fashion and consequence, under whose protection she might not only have travelled with the utmost ease and elegance, but, since she was directed to do so, by her husband, with the greatest propriety. — 'Such,' said Miss Waverly, 'is the representation that has been made to my mother, and which, added to her own dislike of Geraldine's coming hither at this time, has irritated her so much against my sister, that she will hear nothing I can say in her excuse. — She has even forbidden me to see her: I shall not, however, obey her in that respect; but I dare not so directly violate my mother's cruel injunctions, as to meet her on her arrival. — Yet how will her already half broken heart be wounded, when, instead of a friendly reception from a sister who fondly loves her, from a mother who ought to protect her, she finds, awaiting her arrival, a harsh letter from that mother, filled with remonstrances and complaints.'

'She shall at least,' said I, as soon as I could recover from the pain this intelligence gave me, 'she shall at least find one friend ready to receive her. I will wait myself her coming, and soften as much as I can, the inhuman conduct of Mrs Waverly: forgive me Miss Fanny, I think it most inhuman.'

'I was about,' answered she, 'to solicit that friendly assistance which you now so generously offer. — Without some such interference, the blow will quite overwhelm my unhappy sister. — By what means my mother has got such intelligence, I cannot imagine. — Her usual informer, one whose visits I always dreaded, is no longer here, and if she were, I cannot discover how Desmond's abode in England, which was a secret to his most intimate friends, should be known to her. — I own, Mr Bethel, I wish he had forborne to visit the country, where Geraldine resides, with an air of secrecy; — for though she assures me, (and she is truth and candour itself,) that in doing so, he was actuated by very different motives from those which my mother's informer has dared to impute to him; yet assuredly, such a circumstance happening to a young and beautiful woman, apart from her husband, will receive, from the generality of the world, a very different interpretation.'

It would be difficult to describe with the pen, the manner and voice in which Fanny Waverly uttered this — her countenance I could not see, for she turned from me, and had her handkerchief to her eyes. — Her emotion was however extremely affecting. I did all I could to re-assure her, and promised, that I would see Geraldine composed and easy, before I left her, in her new lodgings, (where she was expected that afternoon,) and give early intelligence of her state of health and spirits to the anxious Fanny.

'Alas' said she, 'it is all the comfort I shall have about her to day; for my mother has made an engagement with the Fairfax's, from which, I have in vain attempted to excuse myself. — Pardon me, Mr Bethel — they are relations of your's and are soon to become relations of mine, but I shall never love them, for I detest pride and selfishness wherever I meet them: above all, I detest them, when they are poorly concealed under the ill managed affectation of refined sentiment, and superior information.

I could not forbear a smile at the little asperity, with which this sarcasm (you will call it truth) was uttered; and soon after, as Fanny had made some excuse to her mother, which she feared, would be de-tected as an excuse, if she staid too long, we parted, and I prepared for the painful scene I was to go through in the afternoon. I thought it however best, as I was known to be so much connected with you, not to wait her arrival at the inn; but to leave a note for her, entreating permission to attend her, as early as she could admit me.

About half past five o'clock, I received from her, the following card.

'Mrs Verney is infinitely obliged to Mr Bethel, for his early and most welcome attention: being unable from indisposition, to remain at the Bear without great inconveniences, she is already removed to her lodgings in Milsom-street, where she expects, with impatience, the satisfaction of seeing Mr Bethel.'

I hastened thither instantly; and was shewn into a small dining-room, where I saw the two eldest of her lovely children playing on the carpet: the door of the adjoining room was a-jar, and I had hardly spo-ken to George, before Geraldine entered.

Such an expression of despondence and woe was on her counte-nance, that I started as I saw her. — She forced, however, a melan-choly smile, as she held out her hand to me; and said, in a faultering voice, 'This is kind indeed, and like my friend Mr Bethel.'

I endeavoured, in my turn, to speak chearfully; but it would not do. — She waved her hand for me to take a chair, but seemed afraid of trusting her voice with another sentence. — There was evidently such a painful struggle to conceal her agitation and check her tears, that to have seen her weep would have been less affecting. — I expressed my fears, that she was a good deal fatigued by her journey — she answered, 'I am, indeed: travelling with three very young children, with only one servant, and in some uneasiness of mind, has been altogether a little too much for me. — The sight of a friend like you, Mr Bethel, is, however, reviving; and makes me as much amends as any thing can now make me, for the want of kindness I experience from my own family.' This cruel reflection was insupportable — her voice failed her; and she drew her handkerchief from her pocket, to conceal the tears she could no longer restrain.

After yielding to them a moment, however, she endeavoured again to repress them; and said inarticulately, 'I beg your pardon, for attempting to conceal any thing from you; and to distress you by the sight of sorrow that must appear extravagant. — But read this letter from my mother — from my only parent — from her, in compliance with whose wishes ——' She could not go on — I took the letter from her hand, which I could willingly have pressed to my heart. — I was too much agitated to read it very distinctly then; but I enclose it to you, for she gave me leave to put it in my pocket.

'You see, Mr Bethel,' said she, when she regained her voice — 'You see, that the coldness of my family is not judged punishment enough; but that they accuse that most generous and noble-minded of men, your friend Desmond, of attachments — of views, which, I am sure, he never entertained; and thus rob me of the only friend, except yourself, that my cruel destiny has left me. — But I will submit to it in silence — I will not trouble my mother with the unwelcome sight of a daughter, whose misfortunes are her faults — I will go — but yet I know not whither! — they will allow me, I hope, a short respite here till I can determine.'

I need not, surely, say to you, that I said every thing I could imagine, to console this lovely, injured mourner. — I told her that her sister had sent me, to assure her of *her* unfailing tenderness, and of her determination, that no injunctions from her mother, should prevent her seeing her the next day. I endeavoured to persuade her, that the ideas Mrs Waverly had taken up about you, were owing to the forgeries of malice and malignity — that she would soon be convinced of their falsehood — and that all would be well. — She shook her head — 'Ah! never!' said she, 'in this world for me — my destiny cannot be changed — it must, therefore, be supported. — But, however, no state of mind, so cruelly painful as that I have endured since I received, two hours ago, my mother's letter, can last long.'

A silence of some moments ensued, for I had exhausted every proper topic of consolation. At length, she said — 'Notwithstanding all this, I am so conscious of the rectitude of my own heart; and so perfectly convinced of Mr Desmond's honour and integrity towards me, that I shall not affect to have any reserve about naming him; for to do so might intimate that I blushed at knowing how highly he honours me with his esteem, which I rather glory in. Have you heard from him, Mr Bethel, since he has been in Kent? — Is he well? — and does he talk of returning soon to France?' — I replied, 'that I was not, at present, informed of your intentions; but should, probably, soon see you at your own house; where, I imagined, you would stay, at least a month.' — She sighed — 'We shall lose you then,' said she to me; 'that loss will be irreparable.' I assured her, that, as long as my continuing at Bath would be of use to her, in the smallest degree, I would not suffer even my wish to see you, after so long an absence, to have any weight with me. — I could have added, that I knew I could not oblige you so much as in remaining where my presence could contribute to her satisfaction.

She was not able to thank me; or, for some time, to speak. — Recovering herself, she said — 'you are too good, Mr Bethel! — The voice of kindness and sympathy, overcomes me more than the cold and cruel reserve of my family, because I cannot help making continual comparisons! — My Fanny! — she too forsakes me! — yet I would not have her disobey my mother, however I may languish to see her.'

Again I assured her, her sister would fly to her, at all hazards, the moment it was possible; and after some farther conversation, I had, at length, the pleasure of leaving her much more composed than I had found her. — She spoke, however, with extreme anxiety, about her youngest child, whose constitution is, she fears, quite ruined by the uneasiness that has been preying upon her own, while she has been nursing him.

As to Geraldine herself, she looks most beautiful. — Less dazzling than she once was — she is a thousand times more interesting than in the most luxuriant bloom of early beauty. — I never saw a face that gave me so much pleasure in the contemplation of it, as her's does; and yet I have seen many more regular. — The reason of this, I believe, is, that there is so much sense blended with so much sweetness in every expression of her countenance. — I have often seen both separately; but, in faces, where one predominates, there is frequently a want of the other. — Her form, too, is, in my opinion, the very perfection of feminine loveliness; yet it seems to owe all its charms to her mind: the dignity of the one heightens every grace of the other. See! if your inexorable Mentor, as you have often called me, is not writing an eulogium on the very charms for which he condemns your adoration. — But I am now too well convinced that nothing can divest you of your attachment; and the justice of my praises cannot encrease it. — All I shall henceforward attempt to do, will be to keep it within those bounds of prudence, which you cannot pass without doing the most fatal injury to its object — Prudence in which, my friend, you most cruelly failed in your journey into Wales. I own I am much disturbed at the information Mrs Waverly has obtained of the circumstances of your abode in a place, where I thought it quite improbable that you could be known. I am still more disturbed at the construction she has been taught to put on your visit.

I have just had a note from Miss Waverly: she will be with her sister to-morrow morning at seven o'clock — This evening, her mother has taken care to render it impossible.

I will write again in a few days, till when and ever I remain,

My dear friend, your's faithfully,

E. BETHEL

LETTER IV

TO MRS VERNEY

Bath, Thursday

DAUGHTER VERNEY,

I hear, with great concern, and indeed amazement, of your intended arrival at this place. I wish you had acted more prudently, as well as properly; and am surprised, that in your situation, you should think it right or becoming, to receive visits from Mr Desmond, or any other person, not authorised by your family; and, at the same time, refuse to comply with your husband's request, in going abroad, under the care of the nobleman, whom he had engaged to see you safe to him. — I am very much alarmed for the consequences of all this; and, indeed, those of my particular friends, whose judgment I rely on, have given me great reason to be so, by the representations they have made to me of the opinion the world will form upon such conduct. — Encouragement or countenance from me, it will not receive; and, as to supporting the expence, it is quite out of my power. — You will do well, therefore, to consider, whether you had not better determine to go to France, where, I understand, your husband is likely to be handsomely supported, till his affairs can be settled; and to accept the polite and handsome offer made by the foreign Duke, before it is too late. — You remember, to be sure, as you are fond of poetry, the line your poor father, on former occasions, has quoted from Milton or Shakespeare, or some of your favorite authors —

'The wife, where danger or dishonor lurks,
Seemliest and safest by her husband stays.'[3]

At present, your separation from Mr Verney is altogether voluntary, and, therefore, highly improper; and quite inconsistent with the prudent line of behaviour, which I expect from a daughter of mine — such, indeed, as lays me under the necessity of saying to you, though it may appear harsh, that I cannot let my daughter Frances see you, nor consent to receive you myself, till I find you have determined to embrace the proper conduct of going to your husband — as to do otherwise, would be to encourage both, in what is in my own opinion, quite wrong; and give fresh occasion for scandal, which has begun to be too busy already.

I hope Mr Desmond will oblige me in forbearing, for the future, to interfere in the affairs of my family; and that I may not hear him named again in the same breath with any of them, unless on quite a different footing.

I desire your speedy determination, as to going abroad; and when you have taken a becoming resolution, you shall not find me backward in kindness. — My circumstances are, a[t] present, much circumscribed, by the necessity I am under to do my best in figure and appearance for your brother's approaching marriage, with a woman, whose fortune and connexions are so proper and desirable for him. — Nevertheless, I will strain a point to grant you any little accommodation for your journey — though, certainly, not to support you in a wilful separation from your husband, which nothing can excuse, and no mother, who has a due sense of propriety, will encourage.

As to your three children, I am glad to hear from Frances, that you have weaned the little one, as that takes off one objection to your travelling. You may leave them all very properly, with some careful person; and, if they are near this place, I will see now and then, that they are well looked after.

I am (if so your conduct shall allow me to subscribe myself)

Your affectionate mother,

ELIZABETH WAVERLY

LETTER V

TO MR BETHEL

Sedgewood, Kent, June 24th, 1791

With what calmness my dear Bethel, do you recount a scene, that I cannot read, without feeling something like frenzy. With how few remarks do you enclose me a letter that deprives me of all patience and —— But it is the mother of Geraldine that writes it, (at least, she has always passed for such, though one would be tempted to fancy there was an exchange made in her infancy) and I will not exclaim against her; but only entreat you to let me know, by the return of the post, whether the lovely persecuted being, to whom it is addressed, has taken any resolution in consequence of it. I dread, least that tender and dutiful sweetness of character, to which her wretched marriage was owing, should again betray her into this detested measure; and that her ideas of obedience to her odious mother, and her worthless husband, should precipitate her into the very abyss of wretchedness. — My hope is, that the proposal — so cool a proposal too, that she should leave her children, will rouse that proper spirit of resistance against usurped and abused authority, which, for herself, she would not, perhaps, exert. — To leave her children, to go herself to such a husband, escorted by a man, to whom, I am persuaded, he has sold her; and all this, by the authority of an unfeeling old woman, who is solicitous for her fame forsooth! — and displeased at my having called at her door, when I happened to be in a same neighbourhood.

One is half tempted to fly out of the world in a fit of despair, when one considers how the farce of it is carried on, and what wretches exist in it, whose whole business seems to be to destroy the few comforts, and embitter the few pleasures which it affords. — I am totally unable to guess to whose cursed officiousness it is owing, that this prudish, narrow-minded old woman (I cannot keep my temper with her) is so well informed of my having been at Bridge-foot; a secret kept even from you, and fancied was unknown to all the world; since I had the precaution not to take even a servant with me. — I could execrate, with a most hearty good will, her informers, whoever they may be; and wish I could draw a drop of blood from their hearts, for every tear this diabolical business has drawn from the eyes of Geraldine. — But a heart that can wantonly injure *her*, can have no warm blood in it — It must be some disappointed prude, or uncharitable pedant. — I know none of either description at all likely to interfere with me — yet if I could discover them, I should be tempted to expose them to something worse than this apostrophe —

> 'I tell thee, damned priest,
> 'A ministering angel shall my sister be
> 'When thou liest howling!' —*

It is in vain, my dear Bethel, for me to attempt calling off my mind a moment from Geraldine; and were it not that my presence might expose her to a repetition of these odious suspicions, I should be now at Bath; whither you knew it was fully my purpose to go when I quitted Herefordshire, had not she been driven thither, and made my going just at the same time improper; though I was then far from dreaming of all the occasion there existed for my precaution.

As it is, I must remain here, at least, till I have your answer; which I entreat you to forward to me as soon as possible; for, till it comes, I can determine on nothing — and there is no situation so irksome as

---

   *   Shakespeare.[4]

the state of suspence I am now in; certain, that however it terminates, I must be wretched, but dreading what is of infinitely greater moment, that Geraldine may be yet more miserable.

Do not encourage me, Bethel, in the idea of her having for me personal regard. — I, who know and adore the unsullied purity of her mind, know, that the admission of such a sentiment, however involuntary, would render her unhappy; and I would not obtain all the happiness imagination can conceive, at the expence of giving her heart one reproachful pang. — You think this asseveration inconsistent with my rashness, in concealing myself in the neighbourhood of her late residence. — But besides that I had other motives for my journey thither, than it is in my power to communicate to you; I protest to you that had not chance thrown me in her way, I should not have *then* seen her. — This appears contradictory and ridiculous, but I must be content to let you call it so.

How tedious, how irksome is the sort of life I have led the little time I have been here. — I find that the locality of our attachments depends upon the persons that surround us, rather than the places where we are happy. — I have preferred this small estate as a residence, from my infancy; and here the most joyous hours of my life were past. — When I became my own master, I hastened hither; and, as I repaired the old house, and saw the roads mended, and the fences got in order, as I planted my shrubs, and gave directions for the care of my timber, procured modern comforts within the house, and put every thing without in order, a thousand agreeable images returned of my former pleasures; and with the sanguine eye of youthful expectation, I looked forward to greater pleasures yet to come.

I shall meet, said I to myself, as I indulged these charming illusions, with some lovely and amiable young woman, whose taste is congenial with my own — One, who will be more pleased with this place, because I love it, than with my other house; which, though larger and handsomer, is not in so beautiful a country, and to which I have no particular attachment. — That, therefore, I will let, and reside here altogether; and, when the naturally delicious situation is gradually improved, and a new room built for my books, I think, that with such a woman as my imagination has formed, I shall here find happiness — if happiness be ever the lot of humanity.

While I was looking out, therefore, for this 'last best gift of heaven,'[5] I was as busy in my improvements, and as delighted with my future paradise, as ever projector was with some favourite scheme that was to procure him millions. — Alas! destiny, inexorable destiny, was at work not only to destroy my lovely visions, but to embitter their destruction by shewing me that they might have been all realized. — At this period — near four years ago, I first saw Mrs Verney; then only a few months married, and brought down by her husband, for the first time, to his Kentish villa. — The beauty of her person, though that person is exactly what my fancy would form as the most lovely and perfect, made no immediate or deep impression. — She was a married woman, and her beauty was not, therefore, to be considered by a man, looking out, as I was, for a wife, and who never harboured an idea of seducing the wife of another. — Yet, perhaps, I listened with more pleasure to her sentiments, because she was eminently handsome. — I had listened but a little, before I discovered, to my utter confusion, that she was exactly the woman with whom I could be happy; and, in a few months, I found that I could never now be happy at all, for that she could not be mine, and I could think with pleasure of no other woman.

For above two years, under pretence of trying to reason myself out of this prepossession, I cherished it. — The unaffected ease and innocent freedom with which she treated me, fed the flame that was consuming me; but she was totally unconscious of it. — And, though I could see that Mr Verney was altogether unworthy of her, that she was but too sensible of it; and had been married to him merely because it was the will of her family. Believe me, Bethel, that I honoured highly that noble resolution with which I saw she not only bore, but tried to make the best of her lot; and never, in any one instance, attempted to raise a sentiment in my own favour, to the prejudice of the affection which she believed she ought, and which she tried to feel, for her husband. — That husband, who valued so little the blessing he possessed, that, after he had once gratified his pride, by shewing to his libertine friends the most beautiful woman of the time, as his wife, he was accustomed to leave her for weeks and months together; and, while he was dissipating his fortune in every species of extravagant folly, she was either alone at Linwell, or had no other companion than Fanny Waverly, then a wild girl, between sixteen and seventeen — just emerging from the nursery into the delights of succeeding her sister as a beauty: and who, though heartily rejoiced to escape from her mother, seemed then not to be so advanced in understanding, as to be a companion for her, though there was not the difference of two years in their ages.

It was at these periods when Geraldine was so much in solitude at Linwell, that my attachment took so deep root. — I found by her preferring the country even at seasons when she might have been in London — I found by her taste for reading, for drawing, for domestic pleasures, that she was, in every respect, the very woman my imagination had formed. — The more I saw of her, the more I felt this — yet could I not determine to quit her, till your remonstrances and some fears, least with Verney's encreasing follies, my regret and murmurings might encrease also, and to her prejudice, determined me to go abroad. — How successless that expedient has been in regard to curing me of my passion for her, you know too well. — What ill consequences have otherwise attended it, I hope you will never know at all.

But I was about to relate the effect that my former friendly and innocent intercourse with this lovely woman, has on my present frame of mind; and how it touches, with peculiar sadness, every object around me.

This place, though more than six miles from Linwell, and almost as far again from Hartfield, is yet, you know at that distance, which in the country constitutes near neighbourhood. — I was at school at Eaton with Verney, and though on our entrance into life, his pursuits and mine were so different, that no intimacy could subsist between us, yet our acquaintance was of course renewed, when we both came to settle in this country. — I visited equally at the house, whether he was at home or no; and, at length, I was restrained only by my fears of injuring the reputation of Geraldine, from seeing her every day; for all other society was insipid or disgusting.

At that time Geraldine rode on horseback, or drove her sister in a cabriole; and, as she was fond of gardening, I sometimes used to solicit her opinion on the alterations I was making — and when she approved what I had directed, or gave me any idea of her own, I pursued my plans of improvement with redoubled alacrity. — Her presence gave to every object a charm which I now look for in vain! — And the groups of shrubs which were then planted by her direction, now grow and flourish, as if to remind me only of the happiness I have lost — a happiness which one half the world would call chimerical, and the other half absurd and ridiculous — but which nevertheless *was comparative happiness*; for when I knew I could see her at any time in an hour, and that I should pass an hour or two near her, twice or thrice in the course of the week; I repressed, if I could not entirely destroy, the regret which arose on reflecting that her life was dedicated to another.

I have been most decidedly miserable ever since I have been here: every body tires me, and business or conversation alike disgust and teize me. — I fancied that after an absence of twelve months, the former might, for a time, occupy my mind; but Best, who you know I left as a steward, is so intolerably slow and stupid, that it is quite impossible for me to attend to his accounts and his details. — However he is very honest, and all seems right enough — and I have given him his discharges. — The good folks of the neighbourhood have persecuted me every morning — post chaises and whiskies, and cavaliers, have beset my door. — Some of these worthy people I have seen, because I happened to meet them in the grounds, and they were so happy at my return, and so full of obliging hopes that I was coming to live among them, and be a good neighbour, that really I was concerned to disappoint them; especially certain amiable gentlewomen between fifty and sixty, who have daughters between twenty-and-thirty, and who are so good as to be particularly solicitous for my settling in their neighbourhood. — One of these, an acquaintance it seems of my mother's, came in a solemn embassy, like a dowager queen of Sheba, to visit me, whom she praised quite into a Solomon; but, as she piques herself upon speaking her mind freely (and is of course the terror of all her acquaintance) she told me she should not spare *my* faults; for she loved me for the sake of her old friend, my dear mother, and knew I had too much sense not to understand she spoke out of sincere regard; when she pointed out some errors in my conduct, which so good and promising a young man, *one who was such a credit to the times*, would do well to correct.[6]

I cannot say I much liked this exordium, — Conscience told me I had committed errors enough, which such a sybil might strike at; but I felt the most uneasy in a matter where my conscience totally acquitted me. — I figured to myself that she might allude to my journey into Wales; and, I believe, my countenance betrayed my apprehensions, for she cried — 'Oh! but my dear Sir, don't blush so — I shall not touch upon family secrets (nodding significantly) — No, no — I only mean to ask you, how you *can* like to go so often to that odious France, which, at all times, was the ruin of all the fine young men that ever went there in my memory, and now must be much worse; for, I understand, they have neither church nor king — neither money nor bread — a sad race of people always; and nothing ever seemed to me so absurd as sending an English gentleman among them. — As to you, I don't, indeed, see any great change in you yet, except that you have lost your English complexion — but I heartily hope you'll go no more — but sit down quietly and creditably at home, with a good discreet young woman for your wife, and have no hankerings after these foreign doings. — There was a report got about, that you had either been married in France, or got a French mistress. — I am heartily glad to find there's no truth in such a rumour — Indeed I always said — No, no, says I, Mr Desmond, if I understand him at all, has better notions. — Take *my* word for it, who have known him ever since he was an infant, that he has good sound honest English principles at bottom, and loves his own country, and his own country folks, and we shall see him come and settle among us — a yeoman of Kent: which is better than any French duke or marquis, or grandee of them all.' — To the truth of this position I heartily assented; and felt relieved that nothing had alarmed this truly British matron, more than a friendly dread of my having imported a French mistress. — She did not, however, end her very long visit, till she had again most seriously exhorted me to put away all foreign vanities, and come to see her. — She assured me her daughter, Dorothy, was returned from visiting her aunt in the North, quite altered for the better in her health, and longing to see her old play-fellow, Mr Desmond — and that her youngest, Marianne, was grown out of my knowledge, and quite a fine young woman. — What could defend an heart thus strongly beset, but a predilection, against which neither Dorothy nor Marianne can contend?

My dear Bethel, I expect your next letter with an impatience that is beyond the power of words to describe: five days must pass before I can be relieved — but keep me not in suspense an hour longer. — Day after day I linger here in tortures, even greater than you are aware of: I rise in a morning only to count the moments, till the return of the messenger I send for letters; and then to become splenetic for the rest of the day, if he does not bring me letters from you or from some other person who can name the situation of Geraldine.

She did, indeed, promise to write to me herself; and I have expected her performance of that promise with torturing inquietude. — But now I can too well account for her having failed in it; and, since these infernal gossips have raised such suspicions, I shall not hear from her at all. — Oh! I could curse them — but you will have no patience if I suffer myself to relapse into the useless execrations of impotent rage.

I wander about like a wretched restless being — now trying to sit down to books of which I know not one word, though I pore over them for hours; now hiding myself in the woods from the horrible importunity of visiters whose kindness I cannot return.

Relieve me soon, dear Bethel, from this miserable state, or in a fit of desperation, I may set out for Bath.

LIONEL DESMOND

LETTER VI

TO MR DESMOND

Bath, June 28th, 1791

I have this moment your letter of the 24th, which distresses, but does not amaze me. I expect to have you enacting very soon the part of an English Werter; for you seem far gone in his species of insanity; and I fear what I have to say to you to-day, will only feed this unhappy frenzy.[7] — You tell me, however, that if you do not hear from me exactly at the time you expect, (without ever considering that many circumstances, quite immaterial to the cause of your solicitude, may prevent my being so very punctual) you may, perhaps, set off to Bath, in a fit of desperation. — I write, therefore; for though sure to inflict pain, by all I have to say, it will (if you have a yet a shadow of reason left) prevent a greater evil. — Your coming now to Bath would be absolute madness; and absolutely useless as to any service you could render Geraldine — If in this disposition of mind, you can attend to the most extraordinary events, that do not immediately belong to its cause, you, perhaps, may have heard the news of the flight of the King of France and his family, which arrived here yesterday.[8] — The same post brought letters to Geraldine from her husband, written in great haste, and with great exultation. — He seems to doubt, from the purport of de Romagnecourt's letter, after his first interview, whether she would accompany him; and therefore sends to the Duke's agent, in London, a letter to her, containing more positive injunctions; and bills for sixty pounds, with which, in case the Duke should be departed, he directs her instantly to set out for Paris, by way of Dieppe and Rouen; and, if she *must* have it so, to bring her children; but at all events, to begin her journey immediately. — He tells her, that though he is, at present, in Austrian Flanders, measures are so arranged, that his friends will, in a very short time, return in triumph to Paris, where he is assured of a splendid support; and the immediate means of retrieving his affairs. — This letter, which is couched in the most positive and forcible terms he could devise, was forwarded by the agent of the Duke, who, it appears, knew that Geraldine was at Bath. — On the receipt of it, she sent for me; and putting the letter into my hands, sat down, and fell into an agony of tears.

I asked her, as soon as I recovered a little from my surprize and concern, what she meant to do? — 'I go,' replied she — 'I have now no longer a reason against it — at least, none that will be attended to; and I must obey —'

'Good God!' exclaimed I, in distress I could not conceal, 'is this a time to order you, unguarded and alone, to undertake such a journey; and to enter a capital, which must, from the present circumstances, be in consternation and confusion? — If you must go, I cannot bear the thoughts of your going unprotected.' — And yet,' said she, 'that is the very circumstance that determines me; for, with such protection as Mr Verney had before chosen for me, I would not have gone.' — She sighed deeply, but dried her eyes. — 'It is over,' added she — 'I took the liberty of troubling you to come to me, Mr Bethel, to ask your friendly advice; but I now see, on a moment's farther consideration, that I have but one part to take; and that I have done wrong to hesitate.'

'Pardon me,' replied I — 'I rather think, my dear Madam, you will be more wrong, should you determine too hastily. Does your sister — does your mother know of this letter; and the *command* it contains?'

'My sister does; for she was here when I received it half an hour ago. — She left me to acquaint my mother with it, whom I have not yet been permitted to see. — But as she has kept me at a distance from her, because she conceived displeasure at my not consenting to go before, she will, undoubtedly, have a stronger reason to insist on my going now. — My brother, Mr Waverly, has, at last, determined on all the preliminaries and preparations for his marriage, which has been so long in suspence. — It is to be concluded on immediately. — I am, I know in the way: they can neither invite me to the joyous festivity with pleasure, or leave me out with decency. — I have now money to go abroad, which my mother will insist upon my using for the purpose my husband designed it; and *she* will be relieved from the apprehensions which I know she has been under, least she should be compelled to advance money for my support here. — Against all these reasons on her part, which she will enforce by the powerful words, *duty* and *obedience* — What have I to offer? — My fears; they will be treated as chimerical — (nor, in fact, do I entertain any): My reluctance! that will be imputed to very unworthy and false motives. — In a word, though I will await Fanny's return, before I begin to make actual preparations for my immediate journey, I am perfectly assured, that my mother's orders will enforce those of Mr Verney; and that I must go.'

At this instant, Fanny Waverly, her eyes swoln, and the tears still streaming down her cheeks, entered the room; and throwing herself into the arms of Geraldine, sobbed aloud, and hid her face in her bosom. — Geraldine, by a glorious effort of resolution, instead of yielding to the anguish, under which I could see she was ill able to support herself, tried to soothe and tranquillize her sister. — 'Come, come, my Fanny,' said she, 'be composed. — I knew, before you went, the message with which you would return — I, therefore, am prepared for it; and I entreat you not to let it thus affect you.'

The agonizing grief of the one, and the tender fortitude of the other, were, to me, equally affecting; and, as I contemplated one sister weeping in the arms of the other, who, by a painful restraint, exerted that fortitude, not to add to her afflictions; I was on the point of taking them both in my arms, and swearing to defend and protect them with my life and fortune. — The scene, however, was too distressing to be endured long. — Fanny continued weeping too much to be able to deliver her mother's message; and Geraldine, who had led her to a chair, hung over her, supporting her head, and holding her hands, with *such* a look! *She*, however, did not now shed a tear;

but her paleness, her trembling, and the expressive look she threw towards me, explained, too clearly, what passed in her heart. — At this moment, the servant, who was not aware of this afflicting interview, entered with the three children. — At the sight of them, I saw that Geraldine's resolution was about to forsake her; and when the little boy ran up to Fanny, and entreated her not to cry, she became absolutely convulsed; and Geraldine, after an ineffectual struggle of a moment, hastily left the room, and waved her hand for the maid and the children to follow her.

I was then alone with Fanny Waverly; but I knew not how to attempt pacifying the violence of her emotions. — She seemed, indeed, incapable of hearing me. — I approached her, however, and took her hand.

'You injure yourself,' said I, 'and your sister, by thus giving way to immoderate sorrow. — Command yourself, my dear Miss Waverly, for her sake; and tell me, I beseech you, if I can be of any use in mitigating distress, which, from my soul, I lament.'

'Oh! Mr Bethel!' answered she inarticulately, 'my mother is so cruel — so very cruel to Geraldine, that it breaks my heart. — She has heard the purport of Verney's letter; and ordered me back to say, that it was not only her opinion that she ought to set out, but her *command* that she should instantly prepare for doing so; on which condition alone she will receive, and give her her blessing. — I own I remonstrated rather earnestly with my mother; but I was so far from obtaining any mitigation, that I was very severely reproved for daring to question the propriety of her decision; and bade to observe, that if I presumed to attempt influencing my sister to act contrary to her duty, so clearly pointed out, it would be at my own peril; and that I must, in that case, be content to share the fate that must soon overwhelm my sister; but, indeed, Mr Bethel, continued she, it is not *that* threat that should deter or frighten me, if I were not too sure that I should be a burthen to Geraldine, and only encrease her difficulties.'

'Do not, however, encrease them now, my amiable friend,' said I, 'by these deep expressions of anguish. — I do assure you, that your sister had anticipated all the purport of the message that distresses you; and that it will shock her less than you imagine. — Try, therefore, to recover yourself — tell her the truth, and assist her in forming such a resolution as is best. — I *own* I think that is, to brave the worst that can happen by staying; and to refuse to set out, at least, till she hears Mr Verney is at Paris to receive her.'

As if relieved, by hearing that this was my opinion, and in the hope that it would influence her sister, Fanny now flew to her. — She and her servant were only in the next room with the children: I waited, a moment, the issue of the conference, and a violent burst of weeping assured me, too well, that it would be most affecting. — This, however, was from Fanny Waverly; for, in five or six minutes, Geraldine re-entered the dining-room, with forced serenity, she even tried to smile, when she said, 'this dear girl is so unfortunately full of sensibility and affection, that it is impossible to pacify her. — She fancies I go to meet anarchy and murder in France; and on seeing me packing up mine and my children's cloaths, that I may be ready to set out to-morrow, she has relapsed into the wildest expressions of sorrow. — I wish you would try, Mr Bethel, since she will listen to and believe you, to reason her out of these groundless apprehensions.'

'I wish,' said I, 'that I *could* set about that without forfeiting my sincerity, but, upon my honor, I do not think, and therefore cannot say, her apprehensions are groundless.'

'*I*, however, have no fears, Mr Bethel — The French, of whatsoever party I may fall among, will not hurt a woman and children! — On admitting it possible, that in some of those popular commotions, that are, certainly, likely to convulse, for some time, a kingdom just bursting into freedom from the grasp of the most oppressive tyranny, I might be involved; (which is extremely unlikely) Good God! what have I to fear? — Not death! assuredly; for there is hardly one situation, in which I can *now* be placed, to which death would not be preferable. — I will be very sincere, my good friend, and say honestly, that after what I know, and what I *suspect* of Mr Verney, I had rather meet death than be in his power. — I had rather meet it than my mother's unkindness — infinitely rather, than to know that I and my poor little ones (her voice almost failed her) should be a burthen to *her*, who is so unwilling to bear it, even for a little while. — Has then death any terrors for me? and can one who fears not death, shrink from danger! — If I get among the wildest collection of those people whose ferocity arises not from their present liberty, but their recent bondage, is it possible to suppose they will injure *me*, who am myself a miserable slave, returning with trembling and reluctant steps, to put on the most dreadful of all fetters? — Fetters that would even destroy the freedom of my mind.' I was excessively struck with the manner in which she spoke this; nor did I imagine that her soft features and dove-like eyes, could have assumed such an expression of spirit — She saw, I believe, I was surprized. — 'Why,' said I, 'do you put on these fetters, if you feel them to be so insupportable?'

'Because,' returned she, 'it is my *duty*; and while I fulfil that, I can always appeal to a judge, who will not only acquit, but reward me, if I act up to it. — The more terrible the task, the greater the merit I assume in fulfilling it; besides that, my mother's inhumanity has lessened its horrors. —

> ————"Thou'dst shun a bear;
> But if thy flight towards the roaring sea,
> Thou'dst meet the bear in the mouth."*

'Well! but,' said I, 'not to speak of Mr Verney, whose conduct is in every way unpardonable; not to speak of the danger that may attend journeying towards Paris, at present; and which may, perhaps, be partly imaginary — give me leave to ask, how are you able, with three young children, and only a maid servant, to encounter the fatigues of so long a journey? — I have heard you say you are excessively affected by sea sickness; and that nothing overcomes you more than hurry: yet here are you about to encounter both the one and the other, with only a young, helpless English girl as a servant, who will be terrified to death every step she takes.'

'Ah! Mr Bethel!' replied Geraldine, shaking her head mournfully, 'you oblige me again to use a quotation —

> ————"When the mind's free,
> The body's delicate; the tempest in my mind,
> Doth from my senses take all feeling else,
> Save what beats there.†"'

---

* Shakespeare.[9]
† Shakespeare.[10]

'What then,' said I, 'for God's sake tell me — what is your resolution? and in what way can I render more easy, any that you will absolutely adopt?'

'My resolution, my good friend, is, to set out very early to-morrow for France, by the *route* Mr Verney has directed. — If there is a possibility of getting, by that time, a female servant, who speaks a little French; and of hiring a man servant, on whom I can depend, I will do both: in these instances, perhaps, your friendly assistance may be exerted.'

'And you are positively determined to go?

'So positively, that I have sent to enquire whether I can have a coach here: if not, I must have two post-chaises, which will be much less convenient; and if I cannot here procure the servants I want, I must take the chance of getting them either from London, whither I shall write this evening, or at Brighthelmstone, where I shall embark; and to which place I shall go, by way of Salisbury and Chichester, without going round by London.'

I now saw, that the most essential service I could render our lovely, unhappy friend, was to set out instantly in quest of such persons and accommodations as she wanted. I knew that it was absolutely necessary for her to have a coach, and not trust to French vehicles — It was equally necessary to procure for her a trusty man servant. — These, therefore, I set about finding; and by a singular piece of good fortune, I found, at the livery stable where I applied, a very good coach, that was left there to be sold, by the executors of a gentleman, who had it made new for his journey to Bath, where he died soon after his arrival. — It was fitted up with many conveniencies for an invalid under the necessity of travelling; and was exactly suited to carry such a family as that for whose use I now purchased it; ordering the man, who had the sale of it, to tell Mrs Verney, 'that he had directions to let it at a price he named; which was to be paid on returning it:' for that I had otherwise managed the matter, was of necessity a secret.

It was infinitely more difficult to procure her a servant, and it was near one o'clock in the morning when I gave up the hope of satisfying myself in this respect. — I could not, however, determine to let her go either without one, or with one with whose character I was not perfectly satisfied; and therefore, after some deliberation, I resolved to send my own man, Thomas Wrightson, with her; as I can do very well without him, till I can find some proper person to send over to her, or hear of her having provided herself with one there. — Thomas, indeed, does not speak any French to signify, though he was once at Paris with me: but he is very honest and active; and, upon my proposing it to him, he said — 'that though upon no other account whatever he would quit me, unless my honour was pleased to discharge him; yet, for such a lady as Mrs Verney, in such a time to be sure, he would go through fire and water, by night or by day.' — I assured him there would be very little water, and I believed, no fire whatever to go through; and having settled the terms which made it a matter of profit, as well as chivalry to honest Thomas, I dispatched, late as it was, a note to Geraldine, to inform her how this was settled; and had the pleasure to hear, in an answer written by herself, that she was extremely well satisfied with the arrangements I had made for her; and had, in the mean time, been lucky in her own endeavours; having made a fortunate discovery of a person between forty and fifty, who had been a governess at a school at Bath, and was desirous of attending any lady to Mante, of which place she was a native, for the consideration of the expences of her journey. — Geraldine added, that as she had been indefatigable in her preparations, every thing would be ready, and she should depart at eight o'clock the next morning; when she intended driving to the door of her mother, to take leave of her, and receive the *promised blessing*; and that she begged of me to meet her a little without the town, to walk back with Fanny (who was to go far in the coach with her) and to receive her last acknowledgments, for what she termed, my unexampled friendship.

I knew that much was yet to be done, of which she was not aware. — I arose, therefore, at five o'clock, and had my banker here called; who gave me a letter of credit on Paris for an hundred pounds; and another to a gentleman at Rouen, to entreat his attention to the travellers, in regard to exchanging their money, or any other little office of kindness; and, thus prepared, I waited impatiently for the hour, when the coach which contained our lovely exile, was to overtake me on the road. — I had proceeded near a mile beyond the place of appointment, when it appeared — It stopped on approaching me. — I found only Geraldine, Fanny and the children in it, for that her last conference with her sister and with me might not be interrupted, the two female attendants were ordered to follow so far on foot, and the coach was to stay for them.

I trembled as I drew near the scene I was to pass through. — Fanny, her face covered with her handkerchief, was sobbing bitterly — Geraldine was pale and trembling; but an artificial composure, seemed to be the effect of the effort she was obliged to make to support herself, soothe her sister, and attend to her children. — The moment I saw her countenance, I saw too plainly written there, the cruel harshness of her mother, but she tried to speak with steadiness, when she begged of me to get into the coach. — I obeyed; but I was infected with the tender sorrows of the party I found there, and could say nothing to console them.

I had, however, no time to lose in indulging useless sympathy: I took, therefore, out of my pocket, the letters I had obtained. — I told her, that by one, she would find herself entitled to a small credit, in case she should want it, which would be no inconvenience to me; and her taking it was the only proof I required of that friendship which she had so often declared she favoured me with — That the other letter was to a gentleman at Rouen, who might be serviceable to her on her way — 'And now, dear Mrs Verney,' said I, 'unless any thing more can be devised for your service, Miss Waverly and I will say farewell; for this parting, this sad parting, will hurt you too much; and, I fear' — 'It is true,' said she, interrupting me, 'that it is wiser to part while we are yet able. — Fanny, my most beloved sister, have pity upon yourself and me, and do not destroy me quite by your affection, which is now almost cruelty.'

Poor Fanny threw her arm round her sister's neck, and, with a deep and convulsive sigh, kissed her, but could not speak. — At the same moment Geraldine gave me her hand, on which fell, as I pressed it to my lips, the only tear I have shed for some years. It was cruel to prolong this scene, and, indeed, almost impossible to bear it. — I therefore opened the coach-door, leaped out, and Fanny Waverly, disenagaging herself from the children with a sort of desperate resolution, followed me. — Geraldine was totally silent, and I dared not look towards her — but the little boy continued to call to his aunt Fanny, and to entreat her not to go from him, till the two women who had, by this time, come up with the coach, were helped in by Thomas. One of them very wisely drew up the coach-window, and on a signal from me, it drove very rapidly away.

I remained standing in the road, supporting Miss Waverly, who was drowned in tears, and choaked by speechless sorrow. — I spoke to her, entreating her to bear, with as much fortitude as she could, a separation that, however painful, would probably be short. — She replied, in a voice broken by sobs — 'God knows how that may be, Mr Bethel, but if I dared follow my inclinations, it should be short indeed.'

'We must none of us,' said I, 'follow out inclinations, when they are in opposition to our duty, my dear young friend.'

'And yet,' cried she, indignantly, 'such behaviour as I have just now witnessed from Mrs Waverly towards my sister, ought, methinks, to dissolve all ties of duty.' — I was glad that her anger restored her to herself — I knew it was justly excited, but how justly I could not have believed, if Fanny had not, by degrees, described to me the whole scene between her mother and Geraldine. — I will not irritate your mind by relating it: suffice it to say, that pride, avarice, and insensibility, never more effectually united to render a woman detestable; nor did ever angel shew a more decided contrast to an evil spirit, than Geraldine at that trying moment formed to her mother.

Well, my dear Desmond, it is over! — Geraldine is gone — To-night she proposed being at Salisbury, to-morrow at Chichester, and on Saturday at Brighthelmstone, time enough for the packet, which is advertised to sail on the evening of that day.

Before you receive this, therefore, she will be embarked; and, however you may execrate the cruel necessity that has compelled her to such a step, or reprobate as chimerical and ill-founded, that sense of duty which urged her to obey this compulsatory mandate of Verney's, you will, now the die is thrown, submit to what is inevitable — and perhaps the certainty that your misfortune is without remedy, (for Geraldine's return to her husband you will certainly consider as a misfortune,) is the only thing that could teach you to bear, or induce you to attempt conquering your regret. — Assure yourself, that as to her journey, she has every accommodation to render it as tolerable as, under such circumstances, it could be made. — The pain of her mind I could not remove; but hope and believe I have exempted her from suffering much personal inconvenience.

And now, Desmond, since I have as gradually as I could, disclosed this sudden and painful transaction, let me speak a word or two from, and of myself. — You are, by this time convinced, that to come hither could answer no purpose as to Geraldine, but it would certainly alarm the old lady, who has got it most invincibly fixed in her imagination, that you have a design upon her daughter, and have influenced her to refuse going to her husband the first time he sent for her. — Fanny Waverly has in vain tried to discover from whom this intelligence came: her mother hears not your name mentioned with patience, and should you now appear here, she is very likely in her *imprudent prudence*, to call it pursuing her daughter and insulting the family. It will be cruel too to poor Fanny, who could only see you either by stealth or by chance. — One would be extremely improper, and the other by no means conducive to the restoration of her tranquillity; for it is easy to see she has entertained a partiality for you, which her good sense and her pride have assisted her to conquer, on the conviction that you are in love with her sister — for that you certainly are so, she is, I can perceive perfectly aware, though she carefully avoids ever hinting at it to me.

Coming hither to meet me, is now quite out of the question, as I shall only be here about six days more — long enough, however, to receive a letter from you, which I hope will tell me, that your mind is more subdued to your fortune, than it was when you wrote last; however, that fortune may have become more perverse, and that you have determined to sit down for some months, at least, quietly in Kent, where I hope you will recover your reason. — Receive for that and every good, the most sincere wishes of,

Your's most truly,

E. BETHEL

P.S. I shall leave Louisa here, as both she and Miss Waverly desire it — and shall return in the Autumn — and then she will go back with me to Hartfield.

LETTER VII

TO MR BETHEL

Sedgewood, July 2, 1791

Geraldine so suddenly gone! and to meet her husband, who, when she arrives at Paris, will probably not be there as he proposed — as the event that has since happened, the King of France's return, must inevitably make an alteration in those plans, whatever they were, that his noble foreign friends had projected for him. — I am in such a state of mind that I know not what to write. — But do not, my dear Bethel, hurry from Bath one day sooner on my account, as I have business which will inevitably call me from hence — and I shall set out to-morrow on an absence of a few weeks, perhaps: but as I do not know exactly where I shall be, and shall have my letters sent after me as soon as I do know, continue to direct hither. — I am extremely interested for Fanny Waverly (though I am persuaded you are mistaken as to her honouring me with her partial esteem) and most heartily do I wish that you could see her in the same light as you wish me to do. She deserves a better fate than she will probably meet with, if her hateful mother is to dispose of her. — Oh! where at this moment is Geraldine? — to what fatigues and perils may she not be exposed? — I thank you, however, for all your friendly attention to her. — Would to heaven I could have been apprized of her going — but that was certainly impossible — and again I thank you for doing all that could be done on such short notice. — Good God! what would have been her situation had you not been at Bath? — I should never have retained my senses, had she departed on such a journey without the accommodations you contrived to collect for her.

If I could divert my mind a moment from this uneasy subject, I should call upon you to rejoice with me, my friend, at the calmness and magnanimity shewn by the French people, on the re-entrance of the King into Paris.[11] — This will surely convince the world, that the *bloody democracy* of Mr Burke, is not a combination of the swinish multitude, for the purposes of anarchy, but the association of reasonable beings, who determine to be, and deserve to be, free.[12] — I would ask the tender hearted personages who affect to be deeply hurt at the misfortunes of royalty, whether if this treachery, this violation of oaths so solemnly given, had been successful, and the former government restored by force of arms, the then triumphant monarch and his aristocracy, would, with equal heroism, have beheld the defeat and captivity of the leaders of the people — and whether any indignities would have been thought too degrading, any punishment too severe for them.[13] — Then would the *King's castles** have been rebuilt, and *lettres de cachet* have re-peopled the dungeons!

I rejoice as a man, that it is otherwise — and I believe and hope, from the present disposition of the people, that a permanent constitution will now soon be established, in which all the power to do good shall be left in the hands of the chief magistrate, but none to become a despot. — Some evils, however, must be felt before this great work can be compleated — and, perhaps, some blood still shed: but when all the ill that has yet happened (allowing even the most exaggerated accounts of it to be as true) is compared with the calamities of only one campaign in America, for a point which at last we did not carry, and ought not to have attempted; I own I am astonished at the effrontery of our ministerial declaimers, who having supported the one, have dared to execrate the other.[14]

Shall you hear of Geraldine? — Are there any hopes of her writing to me? — Did she mention me on the day of her departure? — Oh! what would I not give for one, only one line from her, to say she is safe in France. — Yet how can she be safe any where while in the power of such a man as Verney? — And how could her mother compel her to put herself into it a second time?

You need not apprehend my now visiting Bath, against which, at the beginning of your letter, you remonstrate as gravely as if you supposed I should really set out to see where Geraldine *had* been. — The evil consequences of it I own I cannot imagine; for, as it is known she is not there, it could hardly be supposed I came after her. — However, as you are so soon leaving it, as I have really business elsewhere, and may, perhaps, soon see you in this part of the world, a journey thither now is quite out of the question.

If you write by the return of the post, perhaps your letter may still find me here, for I am not at all well; and though I have had some-

---

* Mr Burke's name for the Bastile.[15]

times thoughts of setting out tomorrow, as I mentioned in the beginning of my letter, yet I now believe it as likely I may defer my journey for some days.

Adieu, my dear Bethel,

Your's ever,

LIONEL DESMOND

LETTER VIII

TO MR DESMOND

July 6th, 1791

Are you quite candid with me, Desmond? — And are you really going, you know not when, you know not whither? — Is it quite like my friend, even under the influence of this unhappy passion, to be so very unsettled in his plans? — It is, however, more unlike him to be disingenuous! — More unlike him, to take a step the most injurious, that can be devised, to Geraldine! — I mean going to France in pursuit of her. — You surely cannot be so indiscreet, nay, I will call it so cruel, as to meditate this. — You tell me, that if I write by the return of the post, you shall, on second thoughts, probably receive my letter at Sedgewood. — I write, therefore; and I conjure you, if you read it in England, let nothing induce you to cross the Channel, till you are assured that Geraldine is with her husband, and till there is no longer any danger of those reports gaining ground, which, (I cannot conjecture how,) have certainly got into circulation here of your attachment to her.

On the supposition, therefore, that you foresee all this, and that the indecision and confusion of your last letter, arose, not from any project of this kind, but merely from the painful sensations occasioned by the first shock of Geraldine's departure, I write, as you desire, by the return of the post, and direct my letter to Sedgewood.

To answer first your questions — Geraldine has not yet written to me; but she assured me she would write the moment her embarkation was certain, and again from Dieppe, by the return of the packet. — These letters, therefore, I hourly expect. — I have very anxiously watched the wind ever since the day, when it was probable, she would reach the coast, and till Thursday, it has been exactly contrary, and so high, that I am persuaded she did not fail before that day, though, from the change since, I have no doubt but that she is by this time far on her way to Paris.

You enquire, whether on the day of her departure, Geraldine spoke of you? — Yes! my friend; but it was with that guarded propriety her situation demanded. — She spoke of her obligations to you; she expressed the most earnest wishes for your happiness, and said, 'When I am settled in France; if, indeed, I am to be settled, I shall take the liberty of troubling Mr Desmond with a letter.' — A faint blush trembled on her cheek, and her voice faultered as she added, 'He spoke, I think, of being soon in France himself, do you think he intends it?'

I replied, that you had talked of it to me in your letter, but that I knew nothing certainly. — I saw that all the consequences of your going when she did, occurred to her; yet, perhaps, she secretly, and without daring to avow it even to herself, wished you might, while she persuaded herself she feared it. — To me, however, she spoke of it no more; but simply desired her compliments and good wishes to you almost the moment she bade adieu to me and her sister. — This I did not mention to you before, nor should I have done it now, but that it is necessary to be sincere when you question me: yet, as you sometimes protest, though, I think, you are not uniformly consistent in your declarations, that you do not even wish she should feel for you a partiality which, by the consciousness of its impropriety, might render her more unhappy; I wonder you should ask what you do not desire to know.

I thank you for your wishes to promote me to the favour of Miss Waverly, but have you sufficiently considered the difference of our ages. — I am, alas! in my fortieth year — I believe Fanny is not two-and-twenty; and if I did not greatly suspect that her little fluttering heart has felt more than mere friendship for you, *I* could never hope to become acceptable to a young woman surrounded as she is, with flattery and admiration; or, admitting it probable, would it be very discreet in me to give Louisa a mother-in-law not above eleven years older than herself. — No, my dear Desmond, *I* must not think of nymphs of twenty-one.

Your uncle Danby, who is the most profound politician that frequents the coffee-houses of this news-demanding and news-affording city, has, within this last fortnight, been very solicitously enquiring of me about you; nor could his curiosity relative to your motions, have been superceded by any thing but his greater anxiety about the motions of the King of France, — Now he is so entirely engrossed by his lamentations over disappointed treachery, and so concerned that the intended evasion of Louis XVI which would have plunged France, if not all Europe, into an immediate war, has failed, that he has not a mind capacious enough to attend to your interests too, and therefore is content to let you be as romantic and absurd as you please, till it is decided whether the French will receive their king again, or immediately declare the nation a republic.

It is, indeed, a speculation important enough to occupy a more enlarged and enlightened understanding than that of the good Major; and never were the eyes of the European nations fixed on a more interesting spectacle.

The Major and I differ less on the subject of politics than on any other, though on that we are far from thinking alike. It is, however, the only kind of conversation I can long hold with him; because, in all that relates to common life, there is in his ideas and expressions, a hardness and coarseness that sometimes shocks and always repulses me. — Swift, I think, in one of his most misanthropic humours, says, while he execrates the human race in general, that he still loves John and Thomas.[16] — There is something in Major Danby just the reverse of this. He would not care if John and Thomas, with whom he has been living in habits of friendly intercourse, were to be hanged to morrow; but he is extremely solicitous for the fate of nations of which he knows not, nor is ever likely to know one individual. — But even there, it is the princes and nobles of the land, for whom his solicitude is called forth; for as for *les gens du commun*, he thinks *they* are by no means worth the attention of a man of sense and fortune; and that the world was made for those only, to whom chance has given the means of enjoying a good table, and certain comforts and conveniences of life, for which he has a very decided relish.[17]

Of course, the present arrangements in France are very obnoxious to him; and he collects round him a little band of minor politicians, who have an high opinion of his sagacity, and who have adopted, from Mr Burke, under his auspices, the opinion, that if some fortunate event, (such as the combination of crowned heads) does not restore to the French their former government, there will be a blank in that portion of the map of Europe that *was* France.

The terrors for the lives of the royal family, which these persons affected to entertain, have now subsided; but the lamentations over their imprisonment, as it is termed, are become more clamorous than ever. — To unprejudiced minds, however, the conduct of the French, on the return of their ill-advised monarch, has certainly something great and noble in it. — I own I am one of those who wish that this magnanimity of character may be followed by a steady and well-directed pursuit of the present great object, the formation of a constitution, that, without its defects, may unite all the advantages peculiar to that of England, which, even with those flaws and imperfections, is undoubtedly the best in the world. — So far, at least, it may be said to deserve that character, as it seems to secure, better than any other, two great objects discordant in their nature, and therefore not very peaceful neighbours — I mean the dignity of the state, and the privileges of the people. — It has not only been long our national boast, but admired and analized by foreigners of the most enlarged and enlightened understanding. — You will tell me, perhaps, that it is beautiful in theory, but defective in practice: and are not even the ordinances of God exposed to a similar objection? — We have, indeed, a marvellous proof that our constitution has inherent excellence in no common degree; when we find it, even in the days of luxury and corruption, so far sufficient for all the great purposes of society; that amidst all our complaints, it may, I believe, be truly asserted, that in no age or country, has there existed a people, to whom general happiness has been more fairly distributed, than it is among the English of the present day.

I believe you are so far gone, my dear Desmond, in what are called (but, I think, improperly called) the *new doctrines*, that you would contest this opinion with me, were you not just now in a state of mind that renders every other concern, but those of Geraldine, indifferent to you. — I am afraid my friend's patriotism is so inert, at present, that he would not care if all the world were enslaved, so Geraldine was but free. — However, you will recollect, that whenever you are able and willing to enter the lists on the other side, I am ready to meet you with all your natural acuteness, and the aid of your French friends, on this ground; the general good of the British constitution — This, surely, does not lessen, in your mind, my zeal for the happiness of the whole human race. — It does not make you suppose, that because I think our form of government good, I do not, therefore, allow, that there may be a better; nor that I am jealous least a neighbouring nation should find that better. — At the same time, I am compelled to say, that the proceedings of the National Assembly, since the death of Mirabeau, give me too little reason to believe they will.[18] — I dread the want of unanimity — the want of some great leading mind, to collect and condense the patriotic intentions and views of those who really wish only the salvation of their country. — The *despotism* of superior ability is, after all, necessary; and it is the only despotism to which reasonable beings ought to submit.

Enough of politics. — Now, again, to domestic concerns. — Though you give me but little hope, in the vague way in which you write, of meeting you in Kent; I shall, in a few days, set out on my return home. In leaving this place, after so long a stay, I regret nobody but my fair Fanny Waverly; yet, indeed, Desmond, I am not in love with her. I shall not, however, go from hence, till some accounts are obtained of Geraldine, which, whenever they arrive, I will transmit to you by the quickest conveyance, notwithstanding all the confusion of that part of your letter which talks of your address. Again, I ask you, are you acting with your usual ingenuous confidence towards your friend?

E. BETHEL

LETTER IX

TO MRS VERNEY

Bath, July 18th, 1791

Where are you, my dear sister? and how shall I quiet my anxiety about you? While Mr Bethel was here, I could endure it better, because he had patience to listen to my eager, and sometimes childish inquiries, and to convince me, by reason and argument, that there was not time to hear from you, or that a thousand circumstances might arise, from winds and posts, to delay your letters: but now that he has been gone two days, I find myself insupportably wretched, and I feel my wretchedness the more, because I am compelled to conceal it.

My brother was married yesterday, and is departed with his bride for Bexley Hill, where his mother and mine, with your unhappy Fanny, are to meet them in a few days. — I am heartily glad the ceremony is over, and this very important matter, which so long occupied and agitated my mother, at length arranged. As her son cannot be unmarried, (which he will probably desire to be before the end of the week, from mere fickleness of disposition) she will now fancy him settled in the world, and I hope be more settled herself, though I have lately learned, that Mrs Fairfax, who, to the last moment, murmured, internally, at giving her daughter to a commoner, (though his fortune reconciled her to the deficiency) is plotting with my mother, and making interest with all her great friends, to procure for Mr Waverly an Irish peerage. — The preamble to the patent will apply with infinite propriety to my brother, when it speaks of *his good services to his country.* — However, in the plentiful showers of new coronets which daily fall, one, I doubt not, will find its way to his head; but, I suppose, a great difficulty will be to determine what title he shall assume. — Every pretty name, and words of elegant termination, in *ville,* and *wood,* and *ton,* and *ford,* and *bury,* and *wick,* seem to be already monopolized and engaged: but, if he were not my brother, I should venture to propose the very *proper* appellation of Baron Weathercock. — Now don't, my dear Geraldine, put on an air of displeasure. I would not be flippant about these relations of ours, (though the whole courtship that preceded this marriage has been to me a course of inexpressible torment) but when I reflect on their behaviour to you, I find it impossible to command myself. — The cold, supercilious insolence of that antiquated piece of affectation, Mrs Fairfax, with whom, there is no crime so great as being in inconvenient circumstances; nor any recommendation so irrisistible as riches and title — the pride and arrogance of her eldest daughter, now my sister-in-law, who, under an affected and over acted mildness of manners, believes that the world was made only to do homage to her charms; and the yet more offensive conceit of Anastatia, whose whipt syllabubs of science she compels every one to taste and to admire, form together such a group, as it is quite impossible not to fly from if one could. — But I, alas! am chained to it — under pain of being 'put into everlasting liberty:' for, I believe, were my mother to know how very much I dislike these people, she would, without much compunction, discard me, and put me to board somewhere or other on the interest of my fortune — and can I wonder at this after her behaviour to you?[19]

You tell me, however, that I ought to bear whatever is inflicted by a parent's hand; and so, my dear Geraldine, I am learning as fast as I can, to check the natural impetuosity of my nature, *and smitten on one cheek, to turn the other.* — I will not indulge any of those satirical sallies that you have so often disapproved, but grow softly, sweetly sentimental, like the amiable Anastatia; and, when she is collecting round her all the men in the room (whether old or young, ugly or handsome, fools or wits) by the pretty languishing airs she gives herself, and totally neglecting every one else, with a rude indifference, as to their opinions, which is often extremely shocking; I will very humbly take my station behind her, and study those inimitable graces which render her so attractive. — She treats me like an insignificant child — and sometimes in the drawling quality tone, which she affects, speaking in the roof of her mouth as if she had lost her palate, she calls me poor, dear little Fanny! — Certainly I have not twenty thousand pounds as she has — nor have I a genius to write charades, songs and sonnets — nor to act plays, and read in public. — I hope, however, you don't think I say all this from envy, for I assure you, that with her humble three thousand pounds, and inferior advantages of every kind, poor, dear, little Fanny, would not change with the accomplished Anastatia. — I never seemed much worth her notice in any way, not even as an object of her contemptuous pity, till Mr Bethel shewed me so much friendly attention, and was so much with me. — Mr Bethel is, you know, related to the Fairfax family, and though it is well understood that he does not intend to marry again, and is, on account of his two children, a man whom Miss Anastatia would not accept of, yet could she not bear the preference he has always shewn me; and has sometimes been unable to repress her indignation at his want of taste. — Since he has been gone, she has perceived the dejection of my spirits, and whenever she has had an opportunity has affected to condole with me on the departure of my *sage lover* — and *my disappointment.* — It is in such conversation, if conversation it may be called, that I am to pass the tedious days of the next month, with the new married couple, and their relations and acquaintance. — Oh! Geraldine, why cannot I dedicate these days to you?

Mr Bethel is gone back to his house in Kent. He told me some time before the cruel event of your being sent for to France, that his friend Desmond was, he believed, coming to Bath: but the most unaccountable circumstance of my mother's suspicions being excited about him, has, as I gather from Mr Bethel's hints, entirely put an end to that project — and he is now gone, his friends knows not whither; but he says, most probably into the North of England (where he has many connexions) for the rest of the Summer.

I own I regret, though perhaps I ought rather to rejoice at, not seeing him here: but do not fancy, my dear sister, that this wish has any thing to do with that partiality for Desmond, which I was once simple enough to indulge, and partly to avow. — No predilection of that sort can last long, after a conviction of its never being returned, and I must have the most perfect conviction of that, in regard to Mr Desmond, whose heart is certainly devoted to another — though who that other is, it is better, perhaps, for neither of us to inquire.

The idle rumours that had been spread on that subject, are now dying away. — Other stories, equally gratifying to the curious malignity of the people, who call themselves the world, have succeeded; and except some sarcasms on the part of Mrs Fairfax — some affected concern on that of Miss Anastatia, and some airs of consequential and mysterious apprehension from the new Mrs Waverly, I have heard nothing about Desmond's Welch expedition, on which you will therefore, I hope, make yourself easy.

One of the stories that for some days engrossed the conversation of the Bath circles, till it was superceded yesterday by the splendid wedding of Mr Waverly, was the sad calamity that has befallen poor Miss Elford. You know, I believe, that six or eight weeks since, she departed from hence in order to make her usual Summer tour among her illustrious friends, for the last time before her marriage; and having staid a week with one friend, and a week with another, and ten days with a third, her lover, Dr M'Dougal, was to have met her at the most northern of these visits, and with no other guard, 'save her own purity' — she was to entrust herself to him to go to Scotland, where his family reside, and where she was to have become Mrs M'Dougal.

As none of those friends, with whom she formerly corresponded, heard from her, they concluded that these arrangements were prosperously succeeding; and within these ten or fourteen days, they have been looking with impatience for an account of the celebration at Edinburgh of these happy nuptials: when suddenly a report among the acquaintance of the Doctor, that on his arrival four or five weeks since, at the seat of his father's from whence he was to have met his future bride at York, he received the very unexpected intelligence, that an uncle who had been many years in the West Indies, where he had a wife and a son, and from whose riches no expectations were therefore formed, had buried both within the course of eighteen months, and at length followed them himself, leaving about forty thousand pounds between Dr M'Dougal and his sister, a widow, not young, and without children — so that it was probable the Doctor would possess the whole. — In consequence of this accumulation of good fortune, report goes on to say, that Miss Elford has lost her admirer, who now feels it unnecessary to unite himself to a woman whom he does not love, in order to forward his interest in his profession — and that the deserted damsel, in the last despair at this disappointment, cannot bear to shew herself in a place which she left with such very different hopes, but has hid herself and her blasted expectations in some remote part of England.

It is at once amusing and mortifying, to remark the secret pleasure with which the *soi-disant* friends of poor Miss Elford relate this. — The day before Mrs Waverly's marriage, an assembly, chiefly consisting of the tabbies, who are the delight of my mother and Miss Fairfax, was held at the house of the latter; and while amid their cards, this fertile subject was introduced, I could not but smile at, while I regret, the fallacy of professed friendship, and the wonderful malignity of human nature. — The good fortune of Dr M'Dougal, raised all their spleen. — Yet I could see that they secretly rejoiced, that their 'worthy friend,' Miss Elford, was not to share it, while, as if to revenge her cause, they loaded the poor Doctor with every abusive epithet which their fertile malice could suggest — and with the most fulsome affectation of pity towards the deserted Ariadne, they expressed a terrible abhorrence of the cruelty of the modern Theseus; who had, as one of them affirmed, left her in a dreary part of Scotland, where he had appointed to meet her; but where, instead of himself, she was saluted by a cold letter, taking leave of her for ever — part of which letter this well informed gentlewoman even repeated.[20]

I observed, that during this conversation, my mother, who in such sort of confabulations is seldom backward, was unusually reserved — she said it *might* be all very true, for she had no intelligence from *dear* Philadelphia to the contrary; but still she was willing to *hope for the best.* — You must agree with me, my dear sister, that my mother is not very apt to keep to herself her knowledge on any topic, particularly when she fancies, or knows, she possesses, on the subject in discussion, more information than those who are speaking of it. — Nevertheless, I am convinced, that she on this knows a great deal more than she chuses to tell; and has, for once, some reason for silence, so strong as to conquer her desire of giving her knowledge to her admiring auditors. — How she should come by this information, indeed, I cannot guess; or why, if she corresponds with her dear Philadelphia, it should all of a sudden be kept so profound a secret. — But conjectures on this head are useless, nor is it a matter that much deserves the trouble of investigation. — My mother, perhaps, having changed her bosom friend (for one, of what the common people call a crony, she must always have) has a mind to dismiss her quietly, and not by joining in any sarcasm against her, irritate her (especially in these very irritable moments) to disclose the purport of those long conferences which she and Miss Elford used to have together; during which, I believe, there was no transaction of her past life that she did not relate to this dear Philadelphia; nor any measures for her future conduct, in regard to her family, that she was not suffered to dictate. — The elderly ladies have a mortal aversion to great intimacy between two girls — and many have been the chidings and remonstrances I have endured, for walking and whispering and gigling, with the young people of my own age, who have happened to be thrown in my way. — 'Twas for no good, my mother used to say, that these violent intimacies subsisted. — I wonder what good ever arises from the caballing of a dowager, and an old spinster. — I dare say, if these conferences could be fairly related, those of the Misses would be found the most innocent of the two; for theirs, I believe, generally turn upon the topic of gaiety, vanity and love — and those of the ladies of a certain age, upon hatred, malice, and all uncharitableness.

Ah! my dearest sister, while I am writing all this where are you? Your short incoherent letter* informed me, indeed, that you were safe as far as Rouen; but what has happened since! — I tremble at every sentence of French news; and the people among whom I live are such

---

* Which does not appear.

inveterate and decided enemies to the revolution, that they exaggerate with malicious delight, all the mischief they hear of, and represent the place whither you are going as a scene of anarchy, famine, and bloodshed. — I have heard stories that I am sure are improbable, and I hope impossible — and when my mother, the other day, was relating one of them 'on the authority of a dear friend, of a dear friend of hers, a Lord somebody, just come through Paris in his way from Italy' — I could not help saying — 'And you believe all this Madam?'

'Believe it girl? — yes to be sure — I not only believe, but know it.' —

'And yet, Madam, it was at such a time, and consigned to such a man as your son-in-law, Verney, that you insisted upon sending your daughter, Geraldine, to Paris.'

I don't know that I ever recollect seeing my mother so angry, nor can I guess when her indignation for my impertinence would have subsided — if luckily for me, the upholsterer had not that moment entered with the patterns of some linens and chintz of which the new furniture at Bexley Hill is to consist. — Her daughter Geraldine, and her daughter Fanny, were in a moment equally forgotten; and she sent in a great hurry for her son to call a council with Miss Fairfax on this important point. — A very serious debate ensued, which, as Mr Waverly was of the party, I knew would not very speedily end: and before they could settle the first question, whether the chintz furniture of the west chamber should be lined with sky blue, or grass green, I made my escape.

I direct this letter to the care of the banker at Paris, who Mr Bethel assures me will know your abode there, and carefully convey it to you. — Oh! how anxiously I long to hear from you — how painfully does my imagination dwell on the difficulties you may encounter, unprotected as you are; yet how decidedly convinced I am, that the greatest evil that can befall you would be meeting with your husband.

It is with a bleeding heart, my dear Geraldine, I say this; and, with a bleeding heart I await your letters, which heaven grant may bring me better accounts of you than my affrighted fancy suggests.

May heaven protect you, and all you love.

FANNY WAVERLY

LETTER X

TO MISS WAVERLY

Meudon, August 16th, 1791

Once more, my dearest sister, I have again a transient respite, after such a series of mental and bodily sufferings as I have not in my former letters*, very fully insisted upon, because it was enough for me to endure them, without tearing to pieces, by the description, the sensible heart of my Fanny.

I will now, however, when I can look back upon these situations and sensations with some degree of calmness, recapitulate briefly my little travels, the account of which must have been broken and disjointed, by the hurried and incoherent letters I wrote from Rouen and Paris.

I need not remind you of the state of languor in which I landed at Dieppe, after what was, they told me, a quick passage of seventeen hours. — I expected, the next morning, to have seen some symptoms, in the town, of the misery, which I was assured, the revolution had occasioned; but every thing is the same as it was when we passed this way to England, six years since, except that, instead of processions of *les Carmes déchaussés, ou les Pères de l' Assomption,* we now see small parties of armed citizens parading the streets, at certain hours, as they go to their exercise, or to relieve the guard; much better looking men, and much fitter to be entrusted with the care of their town than the miserable looking, half-starved soldiers, that I remember to have seen exercising on the walls when we were here before, who seemed likely, from actual want, to pillage, rather than protect the coast.[21] — These, on the contrary, are all men armed voluntarily to defend themselves, their famiies, and their property; and, in a short time, when the advantages of freedom are felt, and the disadvantages of obtaining it by force forgotten, these associations will be as Smollett describes his countrymen, in one of the most beautiful odes that ever was written —

> 'With hearts resolv'd, and hands prepar'd,
> The blessings they enjoy — to guard.'[22]

---

* Which do not appear.

That these blessings are not yet fully felt, seems to be the only complaint that the enemies to the freedom of France can alledge against it; as if, immediately after such a change, all could subside into order, and 'every man sit down under his own vine and his own fig-tree.'[23]

We know, from daily experience, that even in a private family, a change in its oeconomy or its domestics, disturbs the tranquillity of its members for some time. — It must surely then happen, to a much greater degree, in a great nation, whose government is suddenly dissolved by the resolution of the people; and which, in taking a new form, has so many jarring interests to conciliate — A country too, where genuine patriotism having been always a prohibited sentiment, every man, whose property or talents give him weight, has been so long accustomed to consult his own interest, that the sacrifices to be made for general good appear too difficult to the individual, and he shrinks, from private inconvenience, which is certain and immediate, when remote, though general benefit is to be obtained by it.

We began our land journey the next day, save one, after our landing — Some little difficulties occurred about the number of post-horses that were to draw our carriage, on account of six persons being in it; though of those six, three were infants in lap (these arrangements, which seem so strange and teizing to the English, are, I imagine, a remnant of former despotism, which gave the profits of the posts to government at its own discretion).

The country is very fine around Rouen. Hills, resembling the high downs in Sussex, arise immediately around it, but the prospect from the summit of that to which the road led us, is infinitely more beautiful than any I ever saw. — The Seine winding through a lovely vale of great extent, and the port of Rouen crouded with vessels — the town and suburbs — the old and magnificent cathedral — all embosomed in trees, with the finest meadows beyond them, and an infinite number of *châteaux* scattered through the whole landscape, render it altogether such a view as I never saw equalled in England; but, indeed, I have not, in my own country, been a great traveller.

On the summit of the hill, and just as the road led along a chalky hollow, which had been cut to ease the steepness of the acclivity, we were met by a procession of priests, chanting solemnly in Latin, and, as I apprehend, carrying the host to some sick person. — They were preceded by a small party of the national guard, in their uniform, and under arms. — The priests, one of whom carried a large crucifix of silver, gilt, were to the number of eighteen or twenty, all men in the flower of their age, and remarkably well-looking. — I ordered the postillions to stop, and my servants to pull off their hats, while the procession passed, which had in it a solemnity particularly affecting; as the dirge they were singing in excellent voices, fell, or was resumed in aweful responses echoing along the hollow cliffs of chalk. — The mournful music was in uniform with the melancholy temper of my mind; and I involuntarily shed tears, as I apostrophised the departing spirit, to whom these religious men were carrying the sacred wafer, which, in their opinion, secures its future happiness. — 'Poor trembling being!' said I, thou art, perhaps, about to quit, reluctantly, a world, to which some tender connexion, some scenes of promised happiness attaches thee! — With reluctant and fearful heart, thou wilt receive what is to be, in thy opinion, a *passport* to the bosom of thy God! — while I, a wretched wanderer, in a wretched world, would most willingly exchange situations with thee; and with thy faith and thy prospects, lay down, even with pleasure, a life which, according to the course of nature, may be very long, according to all present probability, must be very miserable.'

These thoughts occurred as the figures slowly, and with down-cast eyes, passed close to my coach. — The procession was finished by another small party of the national guard. — 'All religion, however,' said I, 'is not abolished in France — they told me it was despised and trampled on; and I never enquired, as every body ought to do, when such assertions are made — Is all this true?'

As we proceeded, nothing could appear more beautiful than the extensive plains of Normandy, which, under all the disadvantages of bad cultivation, and the tumults existing these last two years, which are certainly inimical to the labour of the husbandman, do, literally, laugh and sing. — This appearance of plenty would convince me of the truth of what Mr Desmond once assured me, if I ever could doubt of facts which I hear from so accurate and candid a judge; I mean that the deficiency of bread, (*la disette du pain*) which, in eighty-nine and ninety, was so severely felt at Paris, was artificial, and created by those, who not only had the power to monopolize for their own profit, but others, who had it in view to reduce the people by famine to obedience — to turn their thoughts from the acquisition of freedom, to the preservation, on any terms, of existence.[24]

It has been affirmed, and never contradicted, that the civil magistrates of Paris, and the intendants of the provinces, had caused the corn to be cut down in the green blade. — The effect of this atrocious wickedness, was, however, exactly the reverse of that which was intended. — The transaction was discovered, and can we wonder it was resented? — The wretched projectors fell victims to the indignation of the people; and the cry of 'du pain, du pain, pour nous & pour nos enfans,*' was loudly urged in the ears of royalty, when royalty was believed to have encouraged such atrocity.

While humanity drops her tears at the sad stories of those individuals who fell the victims of popular tumult so naturally excited, pity cannot throw over these transactions a veil thick enough to conceal the tremendous decree of justice, which, like 'the hand writing upon the wall,' will be seen in colours of blood, and however regretted, must still be acknowledged as the hand of justice.[25]

This excursion into the field of politics, where, for the most part only thistles can be gathered, and where we, you know, have always been taught that women should never advance a step, may, perhaps, excite your surprize. — You will possibly wonder that, under the pressure of those evils which so lately surrounded me, I should, for a moment, find my spirits enough disengaged to enter into disquisitions so little attractive. — The truth is, that whenever I am not suffering under any immediate alarm, my mind, possessing more elasticity than I once thought possible, recovers itself enough to look at the objects around me, and even to contemplate with some degree of composure, my own present circumstances, and the prospect before me, which would a few, a very few months since, have appeared quite insupportable.

It is to my sister, to my second self I write, and from her I do not fear such a remark as was made on some French woman of fashion, (whom I cannot now recollect) who being separated from her husband, changed her religion to that (whatever it was) which he did not profess — 'She has done it,' said a wit, 'that she might never meet her husband either in this world or the next' — Thus it might, perhaps,

---

* Bread, bread, for us and our children.

be said, that I determine never to think on any article (even on these, whereon my age and sex might exempt me from thinking at all) like Mr Verney; and therefore, as he is, he knows not why, a very furious aristocrat, that I, with no better reason, become democrat.

But I do assure you, my Fanny, that however ridiculous Mr Verney's adherence may seem to the cause of persons of whom he knows nothing but their vices and their follies, my inconsequential opinion would not be put in the other scale, were I not convinced, that every principal, all that we owe to God, our fellow creatures and ourselves, is clearly on the other side the question.

This must be from conviction, for it cannot be from the prejudice of education. — We were always brought up as if we were designed for wives of the Vicars of Bray.[26] — My father, indeed, would not condescend to suppose that our sentiments were worth forming or consulting; and with all my respect for his memory, I cannot help recollecting that he was a very Turk in principle, and hardly allowed women any pretentions to souls, or thought them worth more care than he bestowed on his horses, which were to look sleek, and do their paces well.[27]

As to our mother, I am afraid our filial duty, highly as I venerate the principle, cannot conceal from us, that she suffered, in her department, no sentiments to be adopted which did not square with the substantial rules of domestic policy; for every single man of large fortune, though decrepid with age, or distorted by the hand of Nature, though half an ideot from his birth, or rendered worse than an ideot by debauchery, we were taught to throw out encouragement; and, I really believe, if the wandering Jew, or the yellow dwarf, or any other fabled being of hideous description, could have been sent on earth to have personified men of eight or ten thousand a year, we should have found it difficult to have escaped being married to them, if they had offered *good settlements.*[28]

Riches and high birth — (the latter rather because it generally includes the former, than for its own sake) riches and high birth were ever most certain recommendations to the favor of my mother. — Merit unattended by these advantages, we were always taught to shun: she knew that, unless we were blinded by early prejudice, it would force itself irresistibly on unadulterated minds; and against such impressions she was constantly on her guard.

With what vigilance did she contrive, at Bexley Hill, to exclude from all our parties every young man who had nothing else to recommend him, than his deserving to be noticed. — I remember, when a regiment of horse was quartered for some time at Wells, how eagerly she solicited the company of those of the officers, who were reputed to be men of fortune, while, if any subaltern of inferior expectations, was introduced to her table, how cold, how reluctant were her civilities! —

That *I* have been most unhappily the victim of this mercenary spirit, I do not, however, mean to make matter of reproach to my mother. — Happiness, in her estimation, consists in being visited by the opulent; in giving and receiving good dinners; in having at Bath, or in London, the reputation of having fashionable parties, and very full rooms; of curtsying, at church, to all the best dressed part of the congregation; and being looked upon as a very sensible woman, and one who knows the world; of being appealed to by the yellow admirals and gouty generals, as a person of great sagacity in cases, whether of medicine, or cards, or anecdote; and of being considered as a perfect judge of etiquette; and a woman of the highest respectability.

Now, as these circumstances do, in her idea, constitute the *summum bonum*, can you wonder that she endeavoured to procure their certain possession for us?[29] — That she has failed, at least, in regard to me, is not to be imputed to her as an error; her judgment was originally wrong; the fault of the head rather than the heart. — She could not have succeeded, because, had Mr Verney's self-indulgences left me all these blessings, on which my mother sets so high a value, I should, if I had been compelled to have entered into their routine, have been infinitely more miserable than I am now.

But to go on with the brief history of travels, which I have hitherto only related in a vague and disjointed way, I may as well take up the word miserable, with which I concluded the last sentence, and tell you, that miserable, very miserable I was at Rouen: not, however, from finding the country — '*en feu & en sang*,'* as I had been assured I should do, by some emigrants with whom I conversed at Brighthelmstone; but from my own sad reflections, and the uncertainty of what was to be my destiny on my arrival at Paris.

---

* In blood and fire — or, as we say, under fire and sword.

Far from finding my approach to this city (Rouen) impeded by any of the popular confusion of which we have been told so much, I must give you a description of the scene.

It was about half past nine o'clock, when we entered the long double avenue of elms, which begins above a mile from the town. — The day had been very warm, and the evening was deliciously serene. — The moon, nearly at the full, was reflected in long lines of radiance on the silver bosom of the Seine, which is here much broader and clearer than at Paris; and the oars of boats, going up the river, were heard at intervals, as they dashed the sparkling water, mingled with the somewhat mournful, yet not unpleasing, sound of the sailors on the quay above, drawing up their anchors to depart. — As we advanced, the noise of the postillions, who delight in cracking their whips and hooting as they approach a town, interrupted, but could not drown the enlivening notes of the fifes, clarinets, and organs of the Savoyards, to which two or three parties were gaily dancing by the road side, while many others were walking under the trees, enjoying the beauty of the night. — The nearer we approached the town, the more numerous and well dressed were the groups we perceived, till near the former barrier, it might be justly called a croud who seemed to have no object but the pleasure of a gay walk by moon-light after a hot day. — 'And this,' cried I, as I surveyed them, 'this is a specimen of universal national misery — of the fierce and sanguinary democracy so pathetically lamented by Mr Burke!'

The next morning I received from the French merchant, to whom Mr Bethel gave me letters, every attention which I could have claimed on a long acquaintance. He regulated every thing for our future journey in the way, least likely to occasion fatigue to me, and after resting at Rouen one day, we again went forward towards Paris.

Had my mind been less cruelly occupied by the certainty of present evils, or could I have looked forward with more calmness to the scenes that awaited me at Paris, I should have contemplated, with peculiar pleasure, the uncommon charms of the country that borders the Seine near Vernon — a town remarkably dirty and melancholy, situated in a spot of which imagination cannot conceive the beauty.

Around Rouen it is very fine: but, perhaps, as I had passed that country, before, I was less struck with it now, and as I then travelled what is called the upper way to Paris, I did not go through Vernon.

The Seine, along whose banks the road lies for many miles, is here very broad and very rapid — broken by several beautiful little islands, where the willow dips its trembling leaves into the current, and mingled with the darker shade of alders, the poplar rises in luxuriant spires above. — On the opposite side of the river there are coppices edging the water, or green lines of meadow ground — hills resembling the Southern Downs of England, arise beyond these — with here and there a scattered vineyard, the first I had seen in France. — But a little beyond Vernon there are other hills of the most extraordinary forms I ever remarked. — They appear, at the distance from which I surveyed them, like immense circular masses of stone or marble, piled on each other, or assembled in rows, as if some supernatural beings of extraordinary strength had thrown them there. — The singularity of their outline gives to the whole landscape, for some miles, a very romantic appearance; and the road from which it is surveyed is equally wild and picturesque — for it lies under a ridge of high chalk rock, beneath which are a few cottages, partly formed of the rock itself, and half hid with vines.

You will wonder, perhaps, that in the state of mind I was, as I passed through this country, I should be able to give so much attention to it as to make out even this slight description. — But I find, that from a habit of suffering, the mind acquires the power to suffer; and, if it resists at all, becomes every year less acutely sensible. It must at least be so with me; for I now look forward with melancholy composure to events that appear inevitable, of which the bare idea a few years, or even a few months ago, would have driven me, I think, to frenzy. — I see no end of my calamities but in the grave — and having in a great measure ceased to hope, it were ridiculous to fear. — Fate can have nothing worse in store for me than separation from those I love, embittered by poverty and contempt. — Long lingering years, varied only by different shades of wretchedness, is all my prospect. — Torn for ever from my dearest connections, and doomed to be the unresisting victim of a man, whose conduct is a continual disgrace to himself, his family, and his country.

'Regretter ce ceux qu'on amie, est un bien en comparaison de vivre avec ce qu'on hait' — says de la Rochefaucault.[30] — I do not hate Mr Verney — God forbid I should: but yet I own his late conduct, in regard to Monsieur de Romagnecourt, and other circumstances that have accidentally come to my knowledge, have raised in me such a dread of him, that there is no humiliation to which I had not rather submit, than that of considering myself as his slave. — Yet to repeat the words of a pathetic French poem, I was reading yesterday.

'Tel j'étois, tel je suis encore,
'Ne respirant que pour souffrir.'

But I have strangely wandered from the narrative I undertook, to give more connectedly than you can gather it from my former letters.

I pass over the rest of my journey from Vernon to Mante, where we remained one night; and, in which, if there was any thing remarkable, I did not see it — for as I approached Paris my spirits sunk, and every league became more and more depressed. — Yet what I felt was the calm desperation of incurable calamity, and not those sudden paroxysms of anxiety which are yielded to, when hope represents the possibility of redress; and the agitated mind, in the most acute moments of sorrow, looks round for succour. — *I* had nothing to hope — and what I then had to fear was of a nature so dreadful and so peculiar, that I hardly dared to trust my mind with its contemplation.

At length we arrived at Paris, and I saw myself in l'Hotel de Moscovie; for though Mr Verney's letter had ordered me to take up my abode at the magnificent hotel of his illustrious friend, Monsieur le Duc de Romagnecourt, I had, in this instance, and by the advice of Mr Bethel, determined to disobey him. — I had written from Dieppe to Mr Verney, to say I should await his orders at l'Hotel de Muscovie; but there were no letters there for me, [n]or had any person been there enquiring after me. — As I was extremely fatigued, I determined, though it was yet only early in the evening, to do no more that night, than announce my arrival to the banker, to whom Mr Bethel, and his friend, had given me letters; and deferring till the next day, every determination as to a future plan, to endeavour to procure some repose to my children and myself. — In this I succeeded so far, as to see them all well the following morning, and to find my own spirits rather more tranquil than I could expect, when, at nine o'clock, I received a note from Monsieur Bergasse, to whom my letters were addressed, saying that he would wait on me at ten.

I could not avoid explaining to him, though it was with extreme reluctance, the orders I had received from Mr Verney. — I saw at once that he was startled at them, and believed that no husband who either regarded his wife or his honour, would have given such directions. — He informed me, however, that though the Duc de Romagnecourt had quitted Paris some time before the flight of the King, and that the splendid preparations making for his return from England, had been countermanded; yet it was likely that Mr Verney, who might not have received my letter from Dieppe, had sent to the Duke's house his instructions how I should proceed — since the political changes that had happened after his first desiring me to meet him in France, had probably changed his intentions in regard to me and to himself.

To the hotel de Romagnecourt, therefore, Mr Bergasse was so good as to go for me. He very soon returned with a letter from Mr Verney, directing me to remain there till his arrival, and informing me that he was going for a very short time, to the neighbourhood of Avignon, with his dear friends Messieurs de Romagnecourt, de Bellizet and de Boisbelle; the former and latter of whom had just rejoined him — and that, in the mean time, I should find that every accommodation had been directed by the Duke to await me at Paris.

I could see by the whole turn of this letter, which was not, indeed, written with much art, that Mr Verney had calculated that the money he remitted to me for my journey, could do no more than defray the expences of it; and that on my arrival at Paris, necessity must conquer the repugnance I might feel at being thus made over, as an inhabitant of the house of Monsieur de Romagnecourt.

This gentleman also had taken the trouble to write to me; and, with many extravagant expressions of attachment and admiration, expressed his regret at my cruelty in not deigning to accompany him, and his delight at my charming condescension in coming at all; — his *ardent* hopes that his letter, would find me in entire possession of his house at Paris, where he had given directions that his carriages and servants should be at my command; and of all of which he besought me to consider myself as sole mistress.

Oh! Fanny, what would have become of your unhappy sister, but for the kind interposition of Mr Bethel. — Thus forced by my mother's inhumanity into a foreign country, without money or friends, where could I have found refuge for myself and my poor little ones, whose natural protector most unnaturally consigns their mother to a destiny more terrible than the most humble poverty.

Good God! is it possible that I am writing thus of the father of these children, for whose sake only I endure life? — I dare not trust my pen with another line on that subject —

'Oh! that way madness lies; let me shun that,
No more of that' ——*

The determination I at length came to was, to remain at the hotel de Moscovie, where I found very good accommodations, till I heard again from the unfortunate man whose property I am — but on no account to meet him, if I could avoid it, till he had relinquished every idea of compelling me, either with him or alone, to become an inmate in the house of Monsieur de Romagnecourt. — The manner in which I perceived Monsieur Bergasse heard the name of that nobleman spoken of, confirmed, too certainly, all the fears I had of Mr Verney's motive for cultivating an intimacy, from which most husbands would have recoiled — and, if contempt and abhorrence of his principles, could engender hatred against the father of George, of Harriet, and of William, surely I should be justified in feeling it.

Oh! how impossible it is to help relapsing continually into a topic so heavily pressing on the heart. — Let me, however, close the detail of my wandering, till I settle here. — I remarked, in the little time I had to remark any thing, that I never saw so many people, of all ages, scarred and seamed with the small pox, as I had observed since my being at Paris. — I was told that it was owing to the inveterate prejudices inculcated by the priests, who even now persisted in teaching, that to disarm this cruel disease of its malignity, was to offend heaven, which intended that it should blind, cripple, or render spectacles of horror, those whose lives it spared. — I enquired if it was now in Paris — I was answered that it was always in Paris. — Terrified at this intelligence, I sent to my friend Monsieur Bergasse, entreating him to look out for an house at some of the villages around it. — He very obligingly undertook the enquiry, and on Friday informed me, that he had heard of a *maison bourgois*,† but well furnished, and fit to be immedi-

---

* Shakespeare.[31]

† Houses in France were, till now, distinguished by 'maisons bourgois,' fit only for citizens or inferior people — and maisons noble, belonging to men of rank, or to les terres titrés.

ately inhabited, at Meudon. — I entreated him instantly to engage it — he did so; and, on my arrival, I found it infinitely more comfortable than I expected. — Here then I am, my Fanny, waiting in anxiety, but not with impatience, Mr Verney's further orders. — With sensations very different *your* letters are expected by your affectionate

GERALDINE

Have you heard from Mr Desmond? — I thought he would before now have written to me.

Mr Bethel, I hope, is still at Bath — I conclude I might by this time send my compliments to our newly acquired sister; but probably she will readily dispense with that ceremony. — Do you recollect in the novel of Sidney Biddulph (one of the best that we have in our language) how poor Sidney is treated in her adversity by the haughty wife of her brother, Sir George? Perhaps there is a little similarity in our destinies — But *I* have *no Faulkland!*[32]

LETTER XI

TO MISS WAVERLEY

Meudon, Sept. 7, 1791

You ask me, my sister, for a further description of my abode, if that can be called an abode where I am only a transient lodger, and from whence I every moment expect to receive a summons to depart — for — Alas! I know not whither!

You ask, too, my motives for prefering this place, which in my last letter I told you was melancholy, to Versailles or St Cloud, where I could equally have the advantage of gardens — or to Chaillot, Passy, or some other pleasant village, more immediately adjoining to Paris. — My dear Fanny, I prefer this place, *because it is* melancholy, and *because it is retired.*

Here, as I wander over the deserted gardens, I seldom meet any body but the men, who keep them in something like order, and who do not even look back at me, or mark my solitary walks.

There are, at Meudon, two palaces, one of very ancient structure and long, quite uninhabited — The other built, or at least repaired, by the Dauphin, father of the present King, which Louis the XVIth has occasionally inhabited, and which contains many handsome apartments. — They both stand in the same garden, which has never received any modern improvements — and in many parts of it the borders are destitute of their former ornaments; and, of many of the trees and shrubs that remain,

> 'The boughs are moss'd with age,
> And high tops bald with dry antiquity.'*

Adjoining to the most ancient of these royal houses, which terminates a long avenue and a large court, is a chapel with an arched gateway, leading to it from the garden, and surrounded by paved passages and high cloisters — and it is on some broken steps, that near these almost ruinous buildings, lead from the lower to the upper garden, I frequently take my pensive seat, and mark the sun sinking away above the high coppices that are beyond the gardens; (and I imagine form a part of them, though I have not yet ventured to wander so far.) — A yet more chearful seat I have found for my less melancholy moods, on the wall of the terrace on the opposite side, which looks down immediately on the village of Meudon — where, among its pleasant looking houses, they still point out the habitation of the celebrated *Rabelais*.[33] — As I never enjoyed, because, perhaps, I do not understand his works, I contemplate it not with so much pleasure as it would afford those who can admire them. — Of late, my Fanny, I have found this view too *riante*, and have adhered almost every evening after I have put my little ones to bed, to the old steps — where I hear no sounds but the bell of the convent of Capuchins (which is on a high ridge of land, concealed by trees, about half a mile from the old palace) or the wind murmuring hollow through the iron gratings and stone passages that lead round the chapel, from whose windows of painted glass I can fancy the sullen genius of superstition peeps forth, sighing over his departed power, in melancholy responses to the summons, that call the monks to their evening devotions.[34]

I often meet, as I come through the avenue, some of these venerable fathers, who, with slow steps, and downcast eyes, their cowl frequently covering their faces, and their arms crossed upon their breasts,

---

* Shakespeare.[35]

pass me — apparently so occupied by their holy meditations, as not to hold an insignificant being like me, worth even a salutation.

But why should that seem discourteous, which is probably a part of their religion? I ought also to consider, that besides the gloomy austerity of their order, they are now, perhaps, more austere, because they are unhappy. — They believe their altars are violated, and their profession rendered odious. — They fear their subsistence may fail them, and that they may be turned out into a world which is seldom too kind to the unfortunate, and is likely to treat *their* misfortunes with ridicule instead of pity. — I have observed, within this last week, one among them who seems more restlessly wretched than the rest. — I remark him every day pass by the windows of the house where I live, with a basket in one hand, and a staff in the other — his hood always concealing his face, and his tall figure bending as if weighed down by calamity.

After the morning duties are over, I see him glide among the trees in the garden, or among the vines that clothe the declivity towards the village. More than once he has come forth of an evening from the cloistered passages of the chapel, and, with solemn step, crossed near me to attend the last offices of the evening, when he hears the bell from the convent echo among the winding colonades.

There is something particularly affecting to me, in beholding this solitary mourner — whose griefs, though they are probably of a different kind from mine, are possibly as poignant. — Perhaps he was once a gay and thoughtless inhabitant of the world. — He may have seen (for he does not appear to be a young man) these now deserted palaces, blazing in the splendour of a voluptuous court. — Among its vanished glories, he may have lost all he loved; and he has now, it may be, no other consolation than visiting in the *cimetieré* of the chapel, the stone on which time is destroying even the sepulchral memorial of this beloved object.

As I thus make out, in my imagination, his melancholy story, I shed tears; I shudder at the distress I have drawn. — Oh! Fanny! — among all the miseries of humanity, the most insupportable is surely the death of those we love; and yet how full of contradiction is the human heart. — I know there are many, many evils in life to which death is infinitely preferable — I know that I myself prefer it to the continuance of such an existence as has long been mine; yet, to out-live *you*, my *children*, and *one or two of my friends*, presents an idea of calamity which would deprive me of my reason.

How have I been led by the poor desponding Monk into this digression? — I hardly know, and have not now much time to revise what I have written, as a messenger goes to Paris this evening, who is to take my letter. I return, therefore, to my subject as abruptly as I quitted it, to tell you the little that remains to be said about my house — it is just like other French houses; and its only recommendation to me is the melancholy sort of repose, and the solitary walks, which its immediate neighbourhood to the gardens of Meudon afford me.

The windows command great part of the view between this place and Paris, to which, it would be difficult for the pencil to do justice: — with a pen, it were hopeless to attempt it.

The first yellow tints of Autumn are hardly stealing on the trees, encreasing, however, where they have touched them, the beauty of the foliage. — The sky is delightfully serene; and a sun-set in the gardens here exceeds what I ever saw in England for warmth and brilliancy of colouring. — No dew falls, even when the sun is gone, though we may call the evenings now autumnal evenings. — I am generally out with my children till past seven o'clock, and after I have attended them to their beds, I still find it mild and warm enough to allow me to perform *my* vespers in the open air.

You, my Fanny — at least, till your tenderness for me taught it to you — you have never been unhappy, and have never known (O! *may* you never know) the strange and, perhaps, capricious fellings of the *irretrievably* wretched. — Since I have found myself so, I have taken up a notion that I do not breathe freely, while I am within the house; and like the poor maniac, who wandered about in the neighbourhood of Bristol, I fancy 'that nothing is good but liberty and fresh air.'

In consequence of this sensation, I live all-day about the gardens. While the sun is high, Peggy attends me with the three children, in some shady part of them; and George often amuses himself with catching the little brown lizards which abound in the grass, and among the tufts of low shrubs on this dry soil. — He brings them to me — I bid him take great care not to hurt them — I explain to him, that they have the same sense of pain as he has, and suffer equally under pressure and confinement — He looks very grave, as I endeavour to impress this on his mind; and then gently putting them down, cries, 'no! no! indeed! I will not hurt you, poor little things!'

How much a tone, a look, an almost imperceptible expression of countenance will awaken to new anguish an heart always oppressed like mine! — As, liberating his prisoners, he says this — I look round on him, his sweet sister, and his baby-brother, and internally sighing, say, 'Oh! would I were sure, if ever your poor mamma is torn from you, that nobody will hurt you, poor little things!'

What ails me, to be thus unusually weak, this evening? — I believe the heat of the day has overcome me — I will go and walk, as I did last night, when I have finished my letter.

I shall probably meet my fellow sufferer, for such I am sure he is, the solitary Capuchin — I have just seen him walk towards the palace garden. — Well! — and is there not satisfaction in beholding a being, who, whatever may have been his misfortunes, seems to have found consolation and fortitude in religion. — I have often entertained an half-formed wish that he would speak to me. — Perhaps his own sufferings may have taught him that tender sympathy with the sufferings of others, which is often so soothing to the sick heart, and he might speak of peace to me!

I am sadly distressed here for want of books. The few which, with such a quantity of necessary baggage, I was able to bring with me, I have now exhausted; and though my good friend, Monsieur Bergasse, has sent me some from Paris, they happen to be such as I cannot read with any pleasure. — I have supposed it not impossible that the Monk might supply me from the library of his convent.

This deficiency of books has compelled me to have recourse to my pen and my pencil, to beguile those hours, when my soul, sickening at the past, and recoiling from the future, would very fain lose its own mournful images in the witchery of fiction, or in some pursuit; though, alas! it is too true, that the mind will stray from the fingers; and that I cannot find, either in work or in drawing, enough employment to keep me from sad and bitter reflection.

Reason as vainly tells me, that nothing can be worth the unceasing solicitude I feel. — Were it only for myself, I surely should not indulge it; nor would I magnify or dwell upon the actual and possible miseries of my destiny, but for my children! — for those I love so much better than myself! — I cannot help being sensible of such agonizing anxiety as occupation cannot charm, nor reason conquer.

I have found, however, a melancholy delight in describing these sufferings. — I usually take my evening seat on the flight of steps I have described to you. — Sometimes, when I am in more tranquil spirits, I sketch, in my port-folio, the wild flowers and weeds that grow among the buildings where I sit. — In some parts, ivy holds together the broken piles of brick, from whence the cement has fallen. — The stone-crop, and the toad-flax, cover or creep among the masses of dis-jointed marble; several sorts of antirhinum still wave their pink and purple blossoms along the edges of the wall; and last night I observed, mingled with them, a root of the field poppy, still in flower. — On the qualities of this plant I fell into a reverie. — To you, my Fanny, and to you only, I entrust the little wild ode — almost, indeed, an impromptu, which this contemplation produced.

ODE TO THE POPPY

Not for the promise of the labor'd field,
Not for the good the yellow harvests yield,
    I bend at Ceres' shrine;[36]
    For dull, to humid eyes appear,
    The golden glories of the year;
Alas! — a melancholy worship's mine!

I hail the Goddess for her scarlet flower!
    Thou brilliant weed,
    Thou dost so far exceed,
The richest gifts gay Flora can bestow;
Heedless I pass'd thee, in life's morning hour,
    (Thou comforter of woe,)
'Till sorrow taught me to confess thy power.

    In early days, when Fancy cheats,
        A various wreath I wove;
    Of laughing springs luxuriant sweets,
        To deck ungrateful love:
    The rose, or thorn, my numbers crown'd,
    As Venus smil'd, or Venus frown'd;
But Love, and Joy, and all their train, are flown;

E'en languid Hope no more is mine,
  And I will sing of thee alone;
Unless, perchance, the attributes of grief,
  The cypress bud, and willow leaf,
Their pale, funereal foliage, blend with thine.

  Hail, lovely blossom! — thou can'st ease,
  The wretched victims of disease;
Can'st close those weary eyes, in gentle sleep,
  Which never open but to weep;
    For, oh! thy potent charm,
  Can agonizing pain disarm;
Expel imperious memory from her seat,
And bid the throbbing heart forget to beat.

Soul-soothing plant! — that can such blessings give,
  By thee the mourner bears to live!
  By thee the hopeless die!
  Oh! ever 'friendly to despair,'[37]
  Might sorrow's palid votary dare,
Without a crime, that remedy implore,
Which bids the spirit from its bondage fly,
I'd court thy palliative aid no more;
  No more I'd sue, that thou shouldst spread,
  Thy spell around my aching head,
  But would conjure thee to impart,
  Thy balsam for a broken heart;
  And by thy soft Lethean power,
    (Inestimable flower)
Burst these terrestrial bonds, and other regions try.

GERALDINE VERNEY

LETTER XII

TO MR BETHEL

I have been long in writing to you, Bethel, and now hardly know whence to date my letters, as I am, and have been, and shall be, upon the ramble for some time. — I am unhappy, and the unhappy are always restless.

What a challenge on political affairs does your last letter contain! — In the present state of my spirits I cannot contend with you, were I disposed to do it; but I am willing to allow, that much of your eulogium on the constitution of England is just; and that it is so good, that it ought to be better.

If we see an individual who has a thousand good qualities that excite our esteem and admiration, and yet know he has two or three failings that render all his virtues of little avail, we very naturally say, what pity that this man, who is so brave, so sensible, so humane, should, by a strange inconsistency of character, be so corrupt, so easily led away by objects unworthy of him — so warped by prejudice, so blind to his own interest — And thus it is with all the affairs of life, perhaps; that any degree of perfection makes us regret that the object in which it exists is not perfect.

Of this nature is the regret I feel in regard to my country. — I would have our boast of her excellence just — I would not have it the mere cant which we have learned by rote, and repeat by habit; though, when we venture to think about it, we know that it is vanity and prejudice, and not truth, when we speak of its wonderful perfection; and that even those who are its most decided partizans, are continually betrayed into an acknowledgement of its defects. — Boswell, in his life of Johnson says, that 'in the British parliament, any question, however unreasonable or unjust, may be carried by a venal majority.'[38] — This is acknowledged truth; and it follows, that while the means of corruption exist to an extent so immense, there must be a venal majority; and, of course, every question, however ruinous, will be carried. — While this is the case, and while every attempt to remedy this *original sin* of the constitution is opposed (though the necessity of that remedy has been allowed by the greatest statesman of our country) while every proposal to make it *really* what it is only *nominally*, raises a cry as if the subversion of the whole empire was intended — I cannot agree to unlimited praise — though most certainly willing to allow to you, that a greater portion of happiness is diffused among the subjects of the British government, than among any other people upon earth. But this rather proves that *their* condition is very wretched, than that ours is perfectly happy. — Carried on a little in the same way, was the argument that I heard not long since, *against* the abolition of the detestable Slave Trade.[39] — I was pleading *for it* with a *member of parliament*, who *has an estate in the West Indies*, and who has been there himself, some years ago, when he commanded a man of war. — I talked warmly (for I had just been reading the reports of the committee) and I talked from my heart. — My adversary, well hackneyed in the ways of men, treated all I could say as the ill-digested speculation of a hot-head enthusiast, who knew nothing of the matter. — 'You are young, Mr Desmond,' said he, 'very young, and have but little considered the importance of this trade to the prosperity of the British nation: besides, give me leave to tell you, that you know nothing of the condition of the negroes neither, nor of their nature. — They are not fit to be treated otherwise than as slaves, for they have not the same senses and feelings as we have. — A negro fellow minds a flogging so little, that he will go to a dance at night, or at least the next day, after a hearty application of the cat. — They have no understanding to qualify them for any rank in society above slaves; and, indeed, are not to be called men — they are monkies.' 'Monkies! Sir!' exclaimed I, 'that is, indeed, a most extraordinary assertion. — Monkies! I believe, indeed, they are a very distinct race from the European — So also is the straight-haired and fine formed Asiatic — So are the red men of North America — But where, amid this variety, does the man end, and the monkey begin? I am afraid if we follow whither this enquiry will lead us, that we shall find ourselves, more degraded then even by the whimsical system of Lord Monboddo.[40] — If the negro, however, is a monkey, let me hazard one remark — that their very near affinity to us, is too clearly ascertained by the alliances we have formed with them. Nay, I have even heard that captains of our ships of war, have often professed that they prefer the sable nymphs of Africa to the fairer dames of Europe —

'The pale unripen'd beauties of the North.'[41]

'And, if I recollect aright, Sir, I have formerly, in moments of un-guarded conviviality, heard you say, that when you were a young man, and in the sea service you had yourself indulged this partiality for these monkey ladies.'

This parried, a little, the round assertion that negroes were not men: but he still insisted upon it that they had little or no feeling. It was not, however, very difficult to prove, as far as proof can on such a point be brought, that their physical and moral sensibility is more acute than ours. — I will not lengthen my letter by repeating these proofs, be-cause I am persuaded you are not disposed to dispute them; but go on to say, that after I had carried almost every article against him, my adversary was compelled to take shelter under such an argument as yours.' — 'Perhaps,' said he, 'the negroes *are* sometimes beat, but not half so much as our soldiers are — The punishment inflicted on sol-diers is infinitely more severe.'

'Does not that, Sir,' said I, 'rather prove that our military punish-ments are inhuman, than that the negroes have nothing to complain of?'

Thus, my dear Bethel, it seems to me, that instead of proving that we are extremely happy, you prove only that we are comparatively so; and, for my part, I never could, as many people do, derive consola-tion from the reflection that the existence of evil in the person of an-other, diminished the sense of what I felt in my own.

Do not, however, misunderstand me: I think that our form of gov-ernment is certainly the best — not that can be imagined — but that has ever been experienced; and, while we are sure that practice is in its favour, it would be most absurd to dream of destroying it on theory. — If I had a very good house that had some inconveniencies about it, I should not desire to pull it down, but I certainly should send for an architect and say, alter this room — it is too dark — remove those passages — they are too intricate — make a door here, and a staircase there; make the kitchen more habitable for my servants, and then my house will be extremely good. — But I should be very much startled if my architect were to say, 'Sir, I dare not touch your house — if I let in more light, if I take down those partitions, and make the other changes you desire, I am very much afraid that the great timbers will give way, and the *party-walls* crush you beneath their ruins.'

As I do not know when I shall see you, I shall continue to write

— and wish very much to hear from you often. — If you send your letters to Messrs Sibthorpe and Griffith, bankers in London, on whom I draw for money as I want it, they will always be able, during the rest of my ramble, to trace my route by my drafts and letters on business.

Adieu! dear Bethel,

Ever your's faithfully,

LIONEL DESMOND

LETTER XIII

TO MR DESMOND

Hartfield, Sept. 10, 1791

I stifle, I repress all curiosity, Desmond. — I have often told you I never desired to interfere with your affairs, farther than you wished me to do so — farther than you thought I could be useful to you: and therefore, though I read, with wonder and concern, a letter not dated, either as to place or time — a letter, in which the name of Geraldine is not mentioned; and in which you seem not to know either where you are or where you shall be — I will not say more upon it, than that I am always glad to hear of you, upon your own terms.

When will the time come to which I have so long and so vainly been looking forward? — When shall I see you living in Sedgewood, in that most respectable of all characters, the independent English gentleman? — I never wanted your society so much as I do now; but, perhaps, never was so unlikely to have it; and all that I find here, is so little to my taste, that I shall be glad to return to Bath, which it is judged necessary for me soon to do.

This dislike of society, however, arises not from its quantity, but its quality. — Since Sir Robert Stamford has settled in the neighbourhood, his house, which is almost always full, supplies the market-town with idle or curious morning visiters; and at the coffee-house, where I very seldom go, I happened, on calling yesterday, to meet your Uncle, Major Danby, and I learned that, attracted by the reputation of Epicurean living, he had accepted the invitation often given by his old acquaintance Sir Robert, and was on a fortnight's visit at Linwell.

I found the Major had collected round him the Curate, the Attorney, the Attorney's Clerk, the Riding Surveyor, the Master of Academy, 'where youth are *genteelly* educated,' and two or three of the principal tradesmen of the town: and that, from a very long oration on politics, which they had heard with conviction and admiration, he had glided away on a descriptive tour to his own seat, near Bath; and was giving a *catalogue raisonée* of its conveniences, obliquely preferring them all to the accumulations of the same luxuries at Linwell.[42]

'I own,' said he, 'Sir Robert has been at a great expence, an immense expence — but the thing, my dear Sir, (addressing himself to the Attorney) the thing is judgment — judgment in laying out money is every thing.'

'Aye, Sir, to be sure,' answered this gentleman, (who was, I found, an enemy of Sir Robert's, because he was employed in election matters by a great man of the opposite party) — 'aye, certainly; and, as you say, how should Sir Robert Stamford have this judgment? — seeing, that it was but a few years ago that he knew more of a *fi, fa* and *latitats, John Doe* and *Richard Roe*, than about raising foreign fruits and ice creams.[43] — I don't wish to speak in disparagement of the profession neither — for an honest attorney is a very honourable thing.'

'And, I am sure, it is a very rare one,' interrupted a blunt tradesman, in a smooth black wig, and leather breeches — 'a very rare one — and, for aught I ever saw or heard to the contrary, you may put all the honest lawyers that ever was in your eye, and never see the worse.'

'That's not so civil a speech, Sir,' said Mr Grimbold, the Exciseman. 'Sir Robert Stamford, Sir, my worthy patron, is a man of honour, Sir, and a gentleman, Sir; and as for his having practis'd the law, Sir, and thereby raised himself to his present rank, it does him credit, Sir, and shews that this government and administration fairly and justly rewards merit, Sir.'

'Come, come, Mr Grimbold,' cried the Attorney, 'we know very well that the greatest merit Sir Robert has in your eyes, is his having rewarded *your* merit, and made you a riding-officer; because of the votes for this here borough of ours, that are in your family, Mr Grimbold —'[44]

'Yes! yes!' said Mr Doughty, another tradesman, 'we understand trap, and so does our good neighbour. — As to me I am free to speak without favour or affection — We all know what Sir Robert Stamford — What then! — which of us that had been as much in luck would not have done the same thing? — I have nothing to say to that. —

Whatever a man can make in the way of business, whether it be as a lawyer, or a tradesman, or as to a place at court, is all fair enough; and I, for my part, don't want to cry Sir Robert down, though he does not deal at my shop. He went to Gill's when he settled here — for why? 'Twas natural enough, Gill could command three votes — certain I have but one: but Sir Robert, though he is not a constant customer, lays out a good deal of money with me, and I've no fault to find,'

While this conversation, so expressive of the candour and disinterested conduct of British electors, went on, I stood *perdu* behind Mr Grimbold; a tall personage, whose broad shoulders, however, just permitted me to peep over at the Major, who had not yet espied me.[45] — I saw he became extremely restless at being compelled to hear so much of the consequence of his friend Sir Robert, when he was thinking only how he might best display his own. — Not very curious in his auditors, he is well contented to be heard; and detests a man who interrupts him worse than a pick-pocket.

He now raised his voice in the vain hope of being still attended to. — The worthy Burgesses of W——— had got upon a topic much more interesting to them, than a description of pastures, the beef of which they should never partake, and of pineries, the produce of which, not even an election could send them a share; and he therefore bustled up to quit the circle, when perceiving me, he advanced, and very cordially shook hands with me. — We walked away together, and fell into conversation on the views, and the soil, and the husbandry in this part of the country; which, he said, was very much inferior to that tract of the county of Somerset, round his house at Ashford-hall.

This uncle of yours has, to a very extravagant degree, a trait of character which I have, in my way through life, once or twice remarked before. — Whatever he does, is better done than any other man living could have done it — whatever he says is without appeal — whatever he possesses is more extraordinary, more excellent, than are the same things in the possession of his neighbours.

His house and gardens are the best in the county — his men do more work — his crops are more luxuriant — and so fond is he of being always the most active and the most important, that I have heard him boast of having, in his judicial capacity for the county of Somerset, committed, in the course of one year, more prisoners to the county jail, than any three of his brethren of the bench.

You know, that being an old bachelor, and somewhat of an epicure, he is at home, what the vulgar call a cot; and has laid down his spontoon for the tasting spoon, converted his sword into a carving knife, and his sash into a jelly bag. — It is not her youth or her beauty, that recommended his present favourite housekeeper; but the skill she had acquired in studying under a French cook, at the house of a great man, who acquired an immense fortune in the American war, by obtaining the contract for potatoes and sour crout.[46] — But even to this gentlewoman, skilled as she is in 'all kinds of made dishes, pickling, potting, and preserving,' and tenderly connected with her, as the prying world supposes the Major to be; he does not leave the sole direction of that important department, his kitchen; which, when he is at home, he always superintends himself. — 'Aye, aye,' said he, in this last conversation, 'let those alone for good eating who know what it is to have lived badly. — *I* remember when we were in camp in Germany, and had nothing to drink but water from a pond that swarmed with vermin, and not enough of that — and nothing to eat but such bread as I would not now give to my hogs — while the money went into the pockets of the contractors.'

'You now live in happier times, Major,' said I.

'Aye, that we do, indeed — these times are very good times, if the damned scoundrels of presbyterians and non-conformists would but let us be quiet that think them good; and not be disturbing the public tranquillity, and be cursed to the round-headed sons of b———s.' Then looking more important, he added, 'To tell you very seriously my thoughts, Mr Bethel, I don't much like the present appearance of affairs — there is a very troublesome mutinous spirit got among the dissenters — These riots that happened in July at Birmingham' —[47]

'Nay, dear Major Danby,' cried I, 'it was not the dissenters who rioted there' —

'No; but it was owing to them and their seditious meetings. — For my part, I rejoice that they fell into the pit they had dug for others. — I wish that they had all been blown up together, and the country well rid of them. — I'll tell you what, Bethel, if I commanded on that occasion, I should have been apt, I believe, to have protected those honest men in what they did against your confounded saints. — Those canting puritans are all water drinkers, fellows that sing and pray — I'd extirpate the whole race.'

'You would really?'

'Yes, by G——— would I, before they do any more mischief. — What business have *they* to mutter, and raise disturbances, and complain of their grievances? I hope government will never grant them an ace — let them grumble on, but not influence the opinion of other people. — At present I am a little uneasy at the face of affairs. — I have a stake in the hedge, Mr Bethel, a pretty considerable stake, and I don't desire to see it trampled down.'

'I don't know,' replied I, 'any body that does.'

'Yes, yes, but I do know such. — You are, indeed, a temperate man — a man who has seen a good deal of the world. — You have a stake also of some consequence; so, indeed, and a very valuable one, has my nephew, Desmond — But what d'ye think now of him? — He's as discontented as any Praise-God-bare-Bones of them all. — I can't imagine what possesses the puppy — he's not like any other young fellow of his age. Instead of sporting his money like a man of spirit, on the turf, or with the bones, he goes piping about, and talks of unequal representation, and the weight of taxes, and the devil knows what; things, with which a young fellow of six-and-twenty has no concern at all. — And then, as for his amours; instead of keeping a brace or two of pretty wenches, he goes sneaking after a married woman — to be sued for damages, and, perhaps, run through the body.'

'Sneaking about after a married woman, Sir,' said I, 'pray explain.'

'Come, come, Bethel,' replied your sage uncle, 'don't affect ignorance. — I believe you are a trusty confidant, but here your secresy is a mere joke — the thing is too notorious.'

'I must beg an explanation, Major Danby,' cried I, with some warmth — 'since you think me concerned, it is the more necessary.' 'Why, if I must explain then, can you really now suppose that we don't all know the history of Mrs Verney?' — 'The history of Mrs Verney, Sir! — Upon my honour I must recommend it to you to speak more cautiously of a woman of whom malice itself cannot injure the reputation — A woman who is an example of a blameless wife, to a very worthless husband — and the best mother, daughter, and sister ———'

'Why damn it now, Bethel, how can you fancy all this will do with me? If Mrs Verney has a *penchant* for Lionel, with all my soul. — I know very well that if the stupid puppy, her husband, had as many horns as the beast in the Revelations, he deserves them all, and

Desmond has as good a chance as another, with any woman; but I think he's a fool to be at such a cursed expence about it, and then to fancy himself so snug, like a woodcock that hides its head, and believes itself secure; — Hah! ha! hah!'[48]

'Upon my word, Major, I must still declare myself ignorant of your meaning.'

He absolutely shouted, in his coarse boisterous way, but seeing me look very grave, he at length checked his mirth, and said — 'Why lookee, Bethel, when a young fellow lays down between three and four thousand pounds, to release from execution the effects of a man he despises and contemns; when he goes down *incog.* to the retirement of such a man's wife, and stays near a month in her neighbourhood; when he is known to have declined the most advantageous offers of alliance from the families of some of the finest young women in England on her account; and, when he is actually, at this time, gone abroad with her; or, however, concealed somewhere or other, how the plague can you suppose the world will *not* talk? It is well enough known, that Verney is a savage and a scoundrel, who will sell his wife to the best bidder. — Why don't Lionel offer him her price at once, for now you may depend upon it he'll be sued, and Verney will get devilish damages.'[49] — I was, as you will easily believe, thunderstruck by a speech in which truth was so blended with falsehood, that while I was compelled to allow some part of it to be true, it seemed hopeless, with such a man, to contend, that much of it was an infamous supposition. — How make your uncle Danby believe, that you should, on a system of affection, *merely platonic,* have advanced this money? (of which it is wonderful that he should be informed) *on a system merely platonic,* go and live *perdu* in Herefordshire? *on a system merely platonic,* be now concealed in France, in the neighbourhood of Geraldine — for such I am afraid is the fact. — Dear Desmond! behold the consequences of your indiscretion! — See what cruel (and, as I am convinced) what *unjust* reflections you have been the means of throwing on the woman you love — consider all the consequences that may follow. — However hopeless the undertaking appeared, I endeavoured to convince Major Danby, that in whatever way you might have interfered to be serviceable to Mrs Verney, for whom you had a very great friendship; yet that all this originated, on your part, not from any designs prejudicial to the honour of Mrs Verney, but from your pity for an amiable woman involved in undeserved calamities; that you certainly were not in France now, but in the North of England; and that Mrs Verney was with her husband.'

All the answer I could obtain to this was, 'Pooh! Pooh! — Pshaw! pshaw! we know better.' — I could neither convince the Major of the fallacy of the reports he had heard, or prevail upon him to name the authors. — Tired with the conversation, and heartily vexed, I left him soon after; nor could the account he was again going to begin of his own importance, which is an idea ever uppermost in his mind, prevail upon me longer to attend to him. — I returned home, and he went back to Sir Robert Stamford's, there to entertain the respectable society (among whom I find is Lord Newminster and Sir James Deybourne) with an account of *my* consternation at the knowledge he has of your affairs.

I own to you, Desmond, that this dialogue has occasioned to me very cruel disquiet. — If this letter reaches you before the mischief is irreparable, by the universal dissemination of these reports, so injurious to the peace, perhaps so fatal to the life of Geraldine; appear, I conjure you, shew yourself in England — convince her friends and the world that you have *not* followed her to France; and vindicate, at once, her fame, and the veracity of

Your faithful servant,

E. BETHEL

LETTER XIV

TO MR BETHEL

Bexley Hill, near Wells, Somerset,
Sept. 23, 1791

You lately accustomed me, dear Sir, to confide to you the cruel uneasiness that preyed upon my heart, in regard to my sister Verney; and surely you will forgive me, if I once more intrude upon you — when I am, on her account, infinitely more unhappy than ever, and when I have no friend but you to whom I dare speak of her.

It is now two days since I have been in possession of a sixth letter from her, since she has been in France. It is dated, as the two preceding letters were, from Meudon. It gives me an account of her situation; it describes the scene around her; they are her words — her sentiments — her ideas — and she has even added a beautiful little ode, which as I read it, gave me such a picture of her despondent state of mind, as drew tears from my eyes.

As there were, however, some parts of this letter which I could not, with propriety, shew my mother, as the sentiments might have raised her anger, and the poetry her aversion, I said nothing to her of my having received such a letter. — She, herself, had long ceased to en-quire, earnestly, about my sister; and therefore, in this concealment, or rather silence, I had not to reproach myself with breach of duty and tenderness, in trifling with maternal solitude.

I believed my mother was quite easy about Geraldine, and con-tent not to be at any expence herself, was perfectly satisfied with what-ever dispositions Mr Verney might chuse to make about his wife and his children.

You will suppose then, that I was extremely surprised yesterday. — I was at work in my own room, when my mother, about a quarter of an hour after the arrival of the letters from the post, entered it. I saw immediately that something had discomposed her; but as trifles very often affect her more than things of consequence, I concluded that her maid had made up her Mecklin lace awkwardly, or had put too much starch in her new Japan muslin; and, having vented as much of her anger on the poor girl as it was probable she would bear at one sitting, I was to afford Mrs Waverly entire ease, by listening (as in duty bound) to the *residuum*; which seemed, by its acrimony, to inflame her features, and agitate her whole frame. — 'Daughter Frances,' cried she, 'have you heard lately from Mrs Verney?'

'Yes, Madam.'

'And pray where is she' —

'In France, Madam, at Meudon, where she was when she wrote to you' —

''Tis false' — replied my mother, anger flashing from her eyes, and trembling on her tongue — ''tis a bare-faced, infamous falsehood, *and you know it is.*'

'Good God! dear Madam! you terrify and amaze me! what can you mean?'

'I mean, I mean — I dare hardly trust myself to utter a sentence so disgraceful. — You, Miss, deceitful, worthless, wicked girl, know it, however, but too well.'

'My dear Madam, what do I know? For mercy's sake do not agitate yourself thus! — Whatever I know about our poor Geraldine, I am sure I never made any mystery of: tell me, I beseech you, what do I know?'

'Odious, base, little hypocrite — you know that this disgrace to my blood, this viper who is to destroy the honour of my family, is *not* in France; perhaps never has been there; but has been, and is, I believe, in my conscience, still at that farm-house in Herefordshire, where she lived before — where she has lain-in — yes, Miss, lain-in of a girl, and is the declared mistress of that villain, Desmond, who has been there with her; and, perhaps, is with her yet!'

The moment I could recover from my immediate surprise, the ridiculous impossibility of this story struck me so forcibly, that my terrors were, for a moment, dissipated; and I recolleced myself enough to say (perhaps with a look of too much contempt, considering it was my mother to whom I spoke) 'upon my word, Madam, a very curious legend. — Have the goodness to tell me, to whose admirably fertile invention you owe it. — If *dear, good* Miss Elford had not been quite removed from this part of the world, I should have given her the honour of it.'

I said this quite by guess, and not at all supposing I was right; but I saw instantly, by my mother's countenance, that my conjecture was just, and my alarm subsided still more. — I was now sure, that not only this falsehood, but the facts that happened during Geraldine's real residence at Bridge-foot, came from Miss Elford; and having conquered my first perturbation, I managed the rest of the dialogue so as to procure from my mother's unguarded warmth, all the intelligence I desired; though it has not, on reflection, given my mind all the ease I expected. — Miss Elford has a relation whose residence is at Ross, and to the house of this relation she retired, when overwhelmed with anguish and disappointment, by the sudden desertion of her mercenary lover. — The inn where the French nobleman and his *suite* put up, was exactly opposite this her melancholy retirement. — A group much less marked by singularity of appearance, would have attracted the attention of an insulated being, eagerly attentive to every occurrence that afforded any thing to gratify her natural love of malicious enquiry, now sharpened by internal wretchedness and discontent. — The foreigners no sooner appeared, than Miss Elford became stationary at her window, and she saw an Englishman with them, in whom she immediately recollected the person of Mr Desmond.

The chambermaid of the inn was well known to her. She contrived to send for her over, to pick out all she knew then of the guests, and to engage her to make farther enquiries — in consequence of which the woman soon informed her, that Mr Desmond had been living some time at the cottage at Bridge-foot, very near the residence of Mrs Verney; that he returned thither before the foreign gentleman, and afterwards accompanied Geraldine to Gloucester. — All this, with some additions of her own, was transmitted to my mother, under the strictest injunctions of secrecy. — This explains all those circumstances that gave me such pain and astonishment, when my mother had taken such a sudden antipathy to Mr Desmond, and so strenuously insisted on Geraldine's going to her husband.

But how shall I account for what, on the same authority, my mother has now heard, that my sister, attended by a gentleman, the description of whom answers to the person of Mr Desmond, returned to Bridge-foot about three weeks since, where she was, in a few days, delivered of a daughter; that her attendants, consisting of two women, are French, who cannot speak a syllable of English. — The gentleman, who accompanied her, left the place about ten days ago; but the lady is supposed to be still there.

I know, that were not Geraldine incapable of such conduct, unversed in deceit, and possessing a heart as free as from guilt as her mind is ingenuous and candid, there are numberless other objections to the probability of her being so situated. — Yet, as Miss Elford had most certainly truth for the general ground of her former assertions, how is it possible to convince my mother that all she relates now is mere fabrication? — How is it possible to convince the malicious, prying world of this? — Indeed the particulars are so minute which Miss Elford has sent, it is almost impossible to suppose, that with all her art, or all her malice, she could have the cunning to invent, or the effrontery so boldly to assert them, and to dare any one to disprove facts; which she assures my mother, only her tender regard for her could induce her to bring forward so positively. — 'My heart, *dear, dear,* Mrs Waverly,' says the canting prude, 'my heart bleeds for every pang which justice and truth oblige me (to prevent your being deceived and imposed upon) thus to inflict on your's!'

Dear Sir! what am I to think of all this? — That my sister Geraldine, whom I know to be in France, should be at this village in Hereford-shire, I know is impossible. — I own it is much more likely that Miss Elford, through malice or error, or both, has invented the story, or taken some other person for her. — Yet, as the report will not only be inju-rious to the fame of my beloved sister, but may be attended with con-sequences fatal to the life of *your* beloved friend — I own, that though I despised it at first, I now feel most completely alarmed; and entreat you to have the goodness to tell me, by the return of the post, whether you know where Mr Desmond is; and whether you think any meas-ures ought to be pursued; and what to prevent the farther progress of a calumny, from which so much mischief is to be apprehended.

Imagine with what impatience I wait to hear again from my sister — and how often I have examined and re-examined the contents and the post-marks of those letters I have already received from her. — When an evil, of whatever nature, is certain, the mind, by degrees, acquires firmness to endure it; but the pain of uncertainty and conjec-ture, like what I now suffer, is, of all others, the most intolerable. — I have not closed my eyes during the last night; [n]or have I had one moment's tranquillity of mind since my mother's angry communica-tion. — To add to my excessive vexation, she has related the whole, in the most unguarded way, to Mrs Fairfax and her daughter, to my brother and his wife, and to a certain Lord Fordingbridge, who is here on a visit to Mr Waverly; and, I think, the lover of Miss Anastatia. — There are, therefore, no hopes of stifling the report; and if I can judge by the manner of the ladies, there is not one of them who fails to hope it may be found true. — Geraldine is too lovely, and has been too much admired, not to be disliked by women who are so remarkable for their wish to monopolize all admiration; and they are glad of an opportunity to exclude from the family a part of it, who might, they apprehend, in consequence of Verney's mad dissipation, be, at some time or other, a weight on the pecuniary interest of the rest.

Lord Fordingbridge met with Desmond abroad, and seems to have conceived some personal dislike to him. — My brother has been de-bating, whether he ought not to apply to him for immediate satisfac-tion; but of his pursuing that idea, I should not have very acute apprehensions, if I did not see that Lord Fordingbridge, towards whom he looks as to an oracle, (for he is reckoned a young man of eminent abilities) did not seem very much inclined to urge him to such a step. — The whole conversation of the circle here, has been engrossed by this affair ever since yesterday; of course, it is terribly painful to me: but I dare not absent myself from it long together, and have stolen the time I have been writing this from my pillow, though not from my repose; for, till I am less distracted by conjectures and apprehensions, I have no hope of obtaining any. — Pardon, dear Sir, this incoherent letter. — I really do not know what I am about; and never in my life had so much occasion for that friendly advice, with which you have so often honoured and obliged,

Sir,

Your most grateful and obedient servant,

FRANCES WAVERLY

LETTER XV

TO MISS WAVERLY

Hartfield, Sept. 28th, 1791

It was late last night, dear Madam, before I received your letter. — However I am flattered by being thus honoured with your confidence, the purport of it has given me extreme uneasiness — the more so, as what I have to say, in reply, will not, I fear, relieve you from any part of your's.

I agree with you, however, in opinion — opinion, surely, founded on the securest ground; that our dear Mrs Verney is incapable of the conduct which is, by Miss Elford's representation, and Mrs Waverly's credulity, imputed to her. — Yet, convinced as I must, on reflection, be of this, I am, at the same time, compelled to acknowledge, that there is an air of mystery in the letters of Mr Desmond to me, so unlike his usual style of confidence and candour, that I account for it no otherwise than by supposing there is something in his situation, which it is necessary to conceal even from me.

These letters are not dated, so that I know not whither they come from, or how long they are written before I receive them. — But it is probable that Desmond is at a great distance, as he receives my letters, which are sent to the care of his bankers in London, very long after they are written.

I will own to you, that this reserve of my friend's, which I never, till lately, experienced from him, has hurt me extremely. — Yet, perhaps, I am wrong; there are circumstances and situations, which a man of honor cannot, and ought not, to reveal to his most intimate friends.

I thought, however, that, upon the footing we always have been together, I, who can have no object in view but his service, might attempt to discover how I might more quickly convey my letters to him, particularly as some affairs, relative to one of his estates, required his immediate answer. — I, therefore, wrote to the second partner in the banking-house he is connected with, who is more particularly entrusted with his concerns, and begged an address to Mr Desmond, stating my reasons for asking it. — I received last night a very polite answer from this gentleman, assuring me, that he would convey any letter to Mr Desmond, as safely and expeditiously as possible; but, that to give his address, even to me, would be a breach of a promise solemnly given, which, he was sure, I would not ask him to commit.

What am I to think of this? — and why should Desmond's residence be a secret to me, unless —— but I will not torment you or myself, dear Miss Waverly, with conjectures, which I stifle as soon as they arise. — Perhaps I may have a letter from him to-day; but, as I send this to the post, at six miles distance, by the messenger, who brings back my letters, I cannot, if I wait the man's return, answer your's so soon as you desire. — All I can now do, therefore, is to assure you, that I will send you the earliest intelligence I receive; and if such difficulties should arise, as make my being near of any use to you, in your present state of solicitude, in regard to friends so dear to us both, I will hasten my journey to Bath. — If I have any news of Desmond by the post of this day, I will write to-morrow.

> I have the honour to be,
> Dear Madam,
> With great esteem,
> Your most obedient and faithful servant,
> E. BETHEL

LETTER XVI

TO MISS WAVERLY

Hartfield, Sept. 29th, 1791

DEAR MADAM,

In pursuance of my promise, in my letter of yesterday, I enclose you a pacquet I received from Mr Desmond, by the return of my messenger — though it is wholly foreign to the topic that so deeply interests us, and can serve, perhaps, only to encrease uneasy apprehensions; for it must be remarked with wonder, that Desmond, who, with whatever subject he began his letters, generally spoke more of Mrs Verney than any other, now seems to force himself upon political affairs, (about which, till a few months since, he was totally indifferent) in order to escape from naming her who once engrossed all his attention.

The letter came, as usual, from his bankers in London; and, I own, serves rather to irritate than appease my uneasiness. I await your farther commands with impatience —

And am,
Dear Madam,
With perfect esteem,
Your most obliged servant,

E BETHEL

From some passages of the enclosed letter, one would conjecture that Desmond is in France. — I know not what to think of it.

LETTER XVII

TO MR BETHEL

I thank you, dear Bethel, for your account of my worthy uncle, whom you seem, indeed, to have studied more than I have done. — Perhaps, according to worldly maxims, I have done wrong to have neglected him so much; but, to the overbearing and dictatorial consequence he assumes, I never could submit, even if I had happened to *want* the advantage I might have acquired by it. — The gross epicurism in which he indulges himself, while he repeats, with exaggeration, the vices of others, are traits of character so offensive to me, that whenever we meet, I am far from gaining his good opinion by flattery and acquiescence; and find it as much as I can do, to conceal the disgust I feel. — As we see each other, however, so seldom, and I levy no tax either on his affections or his pocket, I could wish he would not remember our relationship only to make me the object of his enquiries and his comments. — What business has he to talk of Mrs Verney? — he, who never in his life was sensible of an attachment to a woman of honour, nor was ever capable of understanding such a character as hers. — The gross and odious reflections which he has taken the unwarrantable liberty to utter, I should find it impossible to avoid resenting, were he still nearer related to me. — I hope, therefore, before I see him again, that he will be furnished with some other topic of conversation, by his coffee-house friends at Bath; — men who having once had active bodies and inactive minds, are now deprived, by disease, of the former advantage, and are compelled to give to their shallow understandings obnoxious activity, to prevent a total stagnation of existence; or by the silly women, at whose card parties he passes his evenings, many of whom owe the prodigious virtue on which they value themselves, to that want of personal beauty, which prevented their ever being in danger.

'Casta est, quam nemo rogavit,'[50]

says the proverb. — Heaven forgive me, if I judge uncharitably; but I very much suspect, that in common minds among the sex, this extreme and exquisite sense of delicacy, which always acquires peculiar energy after thirty-five, is much oftener the offspring of disappointed pride, than angelic purity. — Among the good matrons and virgins of this description, my uncle is a very oracle. — Among them he retails the conversation of the morning, and they make up together, in their evening vigils, those scandalous anecdotes, from even which Geraldine cannot escape, though, if they had not the power to give her a moment's pain, I am sure they would not give me a moment's thought. — Now, however, she is in France, and these arrows 'dipped in double poison,' will not, I trust, reach her, unless some 'd———n'd good natured friend'* should take the trouble, in *pure kindness*, to feather the shafts so as that they may reach her.

---

* The Critic.[51]

I remember, that when I used to see more of Major Danby than I have now done for these last years, I used to consider, with some degree of wonder, the odd construction of his mind, which nature intended to be a good, plain, common mind; but having acquired a roughness, from being early in life a soldier of fortune, he saw himself in unexpected affluence, at a middle period of life, when he had learned the value of money, by having struggled with the want of it — And the moment he quitted his profession, he lost the open, manly character it gives, and acquired nothing meritorious in place of those qualities; for he became a little of a literary man — a little more of a politician — still more of an epicurean — and above all, a man of great consequence to himself. — His mind now resembles a quilt I have seen at an inn, composed by the industrious landlady, in a sort of work, which, I believe, the women call patchwork; triangular or square shreds sewn together to form a motley whole — here a little bit of chintz, surrounded by pieces of coarse and tawdry cotton; there a piece of decca work, joined to a scrap of dowlas; in one place a remnant of the fine gown of the Lady of the Manor; in the next, a relict of the bed-gown of her house-maid. — So oddly, in the composition of my good uncle, is a fragment of gentleman-like qualities tacked to great patches of obsolete principles and hard prejudices — to an obstinate adherence to his own gratifications, and a prodigious attachment to his own imagined consequence. — But a truce with the Major: — I have bestowed more words upon him than ever I recollect to have done before, and more than, perhaps, I shall ever do again.

In wandering round the world, I hear more of politics than of any other subject — and I am always glad to attend to them, when the events under discussion are of consequence enough to attract my attention, and detain it a little from the internal wretchedness I bear about me.

The enemies of the French revolution are, at present, in dismay — for the King has signed the constitution, and they begin seriously to fear that the liberties of France will be firmly established.[52] — Their great hope, however, is in the confederacy of 'the kings of the earth' against it, particularly that of the Northern powers; which, if they do unite, will be the first instance, in the annals of mankind, of an union of tyrants to crush a people who profess to have no other object than to obtain, for themselves, that liberty which is the undoubted birth-right of all mankind.[53] — I do not, my friend, fear that all 'these tyrannous breathings of the North' will destroy the lovely tree that has thus taken vigorous root in the finest country of the world, though it may awhile check its growth, and blight its produce; but I lament, that in despite of the pacific intentions of the French towards their neighbours, its root must be manured with blood.[54] — I lament still more, the disposition which too many Englishmen shew to join in this unjust and infamous *crusade* against the holy standard of freedom; and I blush for my country!

I must, however, remark, that those in whom I have observed this disposition, are all either courtiers themselves, or connected with courtiers — And I know not whether to admire most their *English* sentiments or *their English* versatility; for among them, I recollect, are some gentlemen, who, three years since, when the speeches of Mr Burke were said to press so hardly on a gentleman then, and still before the highest tribunal of his country, exclaimed against the proceedings of that great orator with the utmost indignation.[55] — They then declared, in all companies, that he prostituted his eminent talents to the purposes of party — and, to the purposes of party, sacrificed his veracity.

But now, when in the book written against the patriots of France, he has done the same thing — when he advances opinions, and maintains principles absolutely opposite to all the professions of his political life — when he dresses up contradictions with the gaudy flowers of his luxuriant imagination, in one place, and in another, knowingly misrepresents facts, and swells the guilt of a *few*, into national crimes; to prove the delinquency of a whole people struggling for the dearest rights of humanity, Mr Burke is become, in the opinion of these my courtier acquaintance, the most correct, as well as the most eloquent of men— for he is of their party — he is become the champion of the placeman — and the apologist of the pensioner.[56]

As for his political adversaries, who have taken up the gauntlet, he has chosen to throw down — What have they done to excite such a terrible outcry? — They have exhibited to view many prejudices, which we have been so accustomed to, that we never thought of looking at them.

They have endeavored to convince us of the absurdity and folly of war — the inefficacy of conquest — the imposition which all European nations have submitted to, who have, for ages, paid for the privilege of murdering each other. — These writers have told us what, I apprehend, Locke, and Milton, and Bacon, and (what is better than all) common sense has told us before, that government is not for the benefit of the governors, but the governed; that the people are not transferable like property; and that their money is very ill bestowed, when, instead of preventing the evils of poverty, it is taken from them, to support the wanton profusion of the rich.[57] — And what is there in all this, that in other times, Mr Burke himself, and Mr Burke's associates, have not repeatedly re-echoed through their speeches? — Once, it is certain, these gentlemen seemed to agree with Voltaire, who somewhere says,

'A mesure que les pays sont barbares, ou que les cours sont faible, le cérémonial est plus en vogue — La vraie puissance, & la vraie politesse, dedaignent la vanité.'*

But let us allow, in contradiction to Mr Burke's former opinion, (who once wished to see even the sun of royalty shorn of his superfluous beams) let us allow, that a very great degree of splendour should surround the chief magistrate of a great and opulent nation — Let us allow, that the illustrious personage, who now fills that character, has, from his private and public virtues, a claim to the warmest affections of his people; that towards him and his family, the greatest zeal and attachment should be felt, and every support of his dignity chearfully given; yet, can it be denied, that the people are enduring needless burthens, with which all this has nothing to do?

Let any man whose name neither is, nor is ever likely to be in the court-calendar (the red book) look deliberately over it — let him reckon up the places that are there enumerated — a great many of which are sinecures — let him enquire the real amount of the salaries annexed to them, (for *they* are *not* enumerated) and the real services performed — then let him consider whether these places would exist, but for the purposes of corruption — let him reckon of how many oppressive taxes the annihilation of these places, would preclude the necessity.[58]

---

* In proportion as countries are rude, or their governments feeble, ceremony is more requisite — True power and true politeness, alike disdain pageantry and vanity.[59]

I might add, that the list of pensioners, could it ever be fairly got at, might come under the same consideration — Is there upon that list *many*, are there *any* names, that have found a place there because their owners have grown old, without growing rich in the service of their country? — Does deserted merit? does indigent genius find, in the bounty of that country, an honourable resource against unmerited misfortune? Alas! no! — To those who have only *such* recommendations, the pursuit of *court favor* is hopeless indeed. — But the meretricious nymph receives, with complacent smiles, the superannuated pander of a noble patron, his cast mistresses, his illegitimate children, his discarded servants, his aunts, great aunts, and fifth cousins. — If the nobleman himself is a sure ministerial man in the upper house, he is sure of some degree of favour; but it is measured to him in proportion to the influence he has in the lower; and it is to reward *such men*, to gratify their dependents, that the poor pittance of the mechanic is lessened — the prices of the most necessary articles of life raised upon the 'smutched artificer,' and a share of his fourteen pence a day 'wrung from the hard hands' of the labourer.[60]

Either these things are true, or they are not. — If they are *not* true, the persons who are interested in the refutation of them, are marvellously silent! — If they *are true*, can your most enthusiastic admiration of our present glorious establishment, conceal from you, that they should be put an end to?

You say, my dear Bethel, that you wish for my society in our favourite county. — If ever I should return thither, to meet you, would be my principal, indeed only inducement; but, alas! warm and sincere as my friendship for you is, it cannot alone replace, it cannot make amends for all I have lost. Yet, I know, you will say I have lost nothing that I ever possessed; and that if I could once determine to look out for some other enjoyments than those my romantic fancy had described, I might yet find as reasonable a portion of happiness as any human being has a right to expect. — All this may be very true, and very reasonable; but I have, unhappily, a degree of felicity, impressed on my mind, *which was once attainable*; and though I know it is attainable no longer, I am like the unhappy man who is said to have died in consequence of the love he had conceived for a picture, which, after many enquires, proved to be that of the fair Gabrielle. — I know there are a hundred, nay, a thousand other plans and people, with whom other men might sit down contented; but I have made up a 'fair idea,' and losing that, all is to me a blank.[61]

You are always lamenting, in the warmth of your friendly zeal, that my prospects are thus blasted on my entrance into life; but why? — What do you call their being blasted? — I might, it is true, be a member of parliament, and give a silent vote for, or make an unregarded speech against government, which my slight influence could not render better or worse. — I might have married some fine lady, with a fine fortune, who would have done me the honor to bear my name abroad, and render me completely wretched at home; and this you call, my good friend, following my prospects. — Alas! I would not recall uneasy recollections to your mind, but I must ask, — Did *you* find happiness, in this career, which you now lament my neglecting to pursue? — Or, can you decide, whether I shall finally be wrong or right in following one very opposite?

It is amazing to me, that with your mind, you cannot comprehend the delight of living only for one beloved object, though hopeless of any other return than what the purest friendship may authorise. — It is still more wonderful that you cannot understand this, when this object is Geraldine, of whom you think so highly. — Oh! Bethel! is it possible you can have seen her in those scenes which have called forth all the perfections of that lovely mind, and not allow me to be right, when I say with Petrarch —

'Pur me consola, che languir per lei
Meglio e, che gioir d'altra —'[62]

Adieu! my friend, continue to write to me; and be assured ever of the truest attachment and regard of

Your's

LIONEL DESMOND

LETTER XVIII

TO MR BETHEL

Bath, Oct. 3, 1791

DEAR SIR

A slight indisposition that my mother has had, and the sudden departure of Mr and Mrs Waverly, to visit some distant friends of the Fairfax family, brought us back to Bath sooner than we intended. — Your last letter followed me hither; and, in thanking you for it, and for that it enclosed from Mr Desmond, I have to inform you of some very singular circumstances that have happened since our return.

I was surprised yesterday morning, by the servant's informing me that a French gentleman was below, and desired to speak to me. My mother was in the room, and I could not conceal my apprehensions, that this stranger brought me some intelligence of Geraldine. — I trembled as I asked her whether she would be pleased to admit him?

'What kind of a man is he?' enquired Mrs Waverly, sternly, of Matthew.

'Lord, Madam,' replied he, 'quite a gentleman-like, handsomish-kind of a man; really a good-looking person, considering he is a foreigner.'

'Let him be shewn up,' answered my mother, who had not so much intended enquiring after his good looks, as whether they were the looks of a visiter, or of a solicitor of charity — 'I cannot speak to him,' said she, 'you must make out, child, what his business is.'

I had not time to analyse the confused emotions I felt, before a gentleman entered the room, who appeared to me one of the most elegant men I had ever seen. — If his person prejudiced me in his favour, you may believe that favourable prejudice was not lessened, when he announced himself to be Monsieur de Montfleuri; the intimate and beloved friend of Desmond.

I felt instantly as if I had known him for ages, and was sorry I could not acquire courage to tell him so in his own language: yet he spoke English extremely well, and divided his attentions with so much true politeness between my mother and me, that though she was prepared to dislike him, first, because he was a foreigner, and secondly, because he was the avowed friend of Desmond, she insensibly relaxed into a smile; then gave him a general invitation to her house during her visit to Bath; and, before he took leave, even pressed him to make her house his most usual home. — He answered, that his stay at Bath would be short, but that he should most undoubtedly avail himself of her obliging permission to pay his respects to her.

He left us — and during his visit had never named Mr Desmond, but in his introductory speech. — I longed to ask him where he was, but was with-held by a thousand fears that have since appeared ridiculous. — I would have asked him in French, but as he spoke English so well, it would have been unpolite: yet I suffered inconceivable anxiety all evening, when I was engaged to go to a ball, at the upper-rooms, where, I flattered myself, I should meet him. — I was not disappointed. — Montfleuri was the first person I saw on entering the room. — He immediately came up to me; and as he did not think himself qualified to join in English country dances, and as I was the only person in the room with whom he was acquainted, I disengaged myself from the gentleman with whom I was going to dance, and had a great deal of conversation with Monsieur de Montfleuri, which, of course, turned principally on Mr Desmond.

You will easily imagine, dear Sir! how earnestly I wished to ask him several questions about his friend; but, though he spoke in the most unreserved terms of the good qualities of Desmond, and of their long friendship, I observed, that he carefully avoided saying much of his present situation or prospects. — At length, I ventured to ask him where his friend now was? — He replied, that he did not certainly know, as it was some time since he heard from him. — 'Is he,' said I, afraid of pressing too far on a subject, from which he seemed to recede, 'is he in France or in England?'

Monsieur de Montfleuri, whose eyes are the most penetrating I ever saw, looked at me as if he would read my very soul. — I shrunk, I believe, from his enquiring and piercing eyes; for, I own, they distressed me extremely — nor did what he said serve to relieve me. — 'Desmond,' said he, 'is a very fortunate man, to occasion you, Mademoiselle, so much friendly solicitude.' — I believe I looked very foolish; and, though I hardly know why, I was discouraged from repeating my question.

But, on consideration, after I returned home, my anxiety was by no means abated by an interview, which, I had hoped, would entirely subdue it. — The more I considered the conversation I had with Monsieur de Montfleuri, the more I was persuaded, that there was some mystery hung over the present situation of Desmond. — I have seen Monsieur de Montfleuri this morning; he dines with us to-day; and says, that though he came to Bath with no other intention than to pay his compliments to us, and a family from France, with whom he is acquainted; yet he is so flattered by the civility he has received, and so happy in being allowed the honour of cultivating our acquaintance, that he shall prolong his stay, and not return to France, for, at least, a fortnight.

Dear Sir! how shall I remain so long in suspense about this odious report? — Yet I feel it to be impossible to speak of it to Monsieur de Montfleuri, nor do I dare entrust my mother with such a delicate negociation; for, it is but too probable, that she would speak of Desmond, perhaps of my sister, with an asperity that would be extremely improper, and would defeat her purpose.

I have reason to believe that her intelligence fails, either by the removal of Miss Elford, or the disappearance of those objects, whoever they were, that gave her ground for her report; for, within these few days, my mother has not renewed the conversation; but seems again occupied by some scheme for the aggrandizement of Mr Waverly.

In the mean time, I have observed, with wonder, the favour Monsieur de Montfleuri has obtained in her sight. — For him, she seems to have conquered her aversion to foreigners; and her peculiar aversion to Frenchmen — nay, she is almost persuaded, that since he is a partizan of the French revolution, it cannot be quite so dreadful a thing as people have represented it. — I never observed so strong and prompt an effect, from elegance of manners, (which he certainly possesses in an eminent degree) as in this sudden impression Montfleuri has made on my mother. — But it must, however, be added, that she has pretty good intelligence as to his fortune, knows it to be a very large one, at present, and likely to be much encreased by his accession to the estate of the Count d'Hauteville, his uncle, whose only heir he is. — You know my mother well enough to understand, that were Monsieur Montfleuri a Cherokee, or a Chicksaw, his country would be no objection to a place in her esteem, if he had a *good property*; and his manners and understanding, though they were the first in the world, no recommendation to her favour without it.

But I am writing on, as if you had nothing else to do but to attend to my letters. — Pray pardon me; and recollect, in my excuse, that I have not, in the world, any other person to whom I can open my heart on the cruel subject which weighs upon it.

What I meant to ask of you, (though I have made so many digressions, still unwilling to intrude upon you with what may, perhaps, be an improper request) is, whether there would be any impropriety in *your* writing to Montfleuri, to ask intelligence about our friend. — Perhaps this is impracticable — if it is, pray forget my asking; and forgive it, in consideration of the excessive anxiety I feel. — I have had no letter from Geraldine; and every hour encreases that solicitude, which I can neither satisfy or repress.

Whatever you have learned, I beg to hear by an early post; and that I may be allowed to remain,

Sir,

Your much obliged,

And most obedient servant,

FRANCES WAVERLY

I enclose, in one of the franks that brings this voluminous letter, a billet from dearest Louisa, who impatiently expects your return to Bath. — I have not once broken your injunction, not to take her to a ball, or any public meeting, till you come.

LETTER XIX

TO MISS WAVERLY

Hartfield, Oct. 7th, 1791

DEAR MADAM,

It is, indeed impracticable for me to apply to Mr de Monfleuri, to enquire into the past conduct or actual situation of Mr Desmond. If there are any circumstances in that conduct with which he has chosen rather to confide to M. de Montfleuri than to me, you will see at once, the impropriety of *my* expressing any curiosity on affairs with which he did not himself think proper to entrust me. — I lament that I cannot, in this instance, obey your commands with that alacrity which it would, on almost any other occasion, be my pride to shew.

As to the report which you have traced to Miss Elford, and which has given you so much disquiet, perhaps it is best to let it die of itself. — I shall, in a few days ... I was here interrupted by the arrival of a messenger from W. bringing the inclosed extraordinary letter; which, from the direction — 'to be forwarded instantly' — the post-master sent over, without waiting for the arrival of the servant I usually send. — I am too much confused, by the contents of this letter, to be able to make any remarks on it; or, indeed, to advise what should be done.

Let me hear as soon as you have received and considered it; and, if I can be of any use, I will instantly set out for Bath — though I know not what good I can do; or, indeed, what can be done at all.

I am, dear Miss Waverly,
Your faithful servant,
E. BETHEL

LETTER XX*

TO MR BETHEL

Paris, Oct. 1, 1791

It were vain to attempt secrecy any longer. — She is gone! — She is gone to meet that very fate from which I have, with watchful affection, been endeavouring to save her. — I left her only for one day on indispensable business. — I found, on my return, that she was set out on a moment's notice for the South of France, by the direction of her husband. Alone! — she is gone alone! and has not taken even a servant with her. — Her children, to whom she has always been so tenderly attached, she has left at Meudon, to the care of servants; and in such haste did she depart, that she gave no direction whether she should be written to. — It is some infamous stratagem of De Romagnecourt's to get her into his power — And I, fool that I was, have been afraid of openly avowing myself, of taking those measures which would have saved her; and now, perhaps, now it is too late! — Whither can I turn me? what can I do? — To sit down quietly under the apprehensions that crowd upon my mind, is impossible.

---

* This letter was enclosed to Miss Waverly by Mr Bethel.

I am this moment returned from Meudon, where, by a mere acci-dent, I witnessed the distress of her servants, left with the children in such a state of anxiety and suspence. — She gave to the young woman, who has long lived with her, all the money she had about her, and an order on Bergasse for more. This has given me the only ray of comfort I have received. — Bergasse may inform me whither she is gone, and I will instantly follow her whatever may be the consequences. — She said to the servants, that Mr Verney was wounded in a quarrel, and lay very ill in the neighbourhood of Avignon; and that thither she was going to him. — But it is not so; it is a *finesse* of Romagnecourt's, to which her husband has lent his name.[63] — It is impossible to describe to you what I feel — I will leave my letter open till I return from speak-ing to Bergasse. (Three o'clock) — I have seen him. All he could in-form me was, that about five, yesterday evening, Mrs Verney came to him in great apparent distress. — She read to him part of a letter, writ-ten by Mr Verney, in an hand legible, which informed her of his hav-ing been wounded in a scuffle in the streets of Avignon, and laying in great danger at a cottage about two miles from the town, where he entreated her to hasten to him, that he might put into her hands the means of securing his remaining fortune to his children; and ask and obtain forgiveness for all the injuries he had done to them, and to her-self.

Bergasse assured me, he endeavoured to dissuade her from setting out alone, on such an occasion, and for a part of the country, where to travel, is really hazardous. — She answered, should Mr Verney die, without having seen her, she should never forgive herself, or ever taste again one moment's content: — That to personal danger, she was to-tally indifferent, and only entreated him to supply her family at Meudon with money; and if she did not return within a month, to send them back to England, to the care of her mother. —

'I never saw,' said Bergasse, 'so lovely a woman, nor ever felt so interested for any one before. — I would have laid down my life, at that moment, to have served her; but what could I do? — she would not hear of sending any other person to enquire into the real situation of her husband; she would not hear of my procuring any person to accompany her, who would she said, be of no use to her. — All that she would suffer me to do, for her service, was to hire a chaise, as lighter and more expeditious than the coach she came in from England — I saw her get into it. — She promised to write to me the instant she got to the place described by Mr Verney's letter. — I saw her depart.'

Though it was very true, that Mr de Bergasse could do no more, I could, in the agony of mind I was in, have cursed him, for not stopping her. — I gave him however, a draft for money, that her children may be assured of a supply; and I now write this, my dear Bethel, while Warham is gone for the post-horses, on which I will instantly follow this dear unhappy, but ever adorable woman. — Good God! — my senses forsake me, when I reflect on the hazardous journey she has undertaken; when I reflect that she has perhaps thrown herself into the hands of an unprincipled monster, in a country where he has probably power to execute whatever he undertakes, and where, the confusion it is in, may give him unquestioned opportunity to commit any outrage with impunity —

Warham is at the door with the horses — I fly to overtake her — that may not yet be impossible — this hope alone animates me—

I would write to Fanny Waverly, and to Montfleuri, for all mystery must now be at an end. — But I know not, very exactly, where Montfleuri is; and if you send this, or the purport of it, to Miss Waverly, it will save time. — God bless you my dear friend? — Oh! would you were here to assist me, in the pious office of saving the most perfect of human beings, from a fate so dreadful, as that, which I am persuaded, awaits Geraldine.

LIONEL DESMOND

LETTER XXI

TO MR DESMOND

Bath, in England, this
18th Oct. 1791

There is nothing, you have told me sometimes, more singular than I am — You might have added, unless it be yourself. — But I am going to give you, my friend, a new proof of eccentricity; for after having escaped till now, and having borne away an unwounded heart, from eyes, the brightest that France, or England, or America could produce, I am desperately in love — Mad! for your Mrs Verney's sister, and shall most certainly marry the lovely little Fanni, if she will accept of me.

— Why did you not give me notice of the danger that awaited me in coming here? — It was not right to suffer me to run into an embarrassment that you know, I have always had the presentiment, would be a very serious one if ever it came to me. — I have vowed a hundred times never to marry, but this beautiful little Englishwoman who can resist? — My affairs however, are in a prosperous train. — The good mamma looks kindly upon me, and my charming Fanni, does not hate me, if there is any trusting to the language of the eyes. — There is a brother it seems to be consulted; but I imagine, if my goddess and I agree, we shall neither the one or the other, pay great attention to his opinion. — I do not love to be long in suspense, and, when I determine to commit a folly, I like to have it over at once. — So I go this day to Mistress Waverly, to make my overture in form, for to tell the truth, I have already secured the fair Fanni, who is a little afraid the mother may make some objection, on the account of religion; but I am much in a mistake, or the idol of *her* worship is money; and, if she does not fancy, that since the revolution, all the lands in France have agreed not to bear corn, wine, and oil — I persuade me that I can make out an account of my estate, which will satisfy all her scruples about the *soul* of her daughter, which assuredly, I shall not lead out of the path that has been followed by the *souls of her ancestors,* or divert, from any other, it may like better to follow — *My* ambition lying quite in *another line.* — If I bring matters to a speedy conclusion, I shall be married like a good Lutheran or Calvinist, or whatever is orthodox in the British church — and, having secured my sweet little English woman, according to her own ritual, shall set forward immediately for France. — This, I suppose, is the only thing I have done these four years, that will please Monseigneur le Comte d'Hauteville, to whom I mean to announce it in due form. — He may now flatter himself that his family will not be utterly extinguished; but what signifies it, when they will be under the cruel necessity of being only *Messieurs*, and not *mes Seigneurs.* — My good uncle, however, lives in hopes of a counter-revolution, and piously puts up his orisons for an invasion of his native country by Austrians, Russians, and Prussians, to restore Frenchmen to their senses and their *seignories.* — The remedy, it must be confessed, is somewhat violent.

I pray you, Desmond, to write to me immediately, and tell me what part of France I shall find you in. I hope you are made quite content by the purport of my last letter, as to the subject of our long and mutual inquietude. — Nothing but silence and prudence are wanting now to put an end to all farther pain upon this affair; and I differ so much from all the rest of the world in such circumstances, that, I think, I have done much better than if I had killed my friend, or been killed myself, because he was amiable, and my sister was a woman. — An Epicurean is, at least, a peaceable animal. — Poor Josephine is quite well in London; and, by this time, you have seen Madame Verney in possession of her charge. — If Boisbelle should have his head broke,* as I think it very likely he may, we might make a double wedding — if, however, Josephine should alter her mind — Unless that happens, I hope you will never meet, though I have no great notion that her convent scheme will hold long.

I direct this to you by your usual address at Paris. — I expect an immediate answer — and your felicitations on my having, at last, taken a resolution to marry, and become an honest man, which you have so often recommended. I hope I shall not repent it — but I have doubts about the wisdom of it sometimes. — If my wife should be ill tempered, I shall run away from her. — If she should be dull, I shall be weary of her — fatigued, if she have the folly to be jealous of me — and if she be very much a coquette, I shall be jealous of her. — How many rocks are here, in this perilous voyage, on which to wreck one's happiness! — but never mind! — courage! — I am determined to venture — My Fanni is a little angel, and I must have her. — There are a good many chances of being reasonably happy with her, at least, for three or four years, and that is as much as any body has a right to expect. — I find I am unreasonably unhappy without her, and every time I see her I become more and more intoxicated with my passion. How, if our good mamma should refuse her consent? — I do believe that if such a perverse accident should arrive, I have interest enough with my nymph to persuade her to trust herself with me without it, and take our chance for forgiveness afterwards. — But this is unlikely.

---

* A broken head in England conveys a very different idea, but '*lui casser la tête*' — means, in the French idiom, to shoot a man through the head, or kill him.

— I shall give the old lady a *carte blanche,* and let her name her own trustees — *O! Ca ira! — Ca ira!*[64]

Ever devotedly your's,
My dear friend,
JONVILLE DE MONTFLEURI

Do you not think I improve in my English? — Since I have been acquainted with my Fanni, I have thrown away my dictionary.

I have undone my letter again, to say to you, that I have Mrs Waverly's full consent, and am the most happy of men.

Evening of Wednesday,
7 o'clock

Still I have to add — My Fanni has received the letter you wrote from Paris, the first of this month, which you sent to that Mr Bethel, who is to be her trustee. — This hastens our marriage. — It is fixed for Sunday; and we come to France instantly. — I am almost as uneasy as my dear girl is, who has done nothing but weep ever since, at the fate of her sister. Desmond, you have not ever been quite so ingenuous with me about Mrs Verney, as I had, I think, a claim to expect. We shall go immediately to Meudon, to the four children who are there; and, surely, by the time of our arrival, there will be received some account of what is become of you and Mrs Verney. Her husband too! — I did not think any thing could have given me so much concern.

LETTER XXII

TO MR BETHEL

Oct. 23, 1791

Never, my dear Bethel, did the most feverish dreams of fiction produce scenes more painful, or more terrific, than the real events to which I have been an actor, since the date of my last letter. — They are far from being yet at an end. — With anxiety, such as it is impossible to describe, I await the catastrophe! — but I owe it to you, to put you, as soon and as much as I can, out of the suspense and uneasiness in which my last letter involved you, though, possibly, it be only to give you new suspense and new uneasiness. — Before this letter reaches you, however, my fate, must probably be decided.

I write from the cabin of a Vigneron, at Salon, near Avignon. — attended my journey, I will endeavour to collect my agitated and scattered thoughts enough to tell you.

As well as I remember, I wrote to you very hastily from Paris, in consequence of Mrs Verney's sudden departure, who was then gone forward alone, to attend her husband; who represented himself wounded and dying in the neighbourhood of Avignon. But that you may more clearly comprehend the whole of the subsequent narrative, it may, perhaps, be necessary to tell you how I came so well acquainted with the situation and sudden removal of Geraldine.

You have remonstrated with me so often and so vainly, on my passion for her, that the subject was sometime since exhausted between us. — I could not, however, so candidly reveal to you my purpose, as I had, on almost every occasion of my life, been accustomed to do, for reasons, with which she had no concern. But if I did not relate my actions, I attempted not to put on them any false appearance; and since I could not tell you the truth, I forbore to date my letters, and would not mislead you by misrepresentations; which, had I not abhorred every kind of deception, might have been easily done. — I must now, however, relate as much as concerns my own wanderings — undertaken from a motive which, however blameable it might appear, I could not contend with. — The event has shewn that, where the *intention* is perfectly pure, it is not always wrong to follow the dictates of the heart, even when they impel us to act contrary to the maxims of the world, and even in defiance of its censure.

Know then, my dear Bethel, that when you sent me intelligence of the sudden departure of Geraldine for France — when I heard, that the persevering infamy of her husband, and the unfeeling brutality of her mother, contributed to drive her into the snare from which I believed, I had seen her secured, when she quitted Herefordshire — I could not patiently await the event. — I determined, though with anxiety of a very different kind upon my mind, to follow her, and to protect her, if possible, from the wretch, who would thus basely avail himself of his legal right to render wretched, this most lovely and injured woman. — Compared with her safety, every other consideration on earth was insignificant: yet I was conscious that, were it known, even by her own family, that I had followed her to France, some part of the inconvenience, from which it was the wish of my life to save her, would be incurred; and that conviction, added to other circumstances, compelled me to conceal my intentions even from you.

I sat out for Brighthelmstone the very next day after I had intelligence of her departure, and travelling along the coast, I reached that place late in the evening of the next day. — Geraldine and her family were at the Old Ship waiting for a wind. — I dared not, therefore, go to that house, which I on other occasions used to frequent, but I took a private lodging; and ordered my servants, who were known, because they have both lived with me so many years, to keep out of sight.

The wind was so high and so contrary for three days, that the packet she was going in could not get out. — It was not possible for me to engage my passage in the same vessel — Others were on the point of sailing with the change of the wind; but, as these might wait for passengers, and I might thus be detained after her, I chose rather to hire one of the largest fishing boats, the master of which, for a certain consideration, was to convey me to Dieppe, and to sail immediately after the packet. — The air of mystery I was compelled to observe, and the high terms I was willing to give for a conveyance so apparently inferior to the packets, excited in the fishermen, with whom I opened my negociation, much surprize and many conjectures; the most favourable of which, to me were, that I had been engaged in a duel, and, from its fatal consequences, was compelled to make my escape; or, that I was employed by Government to carry on some negociation with the French aristocratic party, and was going to Paris *incog.* for fear of the *reverbere* of the democracy: yet, I am persuaded, notwithstanding the credit I obtained for these gentlemen like motives, that if there had, just at that time, happened to have been any delinquent sought for by public justice, who was supposed likely to attempt escaping to France, I should have stood a chance of being carried to Lewes, and committed for farther examination.[65]

After thirty-six tedious hours, during which I never ventured out but of a night, for a solitary walk along the westward shore, where there was the least danger of my meeting any of my acquaintance, (of whom I found the place was full;) the wind changed, and a steady gale springing from the north east, the packet came out of harbour in the evening of the second day; and, at seven o'clock in the evening, I had notice from Warham, whom I had sent to *reconnoitre*, that the passengers were about to embark.[66]

I would have given the world to have dared to assist the beautiful and interesting exile, whom I could only watch at a distance. — I buttoned a horseman's coat round me, pulled my hat over my eyes, and in a crowd of French and English who were bustling around the door of the ship tavern, to get their baggage down to the shore, I ventured to pass quite close to the lovely but melancholy group, for which my anxious heart was so deeply affected. — I saw Geraldine pale, languid, and dejected, yet forcing herself to appear calm and chearful, in order to quiet the apprehensions of her English servant, Peggy, who had never seen the sea before, and now hung back, afraid of venturing on an element which she had beheld a few hours before, black with tempests that threatened destruction. — The poor girl, who was weeping bitterly, had the youngest child in her arms; the old Frenchwoman carried little Harriet; and the eldest boy was led by his mother, who endeavoured to quiet his eager enquiries of what they were going to do?

They proceeded thus down to the sea. I still remained within hearing, for I observed that Geraldine was too much absorbed in attention to her children, to make many observations on the objects around her; and, I believed, it was impossible for her to know me. — I saw her, Bethel, with calm resolution step forward to meet her destiny; for herself she seemed to suffer nothing, but towards the sea, which was still high, and the rough waves breaking at her feet, she seemed to cast her imploring eyes, and then turned them, humid with tears, which she yet struggled to suppress, on her children. — George, who had been very silent for a moment, now asked, whether they were all to go on that great pond? — His mother, in a faultering voice, replied — 'Yes, my love, I hope you are not afraid?' — 'No;' replied the dear little fellow, 'not afraid, Mamma, of going, if you go — but see how frightened poor Harriet is, let us not take her if she is so frightened.'

The little girl, terrified at the noise of the people, and the rushing of the water, now reached out her arms to her mother, who soothed her, as she hid her face in her bosom. — This obliged her to disengage her hand from George, who alarmed at the privation, clung to her gown, fixing his expressive eyes eagerly on her face, and refusing the attention of your servant, honest Thomas, who would have taken him up in his arms. — Had a painter been there, who could have been indifferent enough to the scene to have exercised his art, he might have made a sketch of this group that would have spoken most forcibly to the heart — what then must I have felt, who was within ten yards of Geraldine, and dared not to speak to her?

The baggage was now stowed, and the boat ready to put off. — I had need of all my resolution at that moment, and all the consideration of the ill consequences that might attend my rashness, to prevent my stepping forward to take her in my arms to the boat; but a gigantic son of the ocean, stalked in his sea boots through the waves like another Polypheme, and seizing her and her child, which clung shrieking to her bosom, lifted them into it; while another, with as little ceremony, carried off Peggy and the infant she had the charge of; your good old Thomas took care of the little boy, whom he placed close to his mother; the French gentlewoman followed, and all the passengers being now embarked, the boat, with a furious crash, put off from the shingles — the spray flashed over it, and I saw, in the pale and dismayed countenance of Peggy, that she gave herself up for lost.[67] — Geraldine, I believe, was sensible of nothing but the terrors of her children, whom she now collected round her, having the two youngest of them in her arms, and the eldest clinging to her. — I saw her countenance as she hung over them — and never, never shall I lose the impression it made on my heart.

The boat now made its way quickly towards the packet. — I sent Warham away to order my honest fisherman to be ready; and, while my boat was preparing, I went up to the high cliffs on the eastern end of the town, to mark the progress towards the packet, of that, which contained the being to whom my heart is devoted.

Had I not before determined to follow her, I should now have done it; so terrible did the encreasing distance appear, as leaning over the cliff, I parodied the speech of Imogen, and as the boat lessened to my view, I could, like her, have

'Turn'd mine eyes and wept.'[68]

But it was now more to the purpose to hasten after her; I saw the men were ready. Warham and John had brought and stowed my baggage. I went down to the shore and threw myself into the boat; and desiring the men to set all the canvas they had, the light vessel overtook and passed the packet before it was quite dark, and at four o'clock the next morning I landed at Dieppe, some hours before the packet.

I might now, perhaps, without any fear of subjecting Geraldine to remarks, have appeared; but I knew so well that though the world should be silent, she herself would be rendered uneasy by it, that I checked myself; and though, on the road, I never was a league distant from her, she had not the least suspicion of my being in the same country.

At Paris I took up my abode in another hotel in the same street, and as she was wholly given up to her children, and never went out, it was not difficult to escape being known. — It was an infinite relief to me to learn, that Mr Verney was not at Paris, and that Geraldine steadily refused to take up her residence at the hotel of Monsieur de Romagnecourt, whither he had consigned her — for about eight days after her arrival, she removed to Meudon; and thither, though it could not be done without difficulty, I determined to attend her.

If your friend, my dear Bethel, had been so disposed, he could, perhaps, have performed the Proteus of intrigue, as well as any modern hero in that line of acting — but, in this instance, so far was I from meditating to injure, that my whole purpose was to protect from injury the object of my tender attachment.[69] — It was, to me, a most flattering and soothing idea, that I was deputed to watch over this angelic woman, with the fond affection of a guardian spirit. — I felt myself ennobled by the charge, and would not have exchanged the sublime pleasure it afforded me, for any less elevated indulgence that the epicurean doctrine might offer. — I know, that with all your good sense, and all your right notions of friendship, you have no more comprehension of this sort of attachment than of the Rosicrusian mystery[70] — Not much more, perhaps, than Montfleuri, who ridicules my platonism as a degree of visionary insanity, and believes nothing about it — Not much more, that my worthy uncle, the Major, who has as little idea of true disinterested love, as he has of patriotism or charity, or rectitude, or of refraining, when it comes in his way, from a good dinner.

As it was less easy to be concealed at Meudon than at Paris; and as I languished for the pleasure of gazing, unperceived, on that lovely countenance, I was compelled to take a disguise; the means of doing so were offered me by the vicinity of the convent of Capuchins. — I need not relate the manner in which, by the help of Warham, I contrived this: it is enough that I succeeded without being at all suspected, and was frequently within a few paces of Geraldine and her children, every hour encreasing my attachment to her, for I every hour saw new occasion to admire the sweetness of her temper, her tender maternal attention — her mild fortitude, and the graces which set off these virtues. — Oh! Bethel! this woman, whose conduct is so irreproachable, while united to such a man as Verney, what would she have been if given to one who felt her value, and endeavoured to deserve her? — If, contending almost ever since her marriage with calamity and regret, she has not only shewn the noblest qualities of the heart, but has cultivated her understanding, and added every ornament to every virtue; what would she have been if the watchful tenderness of unabated love had shielded her from all inconvenience and evil, and left to her only the practice of the milder virtues, and the cultivation of ornamental talents? — But whither am I wandering — in what dreams am I indulging myself? — dreams of what *might have been*; as if to embitter the sad reflection of *what is*; or to irritate the terror with which my soul recoils from the picture of *what may be*.

Yes! my dear friend, at the moment I am writing, and with apparent composure, this long narrative, I know not whether the most miserable destiny is not hanging over *me*; and, at all events, I am certain, that Geraldine must go through as much and as painful suffering as can be felt by innocence. — Guilt and self-reproach can alone inflict incurable anguish.

I will, however, since this state of suspence may, perhaps, last much longer, endeavour to command myself enough to continue my narrative.

While I continued at Meudon, I every day, and sometimes every hour of the day, indulged myself with the sight of Geraldine. — I saw her morning walks, in pensive meditation, and heard the sigh which anxiety drew from her bosom as she turned her lovely eyes to heaven, to implore its protection for her children. I watched her as she sought the shade at noon, when she sometimes tried to beguile her pain, by playing with them on the grass, or by contemplating the wonderful structure of the leaves and flowers, which they gathered and brought to her. — Sometimes I saw her attempt to read; but her thoughts seemed to wander from her book; and her own situation was too uneasy and uncertain to allow her to attend to the fictitious distress of novels, or moralize on the real miseries represented by history. — Her evening walk was always towards the upper gardens, from whence she descended a long flight of steps adjoining the chapel of the old palace, which led to the lower; and there, after her children were gone to their repose, I have seen her sit whole hours; sometimes employed with her pencil, and sometimes apparently absorbed in thought — and failing to recollect it was necessary to return home, till reminded of it by the surrounding darkness.

Oh! what would I not then have given to have dared to approach her? what, to have been sure, that one of those anxious thoughts which crouded on her mind, was fraught with good wishes and good will towards me? — yet, though in these respects I could not be satisfied — indeed, Bethel, I enjoyed, during this period, comparative happiness. — I saw her in present safety, and every hour rendered less the probability of her husband's schemes being carried into effect; as the return of his friends to their former oppressive power became every day less probable. — I saw her health, which had been very much injured by long solicitude, now visibly amending; for though that solicitude was far from being at an end, the comparative repose she enjoyed, aided by the fine air of this country, had already a visible and happy effect on her frame. — The pale rose returned to her cheeks; and her eyes, though they were often filled with tears, regained their mild lustre. — Those lovely arms which had lost their beautiful *embonpoint*, when I saw her at Bridge-foot, were now '*blanc* & *potelé*,' as when they first attracted my admiration.[71] — But plain prose cannot do justice to her personal beauty; and, I am afraid, if I run into poetry, you will find (if you have not found it already) new cause to doubt of, and to ridicule my professions of platonism.

Yet, very certain it is, that if I could have seen her perfectly freed from all her apprehensions of future difficulties — if I might have been allowed to converse with her a few hours every day — have been admitted to a place in her heart, as her friend and her brother, I should have been well content, nor ever have wished (at the expence of disturbing her tranquillity) for any other happiness the world could afford — So, entirely, do I subscribe to the opinion of a French moralist, who says,

'Etre avec des gens qu'on aime, cela suffit; rever, leur parler, ne leur parler point; penser à eux, penser à des choses plus indifferent, mais auprès d'eux; tout est egal.'*

An event, however, happened, that I had long expected, and which relieved my mind from a weight of anxiety and pain. — It was nothing that related to Geraldine; but it made my presence at Paris necessary for some hours. — I went thither, therefore, on the noon of Wednesday; and on my return, on the following morning, about twelve o'clock, I repaired, still as a capuchin, (though I now intended, in a few days, to throw off my disguise) to the spot where, at that hour of the day, I usually saw Geraldine with her children — Alas! there was now no Geraldine! — But after waiting about a quarter of an hour near the spot, I saw the children approach with their maid, and perceived that the poor girl was in an agony of tears, sobbing audibly as she vainly attempted to pacify and appease the dear boy, who was eagerly insisting on being suffered to go to his mamma.

The idea that illness or accident had befallen Geraldine, dissipated, in a moment, all my resolutions of precaution and concealment. — Without even attempting to disguise my voice, or conceal my features, I spoke hastily to Peggy — 'Good God,' said I, 'what is the matter, and where is your mistress?'

The sudden sight of me, in such a place, and in such a dress, added to the terror and confusion of the poor girl, whom I was obliged to support to a seat, where she fell into a sort of fit; and I never felt, I think, more awkwardly and uneasily situated than I did, for some moments, while I endeavoured to reason her into some degree of recollection, and to soothe the eldest boy, who continued to entreat her to take him to his mother; and who, at first, shrunk from my melancholy and uncouth appearance. — At length I learned, to my inexpressible terror, that at two o'clock, the day before, an express had been sent to Geraldine by Mr Bergasse, with a letter, which he had received from the Hotel de Romagnecourt. It was from Verney, and related, that having, with a party of his friends, joined the aristocratic side in the disputes existing at Avignon, he had been wounded in a skirmish, where many of his friends were killed — that he lay at a miserable

---

*   La Bruyere.[72]

auberge, at the village of Salon, near two leagues beyond Avignon, whither he had, with difficulty, escaped — that de Romagnecourt and Boisbelle had fled farther, and were gone he knew not whither and that thus deserted, in a place where there was no medical assistance, he entreated her to send him money, and some friend, who might receive his last directions in regard to his family.[73] — He added — 'I should ask you to come yourself, if I did not feel conscious that I have not deserved your kind attention: otherwise, it would be the only consolation I could receive in dying; or, if I live, you would be entitled to my everlasting gratitude.'

It was this sentence which determined Geraldine to set out immediately. — Listening to nothing but what she believed to be the voice of duty, she gave herself no time to reflect on danger which affected only herself; and, without any other preparation than putting up a small quantity of linen, giving orders about her children, and providing for their subsistence during her absence, she set out for Paris; and, I believe, I related to you, in my first hurried letter, her departure from thence, in despite of the remonstrances and entreaties of Bergasse, who, seeing her so determined, could do no more than facilitate and render easy the journey she was resolved to undertake.

Geraldine, unattended, even by a servant, had been gone near twenty hours, when I began my journey. — Every body at Paris told me, that the Southern Provinces were infested by associations of aristocrats; who, encouraged by the hopes of being speedily restored to their former situation, by the armies which were assembling under the exiled princes, had, *en attendant mieux*, armed those who were content still to remain in vassalage, and had fortified their castles, from whence they sent out parties to attack and destroy all whose religious or political creed differed from their own; and that it was supposed to be under the auspices of these great men, that many parties of banditti ravaged the provinces, carrying with them terror and devastation; miseries which were often imputed to those who had armed only in defence of their families and their freedom.[74] Oh! Bethel! — judge what cruel apprehensions these accounts raised for the safety of Geraldine. — They were, indeed, such as drove me almost to distraction; but though I almost despaired of overtaking and saving her from the horrors into which she had rushed from a mistaken principle of duty; the desire of being serviceable to her was the only sentiment I could attend to; and I therefore added to my own English servants, a Swiss, who was recommended to me for his honesty and resolution, and a Frenchman, who had formerly served me as *valet de place*, and of whom I had a very good opinion.[75] — These four men were completely armed, as I was myself, with two brace of pistols each, and a *couteau de chasse*; and as I surveyed my little troup, I thought, that if we could once overtake Geraldine, we should be able, at least, to convey her in safety to the place of her destination.[76]

Just as I was on the point of departure by the straight road to Lyons, Bergasse recollected, that Verney had directed his wife, in case either she or any friend came to him, that they might travel through Clermont, instead of the usual route, because, if he was able to be removed, he hoped he might reach the *chateau* d'Hauteville, in Auvergne, where a great number of his friends had agreed, by the consent of the Count, to a rendezvous. — In this case, a letter was to be left at the post-house at Clermont, to inform her of his being at Hauteville. Though this information served only to strengthen my prepossession that this was altogether an infamous and treacherous contrivance to put Geraldine into the power of the Duc de Romagnecourt, I determined, at all events, to pursue this road. — At the *chateau* d'Hauteville, I thought I should, at least, have some little interest on the strength of my friendship with Montfleuri; and, upon the whole, I considered this rather as a circumstance in my favour than otherwise; for though it did not make me less apprehensive of the danger Geraldine might incur, it seemed to lend probability to my hopes of being a protection to her.

I find she has herself, since the present suspence, dreadful as it is, has given her leave to look back on the past; related to her sister the circumstances of her journey; and as Fanny will send you that letter, and I had rather you would learn what passed from any hand than from mine, I will only add to this great packet, an assurance, that if it leaves you, my friend, in doubt, as to my fate, and that of Geraldine; that uncertainty must, in a very few days, a very few hours, be terminated; and that exquisite happiness, or irretrievable misery, must be the decided lot of

Your's, ever faithfully,

LIONEL DESMOND

LETTER XXIII

TO MISS WAVERLEY

Oct. 29, 1791

What scenes, my dear sister, have passed since I wrote to you last! — In what a scene do I now write! — When I look back upon the past, or consider the present, I sometimes wonder to find myself living, oftener doubt my existence! — and ask, whether the sufferings I have lately experienced, are not the hideous paintings of disease on the disordered brain of a wretch in a fever? — I am now, however, for the first time since I left Meudon, collected enough to attempt giving you an account of all that has befallen me.

Perhaps I was rash in plunging into danger, which, before my departure from Paris, Monsieur Bergasse forcibly represented to me. — I hardly dare investigate the real motive of this — for were I to examine too narrowly my own heart, I might, perhaps, find that right actions do sometimes arise from wrong feelings. — Had I loved Mr Verney, as the possessor of my first affections — as the father of my children — in short, as almost any other man might have been beloved, I should not, perhaps, have felt so very strongly the impulse of duty *only*, and should not have been urged, by its rigid laws, to incur dangers, against which, the service of pure affection, though the strongest of all motives, could hardly fortify the heart.

Being now, however, but too sensible, that whatever share of tenderness my young heart once gave him, he had long since thrown it away; and that duty alone bound me to him, I determined to fulfil what seemed to be my destiny — to be a complete martyr to that duty, and to follow whithersoever it led.

A wretch, who is compelled to tremble on the brink of a precipice, has often been known to throw himself headlong from it, and rush to death rather than endure the dread of it. — This sort of sensation was, I think, what I felt; and as to my powers of endurance, I was like a victim, whose limbs being broken on the wheel, is, awhile, released from it, that he may acquire strength to bear accumulated tortures. — The short respite I had felt at Meudon, after all my apprehensions on setting out for Paris, had just this effect — my spirits had acquired energy enough to enable me to suffer, without sinking entirely under them, the horrors that overtook me.

Hardly knowing what I did, and impressed only with the predominant idea, that I ought, at all hazards, to attend my husband, that I might contribute to his recovery, or receive his dying injunctions, I left Paris, by the road he had directed, without even a servant, and taking with me only a small packet of linen, and money enough for my journey — I travelled in a state of mind, I cannot describe, during the first day, and would have continued to pursue my route during the following night, if my desolate and helpless appearance had not encouraged the resistance of the people at the post-houses and the postillions. — I had no means of enforcing my wishes; and was under the necessity of submitting to remain in a miserable post-house, at a village called La Briare, where I arrived at night-fall. — There were, however, women in the house of decent appearance: they seemed desirous of contributing, as well as they could to my repose — I obtained, from excessive fatigue, a few hours sleep; and by day-break, the next morning, I proceeded on my way, sustained by a sort of desperate resolution which I had never before felt.

The second and third day passed nearly as the first. — I travelled as far as I could find people willing to convey me, and then, in any house that would give me a shelter, lay down in my cloaths.

On the fourth, they told me I was in Auvergne; and, towards evening, I stopped at a solitary post-house, situated on the edge of an extensive forest, and in a country, where, hardly any traces of civilization appeared. — The people who came out, upon my asking for horses, had a wild and savage appearance. — A tall, swarthy, meagre figure, presented himself at the door of my carriage, and told me he was the post-master. — I begged of him to let me have horses to go on towards Clermont — he told me he had none — that a company of banditti, whom, in the present state of the police, justice had not been able to disperse, had been, for many days, ravaging the country, and had taken from him all his horses. — Then it was that, for the first time during this melancholy journey, I was sensible of fear. — I looked round me, and saw only faces which seemed to me to belong to the banditti the man described; and his own had, beyond any I ever saw, the terrific look which Salvator gives to his assassins.[77] — The country around was more dreary than the wildest heath in England.

— It was a wide uncultivated plain, surrounded with woods, which seemed to be endless. — I knew not, whether to prefer venturing into them, or to remain at the gloomy and miserable habitation before me. — Any debate however, on this point, was soon put an end to, by the declaration of the postillion who had brought me hither, that he could go no farther.

I now certainly felt, in all its force, the horrors of my situation, and fancy even augmented them. — There was, I thought, a sort of savage pleasure on the countenance of the man who called himself the post-master, as he opened the door of the chaise. — I entered trembling, and hardly able to support myself, into a kind of kitchen, which seemed to serve for every purpose, to the groupe of hideous figures that were assembled in it. — If I had before shuddered at the looks of the men, who surrounded my chaise, those of three women, who now crowded about me, gave me infinitely more alarm. I know not how, under the immediate impression I felt, I was able to make such observations; but the elder of them struck me, as being an exact representation of Horace's Canidia.[78] — The two others were younger, and more robust, equally hideous however, and more masculine. — They spoke to each other, as they examined my dress, in a language of which I understood only a few words, repeating often the word, *Anglaise!* with an air of derision. — A fire of vine stalks and turf was made in the chimney of the room, which was floored only with earth, or rather with mud — and never will the circle, that gathered round it, be erased from my recollection — The blaze of the fire, threw catching lights upon their harsh features; and, as all their eyes were fixed on me, I fancied myself surrounded by daemons. — My imagination flew back to my children: it represented my lovely cherubs calmly sleeping, unconscious of the situation of their unhappy mother; who was now, I thought torn from them for ever. — Their poor father too, occurred to me — dying, perhaps, in a place equally wretched; among people equally savage. — That I had put myself into the present danger from a motive of duty to him, was the only consideration that supported me. — What would have been my reflections if the pursuit of any guilty attachment had led me hither?

Though I did not entirely understand the *patois* in which these rude people conversed, I yet heard enough to make me comprehend they were waiting for somebody. They looked frequently at me, and repeated, '*cette Angloise*,' and '*nos Messieurs*.'[79] — The women some-times laughed immoderately, and sometimes one of them went to the door, as if to look for the arrival of the people they expected — this scene lasted above an hour. — One of the women began to prepare supper. A coarse cloth, disgustingly dirty, was spread on a board that reached the whole length of the kitchen. — The pot *au feu* was brought forward to receive a supply of leeks; a large dish of onions and garlic was heated, with something they called beef; and all this was, I learned from their conversation, for *les Messieurs*, whose arrival they awaited.[80]

I felt myself sinking fast under the horrible apprehension, that these expected guests were the banditti of whom I had been told, and that this was an house of rendezvous. — The dreadful stories of murders and assassinations that I had heard, or read of, now crowded on my imagination. — I found it would soon be impossible to support my-self, and a state of insensibility, at such a period, might subject me to the most hideous insults. — I begged one of the women to give me a little wine — she brought some, which I drank; and, on her request for money, I took out a parcel of *assignats* I had in my pocket.[81] — She immediately seized them, and carried them to one of the men, who looked at them by the fire-light, then turned towards me his hid-eous countenance, and grinning horribly, nodded to me, and thrust them all into his pocket.

This seemed as if it would have been the signal to plunder me, if some other project had not been in agitation. — I have since been amazed how I retained my senses and recollection under such circum-stances of horror! which had now, indeed, continued till my aggra-vated apprehensions were arisen to a height it was impossible long to endure.

But now the feet of several horses were heard upon the *pavé* — An exclamation from the people within the house — '*Eh! voila donc nos, Messieurs!*' left me no doubt that these were the troop of ruffians who scoured the country for prey.[82] — They seemed, however, to be in con-tention, for voices were heard very loud, and three pistols went off very quickly. — My ears were then invaded by dreadful groans, as of a per-son killed; groans so loud, that they were distinguishable amidst the clamour of several harsh voices, which was now increased by the hallooing of the men, and the shrieks of two of the women who had gone out from the hovel; where I sat in a state I have not language to describe; the beldam alone remaining with me, who fixed her terrible eyes upon me, and approached me in an attitude as if she were about to strike me, with a long knife, which she had been using over the fire. — I arose to avoid her, when a figure, covered with blood, rushed into the room, staggered towards the chimney, and fell at my feet. At the same instant, a very loud voice cried in English — 'Sir! Sir! Mr Desmond! for God sake! Mr Desmond!' — My senses then forsook me.

When I recovered them it was yet dark. By the single candle, on a table near, I found myself on a sort of bed in a wretched room; around which, as I cast my eyes, all the terrors I had passed through rushed upon my recollection. — There was a rug hung up on one side the bed, which concealed some person behind it. An impulse of fear made me put it hastily aside — and I saw, not the hag who had apparently attempted my life; not one of the ruffians from whom I had dreaded greater horrors, but Desmond himself. — 'Thank God!' cried he, 'she lives!' — Oh! Fanny, the sound of that voice, those words, the suddenness of beholding such a friend protecting me — Is it possible? — Ah! no, it is not; to convey, by language, any idea of my sensation at the moment. — I have, indeed, no very clear recollection of them myself, for in a short time my faintness returned. — I only remember that I gave both my hands into those of Desmond, who hung over me; and, telling him I was dying, recommended my children to him — bade him carry them to England, to put them under your care — blessed him for his friendship — and then closed my eyes, in the persuasion that I should open them no more.

Again, however, the tender attention of this inestimable friend restored me to life. When I became sensible the second time, he was on the other side of the bed, bathing my temples with brandy, and chaffing my hands. Behind him stood an Englishman, whom I knew to be his servant, and whose appearance, the moment I recovered myself enough to remark it, struck me with new fear. — His cheek was cut across, and his cloaths stained with blood: he held under one arm a case of pistols, and a hanger was slung to the wrist of the other. On a table, close to the head of the bed, lay another case of pistols, and Desmond had put a broad sword on the bed. — I turned my enquiring looks on him — he did not seem to be wounded, but his whole appearance indicated that something very extraordinary had happened — he was pale, his eyes were swoln as with extreme fatigue; and, I observed, that he cast them eagerly towards the door of the room, and listened anxiously to every noise.

When he saw me again sensible, he besought me to swallow some wine which he offered me. — I obeyed in silence; for I was not, at that moment, able to speak. — I found, however, my strength and recollection returning; and, at length I asked him the meaning of all I saw.

'Will you, dearest Mrs Verney?' said he, 'will you only oblige me so far as not to ask till you are in a place of safety?' — 'Am I not safe,' cried I, 'any where with you?' — 'You should be,' answered he, 'if my arm, or those of my servants could serve you — if we were sure of being able to protect you against numbers, our lives would be held well sacrificed in the attempt. But the men with whom we engaged last night at the door of this cottage, little knowing the dear invaluable life it contained, are free-booters; men, who having been armed by the resisting aristocracy against the *liberties* of the country, have thrown off their allegiance to their employers, and now prey upon its *property*. — In reaching this post-house we met a party of eight of them, who immediately attacked us: we disarmed and wounded two — I hope not to death. — The other six, after a faint attempt to revenge their comrades, in which I am afraid a third was desperately wounded, fled to the woods; and we easily repelled the endeavours of the people here, who are their associates, to assist them. — The sudden sight of you, to all appearance dead, put every thing out of my head but the necessity of securing these people; which, with my small party, I could not so effectually do, but that one of the men is escaped, who, together with the wretches who attacked us, will most certainly return hither; and though in such a cause it is, I think, no boast to say, I feel myself an host; yet I own I dread worse, ten thousand times worse than death, the consequences to you, if superior numbers should render my endeavours to guard you fruitless.'

Oh! Fanny! what images of distracting terror did this set before me? — The most dreadful of them was, that of Desmond sacrificing his life to save me. — I was no longer sensible of that weakness which, a moment before, lay heavy on me like the hand of death; but starting up I exclaimed — 'Oh! Desmond! for God's sake let us go! I am able to go in any manner, indeed I am — only do not leave me, and my strength will not fail me, whatever it may be necessary for me to undertake.'

'Do you then think,' said he, 'you could be removed in the chaise?'
— I hurried from the bed, protesting I could. — He then told me he
had three servants below — one of whom, on his calling aloud, came
up — He bade him instantly harness to the chaise whatever horses he
could find. — He did so; and, in a few moments I was, I know not
how, seated in it with Desmond; who, I believe had, with the aid of
one of his servants, lifted me down the ladder which led to the lower
room; for I recollect, that on attempting to descend, my strength and
spirits again wholly failed me.

One of Desmond's servants, a Swiss was mounted as postillion; two
English and a French servant rode by its side; and Desmond himself
was in the chaise, only preventing my falling to the bottom by supporting me in his arms. — With my returning senses, however, the
consciousness returned of the exertion I ought to make, that so much
friendship might not be rendered abortive; and that I might not, by
being needlessly burthensome to him, endanger his life. — I struggled then against the sick languor which had been occasioned by the
dreadful scene I had passed — and again enquired, 'to what fortunate
circumstance I owed the protection he had afforded me.'

'Stay,' answered he, 'my dear friend, stay still you see whether that
protection has been effectual! — Let it not now dwell upon your
spirits, when they may be required for greater exertions.' — 'You
apprehend danger then?' enquired I. — 'Less and less,' replied he,
'every step we advance; but still, perhaps, there is some. — My servants, however, are well armed and resolute, and if the worst should
happen' —

I dared not ask what — what if the worst should happen? — I
cast my eyes around — the dawn just afforded light enough to shew,
that we were travelling across an extensive plain, towards the woods
that on all sides surrounded it — Into these woods we entered. —
Desmond looking anxiously from the windows, and directing the driver
which road to take — 'Whither do we go?' said I, 'and is there not
danger of meeting these dreadful men again?' —

'There certainly is,' answered he — 'but the danger would have
been greater to have remained where we were. — It is now possible
we may escape them, and reach the little village of Aiqueperce, which
I know is within a league of these woods, and not above six from the
château d'Hauteville.

'It is thither,' said I, 'that Mr Verney thought it possible he might be well enough to remove —'

'And yet,' interrupted Desmond, 'it is a very long journey from the neighbourhood of Avignon, where his letter is dated, to the house of Monsieur d'Hauteville.'

I cannot, my Fanny, relate all the conversation which was held by fits and starts — Desmond rather declining it, and trying rather to soothe my enquiries, than to satisfy them — While the more I reflected on his arrival at such a place, and at such a time, the more wonderful appeared the intervention of Providence in my favour.

I saw that Desmond had some strange suspicions on his mind, which were raised by the directions I had received from Mr Verney, to take such, and so dangerous a circuit to reach Avignon, when the most obvious way was by Lyons — and I felt, too cruelly felt, that Mr Verney's former conduct too well justified those suspicions. — Present terror, in some measure, deprived me of reflection, or it must have struck me as strange, that if Desmond apprehended any danger at Hauteville, he should rather bend his course thither than towards Clermont, which he told me was a large town, not much farther distant.

We travelled on through the woods for some miles: it was one of those cold, damp, gloomy mornings, which impresses a dreary idea that the sun has forsaken the world. — The wind sighed hollow among the half-stripped trees; and the leaves slowly fell from the boughs, heavy with rain. — The road, rough, and hardly passable, seemed leading us to the dark abode of desolation and despair: yet, when I saw, as I reclined my head against the side of the chaise, that Desmond was with me — as I found his arm sometimes supporting me — and heard his voice speaking of hope and comfort, I found that all local evils were unheeded; and that nothing had power to produce again the stupor from which I had so lately recovered, but the dread of seeing his life in danger. — My sister! if such a sentiment should be deemed culpable in a married woman, let the circumstances, under which it was felt, be at least considered before she is condemned.

At last we emerged from the fearful solitude, and approached a lone village, which Desmond believed to be Aiqueperce: it was not that, however, but another, a league from it. — But, as the people seemed inoffensive and hospitable, he determined to stop there for such refreshment as it afforded. — He would have persuaded me to have gone to bed for some hours, assuring me that he would become a sentinel without the door of my room, to guard against every alarm — but, besides that, I should have found it impossible to obtain any repose, I thought it better not to lose a moment in pursuing our journey, and getting as far as possible from the part of the country which was described as being infested with banditti. — We were yet above seven leagues from Hauteville: the greater part of our route lay, according to the account of the villagers, through a country as dreary in itself, and as dangerous from the parties of unlicensed free-booters that frequented it, as that we had already passed. — After a slight refreshment, therefore, we hastened on; meeting, indeed, with no impediments but those of dreadful roads. — The horses were quite tired; and though we again stopped to give them food and rest for above two hours, they were so exhausted, that it was with the utmost difficulty, and only in a foot pace, that they crossed the great and wild plain which, as Desmond told me, lay before the avenue to the castle of Hauteville; but it was now dark, and I could discern nothing. — My spirits were quite worn out, and my heart sunk in utter despondence: never, indeed, could be imagined a situation so strange as mine. — I was going, I hardly knew with what hope, to a place where Desmond, while he conducted me thither, seemed to apprehend that dangers and distresses, of which, however, he evaded explaining the nature, awaited me: but he agreed with me in thinking, that as I had there a probability of being informed of the situation of Mr Verney, I acted right in going. — He sighed deeply as he assented to my reasons, and generally concluded the short conversations, which were frequently renewed on this subject, with saying — 'At least, while you will allow me the honour of remaining with you, I will defend you with my life.'

At length a distant and faint light, glimmering through the trees, told us we were very near the castle. As we approached it the light disappeared — and the night was so dark, that the Swiss who drove us, could no longer discern whither he was going. — On a sudden, one of the three horses fell into what appeared to be a deep *fossé*. The harness of ropes fortunately gave way, or the chaise must have been dragged after him — the other horses, however, though down, were disengaged from this, by the breaking of the tackle; and Desmond, leaping from the chaise, snatched me out — and having seen me safe on the ground, advanced with the other three men to the assistance of the postillion.

I was unable to stand. — I staggered to a tree against which I leaned, so overcome with fatigue and terror, that I feared my senses would again forsake me. — Desmond having disengaged the remaining horses from the chaise, and sent the French servant forward to try to obtain a light, that the other poor animal might be relieved, came to me; but he was obliged to find me by my voice, for it was impossible to see even the nearest objects. — 'Good God! how cold you are — how you tremble!' cried he, as he took my hand — 'are you able, no surely you are not, to walk forward? — and yet, perhaps, if you are, it will be unsafe to venture. — Since I was here last, some rude kind of fortification seems to have been made. — There was no ditch around the castle before — and I know no longer how to guide you safely' — I was unable to answer him. — He was terrified at my silence; and supposing me again in the situation in which he had so lately seen me, he called aloud for lights and for assistance. — One of the servants came up to him; two of the others were by this time gone to endeavour to obtain admittance into the castle, and the fourth remained with the horses.

The anguish that Desmond seemed to feel for me, roused me from the state into which I had fallen. — I assured him I was able to walk on; and he supported me, as step by step, his servant Warham going first, we endeavoured to find, or rather to feel our way towards the house.

Every way, however, in front, where Desmond said there was formerly only a rail, a deep *fossé* intercepted our passage. — The heavy clouds which had occasioned darkness so total, were now driven away by the sudden rising of the wind; and we could just discern the *château* before us — and attempt to cross the ditch in some other place by going round it.

When I reflected whither I was going, and to what purpose Desmond was, on my account, incurring so much fatigue and so much hazard, I cannot describe the emotions that arose in my mind; nor do I know how I found strength to traverse this melancholy place, still finding it inaccessible. — Desmond now hallooed in hopes his own servants would hear and answer him. After near a quarter of an hour, one of them came towards us, but still on the other side of the *fossé*. He said that he had fallen into it in endeavouring to find his way to the house, and that it was half full of water; but that he had scrambled up on the other side, and found one of the entrances to the castle, where he had knocked and called in vain for some time; that he had then attempted to force the door, which seemed, by some accident, to be incompletely fastened; that he had entered a great hall where the embers were yet a light on the hearth, but that he could make no one hear, and was afraid of going any farther.

Desmond now enquired where he could pass the *fossé*, and bade his servant walk round it, as there must somewhere be a bridge. — Within a few paces a slight drawbridge was found, which the man easily let down. — We passed it; and he led us to the door by which he had himself entered.

Never was so dismal a place so long and eagerly sought for. — The faint embers served just to shew that it was a large and high vaulted room; but as my cloaths were wet through, for it had rained, at intervals, the whole evening, Desmond was so glad to find a fire, that he seemed, in his eagerness for my immediate relief, regardless of all that did not tend to that object. — By this time the English groom, who had also been sent to the *chateau*, had found the same door; and after having helped to make up the fire, and light a candle, he went out with Warham, to assist the Swiss, who remained with the horses, and to shew him the way over the drawbridge; the Frenchman only remaining with us.

I now saw, in the countenance of Desmond, an expression of doubt and uneasiness, which alarmed me more than any fears he could openly have expressed. — I endeavoured first to convince him that I was less incommoded by my wet cloaths than he seemed to apprehend; and then to enquire what he thought of our situation. — 'The people you expected to find,' said I, 'the people whom my letter gave me reason to suppose might be here, are certainly not here' — 'God knows,' replied he; 'perhaps these men have fallen into the snare they have laid for others. — The desperadoes, whom they have armed against their country, have, perhaps, turned those arms against themselves. — The ruffians have, possibly, driven out the owner of this castle, or his friends, for I do not believe he has been lately here himself; and it may be in possession of some such wretches as those we escaped from. — It is better, however, to know at once.'

'You will not leave me?' said I, terrified at the idea of his going on this search. — 'Never,' replied he, 'but with my life; but, when the other men arrive, we will, some of us, go round the rooms of the castle. — That there are inhabitants, the light we saw in the windows, and unextinguished embers of fire, ascertain; that there has existed some necessity for defence, the works around the house, which were certainly not here before, leaves no manner of doubt. What Mr Verney said to you, is evidence enough that here the aristocratic party of these provinces had a rendezvous: yet, if it were still assembled here, it is improbable the members of it should be so little on their guard, or that the noise we have made should not have alarmed them.'

From this conversation I discovered, that Desmond apprehended the place we were in, was in the possession of ruffians and banditti — a circumstance infinitely more terrific than any other that could be imagined. — I observed that he listened to every noise — kept his pistols in his hand, and enquired solicitously of the French servant whether his fire-arms were properly charged? — I do not believe that a quarter of an hour was ever passed in a more uneasy state; for so long it was before the other three men came to us. — When they arrived, Desmond questioned them whether they had seen any signs of inhabitants while they remained within view of the whole front of the castle — they answered none.

Desmond then told them, he wished to enquire, by some persons going round the rooms, whether there were any women who could prepare a bed for me; but none of them knew the way — and none of them seemed very desirous of undertaking the exploit without him — while I was as resolutely determined not to remain behind, if he went. — On surveying the room where we were, it appeared to be a sort of servants hall. — Every thing in it was dirty and in disorder. — The piece of candle which one of the men had found, was nearly extinguished, and we saw no means of renewing the light when it was burnt out. — My fears were so much greater of the people that Desmond seemed to apprehend were within the house, than of any fatigue I could encounter without it, that I could, most willingly, have left it without any farther enquiry; but, besides that, the horses were incapable of going farther, he, probably, knew that our escape was impossible — for that, if such were the inhabitants of the *chateau* d'Hauteville, detached parties of them were in the woods, with whom we should infallibly meet. — I saw, with dreadful alarm, the debate he held with himself, what it would be best to do. — At length he determined to see who was in the house; and, securing the door by which we had entered, he determined that we should all go on this enquiry.

He directed Warham to go first with the candle. — I trembled like an aspin leaf, as he took my arm within his, to lead me along — the other three servants followed. — 'Be not so alarmed,' said he, as we crossed a long stone passage, 'there are five of us; and, I think, any nearly equal number must be fortunate if they gain any advantage.' — We now entered a dark and gothic hall. — Warham stumbled over something, he stooped and took it up; it was one of those caps to travel in of a night, used sometimes in England, but oftener in France; a bullet had pierced it, and it was on one side covered with blood. — Warham, with a countenance where terror was strongly marked, shewed it to his master. — I felt that he grasped my arm closer within his, but betrayed no other signs of fear, and calmly bade Warham go on.

We ascended the stairs, and came to a corridor: in one of the rooms opening into it, Desmond told me he had formerly slept. — The corridor was long, and several rooms adjoined to it. — Desmond thought he heard a sound — he bade us listen! — What a pause of horror! — We distinctly heard the loud breathing of some person or persons — 'We will know,' said Desmond, 'at all events, who they are.'

You know that, in France, it is impossible to open a door, from without, but with the key. — Desmond, therefore, did not hesitate, having once taken his resolution, but, with a violent blow against the door, he aroused the person who slept in the room.— A loud, masculine voice enquired what he wanted, and he bade him instantly open the door.

I shrunk back with dread — for, in a moment, a hideous figure appeared at it, who asked, why such haste, and whether they had brought any prisoners? — This sufficiently convinced me that Desmond's conjectures were true; and I know not how I sustained my trembling limbs, while Desmond, without giving the man time for recollection, disengaged himself from me, and sprung upon him like a lion — 'Villain!' said he, 'what prisoners! — Your life is at my mercy — Tell me instantly — Where is the Count d'Hauteville? and in whose possession is his house?'

The man appeared to me to be twice as tall and athletic as Desmond; but guilt and fear are inseparable. — He either was incapable of making, or feared to make any resistance, but called for mercy with the most abject supplications. — Desmond told him it would be granted, on condition of his immediately informing him by what authority he was in that house — who was there with him — and to whom he belonged.

The man said that he was one of a troop armed for the defence of the castle, by the order of the Count d'Hauteville, who was, himself, gone to Italy — That other noblemen, friends to the cause, had fortified it against the municipal guard, to whom they were determined never to submit — That these noblemen had, within a few days, left the place; and that the vassals they had left behind, had continued, by their orders, in the castle, from whence they had, occasionally, made excursions against the national guard.

'And against travellers,' said Desmond vehemently, interrupting him, 'whom you have robbed and murdered — Is it not so?'

The man denied their having murdered any one, but owned, that they thought themselves justified in plundering the partizans of democracy, who were endeavouring to plunder the noble persons, by whom they were employed and paid. — The eyes of Desmond flashed fire at this information. —'Tell me instantly,' cried he, 'what number of men there is in the house?' — 'Only myself,' answered he, 'and one more, with some women that belong to us. — The rest of our gentlemen are out, and when you came, I believed it to be them.' — 'And how many are there of these *gentlemen* out marauding.' — 'There are eight.'

Desmond, with admirable presence of mind, sent two of the men to secure the companion to this worthy person, who was, he said, in the next room. — Both these ruffians had been so intoxicated the preceding evening, that they were, perhaps, incapable of resistance — They made none. — Desmond's servants conveyed them to a room in the most ancient part of the castle, which was, when the feudal system was in all its force, a place of confinement for the wretched vassals, over whom those barbarous customs gave the *seigneur*, the power of life and death. — It was still stronger secured; for the privilege, though not so often exerted, had never been given up. — While these men were securing in one part of this building, Desmond, with his trembling companion still hanging on his arm, went with the other men and drew up the bridge, thus preventing the entrance of the eight ruffians, who it was likely would immediately return. — Four women were now assembled in extreme terror. — Desmond assured them that he waged no war against them, but that he must insist upon their not attempting to give any intelligence to the persons without, and upon their furnishing me with assistance and refreshment.

He then, as we seemed to be now in a tolerable state of security, would have had me take some repose, for he saw that I was hardly able to support myself. This, however, I refused; for I knew that to attempt sleeping in such circumstances would be to no purpose. — As one of his servants had found his way across the *fossé*, of the depth of which he was ignorant, the men who were out for the purposes of robbery, were certainly able to cross it. — I saw still the possibility, nay the probability of danger to him, and of such scenes as my soul sickened at. The cap which Warham had picked up now lay on a great table in the room to which we had returned — and the idea that the murdered body of some unhappy person to whom it belonged, might be concealed in the house, made me shudder as I surveyed it. — Suddenly the supposition that it was, perhaps, Verney himself, occurred to me. — Gracious heaven! what horror accompanied that thought! — Involuntarily I caught the hand of Desmond, who sat anxiously watching my countenance — He enquired eagerly what was the matter. — 'Oh! Desmond!' said I, hardly, indeed, conscious of what I said — 'Verney is here, I am persuaded he is. He came hither by appointment of his perfidious friends — they were called away before his arrival, and these their retainers have destroyed him.'

He endeavoured to argue me out of a supposition which he saw shook my whole frame. — 'If you have any impression of this sort,' said he, 'I will interrogate the men below; I will myself search the whole house.' — 'Oh! no, no,' replied I — 'send your servant to do this, but for heaven's sake do not yourself leave me!'

Warham was then sent with the Swiss round the house. There was no appearance of any person concealed in it, either dead or alive. — The men who were in confinement below, protested that the cap belonged to one of their own people, who had been fired at in retreating before a party of the national horse, and wounded in the cheek. — On this assurance I became easier; but as I still persisted in refusing to go to any bed above stairs, Desmond desired the women to bring down one and lay it on the floor of the room where we were: they did so, and he prevailed upon me to lie down. The mere change of posture after so many hours of fatigue and terror, was extremely refreshing. — He had before made me eat of some provisions the women produced, and drink some warm wine. — He now assured me his men were so placed that the people from whom we apprehended danger could not surprise us. — 'We are,' said he, 'five men, resolute and well armed; we have heaven on our side; we have your safety to contend for — and can you imagine that we should be easily conquered?'

'Oh! no,' replied I, 'I do not imagine it; but the terror of such a scene! — to shed the blood even of the misguided wretches whom we fear is so horrible! — Your danger — danger for me too!' — Tears, the first I had been able to shed for many days, now burst from my eyes. I found myself greatly relieved by them — and since I saw how much he wished me to attempt it, I endeavoured, while he sat by me, to rest. — I even fell into a kind of half slumber, from which I started in terror, fancying I heard fire-arms, and saw the horrid visages of the ruffians; but I found Desmond only by me, assuring me that all was perfectly safe and quiet, and I sunk once more into something like sleep — and when I again recovered my recollection, it was morning. — Never was the light of day more welcome — for it shewed me Desmond, my generous protector in safety; and I saw his countenance lighten with friendly pleasure, when he found me so much restored. — The women, by this time convinced that we meant nothing hostile to them, or even to the men who had been in possession of the house, if we were not molested, were now in hopes that we should quietly depart: they were assiduous, therefore, in assisting me. — My cloaths, about which I had never thought, were enquired for in the chaise, and the small portmanteau I had was produced untouched. — Desmond waited without the door, while I, with the assistance of the women, changed my cloaths. — A very few moments, you may believe, sufficed me; for I found he was now impatient to pursue the plan which he had settled for me, which was to go on, notwithstanding all passed dangers, to the village where Verney had informed me he was, though this journey was above seventy leagues. — Every consideration of prudence and safety urged our immediate departure. The men were sufficiently refreshed, and the horses able to proceed, all but the poor animal which had fallen into the *fossé* — which was so much injured, that Desmond in mercy ordered it to be shot, and it was replaced by that which he had rode himself — and which one of the men had led.

Before seven in the morning we left this dismal abode. It was three leagues to Clermont — but we arrived there without meeting the party we had so much reason to apprehend, and I once more saw my invaluable friend in safety, after all the perils he had, on my account, hazarded; and here I agreed to take some hours repose, on condition that he would, in the mean time, attend to himself.

Early on the following morning we proceeded, Desmond having hired two men with fire arms to accompany us; which made the party, he thought, so strong as to preclude any apprehensions from the troops of marauders, of which we were still told. — He went himself to the municipality at Clermont, and informed them of the situation of the *château* d'Hauteville; where it is probable the two prisoners were released by their female friends, as soon as we had left them.

I will not, my dear sister, speak of any circumstances of our five days journey from Clermont to Lyons, and from thence to this place. — We met with nothing worth relating after such scenes as I have just described; but the conversation I had with Desmond I will repeat as ingenuously to you, Fanny, as I repeat it involuntarily to my own heart.

Conscious as I am of the ties I am bound by, and shrinking from every idea of their violation, I will now own to you, that I have long been unable to conceal from myself, Desmond's regard for me, though he never avowed it; but, on the contrary, has entrusted me with connexions he has formed, that were wholly incompatible with such an attachment, if he ever meant to acknowledge it. — I am, however, persuaded he never did; and only the singular circumstances of my destiny have made my affected ignorance difficult, and, at length, impossible to be supported.

Fanny — though I certainly should have preferred Desmond to every other man in the world, had it been my fortune to have been acquainted with him before I became irrevocably another's — though I have received from him the most extraordinary instances of generous friendship — though he has more than once hazarded his life for me — and once — Oh! how lately, and how wonderfully, rescued me from death! — perhaps, from worse than death! — Yet, believe me, when I declare to you, that never have I, even in thought, transgressed the bounds of that duty, which, though it was imposed on me when I was not a competent judge of the engagement I entered into, I feel to be equally binding; and whether my unhappy Verney lives or dies, I have the comfort of knowing, that towards him, my conduct has been irreproachable. — I break my melancholy narrative to say this, because I owe it to truth, I owe it to myself. — Indulge me then with yet a word on this delicate and painful subject, because I may, perhaps, speak upon it now for the last time.

I learned then, in our conversation, which became less interrupted and confused, after we left Clermont, that Desmond had never lost sight of me after I quitted England; that he had followed me to Paris, and lived in disguise at Meudon — that a circumstance of a very peculiar nature had obliged him to go to Paris, the day I so suddenly received a summons to attend Mr Verney; but that on his return, finding me gone, and learning, by Mr Bergasse, by what route, he had pursued me, and but for an accident that happened on the road, he would have overtaken me long before that dreadful night, when he most providentially delivered me from a situation so very terrible, that in reflecting on it, I sicken with the terror it yet impresses. — When all this, my Fanny, was added to the recollection of the circumstances that happened at Bridge-foot, and some (which, though I never thought them of much consequence, it was not in my power to obliterate from my mind) that happened much earlier in our acquaintance, it would have been falsehood or affectation, had I pretended to have been ignorant that Desmond's attachment to me was not a common one. But, while all its consequences had been to me only good; while he preserved for me the most inviolate respect, and even promoted my executing towards Verney, what he knew to be my duty, it would have been folly and ingratitude, had I affected resentment which certainly I did not feel.

Still I am aware, that my situation was very strange and very improper, travelling under the protection of a man, who I knew felt for me a regard which I ought not to encourage, and dared not return — so much obliged to him — esteeming him beyond any other human being; every step I took, being conscious, that I owed to him that I existed; and all this, while I knew not but that my unfortunate husband was dying, or, possibly, dead — Alas! I am not a stoic — perhaps my heart is but too susceptible of gratitude and tenderness. — How ill my early affections had been replaced, you know but too well! — But when my husband disdained them, they found refuge with my children and with my sister — Ah! Fanny! but for these resources, should I have been less culpable than so many other young women have been, who have been as unhappily married? — and should I now have possessed what softens the misery of my destiny? — the consciousness of not having deserved it.

Let me still possess this consoling consciousness. — I will tell you, Fanny, what I have done to secure its possession still. — When I found, too certainly, that Desmond had placed his whole happiness in testifying to me, by his conduct rather than his words, how much he was attached to me, I endeavoured, for his sake and for my own, to convince him, that the continuance of that regard, unless it was under the regulation of reason, would be only a source of misery to us both. — 'If Verney should be no more,' said I, 'or if my earnest endeavours to contribute to his recovery, should fail — what have I either in my heart or my person, to repay such affection? — Alas! nothing; — the bloom of both are gone. *You*, Sir, are in a situation of life to expect the undivided tenderness of the most lovely and fortunate of women. — I have nothing but a spirit weighed down by long anxiety — a person no longer boasting of any advantages — and a heart trembling for the fate of three little, helpless beings, who, if my fears do not exaggerate, have but little to trust to from the wreck of their father's fortune. — Let me, Desmond, as your grateful friend, point out where, without any of these drawbacks, all the little advantages you found or fancied in me, may be met with. — My Fanny possesses them all; and with them an heart worthy of your's, uninjured by calamity, and untainted by sorrow.' — I will not tell you, my sister, his answer: it was expressive of the high sense Desmond has of your merit. — I felt that I had acquitted myself; and while my eyes overflow with tears, I still feel it; for indeed, I think, I could die happy, if you were married to Desmond; if I knew that you united in giving to my luckless little ones that generous tenderness you are both so capable of feeling; and sometimes, in deploring together, with the soothing sympathy of kindred minds, the fate of your lost Geraldine!

This is the only plan I, at this moment, look forward to with any degree of satisfaction. — If poor Verney survives — Alas! I would very fain, but cannot flatter myself, that he will be changed. — If he dies — I will retire to some cheap country with my children, and never, with my poverty and theirs, embitter the affluent and fortunate situation of Desmond.

But it is time to close my long and distressing narrative; and if I yield to these overwhelming sensations, I shall not be able! — My tears have rendered the last page illegible!

We arrived then, without any very alarming occurrence, at the village, from an *auberge* in which Verney's letter had been written — Oh! what was my breathless agitation, as I stopped in the chaise, while Desmond went to enquire for him, I cannot describe; for I could not discriminate such a combination of distracting emotions as at that moment assailed me. — In about a quarter of an hour Desmond returned, and I saw, by his countenance, that I was to expect something very dreadful. — 'Verney,' cried I, 'my husband, is he there? — is he living?' — 'He is there,' replied Desmond; 'and I am shocked at myself for having supposed that he was engaged in a scheme of dishonourable treachery, while he lay in all the miseries of indigence and sickness.' — I had heard enough, and attempted to open the chaise door — 'Let me go to him,' cried I, 'this moment — let me go.'

'Be calm, dear Madam,' replied Desmond; 'you will need all your fortitude, do not, therefore, exhaust your strength.' — 'I will go, however,' exclaimed I, 'nothing shall stop me. — Have you seen him yourself?' — 'I have.' — 'And does he know that I am here?' — 'He does — I told him that meeting you by a strange accident, encompassed by dangers, into which you had hurried in your anxiety to attend him, I could not quit you till I had seen you hither. — He expressed, as well as he was able to express, gratitude towards me, and affection towards you.'

Oh! my sister, judge of what I must have felt, when Desmond, after a little more preparation, led me into the room — a miserable room, where lay the father of my children, in a situation which I have not the courage minutely to describe. — His associates had deserted him — his wounds, one of which was, at first, supposed to be fatal, had never been properly dressed, and *now* still (though we instantly procured better assistance) it threatens a mortification. Besides this, the bones of his leg had been broken; and it was so ill set, that, on Desmond's procuring a surgeon, he was under the necessity of breaking it again. — In a condition, which I will not shock you by painting distinctly, had Verney lain near five weeks, without any money, but what his arms and watch had sold for; nor any attendance, at first, but what the reluctant charity of a woman in the house had afforded him: but as his money failed, that declined also; and had it not been for one of *les soeurs de la miséricorde*, who had left her convent, but still exercised the most noble part of her profession, he told us that he must have perished. — Such was the bigotry of the people in this part of France, that this worthy woman was reproached for her humanity by the savages of the village, and told, that in trying to save the life of an *heretic*, she offended God — though this heretic had fallen in a *defence* (from whatever motive) of the very party which so piously consigned him to death, for differing, as they supposed, in opinion. — Alas! poor Verney had never any opinion at all; and now had hardly expressed, in a languid and indistinct voice, his gratitude for my attendance, before he besought me to prevent the *curé* of the parish from persecuting him hourly with his visits and exhortations. Desmond undertook to do this; but the charitable nun came every day; and, indeed, without her assistance, I should have sunk under the fatigue I have endured ever since I have been here, now four days.

I need not remind you of the unhappy propensity Verney has long had to intoxication. — In this habit he has indulged himself ever since he has been told that it endangers his life; and when he is absolutely denied it, he sinks into a sullen or torpid state, and complains that I will let him die of faintness and dejection.

Oh! Fanny! when I see him suffer, and trace in his countenance, distorted, pale, and disfigured as it is, the likeness my dear boy bears to him, I forget all I have suffered — I pardon all his faults — I endeavor to apologize even for those which I fancied he intended to commit — and I pray to heaven for his life — and that he may be happy with his children. — That Being alone, in whose hands are life and death, knows what is best. — My only resource against the long anxiety I have gone through, against that which is to come, is in the consciousness of having done my *duty*. — I am, in some measure, rewarded, even now, by the unwearied, the generous, and surely the disinterested conduct of Desmond, who, whatever *may* have been his motives, or his wishes, *respects that sacred duty*, and never has, since my arrival, uttered one word that could make me reproach myself with having listened to him.

Oh! what a heart is his! — how truly brave! how manly! — how generous! — Though he has no reason to love Verney, the tenderest friend, the most affectionate brother, could not shew more constant attention to his ease. — Yesterday, overcome with the fatigue of sitting up two nights, in order that the directions of the surgeon, after the last horrible operation, might be strictly followed, I lay down, for a few hours, in my cloaths, leaving the young woman-servant of the house in the room, who promised to call me if Mr Verney wanted any thing. — Desmond was gone to the place where he lodges, to write letters to England, which he was promised an opportunity of sending that afternoon, or this morning. — Quite exhausted by excess of fatigue, sleep fell heavier upon me than it has done for many, many days, and when I started from my unquiet dreams which still haunted me, I found it was five o'clock.

I stepped softly towards the room where Verney lay, where I heard him talking in a loud and peremptory voice. His face was flushed even to a purple hue; and he was arguing angrily with Desmond, who hung over him, speaking soothingly to him, and entreating him to be patient! — to be pacified! — As I approached, I saw that Verney darted towards me a look of anger and reproach, while Desmond had a countenance so expressive of concern for us both! — Ah! Fanny! I found that the poor, imprudent patient had bribed, by a promise of a crown, the foolish girl that had been left with him, to bring him wine and brandy, of which he had drank so liberally, that the fever which we had, to all appearance, baffled, by compelling his abstinence, threatened to return. — It was, indeed, returned, and a delirium succeeded. This lasted till towards morning, during all which time, Desmond sat by him, often keeping him, by force, in bed, from which he would otherwise have rushed, notwithstanding his fractured limb. — The scene was often too much for me. — At four o'clock he became more calm, and then Desmond prevailed upon me to leave the room, promising to remain with him.

This morning he seemed a great deal better — declares himself sensible of his folly, and assures us he will be governed. — He no longer complains of pain, and, I think, I have never seen him so composed as since eight o'clock to-day; it is now ten at night. — The surgeon has not been here to-day: but Verney has been so cool and rational, and slept so much, that I have been enabled to finish this letter, which

I began yesterday morning.

I own I now have less apprehensions of him than I have ever had. — His age — his naturally good constitution, are strong circumstances in his favor; and I may remark, my Fanny, I hope not unkindly remark, that Verney does not suffer, as many people do, great irritation of spirits, from excess of sensibility; and if he is tolerably free from bodily sufferings, feels no injury from the emotions of the mind.

Still his condition is, I know, precarious — Still I have much to suffer with him, and for him. — I am, however, relieved, by having thus disburthened my poor heart to you! — Pray for me, my Fanny — for my children — and for the poor unfortunate sufferer their father. — Perhaps, before you receive this, for it is a long way from hence to England, he will be well — perhaps he may not need your prayers! I will contrive to write, from day to day, but now I must close my letter, as this is the only chance of sending it off for some time.

That heaven may watch over the happiness of my dear Fanny, is the warmest wish of her

GERALDINE

LETTER XXIV

TO MR BETHEL

Salon, Nov. 10, 1791

It is all over, my friend — Verney is gone! — The torpor and tranquillity which I described to you in my last letter,* were the beginning of a mortification, which proved fatal twenty hours afterwards — He died yesterday morning. — I will not attempt to describe the behaviour of his angelic wife, nor the comfort it is to me to reflect, on the exact and rigorous attention she has been enabled to give to this unfortunate man at the close of his life, so that her gentle heart, when the first shock has lost its force, will be restored to its tranquillity, and may taste of happiness which no self-reproach will interrupt.

Peace to the ashes of poor Verney! and may his faults be forgotten by the world, as his divine Geraldine has forgiven them. — Bethel!

---

* Which does not appear.

his last act of his life should plead his pardon for every folly with which it was stained. — He was not, till a very few hours before his death, convinced that there were no hopes: he then seemed to collect himself as if to shew how much better he could die than he had lived.

He suffered no pain, and was in perfect possession of his senses: he bade Geraldine leave him alone with me, and thus spoke to me —

'Desmond! I know that your friendship for me cannot have been strong enough to induce you to make all the kind exertions for me, which you have done since you have been here; nor, indeed, to bring you hither. — I have been told, by several people, that you have always been in love with my wife. — Perfectly secure of her honour, more so than I deserved to be, not naturally of a jealous temper, and engaged in the pleasures of the world, as long as I had money to enjoy them, I never heeded this; and, if my informers mean maliciously, they lost their aim. — I am now dying, and I owe it to you, that death comes not with all the aggravated horrors of poverty and wretchedness. — I know you to be a man of honour, and if Geraldine marries again, as there is certainly reason to believe she will, it is to you, rather than to any other man, that I wish to confide her and my children.'

It would be very difficult for me, Bethel, to describe my sensations while this passed. — I answered, however, ingenuously and with truth — 'that I certainly had always preferred Mrs Verney to every other woman, but that my attachment had been unknown to *her*, and never would have led me to transgress the bounds of honour towards *him*; but that if she ever was at liberty, I should deem the happiness of becoming her protector the first that fate could give me.'

'Let me,' said he, 'while I am yet able, make a will in which I will give you, jointly with her, the guardianship of my children. — Poor things! I have nothing to give them; but the settlements made on my marriage have prevented my making them entirely beggars. — Perhaps, my dear friend, my death may be, for them, the most fortunate circumstance that could happen. — I have been miserably cheated: perhaps some of my affairs may be retrievable.'

He then desired me to call up my two English servants, before whom he dictated to me a memorandum, in which he left his wife and his children to my care, appointing her executrix, but requesting that I would be the guardian of his children, jointly with her; and expressing his wishes, that if ever she took a second husband, it might be his friend Desmond. — This he signed: it was witnessed in due form, and when that was done, he gave it me and bade me keep it. — He was fatigued, and asked for a medicine which Geraldine came in to give him — he then fell into a sort of stupor, rather than sleep. — When he awoke Geraldine was alone with him. — I know not what passed, but when she sent for me I found her drowned in tears, and Verney evidently dying. — In a few moments he expired in her arms. — Bethel, if I had not hopes of living with her, such a death would excite my envy.

There was no affectation of violent affliction in his lovely widow. — The natural tenderness of her heart, the thoughts of her children, and the circumstance of their father's dying so far from his country, and in consequence of his unhappy connections, were enough to produce those severe paroxysms of grief in which I saw her for the first twelve hours. — At the end of that time she became more calm. — As I found it was her wish that the remains of her husband should be conveyed to England, I determined that it should be done, and gave orders accordingly.

Mournful as the scene was, I reflected on what the situation of Geraldine would have been had I not been with her; and felt a degree of satisfaction which the possession of worlds could not bestow.

It is now time to consider of our return to Meudon. — I have been entreating her directions: but I see the circumstance of going, so recently a widow, with a man of whose attachment to her she cannot now be ignorant, is very oppressive to her delicate sense of propriety: yet, very certain it is, that the whole world united to censure it, should not induce me to quit her an instant. — Hitherto her mind, weakened by long anguish, has not recovered firmness enough to decide. — She weeps, and tells me in a voice rendered inarticulate by her tears, that she leaves the direction of all to me.

Adieu! dear Bethel, as soon as I know our route, I will write again, in the hope that that you will continue to let me hear from you. — Will it seem unfeeling if I *say* that I am a *happy* fellow? I do not know — but I am sure I should be very *stupid* if I did not feel that *I am so* — I mean, however, only comparatively happy, for I intend to be a great deal happier; but I know that it must be many tedious months first.

I had sealed my letter, and was dispatching it by a messenger to England, with several from Geraldine to her family, when I was amazed by the sudden appearance of my friend Montfleuri, who, rushing into a lower apartment of the poor house I inhabit in this village, threw himself into my arms; and, before I could recover my surprize, disengaged himself, and put into them his wife; on whom, with undescribable astonishment and pleasure, I recognized Fanny Waverly, the sister of my Geraldine.

I was very glad that this unguarded introduction was not made to her instead of to me; for in her present state of mind I know not what might have been the consequence.

I contrived that the knowledge of her sister's being here, of whose marriage she was entirely ignorant, might not reach her so abruptly. — I had the inexpressible happiness to find that she considered this arrival as the most fortunate circumstance that could have befallen her. — With what delight does she gaze on her sister — how affecting, how interesting is the tender friendship between them.

Montfleuri and I have now settled every thing for our journey immediately. — We shall quit this place on the day following to-morrow; and he is to send some of his own servants, with two of mine, in whom I can confide, to attend the last offices that can be done for poor Verney. — This sad ceremony being over, we go to Montfleuri, and from thence to Paris, or rather to Meudon. — Now, there is nothing wrong or improper in my attending Geraldine — blessings on the lovely little Fanny for coming hither. — If Montfleuri should forget his good resolutions, and relapse into that libertinism which was his only fault, I shall not forgive him; but, at present, he seems that most truly happy, as he is always the gayest creature in the world.

LETTER XXV

TO MR BETHEL

Meudon, Dec. 26, 1791

MY EXCELLENT FRIEND,

For so, I persuade myself, I may call you — I write to you by the express wish of our dear friend, Desmond, who begs me and *ma douce*

Fanni, to tell you what he thinks we can say better than he can himself.[83]

And, indeed, he is so occupied with his love and his hopes, distant as they must be, that he sometimes seems to lament the necessity of acknowledging that any other persons in the world have a right to share his thoughts or his affections. — If he can sit whole hours, silent, in the room with Geraldine, he is content. — If he knows she is engaged, or unwilling to be in company, he takes her children in his arms — he plays with, he caresses them; and still he is content. — I thought I had been tolerably in love, when I determined on an affair, so entirely out of my way, as marrying; but my love is really of so humble a species, when put by the side of this sublime passion of my friend's, that I am afraid my amiable *Fanchon* will discover the difference, and be discontent with me.

But all this is wandering from my purpose, which is to tell you, that we are hastening to England, where we hope to be within this month.

I hate writing long letters; and therefore I will only relate what Desmond tells me he wishes you to know. — You have, before now, received commissions with which he troubled you about poor Verney, and we are satisfied will execute them.

We bring with us four children; and that there may be no more mystery about this; that Geraldine's reputation may not suffer, which otherwise it might do, even in your eyes, I will confide to you the truth.

I was so indiscreet and thoughtless as to encourage, in the gay and unguarded heart of my sister de Boisbelle, an affection for Desmond, while he was at my house, little imagining the cruelty I was guilty of towards them both. — Indeed, I knew, that Josephine had been married against her inclination; and had an attachment, almost from her infancy, to a naval officer, a near relation, which, I supposed, guard enough against any other impression; and though I used to rally her about Desmond, I was so prepossessed with this idea, that the possible consequence of encouraging her apparent preference to him, never occurred to me. — When he was wounded at Marseilles, I flew to him, and Josephine went with me. — We attended him through his alarming illness, and when political business called me away, I delegated to my sister the task of taking care of my friend.

No part of the event was to be wondered at, unless it was the greatness of mind which Josephine evinced. — As soon as she became to[o] well assured that the consequence of her indiscreet attachment could not be finally concealed, she determined to save Desmond from any resentment which I might have felt, by declaring to me, that it was her own ungaurded folly, and not to any art or deception on his part, that the blame was owing. — She told me she had promised nothing; that he used no art to betray her; but, on the contrary, had told her that his whole soul was dedicated to another. — Should I have been wise, under these circumstances, to have destroyed my friend? or to have given him a chance of destroying me? — I think it was much more rational to endeavor to conceal what could not be amended. — I did so; and it was *Josephine*, whom *I* attended, that caused such speculation at Bridge-foot; and who, being taken for Geraldine, occasioned to my wife all the terror and uneasiness she has since described to me.

Her going thither was concerted between Geraldine and Desmond; and it was to the generous tenderness of Geraldine, that my sister consented, and Desmond determined to confide their child.

My sister, as soon as she recovered, went to London; and I took care that her infant, which was a girl, should be conveyed to Paris, as Desmond seemed anxious, that wherever Geraldine was, the little creature might be put under her protection. — It was to meet and convey this charge to her, that Desmond left Meudon on the day that Geraldine so abruptly quitted that place. — My sister is since gone to Italy, and is now under the protection of Monsieur d'Hauteville. — Her husband has not been heard of since the night in which Verney received the wound that cost him his life. — If he is dead, and my relation, de Rivemont, ever returns from the East-Indies, where he has, for three years, been stationed, it is probable that their first attachment will end in a marriage; but I shall never deceive him as to what has happened in his absence.

Thus, my dear Sir, I have acquitted myself in informing you of what, though Desmond owned it was necessary you should know, he could not prevail on himself to relate to you.

Have you not heard in England, that Mr Verney, an English gentleman, travelling for his amusement, has been inhumanly fallen upon by a party of the national troops, and killed? — This is, I understand, the report that has universally gained credit: yet, I beg to assure you, that it was in attempting to drive the French from Avignon, which, in a fit of desperate valour, his party undertook; and not in any tumult, or even by the hands of ruffians, who are equally the dread and scourge of all parties, that Verney fell; and that, as I believe, Boisbelle has fallen also.

But thus it is, that, throughout the revolution, every circumstance has, on your side the water, been exaggerated, falsified, distorted, and misrepresented, to serve the purposes of party; and thus I, as well as Desmond, fear it will continue to be. — Probably much more cause will arise for it than has yet arisen; for, according to every present appearance, the hydra, despotism, is raising in every country of Europe one of its detestable *heads* against the liberty of France.

Should this arrive, it is true, I shall be torn from a circle of friends, where the happiness of my *life* is placed, to draw the sword once more. But he must be a despicable wretch, who, in such a cause, would refuse to sacrifice his life itself.

In the mean time, however, let us not waste the moments, as they are passing, in dark speculations on the future; which, after all, we cannot arrest or amend. — It is still more foolish to embitter the present with useless regret; and, as to the past,

> 'Mortels! — voulez-vous tolérer la vie?
> Oubliez, & jouissez,*'

is a very good maxim.

Dear Sir! I wish you all happiness with your amiable family — And am, with sincere respect,

Your most faithful
And devoted servant,
JONVILLE DE MONTFLEURI

LETTER XXVI

TO MR BETHEL

Bath, Feb. 6, 1792

Come, my dear Bethel, I beseech you come hither, and render by your presence, still more happy, those friends for whom you have ever been so generously interested — Come and see Geraldine restored to her

---

* Voltaire.[84]

tranquillity, and your happy friend every day more tenderly attached to her; and reckoning (with impatience he vainly endeavours to stifle) the months that must yet elapse before she can be wholly his. — Oh! were you to see her — were you to witness, in addition to all her former charms, her behaviour to a mother, who was once so harsh, so ungenerous, so cruel to her; were you to see the compassionate attention with which she treats her old friend, Miss Elford, whose malicious representations cost her so dear; were you to behold the tender solicitude which she bestows equally on her own children, and on my little girl, you would love her a thousand — oh! a million times better than ever; and would, with me, bless the hour when I did not, when, indeed, I found *I could not*, take your advice and *forget her!*

Bethel, my dear friend, come to me I beseech you, that I may have somebody to whom I can talk of Geraldine when I do not see her — Montfleuri is too volatile; he loves his wife passionately, but my adoration for her sister he cannot comprehend; and, by the rest of the people, I see it would be understood still less.

And yet there are many, many hours when I am obliged (by these detestable rules, to the observance of which we sacrifice so many days, and hours, and years of happiness) to be absent from her. — Oh! 'twould be an alleviation of their insupportable tediousness, if you would let me talk to you about her, and hear all the plans I have laid down for happiness. — If you will come only for a fortnight I will return with you into Kent. It will be some amusement to me now, to settle an house which, in eight, or *at farthest* ten months (for it is now above three since she has been a widow) Geraldine may inhabit. — I can waste a month or six weeks there. — She seems to wish it; for, I believe, I sometimes frighten her by my restless and vehement temper — yet she may do with me what she pleases: it is only when I am divided from her, to comply with some ridiculous whim of some formal and ridiculous old woman, that I lose my temper. — When I am with her I am patient and tranquil — unless an idea crosses me, as it does now and then, that I am unworthy of the excessive happiness of being her husband, and that some dreadful event will tear her from me! — If she looks pale, though only from some slight cold or accidental fatigue, I fancy her about to be ill, and weary her with my apprehensions and enquiries. — She bears with all my folly patiently; or if she chides, it is with a sweetness that makes me almost love to be chidden.

Will this lovely, this adorable woman, be indeed mine? — Did I tell you, Bethel, how successfully I had managed the affairs of her children? — Scarsdale seemed disposed to give me a great deal of trouble, but now it is all settled. — Those dear infants will be less injured by their father's imprudence than I apprehended; and for their future destiny, as to pecuniary concerns, their beloved mother is no longer anxious.

Heavens! dare I trust myself with the rapturous hope, that on the return of this month, in the next year, Geraldine will bear *my* name — will be the directress of *my* family — will be my friend — my mistress — my wife! — I set before me these scenes — I imagine these days of happiness to come — I see the beloved group assembled at Sedgewood: — My Geraldine — You, my dear Bethel — your sweet Louisa — my friend Montfleuri, and his Fanny. — I imagine the delight of living in that tender confidence of mutual affection, which only such a circle of friends can taste. — I go over in my imagination our studies, our amusements, our rural improvements; a series of domestic and social happiness, for which only life is worth having. — I believe, I trust it will be mine, and I exclaim —

Viver cosi vorrai,
Vorrai morir cosi![85]

Heaven grant it! — But till that hour arrives, when the assurance of such felicity is more completely given me — Oh! lend me, dear Bethel, some of your calm reason to check my impatience; and soothe, with your usual friendship, the agitated heart — which, whatever else may disturb it, will ever be faithfully grateful to you, while it beats in the bosom of your

LIONEL DESMOND

THE END

NOTES

PREFACE

1 conversations to which I have been a witness, in England, and France, during the last twelve months: *Desmond* was written during Smith's residence at Brighton. At the time, the fashionable seaside resort was both a gathering place for French émigrés, most of them aristocrats who had left their country after the National Assembly decreed the abolition of titles on 19 June 1790, and a popular place for distinguished and literary English people, among them many supporters of the French Revolution. Undoubtedly the debates among these Brighton literati were an inspiration to Smith; friends certainly noted her increasing radicalization. In a memo to a letter Smith wrote him on 27 November 1791, Thomas Lowes remarked critically: 'I saw a great deal of Charlotte Smith one autumn at Brighthelmstone & acting (beting?) a democratic twist (which I think detestable in a woman). I liked her well enough for some time, but she disgusted me completely, on the acct arriving of the Massacre of the Swiss Guards at the Tuileries by saying that they richly deserved it: I observed that they did merely their duty ... After this I never wd see Charlotte ... Not long after this Augusta married an emigrant French nobleman, & I understand that her style both in her conversation & novels altered considerably.'

   I have found no support for Smith's claim that she visited France in the years 1791 or 1792, and it appears that the only time she was there was 1784/5 when she and her husband Benjamin Smith fled to Normandy to avoid English creditors. They spent a miserable winter in an isolated, dilapidated chateau near Dieppe where, under harrowing circumstances, Charlotte gave birth to her twelfth child, George.

2 it was in the *observance*, not in the *breach* of duty, *I* became an author: Charlotte Smith continually stressed that she published profusely not for reasons of self-aggrandizement but for money to support and educate her nine surviving children.

3 'The proud man's contumely ...': Shakespeare, *Hamlet*, iii. i. 70–2 (slightly misquoted).

4 'hope delayed maketh the heart sick': Proverbs 13:12: 'Hope deferred maketh the heart sick: but when the desire cometh, it is a tree of life'; 'Adversity ———...': Shakespeare, *As You Like It*, ii. i. 12.

5 friends among those, who, while their talents are the boast of their country: Smith counted among her patrons the famous poets William Cowper and William Hayley.

6 a female friend, to whom I owe the beautiful little Ode: Henrietta O'Neill (1758–93). Her popular 'Ode to the Poppy' was written at the request of Charlotte Smith and first published in *Desmond*. In *Elegiac*

Sonnets Smith had addressed her friend in no. XXXVII 'Sent to the Honorable Mrs. O'Neill, with painted flowers.' A memorial poem, 'Verses, on the death of [Henrietta O'Neill], written in September, 1794,' originally appeared in *The Banished Man* (1794) as the work of the fictional character Charlotte Denzil, Smith's most frank self-portrait as a writer. The poem was later included in the 1797 edition of *Elegiac Sonnets and Other Poems*, vol. II.

VOLUME I

7   at court on the birth-night: court festival held on the evenings of a royal birthday.

8   *mauvaise honte*: 'false modesty, bashfulness.'

9   *penchant*: 'liking.'

10 'the very first world': Christopher Anstey, *LETTER X. Mr Simkin B— n—r—d to Lady B—n—r—d, at —Hall, North*, l.76.

11 The original reads 'effection.'

12 hazard: a gambling game played with two dice.

13 I was compelled to pay five thousand pounds: refers to a suit for criminal conversation in which a husband could sue and claim damages from the lover of an adulterous wife.

14 instead of selling, at a general election, the two seats for a borough which belonged to me: refers to a pocket borough, an election district that was under the absolute control of one person or family. It could thus be disposed of to the highest bidder.

15 chiltern hundreds: a nominal office for which a Member of Parliament applies in order to resign his seat.

16 *mal de famille*: 'family disease.'

17 This decree ... National Assembly: on 17 June 1789 the representatives of the Third Estate and their allies in the Estates-General declared themselves the 'National Assembly.' This National, or Constituent, Assembly drew up France's monarchical constitution and acted as the provisional legislature from 1789 until 30 September 1791, when it was replaced by the Legislative Assembly. The primary move of the National Assembly had been to destroy the feudal regime in France. On 11 August 1789 it proclaimed the abolition of personal privileges, the end of any remaining serfdom, and the suppression of the tithe. In its efforts to establish civic equality, the Assembly decreed the abolition of all aristocratic titles on 19 June 1790.

18 *mezza voce*: 'in a low voice.'

19 *gens comme il faut*: 'respectable people.'

20 *pas*: 'pace, precedence.'

21 *bouleversement*: 'upheaval, upset.'

22 The original reads 'too.'

23 *les terres titrès*: 'titled estates.'

24 'As who should say I am Sir Oracle': Shakespeare, *Merchant of Venice*, I. i. 94.

25 depriving the church of its revenues: the Catholic Church had already suffered considerable financial losses by the reforms of summer 1789 (see note 17), which decreed the abolition of all feudal dues and the tithe. Then on 2 November 1789 the National Assembly confiscated all church property to settle the national deficit. In return, the government took over the administration of education and charity and put the clergy on salaries.

26 the meretricious scarlet-clad lady of Babylon: an allegorical figure in the Revelation of John, 17: 'Then one of the seven angels ... came and spoke to me and said, "Come, and I will show you the judgement on the great whore, enthroned above the ocean ..." In the Spirit he carried me away into the wilds, and there I saw a woman mounted on a scarlet beast which was covered with blasphemous names and had seven heads and ten horns. The woman was clothed in purple and scarlet ... and written on her forehead was a name with a secret meaning: "Babylon the great, the mother of whores and of every obscenity on earth.".'

27 wheat-ears: small northern songbird.

28 The original reads 'their was neither game gravy, ...'

29 our game-laws: English game laws, which restricted the right to kill game to substantial landowners or long-lease holders, were frequently targeted by radical writers as manifestations of a constitution founded on systematic social and legal oppression. In *A Vindication of the Rights of Men* (1790) Mary Wollstonecraft protested: '[W]ho shall dare to complain of the venerable vestige of the law that rendered the life of a deer more sacred than that of a man? ... In this land of liberty what is to secure the property of the poor farmer when his noble lord chooses to plant a decoy field near his little property? Game devour the fruit of his labour; but fines and imprisonment await him if he dare to kill any — or lift up his hand to interrupt the pleasure of his lord. How many families have been plunged, in the sporting countries, into misery and vice for some paltry transgression of these coercive laws, by the natural consequence of that anger which a man feels when he sees the reward of his industry laid waste by unfeeling luxury? — when his children's bread is given to dogs!' (Mary Wollstonecraft, *Political Writings*, ed. Janet Todd [Oxford: Oxford University Press, 1994], p. 16). Wollstonecraft's description of the legal iniquities suffered by the English farmer closely resembles Smith's depiction of feudal oppression under the *ancien régime* in Letter XIV.

30 a zeal Ernulphus might envy: Ernulphus (1040–1124), bishop of Rochester, who is thought to have anthologized the papal decrees, laws, and documents relating to the Church of Rochester known as the *Textus Roffensis*. In his collection Ernulphus included an exhaustive curse or excommunication, a transcript of which can be found in Laurence Sterne, *The Life and Opinions of Tristram Shandy* (1759–67), vol. III, ch. 11.

31 chicken-turtle: an edible freshwater turtle found in south-eastern regions of the United States. Mr Sidebottom evidently derives his wealth from a slave estate. Like many of the liberal authors of her time, Charlotte Smith condemned the inhumanity of the slave trade in her writings (see, for example, *The Wanderings of Warwick* [1794], pp. 45–66). At the same time however, Richard Smith's legacy to her children, over which Charlotte Smith fought a court battle, unyieldingly and for more than thirty years, proceeded from Barbados sugar plantations.

32 turkey powts: obs. for 'pout' (young bird) (*OED*).

33 join the fish-women: in autumn 1789, tension among the citizens of Paris was running high. Food was short in the capital, and the King was massing loyal Flanders troops at Versailles. During a royal banquet for the officers the tricolour cockade was insulted. This sparked the public incident that filled both Edmund Burke *and* Mary Wollstonecraft with horror: on 5 October, an infuriated Paris mob, mostly women, marched to Versailles. The next morning the palace was invaded and Louis XVI was forced to announce his return to the capital and order the release of grain supplies. In *Reflections on the Revolution in France* (1790) Burke depicted the event as follows: the heads of two of the king's body guard 'were stuck upon spears, and led the procession; whilst the royal captives, who followed in the train, were slowly moved along, amidst the horrid yells, and shrilling screams, and frantic dances, and infamous contumelies, and all the unutterable abominations of the furies of the hell, in the abused shape of the vilest of women' (ed. Conor Cruise O'Brien [London: Penguin Classics, 1986], pp. 164f). In her *Historical and Moral View of the Origin and Progress of the French Revolution* (1794) Wollstonecraft voiced similar revulsion at the coarseness of the women initiating the march, whom she described as the 'lowest refuse of the streets, women who had thrown off the virtues of one sex without having power to assume more than the vices of the other' (*Political Writings*, p. 343). The sympathetic portrayal of the French beggar woman, together with Smith's later justification of the violence committed on the morning of 6 October (pp. 310f), testify to the radical quality of Desmond.

34 get under *weigh*: a common variant spelling of 'under way,' from erroneous association with the phrase 'to weigh anchor' (*OED*).

35 the animating spectacle of the 14th: on 14 July 1790, the first anniversary of the storming of the Bastille, festivities all over France celebrated the Revolution. In Paris the *Fête de Fédération* was held on the Champs de Mars (today the site of the Eiffel Tower). About 400,000 persons assembled, among them representatives of the National Guard from every part of the country, to witness Louis XVI take the national oath. For a description see the opening chapters of Helen Maria Williams's *Letters from France*, vol. I.

36 *ci-devant*: 'former aristocrat.'

37 the furious manner in which the carriages of the *noblesse* were driven: the dangers of Paris streets were common-place in eighteenth-century travel literature. Arthur Young, the agriculturalist, reported: 'The coaches are numerous, and, what are much worse, there are an infinity of one-horse cabriolets which are driven by young men of fashion and their imitators, alike fools, with such rapidity as to be real nuisances, and render the streets exceedingly dangerous without an incessant caution. I saw a poor child run over and probably killed, and have been myself many times blackened with the mud of the kennels' (*Travels in France during the Years 1787, 1788, 1789* [1792], entry for 25 October 1787).

38 'Methinks I see in my mind ...': John Milton, *Areopagitica: A Speech for the Liberty of Unlicenc'd Printing* (1644).

39 *Palais Royale*: amusement area with theatres, shops, and coffee-houses. The arcades of the Palais Royal became the centre of revolutionary excitement in Paris; pamphlet shops churned out up to sixteen new political tracts every day and crowds flocked to the coffee-houses to listen to the public orators and debate the latest political events. At the Palais Royal there was free speech, since it belonged to the Duke of Orléans, a cousin of Louis XVI and supporter of the Revolution, and the police could not interfere without his permission. See Young, *Travels in France*, entry for 9 June 1789.

40 that negligence which many of his countrymen have lately affected: to dissociate themselves from the lavish aristocratic culture of the *ancien régime* many revolutionaries deliberately dressed in a plain, even slovenly, manner. The celebrated painter Jacques Louis David went so far as to design and propagate a republican dress, consisting of a jacket with tight trousers, a coat without sleeves, a short cloak, a belt, and a round hat and feather. See John Moore, *Journal during a Residence in France* (1793), entry for 28 September 1792.

41 new regulations: on 13 February 1790 the French National Assembly decreed the abolition of monastic vows. This meant that anyone wishing to leave monasteries was free to do so.

42 *fier aristocrate*: 'proud aristocrat.'

43 hotel: (in French use) 'large private residence, town mansion.'

44 *bel esprit*: 'man/woman of wit.'

45 Clovis: Clovis I (466–511), Merovingian founder of the Frankish kingdom and the first barbarian king to convert to Catholicism.

46 Louis VII (1120–80), Louis XI (1423–83).

47 *curés*: 'parish priests.'

48 a little French pamphlet, entitled, '*Lettre aux Aristo-theocrate Français*': I have been unable to locate either this pamphlet or the '*Histoire d'un malheureux Vassal de Bretagne, écrite par lui-même*,' to which Smith later refers in Letter XIV. Interestingly, the French translation of *Desmond*, *Desmond ou l'Amant Philosophe* (1793), mentions neither of these pamphlets. This could be the result of a slipshod translation but it might

also be taken as an indication that Smith fabricated these two pamphlets to lend greater documentary realism to her narrative.

49   vows, made at a time of life when no civil contract would be binding: in 1768 the *Commission des Réguliers* had raised the minimum age for girls taking their vows from sixteen to eighteen and for men to twenty-one.

50   Louis le Debonair: Louis I (778–840).

51   Millot: Abbé Claude François Xavier Millot, *Elements of the History of France* (1771), vol. I, 'Louis I.'

52   *couvert*: 'place at a table, meal'; *haut clergé*: 'higher clergy.'

53   *canaille*: 'masses, mob.'

54   *taille*: as the key source of royal revenue the *taille* was one of the institutions most fiercely attacked by critics of the *ancien régime*. Since it was devised as a financial equivalent for military service, both the nobility who fought and the clergy who did not have to fight were exempted from the tax. Also not subject to the *taille* were certain judicial and financial executives and, in the eighteenth century, the citizens of large towns. This meant that to an increasing extent the rising expenses of the *ancien régime* were borne exclusively by the rural population. The National Assembly decreed the abolition of the *taille* in 1789. The *gabelle* was a tax on salt. In most regions in France the government of the *ancien régime* held the monopoly on salt. It was being sold at an exorbitant price and each inhabitant, with the exemption of the aristocracy, the clergy, and certain other privileged persons, was required to buy a specified amount from licensed merchants. The *gabelle* was abolished in March 1790.

55   *fermiers-general*: 'Farmers General,' a syndicate appointed to collect taxes.

56   *marechaussées*: corps of mounted constabulary under the *ancien régime*, replaced by the *gendarmerie* in 1790. A *lettre de cachet* was a warrant signed by the king and counter-signed by a minister of state which could imprison anyone without a trial, without means of redress or release.

57   'Ce gouvernement serait digne des Hottentots…': Voltaire, *La Voix du Sage et du Peuple* (1750).

58   *ennuyant*: 'boring.'

59   Luxembourg Gardens: the Luxembourg Gardens form a suitable backdrop to Montfleuri's attack on the politics of the Catholic Church in Letter IX. The Luxembourg district of Paris was still a stronghold of clericalism. Stephen Weston, an antiquary, described his visit to the Luxembourg Gardens thus: 'Here you are sure to meet the disappointed band, and the whole tribe of the counter-revolutionists: it is here only that they hold up their heads, and display their orders. Clergy, Nobility, Monks of all colours, and Friars of all sizes: every order knows its own place, and falls naturally into the rank to which it belongs — the Clergy excommunicate in the Alley des Chartreux, the Nobles and the Military plan their battles in the alley of the Carmes …' (*Letters from*

Paris during the Summer of 1791 [1792], entry for August 1791). It was also here, in the Luxembourg Gardens, where the *Septembrisades* of 1792 were sparked off when an anticlerical mob massacred more than a hundred refractory Catholic priests who had been taken into custody because of their refusal to swear the oath on the Constitution.

60 *petit maitre*: 'fop, coxcomb.'

61 'Still to my country ...': Oliver Goldsmith, *The Traveller; or, a Prospect of Society* (1764), ll. 9–10 (slightly misquoted). See also *Citizen of the World* (1762), Letter III: 'The farther I travel I feel the pain of separation with stronger force, those ties that bind me to my native country, and you are still unbroken. By every remove, I only drag a greater length of chain.'

62 Our national character, a character given us by Caesar ...: Julius Caesar, *De Bello Gallico* (52–51 BC): 'Nam ut ad bella suscipienda Gallorum alacer ac promptus est animus, sic mollis ac minime resistens ad calamitates prefendas mens eorum est.' ['For while the temper of the Gauls is eager and ready to undertake a campaign, their purpose is feeble and in no way steadfast to endure disasters'].

63 Henry the Fourth: Henry IV, Henry of Navarre (1553–1610), a Protestant. To end more than thirty years of violent religious conflict and reunify the country, Henry IV converted to Roman Catholicism in 1593. Under his reign France was pacified and prospered; in 1598 he passed the Edict of Nantes, which terminated the persecution of Huguenots and guaranteed their religious liberty. Louis XIV (1638–1715), the 'Sun King,' who ruled his country from his extravagant court at Versailles, epitomized absolutist rule. The Edict of Nantes was revoked by him in 1685.

64 House of Valois: dynasty that ruled France from 1328 and died out with Henry III in 1589. The massacre of French Protestants in Paris starting on 23 August 1572, the eve of the feast of St Bartholomew, was committed under their reign. To cover up her complicity in the attempted murder of the Huguenot leader Coligny, Catherine de Medicis, mother of King Charles IX, ordered the assassination of the Protestant nobles who were attending the wedding of her daughter Marguerite to Henry of Navarre. It is estimated that in Paris alone, more than 3,000 Huguenots were slaughtered. Soon the killings had spread to the provinces and the bloody conflict between Catholics and Protestants flared up anew.

65 Ravaillac: François Ravaillac, a fanatic, who stabbed Henry IV in 1610.

66 Duc de Sully: Maximilien de Béthune (1560–1641), Duke of Sully, loyal Protestant minister of Henry IV. As director of the king's Council of Finance, he put an end to abuses in tax collecting, reorganized the state finances, and stabilized the economy.

67 Louis the Thirteenth: Louis XIII (1601–43), whose reign was overshadowed by the continual political conflicts with his mother Marie de

Medici and her allied nobles. Owing to Louis's chronic ill health and mental instability, his chief minister, Cardinal Richelieu, quickly became the most powerful figure in French government. The *états généraux*, or 'Estates-General,' was a consultative assembly composed of the three orders, the nobility, the clergy, and the commons. It was generally summoned to grant subsidies or advise the Crown. Louis XIII was the last monarch to convoke the Estates-General before the Revolution; the procedure was abandoned during the absolutist 17th and 18th centuries. In 1789 Louis XVI summoned the Estates-General once again to consider taxation and state expenditure, and it was the meetings of this body that led to the formation of the 'National Assembly.'

68 the Conchinis: Concino Concini, Marquis d'Ancre (?–1617), an unscrupulous Italian adventurer. After the murder of Henry IV in 1610, Concini and his wife Leonora acted as Marie de Medici's chief advisers and set about lining their own pockets. Two aristocratic rebellions raised against them failed, but in 1617 Concini was assassinated. His widow was accused of witchcraft and beheaded and her body burned three months later.

69 continual wars on the subject of religion: the Wars of Religion between Huguenots and Catholics in France had lasted, with intermittences, from 1562 until 1598, when Henry IV decreed the Edict of Nantes which granted the Huguenots their civil and religious liberties.

70 Richelieu: Armand-Jean du Plessis, Cardinal and Duke of Richelieu (1585–1642), dominated French state politics as chief minister to Louis XIII from 1624 until his death. His aims were to destroy the Huguenot cause, consolidate royal absolutist power in France, and break the Spanish-Hapsburg hegemony in Europe.

71 Huguenots: name applied to French Protestants.

72 Mary of Medicis: Marie de Medici (1573–1642), second wife of Henry IV. After his assassination in 1610 she was proclaimed regent for her son Louis XIII. Under the influence of her adviser Concino Concini, Marquis d'Ancre, she squandered France's finances and refused to resign government when her son Louis XIII came of age in 1614. An ally of Louis XIII arranged the assassination of Concini in 1617 and she was consequently exiled. After organizing two unsuccessful rebellions, the Cardinal Richelieu negotiated the peace between her and Louis XIII. After a clash with the Cardinal, Marie de Medici was once again banished from court. She died penniless in Cologne in 1642.

73 Galileo: Galileo Galilei (1564–1642), Italian astronomer and physicist. His astronomical observations supporting the Copernican system brought him into conflict with the Inquisition, which imprisoned him in 1633. Descartes: René Descartes (1596–1650), mathematician, scientist, and philosopher. The metaphysical foundation of his philosophical doctrine was a principle of 'methodological doubt.' Only his most famous axiom, 'I think therefore I am' could be considered an indubi-

table certainty. For fear of the Inquisition he had to publish his first works anonymously.

74 *devoté*: 'staunch believer,' (pej.) 'bigot.'

75 revocation of the edict of Nantz: the Edict of Nantes that was decreed by Henry IV on 13 April 1598 had granted full civil rights to the Huguenots and guaranteed their freedom of worship. Louis XIV abolished the law on 18 October 1685; the revocation of the Edict of Nantes, accompanied by severe religious persecution, caused more than 400,000 Protestants to emigrate, depriving France of its most productive mercantile and artisan classes. In 1789 the National Assembly declared religious tolerance and admitted Huguenots to all posts and professions.

76 disgraceful and ill-managed wars: War of the Polish Succession (1733–8), War of the Austrian Succession (1740–8), and the Seven Years' War (1756–63).

77 'There I visited, the celebrated Galileo, …': John Milton, *Areopagitica*.

78 Louis the Fifteenth: Louis XV (1710–74), whose reign contributed to the decline of the monarchy's political and moral authority. His government was ineffectual and his private life extravagant and dissolute; isolating himself at Versailles, he diverted himself with a succession of mistresses, many of whom, such as Madame Pompadour, gained considerable political influence.

79 La vie privée de Louis XV: Mouffle d'Angerville, *La Vie privée de Louis XV ou principaux Evénements, Particularités, et Anecdotes de son Règne* (John Peter Lyton, 1781). The author is anonymous and the imprint false. The work was published on the Continent.

80 Montesquieu: Montesquieu, Charles-Louis de Secondat (1689–1755), social and political philosopher. In his *De l'Esprit des Lois* (1748), an analysis of different political systems and a theory of the separation of powers, he advocated a liberal constitutional monarchy after the English model.

81 Voltaire: pseudonym of François-Marie Arouet (1694–1778), dominant Enlightenment polemicist, satirist, dramatist, novelist, and historian. His defence of the rights of the individual and his relentless mockery of the injustice of civic and ecclesiastical institutions led to his incarceration in the Bastille in 1717 and his exile to England in 1726–9. Rousseau: Jean-Jacques Rousseau (1712–78), influential theorist in the fields of political and social philosophy, education, theology, and music, and acclaimed writer of sentimental fiction and autobiography. He was an adversary of the Enlightenment faith in progress and science, defending the innocence of primitive man in a 'state of nature.' In contrast to Voltaire's satiric and witty works, Rousseau's writings were characterized by his emotional nature and extreme sensibility.

82 Turgot: Anne-Robert-Jacques Turgot (1727–81), administrator under Louis XV and controller-general of finance under Louis XVI. A physiocrat, Turgot believed that the nation's economic wealth depended

on a free economy based on agriculture, but his efforts to reform feudal privileges caused the aristocratic factions at court to bring about his dismissal in 1776. Mirabeau: Honoré-Gabriel Riqueti, Count Mirabeau (1749–91), was an advocate of a constitutional monarchy who had abandoned his title and joined the commons in the meetings of the Estates-General. An energetic man, whose past testified to the injustices of the *ancien régime* — he fought a long legal feud with his own father who forced him into exile and had him imprisoned by *lettres de cachet* — he soon became the most eloquent orator of the French Revolution. Despite his fervent defences of political reforms and his presidency of the National Assembly to which he was elected in January 1791, he played a double game, acting as secret adviser to Louis XVI from May 1790 onwards. With his sudden death on 2 April 1791 the moderate forces of the Revolution lost their most prominent leader.

83 ministry sent our soldiers into America: from 1776, when the American Congress voted for independence, until 1778 the American Revolution had been a civil war within the British Empire. During that period France had furnished the colonies only with supplies and funds; on 2 February 1778, however, in order to prevent America's acceptance of Lord North's offer of a dominion status, the French government signed a treaty to supply military and naval support.

84 'For, when God shakes a kingdom, …': John Milton, *Areopagitica*.

85 'bear a charmed heart': probably based on Shakespeare, *Macbeth*, V. viii. 12: 'I bear a charmed life.' Possibly Charlotte Smith confused 'Melthorpe' with Samuel Jackson Pratt, alias Courtney *Melmoth*, who wrote *Travels for the Heart* (1777), a rather poor imitation of Laurence Sterne's *A Sentimental Journey through France and Italy* (1768) with sexual allusions far less subtle than in Sterne's original.

86 'I scorn the beauties…': James Hammond, *An Elegy to a Young Lady in the Manner of Ovid*, l. 7 (slightly misquoted).

87 'the bowed roof': James Thomson, *Liberty*, pt V, l. 127.

88 arbeal: obsolete spelling of 'abele,' the white poplar tree.

89 speculations: 'exercise of the faculty of sight, the action, or an act of seeing, viewing, or looking on or at, examination or observation' (*OED*).

90 Knox's Essay No.150, entitled, 'A Remedy for Discontent': Vicesimus Knox, *Essays Moral and Literary* (1778), vol. II.

91 *soi-disant*: 'so-called, self-styled.'

92 Don Quixote: *Don Quixote de la Mancha* (pt I 1605, pt II 1615), Miguel de Cervantes's satire on the ballads and romances of chivalry. *Gil Blas* (1715–35) was a picaresque novel by Alain-René Lesage.

93 'Pass to a scrivener, …': Alexander Pope, *The Second Satire of the Second Book of Horace Paraphrased*, l. 178 (slightly misquoted).

94 *etourderie*: 'carelessness, careless mistake.'

95 'in these sportive plains …': Laurence Sterne, *Tristram Shandy*, vol. VIII, ch. 1.

96 'make not the heart sore': Laurence Sterne, *A Sentimental Journey* (1768), 'Le Dimanche, Paris.'

97 had you been a descendant of Lord Chesterfield's: Philip Dormer Stanhope, 4th Earl of Chesterfield (1694–1773), statesman and diplomat. He is chiefly remembered for his *Letters* (1774) to his son Philip Stanhope (1732–68) which, though intended as a handbook of etiquette and good manners when published, came increasingly under attack because of its sexual immorality. In his letter of 15 April 1751, he advised his eighteen-year-old son to seduce a woman of whom he knew nothing but her beauty and her marital fidelity: 'A propos, on m'assure que Madame de Blot, sans avoir des traits, est jolie comme un coeur, et que nonobstant cela, elle s'en est tenue jusqu'ici scrupuleusement à son mari, quoi-qu'il y ait déjà plus d'un an qu'elle est mariée. Elle n'y pense pas; il faut décrotter cette femme-là. Décrottez-vous donc tous les deux réciproquement. Force, assiduités, attentions, regards tendres, et déclarations passionées de votre côté, produiront au moins quelque velléité du sien. Et quand une fois la velléité y est les oeuvres ne sont pas loin.'

98 'Your heart …': Shakespeare, *Henry VIII*, ii. iv. 110.

99 'I wish it may answer': Laurence Sterne, *Tristram Shandy*, vol. IV, ch.8.

100 Carmelite: on her journey to Rouen, Helen Maria Williams paid a visit to a Carmelite convent and gave a chilling description of its austere regulations: '[the] Carmelites rose at four in the morning in summer, and five in the winter:- … they slept in their coffins, upon straw, and every morning dug a shovel-full of earth for their graves; … they walked to their devotional exercises upon their knees; … when any of their friends visited them, if they spoke, they were not suffered to be seen; or if they were seen, they were not suffered to speak; … with them it was *toujours maigre*, and they only tasted food twice a day' (*Letters written in France in the Summer of 1790* [1790], vol. I, pp. 118f).

101 Louis *ci-devant le Grand*: Louis XIV.

102 *d'un manière la plus opiniatre du monde*: 'in the most wilful manner.'

103 *Chapeau à le Nevernois*: see Christopher Anstey's poem *LETTER X. Mr Simkin B—n—r—d to Lady B—n—r—d, at —Hall, North* from which Smith quoted earlier: 'But what with my Nivernois' hat can compare, / Bag-wig, and lac'd ruffles, and black solitaire?' (ll. 59–60).

104 *roturier*: 'commoner.' Not italicized in the original.

105 *cour d'honneur*: 'main courtyard.'

106 *salle à compagnie*: 'drawing room.'

107 *croisée*: 'casement.'

108 'thick-coming fancies': Shakespeare, *Macbeth*, V. iii. 38 or William Hayley, *The Triumphs of Temper* (1781), Canto I, l. 244.

109 'the wisest aunt telling the saddest tale': Shakespeare, *A Midsummer Night's Dream*, ii. i. 1.

110 Niobe: in Greek mythology Niobe, the daughter of Tantalus, boasted of her fertility to Titan Leto who only had two children, Apollo and

Artemis. Plotting revenge, Apollo killed Niobe's six sons, Artemis her six daughters. Mourning for the death of her children, Niobe became the archetype of the bereaved mother.

111 *bosquets* and *treillage*: 'coppices' and 'trellis.'

112 *cimetière*: 'graveyard.'

113 'Where heaves the turf ...': Thomas Gray, *Elegy written in a Country Church-Yard* (1751), l. 13.

114 The original reads 'Letter XII.' The numberings of the ensuing letters have been amended.

115 'children of an idle brain...': Shakespeare, *Romeo and Juliet*, I. iv. 97f.

116 *triste*: 'sad, bleak'; *ennui*: 'boredom.'

117 Lusignans and Tancreds: the Lusignans were an aristocratic family of Poitou which generated several crusaders and kings of Jerusalem. Tancred of Hauteville (?–1112), Regent of Antioch, was one of the leaders of the First Crusade.

118 the vain honour of the flag: (naut.) 'to make an acknowledgement of supremacy by striking the flag to another' (*OED*).

119 Peter the Hermit: Peter the Hermit (1050–1115), an ascetic, and one of the key figures in the launching of the First Crusade.

120 Charlemagne: Charlemagne, or Charles the Great (742–814), who conquered nearly the whole of Christian western Europe and ruled it as Holy Roman Emperor during the years 800–14.

121 Desmond's answer echoes John Locke's argument in *Two Treatises of Government* (1690), bk I, § 43: '... all this would not prove that Propriety in Land, ..., gave any Authority over the Persons of Men, but only that Compact might; since the Authority of the Rich Proprietor, and the Subjection of the Needy Beggar began not from the Possession of the Lord, but the Consent of the poor Man, who preferr'd being his Subject to starving.'

The figure of the footman figured prominently in eighteenth-century debates on egalitarianism. On a visit to the republican historian Catherine Macaulay, the Tory Samuel Johnson mocked his host: '"Madam, I am now become a convert to your way of thinking. I am convinced that all mankind are upon an equal footing; and to give you an unquestionable proof, Madam, that I am in earnest, here is a very sensible, civil, well-behaved fellow-citizen, your footman; I desire that he may be allowed to sit down and dine with us." I thus, Sir, shewed her the absurdity of the levelling doctrine' (James Boswell, *Life of Johnson*, entry for Thursday, 21 July 1763).

122 The defender of the family of Calas; the protector of the Sirvens: on 13 October 1761, the eldest son of Jean Calas, a Huguenot cloth merchant in Toulouse, hanged himself in his father's shop. In an outburst of anti-Protestant hysteria, Calas was arrested and accused of murdering his son to prevent his conversion to Catholicism. In spite of the fact that there was little evidence to support the charge and Calas insisted on his inno-

cence even under torture, he was found guilty, publicly broken on the wheel, hanged, and burned on 10 March 1762. Several of the Calas family were sentenced as accomplices to the murder, their property was confiscated, the son Pierre was exiled, and the two daughters were imprisoned in convents on the authority of royal *lettres de cachet*.

The circumstances of the case of Pierre Paul Sirven (1709–77) were similar to the Calas affair: early in 1762 he and his Huguenot wife were likewise charged and found guilty of murdering their convert daughter who had thrown herself down a well. Voltaire involved himself in the campaigns to rehabilitate the Calas and Sirven families; he offered shelter to Jean Calas's widow and daughters, published an account of the two cases, exposing the factual and judicial blunders committed, and then followed it up with the *Traité sur la Tolérance* (1763), a powerful plea for religious tolerance and a challenge to State power in the name of the individual's right to justice. Judgements in both the Calas and the Sirven affair were eventually annulled.

123 Those who say …: Voltaire, *Essai sur les Moeurs et l'Esprit des Nations et sur les principaux Faits de l'Histoire depuis Charlemagne jusqu'à Louis XIII*, Chapitre XCVIII, 'De la Noblesse.'

124 *Les manières de la vielle cour*: 'manners of the old court.'

125 *auto da fé*: 'act of faith,' the public burning of heretics.

126 *la vieille cour ecclesiastique*: 'the old ecclesiastical court.'

127 decree of the nineteenth of May: in fact the abolition of nobility was decreed on 19 June 1790.

128 *Louis le Gros*: Louis the Fat, Louis VI (1081–1137).

129 'Great names degrade …': La Rochefoucauld, *Réflexions ou Sentences et Maximes morales* (1665), Maxime XCIV. Smith refers to the following maxime, 'Les Rois font des hommes commes des pieces de monnoie …' as Maxime CLVIII, which means she was using either the second (1666), the third (1671), or the fourth (1675) edition of Rochefoucauld's *Maximes*. In the first edition of 1665 this maxim bears no. CLXV and in the fifth, definitive edition (commonly used today) this maxim had been replaced with 'La flatterie est une fausse monnaie qui n'a de cours que par notre vanité.'

130 had his looks possessed the power imputed to those of the Basilisk: mythological reptile that drove away all other serpents with its hissing and, more to the point here, killed with its look.

131 Joseph Priestley, *Letters to a Philosophical Unbeliever. Containing an examination of the principal objections to the doctrines of natural religion and especially those contained in the writings of Mr. Hume* (1780).

132 'From my own windows …': Shakespeare, *Richard II*, ii. i. 24.

133 *Vale-Vale et me ama*: 'Farewell and love me.'

134 Laurence Sterne, *Sentimental Journey*, 'Montriul.' Parson Yorick on the past of his servant, La Fleur: '… he retired *à ses terres*, and lived *comme il plaisoit à Dieu* — that is to say, upon nothing.'

135   qualified: 'to moderate or mitigate ... esp. to render less violent, severe, or unpleasant' (*OED*).
a campaign or two against the English: one of the main aims of America and its European allies was to break Britain's naval power.

136   privateer: an armed vessel that is privately owned but commissioned by government for war service.

137   to be fed by contract, ... to be buried by contract: in the eighteenth century common jails were run as private profit-making ventures whose administration was rife with corruption. Since the office of jailor was generally unsalaried they lived by lawful fees extracted from prisoners committed to their custody or by downright extortion. The provision of food given out of the county funds was frequently pilfered by them, as were charitable donations. John Howard, a philanthropist who went on lengthy travels through Britain and Europe to catalogue prisons, published *The State of the Prisons* (1777–84), which detailed the conditions suffered by French prisoners of war held at county jails in Forton and Pembroke: 'On that day the meat was very bad ... Most of the six-pound loaves wanted weight ... The straw, by long use, was turned to dust in the mattresses, and many of them here, and at other places, had been emptied to clear them of vermin ... Most of them [French prisoners] had no shoes or stockings, and some were also without shirts.' The French prisoners of war seemed to fare much worse than the Americans whose subsistence was largely secured by the commissionaries' care and the weekly allowances they received from the States. Howard declared he wished 'that the gentlemen concerned for the American prisoners, had extended their regards also to the French, and by their attention and visits had obliged the contractors to be more careful in discharging their duty' (London: Dent, 1923, pp. 143f).

138   *N'importe*: 'it does not matter.'

139   *fossé*: 'ditch, trench.'

140   animal spirits: a vital force believed to be dispatched by the brain to all points of the body.

141   the combined fleets in the Channel: in 1779 the united fleets of Spain and France gained command of the Channel and threatened to invade Britain. Luckily for the British, storms and diseases among the allied troops put an end to the scheme.

142   Fiscal: a public prosecutor. proces verbal: 'official report, record of evidence.'

143   pamphlet, entitled, 'Histoire d'un malheureux Vassal de Bretagne, écrite par lui-même': see note 48.

VOLUME II

1   the October meeting: annual horse race held at Newmarket.

2   Lavater's system: Johann Kaspar Lavater (1741–1810), Swiss philosopher, theologian, and founder of physiognomics. His *Physiognomische Fragmente zur Beförderung der Menschenkenntnis und Menschenliebe* (1775–8, Engl. translation *Essays on Physiognomy*, 1789–98), a book written in collaboration with Johann Wolfgang von Goethe, set forth the theory that the human soul is manifested in the features of the face and the shape of the skull.

3   *avanturier*: 'adventurer.'

4   In the original the words 'my esteem, I know' were italicized.

5   what some celebrated author has said: Jonathan Swift, *Thoughts on Various Subjects* (1706): 'A very little wit is valued in a woman, as we are pleased with a few words spoken plain by a parrot.'

6   Tattersall's: Richard Tattersall, a former groom to the second Duke of Kingston, began auctioning horses in 1766. At his establishment near Hyde Park Corner, customers could buy horses, coaches, and hounds, place bets on races, and gamble.

7   As long as I keep the reversion of the sinecures: refers to the reward Lord Newminster receives for delivering votes perennially.

8   *piquant*: 'piquant.' *agaçant*: 'provocative, saucy' (obs.).

9   'With all the nurse …': Alexander Pope, *Rape of the Lock*, (1712), i, l. 30.

10 The original reads 'scite.'

11 the sanguinary witch: Catherine II, the Great (1729–96), Empress of Russia. She came to power in 1762 when she raised a rebellion against her husband Peter III who was deposed and later assassinated by her supporters. In her youth she had been a follower of Enlightenment philosophy and an advocate of liberal reforms, but over the years her rule became ever more despotic, extending and strengthening the system of serfdom, and silencing advocates of political reform.

12 the book lately published by Mr Burke: Desmond's letter is dated January 8, Edmund Burke's *Reflections on the Revolution in France* had been published two months earlier, on 1 November 1790.

13 *a thousand pens will leap from their standishes*: the account of the Paris women's march to Versailles on 5/6 October 1789 constitutes the melodramatic centrepiece to Burke's *Reflections*. Recalling the young Marie Antoinette 'glittering like the morning-star, full of life, and splendor, and joy,' he mourned her downfall and the loss of the chivalric spirit. 'I thought,' he went on, 'ten thousand swords must have leaped from their scabbards to avenge even a look that threatened her with insult' (*Reflections*, pp. 169f).

14 Sir Robert Filmer in that treatise: Robert Filmer's *Patriarcha. The Naturall Power of Kinges Defended against the Unnatural Liberty of the People*, written between ?1631–48 and published in 1680 was a categorical defence of the divine right of kings. John Locke's *Two Treatises of Government* (1690) were written in response to Filmer's *Patriarcha*.

While the *First Treatise* is primarily concerned with a close scrutiny of Filmer's wilful distortion of Scripture, the *Second Treatise* is a work in defence of the liberal concepts of liberty, equality, and the sovereignty of the people.

15 'Man, not being born free ...': John Locke, *Two Treatises*, bk I, §5.

16 'When fashion, has once sanctioned ...': John Locke, *Two Treatises*, bk I, §58.

17 Mr Burke now loads them ... with every other crime he can imagine: Burke's depiction of the revolutionary events sometimes bordered on the hysterical. The two main revolutionary events that had taken place at the time of the publication of *Reflections* — the storming of the Bastille and the march to Versailles — had cost comparatively few lives, but Burke exaggerated the violence. Charging the National Guard and their leader General Lafayette with a list of crimes including murder, he arraigned the supporters of the Revolution of 'authorizing treasons, robberies, rapes, assassinations, slaughters, and burnings throughout their harrassed lands' (p. 127).

18 'This concerns not their children...': John Locke, *Two Treatises*, bk II, §189.

19 'That fate repine ...': probably based on Matthew 7:6: 'Give not that which is holy unto the dogs, neither cast ye your pearls before swine, lest they trample them under their feet, and turn again and rend you.'

20 I shall not be compelled to wean him: anxiety and distress in a mother were thought to affect her milk and thus the child she was suckling.

21 Paine: Thomas Paine (1737–1809), English writer and pamphleteer. Paine was the son of a Quaker stay-maker and had only a rudimentary education. He went to America in 1774 where he began to publish political articles. He rose to fame during the American Revolution with his pamphlet *Common Sense* (1776), the arguments of which contributed considerably to the Declaration of Independence ratified six months later. Back in England, he wrote *Rights of Man* (1791), a bestselling refutation of Burke's *Reflections*. In it Paine advocated republicanism and outlined a welfare system which included plans for a national education, relief of the poor, pensions, and public works for the unemployed. In an attack on linguistic elitism, Paine countered Burke's pompous prose and courtly rhetoric with plainness of diction, using language designed to appeal to the middle and working classes. For this Paine was criticized by many of his contemporaries; his prose was dismissed as coarse and vulgar, and even the liberal *Monthly Review* (May 1791, 93) disapproved of his 'desultory, uncouth, and inelegant' style.

22 'mouth of honour': Shakespeare, *Henry VIII*, I. i. 137.

23 'We know the thing is neither new nor rare ...': Alexander Pope, *Prologue to Satires to Arbuthnot* (1735), ll. 171–2.

24 Octavia: Octavia (69 BC – 11 BC), sister of the emperor Augustus and wife of Mark Antony. Despite the fact that Antony divorced her and

carried on a public love affair with the Egyptian Queen Cleopatra, Octavia remained the paragon wife, faithful and devoted, raising his children by Cleopatra together with her own.

25 'To spread / A guardian glory round her ideot's head': William Hayley, *The Triumphs of Temper* (1781), Canto V, ll. 551–2: 'When time remov'd delusion's veil by stealth, / And show'd the drear vacuity of wealth; / When sad experience prov'd the bitter fate / Of beauty coupled to a senseless mate: / These gentle wives still gloried to submit; / These, tho invited by alluring wit, / Refus'd in paths of lawless joy to range, / Nor murmur'd at the lot they could not change: / But with a lively sweetness unopprest, / By a dull husband's lamentable jest, / Their constant rays of gay good humour spread / A guardian glory round their ideot's head.'

26 'A blessing on him... ': Smith probably quotes this passage from Laurence Sterne, *Tristram Shandy*, vol. IV, ch.15, where it reads: 'God's blessing ... be upon the man who first invented this self-same thing called sleep — it covers a man all over like a cloak.' In Tobias Smollett's translation of Cervantes's *Don Quixote*, an edition Smith would have been more likely to use than Thomas Shelton's seventeenth-century translation, Sancho Panza remarks: 'praise be to him who invented sleep, which is the mantle that shrouds all human thoughts, the food that dispels hunger, the drink that quenches thirst' (vol. II, bk IV, ch. XVI).

27 '*and reconcile man to his lot*': William Cowper, *Verses supposed to be written by Alexander Selkirk during his solitary abode in the island of Juan Fernandez* (1782), l. 56.

28 a spinster: Laurence Sterne, *A Sentimental Journey*, 'The Act of Charity, Paris.'

29 'Withering on the virgin thorn ... : Shakespeare, *A Midsummer Night's Dream*, I. i. 77f (slightly abridged).

30 the Mentor, instead of always being your Telemachus: in Greek legend, Mentor, the faithful friend of Odysseus, served as the guardian and teacher of Telemachus, Odysseus's son, while Odysseus fought in the Trojan War.

31 'Benedetto sia 'l giorno ...': Petrarch, *Sonnet LXI* ['Blessed may be the day, the month, the year, / And the season, the time, the hour, the point, / And the country, the place where I was joined / By two fair eyes that now have tied me here' in: Petrarch, *Sonnets and Songs*, trans. by Anna Maria Armi (New York, 1946)].

32 'Small things make mean men proud': Shakespeare, *Henry VI*, pt. 2, ii. i. 59.

33 swinish multitude: Desmond's censure of Sir Robert Stamford's husbandry associates it with one of the most notorious passages in *Reflections*, in which Burke had referred to the common people as a 'swinish multitude': 'Nothing is more certain than that our manners, our civilization, ... in this European world of ours, depended for ages upon two

principles; and were indeed the result of both combined; I mean the spirit of a gentleman, and the spirit of religion. ... Happy if they had all continued to know their indissoluble union, and their proper place! Happy if learning, not debauched by ambition, had been satisfied to continue the instructor, and not aspired to be the master! Along with its natural protectors and guardians, learning will be cast into the mire, and trodden down under the hoofs of a swinish multitude' (p. 173).

34 vilify his private life: the government of King George III appointed George Chalmers, alias Francis Oldys, to write a hostile biography of Thomas Paine. In *The Life of Thomas Paine* (1791) Chalmers dug up obscure details of Paine's private life, branding him as an uncaring husband and son, an atheist, failed shopkeeper, and corrupt exciseman. See John Keane, *Tom Paine. A Political Life* (London: Bloomsbury, 1995), pp. 320f.

35 *les gens sans culottes*: a republican of the poorer classes in Paris, gen. an extreme radical.

36 'wordy war': several possible sources but the most likely are James Thomson, *Liberty*, pt IV, l. 978 and Alexander Pope, *The Iliad of Homer*, bk 20, l. 301, *The 1st Book of the Odyssey*, l. 467, *The 12th Book*, l. 520, or *The 18th Book*, l. 40.

37 *gratis*: 'free (of charge).'

38 the Corinthian pillar of polished society: Edmund Burke, *Reflections* (p. 245): 'Nobility is a graceful ornament to the civil order. It is the Corinthian capital of polished society.'

39 "fare sumptuously every day": In *A Vindication of the Rights of Men*, Mary Wollstonecraft insisted that the aristocratic and rich could not develop into virtuous, useful human beings: 'Health can only be secured by temperance; but is it easy to persuade a man to live on plain food even to recover his health, who has been accustomed to fare sumptuously every day?' (*Political Writings*, p. 42).

40 "The horrors of a gloomy gaol ...": James Thomson, *The Seasons*, 'Winter,' ll. 361–4 (slightly misquoted).

41 "Take physic, pomp...": Shakespeare, *King Lear*, iii. iv. 33.

42 "On ears polite": Alexander Pope, *Moral Essays* (1731), iv, l. 150: 'Who never mentions Hell to ears polite.'

43 let us go on till the building falls upon our heads: Charlotte Smith incorporates into Desmond's argument the emblematic castle of which Edmund Burke had made extensive use in *Reflections*. Accusing the National Assembly of doing irreparable damage to the French monarchy, Burke had couched his criticism in architectural metaphors: 'Your constitution, it is true, whilst you were out of possession, suffered waste and dilapidation; but you possessed in some parts the walls, and in all the foundations of a noble and venerable castle. You might have repaired those walls; you might have built on those foundations' (p. 121).

44 "Shakes her encumbered lap ... ": William Cowper, *The Task*, 'The Winter Evening,' ll. 498–9.

45   they give up yearly to the hands of the executioner greater numbers than die the victims of public justice in all the other European countries: by the end of the eighteenth century the English Bloody Code included more than two hundred crimes bearing the death penalty, the vast majority of them crimes against property. And, though the ratio of executions to capital convictions actually fell after 1750, the number of criminals condemned to death and hanged in England was nevertheless high compared to other European nations. In the 1780s in Amsterdam, a city with a population about a third of that of London, less than one convict a year was hanged; barely 15 were executed annually in Prussia in the 1770s, and a little over 10 in Sweden in the 1780s. Only 32 people were executed in Paris in the years 1774–7, against 139 in London; and the number of criminals hanged in London even increased from an annual average of 48 in the 1770s to 70 in the years 1783–7. See V.A.C. Gatrell, *The Hanging Tree* (Oxford: Oxford University Press, 1994), pp. 7–9.

46   "In this rank age, ... *every man within the reach of right*": James Thomson, *The Seasons*, 'Winter,' ll. 382–8.

47   "Disguise the thing I am, ... ": Shakespeare, *Othello*, ii. i. 24 (slightly misquoted).

48   'chastised by fear': Alexander Pope, *The Iliad of Homer*, bk 6, l. 619.

49   'in a rivulet of text running through a meadow of margin' in the soft semblance of letters 'from Miss Everilda Evelyn, to Miss Victorina Villars': perhaps a satirical reference to Fanny Burney's *Evelina* (1778), an epistolary novel told in the correspondence between the young heroine Evelina Villars and her guardian.

50   Triumphs of Temper: Serena, the heroine in William Hayley's poem, is subjected to a series of harassing trials but always proves a paragon of feminine docility and gentleness.

51   satirical Sybil: Sibyl, or Sibylla, a prophetess in Greek legend, traditionally represented as a very old woman proclaiming her prophecies in a frenzied delirium.

52   ordered by the Divan: originally an Oriental council of state, specifically in Turkey the privy council of the Porte, presided over by the Sultan; in a transferred sense a council in general (*OED*).

53   Ranelagh: fashionable pleasure grounds in Chelsea that opened in 1742 and were demolished in 1805. Inside the large rococo rotunda there were stalls for eating and drinking; concerts, masquerades, and fireworks were held in the gardens.

54   condemned with less mercy, than the curate and the barber shewed to the collection of the Knight of the sorrowful Countenance: in Cervantes's *Don Quixote* the barber and the curate secretly raid the hero's library and burn all books of chivalry, poetry, and romance to cure Don Quixote of his fantastic aspirations to knight-errantry.

55 'a plentiful lack': Laurence Sterne, *Tristram Shandy*, vol. III, 'Author's Preface': 'plentiful a lack.'

56 Père de Famille, l'Indigent, le Philosophe sans le scavoir: Denis Diderot, *Père de Famille* (1758); Michel-Jean Sedaine, *Le Philosophe sans le savoir* (1766), *L'Indigent* (1785). All three are prototypes of sentimental bourgeois drama. 'Home to the business and bosoms': Francis Bacon, *Essays* (1625), 'Dedication to the Duke of Buckingham.'

57 'Il n'y a que la raison qui ne soit bonne à rien sur la scene': Jean-Jacques Rousseau, *Lettre à M. d'Alembert sur son Article Genève* (1758). In an article on Geneva, Jean d'Alembert, probably at the instigation of Voltaire, had proposed the establishment of a theatre there. Rousseau replied, arguing that a theatre was not an agent of moral improvement: it would distract the citizens of Geneva from fulfilling their personal and civic duties, ultimately resulting in the dissolution of the town. Passages in Rousseau bear great resemblance to Smith's; Geraldine, for example, states: 'A reasonable man would be a character insupportably flat and insipid even on the French stage, and on the English, would not be endured to the end of the first scene.' In Rousseau it reads: 'Un homme sans passions, ou qui les dominerait toujours n'y saurait intéresser personne; et l'on a déjà remarqué qu'un stoïcien dans la tragédie, serait un personnage insupportable: dans la comédie, il ferait rire, tout au plus' (Paris: Gallimard, 1987, p. 161).

58 'obedient — very obedient': Shakespeare, *Othello*, iv. i. 266.

59 'sad import': William Cowper, *The Task*, 'The Time-Piece,' l. 300.

60 'And on the heat and flame …': Shakespeare, *Hamlet*, iii. iv. 123 (slightly misquoted).

61 'sinuous course': William Cowper, *The Task*, 'The Sofa,' l. 165.

62 'That realm he rules …': William Hayley, *Triumphs of Temper*, Canto III, l. 294.

63 'No tree in all the grove… ': William Cowper, *The Task*, 'The Sofa,' ll. 307–17.

64 'Primavera candida e vermiglia…': Petrarch, *Sonnet CCCX* ['Zephyr comes back and brings the lovely weather, / Flowers and grass, its sweet family ties, / And Philomela warbles, Procne cries, / And spring returns, the white and the pink feather'].

65 'Gorgons and Hydras, and Chimeras dire': John Milton, *Paradise Lost*, bk II, l. 628.

66 'Along the waste, …': Oliver Goldsmith, *The Deserted Village* (1770), l. 137 (slightly misquoted).

67 'The tender rose': Moschus, *Lament for Bion*. Moschus and Bion were both Alexandrian pastoral poets. There has been considerable argument over who was the senior; it is generally agreed that Moschus was at work at circa 150 BC and Bion circa 100 BC. This means that the *Lament for Bion* cannot be Moschus's; it is ascribed to a disciple of Bion.

68 'Passages that lead to nothing': Thomas Gray, *A Long Story*, l. 8.

69　'With flowers and fennel gay': Oliver Goldsmith, *The Deserted Village*, l. 234 (slightly misquoted).

70　The words 'I have' were missing from the second edition.

71　'planetary fires': Ann Radcliffe, 'Night,' l. 3 in *The Romance of the Forest* (1791).

72　Lovelace: libertine hero of Samuel Richardson's *Clarissa*, who lures the chaste heroine from her father's house and rapes her. Helen: In Greek legend Helen, daughter of Zeus, was the most beautiful woman of Greece. She was abducted by Paris; her husband Menelaus and his elder brother Agamemnon led the Greek army to Troy to recover her in the ten-year Trojan War.

73　'Are not these woods … ': Shakespeare, *As You Like It*, ii. i. 3.

74　'To make the worser seem the better reason': John Milton, *Paradise Lost*, bk II, l. 114.

75　The original reads 'cieling.'

76　'There are but two divisions of the world, that where Julie is, and that where she is not': Jean-Jacques Rousseau, *Julie, ou La Nouvelle Héloïse* (1761): 'Le monde n'est jamais divisé pur moi qu'en deux régions: celle où elle est où elle n'est pas. La première s'étend quand je m'éloigne, et se resserre à mesure que j'approche, comme un lieu où je ne dois jamais arriver' (Paris: Flammarion, 1967, p. 313).

77　*suite*: 'train, household.'

78　*debauché*: 'debauched person, libertine.'

79　*avec la charmante femme*: 'with the charming woman.'

80　*toujours couleur de rose*: 'always rosy.'

81　a French Sir Hargrave Pollexfen: rakish character in Samuel Richardson's *Sir Charles Grandison* (1753–4) who falls in love with the virtuous heroine Miss Byron and abducts her to compel her into marrying him.

82　*au desespoir*: 'to be desperately, deeply sorry.' *pays triste et morne*: this 'sad and bleak country.'

VOLUME III

1　'Lo I have sinned against heaven …': Luke 15:21: 'And the son said unto him, Father, I have sinned against heaven, and in thy sight, and am no more worthy to be called thy son.'

2　'There certainly is such a distemper …': Henry Fielding, *Tom Jones* (1749), bk I, ch. 13.

3　'The wife …': Conveniently, Geraldine's mother chooses to ignore the rest of Milton's quotation, which would hardly have applied to Verney's conduct: 'The wife, where danger or dishonor lurks / Safest and seemliest by her Husband staies, / Who guards her, or with her the worst endures.' John Milton, *Paradise Lost*, bk IX, ll. 267–9.

4　'I tell thee, damned priest …': Shakespeare, *Hamlet*, V. i. 263 (slightly misquoted).

5 'last best gift of heaven': John Milton, *Paradise Lost*, bk V, l. 19.

6 dowager queen of Sheba: according to the Old Testament the Queen of Sheba visited the court of King Solomon to probe his legendary wisdom by 'test[ing] him with hard questions.' She came to Jerusalem 'with a very large retinue, camels laden with spices, gold in great quantity, and precious stones' (1 Kings 10). Solomon, succeeding his father David, ruled the united kingdoms of Israel and Judah from about 961 to 920 BC. He was renowned for his wisdom, great wealth, and numerous harem — the Old Testament mentions 700 wives and 300 concubines.

7 English Werter: in 1774 Johann Wolfgang von Goethe published his semi-autobiographical epistolary novel, *The Sorrows of Young Werther*. It told the melancholy story of the life and suicide of the feminized sensitive artist Werther, uncomfortable in society and hopelessly in love with a woman engaged to someone else. The publication of this work resulted in a sensational cultural phenomenon, for it inspired an imitation of Werther's costume of blue coat and yellow waistcoat and an emulation of his despairing high feelings of alienation and self-loathing. Whether 'Wertherism' also generated a wave of copy-cat suicides is, however, doubtful.

8 the flight of the King of France: on the night of 20 June the royal family made an attempt to escape from the Tuileries and reach the counter-revolutionary armies in Metz. The following evening the King and Queen were recognized and arrested by the National Guard in Varennes. It was this flight that sealed the fate of Louis XVI; it proved his opposition to the French revolutionary government and demonstrated his readiness to desert the nation and enter into an alliance with the enemy Austrian forces.

9 "Thou'dst shun a bear …": Shakespeare, *King Lear*, iii. iv. 9.

10 "When the mind's free …": Shakespeare, *King Lear*, iii. iv. 11.

11 the re-entrance of the King into Paris: the royal family were escorted back to the capital where they arrived on 25 June. There are many accounts of the event but all agree that the King was received by silent crowds. Louis XVI and his family were taken to the Tuileries, where they were from now on kept under close guard.

12 *bloody democracy* of Mr Burke, the swinish multitude: see vol. II, notes 17 and 33.

13 violation of oaths so solemnly given: during the *Fête de la Fédération* on 14 July, the festival celebrating the first anniversary of the storming of the Bastille, Louis XVI had sworn the civic oath: 'I, King of the French, swear to the Nation to employ all the power which is delegated to me by the Constitutional Law of the State, to maintain the Form of Government decreed by the National Assembly, and accepted by me, and to enforce the execution of the Laws' (*The Times* for 19 July 1790).

14 ministerial declaimers, who having supported the one, have dared to execrate the other: making another bold attempt to justify the violent

events of the summer of 1792, Smith would once more take up this argument in her next novel *The Old Manor House* (1793). Condemning the British policy in the War of Independence of inducing the Native Americans to fight on their side, she declares: 'The happy effects of this barbarous policy never appeared. Of the tragical scenes it occasioned, the reader, if he or she delight in studying the circumstances in this war redounding to the honour of British humanity, is referred to the Annual Register for 1779 ... Those who have so loudly exclaimed against a whole nation struggling for its freedom, on account of the events of last summer (events terrible enough, God knows!), are entreated to recollect how much the exploits of this expedition (even as related by our own historian) exceed any thing that happened on the 10th of August [the storming of the Tuileries], the 2d of September [beginning of the September massacres], or at any one period of the execrated Revolution in France — and own, that there are savages of all countries — even our own!' *The Old Manor House* (Oxford: Oxford University Press, 1989), p. 360n.

15 *the King's castles*: in his *Reflections* Burke had incriminated the French guards who had assisted in demolishing the Bastille: 'The soldiers remember the 6th October. They recollect the French guards. They have not forgot the taking of the King's castles at Paris, and at Marseilles. That the governors in both places, were murdered with impunity, is a fact that has not passed out of their minds' (pp. 333f).

16 Swift, in one of his most misanthropic humours: Jonathan Swift to Alexander Pope, 29 September 1725: 'I have ever hated all nations, professions, and communities, and all my love is toward individuals: for instance, I hate the tribe of lawyers, but I love Counsellor Such-a-one, and Judge Such-a-one: so with physicians — I will not speak of my own trade — soldiers, English, Scotch, French, and the rest. But principally I hate and detest that animal called man, although I heartily love John, Peter, Thomas, and so forth. This is the system upon which I have governed myself many years, but do not tell, and so I shall go on till I have done with them.'

17 *les gens du commun*: 'common people.'

18 the death of Mirabeau: see vol. I, note 80.

19 'put into everlasting liberty': Shakespeare, *The Merry Wives of Windsor*, iii. iii. 31.

20 deserted Ariadne: in Greek mythology, Ariadne, the daughter of King Minos, fell in love with the Athenian hero Theseus and helped him escape the Cretan Labyrinth after he had slain the mythical Minotaur. From here the legends vary but they all agree that Ariadne was eventually abandoned by Theseus.

21 small parties of armed citizens: the National Guard was formed in Paris on the eve of the storming of the Bastille and put under the command of General Lafayette, a veteran of the American War of Independence.

Throughout France towns followed the example and formed similar units of citizen-soldiers; this civic militia quickly developed into a national army, whose duty was to maintain order and guard against counterrevolutionary activities.

22 'With hearts resolv'd ...': 'Ode to Leven-Water' in Tobias Smollett, *Humphrey Clinker* (1771), Bramble to Dr. Lewis, 28 August.

23 'every man sit down ...': Micah 4:4: 'But they shall sit every man under his vine and his fig tree; and none shall make [them] afraid: for the mouth of the Lord of hosts hath spoken [it].'

24 the deficiency of bread: the history of eighteenth-century France, and in particular the phase of the Revolution, seethes with rumours of 'famine plots,' conspiracies instigated by the nobility and the royal family to starve the people into political submission. In 1789 the 'Great Fear,' a mass hysteria, gripped the French rural population: the harvest had been spoiled by hailstorms and reports spread of bandits in the pay of aristocrats who were coming to destroy homes and seize food. Royal decrees to relieve the corn shortage only aggravated the food crisis: bonuses that had been authorized on imported grain led to speculators buying up French supplies and reimporting them for a profit. The bread shortage in the capital in autumn 1789 prompted the women's march on Versailles, in order to bring back to Paris, as they termed it, 'the baker, the baker's wife, and the baker's boy.' See also vol. I, note 33.

25 'the hand writing upon the wall': Daniel 5: King Belshazzar's feast is interrupted by a mysterious message written by 'fingers of a man's hand' against 'the candlestick upon the plaister of the wall of the king's palace.' The king sends for Daniel who explains the foreboding in the writing: 'This [is] the interpretation of the thing: MENE; God hath numbered thy kingdom, and finished it. TEKEL; Thou art weighed in the balances, and art found wanting. PERES; Thy kingdom is divided, and given to the Medes and Persians.' King Belshazzar was slain the same night.

26 the Vicars of Bray: 'one who readily changes his principles to suit the times or circumstances.' According to the *OED* the Vicar of Bray 'held the benefice from the reign of Henry VIII to that of Elizabeth, and was twice a Papist and twice a Protestant.' In a popular eighteenth-century song the time-serving parson accommodates himself to the religious views of the governments from Charles II to George I, and boasts that 'whatsoever king may reign' he will remain Vicar of Bray.

27 a very Turk in principle, and hardly allowed women any pretensions to souls: the very low status accorded to women in Islamic religion gave rise to the widespread Christian misconception that they were denied the possession of souls.

28 the wandering Jew: the wandering Jew is a mythical figure who, for having insulted Jesus on his way to the Cross, was condemned to wan-

der the earth until Judgement Day. The yellow dwarf is a ferocious and ugly character in medieval French fairy tales.

29 *summum bonum*: 'the supreme good, the end to which all conduct must be subordinated.'

30 'Regretter ...': this is not a quotation from La Rochefoucauld, as Smith states, but from La Bruyère, *Les Caractères, ou Les Moeurs de ce Siècles*, 'Du Coeur': 'Regretter ce que l'on aime, est un bien en comparaison de vivre avec ce que l'on hait.'

31 'Oh! that way madness lies ...': Shakespeare, *King Lear*, iii. iv. 21.

32 in the novel of Sidney Biddulph: a reference to Frances Sheridan's ill-starred heroine in *The Memoirs of Sidney Bidulph* (1761). Unlike Geraldine, who meets the deserving hero Desmond only after her marriage to Verney, the virtuous Sidney is engaged to her lover Orlando Faulkland. Their happiness is ruined when Faulkland's earlier involvement with a young orphan is revealed and Sidney's mother, a well-meaning but domineering and strictly moral woman, persuades her to break off the engagement. Sidney is then pushed into marriage with a Mr Arnold who soon proves to be unfaithful and deserts her for his mistress. Like Smith's hero Desmond, Faulkland continues to watch over the woman he loves, saves her from a fire, and selflessly brings about a reconciliation between Sidney and her repentant husband. And though Mr Arnold is far from being the ruthless rascal Smith's Verney is, his extravagance likewise contributes to his financial downfall and eventually leaves Sidney a young widow with two young children and no provision. Then follows the passage referred to by Geraldine: in her despair Sidney applies to her sister-in-law Lady Sarah, a wealthy but proud aristocrat, who denies her any assistance. Faulkland proposes once more but Sidney steadfastly refuses, urging him to marry the mother of his illegitimate child. In the end he yields to her entreaties, with disastrous consequences to everyone involved. His young wife, not the seduced innocent everyone had taken her for but a cunning libertine, soon after has an affair. Faulkland kills her lover in a scuffle and flees to the continent where he commits suicide. Sidney meekly submits to her fate, as she has done throughout her life, 'shewing' as she puts it, 'a perfect resignation to His will.'

33 *Rabelais*: François Rabelais (c.1494–c.1553), French Renaissance humanist, physician, and writer whose satiric prose is famed for its parody, wit, and obscenity.

34 *riante*: 'happy, pleasant.'

35 'The boughs ...': Shakespeare, *As You Like It*, iv. iii. 105.

36 Ceres: Roman goddess of crops.

37 'friendly to despair': John Dryden, *Sigismonda and Guiscardo*, l. 624.

38 'in the British parliament ...': James Boswell, *The Life of Samuel Johnson*, entry for Tuesday, 23 September 1777. It was a well-known fact that the Crown secured its influence in Parliament through the disposal of

civil, military, and ecclesiastical office, and of pensions and honours raised by taxation. Boswell would return to the issue of corruption in the House of Commons at one of their 'Literary Club' dinners held several months later, when he remarked that there surely always was 'a majority in parliament who have places, or who want to have them, and who therefore will be generally ready to support the government without requiring any pretext.' This view gained backing in an unforeseen quarter, for it was Edmund Burke who answered him with a '[t]rue Sir; that majority will always follow "*Quo clamor vocat et turba faventium*"' ['Whither the shouting calls us and the applauding populace'] (entry for Friday, 3 April 1778).

39 abolition of the detestable Slave Trade: the eighteenth-century culture of sensibility gave rise to a host of philanthropist campaigns, among them the abolitionist movement. The Anti-Slavery Society, founded by the evangelical politician William Wilberforce in 1787, fought a determined battle to effect reforms in the slavery legislation. The abolition of the slave trade in the British colonies in 1807 was their first success but the Slavery Abolition Act, decreeing the emancipation of all slaves, was not passed until 1833.

40 'the whimsical system of Lord Monboddo': James Burnett, Lord Monboddo (1714–99), Scottish judge, pioneer anthropologist, and admirer of Rousseau with whom he agreed that civilization caused corruption and degeneracy. His keen interest in man's relation with the orangutan and his belief that children were born with tails earned him a reputation as an eccentric.

41 'The pale unripen'd beauties of the North': Joseph Addison, *Cato*, i. 4. 142.

42 *catalogue raisonné*: 'descriptive catalogue.'

43 he knew more of a *fi, fa*, and *latitats, John Doe* and *Richard Roe*: latitats were 'writs which supposed the defendant to lie concealed and which summoned him to answer in the King's Bench.' The name given to the 'fictitious lessee of the plaintiff in the (now obsolete) mixed action of ejectment' was John Doe, with the fictitious defendant being called Richard Roe (*OED*).

44 made you a riding-officer: the aristocracy influenced county and borough elections in order to protect the interests of the Lords in the House of Commons. Votes were bought with money, an office in the excise for individuals, or even favours from the Admiralty and the Army for a whole town.

45 *perdu*: 'lost.'

46 obtaining the contract for potatoes and sour crout: throughout the American War of Independence the British army derived the bulk of its provisions from Great Britain. The Treasury took out contracts with army victuallers, many of whom resorted to fraudulent business methods to enrich themselves. Much of the food supplied was of such poor

quality it was simply inedible, and the official records abound with complaints about maggoty meat, worm-eaten peas, rancid butter, mouldy bread, and ship biscuit so hard it had to be broken up with a cannon ball. Contractors cheated the government not only by supplying spoilt provisions but sometimes by mixing sand with the flour or sending barrels of food weighted with stones. See Edward E. Curtis, *The Organization of the British Army in the American Revolution* (New Haven, 1926). In her next novel, *The Old Manor House*, Charlotte Smith launched a more forthright attack on unscrupulous contractors and corrupt government: 'The provisions on board were universally bad; and the sickness of the soldiers was as much owing to that cause as to the heat of climate. Musty oatmeal, half-dried pease, and meat half spoiled before it had been salted down, would in any situation have occasioned diseases; and when to such defective food, their being so closely stowed and so long on board was added, those diseases increased rapidly, and generally ended fatally. But it was all for *glory*. And that the ministry should, in thus purchasing glory, put a little more than was requisite into the pockets of contractors, and destroy as many men by sickness as by the sword, made but little difference in an object so infinitely important, especially when it was known … that messieurs the contractors were for the most part members of parliament, who under other names enjoyed the profits of a war, which, disregarding the voices of people in general, or even of their own constituents, they voted for pursuing' (p. 348f).

47 riots that happened in July at Birmingham: the Unitarian Joseph Priestley, a distinguished scientist and theologian, was the main target of the violent Birmingham riots on 14 July 1791, one of the most serious of the 'Church and King' disturbances. Priestley, an enthusiastic supporter of the French Revolution, was also actively involved in the campaign to repeal the Test and Corporation Acts which still excluded all non-Anglicans from public office and Parliament. After a dinner celebrating the first anniversary of the storming of the Bastille, the anger against the liberal Dissenting community erupted: loyalist crowds attacked the diners, and then moved on to wreck several Unitarian meeting houses and burn Priestley's house and laboratory.

48 as many horns as the beast in the Revelations: i.e., ten, see vol. I, note 26.

49 'Verney will get devilish damages': refers to a suit for criminal conversation, see vol. I, note 13.

50 'Casta est, quam nemo rogavit': 'She is chaste, whom no one has asked.'

51 arrows 'dipped in double poison': Dr. Joseph Warton, *The Dying Indian*: 'The dart of Izdabel prevails! 'twas dipt / In double poison'; will not reach her unless some 'd—n'd good natured friend' should take the trouble: Richard Brinsley Sheridan, *The Critic or a Tragedy Rehearsed* (1779), i. 1. ll. 355–7: 'To be sure — for if there is any thing to one's

praise, it is a foolish vanity to be gratified at it, and if it is abuse — why one is always sure to hear of it from one damn'd good natur'd friend or another.'

52 the King has signed the constitution: on 14 September 1791 Louis XVI swore an oath of loyalty to a revised Constitution.

53 'kings of the earth': John Milton, *Paradise Regained*, bk II, l. 44. Northern powers: after the arrest of the king at Varennes, Emperor Leopold II of Austria issued a proposal to the European sovereigns that they take up concerted action to save the French monarchy. The only monarchs to agree instantly were Catherine of Russia and King Gustavus of Sweden.

54 'tyrannous breathings of the North': Shakespeare, *Cymbeline*, I. iii. 36.

55 speeches of Mr Burke were said to press so hardly on a gentleman then, and still before the highest tribunal of his country: in 1787, Warren Hastings, governor general of Bengal, who dominated Indian affairs from 1772 to 1785, was impeached at Edmund Burke's instigation. After a trial before the House of Lords which lasted seven years, Hastings was eventually acquitted on all charges.

56 principles absolutely opposite to all the professions of his political life: Edmund Burke's earlier championing of American Independence and Catholic emancipation had earned him the reputation of a liberal.

57 Locke: John Locke (1632–1704), foremost political and educational philosopher of the Enlightenment. His *Two Treatises of Government* (1690) describe the origins of the civil state as founded in contract and contest absolutist notions of government and the ideology of the divine right of kings. In Locke's theory the sovereignty lies with the people who have the right to oust a government that fails to fulfill their trust, i.e., fails to secure the public good. Milton: John Milton (1608–74), poet, historian, pamphleteer, and civil servant for the Puritan Commonwealth. Among his many political tracts, all written in defence of religious, political, and domestic liberties, are the *Areopagitica* (1644), his famous vindication of the freedom of the press, and his several pamphlets (1643–5) in support of divorce. Bacon: Francis Bacon (1561–1626), lawyer, courtier, statesman, scientist, philosopher, and essayist. His philosophical work, which outlined a detailed systematization of all categories of human knowledge, was a major influence on French Enlightenment Encyclopaedists. In his political and legal writings Bacon aimed to detach the state from religion.

58 the court-calendar (the red book): an 'almanac or annual hand-book of royal families and their courts' (*OED*). See also note 44.

59 'A mesure que les pays sont barbares... ': Voltaire, *Dictionnaire philosophique*, 'Cérémonies, Titres, Prééminence, etc.'

60 'smutched artificer,' William Cowper, *The Task*, 'The Time-Piece,' l. 491. 'wrung from the hard hands': Shakespeare, *Julius Caesar*, iv. iii. 74.

61 '*fair idea*': several possible sources, the most likely are James Thomson, *Liberty*, pt iv, l. 118 and Alexander Pope, *Epistle to Jervas*, iii, 43.

62 'Pur me consola, ...': Petrarch, *Sonnet CLXXIV* ['Yet I am soothed by this, to grieve for her / Is better than another to enjoy'].

63 *finesse*: 'trick, cunning.'

64 *carte blanche*: 'free hand, unlimited powers.' *Ça ira-Ça ira*: 'it will go' or 'it will happen.' It was part of the refrain of a popular song during the French Revolution, followed by the phrase '*Les aristocrates à la lanterne*.'

65 *reverbere*: 'to reverberate, beat back.'

66 *reconnoitre*: 'to reconnoitre.'

67 Polypheme: in Greek mythology the most famous of the Cyclops and son of Poseidon, god of the sea.

68 'Turn'd mine eyes and wept': Shakespeare, *Cymbeline*, I. iii. 22: 'Follow'd him, till he had melted from / The smallness of a gnat to air, and then / Have turn'd mine eye and wept.'

69 Proteus: one of *The Two Gentlemen of Verona* in Shakespeare's play, a fickle and changing character.

70 Rosicrusian mystery: the Rosicrucian order, a secret worldwide brotherhood whose origins are obscure but which was first mentioned in 1614. Its members claimed to possess various forms of esoteric and magic knowledge handed down from ancient times through initiates, which would ultimately enable the Rosicrucians to control the forces of the universe.

71 *embonpoint*: 'plumpness, fullness of figure.' *blanc & potelé*: 'white and plump.'

72 'Etre avec des gens qu'on aime...': La Bruyère, *Les Caractères*, 'Du Coeur.'

73 *auberge*: 'inn.'

74 *en attendant mieux*: 'meanwhile.'

75 *valet de place*: 'manservant.'

76 *couteau de chasse*: 'hunting knife.'

77 Salvator: Salvator Rosa (1615–73), Neapolitan baroque painter whose sublime landscapes present wild and desolate scenes of remote valleys, towering mountains, craggy cliffs, torrents, and violent thunderstorms, characteristically peopled by witches, monsters, soldiers, bandits, and wolves. In England his romantic landscape paintings were frequently associated with the description of natural scenery in Ann Radcliffe's Gothic novels.

78 Horace's Canidia: Canidia, a Neapolitan courtesan and Horace's lover. After she deserted him he abused her as a sorceress in his *Epodes* v and xvii and in his *Satires*, i.viii.

79 *patois*: 'provincial dialect, jargon.' *cette Angloise*: 'this Englishwoman.'

80 pot *au feu*: 'stew.'

81 *assignats*: paper money issued by the French revolutionary government.

82 *pavé*: 'cobblestone.' '*Eh! voilà donc nos messieurs*': 'there they are our menfolk.'

83 *ma douce*: 'my sweet.'
84 'Mortels!…': Voltaire, *Dictionnaire philosophique*, 'Frivolité.'
85 'Viver …': 'You will want to live like this, / You will want to die like this!'

Appendix A

Extract from Edmund Burke,
Reflections on the Revolution in France
(1790)

... History will record, that on the morning of the 6th of October 1789, the king and queen of France, after a day of confusion, alarm, dismay, and slaughter, lay down, under the pledged security of public faith, to indulge nature in a few hours of respite, and troubled melancholy repose. From this sleep the queen was first startled by the voice of the centinel at her door, who cried out to her, to save herself by flight — that this was the last proof of fidelity he could give — that they were upon him, and he was dead. Instantly he was cut down. A band of cruel ruffians and assassins, reeking with his blood, rushed into the chambers of the queen, and pierced with an hundred strokes of bayonets and poniards the bed, from whence this persecuted woman had but just time to fly almost naked, and through ways unknown to the murderers had escaped to seek refuge at the feet of a king and husband, not secure of his own life for a moment.

This king, to say no more of him, and this queen, and their infant children (who once would have been the pride and hope of a great and generous people) were then forced to abandon the sanctuary of the most splendid palace in the world, which they left swimming in blood, polluted by massacre, and strewed with scattered limbs and mutilated carcases. Thence they were conducted into the capital of their kingdom. Two had been selected from the unprovoked, unresisted, promiscuous slaughter, which was made of the gentlemen of birth and family who composed the king's body guard. These two gentlemen, with all the parade of an execution of justice, were cruelly and publickly dragged to the block, and beheaded in the great court of the palace. Their heads were stuck upon spears, and led the procession; whilst the royal captives who followed in the train were slowly moved along, amidst the horrid yells, and shrilling screams, and frantic dances, and infamous contumelies, and all the unutterable abominations of the furies of hell, in the abused shape of the vilest of women. After they had been made to taste, drop by drop, more than the bitterness of death, in the slow torture of a journey of twelve miles, protracted to six hours, they were, under a guard, composed of those very soldiers who had thus conducted them through this famous triumph, lodged in one of the old palaces of Paris, now converted into a Bastile for kings.

... Influenced by the inborn feelings of my nature, and not being illuminated by a single ray of this new-sprung modern light, I confess to you, Sir, that the exalted rank of the persons suffering, and particularly the sex, the beauty, and the amiable qualities of the descendant of so many kings and emperors, with the tender age of royal infants, insensible only through infancy and innocence of the cruel outrages to which their parents were exposed, instead of being a subject of exultation, adds not a little to my sensibility on that most melancholy occasion.

I hear that the august person, who was the principle object of our preacher's triumph, though he supported himself, felt much on that shameful occasion. As a man, it became him to feel for his wife and his children, and the faithful guards of his person, that were massacred in cold blood about him; as a prince, it became him to feel for the strange and frightful transformation of his civilized subjects, and to be more grieved for them, than solicitous for himself. It derogates little from his fortitude, while it adds infinitely to the honour of his humanity. I am very sorry to say it, very sorry indeed, that such personages are in a situation in which it is not unbecoming in us to praise the virtues of the great.

I hear, and I rejoice to hear, that the great lady, the other object of the triumph, has borne that day (one is interested that beings made for suffering should suffer well) and that she bears all the succeeding days, that she bears the imprisonment of her husband, and her own captivity, and the exile of her friends, and the insulting adulation of addresses, and the whole weight of her accumulated wrongs, with a serene patience, in a manner suited to her rank and race, and becoming the offspring of a sovereign distinguished for her piety and her courage; that like her she has lofty sentiments; that she feels with the dignity of a Roman matron; that in the last extremity she will save herself from the last disgrace, and that if she must fall, she will fall by no ignoble hand.

It is now sixteen or seventeen years since I saw the queen of France, then the dauphiness, at Versailles; and surely never lighted on this orb, which she hardly seemed to touch, a more delightful vision. I saw her just above the horizon, decorating and cheering the elevated sphere she just began to move in, — glittering like the morning-star, full of life, and splendor, and joy. Oh! What a revolution! and what an heart must I have, to contemplate without emotion that elevation and that fall! Little did I dream when she added titles of veneration to those enthusiastic, distant, respectful love, that she should ever be obliged to carry the sharp antidote against disgrace concealed in that bosom; little did I dream that I should have lived to see such disasters fallen upon her in a nation of gallant men, in a nation of men of honour and of cavaliers. I thought ten thousand swords must have leaped from their scabbards to avenge even a look that threatened her with insult. — But the age of chivalry is gone. — That of sophisters, oeconomists, and calculators, has succeeded; and the glory of Europe is extinguished for ever. Never, never more, shall we behold that generous loyalty to rank and sex, that proud submission, that dignified obedience, that subordination of the heart, which kept alive, even in servitude itself, the spirit of an exalted freedom. The unbought grace of life, the cheap defence of nations, the nurse of manly sentiment and heroic enterprize is gone! It is gone, that sensibility of principle, that chastity of honour, which felt a stain like a wound, which inspired courage whilst it mitigated ferocity, which ennobled whatever it touched, and under which vice itself lost half its evil, by losing all its grossness.

This mixed system of opinion and sentiment had its origin in the antient chivalry; and the principle, though varied in its appearance by the varying state of human affairs, subsisted and influenced through a long succession of generations, even to the time we live in. If it should ever be totally extinguished, the loss I fear will be great. It is this which has given its character to modern Europe. It is this which has distinguished it under all its forms of government, and distinguished it to its advantage, from the states of Asia, and possibly from those states which flourished in the most brilliant periods of the antique world. It was this, which, without confounding ranks, had produced a noble equality, and handed it down through all the gradations of social life. It was this opinion which mitigated kings into companions, and raised private men to be fellows with kings. Without force, or opposition, it subdued the fierceness of pride and power; it obliged sovereigns to submit to the soft collar of social esteem, compelled stern authority to submit to elegance, and gave a domination vanquisher of laws, to be subdued by manners.

But now all is to be changed. All the pleasing illusions, which made power gentle, and obedience liberal, which harmonized the different shades of life, and which, by a bland assimilation, incorporated into politics the sentiments which beautify and soften private society, are to be dissolved by this new conquering empire of light and reason. All the decent drapery of life is to be rudely torn off. All the super-added ideas, furnished from the wardrobe of a moral imagination, which the heart owns, and the understanding ratifies, as necessary to cover the defects of our naked shivering nature, and to raise it to dignity in our own estimation, are to be exploded as a ridiculous, absurd, and antiquated fashion.

On this scheme of things, a king is but a man; a queen is but a woman; a woman is but an animal; and an animal not of the highest order. All homage paid to the sex in general as such, and without distinct views, is to be regarded as romance and folly. Regicide, and parricide, and sacrilege, are but fictions of superstition, corrupting jurisprudence by destroying its simplicity. The murder of a king, or a queen, or a bishop, or a father, are only common homicide; and if the people are by any chance, or in any way gainers by it, a sort of homicide much the most pardonable, and into which we ought not to make too severe a scrutiny.

On the scheme of this barbarous philosophy, which is the offspring of cold hearts and muddy understandings, and which is as void of solid wisdom, as it is destitute of all taste and elegance, laws are to be supported only by their own terrors, and by the concern, which each individual may find in them, from his own private speculations, or can spare to them from his own private interests. In the groves of *their* academy, at the end of every visto, you see nothing but the gallows.

...

Appendix B

Extract from Mary Wollstonecraft, *A Vindication of the Rights of Men* (1790)

... I perceive, from the whole tenor of your Reflections, that you have a mortal antipathy to reason; but, if there is any thing like argument, or first principles, in your wild declamation, behold the result: — that we are to reverence the rust of antiquity, and term the unnatural customs, which ignorance and mistaken self-interest have consolidated, the sage fruit of experience: nay, that, if we do discover some errors, our *feelings* should lead us to excuse, with blind love, or unprincipled filial affection, the venerable vestiges of ancient days. These are gothic notions of beauty — the ivy is beautiful, but, when it insidiously destroys the trunk from which it receives support, who would not grub it up?

Further, that we ought cautiously to remain for ever in frozen inactivity, because a thaw, whilst it nourishes the soil, spreads a temporary inundation; and the fear of risking any personal present convenience should prevent a struggle for the most estimable advantages. This is sound reasoning, I grant, in the mouth of the rich and short-sighted. ...

The imperfection of all modern governments must, without waiting to repeat the trite remark, that all human institutions are unavoidably imperfect, in a great measure have arisen from this simple circumstance, that the constitution, if such an heterogeneous mass deserve that name, was settled in the dark days of ignorance, when the minds of men were shackled by the grossest of prejudices and most immoral superstition. And do you, Sir, a sagacious philosopher, recommend night as the fittest time to analyze a ray of light?

Are we to seek for the rights of men in the ages when a few marks were the only penalty imposed for the life of a man, and death for death when the property of the rich was touched? when — I blush to discover the depravity of our nature — when a deer was killed! Are these the laws that it is natural to love, and sacrilegious to invade? — Were the rights of men understood when the law authorized or tolerated murder? — or is power and right the same in your creed?

But in fact your declamation leads so directly to this conclusion, that I beseech you to ask your own heart, when you call yourself a friend of liberty, whether it would not be more consistent to style yourself the champion of property, the adorer of the golden image which power has set up?

... Security of property! Behold, in a few words, the definition of English liberty. And to this selfish principle every nobler one is sacrificed. — The Briton takes place of the man, and the image of God is lost in the citizen! But it is not that enthusiastic flame which in Greece and Rome consumed every sordid passion: no, self is the focus; and the disparting rays rise not above our foggy atmosphere. But softly — it is only the property of the rich that is secure; the man who lives by the sweat of his brow has no asylum from oppression; the strong man may enter — when was the castle of the poor sacred? and the base informer steal him from the family that depend on his industry for subsistence.

Fully sensible as you must be of the baneful consequences that inevitably follow this notorious infringement on the dearest rights of men, and that it is an infernal blot on the very face of our immaculate constitution, I cannot avoid expressing my surprise that when you recommended our form of government as a model, you did not caution the French against the arbitrary custom of pressing men for the sea service. You should have hinted to them, that property in England is much more secure than liberty, and not have concealed that the liberty of an honest mechanic — his all — is often sacrificed to secure the property of the rich. For it is a farce to pretend that a man fights *for his country, his hearth, or his altars,* when he has neither liberty nor property. ...

Our penal laws punish with death the thief who steals a few pounds; but to take by violence, or trepan, a man, is no such heinous offence. — For who shall dare to complain of the venerable vestige of the law that rendered the life of a deer more sacred than that of a man? But it was the poor man with only his native dignity who was thus oppressed — and only metaphysical sophists and cold mathematicians can discern this insubstantial form; it is a work of abstraction — and a *gentleman* of lively imagination must borrow some drapery from fancy before he can love or pity a *man.* Misery, to reach your heart, I perceive, must have its cap and bells; your tears are reserved, very *naturally* considering your character, for the declamation of the theatre, or for the downfall of queens, whose rank alters the nature of folly, and throws a graceful veil over vices that degrade humanity; whilst the distress of many industrious mothers, whose *helpmates* have been torn from them, and the hungry cry of helpless babes, were vulgar sorrows that could not move your commiseration, though they might extort an alms. "The tears that are shed for fictitious sorrow are admirably adapted," says Rousseau, "to make us proud of all the virtues which we do not possess."

... A government that acts in this manner cannot be called a good parent, nor inspire natural (habitual is the proper word) affection, in the breasts of children who are thus disregarded.

The game laws are almost as oppressive to the peasantry as press-warrants to the mechanic. In this land of liberty what is to secure the property of the poor farmer when his noble landlord chooses to plant a decoy field near his little property? Game devour the fruit of his labour; but fines and imprisonment await him if he dare to kill any — or lift up his hand to interrupt the pleasure of his lord. How many families have been plunged, in the *sporting* countries, into misery and vice for some paltry transgression of these coercive laws, by the natural consequence of that anger which a man feels when he sees the reward of his industry laid waste by unfeeling luxury? — when his children's bread is given to dogs!

You have shewn, Sir, by your silence on these subjects, that your respect for rank has swallowed up the common feelings of humanity; you seem to consider the poor as only the live stock of an estate, the feather of hereditary nobility. ...

What were the outrages of a day[1] to these continual miseries? Let those sorrows hide their diminished head before the tremendous mountain of woe that thus defaces our globe! Man preys on man; and you mourn for the idle tapestry that decorated a gothic pile, and the dronish bell that summoned the fat priest to prayer. You mourn for the empty pageant of a name, when slavery flaps her wing, and the sick heart retires to die in lonely wilds, far from the abodes of men. Did the pangs you felt for insulted nobility, the anguish that rent your heart when the gorgeous robes were torn off the idol human weakness had set up, deserve to be compared with the long-drawn sigh of melancholy reflection, when misery and vice are thus seen to haunt our steps, and swim on the top of every cheering prospect? ...

---

1 The 6th of October.

Appendix C

Extract from Helen Maria Williams,
Letters from France
(1790)

LETTER II

I promised to send you a description of the Federation; but it is not to be described! One must have been present, to form any judgment of a scene, the sublimity of which depended much less on its external magnificence than on the effect it produced on the minds of the spectators. "The people, sure, the people were the sight!" I may tell you of pavilions, of triumphal arches, of altars on which incense was burnt, of two hundred thousand men walking in procession; but how am I to give you an adequate idea of the behaviour of the spectators? How am I to paint the impetuous feelings of that immense, that exulting multitude? Half a million of people assembled at a spectacle, which furnished every image that can elevate the mind of man; which connected the enthusiasm of moral sentiment with the solemn pomp of religious ceremonies; which addressed itself at once to the imagination, the understanding, and the heart.

The Champ de Mars was formed into an immense amphitheatre; round which were erected forty rows of seats, raised one above another with earth, on which wooden forms were placed. Twenty days labour, animated by the enthusiasm of the people, accomplished what seemed to require the toil of years. Already in the Champ de Mars the distinctions of rank were forgotten; and, inspired by the same spirit, the highest and lowest orders of citizens gloried in taking up the spade, and assisting the persons employed in a work on which the common welfare of the State depended. Ladies took the instruments of labour in their hands, and removed a little of the earth, that they might be able to boast that they also had assisted in the preparations at the Champ de Mars; and a number of old soldiers were seen voluntarily bestowing on their country the last remains of their strength. A young Abbè of my acquaintance told me, that the people beat a drum at the door of the convent where he lived, and obliged the Superior to let all the Monks come out, and work in the Champ de Mars. The Superior with great reluctance acquiesced: "Quant à moi," said the young Abbé, "je ne demandois pas mieux."*

At the upper end of the amphitheatre a pavilion was built for the reception of the King, the Queen, their attendants, and the National Assembly, covered with striped tent-cloth of the national colours, and decorated with streamers of the same beloved tints, and fleurs de lys. The white flag was displayed above the spot where the king was seated. In the middle of the Champ de Mars *l'Autel de la Patrie* was placed, on which incense was burnt by priests dressed in long white robes, with sashes of national ribbon. Several inscriptions were written on the altar; but the words visible at the greatest distance were, "La National, la Loi, & le Roi."†

… The procession marched to the Champ de Mars, through the central streets of Paris. At La Place de Louis Quinze, the escorts, who carried the colours, received under their banners, ranged in two lines, the National Assembly, who came from the Tuilleries. When the procession passed the street where Henry the Fourth was assassinated, every man paused as if by general consent: the cries of joy were suspended, and succeeded by a solemn silence. This tribute of regret, paid from the sudden impulse of feeling at such a moment, was perhaps the most honourable testimony to the virtues of that amiable Prince which his memory has yet received.

In the streets, at the windows, and on the roofs of the houses, the people, transported with joy, shouted and wept as the procession passed. Old men were seen kneeling in the streets, blessing God that they had lived to witness that happy moment. The people ran to the doors of their houses, loaded with refreshments, which they offered to the troops; and crouds of women surrounded the soldiers, and holding up their infants in their arms, and melting into tears, promised to make their children imbibe, from their earliest age, an inviolable attachment to the principles of the new constitution.

… The National Assembly walked towards the pavilion, where they placed themselves with the King, the Queen, the Royal Family, and their attendants; and opposite this group, rose in perspective the hills

---

* As for me, I desired nothing better.
† The Nation, the Law, and the King.

of Passy and Chaillot, covered with people. The standards, of which one was presented to each department of the kingdom, as a mark of brotherhood, by the citizens of Paris, were carried to the altar, to be consecrated by the bishop. High mass was performed, after which Mons. de la Fayette, who had been appointed by the king Major-General of the Federation, ascended the altar, gave the signal, and himself took the national oath. In an instant every sword was drawn, and every arm lifted up. The King pronounced the oath, which the President of the National Assembly repeated, and the solemn words were re-echoed by six hundred thousand voices; while the Queen raised the Dauphin in her arms, shewing him to the people and the army. At the moment the consecrated banners were displayed, the sun, which had been obscured by frequent showers in the course of the morning, burst forth; while the people lifted their eyes to heaven, and called upon the Deity to look down and witness the sacred engagement into which they entered. A respectful silence was succeeded by the cries, the shouts, the acclamations of the multitude: they wept, they embraced each other, and then dispersed.

You will not suspect that I was an indifferent witness of such a scene. Oh, no! this was not a time in which the distinctions of country were remembered. (It was the triumph of human kind; it was man asserting the noblest privilege of his nature; and it required but the common feelings of humanity, to become in that moment a citizen of the world. For myself, I acknowledge that my heart caught with enthusiasm the general sympathy; my eyes were filled with tears: and I shall never forget the sensations of that day, while memory "holds her seat in my bosom." ...

Appendix D

Charlotte Smith
The Emigrants
(1793)

To William Cowper, Esq.
Dear Sir, *

There is, I hope, some propriety in my addressing a Composition to you, which would never perhaps have existed, had I not, amid the heavy pressure of many sorrows, derived infinite consolation from your Poetry, and some degree of animation and of confidence from your esteem.

The following performance is far from aspiring to be considered as an imitation of your inimitable Poem, *The Task*; I am perfectly sensible, that it belongs not to a feeble and feminine hand to draw the Bow of Ulysses.

The force, clearness, and sublimity of your admirable Poem; the felicity, almost peculiar to your genius, of giving to the most familiar objects dignity and effect, I could never hope to reach; yet, having read *The Task* almost incessantly from its first publication to the present time, I felt that kind of enchantment described by Milton, when he says,

> The Angel ended, and in Adam's ear
> So charming left his voice, that he awhile
> Thought him still speaking.—
> [*Paradise Lost*, VIII.1–3]

And from the force of this impression, I was gradually led to attempt, in Blank Verse, a delineation of those interesting objects which happened to excite my attention, and which even pressed upon an heart, that has learned, perhaps from its own sufferings, to feel with acute, though unavailing compassion, the calamity of others.

A Dedication usually consists of praises and of apologies; *my* praise can add nothing to the unanimous and loud applause of your country. She regards you with pride, as one of the few, who, at the present period, rescue her from the imputation of having degenerated in

Poetical talents; but in the form of Apology, I should have much to say, if I again dared to plead the pressure of evils, aggravated by their long continuance, as an excuse for the defects of this attempt.

Whatever may be the faults of its execution, let me vindicate myself from those, that may be imputed to the design. — In speaking of the Emigrant Clergy, I beg to be understood as feeling the utmost respect for the integrity of their principles; and it is with pleasure I add my suffrage to that of those, who have had a similar opportunity of witnessing the conduct of the Emigrants of all descriptions during their exile in England; which has been such as does honour to *their* nation, and ought to secure to them in ours the esteem of every liberal mind.

Your philanthropy, dear Sir, will induce you, I am persuaded, to join with me in hoping, that this painful exile may finally lead to the extirpation of that reciprocal hatred so unworthy of great and enlightened nations; that it may tend to humanize both countries, by convincing each, that good qualities exist in the other; and at length annihilate the prejudices that have so long existed to the injury of both.

Yet it is unfortunately but too true, that with the body of the English, this national aversion has acquired new force by the dreadful scenes which have been acted in France during the last summer — even those who are the victims of the Revolution, have not escaped the odium, which the undistinguishing multitude annex to all the natives of a country where such horrors have been acted: nor is this the worst effect those events have had on the minds of the English; by confounding the original cause with the wretched catastrophes that have followed its ill management; the attempts of public virtue, with the outrages that guilt and folly have committed in its disguise, the very name of Liberty has not only lost the charm it used to have in British ears, but many, who have written, or spoken, in its defence, have been stigmatized as promoters of Anarchy, and enemies to the prosperity of their country. Perhaps even the Author of *The Task*, with all his goodness and tenderness of heart, is in the catalogue of those, who are reckoned to have been too warm in a cause, which it was once the glory of Englishmen to avow and defend — The Exquisite Poem, indeed, in which you have honoured Liberty, by a tribute highly gratifying to her sincerest friends, was published some years before the demolition of regal despotism in France, which, in the fifth book, it seems to foretell — All the truth and energy of the passage to which I allude, must have been strongly felt, when, in the Parliament of England, the greatest Orator of our time quoted the sublimest of our Poets — when the eloquence of Fox did justice to the genius of Cowper.

I am, dear Sir, with the most perfect esteem, your obliged and obedient servant,

CHARLOTTE SMITH.

Brighthelmstone, May 10, 1793.

THE EMIGRANTS
BOOK THE FIRST

Book I

SCENE, *on the Cliff to the Eastward of the Town of Brighthelmstone in Sussex.*
TIME, *a Morning in November 1792.*

Slow in the Wintry Morn, the struggling light
Throws a faint gleam upon the troubled waves;
Their foaming tops, as they approach the shore
And the broad surf that never ceasing breaks
On the innumerous pebbles, catch the beams
Of the pale Sun, that with reluctance gives
To this cold northern Isle, its shorten'd day.
Alas! how few the morning wakes to joy!
How many murmur at oblivious night
For leaving them so soon; for bearing thus
Their fancied bliss (the only bliss they taste!),
On her black wings away!—Changing the dreams
That sooth'd their sorrows, for calamities
(And every day brings its own sad proportion)
For doubts, diseases, abject dread of Death,
And faithless friends, and fame and fortune lost;
Fancied or real wants; and wounded pride,
That views the day star, but to curse his beams.
    Yet He, whose Spirit into being call'd
This wond'rous World of Waters; He who bids

The wild wind lift them till they dash the clouds,
And speaks to them in thunder; or whose breath,
Low murmuring o'er the gently heaving tides,
When the fair Moon, in summer night serene,
Irradiates with long trembling lines of light
Their undulating surface; that great Power,
Who, governing the Planets, also knows
If but a Sea-Mew falls, whose nest is hid
In these incumbent cliffs; He surely means
To us, his reasoning Creatures, whom He bids
Acknowledge and revere his awful hand,
Nothing but good: Yet Man, misguided Man,
Mars the fair work that he was bid enjoy,
And makes himself the evil he deplores.
How often, when my weary soul recoils
From proud oppression, and from legal crimes
(For such are in this Land, where the vain boast
Of equal Law is mockery, while the cost
Of seeking for redress is sure to plunge
Th' already injur'd to more certain ruin
And the wretch starves, before his Counsel pleads)
How often do I half abjure Society,
And sigh for some lone Cottage, deep embower'd
In the green woods, that these steep chalky Hills
Guard from the strong South West; where round their base
The Beach wide flourishes, and the light Ash
With slender leaf half hides the thymy turf!—
There do I wish to hide me; well content
If on the short grass, strewn with fairy flowers,
I might repose thus shelter'd; or when Eve
In Orient crimson lingers in the west,
Gain the high mound, and mark these waves remote
(Lucid tho' distant), blushing with the rays
Of the far-flaming Orb, that sinks beneath them;
For I have thought, that I should then behold
The beauteous works of God, unspoil'd by Man
And less affected then, by human woes
I witness'd not; might better learn to bear

Those that injustice, and duplicity
And faithlessness and folly, fix on me:
For never yet could I derive relief,
When my swol'n heart was bursting with its sorrows,
From the sad thought, that others like myself
Live but to swell affliction's countless tribes!
—Tranquil seclusion I have vainly sought;
Peace, who delights in solitary shade,
No more will spread for me her downy wings,
But, like the fabled Danaïds—or the wretch,
Who ceaseless, up the steep acclivity,
Was doom'd to heave the still rebounding rock,
Onward I labour; as the baffled wave,
Which yon rough beach repulses, that returns
With the next breath of wind, to fail again.—
Ah! Mourner—cease these wailings: cease and learn,
That not the Cot sequester'd, where the briar
And wood-bine wild, embrace the mossy thatch,
(Scarce seen amid the forest gloom obscure!)
Or more substantial farm, well fenced and warm,
Where the full barn, and cattle fodder'd round
Speak rustic plenty; nor the statelier dome
By dark firs shaded, or the aspiring pine,
Close by the village Church (with care conceal'd
By verdant foliage, lest the poor man's grave
Should mar the smiling prospect of his Lord),
Where offices well rang'd, or dove-cote stock'd,
Declare manorial residence; not these
Or any of the buildings, new and trim
With windows circling towards the restless Sea,
Which ranged in rows, now terminate my walk,
Can shut out for an hour the spectre Care,
That from the dawn of reason, follows still
Unhappy Mortals, 'till the friendly grave
(Our sole secure asylum) "ends the chace."*

---

* I have a confused notion, that this expression, with nearly the same
application, is to be found in Young: but I cannot refer to it.

Behold, in witness of this mournful truth,
A group approach me, whose dejected looks,
Sad Heralds of distress! proclaim them Men
Banish'd for ever and for conscience sake
From their distracted Country, whence the name
Of Freedom misapplied, and much abus'd
By lawless Anarchy, has driven them far
To wander; with the prejudice they learn'd
From Bigotry (the Tut'ress of the blind),
Thro' the wide World unshelter'd; their sole hope,
That German spoilers, thro' that pleasant land
May carry wide the desolating scourge
Of War and Vengeance; yet unhappy Men,
Whate'er your errors, I lament your fate:
And, as disconsolate and sad ye hang
Upon the barrier of the rock, and seem
To murmur your despondence, waiting long
Some fortunate reverse that never comes;
Methinks in each expressive face, I see
Discriminated anguish; there droops one,
Who in a moping cloister long consum'd
This life inactive, to obtain a better,
And thought that meagre abstinence, to wake
From his hard pallet with the midnight bell,
To live on eleemosynary bread,
And to renounce God's works, would please that God.
And now the poor pale wretch receives, amaz'd,
The pity, strangers give to his distress,
Because these strangers are, by his dark creed,
Condemn'd as Heretics—and with sick heart
Regrets his pious prison, and his beads.*—

---

* Lest the same attempts at misrepresentation should now be made, at have
been made on former occasions, it is necessary to repeat, that nothing
is farther from my thoughts, than to reflect invidiously on the Emigrant
clergy, whose steadiness of principle excites veneration, as much as their
sufferings compassion. Adversity has now taught them the charity and
humility they perhaps wanted, when they made it a part of their faith,
that salvation could be obtained in no other religion than their own.

Another, of more haughty port, declines
The aid he needs not; while in mute despair
His high indignant thoughts go back to France,
Dwelling on all he lost—the Gothic dome,
That vied with splendid palaces;* the beds
Of silk and down, the silver chalices,
Vestments with gold enwrought for blazing altars;
Where, amid clouds of incense, he held forth
To kneeling crowds the imaginary bones
Of Saints suppos'd, in pearl and gold enchas'd,
And still with more than living Monarchs' pomp
Surrounded; was believ'd by mumbling bigots
To hold the keys of Heaven, and to admit
Whom he thought good to share it—Now alas!
He, to whose daring soul and high ambition
The World seem't circumscrib'd; who, wont to dream
Of Fleuri, Richelieu, Alberoni, men
Who trod on Empire, and whose politics
Were not beyond the grasp of his vast mind,
Is, in a Land once hostile, still prophan'd
By disbelief, and rites un-orthodox,
The object of compassion[.]—At his side,
Lighter of heart than these, but heavier far
Than he was wont, another victim comes,
An Abbé—who with less contracted brow
Still smiles and flatters, and still talks of Hope;
Which, sanguine as he is, he does not feel,
Andso he cheats the sad and weighty pressure
Of evils present;—Still, as Men misled
By early prejudice (so hard to break),
I mourn your sorrows; for I too have known
Involuntary exile; and while yet

* Let it not be considered as an insult to men in fallen fortune, if these
luxuries (undoubtedly inconsistent with their profession) be here enumerated—France is not the only country, where the splendour and in-
dulgences of the higher, and the poverty and depression of the inferior
Clergy, have alike proved injurious to the cause of Religion.

England had charms for me, have felt how sad
It is to look across the dim cold sea,
That melancholy rolls its refluent tides
Between us and the dear regretted land
We call our own—as now ye pensive wait
On this bleak morning, gazing on the waves
That seem to leave your shore; from whence the wind
Is loaded to your ears, with the deep groans
Of martyr'd Saints and suffering Royalty,
While to your eyes the avenging power of Heaven
Appears in aweful anger to prepare
The storm of vengeance, fraught with plagues and death.
Even he of milder heart, who was indeed
The simple shepherd in a rustic scene,
And, 'mid the vine-clad hills of Languedoc,
Taught to the bare-foot peasant, whose hard hands
Produc'd* the nectar he could seldom taste,
Submission to the Lord for whom he toil'd;
He, or his brethren, who to Neustria's son
Enforc'd religious patience, when, at times,
On their indignant hearts Power's iron hand
Too strongly struck; eliciting some sparks
Of the bold spirit of their native North;
Even these Parochial Priests, these humbled men,
Whose lowly undistinguish'd cottages
Witness'd a life of purest piety,
While the meek tenants were, perhaps, unknown
Each to the haughty Lord of his domain,
Who mark'd them not; the Noble scorning still
The poor and pious Priest, as with slow pace
He glided thro' the dim arch'd avenue
Which to the Castle led; hoping to cheer
The last sad hour of some laborious life
That hasten'd to its close—even such a Man

---

*   See the finely descriptive Verses written at Montauban in France in
1750, by Dr. Joseph Warton. Printed in Dodsley's *Miscellanies*, Vol. IV.
page 203.

Becomes an exile; staying not to try
By temperate zeal to check his madd'ning flock,
Who, at the novel sound of Liberty
(Ah! most intoxicating sound to slaves!),
Start into licence[.]—Lo! dejected now,
The wandering Pastor mourns, with bleeding heart,
His erring people, weeps and prays for them,
And trembles for the account that he must give
To Heaven for souls entrusted to his care.—
Where the cliff, hollow'd by the wintry storm,
Affords a seat with matted sea-weed strewn,
A softer form reclines; around her run,
On the rough shingles, or the chalky bourn,
Her gay unconscious children, soon amus'd;
Who pick the fretted stone, or glossy shell,
Or crimson plant marine: or they contrive
The fairy vessel, with its ribband sail
And gilded paper pennant: in the pool,
Left by the salt wave on the yielding sands,
They launch the mimic navy—Happy age!
Unmindful of the miseries of Man!—
Alas! too long a victim to distress,
Their Mother, lost in melancholy thought,
Lull'd for a moment by the murmurs low
Of sullen billows, wearied by the task
Of having here, with swol'n and aching eyes
Fix'd on the grey horizon, since the dawn
Solicitously watch'd the weekly sail
From her dear native land, now yields awhile
To kind forgetfulness, while Fancy brings,
In waking dreams, that native land again!
Versailles appears—its painted galleries,
And rooms of regal splendour; rich with gold,
Where, by long mirrors multiply'd, the crowd
Paid willing homage—and, united there,
Beauty gave charms to empire—Ah! too soon
From the gay visionary pageant rous'd,
See the sad mourner start!—and, drooping, look

With tearful eyes and heaving bosom round
On drear reality—where dark'ning waves,
Urg'd by the rising wind, unheeded foam
Near her cold rugged seat:—To call her thence
A fellow-sufferer comes: dejection deep
Checks, but conceals not quite, the martial air,
And that high consciousness of noble blood,
Which he has learn'd from infancy to think
Exalts him o'er the race of common men:
Nurs'd in the velvet lap of luxury,
And fed by adulation—could *he* learn,
That worth alone is true Nobility?
And that *the peasant* who, "amid the sons
Of Reason, Valour, Liberty, and Virtue,
Displays distinguish'd merit, is a Noble
Of Nature's own creation!"*—If even here,
If in this land of highly vaunted Freedom,
Even Britons controvert the unwelcome truth,
Can it be relish'd by the sons of France?
Men, who derive their boasted ancestry
From the fierce leaders of religious wars,
The first in Chivalry's emblazon'd page;
Who reckon Gueslin, Bayard, or De Foix,
Among their brave Progenitors? *Their* eyes,
Accustom'd to regard the splendid trophies
Of Heraldry (that with fantastic hand
Mingles, like images in feverish dreams,
"Gorgons and Hydras, and Chimeras dire,"
With painted puns, and visionary shapes;),
See not the simple dignity of Virtue,
But hold all base, whom honours such as these
Exalt not from the crowd†—As one, who long

---

* These uses are Thomson's, and are among those sentiments which are
now called (when used by living writers), not common-place declamation, but sentiments of dangerous tendency.

† It has been said, and with great appearance of truth, that the contempt
in which the Nobility of France held the common people, was remem-

Has dwelt amid the artificial scenes
Of populous City, deems that splendid shows,
The Theatre, and pageant pomp of Courts,
Are only worth regard; forgets all taste
For Nature's genuine beauty; in the lapse
Of gushing waters hears no soothing sound,
Nor listens with delight to sighing winds,
That, on their fragrant pinions, waft the notes
Of birds rejoicing in the trangled copse;
Nor gazes pleas'd on Ocean's silver breast,
While lightly o'er it sails the summer clouds
Reflected in the wave, that, hardly heard,
Flows on the yellow sands: so to *his* mind,
That long has liv'd where Despotism hides
His features harsh, beneath the diadem
Of worldly grandeur, abject Slavery seems,
If by that power impos'd, slavery no more:
For luxury wreathes with silk the iron bonds,
And hides the ugly rivets with her flowers,
Till the degenerate triflers, while they love
The glitter of the chains, forget their weight.
But more the Men, whose ill acquir'd wealth*

---

bered, and with all that vindictive asperity which long endurance of
oppression naturally excites, when, by a wonderful concurrence of circumstances, the people acquired the power of retaliation. Yet let me
here add, what seems to be in some degree inconsistent with the former
charge, that the French are good masters to their servants, and that in
their treatment of their Negro slaves, they are allowed to be more mild
and merciful than other Europeans.

* The Financiers and Fermiers Generaux are here intended. In the present
moment of clamour against all those who have spoken or written in
favour of the first Revolution of France, the declaimers seem to have
forgotten, that under the reign of a mild and easy tempered Monarch,
in the most voluptuous Court in the world, the abuses by which men
of this description were enriched, had arisen to such height, that their
prodigality exhausted the immense resources of France: and, unable to
supply the exigencies of Government, the Ministry were compelled to
call Le Tiers Etat; a meeting that gave birth to the Revolution, which
has since been so ruinously conducted.

Was wrung from plunder'd myriads, by the means
Too often legaliz'd by power abus'd,
Feel all the horrors of the fatal change,
When their ephemeral greatness, marr'd at once
(As a vain toy that Fortune's childish hand
Equally joy'd to fashion or to crush),
Leaves them expos'd to universal scorn
For having nothing else; not even the claim
To honour, which respect for Heroes past
Allows to ancient titles; Men, like these,
Sink even beneath the level, whence base arts
Alone had rais'd them;—unlamented sink,
And know that they deserve the woes they feel.
    Poor wand'ring wretches! whosoe'er ye are,
That hopeless, houseless, friendless, travel wide
O'er these bleak russet downs; where, dimly seen,
The solitary Shepherd shiv'ring tends
His dun discolour'd flock (Shepherd, unlike
Him, whom in song the Poet's fancy crowns
With garlands, and his crook with vi'lets binds);
Poor vagrant wretches! outcasts of the world!
Whom no abode receives, no parish owns;
Roving, like Nature's commoners, the land
That boasts such general plenty: if the sight
Of wide-extended misery softens yours
Awhile, suspend your murmurs!—here behold
The strange vicissitudes of fate—while thus
The exil'd Nobles, from their country driven,
Whose richest luxuries were their's, must feel
More poignant anguish, than the lowest poor,
Who, born to indigence, have learn'd to brave
Rigid Adversity's depressing breath!—
Ah! rather Fortune's worthless favourites!
Who feed on England's vitals—Pensioners
Of base corruption, who, in quick ascent
To opulence unmerited, become
Giddy with pride, and as ye rise, forgetting
The dust ye lately left, with scorn look down

On those beneath ye (tho' your *equals* once
In fortune, and *in worth superior still,*
They view the eminence, on which ye stand,
With wonder, not with envy; for they know
The means, by which ye reach'd it, have been such
As, in all honest eyes, degrade ye far
Beneath the poor dependent, whose sad heart
Reluctant pleads for what your pride denies);
Ye venal, worthless hirelings of a Court!
Ye pamper'd Parasites! whom Britons pay
For forging fetters for them; rather here
Study a lesson that concerns ye much;
And, trembling, learn, that if oppress'd too long,
The raging multitude, to madness stung,
Will turn on their oppressors; and, no more
By sounding titles and parading forms
Bound like tame victims, will redress themselves!
Then swept away by the resistless torrent,
Not only all your pomp may disappear,
But, in the tempest lost, fair Order sink
Her decent head, and lawless Anarchy
O'erturn celestial Freedom's radiant throne;—
As now in Gallia; where Confusion, born
Of party rage and selfish love of rule,
Sully the noblest cause that ever warm'd
The heart of Patriot Virtue[.]*—There arise
The infernal passions; Vengeance, seeking blood,
And Avarice; and Envy's harpy fangs
Pollute the immortal shrine of Liberty,
Dismay her votaries, and disgrace her name.
Respect is due to principle; and they,
Who suffer for their conscience, have a claim,
Whate'er that principle may he, to praise.
These ill-starr'd Exiles then, who, bound by ties,

---

* This sentiment will probably *renew* against me the indignation of those,
who have an interest in asserting that no such virtue any where exists.

To them the bonds of honour; who resign'd
Their country to preserve them, and now seek
In England an asylum—well deserve
To find that (every prejudice forgot,
Which pride and ignorance teaches), we for them
Feel as our brethren; and that English hearts,
Of just compassion ever own the sway,
As truly as our element, the deep,
Obeys the mild dominion of the Moon[.]—
This they *have* found; and may they find it still!
Thus may'st thou, Britain, triumph!—May thy foes,
By Reason's gen'rous potency subdued,
Learn, that the God thou worshippest, delights
In acts of pure humanity!—May thine
Be still such bloodless laurels! nobler far
Than those acquir'd at Cressy or Poictiers,
Or of more recent growth, those well bestow'd
On him who stood on Calpe's blazing height
Amid the thunder of a warring world,
Illustrious rather from the crowds he sav'd
From flood and fire, than from the ranks who fell
Beneath his valour!—Actions such as these,
Like incense rising to the Throne of Heaven,
Far better justify the pride, that swells
In British bosoms, than the deafening roar
Of Victory from a thousand brazen throats,
That tell with what success wide-wasting War
Has by our brave Compatriots thinned the world.

END OF BOOK I.

THE EMIGRANTS
BOOK THE SECOND

Quippe ubi fas versum atque nefas: tot hella per orbem
Tam multæ scelerum lacies; non ullus aratro
Dignus honos: squalent abductis arva colonis,
et curva[e] rigidum falces conflantur in ensem[.]
Hinc movet Euphrates, illinc Germania bellum[;]
Vicinæ ruptis inter se legibus urbes
Arma ferunt: sævit toto Mars impius orbe.

Vergil, *Georgics.* lib. i.505–11

Book II
SCENE, *on an Eminence on one of those Downs, which afford to the
South a View of the Sea; to the North of the Weald of Sussex.*

TIME, *an Afternoon in April, 1793.*

Long wintry months are past; the Moon that now
Lights her pale crescent even at noon, has made
Four times her revolution; since with step,
Mournful and slow, along the wave-worn cliff,
Pensive I took my solitary way,
Lost in despondence, while contemplating
Not my own wayward destiny alone,
(Hard as it is, and difficult to bear!)
But in beholding the unhappy lot
Of the lorn Exiles; who, amid the storms
Of wild disastrous Anarchy, are thrown,
Like shipwreck'd sufferers, on England's coast,
To see, perhaps, no more their native land,
Where Desolation riots: They, like me,
From fairer hopes and happier prospects driven,
Shrink from the future, and regret the past.
But on this Upland scene, while April comes,
With fragrant airs, to fan my throbbing breast,
Fain would I snatch an interval from Care,

That weighs my wearied spirit down to earth;
Courting, once more, the influence of Hope
(For "Hope" still waits upon the flowery prime)*
As here I mark Spring's humid hand unfold
The early leaves that fear capricious winds,
While, even on shelter'd banks, the timid flowers
Give, half reluctantly, their warmer hues
To mingle with the primroses' pale stars.
No shade the leafless copses yet afford,
Nor hide the mossy labours of the Thrush,
That, startled, darts across the narrow path;
But quickly re-assur'd, resumes his task,
Or adds his louder notes to those that rise
From yonder tufted brake; where the white buds
Of the first thorn are mingled with the leaves
Of that which blossoms on the brow of May.

    Ah! 'twill not be:—So many years have pass'd,
Since, on my native hills, I learn'd to gaze
On these delightful landscapes; and those years
Have taught me so much sorrow, that my soul
Feels not the joy reviving Nature brings;
But, in dark retrospect, dejected dwells
On human follies, and on human woes.—
What is the promise of the infant year,
The lively verdure, or the bursting blooms,
To those, who shrink from horrors such as War
Spreads o'er the affrighted world? With swimming eye,
Back on the past they throw their mournful looks,
And see the Temple, which they fondly hop'd
Reason would raise to Liberty, destroy'd
By ruffian hands; while, on the ruin'd mass,
Flush'd with hot blood, the Fiend of Discord sits
In savage triumph; mocking every plea
Of policy and justice, as she shews
The headless corse of one, whose only crime

---

* Shakspeare.

Was being born a Monarch—Mercy turns,
From spectacle so dire, her swol'n eyes;
And Liberty with calm, unruffled brow
Magnanimous, as conscious of her strength
In Reason's panoply, scorns to distain
Her righteous cause with carnage, and resigns
To Fraud and Anarchy the infuriate crowd.—
      What is the promise of the infant year
To those, who (while the poor but peaceful hind
Pens, unmolested, the encreasing flock
Of his rich master in this sea-fenc'd isle)
Survey, in neighbouring countries, scenes that make
The sick heart shudder; and the Man, who thinks,
Blush for his species? *There* the trumpet's voice
Drowns the soft warbling of the woodland choir;
And violets, lurking in their turfy beds
Beneath the flow'ring thorn, are stain'd with blood.
There fall, at once, the spoiler and the spoil'd;
While War, wide-ravaging, annihilates
The hope of cultivation; gives to Fiends,
The meagre, ghastly Fiends of Want and Woe,
The blasted land—There, taunting in the van
Of vengeance-breathing armies, Insult stalks;
And, in the ranks, "Famine, and Sword, and Fire,
Crouch for employment."*—Lo! the suffering world,
Torn by the fearful conflict, shrinks, amaz'd,
From Freedom's name, usurp'd and misapplied,
And, cow'ring to the purple Tyrant's rod,
Deems *that* the lesser ill—Deluded Men!
Ere ye prophane her ever-glorious name,
Or catalogue the thousands that have bled
Resisting her; or those, who greatly died
Martyrs to *Liberty*—revert awhile
To the black scroll, that tells of regal crimes
Committed to destroy her; rather count
The hecatombs of victims, who have fallen

---

  *   Shakspeare.

Beneath a single despot; or who gave
Their wasted lives for some disputed claim
Between anointed robbers: Monsters both!*
"Oh! Polish'd perturbation-golden care!"†
So strangely coveted by feeble Man
To lift him o'er his fellows;—Toy, for which
Such showers of blood have drench'd th'affrighted earth—
Unfortunate *his* lot, whose luckless head
Thy jewel'd circlet, lin'd with thorns, has bound;
And who, by custom's laws, obtains from thee
Hereditary right to rule, uncheck'd,
Submissive myriads: for untemper'd power,
Like steel ill form'd, injures the hand
It promis'd to protect—Unhappy France!
If e'er thy lilies, trampled now in dust,
And blood-bespotted, shall again revive
In silver splendour, may the wreath be wov'n
By voluntary hands; and Freemen, such
As England's self might boast, unite to place
The guarded diadem on *his* fair brow,
Where Loyalty may join with Liberty
To fix it firmly.—In the rugged school
Of stern Adversity so early train'd,
His future life, perchance, may emulate
That of the brave Bernois,‡ so justly call'd
The darling of his people; who rever'd
The Warrior less, than they ador'd the Man!
But ne'er may Party Rage, perverse and blind,
And base Venality, prevail to raise
To public trust, a wretch, whose private vice

---

* Such was the cause of quarrel between the Houses of York and Lancaster; and of too many others, with which the page of History reproaches the reason of man.

† Shakspeare.

‡ Henry the Fourth of France. It may be said of this monarch, that had all the French sovereigns resembled him, despotism would have lost its horrors; yet he had considerable failings, and his greatest virtues may be chiefly imputed to his education in the School of Adversity.

Makes even the wildest profligate recoil;
And who, with hireling ruffians leagu'd, has burst
The laws of Nature and Humanity!
Wading, beneath the Patriot's specious mask,
And in Equality's illusive name,
To empire thro' a stream of kindred blood—
Innocent prisoner!—most unhappy heir
Of fatal greatness, who art suffering now
For all the crimes and follies of thy race;
Better for thee, if o'er thy baby brow
The regal mischief never had been held:
Then, in an humble sphere, perhaps content,
Thou hadst been free and joyous on the heights
Of Pyrennean mountains, shagg'd with woods
Of chestnut, pine, and oak: as on these hills
Is yonder little thoughtless shepherd lad,
Who, on the slope abrupt of downy turf
Reclin'd in playful indolence, sends off
The chalky ball, quick bounding far below;
While, half forgetful of his simple task,
Hardly his length'ning shadow, or the bells'
Slow tinkling of his flock, that supping tend
To the brown fallows in the vale beneath,
Where nightly it is folded, from his sport
Recall the happy idler—While I gaze
On his gay vacant countenance, my thoughts
Compare with his obscure, laborious lot,
Thine, most unfortunate, imperial Boy!
Who round thy sullen prison daily hear'st
The savage howl of Murder, as it seeks
Thy unoffending life: while sad within
Thy wretched Mother, petrified with grief,
Views thee with stony eyes, and cannot weep!—
Ah! much I mourn thy sorrows, hapless Queen!
And deem thy expiation made to Heaven
For every fault, to which Prosperity
Betray'd thee, when it plac'd thee on a throne
Where boundless power was thine, and thou wert rais'd
High (as it seem'd) above the envious reach

Of destiny! Whate'er thy errors were,
Be they no more remember'd; tho' the rage
Of Party swell'd them to such crimes, as bade
Compassion stifle every sigh that rose
For thy disastrous lot—More than enough
Thou hast endur'd; and every English heart,
Ev'n those, that highest beat in Freedom's cause,
Disclaim as base, and of that cause unworthy,
The Vengeance, or the Fear, that makes thee still
A miserable prisoner!—Ah! who knows,
From sad experience, more than I, to feel
For thy desponding spirit, as it sinks
Beneath procrastinated fears for those
More dear to thee than life! But eminence
Of misery is thine, as once of joy;
And, as we view the strange vicissitude,
We ask anew, where happiness is found?—
Alas! in rural life, where youthful dreams
See the Arcadia that Romance describes,
Not even Content resides!—In yon low hut
Of clay and thatch, where rises the grey smoke
Of smold'ring turf, cut from the adjoining moor,
The labourer, its inhabitant, who toils
From the first dawn of twilight, till the Sun
Sinks in the rosy waters of the West,
Finds that with poverty it cannot dwell;
For bread, and scanty bread, is all he earns
For him and for his household[.]—Should Disease,
Born of chill wintry rains, arrest his arm,
Then, thro' his patch'd and straw-stuff'd casement, peeps
The squalid figure of extremest Want;
And from the Parish the reluctant dole,
Dealt by th'unfeeling farmer, hardly saves
The ling'ring spark of life from cold extinction:
Then the bright Sun of Spring, that smiling bids
All other animals rejoice, beholds,
Crept from his pallet, the emaciate wretch
Attempt, with feeble effort, to resume
Some heavy task, above his wasted strength,

Turning his wistful looks (how much in vain!)
To the deserted mansion, where no more
The owner (gone to gayer scenes) resides,
Who made even luxury, Virtue; while he gave
The scatter'd crumbs to honest Poverty.—
But, tho' the landscape be too oft deform'd
By figures such as these, yet Peace is here,
And o'er our vallies, cloath'd with springing corn,
No hostile hoof shall trample, nor fierce flames
Wither the wood's young verdure, ere it form
Gradual the laughing May's luxuriant shade;
For, by the rude sea guarded, we are safe,
And feel not evils such as with deep sighs
The Emigrants deplore, as they recal
The Summer past, when Nature seem'd to lose
Her course in wild distemperature, and aid,
With seasons all revers'd, destructive War.
        Shuddering, I view the pictures they have drawn
Of desolated countries, where the ground,
Stripp'd of its unripe produce, was thick strewn
With various Death—the war-horse falling there
By famine, and his rider by the sword.
The moping clouds sail'd heavy charg'd with rain,
And bursting o'er the mountains['] misty brow,
Deluged, as with an inland sea, the vales;*
Where, thro' the sullen evening's lurid gloom,
Rising, like columns of volcanic fire,
The flames of burning villages illum'd
The waste of water; and the wind, that howl'd

---

*   From the heavy and incessant rains during the last campaign, the ar-
    mies were often compelled to march for many miles through marshes
    overflowed, suffering the extremities of cold and fatigue. The peasants
    frequently misled them; and, after having passed these inundations at
    the hazard of their lives, they were sometimes under the necessity of
    crossing them a second and a third time; their evening quarters after
    such a day of exertion were often in a wood without shelter; and their
    repast, instead of bread, unripe corn, without any other preparation
    than being mashed into a sort of paste.

Along its troubled surface, brought the groans
Of plunder'd peasants, and the frantic shrieks
Of mothers for their children; while the brave,
To pity still alive, listen'd aghast
To these dire echoes, hopeless to prevent
The evils they beheld, or check the rage,
Which ever, as the people of one land
Meet in contention, fires the human heart
With savage thirst of kindred blood, and makes
Man lose his nature; rendering him more fierce
Than the gaunt monsters of the howling waste.

    Oft have I heard the melancholy tale,
Which, all their native gaiety forgot,
These Exiles tell—How Hope impell'd them on,
Reckless of tempest, hunger, or the sword,
Till order'd to retreat, they know not why,
From all their flattering prospects, they became
The prey of dark suspicion and regret:*
Then, in despondence, sunk the unnerv'd arm
Of gallant Loyalty[.]—At every turn
Shame and disgrace appear'd, and seem'd to mock
Their scatter'd squadrons; which the warlike youth,
Unable to endure, often implor'd,
As the last act of friendship, from the hand
Of some brave comrade, to receive the blow
That freed the indignant spirit from its pain
To a wild mountain, whose bare summit hides
Its broken eminence in clouds; whose steeps
Are dark with woods; where the receding rocks
Are worn by torrents of dissolving snow,
A wretched Woman, pale and breathless, flies!

---

    * It is remarkable, that notwithstanding the excessive hardships to which
the army of the Emigrants was exposed, very few in it suffered from
disease till they began to retreat; then it was that despondence consigned
to the most miserable death many brave men who deserved a better
fate; and then despair impelled some to suicide, while others fell by
mutual wounds, unable to survive disappointment and humiliation.

And, gazing round her, listens to the sound
Of hostile footsteps[.]—No! it dies away:
Nor noise remains, but of the cataract,
Or surly breeze of night, that mutters low
Among the thickets, where she trembling seeks
A temporary shelter—clasping close
To her hard-heaving heart her sleeping child,
All she could rescue of the innocent groupe
That yesterday surrounded herf[.]—Escap'd
Almost by miracle! Fear, frantic Fear,
Wing'd her weak feet: yet, half repentant now
Her headlong haste, she wishes she had staid
To die with those affrighted Fancy paints
The lawless soldier's victims[.]—Hark! again
The driving tempest bears the cry of Death,
And, with deep sullen thunder, the dread sound
Of cannon vibrates on the tremulous earth;
While, bursting in the air, the murderous bomb
Glares o'er her mansion. Where the splinters fall,
Like scatter'd comets, its destructive path
Is mark'd by wreaths of flame!—Then, overwhelm'd
Beneath accumulated horror, sinks
The desolate moumer; yet, in Death itself,
True to maternal tenderness, she tries
To save the unconscious infant from the storm
In which she perishes; and to protect
This last dear object of her ruin'd hopes
From prowling monsters, that from other hills,
More inaccessible, and wilder wastes,
Lur'd by the scent of slaughter, follow fierce
Contending hosts, and to polluted fields
Add dire increase of horrors[.]—But alas!
The Mother and the Infant perish both!—
     The feudal Chief, whose Gothic battlements
Frown on the plain beneath, returning home
From distant lands, alone and in disguise,
Gains at the fall of night his Castle walls,
But, at the vacant gate, no Porter sits

To wait his Lord's admittance!—In the courts
All is drear silence!—Guessing but too well
The fatal truth, he shudders as he goes
Thro' the mute hall; where, by the blunted light
That the dim moon thro' painted casements lends,
He sees that devastation has been there:
Then, while each hideous image to his mind
Rises terrific, o'er a bleeding corse
Stumbling he falls; another interrupts
His staggering feet—all, all who us'd to rush
With joy to meet him—all his family
Lie murder'd in his way!—And the day dawns
On a wild raving Maniac, whom a fate
So sudden and calamitous has robb'd
Of reason; and who round his vacant walls
Screams unregarded, and reproaches Heaven!—
Such are thy dreadful trophies, savage War!
And evils such as these, or yet more dire,
Which the pain'd mind recoils from, all are thine—
The purple Pestilence, that to the grave
Sends whom the sword has spar'd, is thine; and thine
The Widow's anguish and the Orphan's tears!—
Woes such as these does Man inflict on Man;
And by the closet murderers, whom we style
Wise Politicians, are the schemes prepar'd,
Which, to keep Europe's wavering balance even,
Depopulate her kingdoms, and consign
To tears and anguish half a bleeding world!—
    Oh! could the time return, when thoughts like these
Spoil'd not that gay delight, which vernal Suns,
Illuminating hills, and woods, and fields,
Gave to my infant spirits—Memory come!
And from distracting cares, that now deprive
Such scenes of all their beauty, kindly bear
My fancy to those hours of simple joy,
When, on the banks of Arun, which I see
Make its irriguous course thro' yonder meads,
I play'd; unconscious then of future ill!
There (where, from hollows fring'd with yellow broom,

The birch with silver rind, and fairy leaf,
Aslant the low stream trembles) I have stood,
And meditated how to venture best
Into the shallow current, to procure
The willow herb of glowing purple spikes,
Or flags, whose sword-like leaves conceal'd the tide,
Startling the timid reed-bird from her nest,
As with aquatic flowers I wove the wreath,
Such as, collected by the shepherd girls,
Deck in the villages the turfy shrine,
And mark the arrival of propitious May.—
How little dream'd I then the time would come,
When the bright Sun of that delicious month
Should, from disturb'd and artificial sleep,
Awaken me to never-ending toil,
To terror and to tears!—Attempting still,
With feeble hands and cold desponding heart,
To save my children from the o'erwhelming wrongs,
That have for ten long years been heap'd on me!—
The fearful spectres of chicane and fraud
Have, Proteus like, still chang'd their hideous forms
(As the Law lent its plausible disguise),
Pursuing my faint steps; and I have seen
Friendship's sweet bonds (which were so early form'd,)
And once I fondly thought of amaranth
Inwove with silver seven times tried) give way,
And fail; as these green fan-like leaves of fern
Will wither at the touch of Autumn's frost.
Yet there *are those,* whose patient pity still
Hears my long murmurs; who, unwearied, try
With lenient hands to bind up every wound
My wearied spirit feels, and bid me go
"Right onward"*—a calm votary of the Nymph,
Who, from her adamantine rock, points out
To conscious rectitude the rugged path,
That leads at length to Peace!—Ah! yes, my friends

---

* Milton, Sonnet 22d.

Peace will at last be mine; for in the Grave
Is Peace—and pass a few short years, perchance
A few short months, and all the various pain
I now endure shall be forgotten there,
And no memorial shall remain of me,
Save in your bosoms; while even *your* regret
Shall lose its poignancy, as ye reflect
What complicated woes that grave conceals!
But, if the little praise, that may await
The Mother's efforts, should provoke the spleen
Of Priest or Levite; and they then arraign
The dust that cannot hear them; be it yours
To vindicate my humble fame; to say,
That, not in selfish sufferings absorb'd,
"I gave to misery all I had, my tears."*
And if, where regulated sanctity
Pours her long orisons to Heaven, my voice
Was seldom heard, that yet *my prayer* was made
To him who hears even silence; not in domes
Of human architecture, fill'd with crowds,
But on these hills, where boundless, yet distinct,
Even as a map, beneath are spread the fields
His bounty cloaths; divided here by woods,
And there by commons rude, or winding brooks,
While I might breathe the air perfum'd with flowers,
Or the fresh odours of the mountain turf;
And gaze on clouds above me, as they sail'd
Majestic: or remark the reddening north,
When bickering arrows of electric fire
Flash on the evening sky—I made my prayer
In unison with murmuring waves that now
Swell with dark tempests, now are mild and blue,
As the bright arch above; for all to me
Declare omniscient goodness; nor need I
Declamatory essays to incite

---

*   Gray.

My wonder or my praise, when every leaf
That Spring unfolds, and every simple bud,
More forcibly impresses on my heart
His power and wisdom—Ah! while I adore
That goodness, which design'd to all that lives
Some taste of happiness, my soul is pain'd
By the variety of woes that Man
For Man creates—his blessings often turn'd
To plagues and curses: Saint-like Piety,
Misled by Superstition, has destroy'd
More than Ambition; and the sacred flame
Of Liberty becomes a raging fire,
When Licence and Confusion bid it blaze.
From thy high throne, above yon radiant stars,
O Power Omnipotent! with mercy view
This suffering globe, and cause thy creatures cease,
With savage fangs, to tear her bleeding breast:
Restrain that rage for power, that bids a Man,
Himself a worm, desire unbounded rule
O'er beings like himself: Teach the hard hearts
Of rulers, that the poorest hind, who dies
For their unrighteous quarrels, in thy sight
Is equal to the imperious Lord, that leads
His disciplin'd destroyers to the field.—
May lovely freedom, in her genuine charms,
Aided by stern but equal Justice, drive
From the ensanguin'd earth the hell-born fiends
Of Pride, Oppression, Avarice, and Revenge,
That ruin what thy mercy made so fair!
Then shall these ill-starr'd wanderers, whose sad fate
These desultory lines lament, regain
Their native country; private vengeance then
To public virtue yield; and the fierce feuds,
That long have torn their desolated land,
May (even as storms, that agitate the air,
Drive noxious vapours from the blighted earth)
Serve, all tremendous as they are, to fix
The reign of Reason, Liberty, and Peace!

Appendix E

Extract from Charlotte Smith,
Personal letter to Joel Barlow[1]

To Joel Barlow[2]   Brighthelmstone Novr 3rd [1792]

I am extremely flatterd, Dear Sir, by your early and very obliging attention to my Letter & indeed have great reason to quarrel with Dr Warner for neglecting an appointment which would have been the means of introducing me to your acquaintance. I read with great satisfaction the "Advice to the Priveledged Orders" and have been, as well as some of my most judicious and reasoning friends here, very highly gratified by the lesser tract, Your Letter to the National Convention which cannot I think fail of having great effect not only where it is address'd, but on those who at present consider themselves as less immediately interested in the questions it discusses. I really pity the advocates for despotism. They are so terribly mortified at the late events in France, and as they had never any thing to say that had even the semblance of reason and now are evidently on the wrong side of the question both in Theory and Practice, it is really pitiable to hear the childish shifts and miserable evasions to which they are reduced.

I am however sensibly hurt at the hideous picture which a friend of mine, himself one of the most determined Democrates I know, has given of the situation of the Emigrants. He has follow'd the progress of the retreating Army in their retrog[r]ade motion, and describes the condition of the French exiles as being more deplorable even than their crimes seem to deserve. The magnitude of the Revolution is such as ought to make it embrace every great principle of Morals, & even in a

---

1   This item is reproduced by permission of The Huntington Library, San Marino, California.

2   The American Joel Barlow (1754–1812) had been a chaplain, editor, and poet; he was now an influential pamphleteer and businessman living in Paris, and well acquainted with all the leading British radicals of his time. For the pamphlet mentioned by Smith, *A Letter to the National Convention*, he was awarded honorary French citizenship.

Political light (with which I am afraid Morals have but little to do), it seems to me wrong for the Nation entirely to exile and abandon these Unhappy Men. How truly great would it be, could the Convention bring about a reconciliation. They should suffer the loss of a very great part of their property & all their power. But they should still be considerd as Men & Frenchmen, and tho I would not kill the fatted Calf, they should still have a plate of Bouille at home if they will take it & not be turned out indiscriminately to perish in foreign Countries and to carry every where the impression of the injustice and ferocity of the French republic[.] That glorious Government will soon be so firmly establish'd that five and twenty thousand emigrants or three times the number cannot affect its stability. The people will soon feel the value of what they have gain'd and will not be shaken by their efforts in arms from without, or their intrigues within (even if they were to intrigue), & many of them have probably sufferd enough to be glad of returning on almost any terms. Their exile includes too that of a very great number of Women and Children who must be eventually not only a national loss but on whom, if the Sins of the Father are visited, it will be more consonant to the doctrine of scripture than of reason.

I not only wish that an amnesty was pass'd for these ill advisd Men, but that their wretched victim Louis Capet [Louis XVI] was to be dismiss'd with his family and an ample settlement made upon him & his posterity so long as they do not disturb the peace of the Republic. I do not understand of what use it can be to bring to trial an Officer for whom the whole nation determines it has no farther occasion. To punish him for the past seems as needless [as] to make him an example for the future, for, if no more Kings are suffer'd, it will avail nothing to shew the ill consequence of being a bad one by personal punishment inflicted on the unfortunate Man who could not help being born the Grandson of Louis 15th[.] Surely it would be great to shew the world that, when a people are determind to dismiss their King, he becomes indeed a phantom & cannot be an object of fear, & I am persuaded there are on all sides much stronger reasons for dismissing than for destroying him. On this occasion, the Republic should perhaps imitate the magnaminity of Uncle Toby, "Go poor devil! why should we hurt thee? There is surely room enough in the World for Us and thee!" [cf. Laurence Sterne, *Tristram Shandy* (1760–67), vol.

II, ch. 12]. It is making this unhappy individual of too much consequence to suppose that his life Can be demanded for the good of people. And when he was reduced to the condition of an affluent private Gentleman, & even that affluence depending on the Nation, I cannot conceive that he would do any harm, but wd sink into total insignificance & live a memento [sic] of the dependence of Kings, not on hereditary and divine right, but on the will of the people[.]

Will you have the goodness to send the Poem by Mr Fingal to Bells, Bookseller Opposite the end of Bond Street in Oxford Street, who will on Teusday or Wednesday forward to me a pacquet of Books[.] I will carefully return it when I have done with it by the same conveyance. I am afraid I shall not be in Town this Winter as my friend [Mrs. O'Neill] with whom I staid last year in Henrietta Street is gone to Lisbon . But if I should see London for a short time it will give me infinite pleasure to wait on Mrs Barlow by whose favorable opinion I am much flatter'd as well as to have an opportunity of assuring you personally of the esteem with which I am,

Sir,

your most oblig'd & obedt Sert,

Charlotte Smith

Extract from Charlotte Smith, Personal letter to Joseph Cooper Walker[1]

To Joseph Cooper Walker[2]

Storrington. 9 October 1793

I have perhaps appear'd negligent in that I have left your last very obliging Letter so long unanswerd. Alas! Dear Sir, if you have not overlook'd in the papers two paragraphs that have lately appear'd there, my apology is already made. Every year of my unhappy life seems

---

1 This item is reproduced by permission of The Huntington Library, San Marino, California.

2 Joseph Cooper Walker (1761–1810), an infirm Irish antiquary and scholar of Italian literature, was one of Smith's regular correspondents and arranged Dublin editions of some of her works.

destin'd to a new course of suffering. The year 1793 and the month of September has been productive of unusual sorrow. My gallant Boy [Smith's son Charles] lost his leg on the 6th before Dunkirk [England had been at war with Revolutionary France since February], & the retreat, which was immediately and rapidly made, compelld them to remove the wounded at the utmost risk of their lives. My poor Charles was remov'd only two hours after his leg had been amputated and not only sufferd extremely in consequence of it but has had the cure much retarded. I received this cruel intelligence on the 11th, and it was a shock almost too severe for me. A few days afterwards I heard from Lisbon of the death of my amiable and invaluable friend Mrs ONeill.[3] Yet I must bear these and probably many other evils—

"We must endure"

"Our going hence, even as our coming hither"—

——My poor invalid, to whom I have sent his next brother, is at Ostend; he has now left his bed and thinks he shall be at home in about three weeks. Nothing can be more dreadful to my imagination than to figure to myself his appearance; a fine active young Man, twenty years old, thus mutilated for life, must appear an afflicting object to a stranger—but to me! I really know not, ardently as I wish to have him at home, how I shall support the sight.

You who have heard much of the perfections of my belov'd friend, tho I think you were not personally acquainted with her, will easily imagine how irreperable her loss must be to all her friends. To me, who have been too long suffering the bitter blasts of adversity and have of course not many friends to spare, it is one of the most cruel blows I could sustain. But let me not dwell too long, dear Sir, on subjects so mournful.

I own that the suffering and injury received by my brave young Soldier appear the more afflicting because his going into the Army was entirely in consequence of the cruel conduct of the Men who call themselves Trustees to his Grandfather's property. There is a considerable living in the family which Mr Smith's Father gave by his Will to any

---

3 Henrietta Boyle, wife of the Irish nobleman John O'Neill of Shanes Castle, was a close friend and had contributed the poem "An Ode to the Poppy" to Smith's novel *Desmond*.

Son of mine who should take orders. As the eldest and the second preferred rather to go to India, Charles was destined for the Church. But when these Men got possession of the property and Mr Smith took the interest of my fortune to live upon, I was unable to keep him at School. I was therefore under the hard necessity of suffering him to remain unemploy'd at home for three years, continually imploring Mr Robinson to allow me wherewithal to place him at a University— or only a part of what would have been necessary: & from year to year hopes were given me that this would be done, but latterly Mr Robinson has not given me any hopes, but on the contrary, tho there is enough to pay all the legacies told me by his Son in Law Lord Abergavenny, that there was for me neither present assistance or future prospect. My literary labour (and yet it has till very lately been incessant) was quite inadequate to the purpose of supporting a young Man at even a Scottish College, but my entreaties and representations were vain, and my poor Charles, being of a spirited and active disposition, at length grew weary of lingering at home in hopeless inaction and told me he would go for a Volunteer unless I could get him a Commission.

I succeeded, Alas! but too well, and tho he has acquired the most flattering character, nothing can make him amends for being thus crippled. I am told that all Government allows is about sixty pounds a year— on which he is to live like a Gentleman if he can; God knows, if this be the case, how I shall manage to procure for him the few indulgencies requisite to soften his sufferings. I must keep him a Servant and a low chair in which he may drive himself. The only consolation I can now feel will be in rendering his life as comfortable as I can; and this consideration has set me to work again on a Novel, which as fast as I write I get my daughters to copy. Perhaps as the MMS will be ready at the same time (in the Month of April if my health is spared), I may be more fortunate in attempting to sell it in Ireland. But I have really given you, dear Sir, so much trouble that I am unwilling to ask your interposition again. Favor me however with your opinion on the subject, and I will write myself to the Bookseller if you think it worth while. I beleive I shall print here on my own account and not sell it to any Bookseller & shall print it at Bath.

You are very good to interest yrself so much in my unfortunate situation in regard to Mr Smith. Tho infidelity, and with the most despicable objects, had renderd my continuing to live with him extremely wretched long before his debts compelld him to leave England, I could have been contented to have resided in the same house with him, had not his temper been so capricious and often so cruel that my life was not safe. Not withstanding all I sufferd, which is much too sad a story to relate (for I was seven months with him in The Kings Bench Prison where he was confin'd by his own relations), I still continued to do all that was in my power for him; I paid out of my book money many debts that distress'd him & supplied him from time to time with small sums so long as he gave me leave, but it is now above seventeen months since I have heard from him, and the few people who know (which I beleive are his Sister Mrs Robinson and one of his friends) have received his instructions not to let me know where he is; I beleive he has another family by a Cook who liv'd with him, and has hid himself in Scotland by another name; so that if I were disposed to commence any process against him to compell him to allow me my own income for his children's support, I know not where to find him.

But I have no such design. My marriage articles, in which there are two flaws that deprive me of any jointure in case of his death, make no provision for a seperation. I was not quite fifteen when my father married me to Mr Smith and too childish to know the dismal fate that was preparing for me. Every thing my Father gave me then (3000£) was settled on him for his life; and £2000 more, which comes to me after the death of my Fathers Widow, a Woman of near 70 years old, is dispos'd in the same manner, So that for me I see no other prospect than being the slave of the Booksellers as long as my health or fancy hold out. Alas! continual anxiety & especially what I have sufferd lately have very much impair'd both: and this precarious resource is very likely to be exhausted.

A Miss Bartar near Derry has requested me to correct a Novel she has written. I own to you that this task is not a pleasant one, for I love Novels "no more than a Grocer does figs," but if I can do any little service to the young Lady in question, I will conquer my repugnance[.] As she seems to be in haste, I shall be much oblig'd to you to send me the pacquet address'd to Cadells as soon as she forwards it.

I have at present every reason to be happy in the marriage of my belov'd Augusta. The Chevalier de Foville [a French emigre officer] is still in my opinion worthy of her, which is saying every thing. But so strong are the prejudices against his Country that not one of her Father's family, and but one of mine can forgive me for consenting to let my daughter make herself happy her own way. This troubles me but little—

Adieu, dear Sir, let me have the pleasure of hearing from you soon, and allow me to remain with sincere regard,

your most obedient and oblig'd Ser^t,
Charlotte Smith

My present residence is in an obscure village
    Storrington, near Petworth, Sussex—
    October 9th 1793—